IMPETUOUS INNOCENT

"Stephanie Laurens is a real find!
She combines outstanding characterization
with action and sensuality, bringing
larger-than-life characters to the page
with such skill and talent that they become
real. All I need is her name on the cover
to make me pick up the book."
—New York Times bestselling author
Linda Howard

*Further Titles by Stephanie Laurens
from Severn House*

THE REASONS FOR MARRIAGE
TANGLED REINS
FOUR IN HAND
A COMFORTABLE WIFE
IMPETUOUS INNOCENT

IMPETUOUS INNOCENT

Stephanie Laurens

This first world hardcover edition published 2013
in Great Britain and in the USA by
SEVERN HOUSE PUBLISHERS LTD of
19 Cedar Road, Sutton, Surrey, England, SM2 5DA,
by arrangement with Harlequin Enterprises II B.V./S.à.r.l.
First published 1994 in the USA in mass market format only.

British Library Cataloguing in Publication Data

Laurens, Stephanie. author.
  Impetuous innocent.
  1. Great Britain--History--George III, 1760-1820--
  Fiction. 2. Love stories.
  I. Title
  823.9'2-dc23

  ISBN-13: 978-0-7278-8313-1   (cased)

All Severn House titles are printed on acid-free paper.

Severn House Publishers support The Forest Stewardship Council [FSC],
the leading international forest certification organisation. All our titles that
are printed on Greenpeace-approved FSC-certified paper carry the FSC logo.

Printed and bound in Great Britain by
TJ International, Padstow, Cornwall.

CHAPTER ONE

"GEORGIE? GEORGIE! Open this door! Aw—c'mon, Georgie. Jus' a bit of a kiss an' cuddle. D'you hear me, Georgie? Lemme in!"

Georgiana Hartley sat cross-legged in the middle of her bed, fully clothed, a small, slight figure in the huge four-poster. The flickering light of a single candle gleamed on her guinea-gold curls, still dressed in an elegant knot. Her large hazel eyes, fixed on the door of her chamber, held an expression of annoyance; her soft lips were compressed into a disapproving line. Charles was becoming a definite boor.

It was her seventh night in England, her fourth at the Place, seat of her forefathers and home of her cousin Charles. And it was the third night she had had to seek the safety of her bedchamber at a ridiculously early hour, to avoid Charles's drink-driven importunities.

She had done it again.

Pulling a pillow across her lap, and wrinkling her nose at the musty smell that arose when she settled her elbows on it, Georgiana berated herself, for what was certainly not the first time and would undoutedly not be the last, for her apparently innate impulsiveness. It had been that alone which had driven her to leave the sunny climes of the Italian coast and return to the land of her birth. Still, on her father's death, it had seemed the most sensible course. With a deep sigh she dropped her chin on to her hands, keeping her eyes trained on the door. All was quiet, but she knew Charles was still there, just outside, hoping she might be silly enough to try to slip out.

James Hartley, painter and vivant, had left his only child to the guardianship of his only brother, her uncle Ernest. Uncle Ernest had lived at the Place. Unfortunately, he had died one month before his brother. Georgiana sniffed. Doubtless she should feel something for her uncle, but it was hard to feel grief on the death of someone you had never met—particularly when still coping with a far more shattering loss. And particularly when circumstances had conspired to land her in Charles's lap. For the news of her uncle's death had not reached James Hartley's Italian solicitors in time to stop her instinctive flight from the beauties of Ravello, her home for the last twelve years, now filled with too many painful memories. She had arrived at the Place to find Charles—Uncle Ernest's son, and a stranger to her—in possession.

The solid oak door rattled and jumped in its frame. Georgiana eyed it with increasing concern. The worn lock and the old iron hinges were all that stood between her and her drink-sodden cousin.

"Aw, Georgie, don' be a prude. You'll like't, I promise. Just a bit o' fun." A loud hiccup reached Georgiana's ears. "It's all right. You know I'll marry you. Lemme in and we'll be married tomorrow. You hear me, Georgie? C'mon, Georgie, open this door, I say!''

Georgiana sternly repressed a shiver of pure revulsion. Marry Charles? Feeling panic stir, she determinedly pushed the horrifying thought aside. Now was no time to go to pieces.

The door bounced, reverberating on its hinges as Charles made a determined assault on the thick panels. Georgiana's eyes grew round. As the thumping continued, she scanned the room for some implement, some weapon. But there was nothing, not even a candelabrum. With a grimace of resignation, she returned her gaze to the heavy oak door, philosophically waiting for whatever came next, confident that, one way or another, she would deal with it.

But the door stood firm. With one last defeated thump, Charles stopped his hammering.

"Damn you, Georgie! You won't get away! You can't escape me. You'll see—you'll have to give in, soon or late.'' A jeering, drunken laugh crept into the room. "You'll see.''

Unsteady footsteps retreated down the passage as Charles took himself off to bed, giggling crazily.

Slowly Georgiana raised her brows. She remained perched on the bed, listening. When five minutes had passed with no sound from beyond her door, she hurled aside the pillow and slipped from the bed. A determined frown settled across her heart-shaped face. She fell to pacing the room. Can't escape?

For five minutes she walked the unpolished boards. The wind whistled and moaned, little blasts worming their way through the ill-fitting shutters to send the curtains skittering. Absent-mindedly Georgiana dragged the patched quilt from the bed and flung it about her shoulders. She reviewed her options. There weren't many. She knew no one in England, had no one to turn to. But one thing was certain—she could not stay here. If she did, Charles would force her to marry him—by hook or by crook. She couldn't hide behind locked doors forever.

With the dogged and purposeful air which had carried her across an unstable Continent unharmed, she threw off the quilt and crossed to the wardrobe. Setting the door wide, she struggled to pull her trunk free. Once she got it to the floor, she tugged the cumbersome corded box to the side of the bed. She opened the heavy lid and propped it against the bed.

A scratching at the door startled her.

Slowly Georgiana straightened and eyed the scarred oak panels with misgiving.

The noise came again.

"Miss Georgie? It's me, Cruickshank."

Georgiana let out the breath she had been holding and went to the door. It was a fight to turn the heavy key. After much tugging, the bolt fell back and she eased the heavy door open. "Cruckers! Thank goodness you've come. I was racking my brains to think of how to get hold of you."

Maria Cruickshank, a thin, weedy woman, tall and lanky, with iron-grey hair tightly confined, sniffed loudly. Originally maid to Georgiana's mother, she was the closest thing to a family retainer Georgiana had.

"As if I'd not come running with all that racket. He

may be your cousin, but that Charles is no good. I told you so. *Now* do you believe me?''

Together they pushed the door shut. Cruickshank wrestled the lock home and turned to face the child-cum-lovely young woman she adored. She placed her hands on her hips and frowned grimly. ''Now, Miss Georgie, I hope you're convinced. We've got to leave this house. It's no place for the likes of you, what with Master Charles as he is. It's not what your father intended, dear me, no!''

Georgiana smiled and turned back to the bed.

Cruickshank's eyes widened. She drew full breath, girding her loins for battle. Then she saw the trunk. Her breath came out with a soft whistle. ''Ah.''

Georgiana's smile grew. ''Precisely. We're leaving. Come and help.''

Cruickshank needed no further urging. Ten minutes later, all of Georgiana's possessions were back in her trunk. While Cruickshank tightened the straps, Georgiana sat on the lid, biting the tip of one rosy finger and plotting her escape.

''Now, Cruckers, there's no point in setting out before dawn, so we may as well get some sleep. I'll stay here, and you go back downstairs and warn Ben. Charles must be dead to the world by now. I'm sure I'll be safe enough.''

Georgiana waited for the inevitable protest. Instead, Cruickshank merely snorted and clambered to her feet.

''True enough. A whole decanter of brandy he poured down his gullet. I doubt he'll be up betimes.''

Georgiana's hazel eyes widened in awe. ''Truly? Heavens!'' She wriggled her toes, then jumped to the ground. "Well, that's all the better. The longer he sleeps, the farther we'll get before he finds out."

Cruickshank sniffed disparagingly. "D'you think he'll follow?"

A worried frown drew down Georgiana's fine brows. "I really don't know. He says he's my guardian, but I don't see how that can be." She sank on to the bed, one hand brushing gold curls from her forehead in a gesture of bewilderment. "It's all so confusing."

Her tone brought Cruickshank to her side, one large hand coming up to pat Georgiana's shoulder comfortingly. "Never you worry, Miss Georgie. Ben and me, we'll see you safe."

Fleetingly, Georgiana smiled, her hand rising to grip that of her maid. "Yes, of course. I don't know what I'd have done without my two watchdogs."

Bright hazel eyes met faded blue, and Cruickshank's stern features softened. "Now, lovey, do you have any notion where you should go?"

It was the question Georgiana had spent the last three days pondering. To no avail. But her tone was determined and decisive when she said, "I've thought and thought, but I can't think of anyone. As far as I can see, the best thing I can do is throw myself on the mercy of one of the ladies of the neighbourhood. There must be someone about who remembers Uncle Ernest or Papa and will at least advise me."

Cruickshank grimaced, but did not argue the point. "I'll be back before first light. I'll bring Ben for the trunk. You get some rest now. Enough excitement for one night, you've had."

Obediently Georgiana allowed Cruickshank to help her into her nightgown, then clambered into the big bed. Cruickshank resettled the quilt and tucked the sheets under the lumpy mattress. Again the maid sniffed disparagingly.

"Even if 'twas your grandpa's house, miss, all I can say is the accommodation leaves much to be desired." With a haughty glance at the aged bedclothes, Cruickshank clumped to the door. "Just to be on the safe side, I'll lock you in."

With the problem of Charles already behind her, and her immediate actions decided, Georgiana's mind slowed. With a sigh, she snuggled deeper into the mattress and curled up tight against the cold. Her lids were already drooping as she watched the door close behind the faithful Cruickshank. The lock fell heavily into place. Georgiana yawned widely and blew out her candle.

"SHHH!" Cruickshank held a finger to her lips and with her other hand indicated a door giving off the dimly lit passage.

Georgiana nodded her understanding and slipped silently past the room where Charles's slatternly housekeeper and her equally slovenly spouse snored in drunken unison. The Pringates were new to the Place, and Georgiana could not conceive how Charles had come to hire them. They seemed to know little to nothing of managing a household. None of the old servants had remained after her uncle's death. Presumably it was hard to get good help in the country. And, even to her untutored eyes, the Place was in sorry condition, hardly an attractive proposition to experienced staff.

Mentally shrugging, she hurried on. The dank corridor ended in a huge stone-flagged kitchen. Cruickshank was struggling with the heavy back door. As she eased it open, the tell-tale sound of a horse whickering drifted in with the wet mist. Galvanised, Georgiana hurried out into the yard, Cruickshank close behind.

Her own travelling carriage, battered and worn after the long journey from Italy, but thankfully still serviceable, stood in the muddy yard, her two powerful carriage horses hitched in their harness. She spared the time to bestow a fond pat on each great grey head before allowing Ben to help her into the coach.

As the door shut, sealing her within, with Cruickshank on the seat opposite, Georgiana settled herself on the padded leather with a weary sigh. She had hoped to enjoy a rest after the jolting roads of the Continent. True, the English roads were in much better condition, but she had looked forward to keeping her feet on firm ground and her bottom on softer seats for some time. Fate, however, had clearly decided otherwise.

The carriage rocked as Ben climbed to his perch. Without his customary whistle, he set the team moving. The coach rumbled quietly out of the yard and turned into the lane.

As the miles fell slowly behind them, Georgiana wondered anew at the oddity of the Place. The old house stood in its own extensive grounds, overgrown and choked with weeds, amid fields and meadows, all lying fallow as far as she had seen. She lifted the window flap and peered through the early morning gloom. There was no sign of livestock anywhere. Fences were broken and gates hung crazily on ruptured hinges. An air of decay hung like a pall across the estate. Heaven knew, it wasn't all that large as estates went. But the Place had hit hard times, and neglect had taken its toll. She was sure her father had not known the state of his family's property. If he had, he would never have suggested she seek refuge there. Or, alternatively, he would have made some provision to restore the Place to its former glory.

As the carriage drew to the crest of a hill which marked the limit of the estate, Georgiana, leaning past the leather flap, caught a last glimpse of the grey roofs of the Place. Then the horses started on the downward slope and trees blocked her view. In truth, from what she had seen in her three days there, she doubted the Place was worth saving.

Her only regret in leaving was that she had failed to unearth the set of paintings her father had told her he had left there. Close to twenty finished canvases, he had said. The only one she was really interested in was a portrait of her mother which he had painted shortly after their marriage. He had always maintained it was the best of the handful of portraits he had done of his wife. Georgiana had looked forward to seeing again the face of her gentle mother, otherwise no more than a misty memory. But Charles had denied all knowledge of the paintings, and her surreptitious searches had failed to find any trace of them. Now, as she didn't fancy staying within Charles's reach, the paintings would remain lost to her. Philosophically, she sighed. She knew she'd made the right choice. But she had so wanted that portrait of her mother.

The lane which led to the Place was long and winding. It followed a strange line, around the boundaries of the holdings of a neighbouring estate, eventually joining a road which ultimately led to Steeple Claydon. The morning mists were lifting by the time the coach trundled into the small village of Alton Rise, no more than a cluster of cottages nestling at the first crossroads. Ben pulled the horses up before the tiny inn. He jumped down from his perch and came to the carriage window.

Georgiana pushed aside the window flap and leant out. "Can you ask where the nearest magistrate lives? If that sounds too far, ask for the nearest big landowner."

Ben nodded and disappeared into the inn. Ten minutes later he was back. "They said best to go on up to Candlewick Hall. It's owned by a London swell, name of Lord Alton. His family's been hereabouts for generations, so it seems a safe bet. The innkeeper's missus thought you'd be safe enough asking for help there."

"Heavens, Ben!" Georgiana looked at her faithful henchman in horror. "You didn't tell them about…?"

Ben shrugged his old shoulders. "'Tweren't no news to them. By all accounts, that cousin of yourn's not much liked."

Georgiana considered this view. It was not hard to believe. Charles, in three days, had proved his colours beyond question. "How far is it to Candlewick Hall?"

"No more'n a couple of miles," said Ben, hauling himself up.

As the coach lumbered forward, Georgiana sat back and rehearsed her explanation. Doubtless she would have to be frank with Lady Alton. She was not sure what she expected her ladyship to do for her. Still, at the very least, surely Lady Alton would be able to recommend a hotel in London where she could safely stay?

The coach had picked up speed on the better-surfaced road. Georgiana's wandering attention was reclaimed by the slowing of the vehicle as Ben turned the horses sharply to the left. Drawing closer to the window, she rolled up the flap and fastened it above the frame so she could gaze unimpeded at the land-scape. And a very different landscape it was. In just a few miles, all evidence of rot had vanished. The fields they now passed were well tended; sheep and cattle dotted the pastures. All was neat and pleasant perfec-tion. As if to give its blessing, the sun struck through the clouds, bathing the scene in warmth and bright-ness.

Georgiana was even more impressed when they reached the park of Candlewick Hall. Two stone ea-gles, perched atop tall gateposts, stood guard. Between them, massive wrought-iron gates hung wide. A neat gravelled drive led onwards, curving away between two lines of beech trees. The horses appreciated the even surface and trotted easily onward. Georgiana looked about her and was pleased to approve. This was how she had imagined an English gentleman's country residence would look, with trimmed shrubberies and manicured lawns falling away on one side to an ornamental lake, a white summer-house perched on an island in the middle. The vista had about it an air of peace and tranquillity. As the coach swept around a bend, she caught a glimpse of colour through the green of the trees—presumably the gardens, which meant the house was near. She scooted to the other side of the coach and looked out.

Her eyes grew round and her lips formed an ''Oh'' of delight.

Candlewick Hall rose before her, its cream stone walls touched here and there with bright creeper. Three storeys of square-paned windows looked down on the gravel court before the front steps. In the morning light, the house was cloaked in a still serenity, a peaceful solidity, which tugged oddly at her. Candlewick Hall embodied everything she had come back to England to find.

The pace of the coach was checked, and they rocked to a stop before the white steps leading up to two massive front doors. Ben swung down and came to assist her to alight. He escorted her up the steps and plied the heavy knocker.

Georgiana faced the heavy wooden doors. It had seemed much easier to claim help from an unknown lady when she had been sitting in her bed last night. But the memory of Charles's ravings stiffened her resolve. As the sound of footsteps drew nearer, she took a deep breath and fixed a confident smile on her lips.

''Yes?''

A stately butler looked majestically down upon her.

"Good morning. My name is Georgiana Hartley. I wonder if I might have a word with Lady Alton?"

Georgiana was pleased with her tone. She sounded confident and in control, despite the fact she was inwardly quaking. If the butler was this starchy, what was his mistress like? She kept her chin up and waited.

The butler did not move. Georgiana felt her confidence draining, dissipating like the morning mist under the intensity of his scrutiny. She wondered if the man was hard of hearing, and was gathering her courage to repeat her request in more strident tones when he smiled, quite kindly, and bowed. "If you will step into the drawing-room, Miss Hartley, I will inform Lord Alton immediately."

Buoyed by her success, Georgiana was across the threshold before she analysed his words. She came to an abrupt halt. "Oh! But it was Lady Alton I wished to see."

"Yes, of course, miss. If you would take a seat?"

Unable to resist the deferential and strangely compelling courtesy of the impeccable butler, Georgiana found herself ushered into a beautifully appointed room and made comfortable in a wing-chair. Having ascertained that she was not in need of any refreshment thus early in the day, the dignified personage withdrew.

Feeling slightly dazed, Georgiana looked about her. The interior of Candlewick Hall did justice to its exterior. Exquisite taste and a judicious eye had chosen and arranged all the furnishings, creating and enhancing a mood of peace and serenity to match that of the gardens. Her hazel gaze wandered over the room, coming to rest on the large painting in pride of place above the mantelpiece. As a painter's daughter, she could not do otherwise than admire Fragonard. She was intrigued, nevertheless, to find a picture incorporating numerous naked female forms so publicly displayed. A more private room would, she thought, have been more appropriate. But then, she reminded herself, she knew nothing of the latest whims of English social taste. And there was no doubt the Fragonard was an exquisite work of art.

The subtle colours of the room slowly eased her tension, seeping into her sight and mind. Georgiana smiled to herself and settled back in the chair. Candlewick Hall seemed designed to calm the senses. With a grateful sigh, she relaxed.

The effects of three late nights dragged at her eyelids. She would close them. Just for a moment.

"THERE'S A YOUNG LADY to see you, m'lord."

Dominic Ridgeley, fifth Viscount Alton, lifted his blue eyes to his butler's face. Around him, on the polished mahogany table, the remains of a substantial breakfast bore mute testimony to his recent occupation. But the dishes had been pushed aside to make way for a pile of letters, one of which his lordship clasped in one long-fingered hand.

"I beg your pardon?"

"A young lady has called, m'lord." Not a quiver of emotion showed on the butler's lined face.

Lord Alton's black brows rose. His features became perceptibly harder, his blue gaze perceptibly chillier. "Have you taken leave of your senses, Duckett?"

Such a question, in such a tone, would have reduced most servants to incoherent gibbering. But Duckett was a butler of the highest standing. And he had known the present Lord Alton from the cradle. He answered the question with an infinitesimal smile. "Naturally not, m'lord."

His answer appeared to appease his master. Lord Alton regarded his henchman with a puzzled and slightly wary frown. "Oh?"

At the prompt, Duckett explained. "It seems the young lady requires assistance with some difficulty, m'lord. She asked to see Lady Alton. She appears to be in some distress. I thought it wise not to turn her away. Her name is Miss Hartley."

"Hartley?" The black brows drew down. "But there aren't any Miss Hartleys at the Place, are there?"

In response to his master's quizzical look, Duckett graciously informed him, "I have heard that Mr James Hartley's daughter has been visiting the Place for the past few days. From the Continent, I believe."

"Staying with frightful Charles? Poor girl."

"Exactly so, m'lord."

Lord Alton fixed Duckett with a suspicious look. "You said she was distressed. She's not weeping and having the vapours, is she?"

"Oh, no, m'lord. Miss Hartley is perfectly composed."

Lord Alton frowned again. "Then how do you know she's distressed?"

Duckett coloured slightly. "It was her hands, m'lord. She was clutching her reticule so tightly, her knuckles were quite white."

Suitably impressed by his butler's astuteness, Lord Alton leant back in his chair, absent-mindedly laying the letter he had been reading on the pile before him. Then he glanced up. "You think I should see her?"

Duckett met his master's eye and did not misunderstand his question. No one who was acquainted with Lord Alton could fail to comprehend the delicacy of the matter. For a young lady to meet a gentleman alone, particularly in the gentleman's house, with no other lady anywhere about, was hardly the sort of behaviour someone as conservative as Duckett would normally encourage. And when the gentleman in question was Lord Dominic Alton, the situation took on an even more questionable hue. But Duckett's perception was acute. Miss Hartley was in trouble and out of her depth. His master could be relied upon to provide the answer to her troubles. And, regardless of his reputation, she stood in no danger from him. She was too young and too green, not his type at all. So, Duckett cleared his throat and said, "Despite the—er—conventions, yes, m'lord, I think you should see her."

With a sigh, Lord Alton rose, stretching to his full six feet. Relaxing, he shook out his cuffs and settled his dark blue coat over his broad shoulders. Then he looked up and wagged an admonitory finger at Duckett. "If this lands me in scandal, old friend, it'll be all your fault."

Duckett grinned and opened the door for his master. "As you wish, m'lord. She's in the drawing-room."

With one last warning glance, Lord Alton passed through the door and crossed the hall.

GEORGIANA'S DREAM was distinctly disturbing. In it, she had transformed into one of the nymphs depicted in the Fragonard canvas. Together with her unknown sisters, she cavorted freely through a sylvan glade, blushing at the cool drift of the breeze across her naked skin. Abruptly, she halted. Someone was watching her. She glanced around, blushing even more rosily. But there was no one in sight. The sensation of being watched grew. She opened her eyes.

And gazed bemusedly into eyes of cerulean blue.

Her gaze widened, and she saw the man behind the eyes. She stopped breathing, no longer sure which was reality and which the dream. For the man watching her, a gleam of undisguised appreciation in the depths of those beautiful blue eyes, was undoubtedly a god. And even more disturbing than her erotic dream. His shoulders were broad, filling her sight, his body long and lean and muscular. His face was strongly featured, yet held the clean lines painters adored. Thick dark hair cloaked his head in elegant waves, softening the effect of his determinedly squared chin. Finely drawn lips held the hint of a disturbing smile. And his eyes, glorious blue, set under strongly arched brows and framed by lashes too long and thick for a man, seemed to hold all the promise of a summer's afternoon.

"Oh!" It was the most coherent response she could muster.

The vision smiled. Georgiana's heart lurched.

"You were sleeping so peacefully I was loath to disturb you."

The deep tones of his voice enclosed Georgiana in a warmth reminiscent of fine velvet. With an effort, she straightened, forcing her body to behave and her mind to function. "I... I'm so sorry. I must have drifted off. I was waiting for Lady Alton."

The gentleman retreated slightly to lean one elegant arm along the mantelpiece, one booted foot resting on the hearth. The blue eyes, disconcertingly, remained trained on her face.

"I'm desolated to disappoint you." The smile that went with the words said otherwise. "Allow me to introduce myself. Lord Dominic Alton, entirely at your service."

He swept her an elegant bow, blue eyes gleaming.

"But alas, I've yet to marry. There is, therefore, no Lady Alton."

"Oh, *how* unfortunate!"

The anguished assessment surprised Dominic. He was not used to such a response from personable young women. His lips twitched and his eyes came alight with unholy amusement. "Quite!"

His tone brought the hazel gaze to his face. But she showed no consciousness of her phrasing. Seeing real consternation in the warm hazel eyes, Dominic rejected the appealing idea of explaining it to her. Clearly, Duckett's assessment of her state was accurate. She might be sitting calmly, rather than indulging in hysterics, as females were so lamentably prone to do, but he had no doubt she was seriously adrift and knew not which way to turn. The expression in her wide hazel eyes said so. In response, he smiled beguilingly. "But I gather you have some problem. Perhaps I could be of help?"

His polite query flustered Georgiana. How could she explain…? To a man…?

"Er—I don't think…" She rose, clutching her reticule tightly. As she did so, her gaze went beyond Lord Alton to the Fragonard. Georgiana froze. What sort of man, with no wife, hung a scandalous masterpiece in his drawing-room? The answer threatened to scuttle what wits she still possessed.

Unknown to Georgiana, her thoughts passed clearly across her face, perfectly readable to the accomplished gentleman watching her. All Dominic's experience told him to accept her withdrawal as the blessed release it doubtless was. But some whimsical and unexpected impulse pushed him to learn what strange story, what quirk of fate, was responsible for depositing such a very delightful morsel on his doorstep. Besides, he didn't entirely like her assumption that he was powerless to help her. He drew himself to his full height and fixed her with a stern eye. "My dear Miss Hartley, I do hope you're not about to say you '—doubt that I can be of assistance—' before you've even told me the problem."

Georgiana blinked. She had, of course, been about to say just that. With the ground cut from under her feet, she struggled to find some acceptable way out.

Lord Alton was smiling again. Strange, she had never before encountered a smile that warmed her as his did.

"Please sit down, Miss Hartley. Can I get you some refreshment? No? Well, then, why don't you just tell me what your problem is? I promise you, I don't shock easily."

Georgiana glanced up, but the blue eyes were innocent. Sinking once more into the wing-chair, she considered her choices. If she insisted on leaving Lord Alton without asking for his advice, where would she go? And, more importantly, how far behind her was Charles? That thought, more than any other, drove her to speak. "I really wanted to ask for some advice...on what I should do, finding myself in the situation I... I now find myself in." She paused, wondering how detailed her explanation need be.

"Which is?" came the soft prompt.

The need to confide in someone was strong. Mentally shrugging, Georgiana threw caution to the winds. "I recently returned to England from the Continent. I've lived for the last twelve years in Italy with my father, James Hartley. He died a few months ago, leaving me to the guardianship of my uncle, Ernest Hartley."

She looked up. Lord Alton's expression was sympathetic. He nodded encouragingly. Drawing a deep breath, she continued. "I returned to England immediately. I...didn't wish to remain in Italy. On my arrival at Hartley Place, I learnt that my uncle had died a month or so before my father. My cousin Charles owns the Place now." Georgiana hesitated.

"I'm slightly acquainted with Charles Hartley, if that's any help. I might add that I would not consider him a fit person for a young lady such as yourself to share a roof with."

His cool, impersonal tone brought a blush to Georgiana's cheek.

Seeing it, Dominic knew he had struck close to the truth.

Keeping her eyes fixed on the empty fireplace, Georgiana struggled on. "I'm afraid...that is to say, Charles seems to have developed a fixation. In short," she continued, desperation lending her words, "he has been trying to force me to marry him. I left the house this morning, very early."

She glanced up and, to her surprise, found no difficulty in meeting his lordship's blue gaze. "I've no one in England I can turn to, my lord. I was hoping to ask your wife for advice as to what I should do."

Dominic's gaze rested on the heart-shaped face and large honey-gold eyes turned so trustingly towards him. For some perverse reason, he knew he was going to help her. Ignoring the inner voice which whispered he was mad even to contemplate such a thing, he asked, "Have you any particular course of action in mind?"

"Well, I did think of going to London. I thought perhaps I could become a companion to some lady."

Dominic forcibly repressed a shudder. Such a glorious creature would have no luck in finding that sort of employment. She was flexing her fingers, her attention momentarily distracted. His eyes slid gently over her figure. The grey dress she wore fitted well, outlining a pair of enticingly sweet breasts, young and firm and high. Her skin was perfect—peaches and cream. As she was seated, he had no way of judging her legs, although, by the evidence of her slender feet, he suspected they would prove to be long and slim. Her waist was hidden by the fall of her dress, but the swell of her hips was unmistakable. If Georgiana Hartley became stranded in London, he could guess where she'd end. Which, all things considered, would be a great shame. Her candid gaze returned to his face.

"I have my own maid and coachman. I thought that might help."

Help? A companion with her own maid and coachman? Dominic managed to keep his face impassive. There was no point in telling her how ludicrous her ideas were, for she wasn't going to hire out as a companion. Not if he had anything to say in the matter. The wretched life most paid companions led, neither servant nor family, stranded in limbo between stairs, was not for Miss Hartley.

"I will have to think of what's best to be done. Instant solutions are likely to come unstuck. I've always found it much more useful to consider carefully before committing any irrevocable act."

Listen to yourself! screamed his inner voice.

Dominic smiled sweetly. "I suggest you spend an hour or so with my housekeeper, while I consider the alternatives." The smile broadened. "Believe me, there are alternatives."

Georgiana blinked. She wasn't sure what to make of that. She hoped she hadn't jumped from the frying-pan into the fire. But he was turning her over to the care of his housekeeper, which hardly fitted with the image revolving in her mind. There was another problem. "Charles might follow me."

"I can assure you this is one place Charles will never look. And I doubt he'd pursue you to London. You're perfectly safe here." Dominic turned and tugged the bell-pull. Then he swung back to face Georgiana and smiled reassuringly. "Charles and I don't exactly get on, you see."

A pause ensued. While Miss Hartley studied her hands, Dominic studied Miss Hartley. She was a sweetly turned piece, but too gentle and demure for his taste. A damsel in distress—Duckett had been right there. Clearly, it behoved him to help her. The cost would be negligible; it would hardly take up much of his time and might even afford him some amusement. Aside from anything else, it would presumably annoy Charles Hartley, and that was a good enough reason in itself. He determinedly quashed his inner voice, that advocate of self-protection at all costs, and returned to his agreeable contemplation of Miss Hartley.

The door opened, and Georgiana came slowly to her feet.

"My lord?"

Dominic turned. "Duckett, please ask Mrs Landy to attend us."

"Yes, m'lord." Duckett bowed himself from the room, a smile of quiet satisfaction on his face.

AFTER A PLEASANT and reassuring hour spent with Mrs Landy, Georgiana was conducted back to the drawing-room. The motherly housekeeper had been shocked to learn of Georgiana's plight and even more moved when she discovered she had missed her breakfast. Now, fortified with muffins and jam and steaming coffee, and having been assured her two servants had been similarly supplied, Georgiana faced the prospect of her interview with Lord Alton with renewed confidence. No gentleman who possessed a housekeeper like Mrs Landy could be a villain.

She smiled sweetly at the butler, who seemed much less intimidating now, and passed through the door he held open for her. Lord Alton was standing by the fireplace. He looked up as she entered, and smiled. Georgiana was struck anew by his handsomeness and the subtle aura of a deeper attractiveness that owed nothing to his elegant attire, but derived more from the quality of his smile and the lights that danced in those wonderful eyes.

He inclined his head politely in response to her curtsy and, still smiling, waved her to the wing-chair. Georgiana seated herself and settled her skirts, thankful she had this morning donned one of her more modish gowns, a grey kerseymere with a fine white linen fichu, edged with expensive Italian lace. Comfortable, she raised expectant eyes to his lordship's dark-browed face.

For a full minute, he seemed to be looking at her and thinking of something else. Then, abruptly, he cleared his throat.

"How old are you, Miss Hartley?"

Georgiana answered readily, assuming him to be considering what employment might best suit her years. "Eighteen, my lord."

Eighteen. Good. He was thirty-two. She was too young, thank God. It must just be his gentlemanly instincts that were driving him to help her. At thirty-two, one was surely beyond the stage of lusting after schoolroom chits. Dominic smiled his practised smile.

"In light of your years, I think you'll find it will

take some time to discover a suitable position. Such opportunities don't grow on trees, you know." He kept his manner determinedly avuncular. "I've been thinking of what lady of my acquaintance would be most useful in helping you. My sister, Lady Winsmere, is often telling me she pines for distraction." That, at least, was the truth. If he knew Bella, she would leap at the opportunity for untold distraction that he intended to offer her in the charming person of Miss Georgiana Hartley.

Georgiana watched Lord Alton's face intently. Thus far, his measured statements made perfect sense, but his patronising tone niggled. She was hardly a child.

"I have written a letter to her," Dominic continued, pausing to draw a folded parchment from his coat, "in which I've explained your predicament." His lips involuntarily twitched as he imagined what Bella would make of his disclosures. "I suggest you take it and deliver it in person to Lady Winsmere in Green Street." He smiled into Miss Hartley's warmed honey eyes. "Bella, despite her occasional flights of fancy, is quite remarkably sane and will know precisely how you should go on. I've asked her to supervise you in your search for employment, for you will be sadly out of touch with the way things are done. You may place complete confidence in her judgement."

Relief swept over Georgiana. She rose and took the letter. Holding it carefully, she studied the strong black script boldly inscribed across the parchment. Her fingers moved across the thick, finely textured paper. She felt oddly reassured, as if a confidence placed had proved to be well founded. After her problems with

Charles, the world seemed to be righting itself. "My lord, I don't know how to thank you. You've been more help than I expected, certainly more than I deserve." Her soft voice sounded so small in that elegant room. She raised her eyes to his, smiling in sincere gratitude.

Unaccountably irritated, Dominic waved one fine hand dismissively. "It was nothing, I assure you. It's entirely my pleasure to be able to help you. Now one more point." He hurried on, strangely unwilling to bear more of Miss Hartley's gratitude. "It seems to me that if Charles is out there scouting about he'll be looking for your carriage, with your coachman atop. I've therefore given orders for you to be conveyed to London in one of my carriages, together with your maid. One of my coachmen will drive you and will return with the carriage. After a few days, when Charles has given up, your coachman will follow you with your coach. I trust such an arrangement is satisfactory?"

Georgiana felt slightly stunned. He seemed to have thought of everything. Efficiently, smoothly, in just one short hour he had cleared the obstacles from her path and made all seem easy. "My lord, you overwhelm me. But surely—you might need your carriage?"

"I assure you my carriage will be…better used conveying you to London than it otherwise would be," Dominic responded suavely, only just managing to avoid a more subtly flattering selection of words. God! Dealing with an innocent was trying his wits. A long time had passed since he had engaged in social discourse with a virtuous young lady of only eighteen summers. It was too abominably easy to slip into the more sophisticated and seductive modes of conversation he used almost exclusively to females these days. Which, he ruefully reminded himself, was a definite reflection on the types of ladies whose company he currently kept.

With another dazzling smile, Georgiana Hartley inclined her head in acceptance. At his intimation, she fell into step beside him, gliding towards the door on tiny, grey-slippered feet.

Still bemused, and with the feeling that events were suddenly moving rather faster than she could cope with, Georgiana could nevertheless find no fault with his arrangements.

Duckett met them in the hall with the information that the coach stood ready.

Dominic could not resist offering her his arm. With gentlemanly courtesy he conducted her to the coach, pausing while she exchanged farewells with Ben, surprising everyone, Ben included, by breaking off her words to give him a quick hug. Then Dominic handed her into the luxuriously appointed coach, wherein her maid was already installed, and stood back. Duckett shut the door firmly. The coachman, Jiggs, gave the horses the office. The coach pulled smoothly away.

Dominic Ridgeley stood on the steps of his manor house, his hands sunk in his pockets, and watched his coach roll out of sight. Then, when he could no longer see the swaying carriage roof, he turned to go inside, pausing to kick at a piece of gravel inadvertently, inexcusably resident on the steps. With a sigh and a pensive smile, as if some pleasant interlude had come to its inevitable conclusion, he went inside and shut the door.

CHAPTER TWO

NIGHT had descended by the time Lord Alton's travelling carriage drew to a halt on the cobbles before the elegant town house of Lord and Lady Winsmere. Georgiana glanced up at the tiers of lamplit windows reaching high above the street. Beside her, Cruickshank sat silent, her lips set in a severe line. The groom swung down and trotted up the steps to jangle the doorbell before returning to help them to the pavement.

A portly butler appeared. One glance at the groom's livery was apparently enough to effect instant entrance for Georgiana and Cruickshank.

Georgiana allowed the butler to remove her pelisse. Then she turned and, in a voice tinged with nervousness, said, "I wish to speak with Lady Winsmere, if you please. I have a letter of introduction from Lord Alton."

Despite the butler's gracious bow and solemn face, Georgiana was instantly aware of his avid interest.

"I will convey your letter to Lady Winsmere, miss. If you would care to wait in the drawing-room?"

Shown into a reception-room of pleasing proportions, Georgiana stopped and blinked. The door shut behind her. Cruickshank had dutifully remained in the

hall. Georgiana scanned the room, then, finding nothing of greater moment to consider, gave her attention
to a careful appraisal of the white and gilt décor. The
room was well stocked with furniture, and every available flat surface sprouted at least one ornament. The
rule seemed to be that if it wasn't white it had to be
gilded. Not even the ornate cornices had escaped. The
effect was overpowering. With a sigh and a shrug for
English fashions, Georgiana chose a stiff-backed, spin-
dle-legged chair, heavily gilded and upholstered in
white damask, and gingerly sat down.

Her gaze roamed the walls once more, but there was
no Fragonard to provide distraction.

She folded her hands in her lap and tried to subdue
the uncomfortable feeling of encroaching upon those
whom she had no right to call on. But Lord Alton had
seemed unperturbed by her request for help. Maybe,
despite her misgivings, there was nothing so very peculiar about her predicament. At least, not to an English mind. Determined to be optimstic, she endeavoured to compose herself to meet Lady Winsmere's
questions. Doubtless, she would have a good few.
What was she making of her brother's letter?

Only then did Georgiana realise she had no idea in
what light Lord Alton had presented her to his sister.
The thick parchment had been fixed with a heavy lump
of red wax, on which the seal of the Viscounts Alton
had been imprinted. Georgiana frowned. A wave of
tiredness rose up to envelop her. Not for the first time
since leaving the comfort of Candlewick Hall, she
wondered at the wisdom of her actions. She was too
impulsive. Often she had landed herself in the suds by

rushing headlong on her fate—witness her flight from Ravello. But it was too late to draw back now. She grimaced. The more she thought of it, the more clearly she perceived her inability to influence the course of events Lord Alton had charted for her. These, presumably, would determine her immediate future. Somehow she had placed herself in Lord Alton's hands.

Georgiana stifled a despondent sigh. She hoped she looked more confident than she felt.

On the floor above, Bella, Lady Winsmere, was in the middle of her toilette, preparatory to attending the theatre. A knock on the door of her boudoir was followed by a whispered conference between her dresser, Hills, and her butler, Johnson.

Distracted from the delicate task of improving on nature, Bella frowned. "What is it, Hills?"

Her black-garbed dresser produced a folded parchment, inscribed to herself in her brother's unmistakable scrawl. Intrigued, Bella immediately laid down her haresfoot. Bits of red wax scattered in all directions as she broke open the seal.

Five short minutes later, she was crossing her front hall in a froth of lacy peignoir, rendered barely respectable by a silk wrapper. Johnson, having anticipated her impetuous descent, stood ready to open the drawing-room door for her.

As the door shut, bringing her guest to her feet, Bella's bright blue eyes, very like her brother's, surveyed her unexpected visitor.

Unconsciously clutching her reticule, once again in a tell-tale grip, Georgiana beheld an enchanting vision, fashionably slender and no taller than she herself was.

But there the resemblance ended. Lady Winsmere was dark-haired, her fine skin was alabaster-white. Her blue eyes Georgiana had seen before. And the elegance of her lacy gown made Georgiana feel awkward and abominably young.

For her part, Bella saw a girl on the threshold of womanhood. Her innocence shone beacon-clear. She was all honey and cream, from the top of her curls, tinged with the sun's kiss, to her delicately tinted complexion. Her golden eyes contained a quality of unusual candour. And she had no more inches than Bella herself. Bella's face brightened. A little sigh escaped her. With a generous and genuine smile, she floated forward, both hands outstretched to capture Georgiana's cold fingers in a warm clasp.

"My dear! So you are Georgiana Hartley! Dominic has written me all about you. You poor dear! What a dreadful thing to happen, and you newly returned to England. You must let me help you."

At Georgiana's murmured, "My lady," Bella broke her stride. But when Georgiana attempted to curtsy, Bella held on tightly to her hands, preventing it.

"No, no, my dear. You're among friends here. You must call me Bella, and I hope you won't think me terribly forward if I call you Georgiana." She tilted her small head to one side, blue eyes twinkling.

Georgiana found her engaging manners difficult to resist. "Why, of course not, my... Bella. But truly, I feel as if I'm imposing dreadfully upon you."

"Oh, pooh!" Bella pulled a face. "I'm always bored; there's so little to do in London these days. I'm positively thrilled Dominic thought to send you to me!

Why—'' she paused, struck by a wayward thought ''—just think. If you'd grown up at the Place, we would have been neighbours.'' Bella waved Georgiana to the chaise and sank to the white damask beside her. ''So, you see, there's no need for you to feel at all bothered about staying with me.''

Georgiana's head reeled. ''Oh! But I wouldn't dream of imposing—''

''Not at all! It's the very thing. You have nowhere to go and we have plenty of room.'' Bella gazed intently at Georgiana. ''Truly, it's no trouble at all.''

''But—''

Bella shook her head. ''No buts. Just consider it as doing me a favour. We'll have such fun. I'll take you about and introduce you to all the right people.''

Despite a sudden tug of impetuosity, urging acceptance of the exciting offer, Georgiana, grappling with the flow of Bella's burgeoning plans, felt constrained to protest. ''But my la... Bella. I don't think Lord Alton can have properly explained. I need to find a post as a companion.''

Recalling the specific instructions contained in her brother's letter, Bella assured Georgiana that he had, indeed, explained fully. ''But my dear, in order to find the right post for you, particularly considering your age, you must first become established in society.''

Bella watched the frown gathering in Georgiana's fine eyes. Before her guest could raise any further objection, she raised one slim, restraining hand. ''Now before you start arguing—and I do so hate people who must forever be sniping and finding fault—I must tell you that you will be doing me the biggest favour imaginable in allowing me to help you. You can have no idea how boring it is to pass the Season with no real purpose. The Little Season is coming up in a few weeks. I implore you to relieve my frustrations and stay with me and allow me to present you. Surely that's not too much to ask?'' Bella's big blue eyes pleaded eloquently.

Bemused by the sudden twist the situation seemed to have taken, with Lady Winsmere now begging the favour of her company, and feeling too drained by the day's events to fight a fate so apparently desirable, Georgiana found herself weakly acquiescing. ''If it's really not too much trouble... Just until I can find a position.''

''Splendid!'' Bella grinned in delight. ''Now the first thing we must do is get you settled in a bedchamber. A hot bath is just what you need. Always so soothing after travelling.''

With a magic wave of one small bejewelled hand, Bella took charge. In short order, Georgiana, her luggage, Cruickshank, dinner on a tray and a large tub together with steaming hot water to fill it had been conveyed to the best guest chamber on the floor above.

An hour later, after she had closed the door of Georgiana's room behind her, having seen her young guest settled in bed, Bella Winsmere's face took on a pensive frown. Slowly she descended the stairs, so deep in thought that she was halfway across the hall towards the front door before she recalled her intended destination. Swinging about, she turned her steps towards the library at the back of the house.

At the sound of the door opening, Lord Winsmere

looked up from the pile of documents he was working on. His lean face lit with a smile of great warmth. He laid aside his pen to reach out a welcoming arm to his wife.

With a quick smile, Bella went to him, returning his embrace and dropping a quick kiss on his greying hair.

"I thought you were bound for Drury Lane tonight?" Lord Winsmere was more than twenty years older than his beautiful wife. His staid, sometimes regal demeanour contrasted sharply with her effervescent charm. Many had wondered why, from among her myraid suitors, Bella Ridgeley had chosen to bestow her dainty hand on a man almost old enough to be her father. But over the years society had been forced to accept the fact that the beautiful Bella was sincerely and most earnestly in love with her eminently respectable lord.

"I was, but we have an unexpected guest."

"Oh?"

His lordship pushed his papers aside, consigning them to the morrow. If his Bella had sought him out, then she had some problem to discuss. He rose and, Bella's hand still in his, led her to the two armchairs stationed before the fireplace.

Bella sat, chewing the tip of one rosy finger, a habit when thinking profoundly.

Smiling, Lord Winsmere seated himself opposite her and waited for her to begin.

"It's really most intriguing."

Inured to his spouse's methods of explanation, Lord Winsmere made no response.

Eventually Bella gathered her wandering mind and

embarked on her story. "Dominic's sent a girl to stay."

At that, Lord Winsmere's brows rose sharply. But the knowledge that, despite his apparent lack of moral concern, Dominic Ridgeley had never permitted the slightest breath of scandal to touch his sister's fair name held him silent.

"She's a would-have-been-neighbour. Her name's Georgiana Hartley. Her father was a painter, one James Hartley. He died in Italy some months ago and Georgiana was left to her uncle's care. Most unfortunately, her uncle, who lived at the Place—you know, it's that funny estate that was made by selling off a piece of Candlewick—well, he died too. Just before her father, only she didn't know that, being in Italy. The long and the short of it is, Georgiana travelled all the way from Italy, only to find her uncle dead and her cousin Charles in charge. It only needs to add that Charles is an out-and-out bounder and you have the picture." Bella spread her hands and glanced at her husband.

"How did Dominic come to be involved?"

"It seems Georgiana was forced to flee the Place at dawn this morning. She doesn't know anyone—no one at all. She asked at the Three Bells, thinking to find a sympathetic lady in residence at a neighbouring estate. Of course, the Tadlows sent her to Candlewick. You know how all our people are about Dominic."

Lord Winsmere nodded sagely, a thin smile hovering about his lips at the thought of the godlike status his far from godly brother-in-law enjoyed on his own lands.

"Well, she went to the Hall and met Duckett. And then Dominic came and persuaded her to tell him all." Bella suddenly broke off. "Oh—are you imagining she must be some encroaching mushroom?" Her ladyship leant forward slightly and fixed her big eyes on her husband. "Truly, Arthur, it is not so. She's the most engaging little thing. So innocent and green and so…so trusting."

Lord Winsmere's fine brows rose slightly.

Abruptly Bella dropped to her knees, draping her silk-clad arms over her husband's knees. She smiled, impish and seductive all at once. "Please, Arthur. Please say she may stay. You know how bored I am. She's perfectly presentable, I give you my word. I could take her about and present her to the *ton*… Oh— I'd have such fun! The balls and parties are so tame, if one's not part of the game. Please, my love. Say she may stay."

Lord Winsmere smiled down into his wife's up-turned face while his mind canvassed the possibilities presented by her unknown guest. Their son and only child was ensconced in the country, happily growing out of short coats. Jonathon's constitution was not sickly but did not cope well with the stale air of the capital. But his own work necessitated his presence in London. Bella, torn between the two men in her life, had chosen to remain by his side. As he doubted he could live without her, he would willingly make any sacrifice to alleviate the boredom he knew she found in the predictable rounds of tonnish entertainment. But an unknown girl? And, if he knew his Bella, she meant to fire the chit off with all flags flying. Not that the expense worried him. But was the girl truly as innocent as Bella, herself not much more experienced for all her matronliness, believed?

He reached out a finger to trace the graceful curve of his wife's brow. Impulsively, she caught his hand and kissed it, then continued to hold it in a warm clasp, her eyes on his face.

"You needn't worry about the cost. Dominic said to charge everything to him."

"Did he, indeed? How very magnanimous, to be sure." Lord Winsmere's mobile lips twitched. Dominic Ridgeley had inherited a fortune of sizeable proportions and could easily afford to underwrite the launching of an unknown damsel into the *ton*. The question that exercised Lord Winsmere's mind was *why* his hedonistic brother-in-law should wish to do such a peculiar thing.

"I think perhaps I should meet this paragon before I allow you to take her under your wing."

Bella's eyes grew round. "Are you thinking she is one of Dominic's paramours? I must admit, I did, too, at first. Well, whoever would imagine him having any contact with an innocent young girl? But I assure you she's just what Dominic says—young and innocent and...and hopelessly lost. I dare say she'll have no idea how to go on, having lived in Italy all this time."

Lord Winsmere's face remained impassive. The possibility that his brother-in-law had sent Bella a lady needing help to cover some lapse of acceptable conduct had certainly occurred, only to be immediately dismissed. Few knew better than himself that, despite Viscount Alton's reputation as a well heeled, insidiously charming and potentially dangerous rake, underneath, Dominic Ridgeley adhered most assiduously to a code of conduct that, if it were more widely recognised, would see him hailed as a pillar of society. But it was the veneer society saw—a façade erected to hide the boredom of a man who had never had to exert himself to win any prize. Born with the proverbial silver spoon tightly clamped between his jaws, and with the compounding assets of a handsome face and an athletic frame, there was little Dominic Ridgeley needed in life. And what he did want came easily. Society adored him. His well born mistresses fell at his feet. With ready charm, Dominic moved through it all, and with the years his boredom grew.

"What, exactly, did Dominic say?"

Bella smiled and shifted to sit at his feet, her hand still holding his, her shining blue eyes turned lovingly on him. "Well..."

Fifteen minutes later, Lord Winsmere felt he was in possession of all the salient facts. The only puzzle remaining was his brother-in-law's motives. A whimsical start? Dominic was hardly in his dotage. Nevertheless, young and girlish and innocent was assuredly not his style. The spectre of Elaine, Lady Changley drifted into Lord Winsmere's mind. Involuntarily, his face assumed an expression of distaste. Lady Changley was definitely not young and girlish, and not by the remotest stretch of the most pliable imagination could she be described as innocent.

Bella saw the disapprobation in her husband's face. Her own face fell. "You don't like the idea?"

Recalled, Lord Winsmere smiled and confessed, "I

was thinking of something else.'' At his wife's fond smile, he continued, ''If the girl is all you and Dominic seem to think, I have no objections to your taking her under your wing. Aside from anything else, she'll have to be terribly innocent to swallow this yarn of yours about the way to securing a position being to make a splash in society.''

Bella met his sceptical look with a bright grin. ''Oh, I'll manage it—you'll see.''

Five minutes later Lord Winsmere returned to his desk to tidy his papers away for the night. The memory of Bella's bright eyes remained with him. She was more animated than she had been in months. Perhaps Dominic's damsel in distress was an angel in disguise. He smiled fondly. All in all, he was looking forward to meeting his wife's protégée.

THE SHARP CALL of the orange sellers woke Georgiana. Bemused, she stared about her, then remembered where she was and how she came to be there. Despite the evidence of her eyes, reality retained the aura of a dream. She was lying propped in her pillows, still wondering, when Cruickshank came bustling through the door with her early morning chocolate.

Georgiana waited silently for her maid's comment. No one could size up an establishment faster or more accurately than Cruickshank.

No sniffs were forthcoming. Not even a snort.

As she accepted the tray across her knees, Georgiana was taken aback to hear the dour maid humming.

Catching sight of her mistress's startled look, Cruickshank smiled. ''A right proper place they keep here, Miss Georgie. No need to teach them anything. Mrs Biggins, the housekeeper, is a tight old bird, but fair, mark my words. Runs the place just as she should. And Johnson—he's the butler—and her ladyship's dresser, Hills, are everything they ought to be. A relief, it is, after the Place.''

"So you're comfortable here?"

At the wardrobe, Cruickshank nodded emphatically. She drew out a violet morning gown trimmed with fine lace and laid it ready across a chair, then went to search for the accessories.

Georgiana sipped her chocolate. As the sweet warmth slid down her throat and heat seeped through her body, she sighed. So wonderful—to have real chocolate again. She closed her eyes and was immediately back on the terrace at Ravello, her father opposite, across the breakfast-table. Abruptly she opened her eyes, blinking rapidly. Enough of that! She had shed all the tears she possessed long ago. Her father had wanted her to get on with her life. He had warned her not to grieve for him. He had had a good life, so he had said, and wanted his daughter to have the same. That was why she was to return to England and the bosom of her family. Some bosom Charles had turned out to be. At the thought, Georgiana wriggled her toes. The idea of Charles scouring the countryside for her, only to return, dusty and beaten, to the damp and musty Place, brought a glow of satisfaction to her honey-gold eyes. Serve him right.

"How long are we staying here?"

Cruickshank came to draw back the covers. Georgiana slid from the bed, busying herself with washing and dressing while she considered how best to answer. She had not discussed her plan to get a position with either of her servants, sure they would veto the idea as soon as they heard it. Come what may, she was determined to keep them with her. They were all that remained of her parents' happy household.

So, standing patiently as Cruickshank laced her gown, she answered airily, "I'll have to discuss the matter with Lady Wins... Bella. She seems to wish us to stay for a while."

Cruickshank snorted. "So I gathered. Still, she seems a real lady; none of your hoity-toity airs about that one."

Georgiana grinned, remembering Bella's fussing the night before. It had been a long time since anyone other than Cruickshank had fussed over her.

After Cruickshank had settled her curls in a knot on the top of her head, Georgiana tentatively made her way downstairs. Johnson found her in the front hall and, gracious as ever, directed her to the breakfast parlour overlooking the rear gardens.

"There you are, my dear!"

Georgiana had the feeling Bella had been waiting for her to appear. Her hostess surged across the Turkey carpet in a cloud of fine-figured muslin. Georgiana returned her smile.

"Are you sure you've recovered from your ordeal?"

Georgiana flushed slightly and nodded. A man, somewhat older than Bella, had risen from the table to watch them, an affectionate smile on his thin lips.

She felt forced to disclaim, "It was hardly an ordeal, ma'am."

"*Ma'am?* I thought I told you to call me Bella." Bella smiled mischievously. "And of course it was an ordeal. Fleeing from horrible Charles was always an ordeal."

Georgiana stopped and stared. "You know Charles?"

Bella's big blue eyes opened wide. "But of course. Didn't I mention it last night?"

When Georgiana shook her head, Bella tucked her arm in hers and drew her guest to the table.

"But we were neighbours; you know that. Of course, Charles came over to play sometimes. But he never got on with Dominic and the other boys, mainly because he was younger and always tried to show off. He used to tease me unmercifully. At least, he did if Dominic wasn't around. So, you see, I know just what it feels like to run away from your cousin Charles. And I can't think he's improved with age."

Standing by the chair beside her new friend, Georgiana shook her head. "I expect you're right." She looked expectantly at the man. He smiled and bowed slightly.

"Permit me to introduce myself, my dear. I'm afraid, if we wait for Bella to remember my existence, we might not be introduced until dinner."

"Oh, fustian!" said Bella, catching his hand and giving it a little shake. "My dear Georgiana, allow me to present my husband, Arthur."

Georgiana dropped a demure curtsy, hiding her surprise. She had not thought about Bella's husband at all, but would never have imagined the youthful Bella married to a man so much older. As she straightened, her eyes met his, grey and kindly, and she had the feeling of being read like a book. But then he smiled, such a sweet smile, and suddenly it no longer seemed so odd that Bella should be his wife.

"Miss Hartley. Might I say how pleased we are to welcome you to our home?"

Georgiana murmured her thanks.

Over breakfast, Lord Winsmere made little comment, but contented himself with listening as Bella and she discussed feminine interests.

"I see you are out of blacks," said Bella. "So fortunate."

Georgiana hesitated, then explained, "Actually, it's only four months since my father died, but he made me promise that I wouldn't go into mourning for him. But—" she shrugged slightly "—I thought greys and lilacs were a reasonable compromise."

Bella's candid gaze assessed her dispassionately. "I must say, if your father was a painter, I can understand why he was so insistent you stay out of black. With your skin, it would certainly not suit."

Georgiana grinned. "I'm not certain that wasn't at the back of his mind when he made his request."

As she turned her attention to her piece of toast, she was conscious of his lordship's grey eyes resting on her with approval.

In fact, Lord Winsmere was pleased to approve of his wife's prospective protégée. Georgiana Hartley, he decided, was a neat little thing. His eye had seen too many beauties to class her as one, but her features were pure and, with the gloss of a little animation, presently lacking, she could lay claim to the appellation of attractive with ease. She was petite, but her figure was full and delicately curved, not unlike Bella's curvaceous form. And, more important than any other quality, the girl from Italy was not missish. Which was just as well, if she was to deal with his forthright Bella. All in all, Bella's assessment had been accurate. Miss Georgiana Hartley was eminently acceptable.

When the ladies left him to his coffee and the morning's news-sheet, he spent some time in a blank study of the parlour door. Undoubtedly, Dominic had done right in sending Georgiana to Winsmere House. There was little hope such an attractive miss could find decent employment without subjecting herself to dangers he, for one, did not wish to contemplate. Dominic's plan to introduce her into society was a wise one. Thus far, the young lady seemed of a most amenable disposition. And, although not highly born, her lineage was not beneath consideration. He had checked for himself in the Register of Landowners. The Hartleys had been an unremarkable family for generations, but they were nevertheless of good stock. She would make some young squire an unexceptionable wife.

However, more importantly from his point of view, her presence would ease Bella's boredom. His darling had talked non-stop since rising this morning, a sure sign of happiness.

With a smile at his own susceptibilities, Lord Winsmere rose and, taking up his unread news-sheet, retired to the library. For once, Dominic seemed to have bestirred himself for purely philanthropic reasons. His scheme was in the girl's best interests and would keep Bella amused. There was no reason to interfere. Bella could entangle herself in the chit's life to her heart's content. Neither would take any ill. As his shrewd brain began to sort through the potential ramifications of his brother-in-law's plan, Lord Winsmere's brows rose. His lips curved slightly. In the end, who knew what might come of it?

"Now, GEORGIE, promise me you won't put me to the blush," said Bella, firmly drawing on her gloves as the carriage drew to a standstill. "I couldn't endure it in front of Fancon. The woman's a terror. Lord only knows what damage she could do to your chances if she heard you asking about the price of a gown."

Georgiana blushed. The slight frown on her friend's face told her Bella was not yet convinced she had won their last battle. Georgiana simply couldn't see the necessity for new gowns for herself. Surely it was not a requirement for a companion to be fashionably dressed? But Bella had been adamant.

"Just wait until you *are* a companion before you start dressing like a dowd."

At Georgiana's instinctive and forlorn glance at her demure grey gown, Bella had been instantly contrite. "Oh, I don't mean that! Your gowns are perfectly acceptable, you know they are. It's just that for going out into society you need more…well, more society clothes. This is London, after all."

Finally, worn down by Bella's arguments, strengthened by the defection of Cruickshank, who had deciphered enough of their conversation to give her a hard stare, Georgiana had consented to accompany Bella to the salon of the modiste known as Fancon. It was her third day in London, and she was beginning to feel at home in the large mansion on Green Street. Lord Winsmere was all that was kind. And Bella, of course, was Bella. Georgiana was overwhelmed by their kindness. But not so overwhelmed that she would consent to Bella's buying her new gowns.

"If I must have new gowns to go about and become known, then of course I'll pay for them." Her calm statement had caused Bella to look at her in concern.

"But, my dear Georgie, gowns, you know...well, they're not all that... I mean to say..." The garrulous Bella had flustered to a halt.

The drift of her thoughts had reached Georgiana. "Oh! Did you think I have no money?"

Bella's eyes widened. "Well, I thought you might not be exactly flush, what with your trip and expecting your uncle to be there to help at the end of it."

Georgiana smiled affectionately. They had thought her a pauper but had still wanted to help. She knew enough of the world to appreciate such sentiments. "Not a bit of it. My father left me reasonably well to do—or at least, that's how my Italian solicitors described it. I don't know what exactly that means, but I have funds deposited here on which I may draw."

To her relief, Lord Winsmere had insisted on accompanying her to the bank her father had patronised. She had little doubt it was his lordship's standing that had resulted in such prompt and polite service. There had been no difficulty in establishing her *bona fides* through papers she had carried from Italy.

While waiting for the carriage to stop rocking, Georgiana glanced at Bella's profile. They had taken to each other as if each were the sister the other had never had. "Only two gowns, mind."

Bella turned, her eyes narrowing. "Two *day* gowns *and* an evening gown." She stared uncompromisingly at Georgiana.

With a wry grimace, Georgiana acquiesced. "All right. *And* an evening gown. But nothing too elaborate," she added, as the groom opened the door.

Together they entered the discreet establishment of Fancon. A woman dressed in severe black glided forward to greet them. Her black hair was pulled back and, it appeared to Georgiana, forcibly restrained in a tight bun. Black eyes, like gimlets, sharp and shuttered, assessed her. This, she soon learned, was the great Fancon herself. Imbued with suitable awe, Georgiana noted a certain restraint in the woman's manner and was careful to give no cause for offence.

Half an hour passed in the most pleasant of occupations. Fancon had numerous gowns to choose from. Georgiana tried on a great many. There were fabrics, too, which could be fashioned to any style she wished. Georgiana found Bella's interest infectious. And she could not resist the temptation to indulge in Fancon's elegant creations. However, true to her word, she chose only two day dresses, one in softest lilac, the other a deep mauve. Both suited her well, their high waists outlining her youthful figure. She feared that Fancon would be irritated by her meagre order, particularly after the woman had been so insistent she try on such a great number of gowns. Yet nothing but the most complete equanimity showed on the modiste's stern face.

Much discussion went into the creation of an evening gown. The styles which favoured her were easy enough to decide. Yet there was nothing suitable made up.

"Your colouring, Miss Hartley, is less pale than the norm. It is no matter. We will decide on the fabric, and I will have my seamstresses work up the gown by tomorrow." With a calm wave of her hand, Fancon summoned her underlings. They brought bolts of fine cloth, in mauves and lilacs. While Georgiana stood, wreathed in fabric, Bella and Fancon studied her critically. Georgiana, too, watched proceedings in the mirror.

"It must show you off to your greatest advantage," declared Bella.

Georgiana seriously doubted that companions were chosen for the picture they made in the ballroom.

Fancon turned and murmured a command. A minute later, a fresh selection of materials arrived. Sea-green gauze, spangled and shimmering, was draped around Georgiana. The assistant stood back, and Georgiana raised her eyes to the mirror. She gasped. Was the slim, slender mermaid she saw there really herself? The green brought out the lights in her hair and eyes, and emphasised the creaminess of her skin. She stood and stared. Then, slowly, she shook her head sadly.

"Not yet. I'm still in mourning, remember?"

Another murmur from Fancon saw a deep topaz silk

replace the sea-green gauze. Again, Georgiana stared. This time she looked almost as worldly as Bella. The silk added an air of allure, of mystery. She looked...enticing. But again she refused.

Apparently resigned to using the purplish hues, Fancon next produced a pale amethyst silk. Georgiana regarded it critically. The colour suited her well enough, making her appear soft and feminine. But the amethyst simply did not do for her what the previous two shades had. In this, she simply looked passably pretty. She turned and looked longingly at the topaz and the sea-green, lying discarded beside her. Still, she couldn't allow herself to be distracted from her purpose. Doubtless ladies who needed companions would approve of the amethyst silk.

"Yes. I'll take this fabric. And the pattern we agreed on."

Georgiana turned in time to catch the look that passed between Bella and Fancon. It was a look that bespoke an understanding, but she got no further clue to assist in its interpretation.

While they waited for the two day dresses to be packed, Georgiana reflected that Madame Fancon had not seemed anywhere near as dragon-like as Bella had led her to believe.

Settled in the barouche, with Fancon's boxes on the opposite seat, Bella leant forward and spoke to her coachman. "Once around the park for luck. Then back to Green Street."

The carriage moved off. Georgiana sat quietly, wondering a little at the revelations of the sumptuous sea-green and topaz silks. Could she really appear like that? Her? Little Georgiana?

Bella also sat quietly, smugly satisfied with the outcome of her scheming. She had been to see Fancon the day before, while Arthur had taken Georgiana to see her banker. The modiste knew her well; she was, after all, one of her best customers. Fancon had been most helpful, particularly after she had let fall the information that a certain peer was most desirous that Georgiana should be well presented, and hence money was no option. Dominic could hardly take exception to that. Bella grinned. She had little doubt Fancon would guess who the gentleman was. Who other than her brother would be likely to leave a young girl in her care?

"Bella, there's been some mistake. We have six boxes instead of two."

Georgiana's words reclaimed Bella's attention. She turned and found Georgiana frowning at the offending extra boxes. "No, no," said Bella. "It's all right. I bought some gowns, too. I couldn't resist after seeing you in them, and we're much of a size." All of which, Bella told her conscience, was perfectly true.

Georgiana raised her brows but said no more.

Bella returned to her absent-minded contemplation of the pavements. Undoubtedly she'd have to argue hard and fast to get Georgiana to accept the gowns she had bought. But none of them were in colours she, so much darker of hair and fairer of skin, could wear. The sea-green gauze and topaz silk would look hideous on her. They were to be delivered tomorrow, along with the amethyst silk. Surely Georgie would see what a waste it would be simply to throw them away?

As the barouche turned into the park, Bella sat up straighter. She looked across at Georgiana, sitting quietly beside her. Demure she might look, but Georgiana Hartley had a mind of her own. Stubborn to a fault, she was sure to balk at accepting what she would probably class as charity. Still, Bella was perfectly certain Dominic would have wanted her to spend his money as she had. She was sure he would approve, when he saw Georgiana in the topaz silk. And, after all, Georgiana should be grateful enough to want to please her brother. She made a mental note to remember Dominic, if she had need of further ammunition to force Georgiana to accept the gowns.

"IT'S MY 'at home' this afternoon." Bella came bustling into the downstairs parlour.

Georgiana looked up from the magazine she was idly leafing through. She felt supremely confident this morning, arrayed in one of her new gowns, a soft bluey lilac cambric. Bella's elegance seemed less daunting now. She caught Bella's eye as it rested pensively upon her. Georgiana raised one fine brow in invitation.

"About the story we should tell about you. To account for your being here."

"What about the truth?" asked Georgiana, not quite sure what her friend meant.

"Well, yes. The truth, of course. But...do you think the whole truth's wise?"

When Georgiana looked her confusion, Bella continued, "You see, if you tell about how you met Dominic, people might get the wrong idea. To support your story, you'd have to explain about Charles. And, my dear, if you're looking for a position, the last person you would want to claim kinship with is Charles."

Bella had put a great deal of thought into how best to broach this most delicate of subjects. Now she watched Georgiana carefully to see how the younger girl took her suggestion. Georgiana was frowning, her thoughts clouding her big eyes.

"You mean...?"

"What I mean," said Bella, candid to a fault, "is that Charles is hardly a gold-plated reference. But there's really no need to mention him at all. All we have to do is decide how you came to stay with me. I think the most sensible thing to say is that we had met, years ago, at Candlewick, before you went to Italy. We became such friends that we've been corresponding ever since. Naturally, when you returned to England and found your uncle dead, you came back to London to stay with me. That should be believable enough, don't you think?" When Georgiana made no reply, Bella pressed her final argument. "And you wouldn't want to put Dominic in a difficult position, would you?"

Put Lord Alton in a difficult position? For a minute, Georgiana could make no sense of her friend's allusion. Then the Fragonard materialised in her mind's eye...and the image of his lordship as she had last seen him, a vision that had not yet faded from her memory.

"Oh."

Of course. Georgiana gave herself a mental shake. She wasn't so innocent that she couldn't follow Bella's drift. While her visit with Lord Alton had been utterly without consequence, society, if it heard of it, might view it otherwise. She raised her gaze to Bella's face. "I'll do whatever you think best. I wouldn't want to cause your brother any trouble."

Bella grinned, entirely satisfied.

"Oh, and one last thing. It will be better, at this stage, if we make no mention of your wish for a position. Such things are better negotiated after you're known."

Georgiana nodded her acceptance, Lord Alton's assurance that his sister knew what was best echoing in her mind.

That afternoon three matrons came to tea, bringing with them a gaggle of unmarried daughters. Georgiana did not succeed in fixing which young ladies belonged to which mama. In the end, it made little difference. To a woman, they accepted Bella's charmingly phrased explanation of her presence. Quick eyes surveyed the latest entrant in the marriage game. The ladies found no reason not to be gracious. Miss Hartley was no beauty.

Miss Hartley had difficulty subduing her mirth. They were really so blatant in their pursuit of well heeled and preferably titled son-in-laws.

To her surprise, Georgiana found conversing with the younger ladies almost beyond her. Used to dealing with the gracious conversation of the Italian aristocracy, among whom she had spent much of her life, used to the subtle ebb and flow of polished discourse, she found it hard to relate to the titters and smirks and girlish giggles of the four very proper English maids. However, she did not make the mistake of attempting to join the matrons. Stoically, she bore her ordeal as best she could.

Bella, watching her, was pleased by her confidence and innate poise. Innocent and trusting Georgiana might be, but she was no mindless ninny, scared to open her mouth in company. Her manners were assured, unusually so for a girl of her age.

When the guests had departed, Bella grimaced at Georgiana. "Witless, aren't they?" She smiled at Georgiana's emphatic nod. "They're not all like that, of course. Still, there are a lot of unbelievably silly girls about." Bella paused, considering her words. "Just as well, I suppose. There are an awful lot of silly men, too."

They shared a grin of complete understanding.

Five minutes later, just as they had settled comfortably to their embroidery, Johnson entered. "Lady Winterspoon, m'lady."

Bella rose. Georgiana was disconcerted to see perturbation in her friend's blue eyes. Then Lady Winterspoon was in the room.

"Bella! Haven't seen you in ages! Where've you been hiding yourself?"

Lady Winterspoon's trenchant accents reverberated through the room. Bella suffered a hug and a hearty kiss and, looking slightly shaken, settled her ageing guest in an armchair. Lady Winterspoon was, Georgiana guessed, quite old enough to be Bella's mother. Who was she?

"Amelia, I'd like you to meet Georgiana Hartley. She's an old friend of mine from the country. Georgiana, this is my sister-in-law."

Georgiana met the clear grey gaze and found herself smiling warmly in response. Lord Winsmere's sister, of course.

"Hartley, hmm? Well, I probably knew your father, if he's the one I'm thinking of. Painter fellow. Jimmy? James? Married Lorien Putledge."

Georgiana nodded, eager to hear more of her parents. She had never before met anyone who had known them in their younger days.

Reading her interest in her eyes, Lady Winterspoon waved one hand in a negative gesture. "No, my dear. I can't tell you much about them; I didn't know them that well. I take it they've passed on?"

Disappointed, Georgiana nodded. Bella promptly stepped in with their agreed explanation for her presence in Green Street. Lady Winterspoon's shrewd eyes remained on Georgiana throughout Bella's speech. Whether she accepted the story, neither young woman felt qualified to say.

"Hmph!" was all the response she made.

After a moment of silence, during which both Bella and Georgiana racked their brains to think of something to say, Lady Winterspoon commented, "Dare say you'll make quite a hit. Not just in the common way. In the circumstances, not a bad thing to be."

Georgiana decided that was meant as a compliment. She smiled.

Lady Winterspoon's lips twitched. She turned purposefully to Bella. "But that's not why I came. Bella, you've got to have a word with that brother of yours. Elaine Changley's becoming entirely too much, with her airs and graces and subtle suggestions she'll be the next Viscountess Alton.'' Lady Winterspoon snorted.

Bella frowned and bit her lip. She cast a slightly scandalised look Georgiana's way. But Georgiana was too engrossed in Lady Winterspoon's disclosures to notice.

''If I thought there was any chance of it coming to pass, I'd insist Arthur break the connection. Elaine Changley! Why, she's...'' Amelia Winterspoon became aware of Georgiana's clear hazel gaze. She broke off. ''Well, you know what I mean,'' she amended, glaring at Bella.

Relieved at the opportune halt to her sister-in-law's tirade, Bella gracefully seated herself on the sofa. ''Amelia, you know I have no influence whatever with Dominic.''

''Pshaw! You'd have influence enough if you chose to use it!''

Bella coloured slightly. ''I assure you I share your concern about Lady Changley, but mentioning her to Dominic is entirely beyond me.''

''Well, Elaine Changley is beyond the pale! Just bear that in mind. You'll look no-how if you wake up one morning to find her your sister-in-law.''

Lady Winterspoon heaved herself up. ''Must go. Just wanted to let you know things need a bit of push from you.'' She fixed her grey gaze firmly on Bella.

Despite her annoyance, Bella could not help grinning back. She rose.

Lady Winterspoon paused to nod to Georgiana.

"I'll see you at Almack's, my dear." She turned to Bella. "I'll get Emily to send you vouchers."

"Thank you," said Bella, taken aback. She had forgotten Amelia had the ear of several of the patronesses of Almack's. She went out with Lady Winterspoon.

Minutes later, returning to the back parlour, Bella found Georgiana staring into space. She shut the door with a click, jolting her guest to attention. "Well!" she said, with determined brightness. "Vouchers for Almack's without even having to charm one of the patronesses. We'll go just as soon as Lady Cowper sends them."

"Yes, of course," said Georgiana. But it was plain to Bella that her friend was absorbed in distant thoughts...thoughts she made no move to share.

CHAPTER THREE

BELLA HEARD the door of her boudoir open and shut, but, absorbed in brushing the haresfoot delicately over her cheekbones, she did not turn around. In her mirror, she saw Hills obediently drop a curtsy and leave. Finally, satisfied with her appearance, she swung about. "Arthur— Oh! Dominic!"

She was out of her chair and across the room on the word.

Half laughing, half frowning, Dominic held her off. "No! Compose yourself, you hoyden. What will staid Arthur think? And I can't have you ruining my cravat as you did the last time."

So Bella had to make do with clasping his hands. "Oh, thank you, dearest Dominic, for sending Georgie to me! We're having such a wonderful time!" She drew him down to plant a sisterly kiss on one lean cheek.

Dominic suffered the embrace, using the moment to cast a knowledgeable eye over his sister. "So you and Miss Hartley have hit it off?"

"Famously!" Bella sat with a swirl of her satin skirts. "But whoever would have thought you'd...?" She broke off, biting her lip.

Dominic's black brows rose. There was a disconcerting glint in his eye, but his voice was gentle when he softly prompted, "I'd...?"

Bella flushed and turned back to her dressing-table, skirts rustling, and busied herself with a pot of rouge. She refused to meet his eye. "That you'd behave so uncommonly sensible, if you must know. From everything I've heard, it must be the first time in weeks!"

"Weeks?" The arrogant black brows rose again. Dominic considered the point for all of ten seconds. "Feels more like years."

Bella, surprised by his weary tone, chanced a glance at him in the mirror. He raised his head at that moment, and she was caught in his chilly blue gaze. "That aside, dear sister mine, you would be well advised not to listen to gossip—about myself, or anyone else, for that matter."

Eyes wide, Bella knew better than to remonstrate. Dominic was ten years her senior and had been the strictest of guardians in the years preceding her marriage. She half expected some more pointed rebuke, but he turned aside, a far-away look settling over his handsome face. To her, that pensive look was far more frightening than Amelia's bluster. Surely he wasn't serious about Elaine Changley?

She waited, but he made no further remark. Finally she asked, "Will you stay for dinner?"

He looked up.

Bella fidgeted with her hairbrush. "Georgie and I are going on to Almack's later, so you needn't fear you'll have to kick your heels in my drawing-room."

Her tone brought a smile to her brother's face, dispelling the withdrawn look which had so concerned her. Still, she was sure he would refuse.

Instead, after a moment's hesitation, she heard him murmur, "Why not?"

As it seemed a purely rhetorical question, Bella made no attempt to answer it.

Dominic shrugged, then turned his sweetest smile full on her. "Since you ask, dear sister, I'll stay. It might be interesting to meet my...*your* protégée."

As Bella reached for the bell-pull to summon Hills, Dominic surveyed a nearby chair through his quizzing-glass. Reassured, he carefully disposed his long limbs in the delicate piece.

"So how came you to get vouchers for the Marriage Mart so soon?"

"Well! It was the most fortunate thing!" Bella seized on the question to lead the conversation on to lighter ground, hoping her intrusion into her brother's private life would be the quicker forgotten. Dominic had never allowed her any speculation on the possible candidates for the position of Viscountess Alton. And she had long ago learned that any mention of his mistresses, past, present or potential, was sure to invite one of his more painful set-downs. Still, after Amelia's warning, and her own unfortunate gaffe, she had felt justified in at least trying to broach the subject.

While Hills informed Johnson of the necessity of setting an extra place and returned to twist her hair into an elegant knot, Bella described the recent history of Georgiana Hartley. As she prattled, she watched her brother's face in the mirror. He sat quietly studying his nails, paying scant attention to her words. His lack of interest worried her. She had hardly expected him to be seriously concerned with Georgiana. After all, he had barely met her and she was certainly not the sort of woman to hold his attention. But his introspection was unusual and disquieting, suggesting as it did the existence of some weightier matter dragging on his mind. Like matrimony. But surely, *surely,* he wouldn't choose Elaine Changley?

It was with relief that Bella finally rose from her dressing-table. What with the distraction of Dominic's arrival, the hour was well advanced. He accompanied her down the wide staircase and entered the drawing-room by her side.

Georgiana was talking to Arthur. Warned by his face that someone unexpected had entered, she turned and was trapped, once again without warning, in the blue of Lord Alton's eyes.

The same eyes that haunted her dreams.

For Georgiana, it was a definite case of *déjà vu.* Her breathing stopped; her heart contracted. Her gaze was oddly restricted, the rest of the room fading away, leaving one strong face to impress itself on her mind. Her stare widened to take in his immaculate evening clothes, and the way his dark hair sat in elegant waves about his head. A cornflower-blue sapphire winked in his cravat, its colour no more intense than his eyes.

Then, thankfully, Arthur moved forward to greet his guest.

The worst was past. Georgiana's natural poise reasserted itself and she could function again. Then Lord Alton turned to take her hand. His clasp was cool and gentle. He smiled and bowed elegantly.

"Miss Hartley. So we meet again. I do hope Bella hasn't been tiring you out with her gadding."

To Georgiana's intense chagrin, her tongue promptly tied itself in knots and her voice deserted her. She managed to force out a weak, "Of course not, my lord," around the constriction in her throat. What on earth was the matter with her?

Luckily, Johnson entered to announce dinner. Inwardly, Georgiana heaved a sigh of relief. But relief died a sudden death when she discovered Lord Alton was dining at his sister's board. Naturally, he sat opposite her. Throughout the meal, which could have been the meanest fare for all she noticed, Georgiana struggled to avoid looking directly at the gentleman opposite, with mixed success. Arthur unwittingly came to her rescue, turning the conversation into political waters. He engaged his brother-in-law in a detailed discussion of the Corn Laws, leaving the ladies to their own interests.

As Bella seemed abstracted, Georgiana confined her gaze, if not her attention, to her plate. As course followed course, and the gentlemen's discourse continued unabated, she was conscious of a growing irritation. Admittedly her awkwardness in the drawing-room had hardly been encouraging, but Lord Alton could at least make the effort to address some remark to her. Perhaps, in England, it was not done to talk across the table, even at family meals.

When the sweets appeared before her, Bella shook herself and glanced about. Only then did she notice that her husband and brother had embarked on a most tedious discussion, leaving poor Georgie to herself. It was on the tip of her tongue to call attention to their lapse of manners, when she recalled that neither gentleman would feel the least inhibited about alluding to her own brown study of the past hour, nor in asking the subject of said study. As she had no intention of once again drawing her brother's fire, she turned instead to Georgiana.

"You see what it is to dine *en famille* in Winsmere House? Pearls before swine, my dear. Here we sit, only too willing to be enthralled, and all they can think of is their political problems." Her eyes twinkled at her husband, sitting opposite her at the head of the table.

Unperturbed by her attack, he smiled back. "In truth, I'm surprised to see you still here. I had thought you were off to Almack's tonight."

Bella's eyes swung to the clock, peacefully ticking away on the sideboard. "Heavens! I'd no idea. Georgie, we'll have to bustle. Come. We'll leave our two fine gentlemen to their port."

Both men stood as she rose.

Georgiana perforce rose too. She could not resist throwing one last glance at the tall figure opposite her. To her confusion, she found he was watching her. But his face bore nothing more than a remotely polite expression. He returned her nod with genial but distant civility.

As the ladies departed the room, Arthur turned to his brother-in-law. "If you have the time, I'd value your opinions on how best to go about this business."

Dominic started slightly, as if his mind had wandered from the matter they had been discussing for the past hour. "Yes. Of course." His usual, sleepily bored smile appeared. "I'd be only too delighted, naturally."

Arthur, not deceived, laughed. "Which means you'd much rather be elsewhere, discussing more enthralling subjects, but you will, of course, humour your host. You, Dominic, are a complete hand. Why you must belittle your efforts in this I know not."

By unspoken agreement, they moved to the door. Dominic waved one languid hand, and a priceless sapphire caught the light. "Perhaps because my—er—efforts, as you term them, are so undemanding as to be positively valueless."

Arthur was surprised into a snort. "Valueless? Who else, pray tell, has succeeded in even introducing the subject in Prinny's presence?"

They entered the library and made for the two large armchairs by the hearth.

"Introducing the subject's hardly the same as gaining His Highness's support." Dominic sank into one chair, stretching his long legs before him and emitting a weary sigh.

Arthur glanced sharply at him. "You know that's not necessary. Just as long as His Highness is aware of how things stand. That'll be more than enough." He handed Dominic a cut-crystal glass filled with his oldest port, then settled comfortably in the chair opposite.

Silence fell, broken only by the ticking of the long case clock in the corner and a sudden crackle as a log settled in the grate. Arthur, who had had plenty of opportunity to observe his brother-in-law over dinner, and to note the arrested expression in those startlingly blue eyes whenever they rested on Georgiana Hartley, continued to watch the younger man, waiting patiently for whatever came next, confident that something, indeed, would be forthcoming.

Finally, Dominic's gaze sought his face. "This Miss Hartley I've foisted on you... I assume you approve?"

Arthur nodded. "Georgiana is exactly the sort of company Bella needs. You have my heartfelt thanks for sending her to us."

The black brows rose. "Seemed the least I could do." Dominic's face showed evidence of distraction, as it frequently had that night. Arthur's lips twitched. He sternly repressed the impulse to smile.

Eventually Dominic shook off his abstraction sufficiently to comment, "Bella was saying she's becoming rather stubbornly taken with this idea of hiring out as a companion. She seemed to think that she, Miss Hartley, might take things into her own hands. That, I need hardly say, will simply not do."

Arthur nodded gravely. "I entirely agree. Also, I have to concur with Bella on her reading of Georgiana's character." He paused to steeple his fingers, and stared into the fire over the top of the structure. "Georgiana is clearly unused to relying on the bounty of others. It irks her, I think, to be living, as it were, on our charity. She has some money of her own, but not, I suspect, the requisite fortune. She has spoken to me about the best way to go about hiring herself out. I returned an evasive and, I hope, restraining answer. Luckily, the fact that she has been out of England for so long makes it relatively easy to make excuses which on the face of it are reasonable, without going into over-many details. However—'' he smiled at Dominic ''—beneath that demure exterior lies a great deal of strength and not a little courage. From what I gather, she made her way to England virtually unaided—not an inconsiderable feat. I seriously doubt she'll accept our vague answers for much longer.''

A black frown of quite dramatic proportions dominated the Viscount's face.

Arthur suppressed a grin. Finally he asked, ''Do you have any ideas?''

Still frowning, Dominic slowly shook his head. Then he glanced at Arthur. ''Do you?''

''As a matter of fact, I do.'' Arthur straightened his shoulders and prepared to explain. His grey gaze rested thoughtfully on Dominic's face. ''Bella, of course, needs distraction. Essentially, that means a companion. But can you imagine how she would feel if I insisted she hire one?''

Dominic's frown lightened.

''Bella has been most assiduous in helping Georgiana and, from what I've seen, Georgiana is truly grateful. I plan to suggest to Georgiana, in confidence, that she become Bella's companion in truth. However, in order to spare Bella's quite natural feelings, the arrangement will be a secret between the two of us. To all outward appearances, which of course must include the servants, she will continue as a guest in this house.'' Arthur's brows rose interrogatively. ''Do you think that'll pass?''

Dominic grinned. ''I'm sure it will. How useful to be able to turn your talents to something other than politics.'' His grin broadened into a smile. ''And no

wonder you're so invaluable in your present capacity.''

Arthur smiled and inclined his head. ''As you say.''
For a moment he regarded the younger man intently.
Then, almost imperceptibly, he shrugged. ''I'll speak
to Georgiana in the morning. It would be wise, I suspect, to ensure she has no opportunity to take the bit
between her teeth.''

''THANK YOU, MY LORD.'' Georgiana curtsied and
watched young Lord Mortlake mince away across the
floor. Still, at least he had danced well.

She flicked open her fan and plied it ruthlessly. The
large, sparsely furnished rooms which were Almack's
were crammed with bodies dressed in silks and satins
of every conceivable hue. The day had been unsea-
sonably warm, and the evening, initially balmy, had
turned sultry. The air in the rooms hung oppressively.
Ostrich feathers wilted. As a particularly limp pair,
dyed puce, bobbed by, attached to the head-dress of
an extremely conscious beauty, Georgiana hid her
smirk behind her fan.

Her eyes scanned the company. Other than Bella,
standing by her side, engaged in a low-voiced conversation with an elderly matron, Georgiana knew
only those few people Bella had thus far introduced
her to. And, she reflected, none of them needed a companion.

As her eyes feasted on the spectrum of colours min-
gling before her, she spared a smile for her sartorial
elegance. By comparison with many about her, she
was underdressed. The pattern of Fancon's amethyst

silk robe was simple and plain, with long, clean lines uncluttered by frills and furbelows. Her single strand of pearls, inherited from her mother, shone warmly about her neck. Originally uncertain, she now felt smugly satisfied with her appearance.

Thoughts of dresses brought her earlier discovery to mind, together with the subsequent argument with Bella. How on earth could she accept the sea-green gauze and topaz silk dresses from Bella, to whom she was already so deeply indebted? Yet it was undeniable that Bella could not wear them. Both dresses were presently hanging in the wardrobe in her chamber. She had been quite unable to persuade Bella to repack and return them. What was she to do about them?

The idea that, if she had been wearing the topaz silk gown that evening, Lord Alton would have paid more attention to her flitted through her mind. Ruthlessly, she stamped on the errant thought. She was here to find employment, not ogle lords. And what possible interest could Lord Alton have in her—an unremarkable country lass, not even at home in England?

Depressed, by that thought and the lowering fact she had not yet made any headway in finding a position, Georgiana determinedly looked over the sea of heads, pausing on the occasional powdered wig that belonged to a previous generation. Maybe, beneath one, she would find someone to hire her?

''Here, girl! Georgiana, ain't it? Come and help me to that chair.''

Georgiana whirled to find Lady Winterspoon beside her. The old lady was leaning on a cane.

Seeing her glance, Amelia Winterspoon chuckled. "I only use it at night. Helps me get the best seats."

Georgiana smiled and obediently took her ladyship's arm. Once settled in a gilt chair by the wall, Lady Winterspoon waved Georgiana to its partner beside her.

"I can only take so much of this place. Too much mindless talk addles the brain."

Georgiana felt the sharp grey eyes assessing her. She wondered whether she would pass muster.

A wry smile twisted Amelia Winterspoon's thin lips. "Just as I thought. *Not* in the common style."

The old lady paused. Georgiana had the impression she was reliving long-ago evenings spent under the candlelight of ballroom chandeliers. Then, abruptly, the grey gaze sharpened and swung to her face.

"If you're old enough to heed advice, here's one piece you should take to heart. You ain't a beauty, but you're no antidote either. You're different—and not just because you're fair when the current craze is for dark. The most successful women who've ever trod these boards were those who were brave enough to be themselves."

"Themselves?"

"Themselves," came the forceful answer. "Don't put on airs, nor pretend to be what you ain't. Thankfully, you seem in no danger of doing that. Don't try to ape the English misses. Don't try to lose your foreignness—use it instead. All you need to make a go of it is to smile and enjoy yourself. The rest'll come easy."

"But—" Georgiana wondered whether she should

explain her situation to Arthur's sister. Maybe she could help her find a position?

"No buts, girl! Just do it! There's no point in wasting your life away being a wallflower. Get out and enjoy yourself." Lady Winterspoon used her cane to gesture at the dance-floor. "Now go on—off you go!"

Despite the conviction that she should feel piqued at such forthright meddling, Georgiana found herself grinning, then laughing as Lady Winterspoon nodded encouragingly. Rising, Georgiana swept a curtsy to her ladyship, now comfortably ensconced, and, a smile lingering on her lips, returned to the throng. She made her way to where she had left Bella.

But Bella was no longer in sight.

Perturbed, Georgiana stood still and wondered what to do. She could go back and sit with Lady Winterspoon, only she would probably drive her off again. English social strictures were not Georgiana's strong suit. Still, she rather suspected she should not wander about the rooms alone. Suddenly she realised she was frowning.

Lady Winterspoon's strong voice still echoed in her mind. "Enjoy yourself!"

Georgiana lifted her head. She had been introduced to Italian society at the age of sixteen. Surely, at the ripe old age of eighteen, she could manage such a simple social occasion as this? Consciously drawing about herself the cloak of social calm her father's female patrons had impressed on her was the hallmark of a lady, she stepped out more confidently to search for Bella—not hurriedly, in a frenzy, but in a calm and dignified way, smiling as she went.

As she moved slowly down the room, truly looking about her for the first time that evening, she heard snatches of conversation wafting from the groups she passed.

"Did you see that Emma Michinford? Making such sheep's eyes at..."

"Well, we all know what *he's* after!"

"She's really rather pathetic, don't you agree?"

"Not that it'll come to anything, mark my words. The likes of him..."

Waspish, biting, cutting gibes... The comments blurred into a melody typical, Georgiana suspected, of the place. Her smile grew.

"Oh!" Her elbow jogged that of another stroller. "I'm so sorry. Pray excuse me."

"Gladly, my dear, if you'll tell me what could possibly be so amusing in Almack's."

The languid tones of the gentleman bowing before her were, Georgiana judged, devoid of menace. He was very neatly and correctly attired, soberly so. His blue coat was well cut, his satin breeches without a crease. Brown hair, stylishly but not rakishly cut, framed a pleasant face. There was nothing one could put a finger on to account for the air of elegance which clung to him.

As he continued to look at her with mild curiosity, Georgiana, Lady Winterspoon's dictum still fresh in her mind, answered him truthfully. "It was merely the conversation, caught in snippets as I walked about. It's—" she put her head on one side as she considered her words "—rather single-minded, if you know what I mean."

A quirky grin twisted the gentleman's lips. "I do indeed know what you mean, Miss…?"

Having embarked on her course, Georgiana dispensed with caution, "Hartley. Georgiana Hartley. I'm staying with Lady Winsmere. I seem to have lost her in the crush."

"Ah, the lovely Bella. I think I saw her over by the door, in earnest conversation with Lady Duckworth. Permit me to escort you to her."

With only a single blink, Georgiana laid her gloved hand on the proffered sleeve. If she was going to be escorted by any gentleman tonight, she was quite content that it should be this one. He hadn't told her his name, but he seemed thoroughly at home.

"From your comment, you seem almost to laugh at the purpose of this great institution. Yet surely you propose to avail yourself of its services?"

This was the sort of conversation Georgiana had cut her social eye-teeth on. "I most certainly intend to avail myself of its services, but not, I think, as you might assume."

Her companion digested this riposte, before countering, "If that means you are not here to snare a title, or a fortune, what possible other use for this place can you have found?"

"Why, that to which I was putting it when you met me."

A pause developed, followed by a great sigh. "Very well. I confess myself stumped. What is it you've discovered within these faded grey walls?"

Georgiana smiled, eyes dancing. "Why, enjoyment, of course. I was enjoying myself." To her surprise, she realised this was true. She turned to glance into her companion's grey eyes. In them, she saw thunder-struck amazement.

"*Enjoyment?* In Almack's?"

Georgiana laughed. "Of course. I'm enjoying myself now. Aren't you?"

Her gentleman stopped stock-still, a ludicrous mixture of horror and humour in his face. "Dreadful! I'll never live this down." Then his face cleared and he smiled, quite genuinely, at Georgiana. "Come, Miss Hartley. Let me restore you to Lady Winsmere. You're clearly too potent a force to be let loose for long."

Perfectly content, Georgiana strolled by his side through the crowd, who, she now noticed, seemed to part before them. Even before she caught sight of Bella's surprised face, she had started to question the identity of her escort. But she was determined not to worry. And, thankfully, whoever he was, her escort seemed to find nothing amiss.

Bella curtsied and chatted animatedly, but Georgiana still heard no name. With a final, *sotto voce,* "Enjoying oneself in Almack's. Whatever next?" the very correct gentleman withdrew.

Georgiana turned to Bella, but, before she could utter her question, Bella was exclaiming, albeit in delighted whispers, "Georgie! However did you do it?"

"Do what? Who is he?" Instinctively, Georgiana whispered too.

"Who? But...don't you know?" Bella stared in disbelief, first at her, then at the elegant retreating back.

"No. No one introduced us. I bumped into him and apologised."

Bella fanned herself frantically. "Heavens! He might have cut you!"

"Cut...? But who on earth is he?"

"Brummel! George Brummel. He's one of society's most powerful arbiters of taste." Bella turned to survey Georgiana appraisingly. "Well! Obviously he's taken to you. What a relief! I didn't know what to think when I saw you with him. He can be quite diabolical, you know."

Georgiana, conscious now of the envious eyes upon her, smiled confidently. "You needn't have worried. We were just enjoying ourselves."

Bella looked incredulous.

Georgiana laughed.

"GOODNIGHT, Johnson."

"Goodnight, my lord."

The door of Winsmere House shut softly behind Dominic. The night continued mild, but the low rumble of distant thunder heralded the end of the unseasonal warmth. Still, Alton House in Grosvenor Square was only five minutes away. Dominic set off, swinging his slim ebony cane, his long strides unhurried as he headed for North Audley Street.

The evening had left him with a sense of dissatisfaction which he was hard put to explain. He had broken his journey to Brighton to check on Miss Hartley, although, to be precise, it was more to relieve his mind over whether Arthur and Bella had been put out over her descent on them. Thankfully, all had turned out for the best. Arthur's scheme would undoubtedly pave the way for Georgiana Hartley to spend the upcoming

Little Season with Bella, after which it would be wonderful if she had not received at least one acceptable proposal. The girl was not a brilliant match, but a perfectly suitable connection for any of the lesser nobility who made up the bulk of the *ton*. He had checked on her antecedents and knew them to be above reproach. Yes, Georgiana Hartley would very likely soon be betrothed. Which was far more appropriate than being a companion.

As he swung south into North Audley Street, Dominic grinned. How typical of Arthur to concoct such a perfect solution to the girl's troubles. And Bella's. Everything seemed set to fall smoothly into place. Which, all things considered, should leave him feeling smugly satisfied. Instead, he was feeling uncommonly irritated. The grin faded. A frown settled over his features.

A watchman passed by unobtrusively, unwilling to draw the attention of such a well set up and clearly out-of-sorts gentleman to his activities. Dominic heard him but gave no sign.

Why should he be feeling so disillusioned, so disheartened? He'd been living this life for the past twelve years. Why had it suddenly palled? The circumstances that had driven him to seek the peace of Candlewick drifted into his mind. All the glamour and glitter and laughter associated with the doings of the Carlton House set. And the underlying vice, the predictability, the sheer falsity of most of it—these were what had sent him scurrying for sanctuary. But even Candlewick had failed to lift his mood. While its serenity had been comforting, the huge house had seemed lonely, empty. He had never noticed it before; now its silence was oppressive.

The corner of Grosvenor Square loomed ahead. Dominic swung left and crossed the road to the railed garden. The gates were locked at sunset, but that had never stopped him strolling the well tended lawns by night. He vaulted the wrought-iron railings with accustomed ease, then turned his steps across the lawns in the direction of his town house on the south side of the Square. Tucking his cane under his arm, he thrust his hands into his coat pockets and sank his chin into the soft folds of his cravat. Doubtless, if he were still in the care of his old nurse, she would tell him to take one of Dr James's Powders. The blue devils, that was what he had.

A vision of honey-gold eyes crystallised in his brain. Why on earth Georgiana Hartley's eyes, together with the rest of her, should so plague him he could not understand. He was not a callow youth, to be so besotted with a female's finer points. He had hardly exchanged two words with the chit, yet, throughout the evening, had been aware of her every movement, every inflexion, every expression.

Leaves from the beech trees had piled in drifts and softly scrunched underfoot. Dominic paused to regard his feet, lightly covered with golden leaves. Then he shook his head, trying to rid it of the memory of curls sheening guinea-gold under candlelight. God! What was this? The onset of senility?

Determined to force his mind to sanity, he removed his hands from his pockets and straightened his shoulders. Ten long strides brought him to the fence, and he vaulted over to the pavement beyond. A few days, not to mention nights, of Elaine Changley's company would cure him of this idiotic fancy. As his feet crossed the cobbles, he commanded his memory to supply a vision of Lady Changley as he had last seen her, reclining amid the much rumpled sheets of the bed he had just vacated. Of course, Elaine's ambitions were on a par with her charms. But as he was as well acquainted with the former as he was with the latter he felt justified in ignoring them. A smile played at the corners of his fine lips as he trod the steps to his front door.

In the instant he raised his cane to beat a tattoo on the solid oak door, an unnerving vision in which Georgiana Hartley was substituted for Elaine Changley flooded his brain. So breathtaking was the sight that Dominic froze. The gold top of his cane, yet to touch the door, remained suspended before him.

The door opened and Dominic found himself facing his butler, Timms.

"My lord?"

Feeling decidedly foolish, Dominic lowered his cane. He sauntered past Timms, one of Duckett's protégés, as if it were perfectly normal for him to stand rooted to his own doorstep. He paused in the hallway to draw off his gloves, then handed the offending cane to Timms.

"I'll be leaving for Brighton early tomorrow, Timms. Tell Maitland to be ready about nine."

"Very good, m'lord."

Frowning, Dominic slowly ascended the gently curving staircase, pausing, as was his habit, to check his fob watch against the long case clock on the landing. Restoring his watch to his pocket, he reflected that, if nothing else could cure him of his disturbing affliction, the decadent amusements to be found within the Prince Regent's pavilion at Brighton would.

BY THE TIME the Winsmere House ladies were handed into their coach for the drive home from King Street, Georgiana had had proved to her, over and over again, the truth of Lady Winterspoon's dictum. If she enjoyed herself, then her partners seemed to enjoy her company. If she laughed, then they laughed, too. And, while such overt behaviour did not sit well with one brought up to the self-effacing manners expected of young Italian girls, it was a great deal better, to Georgiana's way of thinking, than simpering and giggling. Her upbringing clearly had not conditioned her for English social life. Nevertheless, the unrufflable calm she had been instructed was a lady's greatest asset certainly helped, allowing her to cloak her instinctive responses to some of those she had met—like Lord Ormskirk and his leering glances, and Mr Morecombe, with his penchant for touching her bare arms.

"The Sotherbys are holding a ball next week. Lady Margaret said she'd send cards." Bella's voice came out of the gloom of the seat opposite. "After tonight, I've no doubts we'll be kept busy. So fortunate, your meeting with Brummel."

The unmistakable sound of a smothered yawn came to Georgiana's ears. She smiled into the darkness. Despite her tiredness, Bella seemed even more excited by her success than she was. She had originally found her hostess's claim of boredom difficult to believe. Now she could find it in her to understand that, without any special interest, the balls and parties could indeed turn flat. Still, to her, everything was too new for there to be any danger of her own interest flagging before Bella's did. Hopefully Bella would not feel too let down when she found a position and moved away. Into obscurity. Georgiana frowned.

If she had been asked, five days previously, whether she had any ambition to enter the *ton*, she would unhesitatingly have disclaimed all such desire. However, having now had a small sample of the diverse entertainments to be found amid the social whirl, she rather thought she might enjoy being able to savour these, in moderation, by way of a change from the quieter lifestyle she considered her milieu. A saying of her father's drifted past her mind's ear. "Experience, girl! There's nothing quite like it and no substitute known.'

As the clop of the horses' hoofs echoed back from the tiered façades of the houses they passed, Georgiana puzzled over her change of heart. Still, nothing could alter the fact that she would need to earn her way, at least to some extent. That being so, perhaps she should take this opportunity of experiencing the *ton*, of enjoying herself amid the glittering throng? According to Bella, she needed to be known to find a position. So, until she secured one, she could, and perhaps should, follow her father's and Lady Winterspoon's advice.

Bella yawned. "Oh, dear. I'd forgotten what it was like." Another yawn was stifled behind one slim white-gloved hand. Then, "I wonder if Dominic has managed to convince Charles to sell the Place yet?"

The question jolted Georgiana out of her reverie. "Lord Alton wishes to buy the Place?"

"Why, yes. Didn't I mention it?"

Her friend's voice was sleepy, but Georgiana's curiosity was aroused. "No. Why does he want it? From what I saw, it's terribly run down."

"Oh, it is. Run down, I mean. Even when Charles's father was alive... And now..."

Georgiana waited, but Bella's mind had clearly drifted. "But why does he want it?" she prompted.

"The Place? Oh, I keep forgetting you don't know all that much about it." Bella's skirts rustled as she sat up. "Well, you see, the Place didn't exist a hundred years ago. It used to be part of Candlewick. But one of my ancestors was something of a loose screw. He gambled heavily. One of his creditors was one of your ancestors. He agreed to take part of the Candlewick lands in payment. So that was how the Place came about. My spendthrift ancestor didn't live long, much to the family's relief. Ever since then, the family has tried to buy back the Place and make Candlewick complete again. But your family have always refused. I don't know how long it's been going on, but, generally, both families have always dealt amicably despite all. That is..." Bella paused dramatically; Georgiana sat enthralled "—until my father's death. Although he had always talked of rejoining the Place to Candlewick, my father hadn't, as far as Dominic could discover, done much about it. So when he inherited, Dominic wrote to your uncle to discuss the matter. But your uncle never replied. He was, by that time, something of a recluse. Dominic could never get to see him. After a while, Dominic gave up. When he heard of your uncle's death, he wrote to Charles. Charles didn't reply either. Mind you,'' Bella added on a reflective note, ''as Charles dislikes Dominic as much as Dominic dislikes him, I can't say I was surprised at that. Still, from what you've said, the Place is falling down about Charles's ears. I really can't see why he won't sell. Dominic's prepared to pay above the odds, and Charles must know that.''

''Perhaps it's mere stubbornness?''

''Maybe,'' Bella conceded, tiring of her brother's problems. She lapsed into silence, the better to consider the doors the evening had opened for her protégée.

Georgiana puzzled over Charles's behaviour. In the few days she'd had to observe him, her cousin had given the impression of being addicted to the good things in life, or rather, that he had a liking for the finer things but had little of the wherewithal required to pay for them. Which made his refusal to sell the Place, in which he demonstrably took no interest, stranger still.

From consideration of Charles, it was a short step to thoughts of the man so inextricably linked in her mind with her escape from her cousin. The demands of her début at Almack's had precluded her thinking of her earlier meeting with Lord Alton, beyond the wish that she had made a better impression. Undoubtedly she had appeared as a gawky, tongue-tied, awkward child. Where on earth had two years of experience gone? Certainly, nothing in her previous existence had prepared her for the odd effect he had on her. She had never reacted to a man in such a way before. It was both puzzling and unnerving. When it came to Bella's brother, her carefully nurtured Italian calm deserted her. Hopefully, by the time they next met, the peculiar effect would have worn off. She did not wish to be forever appearing as a graceless schoolgirl to the gentleman before whom, more than all others, she wished to shine. Still, no doubt she was refining too much on their meeting. Lord Alton would have seen her merely as a child he had assisted in her time of trouble. She could be nothing more than that to him. The thought that she would like to be a great deal more than that to Lord Alton she ruthlessly decapitated at birth. He was a noted Corinthian and, from what she had heard at the dinner-table, one of the Carlton House set. She had nothing to recommend her to his notice—not beauty, nor fortune, nor birth. To him, she would be no more than a passing acquaintance, one he had perhaps already forgotten.

Besides, it seemed he was on the verge of contracting an alliance, although Lady Winterspoon certainly seemed to think the lady in question was rather less than suitable. But she had heard more than enough in Italy to distrust the conclusions of society. Who knew? Maybe Lord Alton was genuinely fond of Lady Changley. She tried to imagine what the lady Lord Alton was in love with would look like, but soon gave up. She knew so little of him that it was impossible to guess his preferences.

As she ruminated on the twist of fate that had

caused them to meet, Georgiana reflected that it was perhaps as well she would get few chances to be in Viscount Alton's company. He was the stuff schoolgirl dreams were made of. Unfortunately, she was no longer a schoolgirl. And she did not have the capital to indulge in dreams.

CHAPTER FOUR

"MY LORD, I'm most truly sensible of the honour you do me, but, indeed, I cannot consent to becoming your wife."

Georgiana watched as Viscount Molesworth, an earnest young man more at home on his ancestral acres than in a London ballroom, rose awkwardly from his knees.

Dusting off his satin breeches, he sighed. "Thought you might say that."

Georgiana swallowed a giggle and managed to look politely interested.

Seeing this, the Viscount obligingly continued, "Told m'mother so. But you know what women are. Wouldn't listen. Said you'd be bound to accept me. Said you were just the thing I needed. Must say, I agree with her there." He glanced once more at Georgiana. "Sure you won't change your mind?"

Shaking her head, Georgiana rose and put her hand on the Viscount's sleeve. "Truly, my lord, I don't think we would suit."

"Ah, well. That's it, then." Lord Molesworth, heir to an earldom of generous proportions, lifted his head as music drifted from the ballroom down the hall. "Best get back to the dancing, then, what?"

Unable to command her voice, Georgiana nodded. Strolling back into the ballroom on his lordship's arm, she could not keep a happily satisfied smile from her face. She had known the Viscount was bordering on a declaration, had been teetering on the brink for the past week. And, as with her two previous proposals, Georgiana had dreaded having to hurt his feelings. But it had all passed off easily, even more easily than the others. Her first proposal had been from young Lord Danby, who had been truly smitten but so very young that she had felt she were dealing with a younger brother, not a potential lover. Her second offer had come from Mr Havelock, a quiet man of thirty-five summers. She was sincerely fond of him, but in a friendly way, and doubted she could ever think of him other than as a friend. He had accepted her refusal philosophically, and they continued friends, but he had impressed on her that, should she have need of support or even something more, he was forever at her disposal.

Relieved at having weathered yet another proposal with no bones broken, Georgiana gave silent thanks that she had attracted only true gentlemen. Some of the more dangerous Corinthians had certainly looked her over—almost, she had felt, as if she were a succulent morsel they were planning to gobble up. But when they learned she was staying with the Winsmeres they usually smiled and passed on.

However, there were a few who had remained long enough to enjoy a light flirtation, a moment of dalliance. Such a one was Lord Edgcombe, who now approached to claim her for the waltz.

Georgiana smiled and curtsied. "My lord."

His lordship, resplendent in a dark green coat which leant a deeper tinge to his golden locks, bowed easily over her hand. "My lovely." His cool grey eyes flicked to the Viscount, still hovering by her elbow.

Georgiana realised he must have seen them re-enter the room, and wondered how much he guessed. She was now too experienced to take umbrage at his outrageous but calculated greeting. Instead, she spoke confidently, succeeding in distracting his lordship from his contemplation of the hapless Viscount. "I take it that means you approve of my gown?"

Lord Edgcombe's grey gaze swung slowly to her face. His lips twitched. Then, to pay her back for her temerity, he raised his quizzing-glass and embarked on a minute inspection of her person. "Mmm," he murmured. "The style, of course, is superb. Fancon, I trust?"

Georgiana, far from blushing and dissolving into a twittering heap, the prescribed reaction to his behaviour, could not restrain her smile. She understood his lordship's tactics only too well.

Far from being put out by her refusal to succumb, Lord Edgcombe responded with a smile of genuine enjoyment and offered his arm. "Come, sweet torment, the dance-floor awaits and the musicians will soon grow weary."

As she twirled down the room in Lord Edgcombe's arms, Georgiana wondered again at the success, for her part unexpected but none the less flattering, which had resulted in her receiving the attentions of one such as his lordship. He was well born, with a comfortable estate, and could be pleasant enough when it suited him. However, as it only suited him to behave so with a select circle of acquaintances, he was generally thought to be beyond the reach of the matchmaking mamas. Georgiana did not entirely understand his interest in her, but instinctively knew she was in no immediate danger of receiving a proposal from Lord Edgcombe. At least, she amended, as she looked into his smiling grey eyes and correctly divined the thoughts behind them, not a proposal of marriage.

"Relieve my curiosity, my dear. What could possibly be so interesting that you needs must be alone with the noble Viscount?"

Georgiana opened her eyes wide. "Why, we were merely strolling, my lord."

The grey gaze remained on her face for a full minute. Then his lips curved once more. "I see." After a moment he added, his voice low, "I don't suppose you feel like taking a stroll with me."

Georgiana's eyes danced. Keeping her face straight, she shook her head primly. "Oh, no, my lord. I don't think that would be at all wise."

They executed a complicated turn at the end of the room, pausing to allow two younger and more enthusiastic couples to pass by. When they were once more proceeding up the long room, his lordship's attention refocused. "Now why is that, I wonder? Surely you don't mean to say that you fear my company would be less…scintillating than the Viscount's?"

Georgiana laughed lightly, her eyes still holding his. "Oh, no—far from it. My fear is more that your company might prove rather *too* scintillating, my lord."

Lord Edgcombe was no more immune to the flattery of a beautiful young woman than the next man, even if he fully understood her machinations. So he smiled again, sharing in her laughter. ''My dear, you're a minx. But a delightful minx, so I'll let you escape the set-down you undoubtedly deserve.''

Schooling her features to reflect a suitable gratitude, and reducing her voice to a breathless whisper, Georgiana replied, ''Oh, thank you, my lord.''

''Gammon!'' said Lord Edgcombe.

Returning three dances later to Bella's side, Georgiana was given no time to draw breath. Her mentor immediately demanded to be told what Viscount Molesworth had had to say.

Georgiana regarded Bella warily. ''He proposed.''

''And?'' Bella's face was alight.

Georgiana knew it was her friend's dearest wish that she contract a suitable alliance, and Viscount Molesworth was certainly that. But she had no real ambition to marry where she did not love, not even for her best friend. So she drew a deep breath and confessed. ''I refused him.''

''Oh.'' Bella's face fell. ''But why?''

Seeing the real consternation in Bella's big eyes— eyes that constantly reminded her of another—Georgiana was tempted to make a clean breast of it. But the approach of the gentleman to whom she was promised for the next dance reminded her of their surroundings. ''I'll explain later. Not now. Please, Bella?''

Now Bella saw Mr Millikens and smiled and nodded, adding in an undertone for Georgiana's ears only,

"Yes, of course. Later. But Georgie, we really must talk of this."

Georgiana nodded her agreement and moved forward to take Mr Millikens's arm.

The rest of the evening passed in a blur before Georgiana's eyes. She spent much of her time examining and assessing the changes the past two weeks had wrought in her life. Arthur's quietly worded request that she remain in Green Street, theoretically a guest, but in truth as a companion for Bella, had been a turning point. His explanation of Bella's need for purpose in an otherwise frivolous existence had struck a chord of sympathy. After that, she had no longer pursued the idea of finding employment with an older lady. Bella, of course, was kept in ignorance of the arrangement, for it was generally only much older women who had companions.

That first night at Almack's had set the seal on her success. From that evening, a steady flow of invitations had poured into Green Street, and she and Bella had been immersed in a tide of balls and parties, routs and breakfasts. Her popularity, both with the gentlemen and the ladies of society, had made Bella crow. For her part, Georgiana wryly thanked her less than perfect looks. Because she was no beauty, she was not a challenge to the reigning *incomparables*. Thus she was accepted without any great fuss, nor was she the butt of any jealousies. Her natural vivacity, which, thanks to Lady Winterspoon and Beau Brummel, she had discovered, carried her through. In her heart, she strongly suspected it was this, together with her unconventionally un-missish behaviour, which made her so attractive to the gentlemen. Certainly, they flocked about her. And, if she were to be truthful, she could not deny a happy little glow of self-satisfaction whenever she thought of her court. She might not be a hit, or a beauty, but she had her own little niche, her own place in the scheme of things. As Lady Winterspoon had suggested, there were many roads to success.

They were among the last to leave the ball. As she had anticipated, Bella returned to the subject of Viscount Molesworth as soon as the carriage door was shut upon them.

"Why, Georgie? I thought you liked him."

Georgiana leant back against the fine leather upholstery and resigned herself to the inevitable. "Viscount Molesworth is all that is amiable. But truly, Bella, do you think that's enough?"

"Enough? But, my dear, many girls marry with far less than—er—liking for their husbands."

Georgiana stifled a sigh. She would have to try to make Bella understand. "Bella, did you marry like that?"

Bella shifted in her seat, her satin skirts shushing. "Well, no. But...well, you know it's not the done thing, to marry for love. And," she hurried on, "you've no idea the trouble I had, in marrying Arthur. No one could understand it. Oh, it's accepted now. But if Dominic had opposed the match everyone would have agreed with him. Love is simply not a...a determining factor in marriage in the *ton*."

Hearing the sincere note in Bella's voice, Georgiana debated whether to tell her the truth. But, even as the idea formed, she shied away from it. Instead she tried another tack. "But you see, dearest Bella, I didn't come to London to marry. I've given no thought to marrying into the *ton*. I'm not at all sure it would suit me.''

To this, Bella returned a decidedly unladylike snort. ''Not marry? Pray tell, what else are you going to do with your life? Oh—don't tell me you'll be a companion to some old lady. You'll never convince me you would rather be that than married to some nice, considerate gentleman who'll shower you with everything you desire.''

Under cover of the dark, Georgiana grinned. Well, she was a companion, although Bella didn't know it and the lady wasn't old. But would she really prefer to be married, regardless of the man, to have to tend to the comfort and consequence of some faceless gentleman? Georgiana sighed. ''You make it all sound so straightforward.''

''It is straightforward. It's simply a matter of making up your mind to it and then, when a suitable gentleman comes along, saying yes instead of no.''

Georgiana gave a weary giggle. ''Well, if the right gentleman comes along, I'll promise to consider it.''

Bella wisely refrained from further pushing, hopeful that she had at least made her errant protégée think more deeply on her future position within the *ton*. For Bella was quite determined her Georgie should marry well. She was attractive, which was more to the purpose than beautiful. And the gentlemen liked her—as evidenced by three proposals within two weeks. She had held great hopes of Mr Havelock, but Georgie had refused him without a blink. All she could do now was to hope Georgie's elusive right gentleman came along before her protégée got the reputation of being difficult to please.

A GENTLE BREEZE cooled Georgiana's warm cheeks as she accompanied Lord Ellsmere back to his phaeton. She deployed her sunshade to deflect the glances of any curious passers-by as they left the secluded walk and crossed the lawns to the carriageway. Her hand resting gently on his sleeve, she cast a tentative glance up into his lordship's handsome face. He was watching her and, catching her gaze, smiled ruefully.

"Forgive me, my dear, if my actions seem somewhat importunate. You'll have to make allowances for my—er—strong feelings in this matter."

For the first time since that night at Almack's, now more than three weeks ago, Georgiana felt flustered. Only this morning she had been congratulating herself on having managed to keep her earnest suitors from making any further declarations. How could she have guessed what his lordship had planned in the guise of a perfectly decorous drive in the park?

"Oh, yes, of course," she muttered incoherently. She noticed his lordship's slightly smug expression, and her temper, usually dormant, stirred. As she allowed him to help her up to the high seat of the phaeton, she made a heroic effort to pull herself together.

She could hardly claim that no gentleman had tried to kiss her before. But, in Italy, the flowery speeches and extravagant gestures that usually preceded such an attempt gave any lady all the warning she could need, should she wish to avoid the outcome. But Lord Ellsmere had given no indication of his intent. One minute they had been strolling comfortably along a secluded walk, screened by the lush growths of a long summer from the more populated carriageway and lawns, and the next she had been trapped in his arms, quite unable to free herself—not that she had struggled, stunned as she had been. Lord Ellsmere had, unfortunately, taken her lack of reaction for acquiescence and acted accordingly. Then she had struggled.

To give him his due, Lord Ellsmere had immediately released her, only to capture her hand. He had then proceeded to declare his undying love for her, to Georgiana's utter confusion. Her mind had been miles distant before he had acted, and she had struggled to manage even the most feeble disclaimer.

And now, of course, he merely felt he had acted precipitately and swept her off her feet. He had made it clear he did not accept her refusal of his suit. He would, he had said, live in the hope she would, with time, see its advantages.

As he climbed to the seat beside her, Georgiana turned impulsively towards him. ''My lord...''

Lord Ellsmere's eyes followed his diminutive tiger as the boy left the horses' heads to swing up behind them. Then he turned and smiled at Georgiana. ''I'll see you at the ball tonight, my dear. We'll continue our discussion then, when you've had more time to consider.''

His words were kindly, and Georgiana inwardly groaned. This was precisely the sort of situation she had been trying to avoid. But with the tiger behind, she could do nothing other than acquiesce to his lordship's plan.

In truth, as she felt the cooling breeze ripple past, she welcomed the time to marshal her arguments better. Lord Ellsmere was not Mr Havelock, nor Viscount Molesworth. He had every right to expect her serious consideration of his suit. He was eminently eligible—title, fortune, property and connections. Oh, heavens! What would Bella say this time?

Any thoughts Georgiana might have entertained of keeping her latest offer from her friend died a swift death when, re-entering Winsmere House, she made her way to the back parlour. Bella was there, reclining on the sofa, flicking through the pages of the latest *Ladies' Journal*. She looked up as Georgiana entered. And frowned.

"I thought you were driving with Lord Ellsmere."

Georgiana turned aside to lay her bonnet on a chair. "I was."

Bella's frown deepened. "Didn't he come in?"

"No." Georgiana would have liked to add an excuse which would explain this lapse of good manners on his lordship's part, but could think of nothing to the point. Under Bella's close scrutiny, she coloured.

"Georgie! *Never* say it! He's *offered?*" Bella sat up abruptly, the magazine sliding unheeded from her lap.

Bright cheeks made it unnecessary for Georgiana to answer.

"Oh, my dear! *Ellsmere!* Whoever would have thought it? Why, he's..." Georgiana's lack of response suddenly struck Bella. She stopped in mid-exclamation, disbelief chasing elation from her face.

"Oh, no!" she moaned, falling back against the cushions. "You've *refused* him!"

Georgiana smiled weakly, almost apologetically. But she wasn't to be let off lightly. Not this time.

Half an hour later, Bella threw her hands up in the air in defeat. "But I *still* don't understand! Danby was one thing; even Mr Havelock I could sympathise with. But Molesworth...and now, of all men, Ellsmere. Georgie, you'll never live it down. No one will believe you're turning Ellsmere down for the ridiculous reason that you aren't in love with him. They'll start saying there's something wrong with you, I know they will." Bella's voice quavered on the edge of tears.

Georgiana wasn't entirely composed herself. But she endeavoured to keep her tone even as she replied, "But I don't mean to make them propose. I do everything I can think of to avoid it."

Bella frowned, aware this was so. She had watched her protégée like a hen with one chick, and had puzzled over Georgiana's apparent uninterest in her suitors as suitors, rather than acquaintances. To her mind, the offers were coming in thick and fast precisely because, in comparison with most of the other débutantes, the gentlemen found Georgie so comfortable to be with. Then the oddity in Georgiana's declaration struck her. Her head came up. "*Why* don't you wish them to become attached? You can't possibly have decided you can't love any of them. You can't expect me to believe you truly consider the single state preferable to being married."

There was no possibility of avoiding Bella's stern gaze. Georgiana had, in fact, spent the last weeks fantasising on marriage, albeit marriage to one particular gentleman. She felt her cheeks warm as she blushed guiltily.

And Bella, being Bella, and every bit as impulsive as Georgiana herself, immediately leapt to the correct conclusion. "Oh, Georgie!" she wailed. "You haven't formed a...a *tendre* for some unsuitable gentleman, have you?"

Driven to the truth, Georgiana nodded dully.

"But who?" Bella was nonplussed. She had conscientiously vetted those to whom she introduced Georgiana. There had been no one unsuitable. None of the truly dangerous blades had approached her, and, in the circles they frequented, there was precious little chance for any outsider to gain access to her charge. So who was this mysterious man?

"He's not actually unsuitable, exactly," put in Georgiana, anticipating Bella's train of thought. At her friend's interrogative glance, she looked down at her hands, clasped tightly together in her lap, and continued, "It's more a case of...of unrequited love. I fell in love with him, but he doesn't love me."

"Well, then," said Bella, perking up at this, "we'll just have to see to it that he changes his mind."

"No!" squeaked Georgiana. She drew a deep breath and went on more calmly, "You don't understand. He doesn't know I love him."

Bella looked thunderstruck. Then, after a moment, she ventured, "Well, why not tell him? Oh, not in words. But there are ways to these things, you know."

But Georgiana was adamantly shaking her head. "He's in love with someone else. In fact," she added, hoping to shut off the terrifying prospect Bella seemed set on exploring, "he's about to offer for another."

"Oh." Bella digested this unwelcome news, a frown settling over her delicate face. For the life of her, she still could not fathom who Georgie's mystery man could be. In the end, she looked again at Georgiana where she sat on a chair, twisting the ribbons of her bonnet in her fingers, an uncharacteristically desolate look in her eyes.

Bella's kind heart was touched. She had been thrilled at Arthur's scheme to hire Georgiana as her companion and truly grateful for the way Georgie had tactfully gone along with the charade. Inwardly, she vowed she would do everything possible to learn who it was who had stolen Georgie's heart and, if possible, change his mind. Unlike Georgiana, she did not imagine a man about to contract an alliance was necessarily in love with his prospective bride. Hence, she did not consider Georgie's case lost. But, if it was, she must look to protect her friend's best interests. She now knew enough of Georgiana to know she would never consider alternatives until, perhaps, it was too late. So, in a gentle way, Bella asked, "I don't mean to pry, my dear. But do you not feel you could tell me who the gentleman is?"

Georgiana hung her head. Her feelings of guilt were increasing by the minute. How could she repay Bella's kindness in this way? How could she tell Bella she was in love with her brother? Slowly she shook her head. Then, feeling some explanation was due, she said, "You know him, you see. And, as I said, he doesn't know I love him. I...think it would be unfair to tell you—unfair to you and unfair to him.''

Bella nodded understandingly. ''I won't push you, then. But perhaps, in the circumstances, it would be best if I spoke to Lord Ellsmere this evening.'' Georgiana's startled look had Bella hurrying on. ''Oh, I won't tell him what you've told me. But there are ways and means. I'll just hint him away. It would be best, I think, for all concerned if I had a word with him.''

Georgiana thought over this offer. Perhaps, in this case, she would be wise to accept Bella's superior knowledge of how things were done. She raised her eyes to her friend's blue gaze, wishing, for the umpteenth time, that Bella and her brother had taken after different parents in that respect. ''If you don't mind speaking to him...''

''Not at all.'' Bella rose and impulsively hugged Georgiana. ''Now! I'm going to ring for tea, and we'll talk about something quite different.''

Georgiana summoned a smile and tried to tell herself that the peculiar emptiness within was only hunger.

TWO HOURS LATER Georgiana escaped to the sanctuary of her chamber. She did not ring for Cruickshank, wishing only to lie down and rest her aching head.

Quite when it was that she had finally realised she was in love with Lord Alton she could not be sure. Certainly, her social success and the proposals of Lord Danby and Mr Havelock had precipitated her thoughts on marriage. Only then had her feelings crystallised and gained substance. But, given that Lord Alton was so much older than she, and was shortly to marry Lady Changley, aside from having no inkling of her attachment and certainly no reciprocal emotions, she had originally decided her infatuation, for surely that was all it could be, was bound to pass. In such circumstances, and knowing Lord Alton was unlikely to spend much time in his sister's house, or dancing attendance on them, she had not seen her position as Bella's companion to be in any way compromised.

That had been before the shock of this afternoon had opened her eyes. Lord Ellsmere was all any young lady could desire. He was handsome, considerate, worldly and charming. And rich and titled... The list went on. But he was very definitely not the man she desired. When his lordship had taken her in his arms, she had been deep in a daydream in which she was walking with Bella's brother. The disappointment she had felt on realising that it was not Lord Alton kissing her had been acute.

She could no longer delude herself. What she felt for Viscount Alton was what her mother had felt for her father. She had seen them together often enough, laughing happily in a world of their own, to have an innate sense of the emotion. Love. That was what it was, plain and simple.

How had it happened?

Ridiculous it might be. Impossible it might be. But it was real.

With a great sigh, Georgiana burrowed her head into the soft pillow. How she was going to cope when next they met, as it seemed certain they would, she did not know. But cope she would. She had no intention of letting Bella guess the truth, nor of running away and leaving Bella alone. Arthur had offered her a way out of her troubles, and she had accepted in good faith. She would not let him down. Somehow she would manage.

Worn out, she closed her eyes. She needed to rest her troubled mind. And her troubled heart.

THE DUCHESS OF LEWES was holding her Grand Ball three nights later.

"One has to be a Duchess to call your ball 'Grand,'" Bella acidly remarked. "Still, one has to be seen there. It's one of the compulsory gatherings, you might say."

She had arrived in Georgiana's chamber just as that damsel emerged from her bath. Drifting to the bed, Bella fingered the lilac silk gown laid out there. Then, as if making up her mind, she turned to Georgiana. "Georgie, I know your feelings on this, but I really think you should consider wearing the sea-green gauze. You know I can never wear it. Please, wear it to please me."

Georgiana looked up, arrested in the act of towelling herself dry. Golden curls, dampened with steam, wreathed her head. For one moment she hesitated, considering Bella's plea.

"Wouldn't it cause comment, being so soon after my father's death?"

"But your father said you weren't to go into mourning, remember? And although it's common knowledge that your father has recently died, I haven't told anyone how recently. Have you?''

Georgiana shook her head. She considered the seagreen gauze. Stubbornly, she had bought three more evening gowns from Fancon, all in lilac shades, rather than wear the two gowns Bella had surreptitiously bought. But really, what right had she to refuse? It was a simple request and, after all Bella's help, it was a small price to pay. In reality, it was only her pride that forbade her to wear the delicate creations hanging ownerless in her wardrobe. So she smiled, fleetingly. ''If it would please you.''

Bella grinned happily. ''Immensely.'' Her objective gained, she did not dally but whisked off to place herself in the hands of Hills.

Some three hours later, when they had finally gained the ballroom of Lewes House, Georgiana stood beside Bella and wondered why she had not overturned her stubborn pride weeks ago. The approbation in Arthur's eyes when she had entered the drawing-room that evening had assured her that her decision to wear the gown had been the right one. And the unusually intent attention of her court, and of numerous other gentlemen she had not previously encountered, bore testimony to their approval of her change in style.

As she accepted Lord Mowbray's arm for the first waltz, she smiled happily, laughingly returning his lordship's pretty compliments. To her surprise, she had discovered she could preserve the façade of a young lady enjoying her first London Season, free of care and the tangles of love, despite her empty heart. She had never been encouraged to think her own troubles of particular note. Hence, she continued to observe the lives and foibles of those about her with interest. She treated all her court in the same friendly style she had always affected. True, there were few among the débutantes she could yet call friend, but Bella was there to supply that need, for which she would always be thankful.

Georgiana had no idea what exactly Bella had said to Lord Ellsmere. Whatever it was, he had gracefully withdrawn his suit, simultaneously assuring Georgiana of his lifelong devotion. For a whole evening, she had speculated on what Bella could have said. In the end, she decided she didn't need to know.

Despite Bella's fears, her refractory behaviour in the matter of her suitors had not given rise to any adverse effects. She was still "that most suitable Miss Hartley" to the hostesses, and the cards and invitations continued to flood in. She could hardly claim she did not enjoy the balls and parties. Yet, somewhere, some part of her was detached from it all, aloof and unfulfilled, empty and void, waiting. But, as she sternly lectured herself in the long watches of the night, what she was waiting for had no chance of arriving. Lady Winterspoon's dictum had come to her rescue. There was nothing she could do but enjoy herself, thereby pleasing Bella and, as her father would have told her, extending her own experience. So, with typical abandon, she did.

By the end of the third dance, a cotillion, the rooms were starting to fill. Georgiana was escorted back to Bella's side by her partner, Mr Havelock, and he remained beside them, chatting amiably of social happenings. When he finally made his bow and left them, Georgiana turned an impishly animated face to Bella. But what she had intended to say regarding Mr Havelock remained unsaid. In fact the words melted from her mind. Her lips parted slightly in surprise as her gaze locked with Viscount Alton's.

Dominic had made his way to Bella's side through the crush, intending to learn what had become of the golden girl he had left in her care. Only when she turned to face him did he recognise in the exquisite woodland nymph, standing slim and straight in silver-green gauze beside his sister, the same young girl whose heart-shaped face and warmed honey eyes inhabited his dreams. The realisation left him momentarily bereft of words.

It was Bella who came, unwittingly, to their rescue. She uttered a small squeal of delight and, remembering to restrain her impulsive habit of throwing her arms about his neck, grabbed both of Dominic's hands instead. He looked down at her, and the spell was broken. Smoothly, suavely, he raised her hands, first one, then the other, to his lips. "Dear Bella. Clearly in fine fettle."

"But I thought you were fixed in Brighton." Bella received her hands back, but had eyes only for her brother. She saw his gaze had moved past her to Georgiana. When he made no reply but continued to stare at Georgiana, she felt constrained to add, "But you remember Georgiana?"

"Assuredly." Dominic couldn't help himself. His voice had automatically dropped to a deeper register. He smiled into those huge honey-coloured orbs in a manner perfected by years of practice and, taking her small hand, raised it fleetingly to his lips.

Barely able to breathe, Georgiana blushed vividly and sank into the regulation curtsy.

Her blush recalled Dominic to his senses. When she straightened, his face had assumed its usual, faintly bored mien. He turned slightly to address Bella. "As you see, I've decided to exchange the extravagant but questionably tasteful entertainments of His Highness for the more mundane but distinctly more enjoyable pursuits of the *ton*."

"Shhh!" said Bella, scandalised. "Someone might hear you!"

Dominic smiled sleepily. "My dear, it's only what half of the Carlton House set are saying. Hardly fodder for treason."

Bella still looked dubious.

But Dominic's attention had wandered. "Perhaps, Miss Hartley, I can steal a waltz. Judging by the hordes of gentlemen hovering, you have few to spare."

By this time, Georgiana had regained her composure and was determined not to lose it again. "The fruits of your sister's hard work, my lord," she responded readily. She placed her hand on his lordship's sleeve, suppressing by force the shiver that ran through her at that simple contact. How on earth was she to survive a waltz?

Thankfully, Lord Alton seemed unaware of her difficulties. One strong arm encircled her waist, and she was swept effortlessly into the dance. As her feet automatically followed his lead, she relaxed sufficiently to glance up into the dark-browed face above hers.

He intercepted her glance and smiled. "So you've been filling in time with all manner of social gadding?"

Georgiana shrugged lightly. "The pleasures of the *ton* have yet to pall, though I make no doubt they eventually will."

The dark brows rose. "What a very novel point of view." Dominic's lips twitched. "Surely my sister has taught you that all débutantes must, of necessity, profess addiction to all *tonnish* pursuits?"

A small and intriguing smile lifted Georgiana's lips. "Indeed, Bella has tried to convince me of the irreparable harm my lack of long-term enthusiasm might do to my chances. Still, I prefer to hold my own views." Georgiana paused while they twirled elegantly around the end of the room, before continuing, "I find it difficult to imagine being satisfied with a routine composed entirely of balls and parties and such affairs. Surely, somewhere, there must be some greater purpose in life?"

She glanced up to find an arrested expression on the Viscount's face. Suddenly worried she had inadvertently said more than she intended, Georgiana made haste to recover. "Of course, there may be a hidden purpose in such affairs—"

"No. Don't recant." His voice was low and betrayed no hint of mirth. His eyes held hers, unexpectedly serious, strangely intent. "Your views do you credit. Far be it from me to disparage them."

Georgiana was left wondering whether there was,

underlying his seriousness, some fine vein of sarcasm she had failed to detect. But she got no chance to pursue the matter; the music ceased and Lord Alton returned her to his sister's side. With a smile and a lazy flick of one finger to Bella's cheek, and a polite inclination of his head in Georgiana's direction, he withdrew.

On the other side of the ballroom, Elaine Changley shut her ivory fan with a snap. Her cold blue eyes remained fixed upon a head of gold curls just visible through the throng. Surely Dominic hadn't left her for a schoolgirl? Impossible!

The intervening bodies shifted, and Lady Changley was afforded a full view of Georgiana Hartley, slim and elegant at Bella Winsmere's side. The blue eyes narrowed. Her ladyship had not reached her present position without learning to sum up the opposition's good points. There was no doubt the girl had a certain something. But the idea of the charms of a delicate and virginal schoolgirl competing with her own experienced voluptuousness was too ridiculous to contemplate.

Lady Changley's rouged lips set in a hard line. The thought of what her so-called friends would say if, after all her crowing, she was to lose a prize like Dominic Ridgeley to a chit of a girl fresh from the schoolroom was entirely too galling to bear. Perhaps a little reminder of what she could offer was due.

IT WAS PAST midnight when Georgiana slipped on to the terrace outside the ballroom. The last dance before supper was in progress, and the terrace was vacant except for the moonbeams that danced along its length. As the chill of the evening bit through her thin gown, she wrapped her arms about her and fell to pacing the stone flags, drawing in deep breaths of the refreshing night air.

She had yet to become fully acclimatised to the stuffy atmosphere of *tonnish* ballrooms. Feeling the heat closing in on her, she had very nearly suggested to her cavalier of the moment, Lord Wishpoole, that they retire to the terrace. Luckily, a mental vision of his lordship's face expressing his likely reaction to such an invitation had stopped her from uttering the words, and doubtless saved her from the embarrassment of extricating herself from his lordship's unnecessary and very likely scandalous company. Wary of giving Bella any further reason to view her with concern, she had pleaded a slight headache to Lord Wishpoole and headed for the withdrawing-room. Once out of his lordship's sight, she had changed direction. The long windows of the ballroom had been left ajar, but the weather had turned and few guests had availed themselves of the opportunity to stroll on the long terrace.

Georgiana leant against the low balustrade and wished she was not alone. The idea of strolling beside Lord Alton, conversing easily while they took the air, was enticing. Only, of course, there was no possibility of Lord Alton wishing to stroll with her. Unfortunately, reality and dreams did not merge in that way.

The sound of footsteps approaching one of the doors at the far end of the terrace brought her upright. Someone pulled a set of doors wide, and light spilled forth.

Startled, Georgiana looked around for a hiding-place. A tall cypress in a tub stood against the wall. Without further thought, she squeezed herself between the balustrade and the tree.

Through the scraggly branches of the tree she watched as a tall woman glided on to the terrace. The moonlight, resurrected now the doors were again shut, silvered her blonde hair. As she turned and looked towards the cypress, Georgiana caught a glimpse of diamonds glittering around an alabaster throat. The lady's silk dress clung revealingly to a ripe figure; her long, graceful arms were quite bare.

Again light flooded the terrace and was abruptly cut off. Georgiana's eyes grew round.

Dominic Ridgeley's blue eyes were hard as they rested on Elaine Changley. His brows rose. "To what do I owe the pleasure of this meeting, my lady?"

Inwardly, Elaine Changley winced at his tone. *My lady?* Clearly she had lost more than a little ground. But not a suspicion of her emotions showed on her sculpted face as she moved forward to place one slim hand on the Viscount's lapel. "Dominic, darling. Why so cold?" she purred.

To her surprise and real consternation, Lady Changley sensed an instinctive rejection, immediately suppressed, but undeniable. Shock drove her to make a grab, however unwise, for her dreams. Allowing her lids to veil her eyes, she moved seductively closer. "Surely, my love, what lies between us cannot be ended with a simple 'Goodbye'?"

Lady Changley was a tall woman. In one smooth

movement, she pressed herself to Dominic's chest, reaching up to place her lips against his.

Automatically, Dominic's hands came to her waist, initially to hold her from him. But as he felt her silken form between his hands he stopped and quite coldly considered the situation.

He had come to the terrace in response to Elaine's note, intending to make it quite clear that his ''Good-bye'' had meant just that. The problem he was having with Georgiana Hartley, or, rather, with making sense of his feelings towards a schoolroom chit, was his major and only concern. He had almost succeeded in convincing himself that it was merely a passing aberration, that the reason he no longer desired the company, let alone the favours, of the delectable Lady Changley was no more than a function of the natural passage of time and had nothing whatever to do with a slim form in green silk gauze. Almost, but not quite.

And now here was Elaine, providing him with a perfect chance to test the veracity of his conclusions. The acid test. Surely, if he were to kiss her now, a woman he had recently known so well, he would feel something?

On the thought, his hands moved to draw her more firmly against him. Then his arms closed around her and his head angled over hers as he took possession of her lips and then her mouth. He felt the ripple of relief that travelled through her long limbs. Warning bells sounded in his brain. He felt nothing—no glimmer of desire, no flicker of flame. The coals were long dead.

Abruptly he brought the kiss to an end and, lifting

his head, put Elaine Changley from him. "And that, my dear, is very definitely the end. Adieu and good-bye." With a terse bow, he spun on his heel.

Before he could leave, Elaine, desperate, stretched out one white hand to his sleeve. "You can't just walk away from me, Dominic. There's too much between us."

The chill of his very blue eyes as they turned on her froze Elaine Changley's blood. But, when he spoke, Dominic's voice was soft—soft and, to Elaine Changley, quite deadly. "I suspect, my dear, that you'll find you're mistaken. I should perhaps point out that any embarrassment you might suffer upon our separation will be entirely your own fault. And, fur-thermore, any attempt on your part to talk more into the relationship than was ever present will only result in your further embarrassment. So—" Dominic smiled—a singularly humourless smile—and lifted her hand from his sleeve, and thence, mockingly, to his lips "—I will, for the last time, bid you adieu."

Elaine Changley made no attempt to detain him as he strode from the terrace. She was shivering, though not from the cold. Far too experienced to run after her ex-lover, Lady Changley forced herself to stand still until her composure returned. Only then did she follow Lord Alton back into the ballroom.

Georgiana let out a long breath. She emerged from behind the tub, automatically brushing her skirt free of small sticks and needles. She felt as if she had hardly breathed since scuttling behind the tree. That, of course, was the reason she was feeling light-headed. Nothing to do with the revelation that Bella's brother was quite clearly and indisputably in love with Lady Changley. Why else would he have kissed her like that? She had been too far away to overhear their conversation, or to see their expressions, but the evidence of her eyes had been plain enough. Lady Changley had melted into Lord Alton's arms. And he had welcomed her and kissed her as if he intended to passionately devour her.

She knew her love for him was hopeless. Had always known it.

Georgiana shivered. Slowly she looked around the terrace. Her innocent daydream seemed more distant than ever, elusive as the mist which wreathed the treetops. With a deep sigh, she pulled open one of the ballroom doors and re-entered the heated room. She finally located Bella amid a knot of their friends. Pushing through the throng, she made her way to her side, rehearsing her request to leave early on the grounds of a headache which she could now quite truthfully claim.

CHAPTER FIVE

DURING THE NEXT WEEK, Georgiana had plenty of opportunity to develop her tactics for dealing socially with Viscount Alton. Contrary to her expectations, his lordship graced all the functions she and Bella attended. He was politely attentive. There was nothing in his behaviour to feed the flame she was valiantly trying to dampen. To her irration, she found that fact depressing. More than ever aware of the disparity of their stations, she doggedly reminded herself that a thick skin could only be obtained through exposure. Consequently, she did not shrink from contact with Lord Alton. Instead, whenever he asked her to dance—which he invariably did at least once, and, on one memorable occasion, twice—she endeavoured to amuse him with her observations on life in the *ton*. To her surprise, he seemed genuinely entertained by her comments. Indeed, he went out of his way to encourage her to air her opinions. Doubtless, she thought, it ensured he was not overcome with boredom in her otherwise unenlivening company.

Her own motive in maintaining a steady flow of conversation lay in distracting his lordship from the other peculiar responses he awoke in her. Breathlessness, often occurring with a unnerving sense of exhilaration, was the least of these. Sometimes she believed the thudding of her heart would be plainly audible if she weren't covering the noise with her chatter. Thankfully, he had not yet noticed the tremors that ran through her at his slightest touch. She had hoped these would ease with time, with familiarity, as it were. Unfortunately, they were becoming more acute with each passing day; she went in dread of his remarking them.

Absorbed as she was with dealing with his lordship, by the time they climbed into their carriage each night to return to Green Street she was thoroughly worn out. Gradually, the strain grew, until, in order to preserve her defences for the evenings, she found herself forced to forgo the pleasures of the day. When she excused herself from the afternoon's promenade for the second day in a row, Bella's concern became overt.

"Georgie, I simply cannot bear to see you so pulled down." Bella plumped herself down on the *chaise-longue* beside her friend. Georgiana was listlessly plying her needle, setting the occasional stitch in a piece of fine embroidery. Bella glanced anxiously into her face. "You aren't going into a decline, are you?"

Despite her tiredness, Georgiana grinned. "Of course not." After a moment she added, "I assure you I've no intention of pining away. It's just that I find the...the tension of the evening entertainments draining."

Born and bred to such things, Bella could not readily imagine being drained by a ball. However, she was not without sympathy. She frowned as she mulled over the matter. "We could cut down a trifle, perhaps. The

Minchintons' ball is on Friday—we need not go to that, I suppose.''

But curtailing Bella's activities because of her own weakness was further than Georgiana was prepared to go. She was supposed to be Bella's companion, not an inhibiting influence. ''Don't be a goose,'' she replied, her tone affectionate but firm. ''I'm only feeling a bit low, that's all. I dare say if I make a special effort I'll be fine by this evening.'' She paused. ''On second thoughts, perhaps some fresh air would help. If you'll wait, I'll get my bonnet and come with you.''

''Of course.'' Bella smiled encouragingly.

But as soon as Georgiana disappeared through the door, the frown return to Bella's face. Far from reassuring her, Georgiana's rapid about-face convinced her that her friend was endeavouring, however unsuccessfully, to conceal the true effect of her hopeless love. Who knew to what depths of misery Georgie descended when no one was by? Bella fretted over the problem, rendered more acute by the restraint she felt in confiding in anyone. Arthur was her long-time mentor, but in this case Bella felt she would need Georgiana's permission before revealing her friend's state to him.

Georgiana's footsteps sounded in the hall. With a sigh, Bella rose and picked up her discarded bonnet, absent-mindedly swinging it by its long aqua ribbons. She sorely needed advice. Then, in one instant of blinding clarity, she saw the answer. Dominic. He knew all of Georgiana's background. And, after all, Georgiana herself had seen fit, at the very outset, to confide in him.

When Georgiana stuck her head around the door, Bella grinned widely. "Yes, I'm coming," she called and, feeling much more light-hearted, all but tripped from the room.

"PLEASE, DOMINIC. I really *must* talk to you. Privately." Bella put every ounce of sisterly need into her gaze as it rested on her brother's handsome face. But his habitually bored mask showed no evidence of lifting. In fact, she noted, he regarded her even more dubiously than he had before her plea.

"I warn you, Bella, I need no lectures from you."

Far from striking fear into her heart and stifling her request as intended, his precise tones made her relax and give a dismissive smile.

"Not about that! I want to talk to you about Georgiana."

"Oh!" Dominic followed her gaze to the object of their discussion, twirling gaily about the dance-floor in Harry Edgcombe's arms. Then the piercingly blue eyes swung back to Bella. "What about Miss Hartley?"

Bella looked at the knots of people surrounding them. "Not here." She glanced impishly up at him. "Don't you know of an alcove where we might be alone?"

The blue eyes glinted down at her. "Don't be impudent." He caught her hand and drew it through his arm. "As it happens," he said, leading her through the crowd, "I do. But I can't spare too many minutes. I'm engaged to dance with Miss Hartley myself, two dances hence."

"It won't take long," Bella promised.

The small ante-room Dominic led her to was thankfully empty. She sank on to a well padded sofa. Dominic elected to stand, leaning one blue-silk-clad arm along the mantelpiece. "Perceive me all ears, dear sister."

Bella eyed him suspiciously, but could detect no hint of the sarcasm he frequently employed when irritated. "As I said, it's about Georgiana." Now she came to it, she found herself short of the necessary words.

"Has she discovered Arthur's little deception and become difficult?"

"No, no. Nothing like that." Bella frowned, then, sensing Dominic's growing impatience, she abandoned her efforts to find the best phrasing and blurted out, "She's fallen in love."

For a moment, she wondered whether he had heard. His face showed no reaction to her words; he seemed frozen, petrified. Then his black brows rose. "I see." He turned aside, resettling the fine lace on his cuff. "It is, after all, not an uncommon happening. Who is the lucky man?"

"That's just it. She won't say."

Dominic's eyes rested thoughtfully on his sister's dark head. "And you imagine, as she won't divulge his name, he must therefore be in some way unsuitable."

"No, that's not it either." Bella glanced up to find her brother's eyes full on her, irritation fermenting in their blue depths. She hastened to explain. "He's not unsuitable in the way you mean. But it seems she's fallen *irrevocably* in love with a man who's about to offer for another. She says he doesn't know she's in love with him. I've tried to get her to confide in me, but she won't. She says I know him so it wouldn't be fair.''

Dominic digested this information in silence. Then, abruptly, he pushed away from the mantelpiece and paced across the room. Returning, he looked again at his sister. ''How, then, am I supposed to help? I do take it I'm supposed to help?''

Bella smiled, a trifle warily. ''Yes, of course. I wouldn't have told you if I didn't think you could help. I want you to find out who Georgie's gentleman is.''

Dominic's brows flew. ''That all?''

At his tone, Bella's face fell. ''But you must be able to guess. Who is it whom I know is about to marry? Or at least offer for someone. You men always know such titbits before it's common knowledge.''

Pacing once more, Dominic considered his acquaintance. He knew all the gentlemen his sister was on speaking terms with, and would very likely know if any were contemplating matrimony. ''Unfortunately, to my knowledge, no one fits the bill.''

Twisting her fingers anxiously, Bella ventured, ''I had wondered whether it was Lord Edgcombe.''

''Harry?'' Dominic paused, then shook his head. ''Not likely. He does have to marry in the not overly distant future or risk his family hauling him to the altar themselves. But he must marry money, and I doubt Miss Hartley's prospects fit his bill.''

"But couldn't she have fallen in love with him anyway? He's certainly personable enough."

Again, Dominic gave the matter his consideration. Again, he shook his head. "Harry has no plans to marry yet awhile. I doubt he'd even mention the possibility to a young lady circumstanced as Miss Hartley is. And, certainly, he would not have suggested he's about to do the deed." He uttered a short laugh. "Not even to escape a snare would Harry bring up the subject of marriage."

Bella sighed. "So you can't guess either." Disheartened, she stood and shook out her skirts.

Dominic hadn't moved from his stance in the middle of the floor. Now he looked shrewdly at Bella. "What prompted you to ask for help?"

Bella shrugged. "It's just that Georgie's so wan and listless nowadays."

"Listless?" her brother echoed, the vision of Miss Hartley as he had last seen her vivid in his mind. "I've rarely seen anyone *less* listless."

"Oh, not in the evenings. She seems quite lively then. But during the day she's drawn and quiet. Her looks will suffer if she goes on as she is. If *only* she would accept Mr Havelock."

"Havelock? Has he offered for her?"

Bella frowned at the odd note in her brother's voice. It was not like Dominic to be so insultingly disbelieving. "Yes," she averred. "Not only Mr Havelock, but Lord Danby and Viscount Molesworth. *And* Lord Ellsmere, too!"

For once, she had the satisfaction of knowing she

had stunned her brother. Dominic's brows rose to astronomical heights. "Good lord!"

After a moment, his puzzled gaze swung back to her face. "And she refused them all? Even Julian?"

Bella nodded decisively. "Even Lord Ellsmere." She looked down at her hands, clasped schoolgirl fashion before her. "I don't know what I'm to do, for there's bound to be more offers. They can't seem to help themselves."

She looked up to see her brother's shoulders shaking. Bella glared. "It's not funny!"

Dominic waved one white hand placatingly. "Oh, Bella! Would that all women had a sense of humour like Miss Hartley's. I assure you she would see the oddity in such a situation."

Bella was puzzled by her brother's far-away smile. But before she drummed up enough courage to ask what prospect it was that so fascinated him, he came back to earth. "And, speaking of Miss Hartley, we must, I'm afraid, return to the ballroom."

Falling into step beside him, Bella tucked her hand in his arm. "You will try to discover who he is, won't you?"

Dominic's eyes glinted steely blue. "Fear not, Bella mine. I'll give it my most earnest consideration."

And with that Bella had perforce to be content.

IT WAS WELL AFTER midnight when Dominic returned to Grosvenor Square. He let himself in with his latchkey. In the large tiled hall, shadows danced about a single candle burning in a brass holder on the central table. He had long ago broken his staff of their preferred habit of lying in wait for him to return from his evening entertainments. Picking up the candle, he stood at the foot of the stairs, contemplating the broad upward sweep. Then he turned aside and made for a polished door to one side of the hall.

The fire in the library was a glowing mass of coals. He lit the candles in the large candelabrum on the mantelpiece before crouching to carefully balance a fresh log on the embers. After a little encouragement, the flames started to lick along the dry wood.

Standing, he stretched, then crossed to the sideboard. A balloon of fine brandy in one hand, he returned to the wing-chair by the fireplace and settled his cold feet on the fender.

Georgiana Hartley. Undoubtedly the most beguiling female he had met in over a decade on the town. And she was in love with another man. Furthermore, she was in love with a man who didn't even have the good sense to love her. Ridiculous!

Dominic stared into the flames. For what felt like the six hundreth time, he tried to make himself believe that his interest in Miss Hartley didn't exist. But he had travelled that road before and had given up weeks ago. What he had yet to discover was what his interest in Georgiana Hartley portended.

He couldn't believe it was love. Not after all these years. His experience of the opposite sex was as extensive as hers was negligible. And he had never felt the slightest inclination to succumb to any of the proffered lures. Why on earth should he suddenly wish to entangle himself with a young woman barely free of the schoolroom?

Yet he could not get her out of his mind. Her heart-shaped face and honey-gold eyes inhabited his thoughts to the exclusion of almost everything else. He had underestimated the strength of his distraction when he had returned from Candlewick to Brighton. The chit had unexpected depths. Her eyes, like a siren's song, beckoned with a promise he found difficult to resist. Luckily he had realised his state before Elaine had precipitated any renewal of their intimacy. She had, predictably, reacted badly to his withdrawal.

Light from the flames gilded the spines of the leather-covered tomes on the shelves which stretched away into darkness on either side of the fireplace. Dominic took a sip of his brandy, then sank his chin into his cravat, cradling the glass between his hands. He had no regrets about Elaine. In truth, his desire for her had waned before the advent of Georgiana Hartley had banished all thought of illicit dalliance from his mind. A smile of gentle malice touched his lips. Doubtless Elaine would suffer due embarrassment as a result of her posturing. It had been her plan to use public knowledge of their relationship to pressure him into making her aspirations come true. She had been most indiscreet. Lionel, Lord Worthington, his guardian prior to his attaining his majority, had even been moved to post to Candlewick to dissuade him from contracting a *mésalliance,* on account of the bluster of a trollop's long tongue. No, he had no sympathy for such as Elaine Changley.

The fire crackled and hissed as the fresh log settled. With a sensation akin to relief, he turned his mind from the past to contemplate the nebulous future. What did his feelings for Georgiana Hartley mean? Did they amount to anything more than infatuation, regrettable but harmless and, most importantly, transient? Would the lovely Georgiana fade from his mind in six months' time, as Elaine Changley had? These were the questions that tormented him. They had forced him to return to London, to assuage a need he did not wish to acknowledge. Yet, after a week in the capital, he was no nearer the answers.

The only truth he had uncovered was that his normally even temperament was now somehow dependent on Miss Georgiana Hartley's smile.

He dropped his head back against the deeply padded leather. He had tried to tell himself she was too young, little more than a schoolgirl. Any liaison between them would be virtually cradle-snatching. But, whenever he thought along such lines, Arthur's and Bella's happiness would rise up to mock him. And, even worse, Georgiana no longer *looked* like a schoolgirl. Every time they met, Fancon's gowns, or, rather, the delectable shape they displayed, shredded his well rehearsed rationalisations.

But enough was enough. According to Bella, Georgiana was making herself ill over some no-hoper. He had no right to intervene. Not, that was, unless he wished to take their interaction further, to make some positive move in her direction. And that, he was not yet prepared to do.

If Bella, or anyone else, got a whiff of his possible intentions, there would be no chance of wooing her in private. Their every meeting would be watched over by dozens of gimlet eyes. Every word, every expression would be duly noted and analysed. He couldn't subject her to that, not when he wasn't sure what he wanted of her.

Experience, however, was on his side. If he wished, he did not doubt he could create the necessary opportunities to advance his cause, without alerting every gossip-monger in the *ton*. He smiled. There was an undeniable challenge in such an enterprise. The snag was, he was not yet sure. Not sure of what he felt for her. Not sure of what he would do once he was certain the odd feeling in his chest was more than infatuation.

It had taken him three weeks to reach his present state of acknowledged indecision. He had no intention of enduring the situation for much longer, particularly if Georgiana threatened to pine away before his very eyes. Still, how did one test an infatuation? Never having suffered such an emotion before, he had no real idea how to proceed.

The clock in the corner ticked ponderously, marking his heartbeats. His eyes grew unfocused as he stared at the flames slowly dying around the charred log. Finally he stirred. He drained his glass, then rose to return it to the tray. He relighted his bedroom candle at the candelabrum, then snuffed the five long candles it held. In the soft flickering light of the single flame, he made his way to the door.

If he wanted to burn out his obsession with Georgiana Hartley, there was only one way to go about it. He needed to meet with her often, in every possible context, to see all her faults and blemishes, the little incompatibilities which would reduce her status in his mind to one of a mere acquaintance. That was the only way forward.

And, if it proved to be more than infatuation, it was high time he faced up to the truth. And acted.

"I TOLD YOU everyone would be here." Bella stopped on the lawn below the terrace. Tucking her furled parasol under one arm, she retied the strings of her new bonnet in a jaunty bow beneath one ear. "Lady Jersey's entertainments are always well attended, particularly when they're held here."

"Here" was Osterley Park, and the entertainment in question was an alfresco luncheon. To Georgiana, standing patiently by her friend's side, it seemed as if the entire *ton* was gathered on the manicured lawns sloping gently away from the Palladian mansion to the shrubberies and parkland beyond. "Lady Lyncombe is nodding to us. Over there on the left."

Bella turned and bowed politely to the portly matron, who had three gangling girls in tow. "Poor dear. Freckle-faced, the lot of them. She'll never get them off her hands."

Georgiana stifled a giggle. "Surely it can't be that bad. They might be quite nice young girls."

"They can be as nice as they please, but they'll need something more to recommend them to the eligible gentlemen." Bella sighed, in keeping with her worldly-wise pose.

Strolling by her side, Georgiana wondered what it was that recommended her to the gentlemen. Certainly not her looks, for, in her estimation, these were only passing fair. And her fortune was, she suspected, so small as to be negligible. Yet she had received four offers. Despite the fact that she had wished to avoid each one, the very existence of four eligible offers was no small fillip to her confidence.

Smiling and bowing to acquaintances, they strolled the length of the lawn to where three gaily striped marquees had been erected. One housed the beverages; one protected the food. The third was a withdrawing-room of sorts, where ladies feeling the effects of the sun could rest before rejoining the crush.

And it certainly was a crush. The broad expanses were filled with swirling muslins and starchy cambrics, parasols and elegantly cut morning coats dotting the colourful scene. It was difficult to see more than ten feet in any direction. Registering this fact, Georgiana turned to Bella to point out the advisability of staying close together. Too late.

"If you're looking for Bella, she's fallen victim to Lady Molesworth."

Georgiana looked up into Viscount Alton's blue eyes. He was smiling, and she noted the set of small lines radiating from the corners of his eyes. Such a handsome face. Entranced, she forgot her role of sister's companion and smiled warmly back.

Dominic expertly captured her hand and conveyed it to his lips. He caught his breath when she smiled with such guileless joy. For one instant, he could almost believe...

A sudden intentness in Lord Alton's gaze brought Georgiana to her senses. "Oh! Er—where exactly?" She flustered and blushed, and turned away as if looking for Bella, to cover her confusion.

"No, no. This way." Dominic's voice was gentle, softened by an emotion he couldn't quite define.

Georgiana looked where he indicated—to the right—and found Bella deep in discussion with Lord Molesworth's mother—she who had decreed Georgiana could not do other than marry her son.

Dominic recalled Bella's mention of the luckless Viscount. His grin grew. "Perhaps," he said, "as Bella is so absorbed, I could escort you on a ramble by the lake. It's really much more pleasant than being packed amid all this crowd. Unless you're famished?" One black brow rose interrogatively.

"Oh, no," Georgiana disclaimed. She bit her lip. The prospect of a stroll in less cramped surroundings was very tempting. But could she weather such an excursion with Lord Alton? Were her nerves up to it? She glanced up at him and found him regarding her quizzically, as if trying to read her mind. As she watched, a faintly satirical gleam entered the very blue eyes, and his brows rose slightly, as if in challenge. Puzzled, she put aside her misgivings. "If it wouldn't be too boring for you."

With a laugh, Dominic offered her his arm. When she laid one small hand on his sleeve, he covered it with his other hand. "My dear Miss Hartley—or can I call you Georgiana?" He felt the hand under his quiver. His brows rose again. He looked down into her golden eyes. "Oh, yes. Surely, in the circumstances, I can claim that privilege?"

Georgiana had no idea how she should answer. But her nerves were already a-tingle, and she didn't have the capacity to cope with distractions. So she merely inclined her head in assent. "If it pleases you, my lord."

Oh, it pleased him. In fact Dominic felt inordinately pleased with that small success. "As I was saying, my dear Georgiana," he continued, deftly steering her clear of Lord Harrow, another of her present encumbrances, "your company is forever entertaining. Tell me, which of your suitors do you favour?"

Now what on earth was she to answer to that? Georgiana thought quickly, then assumed a bored air. "Why, in truth, I'd not given the matter much thought, my lord." She heard a deep chuckle. "It's all so fatiguing, this marriage game." Lassitude dripped from her every syllable.

Laughing, he countered, "Very neat, my dear. But don't let any of the *grandes dames* hear you espousing such controversial standards. You'll be driven forth, cast out from the bosom of the *ton*."

Georgiana smiled, dropping her pose. "In all honesty, I'm not sure I'm suited to this life."

To mock her words would be the easy way out. Instead Dominic answered seriously. "My dear, it's such as you who keep the *ton* alive."

Her eyes flew to his face.

Reading the question in the golden-lit depths, he explained, "If we did not have people with different ideas, people brought up to different ideas, such as yourself, join us now and then, to refresh our tired fashions, then the *ton* would be an excessively boring and stale society. Instead, if you look about you carefully, you'll see the *ton* encompasses a wide spectrum of tastes and types." He smiled down at her. "Don't worry. You'll fit in. You'll eventually find your place, that niche that has your name engraved on it.''

Shyly Georgiana returned his smile.

They strolled on in companionable silence, around the shrubberies and on to the shore of the lake. A cool breeze lifted off the expanse of grey-green water, flicking little wavelets across the surface. Beeches lined an avenue that followed the bank, golden leaves a carpet beneath the still canopied crowns. There were other guests enjoying the peace, but none intruded on their privacy.

While enjoying the early autumn colours, Georgiana pondered the cause of his earlier satirical look. As she noted the giggling and sighing of more than one damsel they passed, it suddenly occurred to her that Lord Alton might have thought she was questioning the propriety of walking alone with him. Inwardly, she sighed. If only that were her trouble. But she was abysmally aware she was in no danger of receiving any amorous attentions from Bella's brother. Rather, she was more afraid of boring him witless. She cast about in her mind for a suitable topic of conversation.

Far from being bored, Dominic was revelling in the unusual pleasure of strolling in relative peace in a glorious setting with a beautiful woman who was blessedly silent. The only itch to his contentment was the realisation of how deeply contented he in fact was. That, and the strength of his desire to preserve the moment at whatever cost. That unnerved him.

''Do you spend much time with the Prince Regent? What's he like?''

Georgiana's questions broke his train of thought.

Dominic paused, considering, before he answered. "My family have for the past few generations been close to the throne." He smiled down at her. "In the present case, the Regent."

"But…" Georgie hesitated. She had taken in enough of the discussion between Lord Alton and Arthur over Bella's dinner-table to realise the Viscount was more deeply involved in politicking than one might suppose from his pose of arrogantly bored aristocrat. Carefully choosing her words, she ventured, "You discuss politics with His Highness, don't you? Not just…well, social matters."

Inwardly cursing Arthur for his lapse from their normal secretiveness, Dominic attempted to turn her far too perceptive query aside. He laughed lightly. "I assure you, my dear, that—er—social matters are generally dominant with the Regent."

The teasing look he sent her along with his words should have had her blushing. Instead, he saw her beautiful eyes narrow slightly, and knew his diversion had failed. Damn it! She was younger than Bella. She should accept his word without question. And since when did young ladies institute probing inquisitions into a man's politics? She deserved a set-down. Instead, Dominic heard himself say, "However, you're quite right. I do act as a sort of…conduit—a channel of communication, if you like—between certain factions of the Parliament and the Regent." He paused to help her step over a large tree root distorting the even surface of the path. Settling her hand once more in the crook of his arm, he continued, "Despite appearances, Prinny is not entirely insensitive to the problems of the realm. And, while he has limited pow-ers as far as actual law-making goes, his influence can go a long way to seeing changes made where they are desperately needed.''

''And you explain these things to him?''

Dominic laughed. ''Oh, no! I merely act as a form of Greek messenger.''

Georgiana looked her question. Smiling, he explained. ''My task is merely to bring up the subject, to introduce the problem, whatever it might be, to His Highness's notice.'' He grinned. ''That's why I'm back from Brighton with leisure to enjoy your company.''

Georgiana frowned, puzzling this out. ''He didn't like your last problem?''

Her companion's gaze had shifted to the distance, but he was still smiling.

''Not in the least. I'm presently in disgrace, although, of course, that's not general knowledge.''

It seemed to Georgiana that there was quite a deal about the fascinating Viscount that was not general knowledge. But before she could frame any further questions, they emerged from the beech walk and were joined by a gaggle of young ladies and their escorts. Viscount Molesworth was there; so too was Lord Ellsmere. Georgiana caught a look of surprise on Lord Ellsmere's handsome face, followed swiftly by an expression she could only interpret as consideration. However, he said nothing to her, beyond a polite greeting, and fell into step on the other side of Lord Alton, engaging the Viscount in a low-voiced conversation which seemed to have a distinctly pugilistic fla-

vour. In a laughing, chattering group, they made their
way back to the marquees. Bella met them there. To
Georgiana's disappointment, she got no further chance
to converse alone with Lord Alton.

TWO NIGHTS LATER, a masked ball was to be held at
Hattringham House. Bella was thrilled. "It's quite fun,
really. Most people know who you are, of course, but
the masks allow everyone to pretend they don't."

It was the afternoon of the big event, and Bella was
lolling on Georgiana's bed.

Georgiana was frowningly considering her wardrobe. The one evening dress she had yet to wear was
the topaz silk. For some reason, she had resisted temptation, saving it for some undefined purpose. She
rather thought the time for wearing it had come. Why
she should feel so she had no idea. She simply did.
She drew it forth and held it to her.

"Oooh, yes!" said Bella, bouncing up. "I'd forgotten about that one. It's perfect."

"You don't think it's a little too…?" Georgiana
gestured vaguely.

"Heavens, no! A 'little too…' is exactly what one
wants for a masked ball."

"Do you have a mask I can borrow?"

"Heaps! They're in a drawer in my room." Bella
sat up and jumped off the bed. "Come, let's go and
look. Bring the dress."

Five minutes later they had found the mask. A
bronzed affair with elaborate upswept wings, it fitted
snugly across Georgiana's upper face from forehead
to upper cheeks. Her hazel eyes glittered from the

darkened depths of the slanted eye holes. There was no debate on the matter; it was perfect.

When they descended the stairs that evening to twirl joyfully about Arthur in the hall, his face told them they were both visions of delight. ''You won't be able to move for all the beaux at your feet,'' he said, taking one hand of each fair maid and gallantly bestowing a kiss on them both.

As he escorted his two charges to their carriage, Arthur smiled in fond anticipation. He was accompanying them ostensibly because the Hattringham House ball was one of the major events of the Season. In reality, he cared little for the social swim but intended to keep a watchful eye on his youthful wife. Bella too often forgot that what she intended as innocent play might be reciprocated by actions far from innocent. As he rarely had time to devote solely to his wife, Arthur was looking forward to enjoying the evening. He knew Dominic would be there and was quite sure he could leave his brother-in-law to look after Georgiana. In fact, he thought, as his gaze rested on the alluring figure clad in topaz silk seated opposite, he doubted his brother-in-law, in his present state, would have eyes for anyone else.

Georgiana travelled the miles to Hattringham House in an unusual state of nervous anticipation. Nervous anticipation of itself was no surprise—she was accustomed to feeling it grow every time she appraoched the moment she would meet Bella's brother. But tonight the tension was heightened. It was the fault of the dress. If she had known how it would affect her, she would never have worn it. Far from decreasing her anxiety, the realisation tightened the knots in her stomach. Inwardly quivering with trepidation, she accepted Arthur's hand to descend from the carriage to the torchlit steps of Hattringham House. With assumed calm, she glided beside Bella as they made their way through the hall and into the ballroom beyond.

There was no footman to announce anyone, of course. The guests merely entered and joined the shifting throng. Already the rooms were crowded. Glittering jewels winked under the chandeliers. Gay silks and satins swirled, fans fluttered in flirtation, curls bobbed teasingly about artful faces. A hubbub of conversation rose to swamp them; warm air redolent with a heady mix of perfumes and flower scents wrapped them about.

"Phew! What a crush!" exclaimed Bella. "And it's not even ten."

A tall, dark-haired gentleman materialised at Georgiana's side. He bowed elegantly over her hand. "Could I beg the favour of this dance, fair maid?"

Behind the dark mask, Georgiana descried the features of Lord Ellsmere. "I would be honoured, my lord," she replied, rising from her curtsy.

"Now how do you know if I'm a lord or not?" her partner asked as he whirled them on to the floor.

"Given that at least half the gentlemen present must be titled, it seemed a reasonable assumption," Georgiana glibly explained. "And besides, even if wrong, the mistake could only flatter, whereas, if it were the other way about, I could be stepping on toes."

His lordship laughed. "You never step on my toes, my dear."

Abruptly Georgiana wondered whether he had accepted her dismissal of his suit or was, in reality, merely waiting in the expectation that she would change her mind. Held easily within his arm, she was loweringly conscious that she felt nothing—no ripple of excitement, no increase in her heartbeat to betray her emotions. His nearness touched her not at all.

The dance ended and they whirled to a halt. Immediately they were mobbed by a crowd of gentlemen, all wishful of securing a dance with the exciting newcomer. Not everyone recognised her; of that Georgiana was certain. But before she could make sense of all their requests and determine whom it was safe for her to accept, a deep voice spoke from just beside her.

"My claim is first, I think."

Georgiana glanced up, her breath trapped, as usual, somewhere between her lungs and her throat. Her eyes took in the tall, broad-shouldered form at her side, exquisitely garbed, dark hair falling in waves about a dark mask. Blue, blue eyes watched her from the depths of the mask. Even if his eyes and voice hadn't informed her clearly who he was, her senses were screaming it.

"Of course, my lord," she said, drawing again on her inner strength, the only way she could weather the storm of emotions his nearness always unleashed within her. She placed her hand on his proffered arm and allowed him to lead her on to the floor, entirely forgetting the rest of her court.

"Well!" expostulated Viscount Molesworth, left standing by Lord Ellsmere. "If that don't beat the Dutch!" He glared at the broad shoulders of the gentleman whose arms now held the lady in topaz silk. His glare turned to a petulant frown. "Who is he, anyway?"

Lord Ellsmere was watching the couple on the dance-floor, a slight smile on his face. He looked down at the Viscount. "Don't you know?"

Lord Molesworth puffed indignantly. "Wouldn't ask if I did. Stands to reason."

Julian Ellsmere continued to watch the dancers, then, shaking his head in wonderment, left Lord Molesworth without his answer.

Georgiana was struggling to subdue her senses, running riot as usual. As they reached the end of their first circuit, she felt almost in control again. If Lord Ellsmere left her cold, Lord Alton did exactly the opposite. She felt flushed—all over. And the peculiar sensation of weakness she had suffered during their more recent meetings seemed tonight to be intensified. Perhaps it was because he was holding her rather more closely than was the norm. Still, at least her brain seemed to be functioning again.

If she had been more experienced, Georgiana might have wondered at her partner's silence. But, engrossed in her inner struggle, she did not question what it was that kept Lord Alton speechless for the better part of the waltz. Dominic was, in fact, dealing with a revelation of his own. When he had seen Georgiana enter the ballroom at Bella's side her beauty had stunned him to immobility. In his eyes, she was the most ravishing female in the room. A goddess, all gold and bronze. A golden angel, from the topmost gold curl to the tip of her tiny gold slippers. A prize beyond price.

He had watched as she circled the floor in Julian's arms, dazedly waiting until he could approach her. He no longer questioned the effect she had on him; it was now too marked to ignore. But, as he had deftly extricated her from her other admirers, for the first time his full attention had been focused on her. What he saw had effectively knocked him back on his heels. He was far too experienced not to recognise the signs. In all their previous meetings, his mind had been fully occupied in analysing his responses to her, not her responses to him. Now, all his well honed expertise on alert, he let his senses feel for her, and convey back to him her state. Every little move she made was now registered—every indrawn breath, every flicker of an eyelid. The information came in and was automatically assessed, allowing him to respond to her smoothly, easily, encöuraging her, heightening her awareness of him, learning her reactions to his attentions. His instinctive conclusions hammered at his conscious mind. When had it happened? In truth, he didn't care. All that now concerned him was how to capture what was there, how to foster and nurture her feelings, to make them grow to what he desired them to be. And all his experience told him that wouldn't be difficult.

So, with gentle patience, he waited until she had herself in hand once more and could cope with his, "And what might your name be, fair one?"

Georgiana blinked. Surely he recognised her? But then, she reflected, she wasn't sure the others had either. Maybe it wasn't that obvious. She thought quickly, then replied, "I really don't think the purpose

of her ladyship's entertainment would be furthered if
I answered that question, my lord.''

Inwardly, Dominic grinned, but outwardly he was
all dejection. ''But what, then, should I call you,
sweetheart?''

It was a struggle to keep her tone even. '' 'Sweetheart' will do very nicely, my lord.''

Great heavens! Had she really said that? Georgiana
glanced up from under her long lashes and blushed
when she encountered her partner's blue gaze. But he
merely smiled, slowly, and said, ''Sweetheart it is,
then, my dear.''

His deep voice sent tingling shivers down her spine.
What on earth was she doing? What on earth was he
doing?

The music ceased, and Georgiana turned towards
the other end of the ballroom, where she had left Bella.
Her partner detained her by the simple expedient of
tightening the arm that still lay about her waist. ''Oh,
no, sweetheart,'' he said on a soft laugh. ''Hasn't anyone told you?'' At her enquiring look, he explained,
''One of the main—if not the primary—purposes of a
balle masquée is to permit those who wish to…further
their acquaintance to do so without attracting the notice of the tattle-mongers.'' His voice had dropped to
a mesmerising tone. His breath wafted the curls about
her ear as he bent closer to add, ''And I find I very
definitely want to further my acquaintance with you.''

Georgiana gasped. There was no doubting the subtle
invitation couched in those otherwise innocuous
words. Involuntarily, her eyes sought his in the darkened recesses of his mask. The glow she saw in the

blue depths merely served to tighten the iron band that had clamped around her chest, threating to suspend her breathing. "My lord!"

Despite her panic, her words came out in a seductive whisper, quite contrary to her intention. It was as if something stronger than her will was impelling her to accept the challenge she saw in his eyes.

He laughed, softly, his eyes on hers, and Georgiana's bones felt weak. Then he put the challenge into words. "Surely, sweetheart, you're not afraid of what you might learn?"

His head was bent close to hers, his large body overwhelmingly near. His breath felt warm against her cheek; his hands came up to surreptitiously stroke her arms where they were bare above her elbow-length gloves. Georgiana could not repress the shiver of pure delight that coursed through her at his touch.

What on earth was he doing? Dominic mentally sat at a distance and marvelled at himself. He knew— none better—that this was no way to behave towards a gently reared young lady. To experienced courtesans, to the likes of Elaine Changley, his attentions would be perfectly in order. But delicate virgins were apt to flee for cover, to faint or screech if treated to such subtle but strong tactics. Certainly, they wouldn't know how to respond to them. The trouble was, Georgiana Hartley's responses had more in common with those of a courtesan than of the virgin he knew her to be. Fascinated, he waited for her reaction.

Georgiana had no thought of fleeing, fainting or screeching. Her conscious mind was entirely taken up with a fight against her desire to learn what it was his lordship proposed to teach her. Desire won, hands down. She'd deal with reality later.

"Afraid?" she echoed, buying time. "Hardly that. But I do wonder at the wisdom of being seen too much together. Surely our friends, if no one else, will recognise us and think it odd?"

Dominic understood the hidden meaning in her words, but chose to ignore it. He was in no hurry to confirm or deny his recognition of her. "In this mêlée? I doubt any of our friends can even see us. Can you see any of your party?"

He had already seen Bella and Arthur move into one of the adjoining salons, so was not surprised when, after a quick survey of the room, Georgiana shook her head. "I can't see anyone I know."

Smiling, Dominic tucked her hand into his arm. "You see? A *balle masquée* is a time to have fun. So come and enjoy yourself with me." As he steered her in the direction of the terrace, he added for her ears only, "I assure you I have every intention of enjoying myself with you."

To Georgiana's delight, the evening proved to be one of unalloyed pleasure. Initially, she was wary, convinced Lord Alton had not recognised her, and on tenterhooks lest he, not knowing who she was, overstepped the line. Instead, while he certainly drifted very close to the invisible limit of acceptable conduct, he never once gave her cause to rue her deception. For deception it certainly was. What on earth would he think if he ever learnt it was his sister's little protégée on whom he was lavishing his attentions?

To be the object of his attentions was a most sinful

pleasure. Georgiana sparkled, animated as she had not been since her father's death. For one blissful evening she forgot her situation, forgot her cousin, forgot everything beyond the dancing lights in a pair of cerulean blue eyes. They walked through the salons and he pointed out numerous well known identities hidden behind their masks, elaborating on their idiosyncrasies, regaling her with gossip and the latest *on dits,* making her laugh, making her blush. When she confessed to hunger, they found the supper-room and helped themselves to heaps of lobster patties. She had her first taste of champagne, and giggled as it fizzled down her throat. They danced again, waltzing with effortless grace. Georgiana felt as if she were floating, held to earth by the strong clasp of his arm about her waist, drawn to heaven by the warmth in his eyes. Later they strolled on the terrace. She stood at the balustrade and he stood behind her, pointing out the features of the famous topiary gardens, thrown into silvered relief by the moonlight. His breath wafted the curls by her ear; his lips gently grazed her temple. Gently, so gently that she had no strength to resist, his hands lifted to her bare shoulders in a practised caress, skimming down over her bare arms. Ripples of delight shivered through her. He drew her around to face him, lifting one gloved hand and raising it to his lips.

"The evening is gone, sweetheart." His eyes lingered on hers, then dropped to her lips. For one instant, Georgiana wondered if he would kiss her. She hovered, poised on the brink of returning such an embrace, and felt oddly deflated when, in a voice curiously devoid of emotion, he remarked, "Come. Let me take you to find your party."

It was some minutes before Georgiana spied Arthur, Bella by his side, just inside the door to the main salon. She turned to the gentleman beside her, only to find he had disappeared, melting into the still considerable crowd. Suppressing a smile at his tactics, Georgiana went forward to Bella's side.

"Good heavens, Georgie! I was starting to wonder if you'd been spirited away." Bella looked closely at Georgiana, then asked, "Where have you been?"

"Oh, just here and there," replied Georgiana, smiling beatifically. She couldn't help her smile, even though it was making Bella suspicious. Still, with Arthur present, she doubted her friend would seek to interrogate her tonight. And she would handle tomorrow's queries when they came.

Ten minutes later, the Winsmere carriage rolled out along the road back to London.

Dominic Ridgeley watched it go. Pulling on his gloves, he nodded to a waiting footman, who promptly departed to summon the Viscount's carriage. Once comfortably ensconced in soft leather, the excellent springs ironing out the inevitable bumps and jolts, Dominic allowed his mind to coolly assess his involvement with Georgiana Hartley. He placed due emphasis on the "cool"; there had been more than one moment during the evening just past when, for all his experience, he had felt anything but cool. She was an enigma, his golden angel, an innocent who responded with delicious abandon to every practised caress he bestowed on her, who promised to respond with even greater passion to those caresses he had yet to expose her to. A golden angel who had already captured his hardened rake's heart, but, unless he mistook the matter, had yet to realise that fact. A fascinating proposition.

He treated the darkness to a smile of pure delight. Who would ever have believed it?

As the miles fell beneath his horses' hoofs, he relived the evening in his mind. She had accepted at face value his intimation that he hadn't recognised her. Would she still believe that tomorrow? And, if she did, what would she then make of his attentions to an unknown lady? Dominic grimaced. He would have to take the earliest opportunity to disabuse her mind of the idea he had not known who she was. Silly child. He would have known her instantly even if she had worn a full domino. Still, she did not have the experience to know she affected him as much as he affected her. More, if anything. The memory of how hard he had had to fight to refrain from kissing her on the terrace made him groan.

No more anonymous wooing. From now on, he resolved, he would openly court her. Doubtless, eyebrows would be raised. Too bad. His friends were sure to have recognised him tonight anyway. Julian Ellsmere certainly had. And Julian had known which lady he had spent the evening with. Thank heavens she had already refused Julian. The last thing he needed was to have a resurgence of the old story. God knew why the gossip-mongers had never realised that Julian himself bore him no ill will over the affair of Miss Amelia

Kerslake. His black brows rose cynically. Truth, of course, was never of great interest to the gossips.

With a deep sigh, Dominic leant back against the squabs and shut his eyes. Without the slightest difficulty, he conjured up the vision of a pair of big hazel eyes, so brilliant that they seemed to flash with gold fire. His doubts were gone. All considerations of age and station had long since fallen away, discarded as irrelevant in the face of his desire. He wanted Georgiana Hartley. And he intended to have her.

CHAPTER SIX

THE HATTRINGHAM HOUSE masked ball proved a revelation to others as well. While Georgiana waltzed and laughed on the arm of her cavalier, faded blue eyes, pale and washed out, watched her from the anonymity of the side of the room. Under his breath, Charles Hartley cursed. It didn't look promising.

Two weeks he had spent, searching the countryside for his little cousin. Finally he had been forced to conclude that the minx had somehow found her way to London. He had closed up the Place—had been forced to do so. Dismissing the Pringates had been an ugly affair, from which he was thankful to have escaped with a whole skin. But paying them off had severely depleted his reserves. He had hastened to town, reduced to finding lodgings in a mean and dingy street beyond the fashionable areas. Once installed, he had suddenly found himself at *point non plus*. Where would Georgie have gone?

That question had worried him until he was nearly crazed. Luckily, the recollection that her servants had disappeared with her surfaced to lead him from the brink of despair. From what he had seen of them, they would never have countenanced Georgiana doing anything that would bring her into danger. Or ill repute.

Hence, they must have found lodgings in an acceptable quarter.

Days of trudging the streets had followed, calling surreptitiously at the fashionable hotels, hours of drinking in the taverns favoured by the servants of the gentry. Gradually he had been forced to consider the more *tonnish* areas. Finally, his luck had turned. He had seen her in Bond Street.

She had been dressed in the height of fashion, a parasol shading her delicate features, and he had almost missed her. The effect her appearance had had on him, leaving him gaping, had, by sheer luck, saved him from prematurely revealing his presence.

Before he had gathered his wits, she was joined by another female, likewise fashionably elegant. A nagging sense of the familiar had finally crystallised. Little Bella Ridgeley! He had barely made her out, rigged up to the nines as she was, but she was still the little girl he had teased so unmercifully whenever her big brother had not been around.

His eyes had narrowed. So Georgiana had sought refuge at Candlewick Hall—the one place he had not considered looking. Smart of her—or was it pure luck? He had decided on luck, for there was no way Georgiana could have known, and was about to step forward and accost the fair pair, when they were helped into a waiting carriage by a burly footman.

Balked of his prey, the wisdom of reconnoitring the lie of the land was brought home to him. Bella had married a Lord Winsmere. A powerful man. If the Winsmeres were Georgiana's friends, he had better be sure of his strategy before he approached her.

He had followed the carriage through the bustling streets and had seen the ladies set down outside the house in Green Street. They had entered, and he had found an alley close by, from which he could keep the door in view. Georgiana had not re-emerged until the evening, when she had left in the carriage with Bella, both gorgeously arrayed in evening gowns. The sight of those gowns had sent a spasm of sheer fury through him. They had swanned off to a ball while he, half perished with cold, was forced to slink off to his miserable lodgings, with no prospect of a decent meal in sight. He had consoled himself with the thought that at least he now knew where his pigeon had come to roost.

But how to best approach the matter of getting his hands on her once more? With his limited resources, joining the social whirl was a near impossibility. His clothes alone would mark him as pecuniarily embarrassed. The cent per centers were too fly to be taken in by a glib tale; they would advance him nothing. Thanks to the restrictions his father's failings had placed on him, he had no friends among the swells. How to break into the glittering circle?

He had cudgelled his brains for hours. Eventually he had found a young tailor operating on the outskirts of the fashionable districts, one too inexperienced to quibble about his offer of a small down payment with the remainder of the costs to be sent on account. With his most immediate need assuaged, he had turned his mind to gaining an entrée to the balls and parties his cousin frequented.

The Hattringham House masked ball had presented

itself, ready-made for his needs. For the cost of a mask and a deal of studied self-confidence, he had been able to enter the ballroom as a guest, to wander slowly through the salons, carefully studying the female forms present. He had not even had to be covert about this enterprise; most of the young bucks were similarly engaged.

As it transpired, he had not recognised her. It was her voice, gaily answering some sally, which had identified her for him.

Now, as he watched her dance for the third time with the handsome dark-haired man who had monopolised her company for the entire evening, he ground his teeth. He stood no chance of competing honourably with the likes of her present cavalier. And, even from the obscurity of the sidelines, he could sense the rapport which existed between the pair. Damn her! She'd escaped him, only to fall victim to some other aspiring scoundrel. He brushed aside the thought that none but he knew her worth.

Seething, muttering imprecations beneath his breath, he watched helplessly as the dashing cavalier waltzed past, his cousin held securely in strong arms, mesmerised by a smile too experienced for any young damsel to resist.

"Soon," said Charles, entirely to himself. "I'll have to move soon." Having seen quite enough of his cousin and her consort to despair of parting them that night, he left Hattringham House, his brain awash with half-formed schemes.

IT WAS THE NEXT afternoon before Georgiana had leisure to thoroughly examine the events of the Hattringham House ball. Viewed in the calm light of day, she wasn't entirely sure what to make of them. Had he really not recognised her?

Over the weeks, by dint of subtle questioning, she had learnt a great deal more of Bella's brother. For instance, a quiet afternoon spent in the back parlour the previous week had yielded the tale of the initial incident that had given rise to Lord Alton's reputation of being dangerous company for young ladies.

"It happened during the Season immediately following Papa's death. Dominic had missed the beginning of the Season, still tied up with settling the estate." Bella had laid aside her embroidery and stared in concentration at the opposite wall. "I wasn't there, of course, but I've heard the tale umpteen times. Apparently Lord Ellsmere—he's a particular friend of Dominic's, you know—fell desperately in love with a scheming miss from somewhere up north. I forget her name—something like Kertlake. She and her mama had come to town determined to catch the biggest matrimonial prize." Bella turned to Georgiana. "Well, you know how eligible Julian Ellsmere is."

Georgiana had had the grace to look sheepish.

"Well," her preceptress had continued, "Julian fell very heavily, and no one could make him see what she was really like. Apparently she was an out-and-out schemer, flirting with every man, but carefully checking their assets at the same time. Lots of people tried to dissuade him, but he went ahead and proposed and was accepted. Then Dominic returned to town. He saw through Miss Whatever-her-name-was and de-

cided something had to be done. It was too late for
Julian to draw back with honour, so the lady had to
be made to withdraw.'' Bella had paused, eyeing
Georgiana carefully. Georgiana had raised her brows
in question. Bella had grimaced.

''You know what men are. And you've seen what
Dominic's like. So I don't suppose you'll find it hard
to believe that he swept the lady off her feet. He's a
bigger catch than Julian. So the lady broke off her
engagement with Julian, who by now had his eyes well
open. Dominic had managed it so she did it in the
expectation of him offering for her, but he never made
any formal declaration or anything like that. And, of
course, as soon as Julian was publicly free, Dominic
just dumped the girl. The trouble was, not everyone
was in the know. A lot of gossips just saw Dominic
entrapping a beautiful girl and then ruthlessly discard-
ing her. That's what started it all. And, needless to
say, Dominic doesn't give a damn what people think
of him. Naturally, all his friends know the truth.''

At this point, Bella had picked up her embroidery
again. Then she had paused, to add matter-of-factly,
''Of course, later, when he went around seducing all
the bored wives and beautiful widows—the Lady
Changleys of the world, you understand—they simply
painted his reputation blacker.''

Smothering a choking laugh, Georgiana had bent
her head once more over her own embroidery, her
thoughts far removed from *petit point.*

''Mind you,'' Bella had added, waving her needle
in the air to give her point emphasis, ''despite all, he's
never particularly enamoured of them—the women he

seduces, I mean.'' She had frowned, totally absorbed in her subject and no longer conscious of her audience. ''I suspect it's because it's all so easy.'' She had shrugged. ''Just like me, getting bored with the Season—it's all too easy without some purpose behind it.''

They had fallen silent after that, each busy with their own thoughts.

Now Georgiana sat alone in the back parlour, having seen Bella off on a visit to her old nurse. Her thoughts revolved incessantly, driven by an unnerving juxtaposition of longing and uncertainty. The breathtaking thrill of basking in the warmth of his smouldering blue gaze... All the subtle attentions he had paid her throughout the long night of the masked ball... She'd already lost her heart to Lord Alton. Now he seemed intent on leading her on to more dangerous ground. But had he known it was her he was leading? Surely not. Her mind rebelled at the thought. If he had known, then that would mean... No. He couldn't be seriously pursuing her. What on earth could he mean by it, if he was? And what on earth was she to do about it?

She puzzled and worried at her questions, but when Johnson knocked and entered the room two hours later she had still not found any answer.

''There's a gentleman to see you, miss. A Mr Charles Hartley.''

The butler's words effectively banished Georgiana's dreams. Charles? Here? How on earth had he traced her? And why?

The soft clearing of Johnson's throat recalled her

scattered wits. She had enough unanswerable questions without Charles adding to the score. And, secure and safe in Winsmere House, she had no reason to fear her cousin. Johnson, she felt sure, would hover protectively near the door. "My cousin?" It was hard to believe.

Johnson bowed. "The gentleman did mention the connection, miss."

From the butler's stiff tone, Georgiana surmised her cousin had failed to find favour in his shrewd eyes. The observation gave her confidence. "I'll see him in here."

"Very good, miss." Johnson made for the door, but paused with his hand on the knob. "I'll be just outside the door, miss, in case you should need anything."

Georgiana smiled her gratitude as Johnson withdrew.

A minute later, the door opened once more to allow Charles Hartley to enter. In the light streaming in through the long windows, Georgiana studied her cousin as he crossed the room towards her. His appearance had improved considerably since last they had met. She suppressed a grin at the memory. He had been drunk. Now he was clearly quite sober. His clothes were not as elegant as those she had grown used to seeing, but were clean and, unless she much mistook the matter, new. His cravat was tied neatly, if not with flair. A great improvement over the stained and ill fitting togs he had worn at the Place. He was neither tall nor short, neither corpulent nor lanky. Yet his figure was unimpressive compared to the other in her mind. His colouring was much paler and less vibrant than her own. Lank fair hair hung across pallid skin; pale reptilian eyes regarded her with little evidence of emotion. Repressing her instinctive shrinking, she extended her hand as he drew near. "Charles."

As he took her hand and bowed over it, Charles was conscious that his little cousin had somehow changed. The young girl who had fled to her chamber to escape his lovemaking had grown even more lovely. And more confident. But she would never be a match for him. He smiled, struggling to keep his thoughts from showing. She had blossomed into a more delectable piece than he would have predicted. The figure outlined by the bronze silk dress she had worn at the ball was quite real, albeit now garbed in sober grey. Perhaps he would enjoy the role of her husband rather more than he had anticipated.

At his continued scrutiny, Georgiana allowed her brows to rise haughtily.

Recalled to his purpose, Charles assumed a serious face. "Georgiana, I've come to beg your pardon."

Now Georgiana's brows flew upwards in surprise.

Charles smiled tentatively and pressed his advantage. "For my boorish behaviour at the Place. I... Well—" he shrugged and smiled self-deprecatingly "—I was swept away with desire, my dear. I should have told you, of course, of the arrangements that had been made. But I had a hope you would love me for myself and it would not be necessary. I see now I should have explained it to you at the start. You see, my father and your father wanted us to marry." At her instinctive recoil, Charles raised a placating hand.

"Oh, at first I felt as you. You can imagine my dismay, a young man being told his marriage was already arranged. I ranted and raved, but in the end I agreed to do my duty to the family. So I waited for the day your father would send you home. As things fell out, he died before he had brought himself to tell you and send you away from him." Pale eyes carefully scrutinised Georgiana's face. "I can imagine how attached he was to you, and doubtless he sought to keep you by him for as long as possible." Charles smiled meaningfully into Georgiana's eyes. "I can understand his feelings."

To his consternation, Charles could detect no response to his revelations, other than a slight widening of the huge hazel eyes.

"In the circumstances, you can imagine my surprise when I first saw you, first learned of your beauty."

Another smile accompanied this piece of flattery, but evoked no hint of feminine preening.

Charles frowned. Was the child paying attention? He turned the frown to good effect as he continued, "I'm afraid my behaviour was rather wild. I can only ask you to excuse my excesses on the grounds of my incredible relief that, now you were finally here, everything was going to be all right."

Still Georgiana gave no sign of reaction to his tale.

Mentally groping in the dark, Charles put on a humble face and asked, "Georgiana, can you possibly forgive me?"

At the start of her cousin's tale, Georgiana had schooled her features to impassivity. As his story unfurled, she was thankful for the iron control, polished over the weeks of social gadding, that held her silent. She had no doubt that the existence of a long-standing, family-arranged betrothal between them was a fabrication. Her father had always shown particular concern for her eventual state. He had not expected to die suddenly, it was true. But that he had died forgetting to tell her she was formally betrothed was impossible. She resisted the impulse to laugh scornfully, and forced her voice to a cool and even tone. "I suggest your behaviour at the Place is best forgotten."

At his too ready smile, she assumed her most regal manner and forged on. "However, as to this other matter you have raised, of us being betrothed, I'm afraid I must insist that such a betrothal never occurred. Certainly my father never told me of it. Nor were there any documents among his effects to support such a notion. I'm afraid, if your father led you to suppose there was an agreement, then he misled you."

Charles's frown was quite genuine. So much for that idea. He would have to try his second string. He turned slightly and moved away from his cousin, taking a few steps away, then pacing back. His features obediently fell into a look of downcast dismay. He looked straight at Georgiana, an expression of wordless misery on his face. Then he gestured eloquently and turned aside. "Georgiana. My dear, what can I say to convince you?"

If she had not been so sensitive on the subject, Georgiana would have found his histrionics quite entertaining. As it was, she felt no inclination to smile, let alone laugh.

From the corner of his eye, Charles watched her

stony countenance. Intuition told him an avowal of love would fall on barren soil. Instead, he opted for a more avuncular line. ''I would do everything possible to make you happy. Your father's death has left you alone in the world. Please, I beg you, allow me to take on the task of caring for you.''

Georgiana barely managed to keep from laughing in his face. He, to talk of caring for her! He had threatened her—more than threatened her—and under his own roof! She could manage quite well, she felt, without his sort of protection. With perfect composure she replied, ''Please say no more. My mind is quite unalterable on this point. I will not marry you, Charles.''

Yet another proposal, she thought with a wry inward grin. Even less welcome than the others.

Charles sighed dramatically and turned so she could no longer see his face. All in all, he was just as well suited with her decision. It was hardly a great surprise. At least now he had a clear path to follow. After a pained moment, he turned back to her and smiled bravely. ''I knew it was no use. But, you see, I felt I had to try. If I could just ask that we remain friends?''

Georgiana blinked. Friends? Well, it couldn't hurt to make that concession. It meant so little. She smiled gently, somewhat relieved that the episode seemed set to conclude on a much more reasonable note than she had anticipated. She held out her hand, a friendly enough gesture, but still a clear dismissal. ''Friends, then, if you wish it.''

Charles took her hand and bowed over it. As he straightened, his face cleared as if reminded of a pleasant event. ''Ah, I nearly forgot.'' His eyes sought

Georgiana's. "Those paintings you were looking for. At the Place."

Georgiana's heart leapt.

Sensing her response, Charles inwardly smirked. So much for her impenetrable shell.

"Yes?" Georgiana prompted, not bothering to conceal her eagerness.

Charles smiled. "I don't want to get your hopes up, but the Pringates were clearing out the attics when I left. They sent me a message two days ago that they had found some pictures, among other things. I wrote back to ask who had painted them. If they are the ones you seek..." He let his voice trail away.

Breathlessly Georgiana seized the proffered moment to issue the invitation Charles was angling for. "You'll let me know at once? Please, Charles?"

Genuinely pleased, he allowed his smile to broaden. "I'll let you know at once."

Deeming it wise to leave well enough alone, he merely bowed over her hand and smiled encouragingly as she crossed to the bell-pull to summon the butler.

NATURALLY, after she had considered the matter from all angles, Georgiana sought Bella's opinion of Charles's visit and his declaration.

"Friends?" The incredulity in Bella's voice left little doubt of her opinion of Charles. She snorted. "He's a bounder. Always was, always will be."

Georgiana shrugged. "Well, that's neither here nor there." She bent her head over her stitchery. It was the day after Charles's visit and they were in the back parlour, as was their habit of a morning.

Bella stifled a yawn. "Ye gods! I declare I'm infected with your illness."

Georgiana raised an enquiring eyebrow.

"Finding the evenings over-tiring," Bella explained. "I would never have thought a musical supper would be so positively exhausting."

"I rather think that depends on the music," put in Georgiana, with a smile for her hostess. "Besides, from what I saw, you were half asleep through most of the recital."

Bella waved a hand airily. "It's fashionable to nod off. All the best people do it."

With a gurgle of laughter, Georgiana set her work aside. "Seriously, though, do you think Charles will give me my father's paintings back?"

"Don't get too carried away. They might not be your father's at all."

A discreet knock heralded Johnson's entry. "A note for you, miss. There's a messenger waiting for your reply."

Georgiana lifted the simple note from Johnson's salver. It was sealed with a nondescript lump of wax.

Dismissing her butler with a nod, Bella turned to find her friend regarding the missive in her hand with some nervousness. "Well? Open it!"

With a small sigh, Georgiana broke the seal and spread out the single sheet. "It's from Charles," she told the waiting Bella. After a moment, her face brightened. "He's found them! Oh, Bella! They were there after all!"

Seeing the sunshine in Georgiana's face, Bella relaxed and grinned back. "How lovely for you. Is he sending them over?"

Georgiana was reading on. A small frown clouded her brow, then lifted. "Yes and no. He hasn't actually got them yet. He says he's sent to Pringate to bring them to the Hart and Hounds—that's the posting inn, the last before London on the road to Candlewick. I remember stopping there on our way here."

Bella nodded absent-mindedly. "Yes, but why? Why not just bring them to London?"

Georgiana, engrossed in deciphering Charles's scrawl, shrugged aside the quibble. "Charles says he's going to meet Pringate this afternoon to pick up the pictures, and asks if I would like to come too. Oh, Bella! Just think! By this afternoon I'll have them."

"Mmm." Bella eyed her friend with a frown. It would be of no use to tell Georgiana that Charles was not to be trusted. From her face it was clear nothing on earth would stop her from going to fetch her paintings. With a definite feeling of misgiving, Bella held her peace.

While Georgiana penned an enthusiastic reply to Charles's invitation, Bella sat and worriedly chewed her lip. But, by the time Johnson departed to give Georgiana's note to the messenger, she had perked up and was able to listen to Georgiana's excited ramblings with an indulgent smile. It was obvious really. To protect Georgiana from Charles's machinations, all she had to do was precisely what she had always done whenever Charles had threatened. She would tell Dominic.

When Charles called for Georgiana at three, Bella

played least in sight. Charles was high on her list of unfavourite people. She had already surreptitiously dispatched a note to her brother, summoning him to her instant aid. As she watched Charles's small phaeton carry Georgiana away, she struggled to subdue a disturbing sense of disquiet.

Impatiently, she waited for Dominic to call.

ENSCONCED in the comfort of well padded leather, Dominic Ridgeley, Lord Ridgeley, Viscount Alton, man of the world and political intriguer, was deep in consideration of the beauties of nature. Or, more specifically, one particular golden-haired, golden-eyed beauty. The silence of the reading room of White's was punctuated by the occasional snore and snuffle and the crackle of turning pages. Otherwise, there was no sound to distract him from his reverie. The daily news-sheet was held open before his face, but he would have been hard pressed to recall the headlines, let alone the substance of any of the articles. This morning Georgiana Hartley occupied his mind to the exclusion of all else.

He had not seen her for over twenty-four hours. Which fact, he felt, was more than ample excuse for his preoccupation. A political dinner had prevented him from attending Lady Overington's musical supper—a mixed blessing, he was sure. Hence, he had to be content with reliving the events of the masked ball. A slow grin twisted his lips as he recalled his angel's response to some of his more outrageous sallies. He would have to make certain he disabused her mind of her apparent belief that he had not known her identity.

The point niggled, like a burr caught under his collar. It had been a strategic error, to allow her to leave him still thinking he was showering his attentions on a damsel unknown to him. An error he was more than experienced enough to recognise. Still, he would ensure the matter was rectified at their next meeting— tonight, at the Pevenseys' gala. Consideration of her likely reactions to his revelations kept him entertained for some minutes. The sight of her face when the penny finally dropped, her innocent confusion, all unknowingly reflected in her glorious eyes, would afford him untold pleasure.

A soft smile of pure anticipation curved his fine lips.

Seeing it, Lord Ellsmere paused, before clearing his throat meaningfully.

At the sound so close by his ear, Dominic jumped. His eyes met those of his friend in pained surprise.

Julian Ellsmere grinned. ''Interesting thoughts, old man?''

Dominic struggled up out of the depths of his chair. ''Damn you, Julian! I was just—''

''Shhhh!'' came hissing from all corners of the room.

''Come into the smoking-room,'' whispered Lord Ellsmere. ''I've got some news I think you should hear.''

They had been at Eton, then Oxford, together, had shared all the larks and adventures of well heeled young men. And had remained close friends to the present. Which, when they'd found a secluded corner of the smoking-room, allowed Lord Ellsmere to say, ''Don't know how deep your interest goes with your sister's protégée, but I just saw her being driven out of town by a rather rum customer. Tow-headed, pasty-faced bounder.''

The sudden hardening of the lines of his friend's face told Lord Ellsmere more clearly than words just how deeply Dominic Ridgeley's interest in Georgiana Hartley went.

"When?"

"'Bout twenty minutes. Up the North Road."

Dominic's eyes had narrowed. "Tow-headed?" When Julian Ellsmere nodded, he continued, "Medium height and build? Fair skin?"

"That's the man. Know him?"

But Dominic was muttering curses under his breath and heading for the door. When Julian caught him up in the hall, where the porter was scurrying to find his cane and gloves, Dominic turned to him and said, "My thanks."

Lord Ellsmere waved one languid hand. "Oh, think nothing of it. As I recall, I owe you one." He smiled, then sobered to ask, "You'll go after her?"

"Most assuredly. The silly chit should have known better. I'd go bail that's her cousin she's with. And between Charles Hartley and a viper there's not much difference."

The porter returned, and Dominic pulled on his gloves. As he took his cane from the man, Lord Ellsmere, frowning, added, "One other thing. Might be significant. This tow-headed chap... Saw him leaving Hattringham House t'other night."

The chill in Dominic's eyes was pronounced. "You're sure?"

Julian Ellsmere nodded. "Quite certain." After a moment he asked, "Need any help?"

At that, Dominic smiled in a way that made Julian Ellsmere feel almost sorry for Charles Hartley. "No. I've dealt with Charles before. It'll be a particular pleasure to make it clear to him that Miss Hartley is very definitely out of bounds."

Lord Ellsmere nodded and clapped his friend on the shoulder.

With a fleeting smile, Dominic was gone.

A brisk walk saw him entering Alton House. Immediately the door shut behind him, he issued a string of commands which had his groom and coachman running to the mews and his valet pounding up the stairs in search of his greatcoat.

Dominic waited in the hall, frowning, his cane, still in his hand, tapping impatiently against one booted foot. Julian had said he had seen them. That meant an open carriage. Surely Charles wasn't proposing to drive her all the way to Buckinghamshire in an open carriage? No. When dusk fell, the cold would be intense. Presumably the open carriage was just part of his scheme, whatever that was.

Timms's cough interrupted his thoughts. "I don't know as this is the most opportune moment, m'lord, but this note came some time ago from Lady Winsmere."

Dominic's frown lifted. He took the note and broke it open. The sound of his carriage drawing up in the street coincided with his man's precipitate descent with his coat. An instant later, garbed in his many caped greatcoat and clutching his sisters missive in his hand, Viscount Alton climbed into his carriage.

"Winsmere House. Quickly!"

"OH, DOMINIC! Thank God you've come. I've been so worried." Bella's plaintive wail greeted Dominic as he crossed the threshold of her parlour.

"Don't fly into a pucker, Bella. Julian Ellsmere has just told me he saw Georgiana leaving town with a man who sounds like Charles. Has she?"

"Yes!" Bella was wringing her hands in agitation. "She was so set on it, I knew I couldn't stop her. But I don't trust Charles one inch. That's why I sent for you."

Taking note of his sister's unusually pale face, Dominic replied with far greater calmness than he felt. "Quite right." He swallowed his impatience and smiled reassuringly. "Why don't we sit down and you can tell me all about it?"

Haltingly, prodded by gentle questions, the tale of Charles's visit and the subsquent events was retold. By the end of the tale, Dominic was confident he saw the light. He leant forward to pat Bella's hand. "Don't worry. I'll fetch her back."

Bella blinked up at him as he stood. "You'll go straight away?"

"I was setting out when Timms gave me your note. Just as well. At least now I can go directly to the Hare and Hounds." Dominic's blue eyes critically surveyed his sister. At his insistence she reclined on the *chaise*. Her face was too pale and her agitation was too marked, even given the cause. Shrewdly he drew his own conclusions. He had been going to suggest she come with him, to lend propriety to their return to Green Street. But in her present condition he rather thought any further excitement was to be assiduously avoided. And, if truth be known, he would much rather be alone with Georgiana on the drive back to town. He had every intention of reading her a lecture on the subject of herself—care of. Afterwards, he felt sure he would enjoy her attempts to be conciliatory, not to mention grateful. And it would give him a heaven-sent opportunity to correct her mistaken assumption regarding his conduct at the masked ball. Yes, he was definitely looking forward to the return journey. Propriety, in this instance, could go hang.

He smiled again at his sister. "Don't fret. Arthur will be home shortly. You can tell him all about it. I suspect we won't make it back until late, so you'd best send your regrets to the Pevenseys."

"Lord, yes! I couldn't face a party on top of all this."

Dominic grinned, then bent to bestow a kiss on one pale cheek. "Take care, my dear. You burn the candle with a vengeance."

She grimaced at him but refused to rise to the bait.

Dominic crossed the room, but turned at the door to consider the listless figure on the *chaise*. Had she realised yet herself? One dark brow rose. With a last affectionate smile, he left.

CHAPTER SEVEN

JOYFUL ANTICIPATION of seeing her mother's face again carried Georgiana through the streets of London, unaware of the man beside her. However, as the phaeton turned northwards and the more populated streets fell behind, a tingling sense of premonition awoke in her mind.

The afternoon remained fine, a brisk breeze whipping at her cloak and bonnet, promising hard frosts for the morning. As the buildings thinned, the air became perceptibly chillier. Charles's conversation, uninspiring though it had been, had disappeared along with the fashionable dwellings. He seemed to be concentrating on driving the carriage at a slow but steady pace.

Georgiana stared ahead, willing the comforting bulk of the Hare and Hounds to loom on the horizon. But, from Green Street, it would take at least an hour to reach the comfort of the posting inn. A frown drew the golden arches of her brows together. Charles had called for her at three, which, now she came to think more clearly, was surely a little late for an expedition of such distance. It would be dark by the time they returned to Winsmere House. Still, there was little she could do about it now, beyond praying that the plodding nag drawing the phaeton would find its second wind. With a discontented grimace, she gave her attention to their surroundings. She refused to give further consideration to the doubt nagging from the deepest recesses of her mind, the little voice which warned that something was amiss.

Ten minutes later, a surreptitious movement beside her had her turning her head in time to see Charles replace his fob watch in his pocket.

He smiled at her. "Not long now."

Georgiana knew the smile was meant to reassure. It missed its mark. Odd how she had forgotten how Charles's smiles so rarely reached his eyes. Her suspicions, unspecified but now fully awakened, took possession of her mind. The horse's plodding hoofs beat a slow accompaniment to her increasingly trepidatious heartbeat as she reviewed the potential threats she might all too soon have to face.

In the end, she was so preoccupied with her imaginary dragons that she missed the sight of the Hare and Hounds. Only when Charles turned the phaeton under the arch of the innyard did she shake off her reverie to look about her.

She had stopped here on her way to London. But that time she had been travelling in the luxury of Lord Alton's coach, with attentive servants to guard her. Now, as Charles handed her down from the open carriage, she glanced about to see the yard full of people. Ostlers hurried fresh horses out of the stables beyond the yard, while others led weary equines freed of the traces to rest. Stableboys rushed hither and yon, under everyone's feet, helping with the harness and carrying baggage back and forth from the inn. Inn servants stood with jugs of steaming ale and mulled wine, ready to refresh the passengers of the coaches pulled up for the change of horses. At the centre of the commotion stood the southbound accommodation coach, a huge, ponderous vehicle, settled like a dull black bullfrog on the cobbles. The passengers were alighting for their evening meal. Georgiana found herself the object of not a few staring eyes. She was about to turn away when one gentleman raised his high-crowned beaver and bowed.

With a start, Georgiana recognised a distant acquaintance of Bella's and Arthur's. She had been introduced to him at one of the balls. With a small smile, she acknowledged the bow, wondering at the hardlipped, cold-eyed look the man gave her.

Accepting Charles's arm over the uneven surface, more from necessity than inclination, she was about to ascend the two steps to the inn's main door when a sudden commotion on the coach's roof claimed all eyes. Three well dressed youths—roof passengers— were laughingly struggling with each other. At the coachman's loud "Hoi!", they desisted and, shamefacedly realising they were the centre of attention, sought to descend to less exalted positions. Waiting for his companions to climb down the rungs before him, one of the young men looked about the yard and caught sight of Georgiana. Her eyes met his with a jolt of recognition. He was the younger brother of one of the débutantes being presented that Season. She had danced with him at his sister's come-out. His open-mouth stare told Georgiana quite clearly that something was severely wrong.

She had barely time to smile at the young man before Charles tugged her through the inn door. To her surprise, she found that Charles had hired a private parlour for their use. Distracted by the memory of the stares of the two gentlemen in the yard, she paid scant attention to this discovery. As she meekly followed the innkeeper up the wooden staircase, the reason for the stares occurred. Of course! She and Charles shared no more than a fleeting family resemblance. The gentlemen thought she was here, alone, with a man who was no relation. She blushed slightly. There was, of course, nothing wrong with being escorted somewhere by one's cousin. She knew that. It was often the case in Italy, where families were large. She had not thought there was any impropriety attached to her going to an inn with Charles. Surely, if there had been, Bella would have raised some demur? But the disapprobation on the older man's face, and the sheer stunned disbelief in the younger's, stayed with her, banishing all ease.

So, when she heard the click from the parlour door as the latch fell into place behind the burly innkeeper, it was with a heightened sense of suspicion that she surveyed the neat parlour. It was empty. No Pringates. No paintings. Georgiana's heart plummeted. Drawing a steadying breath, she turned to face Charles. "Where are the Pringates?"

Her cousin stood, leaning against the door, watching her with a shrewdly calculating gaze. After a moment, he pushed away from the solid oak panels and strolled towards her. "Doubtless they've been delayed. Let me take your cloak."

Automatically surrendering her cloak, Georgiana forcibly repressed a shudder as Charles's fingers inadvertently brushed her shoulders in removing it. Inadvertently? She risked a quick glance up at his face. What she saw there did nothing for her peace of mind. Quelling the panic rising within, she forced herself to act ingenuously. "Are we going to wait for them?"

Charles straightened from laying her cloak over a chair. Again she was subjected to a careful scrutiny. Georgiana struggled to quieten the hammering of her nerves and face him calmly. Apparently Charles was satisfied with what he saw.

"Having come this far, we might as well wait for a while." His eyes raked her face again. "Perhaps a tea tray would fill in the time?"

Eager to have something to occupy them ostensibly while she considered the ramifications of her latest impulsive start, Georgiana forced a smile of agreement to her lips.

The innkeeper was summoned and, in short order, a buxom young serving girl bustled in with a tray loaded with teapot, scones and all necessary appurtenances. Charles dismissed her with a nod and a coin, holding the door for her.

Under cover of wielding the teapot, Georgiana watched Charles close the door. She almost sighed audibly when she saw he did not bother to lock it.

With renewed confidence, fragile though she suspected it was, she gave her mind over to plotting her moves. The first imperative was to learn what Charles

STEPHANIE LAURENS   177

had in mind. And, she supposed, there was always the possibility that she was inventing horrors where none existed. A slim hope, she felt, with her nerves jangling in insistent warning.

Taking a sip of strong tea to help steady herself, she asked, "There are no paintings, are there?"

Her question coincided with Charles taking a sip from his own cup. He choked but recovered swiftly. His faded blue gaze lifted and fixed on her face, and she had her answer. He smiled, not pleasantly. Georgiana felt her muscles tense.

"How perceptive of you, sweet cousin."

His congratulatory tone purred sarcastically in her ears. For the first time since leaving the Place, Georgiana knew she was face-to-face with the real Charles Hartley. She fought down a wild desire to rush to the door. Charles might not be large, but he was a great deal larger than she was. Besides, she needed to know more. She was sick of mysteries. "Why? Why all this elaborate charade? What do you hope to gain?"

Charles laughed mirthlessly, his eyes never leaving her face. "What I want. Your hand in marriage." Then his gaze slid slowly over her. "Among other things."

His tone made Georgiana feel physically ill. She forced herself to sip her tea calmly, drawing what strength she could from the strong black brew. Her mind wandered frantically amid the pieces of the puzzle but could not make out the picture.

"Not worked it out yet?"

Charles's taunt broke into her mental meanderings. She looked at him coldly.

He smiled, enjoying her obvious discomfort. He

leant back in his chair, balancing it on its back legs. "I'll spell it out for you, if you like."

Georgiana decided that, however distressful, knowing his plans had to be her primary aim. So she allowed a look of patent interest to infuse her features.

Charles's lips twisted in a gloating grin. "My plan is quite simple. We arrived here just as the accommodation coach was unloading. You were seen entering this inn with me by at least two people who know you. That, in itself, will cause only minor comment. However, when we leave here tomorrow morning, while the northbound accommodation coach passengers are breakfasting in the main room downstairs, I feel certain the sight of you leaving at such an early hour with me, without the benefit of maid or baggage, is going to raise quite a few brows."

Georgiana's heart sank as she pictured the scene. He was right, of course. Even she knew what a scandal such a sighting would provoke, regardless of the truth of the matter.

"So, you see, after that you'll have little choice but to accept my proposal." Charles's grin turned decidedly wicked.

Georgiana had had enough. Carefully replacing her cup on the tray, she wiped her hands on the napkin and then, laying the cloth aside, fixed her cousin with a determined stare. "Charles, I have no idea why you are so set on marrying me. You don't even like me."

At that, he laughed. Hand over heart, he bowed from the waist mockingly. "I assure you, sweet Georgie, I'll manage to drum up enough enthusiasm to convince all and sundry of what took place here."

Georgiana shook her head slowly. "It won't work, you know. I won't marry you. There's no reason why I should."

The cynical twist of Charles's lips told her she had not heard all of his plan. "I hesitate to correct you, fair cousin, but, unless you want the Winsmeres mired in scandal, you'll most certainly marry me. It won't have escaped the notice of the gossip-mongers that you're supposedly in their care."

Involuntarily, Georgiana's lip curled. "You really are despicable, you know."

To her surprise, her tone was perfectly controlled. In fact she felt strangely calm. The lack of expression in Charles's cold eyes sent shivers up and down her spine. But now her own, usually latent temper was on the rise. It had been one thing when he had threatened *her;* to threaten her friends was another matter entirely. She folded her hands and met his gaze unflinchingly. "Be that as it may, I repeat, I will not marry you. Unless things have changed rather dramatically in England, I suspect you still need me to speak my vows. That being so, if you persist in your plan to ruin my reputation, then, when I leave here, I will stop at Green Street only long enough to pick up my luggage and servants. I'll return to Ravello." Summoning a disaffected shrug, she lifted her chin and added, "I always meant to go back eventually. And, with me gone, no scandal of any magnitude will touch Bella and Arthur."

For one long moment, Charles stared at her, eyes quite blank. It had never occurred to him, when he had planned this little campaign, that his prey would simply refuse to co-operate. Having seen her riding high in the social whirl, the threat of a catastrophic fall from grace had seemed an unbeatable card. Now, looking into hazel eyes that held far too much calmness, Charles knew he was facing defeat. Typically, he chose to counter with the usual threat of a bully. With a low growl, he rose menacingly, his chair falling back with a clatter on the floor.

Georgiana's eyes widened in dismay. She felt trapped, unable to move, caught and transfixed by the animosity which poured from Charles's eyes. Not until then had she realised just how much he disliked—nay, hated—her. She stopped breathing.

Charles was poised to come around the table, muscles tensed to lay ungentle hands on her, when the unlikely sound of quiet applause broke across Georgiana's strained senses. She turned towards the door.

Deafened by his anger, Charles only turned after seeing her attention distracted.

The sight that met their eyes was, to Georgiana, as welcome as it was unbelievable. The door lay open. Absorbed in their mutual revelations, neither had heard the click of the latch. Leaning against the doorframe, his greatcoat open and negligently thrown over his shoulders to reveal the elegance of his attire, Lord Alton surveyed the room. Having successfully gained the attention of both its occupants, he smiled at Georgiana and, pushing away from the door, strolled towards her.

In a daze, Georgiana stood and held out her hand, bemused by the sudden turn of events. Blue eyes met hers, conveying warming reassurance and something else—something very like irritation. Bewildered, Georgiana blinked.

Dominic took her hand and bowed over it, then placed it on his arm and covered it comfortingly with his own large hand. "Miss Hartley. I am here, as arranged, to convey you back to town."

Georgiana's eyes flew to his and read the silent message there. The warmth of his hand banished her fears. She had complete confidence in him.

With an encouraging smile, Dominic turned and, seeing her cloak, released her to fetch it.

The action broke the spell which had held Charles immobile. His normal pasty complexion had paled at the sight of his childhood nemesis. Now his face flooded with unbecoming colour. "You're out of order, Ridgeley," he ground out through clenched teeth. "My cousin is in my care. And she's not returning to London."

Settling Georgiana's cloak about her shoulders, Dominic raised his brows in fascinated contemplation of the thinly veiled threat. His gaze met Charles's squarely, then wandered insultingly over the younger man's frame. Dominic Ridgeley was a man in his prime, a noted Corinthian, five years older, three inches taller and two stone of sheer muscle heavier than Charles Hartley. And Charles knew it.

To Georgiana's intense relief, he dropped his eyes, blanching, then flushing again. Bella's brother tucked her hand in the crook of his arm and patted it comfortingly.

"Come, my dear. My carriage is waiting."

By some magical machination, Georgiana found

herself escorted gently but firmly out of the inn by a route which exposed her to no one other than the inn-keeper, bowing obsequiously as they passed. Handed into the same luxuriously appointed coach that she had used on her previous visit to the inn, she sank back against the fine leather with a small sigh of relief tinged with disillusionment. The search for her mother's portrait had nearly ended in nightmare.

The evening was closing in. Georgiana glanced up to see Lord Alton's large frame silhouetted by the light thrown by the flares in the innyard. He paused, one foot on the carriage step, and gazed back at the inn, an expression she could not define on his face. Then, abruptly, he stepped back. "Your pardon, my dear. Unfinished business." He frowned and added, "I won't keep you more than a minute."

He shut the carriage door, and Georgiana heard him call up to the coachman to watch over her. Peering out of the window, she saw him stride purposefully through the main door of the inn.

As the minutes ticked by, the conviction grew that Lord Alton's "unfinished business" lay with Charles. Georgiana fretted, frustrated by her helplessness. She had almost reached the point of sending the coachman in search of his master when Lord Alton appeared on the inn steps. As he strode across the yard, Georgiana scanned his person. He was undeniably intact. His greatcoat swung, impeccable as ever, from his broad shoulders. She expelled a little sigh of pent-up breath and hurriedly moved farther along the seat to make room for her rescuer. Then he was in the carriage and they were moving.

To her consternation, Georgiana found travelling in a closed carriage with Bella's brother was almost as much as an ordeal as being in the inn parlour with Charles. But, while with Charles she'd had to subdue her disgust, with Lord Alton it was an entirely different emotion she fought to control. At one level, she revelled in his nearness, in the delicate wafts of sandalwood and leather that subtly teased her senses. Occasionally a deep rut jolted her shoulder against his arm. But the feelings which rose up inside her were too dangerous, too damning. Ruthlessly, she fought to quell them, forcing her breathing to slow and her mind to function.

''Did Bella send you?''

Dominic had been waiting, with what patience he could muster, for her to recover. He frowned into the gathering gloom and turned towards her. ''Both Bella *and* Julian Ellsmere.''

''Lord Ellsmere?''

''The same. He saw you leaving London with Charles—a 'tow-headed bounder' was his description.''

His clipped tones destroyed any impulse Georgiana had to laugh.

''Then Bella sent around a note and told me where to look for you.'' Dominic studied his angel's face in the faint glow of light cast back from the carriage lamps. He could see no sign that she understood the danger she had been in, no comprehension of the fear and worry her impulsive start had visited on him. His tone became noticeably drier. ''I find it hard to understand why, knowing Charles as you do, you consented to this ill advised junket.''

At the clear censure in his voice, Georgiana stiffened. She swallowed the peculiar lump in her throat to say in a small, tight voice, ''I'm sorry if I've caused you any inconvenience.''

Inwardly Dominic cursed. This interlude was not progressing as planned. He was having the devil of a time holding on to his temper, rubbed raw by the troubled speculation of the hour and more it had taken to reach the inn. The impulse to shake her was strong. Yet, in his present mood, he doubted the wisdom of laying hands on her. And, wise in the ways of young ladies, he knew his angel, far from being adoringly penitent, was close to taking snuff. If he gave in to temptation and read her the lecture burning the tip of his tongue, she might well treat him to a deplorable display of feminine weakness. For once, he wasn't sure of his ability to withstand such a scene. With a ''Humph!'', he folded his arms across his chest and stared moodily out of the window.

For her part, Georgiana kept her gaze firmly fixed on the passing shadows, concentrating on subduing her quivering lips and blinking away the sudden moisture in her large eyes. It was really too much! First he had taken charge of her, like a guardian, just because she had asked for help. Then he had not had the sense to recognise her at the masked ball and had made her lose her heart with his wickedly sophisticated ways. Now he was treating her like a child again, upbraiding her, blaming *her* instead of Charles!

Trying not to sniff, Georgiana determinedly dragged

her mind away from its preoccupation with the gentleman beside her and turned it to consideration of something—anything—else.

Lord Ellsmere's actions, for instance. Why had he gone to Lord Alton, rather than directly to Bella? That Bella should have summoned her brother was no surprise, but why had Lord Ellsmere done so? No answer occurred to her. Giving up on that issue, she wondered how to acceptably ask what he had done when he had re-entered the inn. She felt she had a right to know; it might prove important in any future disputation with Charles. Surreptitiously, she glanced at him.

In the light thrown by the lamps of a passing carriage, she saw a bloody scratch across the knuckles of his right hand.

"Oh! You've hurt yourself!" Without a thought for propriety or the consequences, Georgiana captured his hand in hers, holding it closer to examine the wound in the dim light. "You've been...been milling with Charles!" Settling the large hand firmly in her lap, she whipped out her small handkerchief and wrapped it tightly over the cut, tying a small knot in the lace edging to keep it in place. "There was no need, I assure you."

A deep sigh greeted her protestations. "Oh, there was every need. Charles needed to be taught a lesson. No gentleman goes about scheming to ruin a lady's reputation."

"What did you do to him?"

His head back against the squabs, Dominic tried to read her expression. "Don't worry, he still lives." When she continued to wait patiently, he grimaced and added, "He was unwise enough to make a number of suggestions I found distinctly ungentlemanly. I took great delight in making him eat his words."

"But you might have been hurt! You *were* hurt." Georgiana looked again at the hand which still lay in her skirts, gently cradled between hers. Suddenly recalling the impropriety of holding a gentleman's hand in her lap, she reluctantly released it, thankful the dim light hid her blushes.

His lips twisting in a smile he knew she could not see, Dominic equally reluctantly withdrew his hand from where it lay, stilling the all but automatic impulse to reverse the situation and capture her hand in his. He had initially been stunned into immobility by her impulsive actions. When his wits returned, he had seen no reason to shorten a moment which had touched him strangely. Now, sensing her unease, he sought for some comment to distract her.

"Anyway, I doubt you'll be troubled by Charles again."

Georgiana heard and nodded, but, suddenly feeling ridiculously weak, sought refuge in silence. Too many emotions swirled in her breast, conflicting with all the accepted precepts, and his nearness only compounded her confusion. She fixed her gaze on the scene beyond the window, the shadows of trees merging into the darkness. Yet her mind remained centred on the man beside her.

Perceptive enough to sense her turmoil, Dominic smiled into the darkness and, smothering a small sigh of frustration, put aside his plans for furthering his suit. She was nervous and on edge. Doubtless, her recent brush with the despicable Charles had contributed its mite to her state. In fact, now he came to think on it, it was wonderful that she hadn't treated him to the vapours. Most young women would undoubtedly be weeping all over him by this juncture, not concerning themselves with his minor hurts. In the dark, his fingers found the lace edging of her handkerchief wrapped tightly about his hand.

The moment was not right, either, for bringing up the subject of the masked ball. He was far too experienced even to contemplate making love to her now, while she was so touchy. There was, after all, tomorrow. And the day after tomorrow. And all the days after that. For, if nothing else had been settled this evening, he had definitely decided that Georgiana Hartley was not going to be allowed to slip out of his life. Whether she realised it or not, she was there to stay.

He paused in his mental ramblings to glance down at the slight figure beside him. She sat absorbed in her thoughts, her hands tightly clasped in her lap. Another half-hour would see them in Green Street. With another smile for the darkness, Dominic settled his head comfortably against the well stuffed squabs and closed his eyes, the better to indulge his fantasies.

Georgiana sat silently, taking herself to task for her forward behaviour. A lecture on the unwisdom of allowing her fanciful dreams to lead her to read more into Lord Alton's actions than was intended followed. He was very fond of Bella. She should remember that he had come to find her in response to Bella's request—brotherly devotion was the emotion which drove him to protect her, nothing else. Her stern admonitions made her flinch inwardly but did little to ease the tightness around her heart.

Gradually, without conscious direction, her tired mind drifted to consideration of its main preoccupation. Of course he had no interest in her. If he had known who she was at the masked ball, he would have mentioned the fact by now. She knew little of the ways of gentleman rakes, but felt sure a coach trip, together alone, must rate as one of those opportunities too good to let slip. Yet the man beside her remained silent. She stole a glance at him from beneath her lashes. His eyes were closed. Emboldened, she allowed her gaze to skim the contours of his face, the wide forehead and squared chin, his firm, well shaped lips... Finding her mind frolicking in fantasies of how those lips would feel against hers, Georgiana forcibly withdrew her gaze and returned it to contemplation of the darkness beyond the window.

Ravello. The image of the villa there, now hers, materialised in her mind's eye. She seized on it. And was suddenly struck by the obvious solution to her troubles. Charles was a bully and totally unscrupulous. He would continue to threaten her peace of mind while she remained in England. And Bella's brother, too, disturbed her rest and reduced her ability to cope with the daily round of fashionable life. Yet she was not particularly enamoured of the social whirl; it would cause her no great pain to eschew the life completely. It was a pleasant diversion, nothing more.

With sudden conviction, she made up her mind. She would see out the Season with Bella, as she had promised Arthur she would. Then she would return to Ravello, a great deal older and a great deal wiser. She stifled a small sigh and forced herself to promise—when winter set in, she would be in Ravello.

The increasing light coming from street-lamps as they entered the capital made it worth while for Dominic to desert his imaginings in favour of the real thing. He had been watching Georgiana for some minutes, wondering what it was that kept her so serious, when a point which had thus far eluded him surfaced as a question. "Georgiana, do you have any idea why Charles wants to marry you?"

As he said the words, he realised they were hardly flattering. Still, he had a high enough opinion of Georgiana Hartley to be sure she was not the sort of flighty young woman who believed all men who wished to marry her were smitten by her beauty. The memory of her numerous suitors, all of whom were most definitely smitten, himself included, brought a wry smile to his lips.

In the flickering, shifting light, Georgiana saw the smile, and her heart turned to lead and dropped to her slippers. To ask a question like that and then smile condescendingly! Well, if anything was needed to convince her Lord Alton had no romantic interest in her it was that. Doggedly, she forced her mind to concentrate on his query. Frowning with the effort, she shook her head and answered truthfully, "I have no idea."

"It was the same while you were at the Place?"

Georgiana nodded. "Exactly the same." She paused, then decided she might as well tell Lord Alton the whole of it. He knew so much already. Choosing her words carefully, she explained Charles's claim of a long-standing betrothal.

"And you're certain such an arrangement never existed?"

"Quite sure." Georgiana paused, then added in explanation, "My father and I were...very close. He would never have done such a thing and not told me. Not for any reason."

Lord Alton seemed to accept her assurance. He sat silently beside her as the coach rumbled along the cobbles towards Green Street.

Dominic had no doubt that Georgiana's beliefs were true. He only wished he had known of Charles's claim before he had returned to the inn parlour. The tenseness he had felt but not recognised on his drive to the Hare and Hounds had converted to anger once he had got Georgiana safely away—anger that had demanded some outlet. So he had returned to the parlour, to be quite unnecessarily provoked by Charles's animadversions on his cousin. In the end he had administered a thoroughly deserved thrashing. He knew Charles was close to financial ruin—was, in fact, technically bankrupt. Georgiana's small fortune would not come close to meeting his mounting debts. After suggesting Charles would be wise never to approach his lovely cousin again, he had repeated his offer to buy the Place. The sum he named was far more than Charles would ever get from any other, with the Place situated as it was. Charles had only attempted a sneer through swollen and cracked lips.

Dominic contemplated a late-night return to the Hare and Hounds, to pursue further the reason for

Charles's apparent fixation with marrying his cousin. Even less than Georgiana did he believe Charles would act for the good of the family. There was something in all this that he was missing, some vital clue which would make all clear. But Charles would almost certainly have left before he could return to the inn.

He turned the anomalies of Charles's behaviour, both with respect to Georgiana and to the sale of the Place, over and over in his mind. Suddenly, the two connected. Dominic straightened in his seat.

"Georgiana, have you been to see your father's English solicitors yet?"

Dragged from the depths of a series of most melancholy thoughts, Georgiana shook her head. "No. I suppose I should, but there doesn't really seem much point."

"But..." Dominic paused, then decided he was going to interfere even though he theoretically had no right. Right be damned. He was going to marry the chit, wasn't he? "Correct me if I'm wrong, but I seem to recall you left Italy before notification of your father's death was acknowledged by your English solicitors. Is that right?"

"You mean," said Georgiana, brow wrinkling in an effort to get the question straight, "before they wrote back after they got the letter from the Italian solicitors?" At Dominic's nod, she agreed. "Yes, that's right."

"And you haven't seen your father's will?"

"No...no. That was left with the English solicitors. But I always knew I would inherit all Papa's money. And the villa at Ravello." She paused, puzzled by his line of questioning, not sure of what possibilities he saw. "But surely if there had been anything more, or anything unexpected, someone would have told me by now?"

"Who are your solicitors here?"

"Whitworth and Whitworth, in Lincoln's Inn."

"Good. I'll take you to see them tomorrow."

Georgiana turned to look at him in amazement. She had not previously had much exposure to the autocratic side of Lord Alton's temperament. She surveyed the satisfied expression on his face with misgiving. "But...why?"

He smiled at her, and she almost forgot her question.

"Because, my dear Georgiana," he said as he captured her hand and raised it to his lips, "Charles, despite all evidence to the contrary, is not a complete gudgeon. His attempts to coerce you into marriage must have some motive behind them. And, as your kinship with him is the only connection between you, I suggest we start looking for the answer with your father's solicitors."

Despite the clear impression that Lord Alton had a stronger motive for insisting she visit her solicitors, Georgiana got no further chance to question him. He had barely ceased speaking when the carriage pulled up outside Green Street. In the ensuing hullabaloo there was no opportunity to do more than thank him prettily for his rescue and meekly accept his instruction to be ready the next morning at eleven.

GEORGIANA RETURNED Arthur's reassuring smile as the Alton town carriage drew up at the entrance to

Lincoln's Inn. Both she and her host had been taken up by an irresistible force at eleven that morning, their objective being the office of her father's solicitors. Despite her belief that nothing new would be learned from Whitworths, Georgiana was enjoying her first view of an area of London she had not previously had cause to visit.

Lord Alton, sitting beside her, had leant forward to speak to the porter. As he leant back, the carriage lurched forward again, over the cobbles and through the large gate of the Inn. The cobbled yard was surrounded by buildings entirely given over to solicitors and clerks. By each doorway leading on to a stairwell hung the bronze plaques of the practitioners within. The carriage drew up before one such door. Lord Alton jumped down and gave her his hand.

Their destination lay on the first floor. A desiccated clerk of indeterminate years, dressed in sombre grey and sporting a tie wig of decades gone by, bade them seat themselves in the small outer office, ''While I enquire if Mr Whitworth will see you.'' He left Georgiana with the definite impression that to be permitted to see the Mr Whitworths was tantamount to being granted an audience with the Regent.

Minutes later he was back, oozing spurious concern. A Mr Whitworth—the elder, as they later learned—followed close on his heels. A portly man of late middle age, he glanced down at the card he held in his hand, given to the clerk by Lord Alton.

Mr Whitworth looked at the two elegant and eminently respectable gentlemen filling his antechamber and became slightly flustered. "My lord...?"

Dominic took pity on him. "I am Lord Alton," he explained smoothly, "and this is Miss Georgiana Hartley, one of your clients. She is presently in the care of my sister, Lady Winsmere. Lord Winsmere," he added, indicating Arthur for the solicitor's edification, "and I have escorted her here in the hope you can clarify a number of points concerning Miss Hartley's inheritance."

It was doubtful if Mr Whitworth heard the latter half of this speech. His eyes had become transfixed on Georgiana, sitting patiently on a chair between her two protectors. Despite the fact she was now used to being stared at, and knew she looked her best in a soft dove-coloured merino gown with a delicate lace tippet, Georgiana found his gaze unnerving. As Lord Alton finished speaking, and the man continued to stare, she raised her brows haughtily.

Mr Whitworth started. "Miss Georgiana Hartley— Mr James Hartley's daughter?" he asked breathlessly.

Georgiana looked puzzled. "Yes," she confirmed, wondering who else had her name.

"My dear young lady!" exclaimed the solicitor, grasping her hand and bowing elaborately over it. "My dear Miss Georgiana! Well, it's a relief to see you at last! We've been searching for you for months!" Once he had started, it seemed the man hardly paused for breath. "Almost, we had begun to fear foul play. When we couldn't contact you and all our letters were returned unopened and no one seemed to know where you had disappeared to..." Suddenly he paused and seemed to recollect himself. He waved plump hands in sudden agitation. "But what am I thinking of? Please come into my office, Miss Hartley, my lords, and we will sort this matter out at once."

He ushered them into a large office which bore little resemblance to the spartan outer chamber. Here all was air and light, with a rich red Turkey carpet covering mellow polished boards. Through the windows, the branches of the trees in the small lawn in the middle of the yard could be seen, the last yellow leaves tenaciously defying the brisk autumn breeze.

As they entered, a thin, soberly clad gentleman rose from behind one of two large desks. Mr Whitworth, holding the door, proclaimed, "Alfred, Miss Hartley is here!"

The second Whitworth—for, from the similarity of facial features, there was little doubt of who he was—looked startled. He pulled his gold-rimmed pince-nez off his nose, polished the glass, then returned it to its perch the better to view Georgiana. After a moment of rapt contemplation, he sighed. "Thank God!"

Both Whitworths bustled about, arranging chairs for their guests. They set these in front of the large desks which, side by side, faced the room. Once their visitors were seated, they subsided, each behind his own desk.

"Now!" said Whitworth the elder, chins flapping as he settled, hands folded before him. "As you can see, we're delighted to see you, Miss Hartley. We have been trying to contact you since we learned of your father's death, with respect to the matter of your inheritance." He beamed at Georgiana.

"If we might speak frankly...?" enquired Whitworth the younger, his flat tone a contrast to his brother's jovial accents.

Turning to face him, it took a moment before Georgiana understood his query. "Oh, please," she said quickly when light finally dawned, "Lord Alton and Lord Winsmere are my friends. I will be relying on their advice."

"Good, good," said Whitworth the elder, causing Georgiana to swivel again. "Not wise for a young lady so well dowered as you are to be alone in the world."

"Quite," his younger brother concurred drily.

"Now, where to begin?"

"Perhaps at your father's bequests?"

"There weren't many—nothing that interfered with the bulk of the estate."

"A few minor legacies to old servants—the usual sort of thing."

"But the major estate remains intact." Whitworth the elder paused to beam again at Georgiana.

Stifling the impulse to put a hand to her whirling head, Georgiana took the opportunity to quell her impending dizziness. It was like watching a tennis game, the conversational ball passing from brother to brother and back again, before their audience of three. Then his last words registered. "Major estate?"

"Why, yes."

"As the major beneficiary of your father's will, you inherit the majority of his estate."

"Which is to say," Whitworth the elder took up the tale smoothly, "the estate known as the Place in the county of Buckinghamshire…"

"His invested capital," intoned Whitworth the younger. "The house in town..."

"And all his paintings not previously sold."

A pause ensued. Georgiana stared at the elder Mr Whitworth, he who had last spoken. Lord Winsmere, having given up the unequal task of allowing his eyes to follow the conversation, stared out of the window, his lips pursed. Lord Alton, even less enthralled by the vision of the Whitworths, had shifted his gaze long since to the young woman beside him. He showed no surprise at the solicitor's news.

"The Place? But... There must be some mistake!" Georgiana could not believe her ears. "My cousin Charles owns the Place."

"Oh, dear me, no!" said the younger Whitworth. "Mr Charles Hartley is not a client of ours."

"And has no claim whatever on the Place. The estate was not entailed."

"It generally passed through the eldest male..."

"But your grandfather divided his estate equally between his two sons..."

"Your father and his brother, your uncle Ernest."

"Both were given an estate—in your father's case, the Place."

"Unfortunately, Ernest Hartley was a gambler."

"Quite ran through his patrimony, as the saying goes."

"He eventually lost everything and turned to your father for aid."

"Your father was enjoying a great success in London at that time. He had married your mother and was much in demand. Dear me, his fees! Well, quite astronomical, they seemed.'' Mr Whitworth the elder paused for breath.

This time Georgiana could not restrain her need to put a hand to her brow. The world was whirling.

''If we could condense this history, gentlemen?'' Viscount Alton's precise tones jerked both Whitworths out of their rut.

''Er—yes. Well,'' said Mr Whitworth, with a careful eye on his lordship, ''the long and the short of it is, your father and mother wished to spend some time in Italy. So your father installed your uncle as steward of the Place, put his ready capital in the funds, leased the house in London, and left the country. I believe you were a child at the time.''

Georgiana nodded absent-mindedly. The Place was hers. It had never been Charles's property, and he had known it.

''When we heard of your father's death,'' broke in the younger Whitworth, warily eyeing the Viscount, ''we wrote immediately to you at the villa in Ravello. The letter was returned by your Italian man of business, stating you had returned to England before learning of your uncle's demise and had planned to stay at the Place.''

Whitworth the elder opened his mouth to respond to his cue, but caught the Viscount's eye and fell silent, leaving it to his sibling to continue, ''We wrote to you there, but the letters were returned without explanation. In the end we sent one of our most trusted clerks to see you. He reported that the house was shut up and deserted.''

The elder Whitworth could restrain himself no

longer. "No one seemed to know where you'd gone or even if you'd arrived from the Continent."

Following the tale with difficulty, Georgiana saw what must have occurred. Questions hammered at her brain, but most were not for the solicitors' ears. She fastened on the one aspect that held greatest importance to her. "You mentioned pictures?"

"Oh, yes. Your father left quite a tidy stack of canvases—some unclaimed portraits, and others—in England. He always claimed they were a sound investment." The dead tones of the younger solicitor left no doubt of his opinion on the matter.

"But where are they stored?" asked Georgiana.

"Stored?" The elder Whitworth stared at her wordlessly, then turned to his brother for help. But the younger Whitworth had clearly decided this was one cue he would do well to miss. "Er..." said Mr Whitworth, chasing inspiration, "I rather suspect he must have left them at the Place."

"Are you certain they haven't been sold?" Lord Winsmere bought into the conversation. "From what you say, Ernest Hartley sounds the type to hock his grandmother's spectacles. Excuse me, m'dear," he added in an aside to Georgiana.

But the elder Whitworth waved his hands in a negative gesture. "A reformed character, I assure you. After his—er—brush with the Navy, he was so thankful to be pulled free that he was quite devoted to his brother and his interests."

"Devoted?" echoed Lord Alton incredulously. "Have you seen the Place?"

"Unfortunately, Mr Hartley was unsuited to the task

of managing the estate, although he tried his best.''
The younger Whitworth drew his lordship's fire. "We
would seriously doubt he would have sold any of his
brother's paintings. He lived quite retired at the Place
until his death, you know.''

"So,'' said Georgiana, struggling to take it all in,
"the most likely place for my father's pictures—the
ones he left in England—is the Place. But they aren't
there. I looked.''

Both Whitworths shifted uncomfortably but could
throw no further light on the matter.

Eventually Mr Whitworth the elder broke the silence. "Are there any instructions you wish to give
us, my dear, concerning your property?''

Georgiana blinked, then slowly shook her head.
"I'm afraid I'll need a little time to think things
through. It's all been rather a surprise.''

"Yes, of course. No rush at all,'' said the elder Mr
Whitworth, resuming his genial state. "Mr Charles
Hartley will of course be given due notice to quit.''

Then, as there seemed nothing further to say, Georgiana rose, bringing the men to their feet.

"One moment, my dear,'' came Lord Winsmere's
voice. "It's as well to know all the facts.'' He smiled
at Georgiana and then turned to ask, "You mentioned
capital placed in the funds. What is the current balance?''

The elder Mr Whitworth beamed. The figure he
named sent Lord Alton's black brows flying.

An enigmatic smile played on Lord Winsmere's lips
as he turned to a stunned Georgiana. "Well, my dear,

I'm afraid you'll have more than your earnest suitors to repel once that piece of news gets around.''

ARTHUR'S REACTION was echoed by Bella when, over the luncheon table, she was regaled with the entirety of Georgiana's fortune. Arthur told the story; Dominic had declined an invitation to join them, pleading the press of other engagements.

"There's no point in thinking you can hide it, Georgie,'' Bella said once she had recovered enough to speak. "You're an *heiress.* Even if the Place is all to pieces.''

Georgiana was still trying to recover her equilibrium. "But surely, if we don't tell anyone, no one will know.''

Bella felt like screaming. What other young lady of quality, with her way to make in the world, when informed she was a considerable heiress, would act so? Inwardly, Bella railed again at the unknown who had stolen her friend's heart. Dominic had not yet found him; that much was clear. After his successful rescue of Georgiana the evening before, he had stayed to partake of a cold supper. She could well imagine what he had done to Charles, even without the tell-tale handkerchief she had seen him quickly remove from his hand and stuff into his pocket before he thought anyone had noticed. She was more than ready to believe his assertion that Charles would not trouble Georgiana again, and would in all probability not remain over long in England. But, after arranging for Arthur to accompany Georgiana and himself to her solicitors' this morning, her brother had merely bestowed a fond pat on her cheek and left...left her to struggle with the herculean task of convincing Georgiana to forget her hopeless love and choose between her lovesick beaux.

Sudden inspiration blossomed in Bella's mind. "Georgie, my love, we will really have to think very carefully about how you should go on." Bella paused, carefully choosing her words. "Once it becomes known you're an heiress, you'll be swamped. Perhaps it would be better to make your choice now."

Georgiana's gaze rose from her plate to settle on her friend's face. Bella's attempted manipulation was unwelcome, but, seeing the wistful expression in the blue eyes watching her, and knowing that she only meant to help, Georgiana could not suppress a small smile. But, "Really, Bella!" was all she said.

Abashed, Bella retreated, but rapidly came about. "Yes, but seriously, Georgie, what do you plan to do?"

"I'm afraid, my dear," put in Arthur, "that for once Bella is quite right." Bella grimaced at his phrasing. "Once it becomes common knowledge that you have such a fortune, you'll be besieged."

With a sigh, Georgiana pushed her plate away. They had sent the servants from the room to give free rein to their discussion. She rose to fetch the teapot from the side-table. Slipping once more into her chair, she busied herself with pouring cups for both Arthur and Bella before helping herself. Only then did she answer Bella. "I don't know. But please promise me you'll say nothing to anyone about my inheritance?"

Arthur bowed his acquiescence. "Whatever you wish, my dear." His stern eye rested on his wife.

Bella pouted, but, under her husband's prompting, she gave in. "Oh, very well. But it won't help, you know. Such news *always* gets around."

CHAPTER EIGHT

THE ACCURACY of Bella's prediction was brought home to Georgiana before the week was out. Shrewd assessing glances, condescending and calculating stares—the oppressive, smothering interest of the *ton* made itself felt in a dozen different ways. She could only conclude that the clerks in Mr Whitworth's office, or, perhaps, the Mr Whitworths themselves, were less discreet than she, in her naïveté, had supposed.

Bella, of course, behaved as if all the attention was only her due. Her friend continued to hope she would succumb to the blandishments of one or other of her insistent suitors. In fact, thought Georgiana crossly, the entire charade was enough to put anyone off marriage for life. How could she ever hope to convince herself any gentleman was in earnest, that he truly loved her for herself, rather than for the financial comfort she would bring him, when everyone behaved as if her new-found fortune was of the first importance?

With a disgusted little snort, she turned over on the coverlet of her bed, kicking her legs to free her skirts from under her. She had retreated to her room to rest before dressing for dinner and the Massinghams' rout. For the first time since Georgiana had come to Green Street, Bella had also retired for a late afternoon nap.

While she studied the details of the pink-silk-draped canopy, Georgiana considered her friend. Bella certainly seemed more tired these days, though the bloom on her skin showed none of the subtle signs of fatigue. Still, Georgiana couldn't understand how she kept up. Or why. For her own part, the glamour of the balls and parties was rapidly fading, their thrills too meaninglessly repetitive to hold her interest. Now she had no difficulty in understanding Bella's plea of boredom with the fashionable round.

Her eyes drifted to the wardrobe, wherein resided all her beautiful gowns. Bella was always so thrilled when she wore her latest acquisitions. They were worth every last penny just for that. Georgiana grinned. She could hardly deny Bella such a small pleasure when all her friend's energies were directed towards securing her, Georgiana's, future. Nothing seemly likely to turn Bella from her purpose. Her beloved Georgie must marry into the *ton*.

As an errant ray of sunshine drifted over the gilded cords drawing back the curtains of her bed, Georgiana wondered again at the oddity of having a virtual foster-sister. She was fast learning that receiving care and concern laid a reciprocal responsibility on the recipient. But, despite Bella's yearnings, this was one aspect of her life on which she was determined to hold firm. She would marry for love, or not at all.

Just the thought of love, the very concept, brought a darkly handsome face swimming into her consciousness. Vibrant blue eyes laughed at her through a mask, then turned smoky and dark. Resolutely she banished the unnerving image. Dreams were for children.

In truth, if it had not been for Lord Alton's support, she might well have turned tail and fled back to Italy the first day after their discovery at Lincoln's Inn. The puzzle of Charles and his machinations was now clear. Fiend that he was, devoid of all proper feeling, he had decided to marry her before she found out she owned the Place. That way, Dominic had explained, she would likely never have known the extent of her fortune; as her husband, Charles would have assumed full rights over her property.

Dominic. She must stop thinking of him like that, in such a personal way. If she was to preserve her secret, she must learn to treat him with becoming distance. Unfortunately, this grew daily more difficult.

When he had appeared before her at the Walfords' ball the evening after their momentous visit to the Whitworths', she had offered him welcome far in excess of what might reasonably be excused on the grounds that he was her patroness's brother. She hoped he had put it down to a gush of girlish gratitude, no matter how the very thought irked her. But the warmth in his blue eyes had left her with an uncomfortable feeling of no longer being in control, as if some hand more powerful than hers was directing her affairs.

Dominic—*Lord Alton!*—continued to rescue her from the worst of her importunate court. In fact he was now so often by her side that the rest of her admirers tended to fade into the background, at least in her eyes. Georgiana frowned at the wandering sunbeam which had moved to light the bedpost. Now she came to consider the matter, it was almost as if Lord Alton himself was paying court to her.

Another unladylike snort ruffled the serenity of the afternoon. Ridiculous idea! He was merely being kind, giving her what protection he could from the fortune-hunters, knowing she did not like her prominence one little bit. He was her patroness's brother, that was all.

Nothing more.

THE HUM of a hundred conversations eddied about Georgiana, enclosing her within the cocoon of the Massinghams' rout party. The bright lights of the chandeliers winked from thousands of facets, none more brilliant than the sparkling eyes of the débutantes as they dipped and swayed through the first cotillion. Laughter tinkled and ran like a silver ribbon through the crowd. It was a glittering occasion; all present were pleased to be seen to be pleased. The ballroom was bedecked with tubs of hothouse blooms, vying with the ladies' dresses in splashes of glorious colour, perfuming the warm air with subtle scents. A small orchestra added its mite to the din, striving valiantly to be heard above the busy chatter.

Newly entered on the scene, Georgiana had taken no more than three steps before being surrounded by her intrepid admirers, all clamouring for the honour of setting their name in her dance card. With a charm none the less successful for being automatic, she set about her regular task of ordering her evening.

"My dear Miss Hartley, if you would allow me the supper waltz I should be greatly honoured."

Georgiana glanced up and found the serious face of Mr Swinson, one of her earnest suitors, who had become even more earnest over the last few days, hovering beside her. All her instincts cautioned her to refuse his request. The supper waltz, with the implied intention of going into supper on the gentleman's arm at the conclusion of the measure, was the most highly prized of the dances at such a gathering. Whenever possible, Georgiana strove to grant that dance to one or other of her refused suitors, so as not to raise any false hopes among others of her court. But what excuse could she give, so early in the evening? A lie? Resolute, she opened her mouth to deny Mr Swinson, hoping he would accept her refusal without excuse, but was forestalled by a deep voice, speaking from behind her left ear.

"I believe the supper waltz is mine, Swinson."

Swaying slightly with the dizziness his nearness always induced, Georgiana struggled to keep her expression within the limits of the acceptable, and knew she failed dismally. Her eyes were alight, her nerves tingling. She turned and gave her hand to Lord Alton. She didn't even notice Mr Swinson huffily withdraw, eyeing the elegant person of the Viscount with marked disfavour.

Lord Alton bowed low over her hand. "Fairest Georgiana."

His words were a seductive murmur, rippling across her senses. Then, knowing it was unwise, but utterly incapable of resisting the compulsion, Georgiana met his eyes, and the warmth she saw there spread through her, leaving dizzy happiness in its wake.

"My lord."

She retained just enough wit to return his greeting, dropping her eyes from his in a flurry of shyness.

With a gentle smile, Viscount Alton tucked the hand he was still holding into the crook of his arm, thereby making life exceedingly difficult for the numerous other gentlemen waiting to pay court to this most desirable of young ladies. Lord Ellsmere, by his friend's side, grinned. Taking pity on Georgiana, he engaged her in light-hearted conversation.

Georgiana's hand burned where it lay on Lord Alton's silk sleeve. Why was he behaving so? Under cover of paying polite attention to Lord Ellsmere as he related the latest *on dit,* she glanced up to find the Viscount's blue eyes regarding her, an expression she dared not place lighting their depths. Another glance around showed her frustrated court dwindling, leaving only those gentlemen she regarded more as friends than suitors. Unlike those whose interest was primarily pecuniary, none of these gentlemen seemed to find Lord Alton's possessive attitude any impediment to conversing with her.

Possessive? Georgiana's thoughts froze. Then, inwardly, she shrugged. If the shoe fitted… And really there was no other way to describe the way he was behaving. This was the third night in a row he had appeared by her side almost immediately she had entered a room. By his mere presence he eased the crush about her, bringing relief which would doubtless be acute if she could feel anything through the sheer exhilaration of having him so near.

With an effort Georgiana forced herself to attend to the conversation, grateful for the distraction of Mr Havelock, who now joined them. By imperceptible degrees, the circle about them grew as more acquaintances stopped to talk. Gradually the sense of being, in some strange way, identifiably his receded, leaving only a subtle feeling of security.

When Lord Aylesham approached to claim the next dance, Lord Alton relinquished her with no more than a warm smile and a whispered reminder of their later appointment.

Released from the mesmerising effect of the Viscount at close quarters, Georgiana determinedly devoted a large part of her mind to a detailed analysis of his actions and motives. None of her partners noticed anything amiss; she was now too thoroughly practised in the arts of dancing, conversing and general entertaining to need to assign more than a small portion of her attention to these endeavours.

Of all the questions revolving in her head, the most insistent was, *Why?* Why was he doing all the things he was? Why was he behaving as he was? Again and again, only one answer came. It was impossible to attribute his actions to any other cause. *He was making her the object of his attentions.* Delicious shivers ran up her spine when she finally allowed her mind to enunciate that fact. Mr Sherry, whose arms she graced at the time, looked at her askance. Georgiana smiled dazzlingly upon him, completely stunning the poor man.

The next instant her sky clouded again. How could she believe such a magnificent man, with all the advantages of birth, position and fortune, would seriously look in her direction? That he was contemplating anything other than the acceptable was unthinkable. But perhaps he wasn't contemplating anything at all.

Maybe she was just an amusing aside, his sister's protégée who needed looking after. Was she simply a naïve foreigner, reading far more into the situation than was intended? Georgiana forgot to suppress her sigh, and was forced to spend the rest of the dance soothing a ruffled Mr Sherry.

While Georgiana struggled with question and answer, alternating between cloud nine and prosaic despondency, the object of her thoughts strolled about the rooms, stopping here and there to chat as the mood seized him. Dominic was in a state of pleasurable anticipation. To his mind, his course was clear. While it was not one he had followed previously, he did not doubt his ability to carry the thing off. The major problem was time—or, rather, the patience required to see the campaign through.

The necessity for taking things slowly was self-evident. This time the object of his desires was not an experienced woman, capable of playing the game with a facility on a par with his. This time he wanted a green girl, an innocent, an angel whose conquest meant more to him than all the others combined. She needed gentle wooing. So the habits of the last ten years were set aside in favour of the strict dictates of propriety. With a wry grin at no one in particular, Dominic wondered how long he could harness the coiled tension that was growing, day by day, beneath the surface of his suave urbanity.

"Dominic! What ho, lad! Up from the princely delights of Brighton?"

Dominic swung to face the speaker, a smile lighting his face. "My lord." He nodded to Lord Moreton, one of his late father's contemporaries. "As you say, sir, the amenities of Brighton palled."

"Palled before the attractions of the young ladies, eh?"

Unperturbed by the close scrutiny of a pair of sharp grey eyes overhung by bushy brows, Dominic smiled in his usual benign way and agreed. "Oh, Prinny's no competition, I assure you."

Lord Moreton guffawed. Slapping Dominic on the back, he resumed his peregrination through the crowd, allowing Dominic to do likewise.

It was, Dominic supposed, inevitable that people would start to speculate. The very fact that he was here, attending all the balls and parties of the Little Season, rather than pursuing a very different course, in very different company, positively invited the attention of the gabble-mongers. No one was as yet sufficiently bold to put their speculation into circulation, but doubtless that, too, would come. For his part, he didn't give a damn what the gossips said. He'd weathered far worse. But he would need to be vigilant to ensure no disturbing whispers reached his Georgiana's ears. In truth, he was not sure how she might respond. But, with first-hand knowledge of the spitefulness of some among society's civilised hordes, he was not prepared to take any chances.

For the first time, at the ripe old age of thirty-two, he was seriously wooing a young lady. The pace grated. The slowly compounding returns, when set against the constantly high expense in time and restraint, were hard to bear, particularly for one to whom instant gratification of the smallest whim, however

fleeting, had become the norm. And unusual absti-
nence only aggravated his state.

Still, there was at least one shining beacon on the
horizon, holding the promise of safe haven in the end.
He was too experienced not to be able to read the
signs. Her response to him was gratifying, even at
thirty-two. Who would have imagined he would be so
susceptible to such flattery? Dominic allowed a slow
grin to twist his lips. The pull he sensed between
them—that magnetic attraction that drew man to
woman and bound them together with silken strands
of desire—was so strong that he felt sufficently confident to leave her, essentially unwatched, for half the
evening. The other half, of course, would be his. At
least this way the gossip-mongers would have to wait
a little longer for their *on dit.*

"What on earth are you grinning at?"

Startled, Dominic turned to find Bella at his side.
His slow smile surfaced. "Pleasant thoughts, my
dear." His eyes scanned her face, noting the pallor she
had attempted to hide with rouge. "How goes it with
you?"

A small frown worried at Bella's arched brows.
"Oh, so-so." she paused, then went on in a rush, "If
I wasn't so concerned about Georgie, I declare I would
have stayed at home with Arthur. These affairs are
becoming a dreadful bore."

The quavering note in her voice alerted Dominic to
her state. He drew her hand comfortingly through his
arm, stroking it soothingly, a small gesture he had used
since she was a child. It had the desired effect. While
his sister regained her composure, it occurred to him

that time, his present arbiter, was about to place a limit on his courtship. The Season had only two more weeks to run. Then the *ton* would retire to their estates for Christmas and the worst of the winter. He was unsure if Bella had yet recognised her condition. Typically she was not one to coddle herself and could be relied on to fail to consider such possibilities until they became too obvious to ignore. But Arthur was not so sanguine. He would undoubtedly wish to remove from London as soon as the Season ended. Which raised the question of Georgiana's future plans.

On impulse, Dominic turned to his sister. "Incidentally, what are you planning for Christmas?"

Diverted, Bella gave him a clear blue stare. "Christmas?" Then, recovering from her surprise, "I haven't given it much thought." She shrugged. "I suppose we'll go down to Winsmere, as usual."

"Why not come to Candlewick? You haven't spent Christmas there since you married. I want to open the house up—just us, but the place needs warming."

Bella was taken aback by the invitation, but the more she considered it, the more value she could see in the suggestion. While she was very comfortable at Winsmere Lodge, it couldn't compare with the graciousness of Candlewick. Nothing could. "I'm sure Arthur wouldn't mind. I'll speak to him tomorrow."

Dominic nodded. "What about Georgiana?"

Bella's brow clouded again. "I've already asked, but she seems set on returning to Italy. I've tried to talk her out of it, but she's so stubborn!"

His suspicions confirmed, Dominic, repressing a

grin at his sister's disgruntled tone, said, "Leave it to me. I'll see what my persuasions can do."

Big beseeching blue eyes met his. "Oh, Dominic. If you could only persuade her to stay, I just know she'll make a good match once she gets over this horrible mystery gentleman of hers." Remembering her brother's promise, Bella added, "You haven't found out who he is yet, have you?"

It was Dominic's turn to frown. Amid the delights of wooing Georgiana, he'd forgotten the existence of her "secret love". Now, considering the matter carefully, knowing what he did of that young lady, he was hard put to it to credit the notion. If she had ever in truth had a "secret love", then the man was all but forgotten already. The unwelcome idea that Georgiana's partiality could vacillate like a darting sunbeam, now here, now there, awoke in his mind. Resolutely he quashed it. Quite simply, he had no intention of allowing her the leeway neccesary to vacillate. Seeing the worry etched in Bella's face, he yielded to the impulse to reassure her. "Don't worry your head about your protégée. From all I've seen, she's well on the way to achieving a highly creditable alliance."

The glow in Bella's face brought a smile to Dominic's lips.

"Who? Where...? I haven't noticed any particular gentleman... Oh, Dominic! Don't tease! Who is he?"

But Dominic only shook his head, smiling at her chagrin. "Patience, sister, dear. Don't crowd out the action. Just keep your eyes open and you'll doubtless see it all. But," he said, returning to a sterner tone, "believe me, there's no need for you to worry."

Bella grimaced up at him.

Dominic's brows rose, with that faintly supercilious air that warned Bella he was in earnest. Her rejoinder was destined to remain unuttered as Viscount Molesworth approached to claim her for the cotillion just forming.

Free again, Dominic continued his amble, determined to eschew Georgiana's company until the supper dance provided him with adequate excuse. At the door to the card-room, he was hailed by his brother-in-law.

"Thought you were at home," Dominic said, strolling up and nodding to Lord Green, standing beside Arthur.

"Finished my last box earlier than I'd thought. You've seen Bella?"

Dominic nodded. "She's dancing with Molesworth."

"In that case, come and join us."

"Just a quiet hand," put in Lord Green with a smile, "but at least more life than you're likely to find out here."

The smile on Dominic's face broadened. "Not tonight. I have other fish to fry."

"Ah." Arthur's pensive eye met his brother-in-law's bright blue gaze. "And what a shock that must be to the system."

Dominic's lips twitched, but he responded calmly. "As you say."

"Still," said Arthur, his eyes now on the figure of his wife twirling down the set with Viscount Molesworth, "it's worth it in the end."

With a nod and a smile, Dominic moved on. The cotillion had ended, and the dancers were taking their places, with a great deal of noisy laughter, for a set of country dances. His eyes were drawn to where Georgiana was standing, partnered by Julian Ellsmere. Dominic stood unobtrusively between a sofa occupied by two turbaned dowagers and a potted palm and watched the dancers, anticipation growing keener by the minute.

Suddenly the irritation of being stared at caused him to lift his eyes and look over the dancers' heads. Directly opposite, Elaine Changley stood watching him.

She smiled as their eyes made contact. Then, completely ignoring the ladies beside her, she glided across the ballroom in his direction.

It was a bold move. Under his breath, Dominic uttered an oath, completely forgetting the proximity of the elderly dowagers. As he watched her progress between the sets, he allowed himself to examine, as if from a distance, her attractions. Other than as a passing diversion, she had failed to activate his interest. He had never encouraged her to believe otherwise. It amazed him that she could confuse the emotion he felt for the lady he would marry with the fleeting passion he had indulged with her.

Elaine Changley was desperate. Just how desperate, she had not known until she had seen the handsome form of Dominic Ridgeley across the room and realised the smile on his face was caused by the sight of his sister's protégée. Her present play was a gamble. By the time she reached his side, she realised how dangerous a gamble it was.

Dominic greeted her with a formal bow and a cold, "Elaine."

Inwardly, Lady Changley winced, but she kept a bright if brittle smile fixed on her lips and attempted to inject some warmth into her habitually cold gaze. "Dominic, darling," she purred, "how pleasant to find you here. Have you come to alleviate the singular boredom of this party?"

Dominic allowed his gaze, which had returned to the dancers immediately after greeting her, to come slowly about to rest on her face—a handsome face, pale and perfectly featured, but devoid of all softness, all womanly feeling.

The music stopped.

Suddenly nervous, Elaine Changley plied her fan, fluttering it delicately just below her eyes.

Curtly Dominic bowed. "If you'll excuse me, my lady, I am engaged for the next dance."

With that, he left her, aware of the avid interest of the dowagers, and of Elaine Changley's eyes, following him.

Paler than ever, Elaine Changley had no move left on the board. She had perforce to remain where she was, her temper in shreds, and bear the sly feminine whispers of the ladies from across the room and the less subdued cackle of the witches on the sofa beside her. Her apparently impetuous approach to Lord Alton had been designed to draw all eyes. His leaving her after no more than a minute made his uninterest as clear as if the town crier had announced it. And he had gone straight to Miss Hartley's side! Seething and impotent, Lady Changley stood rigid as a post, forced to accept the most comprehensive defeat of her varied career with what very little grace she could muster.

A sudden tingling rippling along her nerves told Georgiana, chatting easily with Lord Ellsmere, that her next partner was close. She turned slightly to find her hand taken in a firm grip and placed, equally firmly, on Viscount Alton's arm. Chancing an upward glance, she found his lordship's blue eyes smiling down at her, that curiously warming expression readily discernible.

"Julian, I believe Arthur is looking for a fourth in the card-room."

Lord Ellsmere laughed at the overt dismissal and, with a smiling bow over Georgiana's free hand, he left them.

There was a slight break betwen the country dances and the waltz, while the musicians retuned their instruments. Lord Alton seemed quite content to spend the time staring at her. Unnerved, and knowing she would very likely dissolve entirely if she permitted him such licence, Georgiana strove to find a suitably distracting conversational gambit.

"All the *ton* seem to be attending tonight. The rooms are quite full, don't you think?" Breathless and quivering, it was the best she could manage.

"Are they?" Lord Alton replied, brows rising, but his gaze remaining fixed on her face. "I hadn't noticed."

The expression in his blue eyes and the seductive tenor of his voice infused his words with a meaning far in excess of the obvious. Georgiana blushed.

Dominic smiled. "But you remind me of something I had to ask you."

"Oh?" Georgiana struggled to reduce their inter-action to the commonplace. If she could only keep talking, and avoid those soft silences that he used so well to steal her mind and her wits and her very soul, she might just survive. "What was that?"

"Why, only that I wondered what your plans for the winter months were." The music restarted, and Dominic drew her gently into his arms and into the swirling drifts of couples on the floor.

Her feet circling dutifully, Georgiana made a des-perate effort to focus her mind on his words. "Ah..." She moistened suddenly dry lips with the tip of her tongue, then tried again. "I... That is to say..." She caught his amused look. A sudden little spurt of anger allowed her to regain her composure. Putting up her chin, she stated calmly, "I expect to be returning to Italy."

A woebegone sigh met her declaration. At her look of surprise Dominic said, "Mrs Landy and Duckett will be so disappointed. I'm sure they would love to see the eminently fashionable young lady you have become, if only to congratulate themselves on their far-sightedness."

Georgiana looked her puzzlement.

Effortlessly guiding her about the turns required to negotiate the end of the room, Dominic waited until they were once more precessing up the length of the ballroom before smiling down into her large eyes. "I have invited Bella and Arthur to spend Christmas at Candlewick. It is my earnest hope you will join us."

Wise in the ways of his Georgiana, Dominic watched her thoughts in her eyes. He waited until the desire to accept his invitation had been overcome by her instinctive fears, and a reluctant refusal was about to leave her lips, before allowing a pained expression to infuse his features. "Before you come to any hasty conclusion, I beg you will consider what a refusal would mean to me, my love."

His evident distress, the unacceptable endearment, combined with her own conflicting emotions, which he had skilfully invoked, left Georgiana's head in a whirl. "What...? Why, what on earth can you mean, my lord?" Her eyes widened. "What did you call me?"

He ignored her last question, and continued in despondent vein, "You must see that it really won't do."

Dizzy, Georgiana made a grab for sanity. She drew a deep breath. "My lord—"

"Dominic."

Georgiana blushed, and was further confounded by his lordship's rising brows and the words, "If I'm to go about calling you 'my love', it's only reasonable for you to use my Christian name."

Georgiana was so flustered that she could think of nothing to say.

"Now where were we?" mused his lordship. "Ah, yes! You were about to accept my invitation to spend Christmas at Candlewick."

Her resolve to flee to the safety of Ravello as soon as she possibly could was melting under the warmth in his sky-blue eyes. "But—"

"No buts," countered Dominic. "Just think of poor Arthur and myself, condemned to a mournful Christmas with Bella all mopey because you've gone off and left her in the dismals again.'' Glancing down into her sweet face, and seeing that desire was winning his battle, Dominic withheld the news of Bella's condition. He would keep that as an ace up his sleeve, in case of future need. "You couldn't possibly be so cruel."

The music ceased, and for one silent moment they stood, eyes locked. Then, suddenly frightened she would see the strength of his desire in his eyes and be alarmed, Dominic smiled and broke the contact. He raised one long finger to caress a golden curl that hung by her ear. The finger, with a will of its own, moved on to trace the curve of her jaw.

At his touch, Georgiana shivered, pure pleasure tingling along already overstretched nerves.

Dominic's eyes widened slightly. His gaze returned to her eyes, large and luminous under softly arching brows. Instinctively he sought to reassure her. "Besides," he said, his voice no more than a whisper, "there's no reason for you to run away."

Georgiana's tired brain accepted the statement, with all its layered meanings. She understood he knew she had no pressing need to return to Italy, but also, in her heart, heard his vow that she would have no cause to flee him.

"Say you'll come. I promise you Christmas at Candlewick will be everything you could wish." Dominic had not the slightest hesitation in making that vow. He had every intention of seeing it fulfilled.

Entranced, with his darkened eyes demanding only one answer, Georgiana found herself nodding.

A brilliant smile was her reward. Warmed through

and through, she allowed him to settle her hand on his arm once more.

The other dancers were leaving the floor, heading for the supper-room. Dominic's appetite had no interest in food, and, from her pensive expression, his Georgiana was not in the mood for lobster patties either. With an imperious gesture he commandeered a footman and sent him on a search for two glasses of champagne.

With the foresight of a man accustomed to success in the field, he had already made arrangments to allow him to appropriate much of the rest of Georgiana's evening without raising any scandalised eyebrows. When the footman returned with their drinks, Dominic handed one to Georgiana and, taking the other himself, steered her away from the crowded supper-room towards the entrance to the ballroom.

With the fizz of champagne tickling her throat, Georgiana held her peace until it became clear he did indeed intend leading her out of the ballroom. Then she raised her face, her eyes meeting his in mute query.

Dominic smiled slowly, allowing just enough time for her to sense his thoughts and blush delightfully, before saying, "I thought you might like to see the Massingham art collection. It's quite impressive, and includes, I'm told, a number of your father's works."

It was, of course, the perfect ploy. Georgiana was all eagerness to view her father's protraits of the last generation of Massinghams. And no one would remark on their absence on such an errand, particularly not when Dominic had had the forethought to request permission from Lord Massingham to show his sister's protégée around the collection, dispersed about the gallery and the large library downstairs.

Delighted with their excursion, Georgiana relaxed entirely in the enjoyment of fine paintings, many of which she, with her tutored eye, could accurately place and appraise. To her surprise, Dominic proved to have a sound knowledge of the painters whose works were displayed. She eventually forced him to admit to an extended Grand Tour, which had included many of the galleries and great houses of Europe.

He did not press her to speak when they stood before one of her father's portraits, but stood back and perceptively left her to her musings.

After long moments of studying again the brush strokes she knew so well, Georgiana sighed and moved on, coming up again level with Dominic, smiling tremulously at his now serious face with its gently questioning look. She allowed him to take her hand. He raised it and, to her surprise, brushed it gently with his lips before returning it to its accustomed place on his sleeve. Strangely comforted, recognising her need only by its relief, Georgiana felt herself curiously but totally at ease by the side of this man who more normally reduced her to quivering mindlessness.

With no need for words, they descended the staircase and crossed the chequered-tiled entrance hall to the library. The door stood open, glasses and a decanter on a tray bearing witness to the Massinghams' care for their guests, all of whom had apparently succumbed to the lure of the lobster patties. The room was empty. Ushering Georgiana in, Dominic quietly closed the door behind them.

The walls boasted two Tintorettos, a Watteau and one Hartley—a small protrait of one of the sons of the house. It hung between two sets of long windows. Dominic appropriated a three-armed candelabrum from a sidetable and placed it on the sofa table beneath the portrait.

Head on one side, Georgiana studied the small picture. Dominic watched her. The flickering candlelight gleamed on her golden tresses, striking highlights deep in the silken mass, like flames in molten ore. His fingers itched to tangle in those glorious curls, to see her golden eyes widen in surprise, then darken with delight. He could not see the expression in those bewitching eyes, but her lips, warmly tinted and full, were pursed in thought, pouting prettily, all but begging to be kissed. Desperately he sought for some distracting thought. If he continued in this vein, he would never be able to resist the temptation posed by the deserted room.

"It's one of his better works," said Georgiana. She smiled up at her companion, so still and silent beside her. His face was a polite mask, telling her nothing of his thoughts, but his eyes, so intensely blue that they seemed, in the weak light, to be almost black, sent skittering shivers along her sensitised nerves. She found herself wishing she had not donned the latest of Fancon's creations—a sheath of bronze satin which revealed rather more of her charms than she was presently comfortable with. She reminded herself to keep talking. "Papa always said that children were especially hard to do. Their features are so soft—almost unformed—that he claimed it was excessively easy to make them look vacuous.''

Dominic, with no interest in anything save the flesh-and-blood woman beside him, asked, ''Are there any portraits of you?''

Alerted by the rasping huskiness of his voice, Georgiana moved slightly, ostensibly to gaze out of the uncurtained window, thereby increasing the distance between them. ''Of course,'' she replied, surprised at her even tone. ''There are three at the villa in Ravello, and there was supposed to be one, done when I was very young, left in England.''

If Georgiana had seen the smile which curved Dominic's lips as she stepped into the window embrasure, she might have recognised the unwisdom of the move. As it was, it was only when, after a moment's silence had further stretched her nerves to tingling awareness, he closed the distance between them, coming to stand behind her, that she realised she was effectively trapped, unable to retreat, her exit blocked by his large body. And he was so close that she dared not turn around.

Dominic's smile was devilish as he moved so that no more than an inch separated them. His hands came up to stroke her upper arms gently, where her ivory skin gleamed bare above her elbow-length gloves. He leant forward so that his lips were close by her ear, and whispered, ''In that case, we'll have to make a special effort to locate these mysterious paintings.'' He grinned at the shiver that ran through her. ''Perhaps, now that you own the Place, you should institute a search.''

''Mmm-mmm,'' murmured Georgiana, her mind far from her father's missing paintings. He was so close! Through the thin satin gown, she could feel the radiant heat of him. His breath wafted the soft curls by her ear, sending all sorts of feelings skittering through her body. The caressing hands, drifting so gently over her skin, had ignited a funny warm glow deep inside her, quite unlike any sensation she had previously experienced. She decided she liked it.

Caught up in her novel discoveries, Georgiana was unaware of her instinctive movement, of leaning back against the hard chest at her back, letting her coiffed head rest against one broad shoulder, exposing the long column of her throat and a creamy expanse of shoulders and breasts to the blue gaze of the man behind her.

Dominic stopped breathing. This wasn't how he had planned it. Suddenly the rules of the game seemed to be shifting, leaving him confused, struggling to control a rampant desire which had somehow slipped its leash. His eyes flicked to hers, and found them half closed, heavy-lidded with the first stirrings of passion. Her lips, luscious and ripe, were slightly parted, her breathing swift and shallow. Full understanding of the effect he was having on her hit him with the force of a sledge-hammer.

A muffled groan escaped him, then, unable to resist, he bent his head and touched his lips to where the pulse beat strongly beneath the soft skin of her throat.

Georgiana stiffened at the intimacy, then, as his lips

moved over her skin, warm and gentle, yet teasing, so teasing, promising more of the delicious delight, she relaxed fully against him, accepting and wanting to know more as the fires within her grew.

The click of the door-latch brought Dominic's head up.

"This place is nice and quiet. So much noise up there, can't hear yourself think!" The old Duke of Beuccleugh stumped into the room, accompanied by two equally ancient cronies. They headed across the room towards the deep armchairs by the hearth, but pulled up to stare at the couple engaged in rapt contemplation of the picture on the wall between the long windows.

"Very nice brush strokes, don't you agree?" said Viscount Alton, gesturing towards the painting.

Georgiana choked.

Dominic turned, as if just realising they were no longer alone.

The Duke peered at him, then recognition dawned. "Oh, it's you, Alton."

"Your grace." Dominic bowed.

"Admiring the view?" enquired the Duke, hard grey eyes glinting.

With an expression of bland innocence, Dominic explained, "Miss Hartley's father painted the portrait."

"Ah." His Grace's grey gaze switched to Georgiana, curtsying deeply. "Painter chappie, heh? Vaguely recall him, if m'memory don't serve me false." He nodded benignly at Georgiana, then recalled his purpose in the room. "Dancing's started again upstairs."

Dominic took the hint. "In that case, we should perhaps return." He turned to Georgiana and offered his arm. "Miss Hartley?"

Very correctly, Georgiana placed her hand on his sleeve and allowed him to escort her back to the ballroom. She was deeply shaken. Never would she have believed she would enjoy such a scandalous interlude. Yet she had not only enjoyed it; even now, with her eyes wide open, and no longer under his hypnotic spell, she was conscious of how deeply she resented the interruption that had brought a premature end to proceedings. Her concupiscence shocked her.

Unknown to Georgiana, her response had also shocked Dominic although, in his case, the feeling was purely pleasurable. On the stairs he recalled his as yet unfulfilled intention of making clear to the beautiful creature on his arm that he had, most definitely, known who she was at the masked ball the week before. Determined to be rid of this potential source of misunderstanding, he waited until they had reached the upper landing before stopping to glance down at a still flushed Georgiana. Unable to resist a knowing smile, drawing sparks from her huge hazel eyes, he chose what he thought was a simple but effective means of conveying his information. "I most heartily approve of that dress, my love," he said, his voice a sensuous murmur. "It will doubtless vie for prominence in my memory with that topaz silk creation you wore at the masked ball."

Georgiana blushed furiously, completely missing the implication in her thoroughly unnerved state. With an enormous effort, she gathered sufficient control to incline her head graciously and say, "I think perhaps we should return to the ballroom, my lord."

A deep chuckle answered her. "I'm sure you're right, my love. You've had quite enough adventure—for tonight."

There was a wealth of promise in his suggestive tone, none of which was lost on Georgiana. She willed her jittery nerves to compliance and, with the most serene expression she could muster firmly fixed on her face, allowed him to lead her back into the cacophony of the ballroom.

NOT UNTIL she was wrapped in the darkness of the Winsmere carriage on the long drive home from the Massinghams' did Georgiana allow her mind to dwell on the events of the evening. Even in the shielding gloom, she felt herself blush as she recalled those long moments in the library. How could she have been so…so positively *wanton?* Easily, came the damning reply. And now he knew. The thought made her shiver. Drawing her cloak more closely about her, she snuggled into its warmth, feeling the silk lining brush across her bare shoulders. These outrageously fashionable gowns of Fancon's hardly helped. Somehow, scantily clad in satin and silks, she was much more aware of a peculiar need to be held, to be stroked and caressed as she had been that evening. Repressing a little snort of derision, she told herself she could hardly claim it was the dresses which made her feel as she did. They simply made it easier to feel so…abandoned.

Jettisoning that unproductive line of thought, she

blushed again as she remembered Dominic's rapid actions when the Duke and his friends had threatened discovery. She had sensed his suppressed laughter and had had to struggle to subdue her own, bubbling up in reply. It was odd, now she came to consider the matter, that she felt no sense of shame, only frustration.

Abruptly refocusing her thoughts once more, she tried to remember what he had said later, before they had gained the ballroom. Her mind promptly supplied the caress in his eyes as they had roamed appreciatively over her face and shoulders before he had complimented her on her gown. What had he said? Something about it being as pretty as her topaz silk.

The carriage jolted over a rut and she slipped sideways on the seat. She resettled herself in her corner, sightlessly watching the house fronts slip past the window.

Then her mind caught hold of the elusive memory, and his words replayed in her head. "It will doubtless vie for prominence in my memory with that topaz silk creation you wore at the masked ball."

Georgiana gasped.

"Georgie? Are you all right?"

Struggling to draw breath, Georgiana managed a reassuring phrase, then, feeling winded, curled up in her corner and gave her full attention to her staggering discovery.

He had known!

Which, as she had long ago worked out, meant... Her mind went completely blank, unable to accept the implication. Yet it was the only explanation possible.

Her heart beating in double time, a host of quivery, fluttery feelings crowding her chest, Georgiana forced her mind to grapple with the unthinkable. He had known, therefore he was... Oh, heavens!

THE NEXT THREE DAYS passed in a haze of happiness. Georgiana hardly dared to believe her deductions, yet, whenever she met Lord Alton, every word, every action, confirmed them. He was paying court to her. Her—little Georgiana Hartley!

Bella seemed quite unaware and, yielding to the promptings of some sixth sense, Georgiana did not explain the source of her sudden elation to her friend. Bella had, certainly, noticed her glow. Uncharacteristically, she had yet to enquire its cause. But Georgiana was too much in alt to worry about such inconsistencies.

She had artfully managed to drop the information that Dominic had invited her to Candlewick for Christmas and she had accepted. Bella had feigned complete surprise, but Georgiana suspected she had known of her brother's intent. The subtle smugness in her smile suggested as much.

It was Lady Chadwick's gala tonight. She would see Dominic there, she was sure. They had yet to meet outside a ballroom, but it had only taken a moment or two to work out his strategy. Young and naïve as she was, even she knew any overt gesture on his part, any attention which could not be credited to a natural assistance to his sister's protégée, would make them the focus of the most intense speculation. She had no wish to figure in the latest *on dit,* and was grateful for his care of her reputation.

So she had to make do with the caress in his eyes every time they met, the gentle promise of his smile, the touch of his fingers on hers. It was nowhere near enough. She contented herself with the thoughts that, when the time was right, he would surely advance their courtship to the stage where the heady delights he had introduced her to in the library of Massingham House would once again be on their agenda.

Bella had retired to rest before the Chadwick gala. Georgiana had come to her room with a similar intention. But her thoughts denied her sleep. Restless, she jumped off the bed and paced the room in small, swirling steps, then broke into a waltz, spinning about as anticipation took hold. Whirling almost out of control, she did not see the door open, and cannoned into Cruickshank as she entered.

"Oh!" Georgiana put a hand to her whirling head. "Oh, Cruckers! What a start you gave me."

"I gave you?" said her dour maid, righting herself and shutting the door firmly. "Now, Miss Georgie, whatever's got into you? Whirling about like a heathen, indeed!"

Georgiana giggled, but made no other reply. She was in love, but she had no intention of letting anyone into the secret. Anyone other than Dominic.

Cruickshank sniffed. "Well, if you're so wide awake, I'll get your bath-water brought up. We may as well spend the time beautifying you."

Georgiana, thinking of the admiration she would see in a pair of bright blue eyes, gladly agreed.

THERE WAS NO supper waltz at the Chadwicks' gala. Dominic had, instead, claimed both the first and the last waltzes of the evening. Twirling down the long ballroom, under the glare of the chandeliers, Georgiana suddenly realised why it was he always chose a waltz. He was holding her far closer than was the norm. And, when she blushed, all he did was laugh softly and whisper, ''As I cannot steal you away, my love, to a place where we might in safety pursue our mutual interest, you can hardly deny this lesser joy.'' The look that went with the words only made her blush more.

At the end of the dance, the last waltz of the evening, she was breathless and very nearly witless. Laughingly declining a most sensually worded invitation to take the air on the terrace—a highly dangerous undertaking, she had not a doubt—she whisked herself off to the withdrawing-room. A glass of cool water and a few moments of peace and quiet were all the restorative she needed. It would never do to let Bella see her return from a dance with her brother in such a state. There was, she felt sure, a limit to her friend's blindness.

When she entered, the withdrawing-room, a large bedchamber on the first floor, was empty of other guests. While she sipped the cool water an attentive maid brought her, Georgiana strolled to the long windows. The cool night air beckoned; Georgiana stepped out on to the small balcony. Behind her, the door of the withdrawing-room opened and shut, but she paid the newcomers no heed.

Not until the words, ''Alton's such a cynical devil.

D'you think he means marriage this time?'' riveted her attention.

Slowly Georgiana turned to face the room. Standing still and silent in the shadows of the billowing draperies, she was concealed from the occupants, two matrons of considerable years and similar girth. They had dropped into two chairs and were busily fanning themselves while they considered the night's entertainment.

"Oh, I should think so," opined one, the fatter, pushing a wilting ostrich plume from over one eye. "After all, why else would he be dancing attendance as he is?"

"But she's hardly his sort," countered the other, resplendent in blue bombazine. "Just look at Elaine Changley. What I want to know is why an out-and-outer like Alton should suddenly succumb to a sweet young thing whose charms can't possibly compare to those he's become accustomed to."

"But haven't you heard?" The fat matron leaned closer to her companion and lowered her voice in conspiratorial fashion. "It's her land he's after." She sat back in her chair and nodded sagely. "Seems she's inherited a section of land Alton's been chasing for years."

"Oh. Well, that sounds more like it. Couldn't imagine what had come over him." The blue bombazine rustled and shuffled, then stood and stretched. "Come on, Fanny. If we don't get back soon, that boy of yours will catch something you'll wish he hadn't."

Frozen, her senses suspended, Georgiana remained on the balcony while the two ladies fussed over the frills on the gowns before departing for the ballroom.

The Place. Georgiana wished she had never heard of it. And, of course, the words rang all too true. According to Bella, it was an obsession of her brother's. Georgiana's heart turned to ice, a solid chilled lump in her breast. Slowly, hardly aware of what she was doing, she came back into the room, pausing to place the glass she was carrying on a side-table.

Then she looked up and caught sight of herself in the mirror above the dressing-table. Huge haunted eyes stared back at her, stunned and distressed. She couldn't go back to the ballroom looking like that.

Drawing a deep breath, Georgiana shook herself, then straightened her shoulders and blinked several times. Pride was not much comfort, but it was all she had left. Determined to think no more about what she had heard until she had the privacy to indulge her tears, she left the room.

Once back in the crowded ballroom, misery hovered, threatening to engulf Georgiana if she relaxed her superhuman effort to ignore the matrons' words. She had to survive the rest of the gala. But Bella, seeing the stricken look in her friend's eyes, was immediately concerned.

"No, Georgie! We'll leave right now. There's no reason at all we need stay for the rest of this boring party."

With a determined frown, Bella silenced Georgiana's protests, and, within minutes, they were ensconced in the carriage and on their way to Green Street.

Bella yawned. "One thing about leaving just that little bit early—you can always get your carriage straight away.'' She stretched and settled herself. ''Now, what's the matter?''

But Georgiana had had time to get herself in hand. She had anticipated the question and strove to deflect Bella's interest. ''Nothing specific. It's just that I seem to have developed a migraine. I find it hard to go on once it comes on.''

''Oh, you poor thing!'' exclaimed Bella. ''You just lie back quietly. As soon as we're home, I'll get Cruickshank to brew a tisane for you. I won't speak to you any further. Now try to rest.''

Grateful for Bella's silence, Georgiana sank into her corner of the seat and gave herself up to her chaotic thoughts. After several minutes of totally pointless recollection, she forced herself to view the facts calmly. First of these was the relationship she knew existed between Lord Alton and Lady Changley. There was no doubt it was real—not just from the gossip, but from the evidence of her own eyes, on the terrace that fateful night. The memory of the passionate kiss Lord Alton had bestowed on Lady Changley was imprinted indelibly on her mind. He had never kissed her—let alone with such ardour. She recalled her early conviction that his attitude to her was merely that of helpful friendship, giving what assistance he could to his sister in her efforts to find a husband for her protégée. And his behaviour at the masked ball? Well, she had always thought he had not known who the lady in the topaz silk was. When had he told her he knew? Only a few days ago, long after he had learned of her inheritance. He could easily have found out what she had worn to the ball—from Bella if no one else. And then, too, Bella's ready acceptance of her sudden happiness could be easily explained if her friend knew her brother was paying court to her.

Georgiana stifled a sob. A few hours ago her world had looked rosy indeed. Now all her hopes lay in ashes about her. She had thought he was different, blessed with all the virtues, strong and steady and protective. Now it seemed he was no different from the rest. His love for her was superficial, assumed, of no great depth, called forth only by her possession of the Place. His main interest in life was status and wealth, with all the trappings. Why, he was not much better than Charles. And Bella thought nothing of Dominic's marrying her to gain title to the land. In all probability, he planned to keep Lady Changley as his mistress, even after they were married.

Georgiana tried to whip up her anger, her disdain. She must despise him, now she knew of his plans. But, as the miles rolled by, a cold certainty crept into her heart. She loved him far too much to despise him. Surely love wasn't meant to hurt so much?

Disillusioned on every front, she huddled into her corner and wept.

CHAPTER NINE

A SLEEPLESS NIGHT filled with hours of crying was no remedy for Georgiana's ailment. Bella took one look at her in the morning and insisted she spend the day in bed. Georgiana was in no mood to argue. But she winced at Bella's last words, floating in her wake as, having insisted on tucking her in, she tiptoed out of her bedroom. "For don't forget, we've the Mortons' ball tonight, and that's one event we can't miss."

Georgiana closed her eyes and let misery flow in. But she knew Bella's reasons for attending the ball, the Mortons being old family friends, and knew she could not avoid going. She had revised her opinion of Bella's part in her brother's schemes. No one who was as kind as Bella could possibly be party to such cold-blooded manipulation. And there was Arthur, too. Try as she might, it was impossible to cast Bella's husband in the light of a hard-hearted character who would idly watch while a young girl was cajoled into a loveless marriage. No. Neither Bella nor Arthur knew of Dominic's schemes. Not that that made life all that much easier, for she could hardly ask them for advice on such a matter. Still, she was glad she had at least two friends she could count true.

The evening came all too soon. Under the combined

ministrations of Cruickshank and the redoubtable Hills, supervised by Bella herself, the ravages of her imaginary migraine were repaired until only her lack-lustre eyes and her pallid complexion remained as witness to her inner turmoil.

Those items were sufficient, however, to immediately draw Dominic's attention to her distress. As was his habit, he gravitated to her side immediately she appeared in the ballroom.

"Georgiana?" Dominic bowed slightly over her hand, his eyes searching her face.

Flustered and weak, Georgiana retrieved her hand immediately, not daring to meet his intent gaze. Her heart was thudding uncomfortably, bruised and aching.

Dominic frowned. "My dear…"

At his tone, desperation flooded Georgiana. She raised her head, but still could not meet his eyes. "I'm afraid, my lord, that my dance card is full."

The silence on her left was complete. She had just entered the ballroom—he must know she was lying.

Dominic felt his face drain of expression. His jaw hardened. The impulse to call her bluff was strong. Then he noticed again her pallor, and the brittle tension in her slim frame, and swallowed his anger.

Stiffly, he bowed. With a cold, "My dear," he forced himself to walk away.

Dominic spent the first two dances watching Georgiana from the side of the room, unsure of his feelings, unsure, for what seemed like the first time in his life, of what to do. What the hell was going on? Then, finding himself the object of more than a few curious glances, he took himself off to the card-room.

He was rapidly inveigled into playing a few hands, but his mind was not on the game, and no one demurred when he left the table and returned to drift idly about the ballroom, keeping an unobtrusive eye on Georgiana. He had been careful enough for their association to have passed for mere acquaintance. If he displayed too overt an interest now, it would be tantamount to a declaration. But the impulse to cross the floor and haul her out on to the terrace and demand an explanation for her extraordinary conduct grew.

If she had betrayed the slightest hint of partiality for any other gentleman, he would have done it, and the consequences be damned. Luckily, she seemed unusually subdued, dancing only with those he knew she deemed her friends, refusing all others.

Slowly, his mind calmed and he started to sort through the possibilities in a more methodical fashion. At the Chadwicks' gala, all had been well, until after their last dance. She had gone off to the withdrawing-room, and he, careful of appearances, had gone to make one in the card-room. When he had returned to the ballroom, he had found the Winsmere party had decamped. That had not surprised him at the time, knowing Bella's condition. But perhaps there had been some other reason for their early departure.

Useless to speculate, when he had no idea what might have occurred. But between that last waltz and this evening, something had happened to destroy the carefully nurtured bond between himself and Georgiana.

Feeling very like hitting someone, but having no idea whom, Dominic scowled and strode out on to the balcony. The cool air brought some relief to his fevered brain. This was ridiculous. He was thirty-two, for heaven's sake! The effect Georgiana's withdrawal was having on him was both novel and highly unnerving. He didn't like it. And he'd be damned if he'd endure it for a minute longer than necessary.

Drawing a deep breath, he frowned direfully at the young couple who, giggling softly, came up out of the secluded garden. Surprised to find him there, arms folded and looking so grim, they fled back to the ballroom. Dominic sighed. If he did not have to be so circumspect, he could have taken Georgiana into the garden and made delicious love to her—

Abruptly he cut off the thought. Right now, it seemed as if she wasn't even speaking to him.

He would have to find out what was upsetting her. From the few comments he had exchanged with his sister, Bella clearly had no idea what had happened— she still had no idea of his interest in Georgiana. He needed to see Georgiana alone. For several moments, he pondered various schemes for attaining this end, finally settling on the one which, although it would not allow the fiction of the avuncular nature of his interest to stand, had the best chance of success.

With his decision made, he left the terrace to lay the necessary groundwork to put his plan into action.

GEORGIANA had no idea how she survived the Mortons' ball. It remained, long afterwards, a dull ache in her memory. She was glad, she kept telling herself, that Lord Alton had accepted her dismissal so readily. It would have been too much to bear if he had insisted she speak with him. Perhaps he had realised she had come to understand his motives and would not be the easy conquest he had expected. Hopefully, he would stay away from her now. Depressed and weary, she slept the sleep of exhaustion, and awoke the next morning, refreshed at least in body, if not in spirit.

Despondent, she trailed into the breakfast-room.

"Georgie! Are you feeling better this morning?"

Bella's solicitude brought Georgiana to her senses. She had no right to wallow in misery and act like a raincloud over her friend. Summoning a wan smile, Georgiana nodded. "Yes. I'm fine."

Bella's face suggested she did not look fine, but, instead of harping on the subject, Bella started chattering about the events that would fill the next week and bring the Little Season to an end. Georgiana listened with half an ear.

As Bella's catalogue ran its course, Georgiana realised she could not just up and flee to Italy tomorrow, much as she might wish to. She had made a bargain with Arthur, who had stood her friend when she had been in need. She could not shrug off her indebtedness. So she would have to see out the rest of the Season with what interest she could muster, trying not to dampen Bella's enjoyment with her own unhappiness.

She apparently returned sufficiently accurate, if monosyllabic, responses to Bella's opinions, for they rose from the breakfast-table in perfect amity.

"Oh, Georgie! I nearly forgot. Dominic noticed you looked a bit peaked last night, so he's coming to take you for a drive this afternoon."

Bella had preceded Georgiana through the door, so did not see the effect her announcement had on her friend.

"It's really a great honour, you know. I can't even remember the last lady Dominic took up for a drive in the park. He doesn't normally do so—says it's too boring. You must wear your new carriage dress; it'll be just the thing."

Reaching the parlour, Bella turned expectantly.

Georgiana had had enough time to school her features to a weak smile. "I really don't know if—"

"Oh, nonsense!" said Bella, dismissing whatever megrim Georgiana had taken into her head. "Some fresh air is just what you need to blow the cobwebs away."

Sinking on to the window seat and taking up her embroidery frame, Georgiana could not think of any reasonable excuse to decline Lord Alton's invitation. At least, not without explaining a great deal more of the situation to Bella. And that she was definitely not up to doing. Quite clearly, Bella was still in the dark regarding the state of affairs between her brother and her protégée.

Throughout the day, Georgiana formulated and discarded a string of plans to avoid the afternoon drive. In the end, her schemes became so wildly far-fetched that her sense of humour came to her rescue. What on earth did she imagine he'd do to her in the sanctity of the park? Besides, she knew him too well to believe he'd do anything scandalous—at least, not with her. She spent a moment in dim regret over that point, then determinedly stiffened her spine. She would go with him and hope to impress on him that she did not wish to see him again. Perhaps, with one major effort, she could avoid having to live with the dread of dancing with him at every evening entertainment, of being held in his arms, with his blue gaze warming her.

With a despairing sigh, she went upstairs to change.

Cruickshank was waiting with the carriage dress laid out. Having seen the sudden change in her mistress, and having more than a suspicion of the cause, Cruickshank fretted and snorted over every pleat in the elegant brown velvet dress with its snug-fitting jacket. Georgiana, knowing she could hide little from her maid's sharp eyes, was thankful to escape her chamber without a lecture. As she descended the curving staircase, the villager hat she had chosen dangling by its ribbons from one hand, Georgiana imagined such a scene, and what Cruickshank might actually say. The possibilities brought a smile to her face, the first for the day.

A sudden tingling brought her head up. Her eyes met blue—bright blue. Lord Alton was standing in the hall below, Bella by his side, watching her. For an instant she froze. Then, drawing what courage she could from knowing she looked as well as might be, Georgiana descended to the hall and placed her hand in his, curtsying demurely.

He raised her and carried her hand to his lips, and there was no doubt of the warmth in his gaze. Georgiana blushed vividly; her heart fluttered wildly. She had forgotten how devastatingly charming he could be.

She turned to Bella, who remained rooted to the spot, an arrested look on an otherwise blank face. But before Georgiana could make any comment, Dominic said, "We'll be back in about an hour, Bella." And, with a nod for his sister, he firmly escorted Georgiana outside.

Handed into a curricle of the very latest design, Georgiana quickly tied her hat over her curls. The breeze was brisk, stirring the manes of the two black horses stamping and sidling between the shafts. A small tiger held their heads. Dominic climbed up beside her and, with a flick of the reins, they were off, the tiger scrambling for his perch behind.

As he threaded his team through the traffic, Dominic realised that his supposedly straightforward plan to have an hour's quiet conversation with his love had already run off the tracks. For a start, there were no horses which could be described as docile in his stables. Until the present, this had not proved a problem. The pair he had unthinkingly requested be harnessed to the curricle were Welsh thoroughbreds, perfectly capable of stomping on anyone or anything they took exception to. And they had not been out for days and would willingly run a hundred miles if he would just drop his hands and give them their heads. Stifling a sigh, he gave them his undivided attention.

Once the park gates were reached, he set the horses to a trot, letting them stretch their legs at least that much. They tossed their heads impatiently, but eventually responded to the firm hand on the reins and accepted their lot. Only then did he turn to view his second hurdle. What on earth had possessed her to wear that hat? He knew perfectly well that the outfit she wore—the very latest in carriage wear—should have been completed by a tight-fitting cloche, perhaps with a small feather or cockade on the brim. The temptation to tell her as much burned his tongue, but he left the words unsaid. At the moment, he did not think a demonstration of his familiarity with feminine apparel was likely to further his cause.

"Someone is waving to you."

Dominic looked about and returned the salutation, ignoring the invitation to draw up his carriage by Lady Molesworth's barouche.

Georgiana's fingers were clutching her reticule so tightly that she could feel the thin metal brim twisting. She wished he would say something, or that she could think of a safe topic to discuss. Finally, sheer desperation drove her to say, "I believe the weather is turning more cold..." only to hear her voice clash with his.

They both fell silent.

Dominic glanced down at the top of her hat and grimaced. Without being able to see her face, he felt he was groping in the dark. He dropped his voice to a softer tone. "Georgiana, my dear, what's wrong?"

His experience with his sister, on top of his extensive expertise in related spheres, enabled him to get the tone just right, so that Georgiana felt that if he said another word in such a gentle way she would burst into tears in the middle of the park and shame them both. She waved her small hands in distress. "My lord... Please..." She had no idea what to say. Her mind wouldn't function, and her senses, traitorous things, were too much occupied with manifestations of his presence other than his conversation. "There's nothing wrong,'' she eventually managed in a very small voice.

Swallowing his frustration, Dominic wondered just what he had expected to achieve with a question like that in the middle of the park. He should have guessed that whatever it was that had upset her would prove too distressing to discuss reasonably in such surroundings. The situation wanted improving, and he would get rid of that hat, too.

Without the least effort, he instituted a conversation on recent events, none of which could be construed as in any way disturbing. Gradually, he won a response from Georgiana.

Grateful for his understanding, and believing the worst was behind her, Georgiana set about recovering her composure, and her wits, eventually contributing her half of the conversation. As they bowled along, the horses' hoofs scattering the autumn leaves, the breeze whisked past her cheeks, bringing crisp colour to hide her pallor. Bella had been right: fresh air was just what she needed. By the time they had completed their first circuit, she was chattering animatedly when, to her surprise, the curricle headed for the gates. They had been out for less than half an hour. ''Where are we going?''

''Back to Green Street,'' came the uncompromising reply. ''I want to talk to you.''

The ride back to Winsmere House was, not surprisingly, accomplished in silence. Georgiana stole one glance up at Dominic's face, but, as usual, his features told her nothing.

The curricle swayed to a halt. Before she could attempt to climb down, he was there, lifting her effort-lessly to the pavement. Breathless, she stood for one moment within the circle of his arms and dared to look up into his face. "There's really no need—"

"There's every need." Dominic's face remained shuttered. His hand at her elbow drew her up the steps.

Georgiana, trembling inwardly with an odd mixture of exhilaration and sheer terror, drew a deep breath and swung to face him. "My lord—"

"Ah, Johnson."

Georgiana turned to find the door open and Bella's butler bowing deferentially. The next instant she was in the hall.

"We'll use the drawing-room, I think."

Borne inexorably over the threshold, Georgiana gave up all hope of avoiding the coming interview and crossed the room, her fingers fumbling with the rib-bons of her hat.

Dominic shut the door and watched with relief as she cast the offending headgear aside. He moved to a side-table and stripped off his driving gloves, dropping them on the polished surface.

"Now—"

The door opened.

"There you are!" Bella came tripping over the threshold, big eyes bright.

Georgiana looked on her with undisguised relief.

Dominic looked on her with undisguised irritation. "Go away, Bella."

Brought up short, Bella turned to stare at him. "Go away? But whatever—?"

"Bella!" The dire warning in his voice was enough

to send Bella about and start her for the door. Then she remembered she was in her own house and no longer needed to heed her brother's orders. She stopped, but before she could turn again a large hand in the small of her back propelled her out of the room.

The drawing-room door shut with a sharp click. Stunned, totally bewildered, Bella turned to stare at its uninformative panels.

Inside, Dominic turned to find Georgiana regarding him with distinct trepidation. Wondering how long his patience was going to last, he crossed the room and took her hands in his, covering her cold fingers with his warm ones. "Don't look at me like that. I'm not going to eat you."

Georgiana smiled weakly.

"But you are going to tell me what's wrong."

Glancing wildly up at him, eyes wide, Georgiana drew breath to reiterate that there was nothing wrong, when she caught his sceptical look and fell silent.

"Precisely." Dominic nodded sternly. "I'm not addle-pated enough to swallow any tale you might concoct, so the truth, if you please."

Standing there, her hands warm in his, the temptation to cast herself on his broad chest and sob out all her woes was dreadfully strong. In desperation, Georgiana sought for some way out, some tale he would accept for her not seeing him again. But another upward glance under her lashes convinced her the task was hopeless.

"It's... It's just that our...our association has become sufficiently marked that people might start talking and..." Her voice trailed away altogether.

She looked up to find an oddly amused expression on Dominic's face.

He smiled. "Actually, our association has, until today, been sufficiently well hidden. However, I dare say they will start talking now."

Distracted, Georgiana frowned. "You mean after our drive in the park?"

Still amused, Dominic nodded. "That. And tonight." At Georgiana's puzzled look, he explained, "It's the Rigdons' ball. And as from now, I'm going to be so very attentive to you that even the blindest of the gossips will know my intentions."

"Your intentions?" Georgiana's voice had risen strangely.

Dominic regarded her with some slight annoyance. "My intentions," he repeated. After a moment he sighed and went on, "I know I haven't proposed, but surely, Georgiana, you are not so scatter-brained you don't know I'm in love with you and intend asking you to marry me?"

Georgiana stared at him. Of course she knew he intended to marry her. But that he loved her? No, she knew that wasn't right. Gently, she tried to ease her hands from his, but he would not allow it.

Dominic frowned. "Georgiana, love, what is the matter?"

Becoming more nervous by the minute, Georgiana shook her head, not daring to look up at him. "I can't marry you, my lord." There, she had said it.

"Whyever not?"

The calm question took her breath away. Inwardly Georgiana groaned. She closed her eyes and wished herself anywhere but where she was. Yet when she opened them again, a pair of large, well formed hands were still clasped firmly around hers. She risked a glance upwards. He was calmly waiting for an answer. Nothing in his face or stance suggested he would let her go without one.

Dominic stood silently and hoped she would hurry up. The effort of keeping his hands on hers, rather than sweeping her into his arms and kissing away whatever ridiculous notions she had taken into her head, was draining his resolution. In the end, he repeated his question. "Why can't you marry me?"

Georgiana drew a deep breath, closed her eyes, and said quite clearly, "Because you're in love with Lady Changley and were planning to marry her."

Sheer surprise kept Dominic immobile and slackened his hold on her fingers.

Instantly Georgiana whisked away and, on a broken sob, rushed from the room.

Even after the door closed behind her, Dominic made no move to follow her. How on earth had she come to that marvellous conclusion? How on earth had she learned of Elaine Changley? Feeling remarkably sane for a man who had just had his first ever proposal thrown in his face, before he had uttered it, Dominic strolled to the sofa and sat down, the better to examine his love's strange ideas.

Within a minute a subtle smile was curving his lips. Another minute saw him chuckling. So that was what all this fuss was about. His ex-mistress. It really was absurd. Undoubtedly Elaine would be thrilled if she ever knew she was the cause of such difficulties. And

Julian Ellsmere would laugh himself into stitches if he ever heard. He spent a moment wondering which busybody had told Georgiana of Elaine Changley, then dismissed the subject from his mind. There were any number of loose tongues about town.

Standing, Dominic stretched, then relaxed. He would just have to arrange to explain to his love the subtle difference between what a gentleman felt for the woman he made his mistress and the emotions he felt for the woman he would make his wife. It was, as it happened, a point he was supremely well qualified to expound. His smile broadened. He had told her he would see her at the Rigdons' that night. As he recalled, Rigdon House had a most intriguing conservatory, tucked away in a corner of the mansion, unknown to most guests. The perfect place. As for the opportunity, there would be no difficulty arranging that.

Strolling to the door, relieved of his strange burden of not knowing what had gone wrong, Dominic felt on top of the world. Then, out of the blue, two phrases, heard at widely differing times, coalesced in his mind. He froze. Georgiana's secret love was a man she had met during her earliest days in London who she believed was in love with and about to marry another woman. He had searched her acquaintance to no avail—there was no such man. Now she had just admitted that she thought *he* was in love with and had been about to marry Lady Changley. *Ha!*

Dominic's smile as he left Winsmere House could have warmed the world.

IT WAS WITH a strange mixture of trepidation and relief that Georgiana entered the Rigdon House ballroom. She had initially felt devastated and drained after her interview with Lord Alton, but a peaceful hour in her bedchamber had convinced her that it was all for the best. At least he now knew she would not accept an offer from him and why. She told herself her problems were over. Yet, deep down inside, she was far from sure he would accept her dismissal. And buried even deeper was the uncertainty of whether she really wanted him to.

She had not left her chamber until, arrayed for the evening, she had descended for dinner. Arthur's presence would, she had hoped, inhibit Bella's ability to question her closely about her brother's strange behaviour. As it transpired, Bella had evinced not the slightest degree of curiosity, even in the privacy of the carriage on the way to the ball. Dimly Georgiana wondered if Bella's brother often did such outrageous things.

After being presented to Lord Rigdon, whom she had not previously met, she and Bella drifted into the crowds of guests, chattering avidly while they waited for the dancing to begin.

Joining a circle of young ladies, many of whom she now knew, Georgiana went through the usual process of filling in her dance card, allocating the vital supper waltz to Lord Ellsmere. To her surprise, he also requested another waltz, earlier in the evening. She was puzzled, for he had rarely danced twice with her since she had refused his suit. Still, she numbered him among her most trusted cavaliers and gladly bestowed on him the first waltz of the night.

It was while she was circling the ballroom in Lord Ellsmere's arms that she first became aware of a change in her status. A number of dowagers sat on chairs lining the walls. From the direction of their sharp glances and the whisperings behind their fans, she realised with a jolt that she was the subject under discussion. A few minutes later, as the waltz ended and, on Lord Ellsmere's arm, she joined a small group of young people, she surprised a look of what could only be envy on the face of Lady Sabina Matchwick, one of the Season's *incomparables.*

Slowly, it dawned that, as Dominic had prophesised, people were beginning to talk. Finding Bella by her side, and momentarily alone, Georgiana could not help but ask, "Bella, tell me. Is it really so very unusual for your brother to drive a lady in the park?"

Bella's candid blue gaze found her face. "Yes. I told you. Dominic's never taken any lady driving before."

"Oh."

At her stricken face, Bella burst into a trill of laughter. Impulsively, she hugged Georgiana. "Oh, Georgie! I'm so happy!"

The approach of their partners for the next dance put an end to any confidences. Georgiana dipped through the cotillion and barely knew what she did. As dance followed dance, she realised the nods and smiles denoted not scandalised horror, but a sort of envious approval. Heavens! Just by taking her for a drive, Lord Alton had all but publicly declared himself. How on earth was she to rectify the mistaken impression? Then Georgiana reminded herself that in a few short days her Little Season would be over. And she would go back to Ravello and forget all about Lord Alton and his very blue eyes.

It was almost time for the supper waltz. Lord Ellsmere came to claim her. By some subtle manoeuvre, he separated her from her court and proceeded to stroll down the long room with her on his arm.

"My dear Georgiana, I do hope you won't forever hold it against me, but I've a confession to make."

Startled out of her abstraction, Georgiana stared at him. "Confession?" she echoed weakly. Oh, dear. Surely he was not going to start pressing her to marry him, too?

As if sensing her thoughts, he smiled at her. "No, no. Nothing to overset you. At least," he amended, frowning as if suddenly giving the matter due thought, "I hope it won't upset you."

Georgiana could stand no more. "My lord, I pray you'll unburden yourself of this horrendous secret."

He smiled again. "It's really quite simple. I engaged you for this waltz in proxy, as it were."

Her heart was beating an unnerving tattoo. "Who...?" Georgiana didn't bother finishing her question. She knew who. And as if to confirm her suspicions, she felt a familiar tingling sensation start along her nerves, spreading from the bare skin of her shoulders and neck in a southerly direction. No, Lord Alton had not accepted his dismissal.

"Ah, here he is."

With a smile and an elegant bow to her, Lord Ellsmere surrendered her to the suavely elegant gentleman who had come to stand beside her.

Georgiana felt her hand being raised and the warm pressure of his lips on her fingers.

"Georgiana?"

His husky tone rippled across her senses. Despite all her intentions, she could not prevent herself from looking up. And she was lost. His eyes caught hers and held her gaze effortlessly. Somewhere in her unconscious the subtle perfection of his attire registered, along with an appreciation of face, form and figure, all apparently designed with her own prejudices in view. But her conscious mind was only aware of the total mastery he exerted over her senses, the hypnotic tug which drew her, unresisting, into her arms. Before she knew it, they were waltzing.

With an effort, Georgiana managed to free enough wit to realise he was smiling at her in amused appreciation, quite certain of his conquest. Then, as her senses probed the ballroom about them, the enormity of his strategy hit her. They might have been waltzing amid a host of other couples, but every eye in the ballroom was on them. She blushed vividly.

This evidence of her sudden awareness drew a deep chuckle. "Don't worry. You look radiantly lovely. Just think what a handsome couple we make."

Georgiana tried to summon enough anger to glare at him, but her overwhelmed emotions were not up to it.

Dominic looked down at her, her golden eyes and creamy skin, the glorious riot of her golden curls filling his vision. More than satisfied with her capitulation thus far, he made a mental note to play on her senses more often—a subtle torture, at present, but so very rewarding.

The music drew to a close, Georgiana waited to be released, but, instead of bowing and escorting her back to Bella's side, Dominic simply tucked her hand into his arm and walked out of the ballroom. Entirely unable to resist, and with a sinking feeling that it would be singularly pointless to try, Georgiana found herself wandering the corridors on Lord Alton's arm.

Suspecting that the amble had more purpose than was apparent, Georgiana turned an enquiring gaze upwards, to be met with a smile of quite dazzling effect.

"I thought, my love, that, given your apparent misconception regarding my feelings towards you, we should find a quiet spot where I might endeavour to disabuse your mind of its strange notion."

Georgiana tried, really tried, to come up with some suitable response, but not a coherent phrase came into her head. At the end of the long corridor, Dominic turned right, opening a glass-panelled door and ushering her through.

Vines and species of *ficus* grew out of large tubs artfully arranged to give the impression of a tropical forest. Cyclamens provided bursts of exotic colour amid the greenery. A small fountain played a lonely tune in the middle of a circular tiled courtyard. Of other humans, there was no sign.

With no real idea of what he meant to say, Georgiana was caught between a desire to hear his words and a conviction that it would be unwise to do so. But she was given no choice in the matter as, smoothly compelling, Dominic led her to a rustic ironwork seat. At his nod, she sat, and he sat beside her, retaining possession of her hand and showing no inclination to release it.

Sensing her skittering nerves, Dominic smiled reassuringly and raised her fingers to his lips, placing a leisurely kiss on each rosy fingertip, his eyes all the while holding hers. He watched as her golden eyes widened and her breathing suspended, then started again, more shallowly and less evenly. Entirely satisfied, he grinned wickedly. "Now where were we, when you so abruptly left the room this afternoon? Ah, yes! You believe I'm in love with Lady Changley and was intending to marry her." He directed a look of patent enquiry at Georgiana, clearly seeking confirmation.

Trapped, in every way, Georgiana coloured.

Smiling again, Dominic continued, his voice light but perfectly serious. "I'm not, I'll have you know, in favour of the idea of a gentleman discussing his paramours with anyone, least of all with his intended bride. Young ladies are not supposed to be cognisant of the sorts of affairs women such as Lady Changley indulge in. However, as you have already heard of her, I'll admit we enjoyed a short liaison, which ended some weeks before I met you."

Dominic paused to allow the full implication of his words to sink in. Georgiana's attention was complete; she was hanging on every word, and he doubted not that she would remember what he said, even should she fail to immediately register its import.

Pensively he began to stroke her fingers with his

thumb. "Like all rich and single peers, I am high on the list of prey for such as Lady Changley. She, unwisely, believed I was besotted enough to offer marriage. At no stage did I do so. You'll have to take my word for that, although you will notice no public charges for breach of promise have been levelled at me. That's because she knows no one would believe I would be so lost to all propriety as to offer to make her my Viscountess.''

To Georgiana his words were every bit as intoxicating as the sensations produced by the insistent pressure of his thumb over the sensitive backs of her fingers. Then his eyes lost their far-away look and his gaze became intent, capturing her own as if to focus her entire being on him. Georgiana felt herself drowning in blue.

Without releasing her from his spell, deliberately, Dominic raised her hand to his lips, but this time turned it to press a warm kiss to her palm. He smiled at the marked shiver the caress produced, but his eyes were nevertheless perfectly serious as he said, ''The feelings I have for you, my love, are far removed from the lust a man feels for his mistress, a fleeting emotion which dissipates, usually in months if not weeks. No man marries his mistress. No man falls in love with his mistress.''

Georgiana could not have moved if the ceiling fell. She was mesmerised—by his voice, by his eyes, by him. Drawing a shuddering breath, she waited for what was to come, knowing she could not prevent him from saying the words, knowing that, once said, they would bind her, no matter how hard she struggled, tying her to him, not by his love, but by hers.

Dominic continued to devour her with his eyes, following her reactions. He waited until full awareness returned to her, then said, "What I feel for you is far removed from mere lust. I can hardly deny I know what that is and can readily define it. What I feel for you is not that. I fell in love with you the first moment I saw you, asleep in my armchair by the drawing-room hearth at Candlewick. You belong there." He paused, knowing that his next move was chancy, but, confident he had gauged her responses, and her temperament, accurately, he smoothly continued, "Regardless of what you may say, regardless of how many times you deny it, I know you love me in exactly the same way I love you."

His words, delivered in a low, deliberate, slightly husky tone, sent shivers up and down Georgiana's spine. He was right, of course, at least in defining her love. Oh, what temptation he posed! Still trapped in his gaze, she knew immediately his attention shifted. His eyes were now fixed on a golden ringlet hanging beside her face. One long finger came up to caress the soft curl, then moved on with tantalising slowness to outline the curve of one brow, then the length of her pert nose, and then traced, oh, so lightly, the full bow of her lips. The roaming finger slipped under her chin and tilted her face upwards. Georgiana's eyelids drooped. His lips touched hers in the gentlest of kisses.

When he drew back, she could barely cope with the sense of loss, could barely restrain herself from throwing her arms about his neck and behaving like a wanton. Again, she blushed rosily, not at his actions but at her thoughts.

Entirely satisfied with progress thus far, Dominic sat back and waited patiently until her breathing slowed, watching her through half-closed lids. When she had recovered sufficiently to glance at him once more, he took up his dissertation. "As you've realised, the rest of the *ton* are now *au fait* with my intentions. Our affairs are thus public knowledge, and should, given your age, proceed with all due circumspection."

He smiled, his eyes lighting with a certain devilment that awoke an answering spark in Georgiana. She found herself smiling back in genuine empathy.

"Thus, you will now be wooed in form. I will drive you in the park every afternoon, weather permitting. I will escort you to whichever evening functions it is your desire to attend. The *ton* will be edified by the sight of me at your pretty feet. Therefore, having attained that position, it will be no great difficulty to propose to you at the end of the Season."

Whereat you'll accept me. And thank God there's only a week of the Season to go! Dominic left his last thoughts unsaid, contenting himself with another warm smile. Dropping a last kiss on Georgiana's fingers, he rose.

"Come, my child. We should return you to the ball before the dowagers start having the vapours."

THE INTERLUDE in the conservatory disturbed Georgiana more than she had believed possible. She had never before been exposed to, let alone been called upon to withstand, anyone as compelling as Bella's brother. The magnetic force he wielded was of a magnitude that rendered mere reason impotent. Settled in her corner of the *chaise* on their way home from Rigdon House, she was conscious that the attractions of Ravello and freedom were dimming in the light of the flame Lord Alton was skilfully igniting.

That he meant to do it, she had not a doubt. Deliberate, calculated, he made no effort to hide his tactics. He wanted the Place. In the darkness of the carriage, Georgiana shivered.

Their discussion had at least relieved her mind of one nagging, guilty worry. He did not and had never loved Lady Changley. Of that, she was certain. She could not decide whether it was the hint of humour that had coloured his voice when he had spoken of his mistress or the coldly unemotional way he had considered her machinations that had convinced her. But convinced she was. Lady Changley might or might not have believed he was in love with her. Whichever way it was, she was only another victim of his lordship's potent charm.

Unfortunately, all that did was prove he had the ability to make women fall deeply in love with him. It hardly proved that he loved her.

The more she considered the matter, the more she doubted the possibility. Why would such a handsome man, so eligible in every way, with all of the last ten years' débutantes to choose from—*incomparables* included—have decided to opt for her? Little Georgiana Hartley, whose head barely topped his shoulder, who knew next to nothing of the fashionable life of England, let alone the political side with which he was so intricately involved. Why had he picked her?

The Place. It was the only answer.

Miserable all over again, Georgiana lay sleepless for a long time after Cruickshank had snuffed her candles. In the dark, she wrestled with demons who all too often had bright blue eyes. He professed love, and she longed to believe him. Yet, when it came down to it, his actions belied his words. Admittedly she had been brought up in Italy, but she couldn't believe national boundaries changed human nature so very much. True love always brought desire in its wake, as was only right and proper. Yet the chaste kiss he had bestowed on her had held no hint of burning passion. And she knew that wasn't how he kissed a woman he desired.

Again and again, her thoughts brought her back to the same depressing conclusion. He was an expert in seduction; she was a novice. Her hand in marriage would secure the Place, so he had calmly set about capturing it. In the world of the *ton,* it would be considered a very fair exchange—her land for the position and wealth he could provide.

As the hours of the night gave way to a grey dawn, Georgiana considered for the first time whether she might be wise to listen to the promptings of her heart, to accept the proposal he had told her was coming, even knowing that her love wasn't shared. She knew he would always treat her well—with respect and affection, if not with the love she craved. She would fill the position of his wife, be able to care for him, bear his children.

A vision of Candlewick swam before her, and she

spent some time imagining what might be. But she could not place him in the picture beside her. Instead, he appeared as a nebulous figure, arriving in the dead of night, leaving with the dawn.

With a sob, Georgiana buried her face in her pillow. No. It was impossible. If she couldn't have his love, the rest was meaningless. She would leave for Ravello as soon as the Season ended.

CHAPTER TEN

"HUMPH!"

The loud snort brought Georgiana awake with a start. Cruickshank stood by the bed.

"You'd better wake up and take a look at these."

With a grim look, Cruickshank drew back the bed curtains. The window drapes had already been opened, letting weak morning sunshine bathe the room. For an instant Georgiana stared uncomprehendingly at her maid, then her attention was drawn to the door. It opened to admit a young girl, one of the parlour maids, all but concealed behind a huge stand of cream roses.

The girl peeked at Georgiana around the delicate blooms, then, with a giggle, crossed to deposit the vase on a table by the window.

To Georgiana's astonishment, her place in the doorway was immediately taken by another maid, similarly burdened. When a third maid entered, with yet more cream roses, Georgiana put her hands to her hot cheeks. Cream roses in October!

Hundreds of cream roses.

By the time the procession of maids had transferred all the blooms delivered to the house by the florist's that morning to her bedroom, Georgiana was speechless. She sat and stared. The sheer outrageous extravagance of the gesture numbed her. About her, the delicate perfume of the flowers took hold, flavouring the air with their subtle enchantment.

She needed no card to tell her who had sent them.

At the Rigdons' ball, he had vowed to woo her formally. His public courtship had started that night, when he had returned her to Bella's side but remained possessively beside her, discouraging all her partners but those he approved of simply by being there. The next day he had swooped down on her morning and taken her driving to Richmond, later producing a picnic hamper for lunch and taking her to the Star and Garter for tea. It was impossible to stand firm against the invitation of his smile. He would accept no denials. Powerless to prevent his whirlwind courtship, she had, unwillingly, reluctantly, been swept along, mesmerised by the blue of his eyes. The following evening she had seen the effects of his strategy. As far as the *ton* was concerned, only the ceremony was required to establish her as the Viscountess Alton.

In the four days that had followed, each filled with unsought joy and a hidden despair, he had succeeded in convincing everyone that theirs would be a marriage made in heaven, until it seemed to Georgiana that only she guessed the truth.

Her moods fluctuated wildly, from ecstatic pleasure when he was with her, to blackest despair when he was not. She was counting the days to the end of the Season, to when Bella and Arthur departed for Candlewick and she could flee to Ravello and safety. She had even tried to sound Arthur out on the possibility of leaving before then. But he had looked at her blankly, seeming not to understand her oblique reference. Incapable of being more explicit, she had been forced to let the matter drop.

Cream roses surrounded her. Her consciousness was filled with him to the exclusion of all else. Georgiana sighed.

Only Cruickshank remained in the room, fussing over laying out her clothes, sharp eyes stealing covert glances, trying to assess her reaction.

Shaking free of despondency, Georgiana slipped out of bed. Cruickshank held up a blue morning dress for her approval. Through narrowed eyes, Georgiana studied its clean lines. Then, abruptly, she shook her head. "No, Cruckers. The new green velvet, please."

Cruickshank's eyebrows rose comically, but she made no comment beyond the predictable snort.

Stripping off her nightgown, Georgiana washed her face and donned her soft muslin undergarments while Cruickshank brought out the latest of her purchases from Fancon. If her association with Lord Alton had taught her anything, it was to value the added confidence appearing before him in new and fashionably elegant gowns gave her. Besides, in a few days' time, she would no longer have the pleasure of appearing before him at all. Despite the heaviness of her heart, weighed down by unrequited love, she was determined to live these last few days as fully as she could, to store away the bittersweet memories to warm the long winter days, and nights, in Ravello.

THE EAST WIND was chilly. Grey clouds scudded low across the tops of the trees, skeletal fingers emerging to trap them as the summer cloaks were stripped, leaf by leaf, away. Everywhere summer was in decline, giving way to the gusts of autumn, chill harbingers of year's end.

Perched on the box seat of Viscount Alton's curricle, Georgiana was immune from the cold. Refusing to face her bleak future, she revelled in the warmth of the moment. Her wind-whipped cheeks glowed and her eyes, when she managed to wrench them free of his lordship's steady gaze, sparkled with life and love. She had left her inhibitions in Green Street and was happy.

Beside her, Dominic was host to a range of emotions, some of which were both novel and, to one of his experience, distinctly disturbing. That he loved Georgiana Hartley, in the complete fullness of the term, he no longer doubted. But that she could invoke in him the full gamut of desire, to the point where his mind became prey to salacious imaginings, was not something he had expected. She was a young, innocent, inexperienced, green girl. A golden angel. Yet, no matter how many accurate adjectives he heaped about her name, nothing detracted from the sensual spell she cast over him. She was learning quickly. But she had no idea, he felt sure, of the risks she courted. His well honed skills, all but automatic, were in danger of carrying them away.

There were few people in the park. The cold weather had kept most of the fashionable indoors. They completed one circuit, then went about again, content to prolong their time in such unaccustomed seclusion. Few words were exchanged. Their eyes spoke, and that was enough.

When the gates hove a second time into view, Dominic acknowledged the passing hours and headed his team for the street. His gaze flicked to Georgiana's face, catching her wide-eyed hazel stare, and he knew she had enjoyed their time together as much as he had. In that instant, he made his decision.

He had postponed asking her to marry him, wanting his courtship of her to be a recognised fact before any announcement. Quick betrothals between men such as he and sweet delights such as she had a way of being remembered and whispered about. He wanted no breath of a question to touch her.

But there were only two more days of the Season to go. And there was no doubt of their state. And no reason at all to procrastinate.

As the park gates fell behind, Georgiana was conscious of the day closing in, of a dimming of her joy. For the past hour she had been happy. It was so easy to forget, to imagine instead how things might have been. But always reality eventually intruded, reminding her of the real reason for his interest in her.

By the time Green Street was reached and he lifted her down she was thoroughly depressed once more. He escorted her indoors, and she inwardly shrank at the coming meeting with Bella. Her hostess, to whom she owed so much, was *aux anges* at the prospect of having her for a sister-in-law.

She was shaken out of her dismal thoughts by the words, ''The drawing-room, I think, Johnson. You needn't inform your mistress that we've returned.''

Before her weary mind had time to do more than register that quite improper order, Dominic had deftly ushered her into the drawing-room and shut the door.

Suddenly conscious of the desirability of putting as much space as possible between them, Georgiana quickly crossed the room. Her heartbeat, which had slowed somewhat since they had left the park, picked up its tempo.

From his stance just inside the door, Dominic viewed her impetuous movement, which had about it the air of flight, and frowned. Then, when he saw the agitated flutter of her small hands, clasping and unclasping before her, a slow smile erased the stern look. She was nervous, no more. A strange rapport existed between them. So she sensed his intention and, true to her age and innocence, was disturbed. His features softened. He crossed to stand beside her.

"Georgiana, my love..."

A small gesture silenced him. Georgiana could stand the strain no more. "Dominic, please," she whispered, infusing every particle of persuasion she could into her tones.

After the briefest of pauses, she continued, "My lord, I am most sensible of the honour you do me, but I cannot marry you."

Dominic suppressed the instinctive retort that he hadn't yet had a chance to ask her and, to his surprise, found himself fascinated, rather than furious. "Why?"

Despite her highly strung state, Georgiana spared a moment to curse silently the incredible evenness in temper that could yield such a mild response. If truth be known, she would infinitely have preferred a more melodramatic reaction. That, she would have known how to deal with. Instead, his deceptively simple question was anything but easy to answer.

In fact, as the minutes stretched, she realised she couldn't answer it at all. In growing panic, she shook her head, dropping her gaze to her nervously clenching fingers.

Dominic sighed. "Georgiana, my love, I should perhaps inform you that I am not one of the school which holds it right and proper that a young lady should refuse her chosen suitor at least three or four times before accepting him, so as not to appear too eager." He waited to see what effect that had, and was not entirely surprised to see her ringlets dance a decided negative.

Allowing silence, so often his ally, to stretch still further, Dominic, close behind her, watched her growing agitation, and chose his moment to murmur, "Sweetheart, I've not got infinite patience."

The gentle tone of his voice cloaked the steel of the words. Georgiana did not miss the implication of either. Her nerves singed by his nearness, she abruptly took a step away, then turned to face him. She had to make him understand the futility of his enterprise.

"My lord, I…must make it plain to you. I will not marry you."

Dominic wasn't really listening. She had not answered his question, which, in itself, was answer enough. He was not in the mood to listen to missish denials, not when her eyes were so soft and her lips, gently parted, just begged to be kissed.

Seeking to impress on him the inevitability of her refusal, Georgiana allowed her eyes to meet his. And,

as had happened so often before, in the warm blue of
his gaze, she felt their wills collide and hers melt
away. Mesmerised, she could barely breathe as he
moved closer, one long finger rising to trace the curve
of her cheek, stopping at the corner of her mouth. Unable to move, she watched as his eyes fixed on her
lips. Unconsciously, her tongue slipped between them
to run its moist pink tip along their suddenly dry contours. He smiled. Then, tantalisingly slowly, his head
drew nearer, his lips hungry for hers.

As her eyelids drooped, panic seized Georgiana. In
desperation, she put her small hands up before her and
met the wall of his chest. She turned her head away.
She felt him hesitate. In that instant she seized the
tattered remnants of her sanity and, on a choked sob,
fled the room.

In utter disbelief, Dominic watched her go. As the
door shut behind her he uttered one comprehensive
oath and, thrusting his hands deep in his breeches
pockets, swung about to glare at the window.

After a moment he glanced around, half expecting
the door to open and for her to return. When nothing
happened, he muttered irritably and ostensibly gave
his attention to a minute inspection of Bella's lace
draperies. What the devil did Miss Georgiana Hartley
think she was playing at? What the devil did she think
he was playing at?

When the ticking of the mantelpiece clock made it
plain any hope of Georgiana's return was forlorn,
Dominic let his head fall back. Scowling at the ceiling,
he vented his disapproval in one sharp and pungent

phrase, then strode purposefully to the door, his face like granite.

Johnson, unperturbed and imperturbable, met him in the hall.

"Dominic!"

In the act of shrugging on his greatcoat, Dominic swung to meet his brother-in-law's sharp gaze.

Arthur stood in the library doorway. Now he took a step back in clear invitation. "I've some information you might find of interest. If you can spare the time...?"

Even from across the hall Dominic could sense the amusement in the older man's voice. He knew Arthur understood his intentions towards Georgiana. And approved of them. With another shrug, he divested himself once more of his coat and, leaving the heavy garment in Johnson's hands, strolled with as much nonchalance as he could muster past his brother-in-law and into the library.

A delighted chuckle was his reward.

Elegantly disposing his limbs in one of the heavily padded leather chairs, Dominic raised eyes limpid with enquiry to Arthur's face.

Sinking into the chair behind his heavy desk, Arthur met the cool blue glaze with one of unalloyed amusement. "You know, for a man of such vast experience, you're being singularly obtuse in your present campaign."

Dominic's black brows rose haughtily. "Oh?"

"From Georgiana's loss of composure and your own black looks, I assume you've offered for her and been rejected."

From narrowed eyes, Dominic surveyed his brother-in-law. They had always got on well. In truth, there was no one he trusted more. So he dropped his reserve and answered with a languid air, "If you must know, I haven't as yet proposed. I have, however, been refused. Twice."

With an effort that was obvious, Arthur swallowed his laughter. Finally, when he was sure he could command his voice, he said, "Well, that's hardly surprising."

The blue eyes watching him narrowed again. After a pregnant pause Dominic murmured, "Arthur, if you weren't who you are, I rather think I'd take exception to that comment."

Far from being cowed, Arthur only smiled. "I didn't think you'd seen it."

A world-weary expression of dutifully waiting to be informed of what "it" was infused Dominic's countenance.

"Why, the Place, of course."

"The Place?" echoed Dominic, bewildered.

"The Place," repeated Arthur. "You know, it's that little piece of land you've spent half of the last ten years trying to buy."

"But..." Dominic stopped. It came as a shock to realise that desire for the Place, an obsession nursed and fed for years, had simply been forgotten, displaced, rendered unimportant by his desire for Georgiana. In fact he hadn't thought of the Place with a view to gaining possession for weeks. Not since he had met Georgiana. He frowned.

Arthur sat back and watched his friend's face as the

pieces fell into place. It wasn't hard to work out the probabilities once the facts had been pointed out. And, despite Dominic's reputation with the ladies, Arthur, remembering the euphoric daydream that had possessed his own sharp wits in the days he had wooed Bella, found nothing odd in the notion that his brother-in-law had completely mislaid his obsession in the whirl of recent weeks.

Eventually Dominic's features relaxed slightly and he glanced up to meet Arthur's grey gaze. "So she thinks I'm marrying her to get my hands on the Place." It was a statement, not a question.

Arthur shrugged. "It's hardly an uncommon event, for men to marry for property. And I doubt she has any idea of the relative value of the Place and your own estates. But I'd go bail Bella's edified her with the tale of your desire for the land." He paused, but Dominic was frowning at the inkstand on the desk. "Has she given you any other reason for her refusal?"

Without looking up, Dominic shook his head slowly. "Not this time. The reason for her first refusal was quite different." He glanced up with a wry grin. "She'd heard the stories of Elaine Changley and had convinced herself I was in love with Elaine."

"And only wanted to marry her for her dowry?"

Dominic looked struck. "She didn't actually say so," he mused, "but I suppose that must have been in her mind. I didn't think further than disabusing her of the idea that I'd ever been truly enamoured of or considered marrying Elaine Changley."

Arthur said nothing.

Then Dominic shook his head. "No, it won't fit. I

started paying court to her at the Hattringhams' ball, before any of us knew she owned the Place.''

''The masked ball?'' said Arthur, tapping one finger against his lips. ''I assume she knew you knew who she was, that night.''

Dominic shifted in his chair. ''No. But I told her I did know later.''

''How later?''

Exasperated, Dominic frowned at his brother-in-law. ''At the Massinghams' rout.''

''*After* our little visit to Lincoln's Inn.''

With a long drawn sigh of frustration, Dominic stretched and crossed his arms behind his head. ''You're right.'' He considered the inkstand again. Then he said, as if talking to himself, ''So I'll just have to remove that little obstacle from my path.''

Perfectly satisfied with the effects of his interference, Arthur leant back in his chair and watched as his brother-in-law planned his next moves. Finally Dominic looked up.

''There are only two more days left to the Season. How long do you plan to remain in Green Street?''

Arthur smiled. ''For as long as it takes you to settle this business.''

A quick smile lit Dominic's face. ''You are coming to Candlewick, aren't you?''

Arthur nodded. ''I've already sent instructions for Jonathon and his nurse to travel direct to Candlewick. The weather's closing in and, as you know, I'm not one to take chances. They should be there by now. I'd thought to send Bella down as soon as she's free of her social activities. Mrs Landy can fuss over her more effectively than anyone else. I'll go to the Lodge and check through business there, then come across before Christmas.''

To all this, Dominic nodded. ''It'll take a day or two to deal with the Place. But once I've cleared that hurdle from my path, I don't expect any further impediment to our affairs.'' He paused, then added with a slightly grim smile, ''I would be obliged if you would inform Miss Hartley that I have some...pressing business to attend to, but will call on her in two days' time to continue our discussion of her future.'' He considered his words, then shrugged and rose. ''With luck, I'll be able to escort both Bella and Georgiana down a few days after that.''

''Good,'' said Arthur. ''The news from the country is that there'll be early snows. I'd feel happier once Bella's safely installed at Candlewick.'' He watched as Dominic crossed to the door, waiting until his fingers were on the handle to say, ''By the by, do let me know if you feel the need for any further assistance in this matter.''

Dominic smiled sweetly. ''My friend, I've often thought it was a good thing for England that you were born an Englishman. God only knows what might have happened if Napoleon and his generals had had you as a quartermaster.''

Arthur laughed.

With a neat bow, Dominic left, closing the door softly behind him.

TO GEORGIANA'S dismay, relief was not her predominant emotion on waking the next morning to no extravagant gifts, no note requesting her company on a drive, nothing. She sighed. She told herself sternly it was how she wanted things to be. He had at last accepted the fact she would not marry him.

Feeling at one with the gloomy morning, close and grey with drizzle, she dressed without interest and wended her way downstairs, wondering what she could do to fill in the bleak hours.

But she had barely left the breakfast-table to join Bella in the back parlour when Johnson came to summon her.

"A legal gentleman, miss. Name of Whitworth."

Brows rising, Georgiana stood and laid aside her embroidery. "In the drawing-room, Johnson?"

The butler bowed and escorted her to where Mr Whitworth the elder waited patiently, his bright eyes darting curiously about the white and gilt room.

As soon as he had bowed to her, Georgiana waved him to a chair. He looked alarmed when it creaked protestingly under his weight. But Georgiana was too puzzled to waste any time reassuring him. She hadn't sent for him. Why was he here?

Apparently agreeing his presence required immediate explanation, Mr Whitworth made haste to answer her unvoiced query. "My dear Miss Hartley, forgive my calling on you unheralded, but we have received a very generous offer for the Place. The buyer is most urgent to settle, so I took the liberty of calling in person."

Georgiana's immediate reaction was of immense relief. She would be rid of her albatross of an inheritance. If it hadn't been for the Place, she would not now be subject to the most deadening melancholy. And she would certainly never want to return there, as close as it was to Candlewick. But, hard on the heels of relief, came a swift understanding of what it would mean to Dominic—no! Lord Alton—if she sold the Place to another. A sharp stab of empathy brought an impulsive denial to her lips. But she bit the words back and forced herself to consider more carefully.

Dominic wanted the Place…wanted it so badly that he would even marry to get it. But, although she loved him, he didn't love her. She would not, could not, allow him to sacrifice either himself or her to the misery of a one-sided marriage. But she could give him what he wanted.

Mr Whitworth stirred uneasily, then cleared his throat.

Before he could launch into one of his long-winded discourses, Georgiana held up a small hand, commanding silence.

Only a moment's thought was required to convince her Dominic would not accept the Place as a gift from her. But there was nothing to stop her offering to sell it to him. He had tried to buy it from Charles, after all.

"What were the conditions offered by this buyer? And who is he?"

Mr Whitworth was only too happy to answer Georgiana's first question, naming a sum which meant nothing to her, but which, he assured her ponderously, was, "Very generous. Exceedingly so!"

After a moment, he went on, "But the thing that moved me to come here in this manner, my dear Miss

Hartley, is that the buyer wishes an answer by this afternoon.''

"This afternoon?'' echoed Georgiana. She looked at her solicitor. His excited urgency was apparent in the way he almost bobbed in his chair. "Surely, that's rather unusual?''

Mr Whitworth pursed his lips, and she feared she was about to be told every case of rapid sale he had ever heard of, chapter and verse. But instead his breath came out in a little whoosh. "Well, yes,'' he admitted. "But whoever has that sort of money to throw down can generally call the tune.''

"Who is this buyer?''

"Ah,'' said Mr Whitworth, eyeing her uneasily. "That's another thing. The man who contacted us is an agent, and he won't reveal the name of his principal.''

So she could be selling to anyone. Georgiana made up her mind. "I wish to consult with my friends on this matter. I will undertake to send my answer to you this afternoon.''

She rose, in a fever to get on with her latest impulsive start.

As if only too keen for her to put the wheels into motion, Mr Whitworth rose too, and rolled forward to take her hand. "Certainly, Miss Hartley. My brother and I will hold ourselves in readiness to act on your behalf as soon as you have communicated your wishes to us.''

With that solemn promise, he bowed low and took his leave.

For some moments Georgiana stood, head bowed,

eyes on the patterned rug. Then, resolutely straight-ening her spine, she crossed the room to the small escritoire. Seating herself before it, she pulled forward a pristine sheet of paper and, after examing the nib carefully, dipped it determinedly into the standish. This wasn't going to be easy, but there really was no alternative.

GEORGIANA'S missive brought Dominic to Green Street at noon. As her note had contained little beyond a summons, he used the time while Johnson went in search of her to pace the drawing-room, pondering the possibilities. Avoiding the little tables Bella seemed to have a peculiar penchant for strewing about her rooms, Dominic had arrived for the third time by the fireplace when he heard the door open.

Entering as calmly as she could, Georgiana wished for the tenth time that morning that she did not have to face Dominic—Lord Alton!—over this particular matter. The very thought of the Place rubbed a sore spot in her heart, aggravating its already fragile con-dition. Thoughts of Lord Alton brought even more pain. But she was determined to go through with it. Unconscious of the worried frown that marred her smooth brow, she pressed her hands together to still their trembling, only to find herself forced, by his out-stretched hand, to surrender one into his clasp.

"My lord." Her greeting was little better than a whisper. Pulling herself together with an effort, Geor-giana raised her head to look into his eyes, steeling herself for the battle to meet his gaze and remain lucid. To her relief, she found it easier than she had anticipated. He was looking at her with undisguised concern.

"Georgiana, my dear, what's the matter?"

And suddenly it was easy to tell him.

"I've received an offer for the Place. A mystery buyer." She paused, temporarily distracted by the sudden intentness in his gaze, and promptly lost her thread. Luckily her rehearsed phrases came to her rescue. "I remembered how keen you were to buy the property from Charles. I wondered if you still wished to purchase it."

Dominic watched as, gently withdrawing her hand from his, Georgiana subsided into one corner of the sofa, lilac skirts softly sighing, and fixed him with her candid hazel gaze. Outwardly he smiled, warmly, comfortingly. Inwardly he wondered where it was that he had left his usual facility for managing such *affaires de coeur*. He had certainly misplaced it. Ever since Georgiana Hartley had magically appeared in his life, his touch had deserted him. He had told his agent to purchase the Place without revealing his name, purely to spare her any undue embarrassment. Instead, having once again failed to predict her reactions to the events he caused to happen, he had forced her to face the very object he was endeavouring to remove from the relationship.

Capturing her eyes with his, he smiled again. "I'm afraid, my dear, I've a confession to make." He could see from her eyes that she had jumped to the right conclusion, but he confirmed it. "I'm the mystery buyer."

"Oh."

Georgiana's eyes fell. She felt decidedly deflated.

Acutely sensitive where she was concerned, Dominic moved to take her hands in his, and drew her to her feet before him. In his present mood he would not trust himself on the sofa beside her. Standing this close to her, holding her hands so he would not sweep her into his arms, was bad enough, feeling as he did. He looked down on her golden head, bent so he could not see her eyes.

"Georgiana?"

But she would not look up. Her eyes seemed to be fixed on her hands, clasped lightly in his. So, with the patience of one who knew all the moves, Dominic slowly raised her hands, first one, then the other, to his lips. Inevitably, her eyes followed...and were trapped when they met his. He smiled, incapable of entirely hiding his triumph. "Sweetheart, do you know why I want to buy the Place?"

With an effort Georgiana tore her gaze from those fascinating eyes. That blue gaze held untold power over her, giving tantalising glimpses of emotions she did not understand but of which she longed to learn more. But she was returning to Ravello. Forcing a tight smile to her lips, she nodded. "Yes. Bella explained."

"I sincerely doubt Bella could explain." He smiled as she turned to him, hope and uncertainty warring in her big eyes. "Oh, I know Bella told you I've always wanted the Place, to return Candlewick to completeness. That has, in the past, been something of an obsession with me. Recently that obsession has been eclipsed by a far greater desire. It had, in fact, completely slipped my mind. Until..." Dominic paused, then decided to leave Arthur out of his explanation. "Until I realised you might misconstrue my interest in you for an interest in your property."

If the matter hadn't been so intensely important, so vitally crucial to him, he would have been amused by the sheer intensity of her concentration. Her huge hazel eyes glowed with hope, tinged with disbelief. He had expected that and did not let it worry him. He would convince her he loved her if it was the last thing he did in life. Despite his firm intentions, he felt himself drowning in her honey-gold gaze, felt the inevitable effect of her nearness start to test his restraint.

"My love, I want to buy the Place so it can no longer stand as a point of confusion between us." Dominic dropped a kiss on her knuckles and decided he had better get out of the room with all speed. If he didn't, she would be in his arms and he had no idea where it would end. "If you agree, send a message to Whitworth and he'll settle it with my man of business." He paused, looking deep into the darkened centres of her wide eyes. Smiling, he released one of her hands, carrying the other to his lips in a parting salute. "Once the sale is finalised, I'll call on you and we can discuss our...mutual interest further."

His look dared her to deny him, but Georgiana was too dazed to do anything but stare.

With a gentle chuckle, Dominic lifted a finger to her cheek in a fleeting caress, then bowed elegantly and left her.

CHAPTER ELEVEN

THE SHARP CRACK as the wax seal broke beneath Dominic's long fingers echoed hollowly in the library of Alton House. Outside, Grosvenor Square lay somnolent under a blanket of fog. The weather had turned with a vengeance, and all who could were making hurried preparations to quit the capital before the roads became impassable. Hurriedly scanning his agent's letter, Dominic put it aside and spread the folded parchment the packet had contained. In the warmth and comfort of his library, in the glow of expensive wax candles, Dominic stared at the title-deed of the Place, which he had longed to hold for so long. It was his. Candlewick was whole once more.

Conscious of a mild elation on that score, Dominic grinned wryly. Far stronger was the relief that now Georgiana could have no more doubts of his love for her, no more excuses to deny his suit.

His eyes narrowed. The recollection that he had on more than one occasion underestimated her ability to misread his intentions surfaced. For some reason, she seemed unable to believe he truly loved her. Incomprehensible though that was, it would be unwise to ignore that particular foible. First his ex-mistress, then the Place—what would the next obstacle in this particular course be?

Unbidden, laughter bubbled up. He had never had the slightest trouble making offers before, although admittedly for less exalted positions. However, to date, his particular concern had always been to ensure the women involved never imagined him to be in love with them. He had never had to convince a woman of his love before. And here he was, getting his feet in a tangle at every step, no doubt providing Arthur with untold amusement. All in all, wooing an angel was proving the very devil of a task.

With a self-deprecatory smile, he put the title-deed in the top drawer of his desk, locking it with a small key from his watch chain.

There was only one way forward. His mind refused to entertain the thought of any outcome bar success. He did not doubt he would win her in the end. It was his patience he doubted. Still, at least this time he was forewarned. And if, instead, she fell into his arms without raising any more quibbles, he would be doubly grateful.

Imagining how he would express his gratitude to his beloved, he settled his shoulders more comfortably against the leather and fixed his gaze on the ceiling. A smile of anticipation curved his lips.

Ten minutes later his reverie was interrupted by sounds of altercation in his hall. The library door flew open.

Bella entered. Timms followed close behind, trying to retrieve the bonnet she still wore.

''Dominic! Thank God you're here! You'll have to

do something. I never imagined she'd do anything so rash!'' Succeeding in tugging her bonnet strings free, she paused only to hand her headgear to Timms before impetuously throwing herself at her brother, who had risen and come forward to meet her. Her small hands grasped his arms. ''You must go after her!''

''Yes, of course,'' Dominic replied, gently detaching her before turning her towards the *chaise*. ''And I undoubtedly shall, as soon as you have calmed sufficiently to tell me where and why.''

His calm, deliberate tones had the desired effect. Bella plumped down on the *chaise* with relief, her bearing losing the frenetic tenseness of a moment before.

''It's just so unexpected. I had no inkling she might do such a thing.''

Dominic forced himself to take the seat facing his sister, reminding himself that any attempt to drag stories out of Bella faster than she was prepared to tell them inevitably took longer than allowing her to proceed at her own pace. Relieved to see her colour improving, and assuming from her words that Georgiana was not in any mortal danger, he contented himself with a bland, ''What's happened?''

''I didn't know anything about it until I came downstairs half an hour ago. We were at the Ranleighs' last night—such a crowd! The rooms were so stuffy, I was quite worn out, so I slept late.'' Bella opened her reticule, hunting through its contents. ''I found this on the breakfast-table.''

Dominic took the single sheet of delicately tinted paper and smoothed it out. As he scanned its contents, his jaw hardened. Undoubtedly, it was past time someone took Georgiana Hartley in hand. The note blithely informed Bella that its writer had decided to ask the tenants of her father's London property whether they had any idea where his missing pictures might be. As she had ascertained that the house was located in Jermyn Street, she did not imagine she would be away long.

"She told me that when she wrote to Mr Whitworth to instruct him to sell the Place she remembered to ask about the London house. Johnson says she received a letter this morning."

"Jermyn Street!" Dominic stood and paced the room, incapable of remaining still. The words, Doesn't she know better? rang in his brain, but he didn't utter them—he knew the answer. There were times when Georgiana Hartley was too much the impulsive innocent for her own good. Over the past ten or more years, Jermyn Street had become the popular address for the well-heeled bachelors of the *ton,* which number included a disproportionate percentage of the most dangerous rakes and roués in England. His gaze returned to Bella's anxious face. "Do you have any idea of the number?"

Bella blushed. Under cover of fossicking in her reticule once more, she explained, "In the circumstances, I thought I should see if I could find the letter from the Whitworths. It was on her dresser." She looked up to hand the plain white envelope to her brother.

Dominic received it with undisguised relief and a fleeting smile for Bella's notions of propriety. "Good girl.'' Then he was reading the fine legal script. ''Seventeen. Who lives at 17 Jermyn Street?''

Bella shook her head, her gaze on her brother's face. He was clearly going through his acquaintance. Then she saw his expression drain.

''Good God!''

Bella paled. ''Who is it?''

''Harry Edgcombe.''

''Oh, dear.'' Bella's wide blue gaze had not left her brother's face. Recognising from uncomfortable experience the emotions flaring in his eyes, she suddenly wondered whether she would have done better by Georgiana to have tried to find Arthur, instead of flying to Dominic.

Abruptly Dominic headed for the door. ''Wait here until I get back.''

Seriously alarmed now, Bella half rose. ''Don't you think I should come, too?''

Dominic paused, hand on the door-handle. ''It would be best if this was done with as little fuss as possible. I'll bring her back here.''

And with that grim promise he was gone, leaving Bella with nothing to do but sink back on the *chaise*, wondering if Georgiana was strong enough to weather both Harry Edgcombe's advances *and* Dominic's temper.

DOMINIC DIDN'T bother with his carriage. As the hackney he'd hired pulled up outside 17 Jermyn Street, he reflected that the anonymity of the hack was an added advantage, distinctly preferable to his carriage with his liveried coachman. Instructing the driver to wait for him, he ascended the three steps to the polished oak door and beat a resounding tattoo. Heaven help Harry if he'd gone too far.

The door was opened by a very correct gentleman's gentleman. Recognising the Viscount, he smiled politely. "I'm afraid his lordship is currently engaged, m'lord."

"I know that. I'm here to disengage him."

And with that the astonished retainer was set firmly aside. Dominic closed the door behind him. His gaze swept the hallway and found Cruickshank, seated in a stiff-backed chair in the shadows. Surprised, she came to her feet.

"Where's your mistress?"

Trained to respond to the voice of authority, Cruickshank immediately bobbed a curtsy. "In the drawing-room, m'lord." With a nod, she indicated the door opposite her chair.

Stripping off his gloves and handing them, together with his cane, to Lord Edgcombe's bemused valet, Dominic said, "I suggest you return to Winsmere House. I will be taking your mistress to meet Lady Winsmere. I would imagine they'll return home in a few hours. Should Lord Winsmere enquire, you may inform him they're in my charge."

Bright blue eyes met faded blue. Cruickshank hesitated, then bobbed again in acquiescence. "Very good, m'lord."

With Lord Edgcombe's valet distracted by Cruickshank's departure, Dominic strolled forward and, after a fractional hesitation, opened the drawing-room door.

The sight which met his eyes would have made him

laugh if he hadn't been so angry. Georgiana was seated in a chair by the hearth and had clearly been listening with her customary intentness to one of Harry's tales. He was leaning against the mantelpiece, negligently attired in a green smoking jacket, his pose calculated to impress the viewer with his particular brand of assured arrogance. Despite himself, Dominic's lips twitched. The door shut behind him with a sharp click. Both fair heads turned his way.

While most of his attention was centred on Georgiana, Dominic did not miss the relief which showed fleetingly in Harry's eyes. Relieved in turn of its most urgent worry, his mind went on to register the expression in Georgiana's hazel gaze. Total innocence. Then, as he watched, she blushed deliciously and, flustered, looked away.

Inwardly, Dominic smiled. He did not make the mistake of imagining her sudden consciousness was due to delayed guilt on being discovered in such a compromising situation. Oh, no—*he* was the cause of Georgiana's blushes, not Harry. Which fact compensated at least in part for his agony of the past ten minutes.

An interested spectator to Georgiana's reaction, Harry pushed away from the mantelpiece, a smile of real mirth lighting his face. "Ah, Dominic. I wondered how long you'd be."

Acknowledging this greeting, and the information it contained, by shaking Harry's offered hand, Dominic turned to find Georgiana rising to her feet.

"I had no idea... I wasn't expecting..."

"Me to arrive so soon?" suggested Dominic. He

advanced upon his love, capturing one delicate hand and raising it to his lips. "I finished my business rather earlier than I had hoped. I take it you've finished yours?"

Georgiana was completely bemused. The last person she had thought to meet this afternoon was Lord Alton. And none of his words, nor Lord Edgcombe's, seemed to make any sense. Entirely at sea, she simply stared into his lordship's blue eyes, traitorously hoping he would take charge.

"No sign of these paintings, I'm afraid," put in Lord Edgcombe, shaking his head. He added in explanation to Dominic, "Moscombe has been with me since I moved here, and he insists the place was completely empty. Even the attics."

Dominic nodded, and tucked Georgiana's hand into its accustomed place in the crook of his arm. "It was a long shot. Still," he added, blue eyes intent on Harry, "no harm done."

Harry's eyes widened in mock alarm. "None in the least, I assure you." Then a gleam of wicked amusement lit his grey eyes. "Mind you, it did occur to me that Miss Hartley might like to view my art collection."

Dominic's black brows rose. "Your etchings, perhaps?"

Harry grinned. "Just so."

"Etchings?" queried Georgiana.

"Never mind!" said Dominic in the voice of a man goaded. He gazed down into wide hazel eyes and wished they were in his drawing-room rather than

Harry's. "Come," he added in gentler tones. "I'll return you to Bella."

Walking beside him to the door, Georgiana struggled to free enough of her mind from its preoccupation with Lord Alton to make sense of what was going on. Emerging into the hall, she looked about for Cruickshank.

"I've sent your maid on." Dominic was beside her, holding her coat.

"Oh," said Georgiana, suddenly aware of a disturbing glint in his lordship's blue eyes. Did that mean she would be travelling in a closed carriage alone with him?

Settling Georgiana's coat over her shoulders, Dominic cast a sharp glance at their host, standing genially beside them. "Harry…?"

Lord Edgcombe's grey eyes met his over Georgiana's head. A slight frown and a shake of the head was all the immediate response Harry made as Georgiana turned to thank him for his trouble. He charmingly disclaimed all effort, bowing with easy grace over her hand. As he straightened, his eyes intercepted Dominic's blue gaze.

"Not a word, I assure you." The grey eyes glinted, amusement in their depths. "You have my heartfelt thanks. Can you doubt it? Any word from me would cook my own goose, after all."

Reassured but puzzled, Dominic raised his brows in question.

Harry grinned and waved an airy hand. "M'sisters are a mite pressed at the moment, it seems. Can you imagine their joy if they learned of—er—what so recently transpired? Why, it would spell the end to my distinguished career." He fixed Dominic with a winning smile. "No, no, m'lad. Rather you than me."

Walking towards the door ahead of the two men, Georgiana, no longer subject to Viscount Alton's mesmerising gaze, tried to follow the gist of their conversation, to no avail. When she turned in the doorway to bid Lord Edgcombe goodbye, it was to see both men cordially shaking hands. Piqued, feeling that something was going on literally over her head, Georgiana tilted her chin a fraction higher and coolly responded to Lord Edgcombe's farewell.

Turning to the street, she majestically descended the steps, but had barely gained the pavement before Lord Alton's long fingers grasped her elbow. A spurt of anger urged her to shake off his hand, but the memory of that odd glint she had seen in his eye undermined her confidence. Before she had time to do more than register the fact that it was into a hackney rather than one of his own carriages he was helping her, she was inside. He followed her, taking the seat beside her. Immediately the driver whistled up his horse and they moved off.

Georgiana strove to quiet her nerves, aquiver with an unnameable emotion. She kept her eyes on the streetscape while she tried to make sense of events. Why had he come to fetch her? Bella? Impulsively, she turned.

"Is Bella all right?"

His face was a mask. At her question, one black brow rose. "As far as I am aware." After a moment he added, "She's waiting at Alton House."

Alerted by the chilled crispness of his tone, Georgiana eyed him warily. ''Did she send you for me?''

Suddenly noticing the tension in his long frame, Georgiana tensed too. But his calmly enunciated, ''Yes. She sent me,'' gave her no clue to the cause of what she suspected was his displeasure.

Irritated by his odd behaviour, Georgiana frowned and asked, ''Why?''

''Because, having learned that you had taken yourself off to visit a house in Jermyn Street, which, to one who knows London, means almost certainly to call on a bachelor alone, she needed someone to rescue you.''

''But I didn't need rescuing,'' declared Georgiana, turning to face him more fully. ''There was nothing the least wrong.''

At his strangled laugh she flushed and went on, ''I admit it was a relief to find it was Lord Edgcombe who lives there, but that just made it easier. And I made sure I took Cruickshank with me so I wasn't alone.''

''When I entered the house, Cruickshank was in the hall and you were most definitely alone with Harry.'' With an effort, Dominic kept his voice even.

Flushing at the censure in his tone, Georgiana swung her gaze to the street. ''Yes, but there wasn't... I was in no danger of...'' Georgiana broke off. Now she thought it over, she was no longer so sure she hadn't been in danger. There had been a rather disquieting gleam in Lord Edgcombe's grey eyes when she had first arrived. However, the more they had talked, the more she had become convinced he was merely slightly nervous over something. Maybe she had misread the signs. Still, he had done nothing to deserve Lord Alton's suspicions. "Lord Edgcombe was most truly the gentleman."

"I would imagine Harry would always act the gentleman he undoubtedly is," Dominic retorted, asperity colouring his words. "But that doesn't mean he isn't a rake and a gamester, and therefore totally unsuitable as private company for a young lady. Such as yourself."

There was no mistaking the anger in the clipped words. Amazed, her own temper flying, Georgiana turned an incredulous face to him. "But you're a rake and a gamester, too. Why is it safe for me to be alone with you but not with him?"

At her question Dominic closed his eyes in exasperation and thought determinedly about his old nurse, about climbing trees at Candlewick—anything to shut out the urge to sweep her on to his lap and kiss her witless. Safe? She was pushing her luck.

Anger growing at his refusal to answer, Georgiana continued, her long irritation with the oddities of English mores finding sudden outlet. "Why did you send Cruckers away? Surely it's not acceptable for me to be riding in a carriage alone with you?"

Forcibly keeping his eyes shut, Dominic answered, "The only reason it's acceptable for you to be alone with me is because we're soon to be married." He waited for her "Oh" of understanding. When no sound came, he slowly opened his eyes.

Georgiana was staring at him in total confusion.

Quickly Dominic closed his eyes. She was definitely not safe.

For long minutes Georgiana could do nothing but stare. But the fact that he had his eyes closed made it easier for her to think. He should have received the deed of the Place that morning. Dominic had said he would visit her once the sale was finalised, *to discuss their mutual interest.* She had no idea what he had meant by that. Now that he owned the Place, she could see no reason why he would still want to marry her.

In real perturbation, Georgiana stared at the handsome face, wishing she could read his motives in the even features. Then, like a beacon on a hill, she saw the light. He had gone too far, too publicly, to draw back now. And that old scandal, the one that had started his rakish career, hung like Damocles' sword, forcing him to offer for her or face the censure of the *ton.*

Which meant she would have to deny him again, one last time. And make it convincing.

She knew he did not love her, not as she understood love. He had shown no fiery passion, uttered no impassioned speeches nor indulged in any melodramatic gestures—all components of love as she knew it. The only time he had kissed her, it had been like a magic caress, so light that she could have dreamt it. But she was in love with him. And, because there seemed to be developing a strange conduit of communication between them, one that did not need words, or even gestures, a sensing that relied on something other than the physical, because of this, she would have to end it now. Or he would know.

And that would be even harder to bear.

Despite his wanting to marry her for her property, something she was honest enough to acknowledge was commonplace in his world, she had always felt safe with him. He had never intentionally done anything to cause her grief. If he ever learned she loved him—not gently, as a well bred young lady should, but to distraction—she doubted he would accept a denial of his suit. He would not cause her pain.

Could he be made to understand that loving him as she did, being married to him, knowing he did not love her in the same way, would cause her even greater pain that if she was never to see him again?

His eyes remained shut. Georgiana could not resist the temptation to study his face, memorising each detail, storing the vision in her heart to last her for a lifetime. She saw his eyelids flicker, then slowly rise. Ill prepared to meet his blue gaze, she straightened and turned slightly away, furiously blinking back the tears which suddenly threatened, pressing her hands tightly together to still their trembling.

Dominic took one look at his love, all but quivering with suppressed emotion, and his anger abruptly vanished.

"Georgiana?"

When she made no answer beyond a small wave of her hand, Dominic drew back, giving her the time she needed to compose herself, ruthlessly stilling the instinctive urge to wrap her in his arms and comfort her. He didn't dare touch her. Frustrated beyond measure, he felt an insane desire to laugh, to catch her to him and kiss her worries, whatever they were, away. Her silence screamed the fact that she was still labouring under some delusion sufficient to make her balk at the very mention of marriage. Her forlorn countenance showed he had his work very much ahead of him.

His eyes on her guinea-gold curls, Dominic sighed. He wanted her, and he was tired of the roundabout the prescribed methods of courtship had put them on.

He waited until her breathing became less laboured, until the pulse at the base of her throat beat less tumultuously. Then he tried again. "Georgiana, my dear, what is it?"

Georgiana put up one small hand in a gesture he found both imperious and, in her present state, endearing.

"Please, my lord. You must let me speak." Her voice was low, urgent and breathless.

"Of course, my dear." Dominic managed a politely attentive tone. He made no move to take her hand, but continued to sit beside her, the flounce of her skirt brushing his boots, his head inclined to watch her face. She did not look up at him, but fixed her gaze on her clasped hands, tensed in her lap.

Georgiana drew a shuddering breath at his easy acquiescence. If only he would remain so calm, she might manage to accomplish her task. But he was near, so near. Speak—she had to speak or her resolution would crumble. "My lord, you must believe that I most earnestly value your friendship, and the...the proper feeling that lies behind your wish to marry me." She paused, reaching deep to dredge the remainder of her strength, before continuing, "I am aware—have always been aware—that my ownership of the Place was fundamental to your interest in me. Now that you own the Place, there is no reason for any further talk of marriage between us." Resolutely she swallowed the sob that rose in her throat and hurried on. "I realise that, if I were of the *ton* and chose to continue living in London, our association these past weeks might give rise to awkward conjecture. However, as I intend returning to Ravello shortly, I beg you will not let such considerations sway you."

Beside her, Dominic allowed his brows to rise. A smile, soft and gentle, curved his lips.

Georgiana drew a deep breath. "My lord, I hope you will see that, in the circumstances, there is no reason for you to offer for me. Indeed," she said, struggling to subdue her treacherous tears, "I beg you will not renew your offer."

"Of course not."

The calm words brought Georgiana up short. One moment she was about to dissolve in tears, the next she had turned and her eyes met his. "I beg your pardon?" she asked weakly.

Smiling sympathetically, Dominic said, "My dear, if my offering for you will cause you distress, then of course I'll not do it. I would never knowingly distress you."

The look which accompanied his words warmed Georgiana through and through, despite the total depression which now hung like a cold black pall over her. He was convinced. He was going to make it easy for her. Tremulously, she smiled.

Seeing this evidence that she had pulled back from

the brink, Dominic smiled back and possessed himself of one small hand.

Georgiana was so relieved that she only just stopped herself from leaning against him, so close as he was. Her head was spinning. Was it possible to feel so cherished and yet know one was unloved? She wasn't sure. In fact she was no longer sure of any number of things. But thankfully he had taken charge. She was sure he wouldn't press her for further words.

Words, especially from his beloved, were very far from Dominic's mind. He had no intention of giving her the opportunity to refuse him again. It occurred to him that there were other routes to his desired goal. The time had come to consider alternatives—his patience was wearing wafer-thin. On impulse, he raised the hand he held and touched it to his lips, then, yielding to a need he was endeavouring to subdue, turned it and pressed a kiss to her palm. He heard the sharp intake of her breath, and glanced up to smile reassuringly at her.

"My dear, you're overset. I give you my word I'll press you to do nothing unless it is your wish, urge you to nothing beyond what is in your heart to do. Remember that."

Georgiana blushed. As a parting speech, it held a note of promise entirely out of place with its supposed intent.

Dominic watched her confusion grow, turning her eyes a deeper shade, like toffee. Repressing the all but overwhelming urge to kiss her, he reluctantly released her hand, adding in a conversational tone, "It's very likely I'll be out of town for the next few days, but

I'll see you before you leave town.'' It would take a day or two to organise his trap, but he had no intention of letting her escape.

The hack turned into a square and pulled up before an imposing mansion. Within minutes Georgiana was ushered inside to find Bella anxiously waiting.

"DUCKETT? What the devil are you doing here?''

Slouched in the armchair before the fireplace, Dominic frowned as his head butler, whom he had supposed still at Candlewick, entered the room. Unperturbed by his greeting, Duckett held a long taper to the fire and proceeded to circumnavigate the room, lighting candles as he went.

"Timms is ill, m'lord. You'd given orders to shut up this house, so the lad very properly sent for me.''

Dominic snorted. Lad? Timms was all of thirty-five if he was a day. But he was one of Duckett's protégés and, provided he obeyed Duckett's guidelines to the letter, would always be assured of the head butler's protection.

Turning the fragile glass balloon he held so that the candlelight caught and reflected from the golden liquid within, Dominic found himself staring at the glowing colour, the same colour as her eyes. With an effort, he withdrew his gaze and found his head butler engaged in the demeaning task of making up the fire.

"Duckett, I have a problem.''

"My lord?''

"A problem with a lady, you understand.''

"I understand perfectly, my lord.''

"I sincerely doubt it,'' replied Dominic. He eyed

his henchman appraisingly. It wasn't the first time he had unburdened himself to Duckett, and doubtless wouldn't be the last. Duckett had started service as a stableboy with his grandfather. He had rapidly progressed through the ranks, reaching his present position shortly after Dominic had attained his majority. They'd been firm friends forever, it seemed, despite a good ten years' difference in age.

"I'd value your opinion, Duckett."

"Very good, m'lord." With the fire blazing, Duckett rose and unobtrusively busied himself, straightening books and stacking magazines.

"The situation," said Dominic, "can only be described as delicate. The lady in question is both young and innocent. The crux of the problem is that she has great difficulty in believing herself to be loved."

Dominic waited for some response, but none came. He turned and saw Duckett flicking the dust from a book before replacing it on the shelf.

"Are you listening, Duckett?"

"Naturally, m'lord."

Dominic let his head fall back against the chair. "Very good." Taking a moment to gather his thoughts, he went on, "This being so, the said lady invents the most tortuous reasons to account for my wanting to marry her, and for refusing my suit. The first was that I was in love with a courtesan and intended marrying her. Having convinced her this was untrue, I then found she believed that I wished to marry her in order to gain title to the Place, which she owns. Owned, I should say, because today I bought it from her. The title-deed now resides in my strong-box and has lost all relevance to the proceedings. The last twist in the tale is that she now perceives that I feel I must marry her because, due to the public nature of my pursuit of her, not to do so would leave her open to the usual opprobrium.'' Dominic paused to take a swig of the fiery liquid in his glass. ''You now have the facts, Duckett. I am presently searching for ways and means of removing her to a suitably isolated locale, sufficiently private to allow me to convince her that I do in fact love her while at the same time rendering her opinion on the subject irrelevant.''

A slight frown marred Duckett's majestic countenance. ''I take it the young lady returns your affections, my lord?''

''The young lady is head over heels in love with me, if you must know.''

''Ah,'' said Duckett, nodding sagely. ''Just so.''

Dominic eyed his impeccable retainer through narrowed eyes. Duckett's gaze was fixed in the far distance. Then, quite suddenly, a smile quirked at the corners of his mouth.

''What are you thinking of, Duckett?''

The soft question brought Duckett to himself with a start. Then he smiled at his master. ''It just occurred to me, m'lord, that now that you own the Place you'd want Jennings and me to put our people through it— to tidy it up, as it were.''

Puzzled, Dominic nodded. ''Yes, but—''

Duckett held up a restraining hand. ''That being so, m'lord, I dare say there'll be personal belongings— things to do with the Hartleys—that we'd need to know what to do with. And, I should warn you, old

Ben says the snows are no more than a few days away.''

Dominic's eyes, vacant, remained trained on his butler's face as the grandfather clock in the corner ticked on. Then, to Duckett's relief, the blue gaze focused. Dominic smiled wickedly. "Duckett, prince of butlers, you're a rascal. I'd be shocked, if I weren't so grateful. No wonder I pay you so well." Struggling upright, Dominic drained his glass and handed it to the waiting Duckett. "We'll set out at first light."

"Very good, m'lord," replied Duckett.

CHAPTER TWELVE

BEING TRULY ALONE again was worse than Georgiana had expected. Bella's brother had come to fill a void in her heart she hadn't even known existed. Until he was gone.

Idly plying her needle over the slippers she intended leaving as a parting gift to Arthur, Georgiana stifled a despondent sigh. The day outside was dull and grey, but no more dismal than the state of her heart. Bella, reclining on the *chaise* in the middle of the room, flicking through the latest *Ladies' Journal,* seemed almost as subdued as she. But, in her friend's case, there was a peacefulness in her quiet which Georgiana, in her tortured state, could only envy.

The Season had come to an end two days before. During the last ball, at Lady Matcham's, there had been much talk of country visits and plans for the annual festivities. Georgiana had listened and tried to summon an enthusiasm she could not feel. To her, the future looked cold and bleak. She waited for Arthur's decision on when they would leave Green Street, Bella and he bound for Candlewick, she for the Continent. He had asked her if she would stay until his business in London was completed, to keep Bella company.

Naturally, she could not possibly refuse such a request. Particularly now that Lord Alton had left London.

He had sent a short note to Bella, simply informing her he had business in the country and would welcome her to Candlewick whenever she chose to quit town.

There had been no word to Bella's protégée.

Casting another glance at Bella, Georgiana couldn't help feeling guilty that she had not been able to satisfy her friend's ambition, and, worse, would not be returning to London to continue their friendship. Arthur would have to find some other distraction for his wife next Season. Georgiana knew she would never return. She would never be able to face Lord Alton's bride. He would eventually marry—an inescapable fate for one such as he. Already she felt a potent jealousy for the beautiful woman who would be his wife. Feeling despair weigh heavily on her shoulders, she forced away her unhappy thoughts and bent over her embroidery.

The door opened.

"A note for you, miss."

Frowning, Georgiana reached for the white rectangle on Johnson's salver, images of Charles and Lord Ellsmere in her mind. But one glance at the strong script emblazoned across the white parchment dispelled those weaker images, replacing them with a handsome, dark-featured face with warm blue eyes.

With the unnerving sensation of having her heart in her throat, Georgiana nodded a dismissal to Johnson and broke open the seal.

"What is it?" asked Bella, struggling to sit up.

Slowly Georgiana scanned the single sheet. Then,

absent-mindedly, she said, ''Your brother wants me to go down to the Place. His people want to know what to do with the furniture and so on.''

Bella, now sitting, nodded. ''Yes, of course. You must tell them whether you want anything set aside.''

''But I don't think there could possibly be anything I would want—'' Georgiana began.

''You can't tell that,'' said Bella seriously. ''Who knows? They might even stumble across those paintings of your father's.''

Bella put her head on one side, the better to view her friend. To her mind, something was not entirely right between Georgiana and Dominic. Why on earth Georgie should fall into such a lethargy just because Dominic repaired to the country for a few days she could not imagine. As she saw it, it was only to be expected that her brother would want to see his affairs at Candlewick organised before he took his intended bride down for a prolonged stay. Despite the fact Dominic had apparently not as yet proposed, Bella was quite sure he would and that Georgiana's plans for removal to Italy would never be realised. She knew her brother well enough to be certain he would view any interference with his schemes in a dim light. But, in this case, her confidence in the eventual outcome was supreme. Consequently, she was waiting with perfect equanimity for the time to come for them to leave for Candlewick.

''When are you to go?'' Bella asked.

''He says he'll come and fetch me tomorrow,'' answered Georgiana, still struggling with conflicting emotions. The note was little more than a polite summons, its wording leaving no room for manoeuvre and even less for escape. Lord Alton would give himself the pleasure of fetching Miss Hartley at ten the next morning. He would undertake to return her to town that evening.

"Perhaps I should come down with you," Bella suggested. "There's nothing to keep me here, and I would like to see Jonathon."

Georgiana readily agreed. In her present state, spending two hours and more in a closed carriage alone with Lord Alton was an undertaking too unnerving even to contemplate.

But when the subject was broached with Arthur that evening he surprised them both by vetoing his wife's part in it.

"I'm afraid, my dear, that I would prefer you to remain in London for the next day or two. As Dominic plans to bring Georgiana back the same day, I really don't think you should leave Green Street just yet."

Put like that, it was impossible to argue the point.

Georgiana retired for the night, trying in vain to quell the entirely inappropriate leaping of her heart whenever she thought of the morrow. All was at an end between Lord Alton and herself. Why, then, did anticipation run in tantalising shivers down every nerve?

PRECISELY AT TEN the next morning, Lord Alton's travelling chaise pulled up outside Winsmere House. Strolling unannounced into his sister's back parlour, Dominic could not repress a smile at the picture that met his eyes. On the window-seat, his beloved sat, perfectly ready, fingers nervously twisting in the ribbons of her bonnet. Her gaze was fixed on the garden, a dull prospect beyond the glass.

His sister lay on the *chaise,* staring at the ceiling, a slight frown puckering her brows. It was she who first saw him.

''Oh!''

With that exclamation Bella sat up, putting up a hand to straighten the wisp of lace she had started experimenting with atop her dark curls. Dominic held out a hand to assist her to right herself, bending to drop an affectionate kiss on her cheek. Then he stood back and eyed her headgear.

Bella held her breath.

After a moment, Dominic's brows rose. ''Has Arthur seen that yet?''

''No,'' said Bella.

''In that case, I suggest you burn it before he does.''

''Oh!'' Spots of colour flew in Bella's cheeks, eliciting a chuckle from her unrepentant brother. ''If you've a mind to be disagreeable, I'll leave you,'' she replied haughtily.

But Dominic only smiled. ''Don't trouble yourself. It's I who am about to leave you. If Miss Hartley is ready?''

Finding herself the object of his calm blue gaze, Georgiana nodded and rose. Within a matter of minutes her cloak had been gently placed about her shoulders and she was settled in the luxury of his carriage, a warm brick at her feet, a soft rug wrapped protectively about her knees.

Taking his seat beside her, and giving the order to

start, Dominic turned and smiled. "The journey should not be too tedious, I hope."

At his smile, all Georgiana's fears dissolved. She smiled back.

They preserved a comfortable silence as the coach wended its way through the crowded streets. Once the outskirts of town were reached, and the power of the four horses began to make itself felt, Dominic turned to Georgiana. "Have you heard of Prinny's latest start?"

She hadn't, of course. Without effort, he entertained her with stories of the *ton* and other suitable anecdotes, until she had relaxed enough to ask some questions of her own. These, not surprisingly, were focused on the Place. Perfectly content with the topic, Dominic described the actual land attached to the Place, and how it related to his own far-flung acres.

"So, you see, the Place all but cuts my holdings in two, at least in that area. It has meant that my people constantly have to route all their movements around the Place, often tripling distances. Aside from being purely a nuisance, it has in recent years become an eyesore—a blot on the landscape. It's been irritating to me, as much as to my farmers, to see good land go to ruin."

Georgiana nodded, the memory of the Place as she had last seen it vivid in her mind.

Dominic paused to glance once more out of the window. The one subject he was most assiduously avoiding was the weather. He had ensured that Georgiana was seated on the left on the carriage, so her gaze, should it wander, dwelt only on the relatively clear skies to the west. On his side the eastern horizon was obscured by slate-grey clouds of the peculiar quality which, to one country-bred, denoted but one outcome. Snow. By nightfall.

The temperature was starting to fall precipitate, even though it wanted half an hour to noon. He did not think Georgiana would notice, wrapped up as she was. Still, it wouldn't do to become too complacent on that score. With a wicked grin, he turned to her once more, his brain making a rapid inventory of the latest *on dits,* selecting those suitable for his purpose.

By his order, the coach took them direct to the Place. It was well after noon when he alighted and handed Georgiana down. His steward, Jennings, and Duckett were there to meet them.

"I'll leave you with Duckett, my dear," Dominic said. "I'll be with Jennings if you need me."

Recognising Duckett, Georgiana was relieved to have his comforting presence beside her as she walked the old rooms of the Place. There was no piece of furniture she remembered with any particular affection. When appealed to, Duckett suggested the vicar's wife, who managed the local charity, and promised to convey the furniture to her.

"There's just one more matter, miss," said Duckett, pausing at the top of the stairs.

Dominic, having finished his instructions to Jennings, approving the steward's suggestion that the Place be made over as a single unit into a farm, came to stand at the foot of the stairs. Spying Georgiana and Duckett in the shadows at their head, he ran lightly up to join them.

"I was just telling Miss Hartley, m'lord, that when our people went through the attics they found one of them sealed up. An old cupboard had been moved across the door. Took three men to shift it. Then it was a struggle to force the door—looked to have been left locked for years. The room inside seems to have been used for painting—bits of rag and dabs of paint all over. There were lots of old paintings stacked by the walls. We didn't know what to do with them, so we left it until you came. Would you care to take a look, miss?"

Her father's paintings? His studio at the Place? Georgiana simply stared at Duckett.

Correctly gauging his love's reaction, Dominic took her hand and drew it through his arm. "Lead the way, Duckett."

Escorted in Duckett's wake, Georgiana drew a deep breath. "Oh, Dominic! If only…"

He glanced down, smiling, inordinately pleased to hear his name on her lips. "Patience. A moment and we'll see."

He helped her up the narrow stairs to the low-ceilinged attics. A white patch on one wall of the first room showed where the old cupboard had been. Now the concealed door stood ajar.

Duckett pushed it open and stood aside to allow Georgiana to enter. Dominic released her and, when she hesitated, gave her an encouraging nudge.

Dazed, she stepped over the threshold, lifting her skirts free of the dusty floor. There was little doubt this had been her father's eyrie. Long windows all but filled the outer wall. Now half covered with creeper, clear, they would have allowed light to flood the large room. An easel stood in the middle of the floor, empty; a paint-stained rag hung on a nail at one corner. Georgiana gazed about. The odd smell of old paints was still detectable, wafting like a ghost about the room.

For one instant, reminded so vividly of the life that had been, she felt the past threaten to engulf her. She struggled to keep back the tears. Then she heard a soft movement behind her and Dominic was there, his hands closing gently on her upper arms, comforting by his touch, by his solid warmth so close behind her. Like an anchor, he held her in the present, defying the past to claim her.

Georgiana drew a deep breath. Calm once more, she put up a hand to touch one of his. Her gaze fell on the canvases, stacked against the side-wall. She moved to touch them and he released her immediately, following her across the floor.

Without words, they set about the task of examining her father's last legacy.

Most of the portraits were of adolescent youths. After a pensive moment, staring at one of a gentle-eyed young man with reddish tints in his hair, Dominic grinned. "Ah! Now I understand."

Patiently Georgiana waited to be educated.

Dominic's smile warned her. "Your father was clearly an astute man. He wanted to leave you something which was sure to retain its value, regardless of the vacillations of fashion. So he left you these." Still Georgiana waited. Displaying the canvas in his hand, Dominic said, "This one's William Grenville as a young man." When Georgiana still looked blank he explained, "Grenville was one of our recent Prime Ministers. His family will pay a small fortune for this. And," he continued, replacing the portrait and picking up another, "unless I miss my guess, this one is Spencer Perceval, another Prime Minister. That one," he said, pointing to another study of an earnest young man, "could be Castlereagh, though I'm not certain." He bent again to flick through the portraits.

There were sixteen in the series, and Dominic could put a name to nine and guess at the others. But the three portraits at the bottom of the pile, once they were uncovered, claimed his and Georgiana's complete attention.

The first was of a young woman, with a sweet face crowned by masses of brown hair. Her eyes, startlingly clear hazel, shone out of the canvas, bright and clear. It was the portrait of Georgiana's mother.

Leaving Georgiana to gaze on her mother's face, Dominic pulled the next from the pile. A young baby rolled playfully on the grass beside the same woman. A gentle smile, full of love, curved the woman's fine lips.

Wordlessly offering this picture to Georgiana, Dominic reached for the last. This showed a young girl, of six or so summers, long golden hair hanging in plaits down her back, honey-gold eyes alight with mischief. A dusting of freckles was scattered across the bridge of her pert nose. Dominic smiled. Turning to Georgiana, he put one finger under her chin and turned her face towards him. After a careful examination, which ignored her brimming eyes, he stated, "You've lost your freckles."

Georgiana smiled tremulously, recognising his attempt to lighten her mood and grateful for it.

Dominic smiled back and released her, gently flicking her cheek with his finger. He glanced about them. "Now that this room has been opened again, I rather think these pictures should be removed from here."

Georgiana looked blank.

"Shall I get Duckett to pack them up and take them to Candlewick? You can decide what to do with them later."

Still dazed by their discoveries, Georgiana nodded her agreement. Duckett began to move about her, carefully stacking the paintings into smaller piles to be carried downstairs by his minions.

"And now," Dominic said, coming once more to stand beside her, "you must be famished. I'll take you to Candlewick, and Mrs Landy can feed us."

Quite forgetting the long trip back to London, Georgiana, happiness filling her heart, and enjoying the novelty of having someone to share it with, allowed herself to be escorted downstairs and into the carriage.

Mrs Landy had a meal waiting. She scolded Dominic for keeping Georgiana so long in the cold, causing Georgiana's brow to rise. But Dominic only laughed.

When they had eaten, he left her in Mrs Landy's care while he went out to talk with his bailiff.

It wasn't until, over tea and scones in the housekeeper's rooms, she noticed the day drawing in that Georgiana started to become uneasy. As the hour dragged by and Dominic did not return, her sense of premonition grew.

The light had faded to a premature dusk when he

finally appeared. He came into the drawing-room, where she had retreated, stamping his feet to restore the circulation. He crossed to the fire and bent to warm his hands. Straightening, he smiled at her reassuringly, but his words dispelled the effect. "I'm afraid, my dear, that we won't be able to return to town tonight. The weather's turned nasty and the roads are freezing. There's snow on the way, and I doubt we'd make the Great North Road before we were stuck in a drift."

At the sight of his satisfied smile, Georgiana's eyes grew round. He'd planned this, she was sure. But why, for heaven's sake?

But her host gave her no opportunity to ponder that vital question. He challenged her to a game of chess, to which she had admitted fair knowledge, and, by the time Georgiana had conceded her king, Mrs Landy was at the door, smiling and waiting to take her to her room to freshen up before dinner. The clouds of worried questions that flitted through Georgiana's mind seemed ridiculous when faced with the solid respectability of that worthy dame.

A sense of unreality hung over her during dinner, eaten in the large dining-room. The huge table, which Mrs Landy had informed her could seat fifty, had thankfully had all its leaves taken out, rendering it a suitable size for household dining. She was seated on Dominic's right, and so attentive was her host that she had no time to question the propriety of the proceedings. The food was delicious, and the wine Dominic allowed Duckett to supply her with was cool and sweet. A discussion of the portraits her father had left her occupied much of their time, until, with the removal of the last course, Dominic pushed back his chair and rose, waving Duckett aside and coming to assist her to her feet. "Come. We'll be more comfortable in the drawing-room."

The presence of Duckett behind her chair had soothed her troublesome conscience, pricking with half-understood suspicion. Now, as the drawing-room door closed and she realised he was no longer in the room with them, her jitters woke afresh. Her nervousness spiralling upwards, she crossed the room towards the *chaise* angled before the big fireplace, conscious that he followed close behind.

"Georgiana."

The single word, uttered in the most compelling of tones, stopped her before the marble hearth. Recognising the futility of attempting evasion, Georgiana turned slowly to meet him. He was closer than she had realised. She found herself enfolded in his arms, like delicate porcelain. Looking up, she felt her eyelids automatically drop as his head lowered to hers and he kissed her, so gently that the caress captivated her senses. This time, the kiss did not end, but went on to steal her breath, and her wits. Her nervousness disappeared, chased away by the warm glow of desire which spread insidiously through her veins. In response to some inner prompting, she slipped her arms free of his hold and twined them about his neck. His lips firmed against hers, until she parted her lips in welcome and, by imperceptible degrees, the kiss deepened.

Suddenly her mind, all alive to every incoming sensation, registered the restraint in his body, the tightness in the muscles holding her so gently, the iron control which stopped him from crushing her to him. She moved closer, letting her body press, soft but firm, against his.

Dominic stiffened with the effort to hold his passions in check. He raised his head to look down into her face. In surprise, he viewed hazel eyes smoky with desire, lips parted slightly in flagrant temptation. The siren he had glimpsed in the Massinghams' library stood within the circle of his arms, her body pliant against his. And it was all he could do to draw breath and, his voice husky, demand, "Marry me, Georgiana."

His words slowly penetrated the fog of desire which swirled through Georgiana's mind. They made no sense. Nothing made any sense any more. He had the Place. This wasn't supposed to be happening. Georgiana ignored his talk and, instead, tightened her hold on him, forcing his lips back to hers.

With a groan, Dominic recognised her state. But he was powerless to resist her blatant demands. His lips closed on hers and he tried very hard to think of other things—anything other than the slim form snuggling so invitingly against him. His plan of gentle wooing had not taken into account the possibility of such responses on her part. In the dim hope that her mind would return presently if he kept their lovemaking in a frustratingly light vein, he rained gentle kisses on her lips and face, ignoring her attempts to ensnare him in a deeper caress. Gradually her flaring passion abated somewhat—enough, at least, for him to try again.

"Georgiana?"

"Mmm." She moved seductively against him, and he caught his breath.

"Marry me, love. Say yes. Now."

"Y... What?" Abruptly Georgiana's eyes focused. Slowly her mind followed. Then, still dazed, she shook her head.

To her amazement, she found herself looking up into eyes darkened with desire but lit by underlying sparks of anger.

"I do hope, my love, that you are not going to tell me you won't marry me."

The clipped accents sobered her. The warmth of his arms still surrounded her, making it difficult to think. Her hands on his shoulders, Georgiana tried to ease from his embrace, only to find the arms holding her so gently were, in fact, made of steel. "I can't think," she murmured protestingly.

"Don't think," came his voice, so close that his breath caressed her cheek. "Just say yes."

Again she shook her head, not daring to meet his eyes. Unequal to this battle, she leant her forehead against his shoulder. She felt his arms come up to draw her closer against him, his solid warmth comforting rather than threatening. Ridiculous, she thought, to feel so wholly at peace in the arms of a man who did not love her.

"Why?"

The question drifted softly, a murmur in her mind.

"Because you don't love me." She answered aloud without realising it.

"What?"

Abruptly he held her from him, staring at her in

stunned disbelief. His eyes searched her face, then his lips twitched. Closing his eyes in exasperation, Dominic drew her head back until it was once again pillowed on his shoulder.

Georgiana snuggled against him, still dazed from his kisses, still wanting more, but not, at this juncture, daring to tempt him further. His insistence on marriage baffled her. Her own responses confused her even more. How wanton she became, with him.

Dominic waited until he had regained some measure of control over his reeling senses before asking, in a perfectly amiable tone, "Do you think, my love, you could explain to me why you think I don't love you?"

The effort required to return their interaction to an acceptable footing was entirely beyond Georgiana. She contemplated attempting to retreat without explaining herself, but doubted she had the strength to win free of his arms, let alone his presence. So when his lips found her ear and nuzzled gently, inviting her confidence, she sighed and said, "You don't really love me, you only say you do. I saw you kiss Lady Changley once. You never kiss me like that."

Put into words, it did not sound particularly rational, but it was the best she could do, with him so close.

Silence greeted her revelation. After a moment she glanced up to find him regarding her, an odd expression in his eyes.

"Do you mean to say that *that* is why you've held me off for so long? Because I *didn't* kiss you the way I did Lady Changley?"

His voice sounded strangled. Georgiana looked up

at him in concern. When she neglected to answer, he shook her slightly. She nodded.

A groan rewarded her honesty. "Georgiana!"

Then she was swept into his arms and ruthlessly kissed, passionately kissed, until her legs collapsed under her and she had to cling to him for support. And still the kiss went on, demanding, commanding and utterly devastating. When at long last she was allowed to emerge, she was shaken to the very depths of her being.

"Oh!"

It was all she could say. She looked up at him, love, joy and wonder dancing in the golden flames of her eyes.

With a wordless groan, Dominic crushed her to him once more, burying his face in her silken curls.

"But why?" asked a dazzled Georgiana. "Dominic, why didn't you kiss me like that before?"

To her amazement, she felt his shoulders shake.

Dominic could contain his laughter no longer. And, although his love struggled in his embrace, he held her tightly until he felt rather less crazed and more capable of answering her sanely. Only then did he ease his hold enough to allow her to look up into his face.

Reassured at seeing her own love reflected in his blue eyes—eyes which held warmth and gentle affection as well as the passion she had not recognised before—Georgiana smiled and waited patiently.

Drawing a deep breath, Dominic sought for words to explain how her innocence had tripped him up yet again. "I was most careful, I'll have you know, not to expose you to my desire, because my sweetest love, it is generally held that innocent young ladies are not—er—sufficiently robust to withstand such raw passions.''

The incredulous widening of his love's innocent stare nearly had him in stitches again.

''Aren't I supposed to like...? No, that can't be true.''

Dominic was nuzzling her ear again. ''I assure you it is,'' he murmured. ''If I'd kissed any of the gentle debs as I've just kissed you, seven out of ten would faint dead away and the other three would have had the vapours.''

Georgiana giggled.

Then she felt the arms around her shift slightly and one strong hand found her chin, tilting it up so that he could gaze into her eyes, his own burning again with the dark lights she now understood. A sensuous shiver ran through her.

A slow and infinitely wicked smile curved Dominic's lips. When he spoke, his voice was husky and deep. ''Enough of the rest of this crazy world. Come, let me see if I can convince you of just how irrevocably I love you.''

His lips closed over hers, and Georgiana, swept away on a tide of passion, gave herself up wholeheartedly to that enterprise.

''Ahem!''

The discreet cough from the doorway brought Dominic's head up. ''What the devil?'' Frowning direfully, he turned his head and located the intruder. ''Duckett?''

At the door, Duckett stood correctly to attention, his

gaze fixed on the far wall. "I'm sorry to interrupt, m'lord, but I thought you'd want to know that Lady Winsmere has just arrived."

"Bella?" Dominic's incredulous question hung quivering in the air, but Duckett had already gone, leaving the door ajar.

Brows flying in disbelief, Dominic looked down at the woman still held securely in his arms. "I suppose we'd better go and see what your chaperon has to say."

Georgiana smiled. "I wonder why she's come."

"Precisely my question. We'd better ask her." Keeping Georgiana within the circle of his arm, Dominic strolled to the door.

In the doorway, they paused to take in the scene. Only one of the large double doors was open, with one of the footmen standing in its protection with a branch of candles, trying to cast some light on to the steps outside. Blasts of cold air hurled into the hall, bringing swirls of snowflakes to flutter and melt on the tiles. On the porch a carpet of snow, already some inches thick, bore witness to the intensity of the storm outside. As Georgiana and Dominic watched, two footmen emerged from the darkness, bearing Bella between them. Duckett followed immediately behind, the shoulders of his dark coat already dusted with snow.

As soon as everyone was inside, the footmen slammed the door shut against the elemental fury ravaging the night.

Immediately her feet hit the floor, Bella glanced about. Her eyes found Georgiana and Dominic, side by side in the drawing-room doorway. "There you are! Really, Georgie, you're going to have to be more careful!'' She bustled up and embraced Georgiana before turning a censorious look on her brother. ''And you, of all people, should have known better!''

Intrigued, Dominic allowed one brow to quirk upward. Holding the door wide, he bowed slightly, ushering both Bella and Georgiana into the drawing-room. He closed the door firmly.

''Now, Bella, cut line. What on earth made you leave Green Street in this hoydenish fashion?''

In response to her brother's crisp question, Bella simply stared.

''*Hoydenish?* Dominic Ridgeley! To call me hoydenish when you've all but compromised Georgiana by unthinkingly bringing her here when you might have guessed the snows were coming on. Why, if I hadn't set out as soon as the first snowflake fell, she'd have had to spend the night here with you unchaperoned. I would have thought with all your experience you would have seen the danger as well as I.''

''Precisely.''

The exasperated tone brought Bella's eyes to his face. Her confidence faltered. ''You knew...'' Bewildered, she glanced from Dominic's face to Georgiana's, then back again. ''I don't understand.''

Dominic sighed. ''Before your arrival interrupted us, Georgiana and I were examining a number of the reasons for our impending marriage. As my affianced wife, she most definitely does not need the services of a chaperon when with me.''

''Oh.'' Bella looked at Georgiana, but her protégée was watching Dominic, a strange little smile on her lips.

Dominic, meanwhile, had crossed to the bell-pull. "Yes. *Oh!* And, what's more, you'll have brought your husband out in these foul conditions—"

"But Arthur doesn't know," Bella interrupted to assure him.

"Most assuredly Arthur didn't know when you left Green Street. However, he will certainly have found out long since and be close behind you. Talking about people who should know better, dear sister, in your condition you have no business to go gallivanting around the country in snowstorms."

Bella gasped. "My condition? Whatever do you—?"

"My lord?"

Dominic turned to the door. "Ah, Mrs Landy."

But before he could give any orders, there came again the sound of the great front doors opening. Voices, all masculine, were heard in the hall.

Bella put a hand to her lips.

Dominic glanced at her but said nothing, his attention returning to the door.

Arthur walked in. One glance was sufficient for everyone to see he was displeased. He nodded a wordless greeting to his brother-in-law, then fixed his wife with a stern eye. "Bella, what's the meaning of this?"

Small hands fluttering, Bella went quickly to his side. "Arthur, you're frozen." When her husband's gaze did not waver, she hurriedly explained, "But really, you must see. If I hadn't come, Georgiana would have been alone here with Dominic."

"My dear, your brother is perfectly capable of managing his own affairs. You're my affair, and I cannot condone your careering across the countryside in this fashion. Not in your condition."

For the second time that evening, Bella was struck dumb.

Before she could recover her wits, Dominic smoothly intervened. "I suggest you let Mrs Landy take you upstairs, Bella. You should get to bed immediately."

"Quite so," agreed Arthur, turning to nod to Mrs Landy, still standing by the door. "My lady is expecting and needs to rest."

Abruptly Bella found her voice. "Whatever do you mean? I'm not—"

"Yes, you are!" said two male voices in emphatic unison.

Bella blinked. Then, as the truth dawned, she smiled beatifically. "Oh," she said.

"Arthur," pleaded Dominic, in a tone of desperation, "take her away. Please?"

Arthur smiled.

Mrs Landy took her cue and bustled forward. "Now if you'll just come along, Miss Bella, we'll get you nicely settled..."

Within a minute, an unresisting Bella had been borne away.

"I'm sure Duckett can organise some dinner for you," said Dominic to Arthur.

Arthur nodded. "If you don't mind, I'll take a tray upstairs with Bella. But first I think I'll go and find some of that excellent brandy you keep in your library.'' The shrewd grey gaze came to rest on Georgiana's face. ''I'm glad to see you've come to your senses, Georgiana. You belong here, my dear.'' With a smile and a nod to each of them, he left.

''Now where were we?'' asked Dominic, as he came to stand once more in front of Georgiana and drew her back into his arms.

Georgiana stared up into his face, her eyes alight with love and laughter. ''Did you really plan to compromise me?''

From under heavy lids, Dominic's blue eyes watched her. He smiled, slowly, knowing what it did to her. ''Mm-hm,'' he assented, nodding solemnly. ''After all, you did beg me not to offer for you. If I couldn't get you to agree any other way, then I was quite prepared to compromise you shamelessly.''

Returning the smile, his golden angel turned into a golden siren and wound her arms about his neck. ''Shamelessly?''

It was the last word Georgiana uttered for quite some time. A log crashing into the stillness of the room finally broke the spell that held them. Dominic raised his head and glanced around to make sure the log had not rolled from the hearth. Turning back, he surprised an impish smile on his love's face. One dark brow rose in question.

Georgiana saw it. She hesitated, then, her smile broadening, she explained, ''I was remembering the first time I saw the Fragonard.'' She inclined her head in the direction of the masterpiece above the fireplace. ''I wondered then what sort of man would hang such a painting in such a place.''

A rakish smile lit his face. "The same sort of man who has two other Fragonards."

Her golden eyes begged the invitation.

"Would you like to see the other two?"

"Mm-hm," Georgiana murmured, one tiny fingertip tracing the line of his jaw. "Where are they?"

"Upstairs," Dominic said, in between dropping tantalising little kisses along her lips. "In the master bedroom."

"Ah," said Georgiana, far more interested in his kisses than in any painting. After a moment she moved closer and asked, "Does that matter?"

With mock-seriousness, Dominic considered the point. One brow rose sternly. "It occurs to me, my love, that, as you have yet to formally accept my offer, such an excursion would be highly improper."

Georgiana smiled, letting her fingertip wander to trace the line of his lips. She glanced up at him through her lashes. "And if I were to accept your offer?"

The blue eyes gleamed. "That, of course, would cast an entirely different light on the matter."

Their gazes locked. For one moment, all was still. Then a slow smile twisted Dominic's lips.

"Georgiana, my love, will you marry me?"

Her face alight, Georgiana squealed as his arms tightened about her. "Yes!" she said, laughing. Then, as his head bent to hers, "Oh, yes."

Much later, curled on his lap, warm and secure and pleasantly intoxicated, Georgiana recalled the paintings. She looked into his face. His eyes were closed, but as she watched they opened. One brow rose in query.

Suddenly shy, she dropped her gaze to where her fingers played in the folds of his cravat. "Will you take me to see the Fragonards?"

As a deep chuckle rumbled through his chest, she blushed vividly. But when she glanced again into his face, his expression was perfectly serious.

"Maybe you should see them. Just so you know what kind of man you're marrying."

His lips twisted into a smile that held a gentle promise. The glow in his eyes thrilled her to the core. Feeling suddenly light-headed, her heart thundering, Georgiana managed to nod her agreement.

A few minutes later they left the drawing-room with some semblance of normality and started up the stairs, Georgiana going ahead. On the landing they met Duckett, on his way down. As he drew abreast of his butler, Dominic paused to murmur, *sotto voce*, "Just remember, Duckett, this is all your fault."

Duckett's rigidly correct demeanour did not alter. He inclined his head. "Very good, m'lord."

Duckett continued down the stairs, pausing at their foot to listen to the soft murmur of lovers' voices, cut off by the closing of a door overhead.

Then he smiled. "Very good, m'lord."

2 6 MAY 2000

WAR
TORN

www.rbooks.co.uk

Also by Andy McNab

Non-fiction
BRAVO TWO ZERO
IMMEDIATE ACTION
SEVEN TROOP
SPOKEN FROM THE FRONT

Fiction
REMOTE CONTROL
CRISIS FOUR
FIREWALL
LAST LIGHT
LIBERATION DAY
DARK WINTER
DEEP BLACK
AGGRESSOR
RECOIL
CROSSFIRE
BRUTE FORCE
EXIT WOUND

For more information on Andy McNab and his books, see his
website at www.andymcnab.co.uk

ANDY McNAB
& KYM JORDAN

WAR TORN

BANTAM PRESS

LONDON · TORONTO · SYDNEY · AUCKLAND · JOHANNESBURG

TRANSWORLD PUBLISHERS
61–63 Uxbridge Road, London W5 5SA
A Random House Group Company
www.rbooks.co.uk

First published in Great Britain
in 2010 by Bantam Press
an imprint of Transworld Publishers

A CIP catalogue record for this book
is available from the British Library.

ISBNs 9780593065266 (cased)
9780593065297 (tpb)

Addresses for Random House Group Ltd companies outside the UK
can be found at: www.randomhouse.co.uk
The Random House Group Ltd Reg. No. 954009

The Random House Group Limited supports the Forest Stewardship
Council (FSC), the leading international forest-certification organization.
All our titles that are printed on Greenpeace-approved
FSC-certified paper carry the FSC logo.
Our paper procurement policy can be found at
www.rbooks.co.uk/environment

Typeset in 11/13.9pt Sabon by
Falcon Oast Graphic Art Ltd.
Printed and bound in Great Britain by
CPI Mackays, Chatham, ME5 8TD

2 4 6 8 10 9 7 5 3 1

Mixed Sources
Product group from well-managed
forests and other controlled sources
www.fsc.org Cert no. TT-COC-2139
© 1996 Forest Stewardship Council
FSC

WAR
TORN

Chapter One

THE SUN HUNG DIRECTLY OVERHEAD, BAKING THE DESERT LANDSCAPE around them. Inside the hot, dark Vector, 1 Section, 1 Platoon had sand up their noses, sand inside their mouths. And when they drank from their Camelbaks, they could feel the grit against their teeth.

The journey across Helmand Province had been long and, despite taking turns on top, the lads had moaned into the sergeant's ear every inch of the way. Rifleman Jordan Nelson had been up there on the GPMG throughout. Now Sergeant Dave Henley joined him for the last leg of the journey.

Dave could see the town just ahead of them. Beyond it, another stretch of flat desert separated them from their destination. The incongruous straight lines and right angles of Forward Operating Base Senzhiri sliced across the distant foothills. The rest of the platoon was behind them, looking less like a convoy than a huge, rolling dust cloud.

1 Platoon was to spend the next six months in FOB Senzhiri. They were the advance party; the rest of R Company would be arriving by air later today. The men sat sweating in the gloom of the Vectors, pinned down by the heat. They fell silent as they approached the town. The men on top watched the ancient mud walls grow higher as they got closer, swelling like bread in an oven.

The trees cowered limply in the sunlight. Nothing moved.

Where was everyone?

Dave could smell danger and feel it in the air.

This town wasn't like the others they'd passed through. It was too empty. Where were the curious kids in dark doorways, tugging against their mothers' *burqas*? Where were those mothers, trying to keep their heads covered as they dragged their reluctant offspring indoors? Where were the people walking home from the bazaar with bulging bags, the old men crouching on steps, chewing and staring?

He felt a sensation of intense heat near his face. Molecules of air and dust ricocheted off his cheek. They had been rearranged by a small mass of such speed and power that it cracked the air as it passed. Dave instantly pushed the safety catch on his weapon. And then enemy fire was bursting and blazing all around him.

The boss gave HQ a sit rep from the Vector behind. 'Zero Alpha, this is Romeo One One. Contact. Wait. Out.'

Noise, dust flying and muzzle flashes everywhere, but when Dave scanned the place for movement, there was none. The walls stared back at him, monumental and impassive. He scrutinized the tops of the palms and fruit trees beyond them for shadows, motion, any unnatural regularity. Nothing. A fire fight was erupting on all sides but the enemy was invisible.

Then, amid the crack and thump of small arms, came the angry boom of a grenade.

'Cover! *Cover!*' Shouts from further down the convoy.

Dave's heart beat faster. Up ahead, buried inside a dark slit in the wall, he had seen something glint. He recognized the dull sheen of a worn weapon, its black surface rubbed away. He didn't take his eyes off it. He focused through spiralling clouds of dust, raised his weapon until the target was in the sights and then fired. He couldn't actually see the result, but he felt a small sense of satisfaction.

'Zero Alpha, this is Romeo One One. Grid . . .' The boss paused. He was at the front of his Vector, his nose probably buried in his map. Dave noticed that his voice was perceptibly higher than normal. And no wonder. The boss had walked more or less straight out of Sandhurst into this shitstorm.

'Grid 883 492. Taking fire. Light weapons. Rocket-propelled grenades. No casualties. Request air support. Wait. Out.'

Far away, in an air-conditioned cabin in the sprawling NATO

base at Kandahar, *Troops in Combat* would be flashing up onscreen. Dave hoped his mate Sam Chandler was on duty and not lounging around in the base coffee shop or beating up a treadmill in the gym. Once a *TIC* showed red on the plasma, Sam or one of his colleagues would be legging it in his flying suit into the wall of heat outside, straight to a waiting Harrier. Dave had watched Sam do this only a few days ago, when R Company had first arrived in Afghanistan. It was a reassuring image.

A voice from HQ, crisp and low-key: 'Roger that. Air support. ETA eight minutes. Out.'

The Vector jerked forward again and the dust thrown up by its wheels thickened into dense clouds. He could smell cordite and hear the ceaseless percussion of gunfire but couldn't see further than the end of his nose. He couldn't see the enemy. And now he couldn't even see the flash of their weapons.

The brown dust seethed between the brown Vector and the brown walls. Dave was firing into a brown void. He paused. Behind him he heard the crackle of the other Vectors' machine guns, fast, urgent, high-pitched against the more sporadic chatter of light weapons. Next to him was the deep thrumming of Rifleman Nelson's GPMG. What the fuck was everyone firing at? Could any of them see anything? Or did it just feel better than not firing?

He listened to the crack of the bullets and the thump as they landed, gauging the gap between the two sounds. He estimated that the enemy were mostly within 100 metres, some very close indeed. But the roar of the Vectors and the echoes around the walls could distort your judgement.

He searched the blank clouds of dust for a target. The Vector rumbled on. And then, without warning, the dust curled in a new direction. Suddenly there was a crack in the brown cloud and he could see through it. Low shop fronts loomed close by him, their metal shutters rolled down, then a narrow side street. Empty. No, it wasn't empty. A figure. Several doorways along, half hidden in the shadows.

Dave took in two things about the man: the way his pale blue robes flowed around him like water, and the fact that he was carrying an RPG. Dave raised his weapon until the optic sight cut into his line of vision. He focused into the post sight. He was

3

aiming at the target's centre of mass: the man's chest. He squeezed the trigger just as the Vector jolted.

Shit.

The man dropped his RPG but did not fall to the ground. He grasped his leg. Then instinct overcame pain and he hopped towards his weapon. Dave's finger curled around the trigger again but the moving parts of his SA80 were suddenly stubborn.

'Stoppage!'

He slid down into the other world inside the Vector, tilting his weapon left as he did so, pulled the cocking handle back and saw the empty case.

Fourteen stone of combat gear at his side moved to take his place. Rifleman Steve Buckle. Capable, fast, reliable.

'Get up there!' Dave yelled. 'RPG down that side street!' The barrel of his weapon was scalding hot. He had brought the smell of scorched metal and cordite into this small, burning space. It clawed at the back of his throat. He blinked. After the blistering light of Helmand Province, midday, it was midnight in here. The enemy rounds bouncing off the Vector's armour sounded as though someone was throwing their money around.

He bent over his rifle. With the working parts back he stuck his finger into the hot weapon. He felt his skin burn as he eased out the empty case and let the working parts slide forward again. Fixed. But too late.

He could make out the faces of his men now. Their bodies were dirty, their necks, their clothes were sculpted out of dirt. Sweat had carved river deltas through the dirt on their faces. Dirt encrusted their lips.

Above, Steve's silhouette was firing in the direction of the RPG.

'Did you slot him?' Dave asked on PRR. Instead of a reply there was a bang. The loudest fucking bang. The most agonized scream. The world's scariest roller-coaster plunging off the tracks. A superhuman force threw Dave to the front of the Vector. His shoulder smashed against the side of the vehicle. He looked up. The sky was a deep, deep blue. Its beauty was punctured by shards of metal.

There was a rag doll flying through the air. The doll looked like Steve Buckle. His body formed a perfect arc, an arc of helplessness. He flew slowly, like an empty suit floating through deep, blue

4

water. When his leg came off, its trajectory had a peculiarly graceful beauty. Then the body was hurtling towards earth and there was
another body falling too. Dave had time to register that this was
Jordan Nelson before he took cover from the hail of fire now
directed at the exposed men in the shattered Vector.

He looked around. How many more men had he lost? But they
were all there, faces bloody and dirty and shocked, looking at him,
waiting for him to lead them.

'You two, get out there, sort them out.' Dave shoved Mal and
Angus towards the casualties. Moments later, blue smoke was
billowing around their twisted bodies. One of them was screaming
in agony. Through the roar of pain, Dave could hear the rage to
live. It had to be Steve.

'3 Section, cover the casualties. 2 Section and the rest of 1 Section
get down that street, clear it and find the bastard with the RPG; he
took a round in the leg.'

Led by Corporal Sol Kasanita, the men headed off down the alley
where Dave had pinged the RPG.

The boss was telling HQ: 'I have times two tango one casualties.
Repeat, times two tango one casualties.'

Dave hoped there was a Chinook ready to go at Bastion. The
emergency team would have to move right now if the casualties
were to make it back to the field hospital inside the golden hour.
Outside that hour, their chances of survival turned from gold to
dust. Just like everything else in this fucking place.

Riflemen Angus McCall and Mal Bilaal were poised over Steve's
body. Where Steve's left leg should have been there was just a massive,
blood-covered cauliflower. Blood flowed from it, blood covered everyone's clothes, blood soaked the fine brown dust of the street.

'Shut the fuck up, you wanker!' Mal shouted at the screaming
victim, who happened to be one of his best mates. He had opened
Steve's thigh pocket now and Dave could see him pulling the big
morphine syringe from it. Angus was holding Steve down.

'I said fucking shut up!' Mal roared over the clamour of the fire
fight. He was shoving the autojet into Steve's remaining leg. Almost
instantly, Steve fell silent.

Steve's body armour was covered with blood and shrapnel. His
clothes were torn, his face lacerated and his helmet pushed back off

his head. With the morphine in, Angus and Mal went to work. Mal's hand found the artery inside the hideous bloody gap at the top of Steve's left leg, scissor clamp at the ready, while Angus tightened the tourniquet.

A medic had reached Jordan Nelson. The rifleman lay still in the dusty street. He looked as though he'd fallen asleep on duty, except that most of his clothes were missing and his lower body was charred almost beyond recognition. A couple of lads from 3 Section and the medic were leaning over him and they were strangely still too. Dave wondered if it was possible to survive burns so severe.

The zap numbers of the casualties had been relayed to the Medical Emergency Response Team at Camp Bastion where the doctor would already be in a Land Rover heading for the helicopter, maybe already receiving details of the casualties' blood groups and allergies on his hand-held. But for the Chinook to get here, the contact had to be over. And it showed no sign of ending. If anything, now that the convoy had been halted, the ambush was more intense.

Dave had found a good firing position inside the ruined hulk of the Vector. He had also found Jordan Nelson's machine gun wedged between a slab of armour plating and a brown mud wall. He grabbed it without hope and was amazed when it worked. Far away, in a second-storey window, across two walls and the yard which they protected, he caught a glimpse of movement. Feeling a surge of satisfaction, he fired. A body slumped from the window.

He glanced up, wondering where the air support was. Eight minutes must have passed by now and the casualties needed to get out of here. The boss had also requested help from A Company, who were currently installed at the FOB and scheduled to leave this evening. Maybe they were too busy packing.

Dave moved around to the side street just as Sol and the lads emerged from it, pushing two prisoners. Jamie Dermott had the RPG – with the grenade removed – and an AK47, mag off and made safe.

'Get those fucking bastards moving,' Dave yelled.

One of the fucking bastards wore long blue robes, now clotted with blood. The man's leathery face was twisted in pain and fear.

His leg dragged. His left leg. A leg for a leg, Dave thought. Fair one.

The firing was deafening now. The enemy seemed to have trebled in number.

A couple more lads followed with a second prisoner. He was younger than the first and more resistant. He treated Dave to a sullen glare and he dragged his feet deliberately slowly through the fire fight, confident of his own safety and exposing his captors as long as possible.

'Get on with it,' Dave roared. He jammed the prisoner in the back with his weapon. He felt angry. In one second Steve's life, Leanne's and the kids' lives had all been changed. Nothing would ever be the same for them. He wished he could shoot the man. Feeling the weapon in his back, the prisoner jumped forward, as if he'd read Dave's mind.

Suddenly, the air support emerged from an empty sky and flew so low that Dave could see the helmeted pilot at the controls. He'd been jumped by Harriers before but it was still impossible to prepare yourself for the intensity of the noise, for the sheer violence and physicality of such a massive tonnage of metal moving at the speed of sound only metres above your head.

Then, when the head and heart of every man on the ground was fit to burst, the Harrier evaporated as suddenly as it had appeared. The roar of its engines melted into the thudding heartbeats of those beneath.

Dave continued to watch the sky. The Harrier was no bigger than a distant bird of prey now, hovering over the faraway hills. Dave waited. Sure enough, after only a few breaths, it was right above their heads again, dimming the sun, screeching over the town in a vengeful fury, cracking the mud walls and shaking the ground.

And then it was gone.

It left a deep silence. Wherever the enemy was hidden, they did not move and they did not fire. The soldiers were still too. The whole town was motionless.

When rotor blades beat the air, the boss talked the Instant Response Team down into a square, maybe a market place, just ahead of them. Before it had touched the ground Mal and Angus were running Steve on a stretcher, two men from 3 Section close behind them with Jordan, to the hot tailgate of the Chinook.

The doctor and his team were waiting. A rear gunner watched over them with a GPMG. Once the casualties were handed over, the medical team's focus was immediate and total and there was nothing for the lads from 1 Platoon to do but return to the convoy. The platoon watched in silence as the thudding blades hauled the big machine into the air. They glimpsed the doctor at work as the Chinook rose and turned for Kandahar.

The A Company team appeared. Dave wanted to say something sarcastic about their late arrival but they were leaving today after countless similar contacts and he guessed thoughts of home must be overwhelming their will to rush into battle. They towed out the mangled Vector and the rest of the convoy started to follow them to the FOB.

Dave was about to jump on board when he saw something lying in the dusty street. Something familiar. He grabbed Steve's leg, tucked it under his arm and leaped into the back of the last Vector as it pulled away.

Except for the boss updating HQ on the net, nobody spoke. Finally, as they neared the FOB, Dave asked about the casualties. He was relieved to hear that they were still both T1s. If either had reached the point where no one could help them, they'd have slipped down the emergency agenda to T4.

He remembered the way Steve's leg had sailed so gracefully through the air. It must only have taken a few seconds but he remembered it in slow motion, as though it had taken an hour. And at the end of the hour, two bodies lying in the street.

Jordan Nelson had recently joined 1 Platoon from another battalion. He was liked, but not yet fully integrated with his new section. He was unmarried but had talked about his family in Watford a lot. He was the oldest of three boys. Or was it four? Jordan talked about his younger brothers as though he was their father. Dave imagined the mother and brothers answering the doorbell, standing in a hallway full of muddy football boots and hooks piled with too many coats. He tried not to think about the silence in the hallway when the Families Officer told them the news.

A Families Officer would also be standing on Steve and Leanne's doorstep back in Wiltshire in a few hours. The other women in the street would be at the window; they'd see the Families Officer ring the bell and fear the worst. Dave's wife Jenny would be sure to see. Leanne and Steve lived right across the road. Sol's wife Adi was a few doors up but she would know, because she always knew everything. Jamie's wife, Agnieszka, who lived up a side street, would probably guess what was going on, even though her English wasn't that good. And like all the others, she'd cry. Both with sadness for Leanne and relief for herself because it wasn't her own husband who was maimed for life.

'You all right, Sarge?' Jamie Dermott asked quietly.

Dave was thinking how only the stoppage in his weapon had brought him down into the Vector just before the bomb had exploded. A few seconds earlier and it would have been him flying through the air to the left while his leg flew to the right. The stoppage had saved him. It had cost Steve his leg and maybe his life.

'Sarge?' said Jamie.

Dave's escape today had been the narrowest. It should have been him. And at this moment, thinking of Steve and Leanne and the twins, he wished it had been him. He shut his eyes.

He said: 'I'm fine.' His throat was so dry the words scratched their way out of his mouth. He imagined his home, in a quiet street in the quiet camp in England. It seemed nearer than Afghanistan. He knew that, in a few days, the madness of Helmand Province would be home and quiet Wiltshire would be some strange, faraway place.

The Vector proceeded to the Forward Operating Base in total silence.

Chapter Two

THE DIFFERENCE BETWEEN JAMIE BEING AROUND AND JAMIE NOT BEING around was that everything went wrong the minute he walked out of the door. The dishwasher had spluttered to a halt before his plane had even landed in Afghanistan. It had been the same with Iraq: the washing machine had stopped, the bathroom pipes had been blocked and the phone had gone kaput within three weeks of his departure.

Agnieszka could cope with the dishwasher because in Poland she had managed without one. But now it was the car. There was a clunk from deep within its bowels. It was the kind of noise you couldn't ignore, the kind which said the car would stop on the motorway just when she was taking Luke to the hospital tomorrow. It was the sort of clunk which said that Jamie had gone and nothing was going to be right until he came back.

So now she was on her way to the garage. She'd shovelled the big pushchair into the back. Luke was crying. And halfway there she realized she should have rung first. Which would have meant speaking on the phone. Which she hated because communicating in English over a phone line was about fifteen times harder than when she could see people pulling their faces into shapes which filled all the gaps in her understanding.

There was nowhere to park at the garage. There was nowhere to park in the road outside. She hovered, wondering what to do. A car hooted behind her.

She drove slowly around the block. Only one parking place, a

10

whole street away. Luke was asleep now. She would wake him if she lifted him into the pushchair and then he would cry again. And she would arrive at the garage and they would say: 'Well, where's the car?' Then they would probably give her an appointment in two weeks.

Agnieszka put her head on the steering wheel and wept. When Jamie was at home, loving her, adoring Luke, taking him when he cried, holding him while he had a fit, fixing broken gutters and unblocking pipes, looking after them both, then life was good. But he never was at home. There had been Catterick, Canada, Iraq, Kenya and now Afghanistan. Afghanistan. Just the word made her cry. It sounded like Pashtu for sadness.

Even after the sobbing stopped, the tears kept falling silently.

She finally managed to pat her face dry and check her makeup. Her mascara hadn't run because she had forgotten to put any on. Good. She reached into her bag, shook the tiny tube and rolled the brush under her eyelashes. She watched herself in the mirror. Despite the tears her eyes had retained their penetrating blue. Her long lashes curled around the mascara.

'You don't need that stuff,' Jamie had told her the first time he saw her putting on her makeup.

'I need for give me confidence,' she said.

She disentangled the feat of engineering that was Luke's pushchair, smoothed the sheepskin liner and lifted him into it very, very gently. At first she thought she had completed this manoeuvre without waking him but then he opened his eyes wide, stared at her and screwed his face into a tight ball. She braced herself. A second later, his roars of displeasure began. Tears burst out of his face like a sprinkler. She hoped he wouldn't have a fit.

She walked towards the garage. By the time she got there Luke was still shrieking. She knew any discussion about the car would be impossible so she kept on walking. She walked around the block. When she passed the plumbing supply shop, someone inside wolf-whistled. Perhaps she had imagined it. But then she glimpsed herself in the tile-shop window. Her legs looked very long today; it was amazing how they seemed to change length. So maybe the whistle had been for her. She flicked her hair back over her shoulders.

Back at the garage, Luke was still wailing so she decided to walk around the block again. This time, as she passed the plumbing supply shop, the whistle was unmistakable. It came during one of the pauses in Luke's cries. She kept right on walking as though she hadn't heard, murmuring a few words to Luke to show that she was oblivious to it.

By the time she reached the garage again, Luke was quiet. Should she go in now? What if his tears came in bursts like her own and he started up again? She decided to walk around a third time.

She glanced surreptitiously into the plumbing shop as she drew near. A young man, tall with a shaven head, grinned at her familiarly from behind the glass. As if he knew her. When all she had done was simply pass his shop a couple of times. She didn't smile back. She found herself blushing. Supposing he thought that she was walking past deliberately again and again?

This possibility was so shameful that she felt she owed a few Aves to the Holy Virgin. Muttering them under her breath she returned to the garage. Luke was fast asleep now.

Hesitantly she pushed him into the dark workshop. A car was raised high on a ramp. A man stood underneath it.

'Erm . . . I bring my car here because . . .' Her voice sounded small in this great cavern of a place. Someone in the corner was spinning tyres on a machine which sounded like a gun firing.

'You shouldn't be in here! Reception's around the side!' the man shouted. The machine-gun noise did not stop. Agnieszka did not understand. She hesitated.

The man gesticulated angrily. 'Round the side!'

She nodded, certain he was telling her to leave, uncertain where to go. Another small humiliation. Until she'd met Jamie, just going into a shop and asking for something was a humiliation. She emerged from almost any situation red-faced, struggling to understand English people and their language. Then along came Jamie and everything changed. When he wasn't away in Catterick, Canada, Iraq, Kenya or Afghanistan.

She walked around the building heaving Luke with difficulty between cars and over kerbs. Then she saw a door and somehow manoeuvred the pushchair inside. This must be the right place. It smelled of workshop but aspired to be an office. The scent of oil and car parts reminded her of her father back in Poland.

He had worked in a small engineering firm until his death.

A man behind the counter discussed a bill with a customer, who was running his finger down the invoice, pausing at each figure. Agnieszka did not care to listen. It was almost summer but she was cold in her T-shirt and it was warm in the office. She closed her eyes and the men's voices sounded like a radio station broadcast from far away in a foreign language. It would be easy to imagine she was in her father's workshop now, a child again, warmed by the brazier, lulled by that comfortable oily smell, falling asleep in her nest of rough blankets while adult words and adult voices washed over her.

The previous customer was leaving, pinning himself against the wall in order to navigate around the pushchair.

'Can I help you?' asked the man behind the desk. She opened her eyes.

'Like to sit down?'

He smiled at her and gestured to a tiny waiting area with a couple of dirty armchairs, a coffee machine and last week's free newspaper. 'You look knackered standing there with your eyes shut.'

Agnieszka stared at him.

'Come on . . .' His face was friendly. 'I'm having a tea; I'll get you one too.'

Agnieszka found herself squeezing into the waiting area and sinking onto one of the chairs. She glanced at Luke. He slept deeply. His head had fallen to the side.

'Milk? Sugar?'

She nodded. A moment later the man handed her a plastic cup, stirring its contents vigorously. He removed the spoon and the tea continued to turn in slowing circles.

The man sat down in the other chair, his hands cupped round his own tea. The two chairs were so close together that it was hard to avoid his legs. Agnieszka swung hers out to the side.

'Now, what can we do for you?'

'My car not working.' Her voice was hoarse. The cup warmed her hands.

'Won't it start?' He sounded as though he knew how your whole day was ruined when your car didn't start.

'It start but it make terrible noise and smell not too good,'

13

she said. 'I think it stop any minute, maybe on motorway.'

'Yeah, in the fast lane, that's when they usually let you down.'

'I go on motorway tomorrow morning to hospital so I think I come this afternoon to get car fixed but maybe you tell me not today. Also, no parking. So my car is far away.'

'Which hospital then, the Prince of Wales?'

'Yes. My baby see specialist at Prince of Wales Hospital.'

'That sounds like a bit of a worry.'

Yes it was. Tomorrow the specialist would ask questions and take notes without smiling. Jamie was in Afghanistan. Her mother was ill in Poland. Her parents-in-law barely spoke to her. The dishwasher was broken. Now the car was planning to stop the moment she got into the fast lane of the motorway. It was all a bit of a worry. It was enough of a worry to make her cry. She did not trust herself to speak so she just nodded.

'How far away is this car of yours?' he asked gently.

'Afghanistan.'

'The car? In Afghanistan?' The man raised his eyebrows and grinned at her so comically that suddenly she felt herself smiling.

'I thought you said how far away my husband is!'

'Oh, he's in the army, is he?'

She nodded. 'Husband in Afghanistan. Car in street that way. Not in first street. Next street.'

'Elm Road?'

She wasn't sure but she nodded.

'Well, let's go and see if we can't sort this problem out. Then you can get to the hospital tomorrow no trouble.'

He stood up, smiled at her again and she smiled back. Here was a good man. Agnieszka felt the same relief she felt when Jamie came home. Everything was going to be all right.

Chapter Three

AS THEY JUMPED OUT OF THE VECTORS EACH MAN STOOD STILL AND felt the silence. No firing. No vehicle noise. No movement.

Dave counted them. As well as himself, the boss and the company sergeant major, there were twenty-six men: three already undermanned sections of 1 Platoon plus a signaller, an engineer, a medic, a sniper and a mortar man. He had counted twenty-eight into the Vectors at Bastion and had expected to count twenty-eight out at FOB Senzhiri. Twenty-six was a bitter number today.

The prisoners remained in one of the vehicles and Dave put a couple of men from 3 Section in charge of guarding them. He took a quick look at the Taliban fighters first.

'Have you seen to his leg?' he asked the medic.

'Yeah, nothing much wrong with it.'

'I thought he took one of my rounds.'

'You missed.'

'Shit. So why all the blood and limping?'

'The limp's what footballers do when the other team looks like they might score a goal. The blood's because you nicked his shin. But it's nothing much.'

Dave stared at the handcuffed prisoners. They stared back at him. Since the contact they had lost some of their fear. Now they tried to muster their dignity. One of them spoke to Dave in Pashtu, spitting out the words like a curse.

'Thank you very much and fuck you too,' Dave said politely.

15

'Make sure they get some water,' Company Sergeant Major Kila told the lads guarding them.

Then he and Dave and the boss strode off into the network of tents and old mud-walled buildings, their feet kicking up little clouds of dust.

The platoon stretched. They breathed the afternoon air deeply. They spoke little. The men who had been in the explosion found the event replaying inside their heads, felt the helplessness of their limbs in the force of the blast again, experienced the same mixture of fear and resignation.

'I thought it was the fucking end,' said Rifleman Mal Bilaal.

'So did I,' said Rifleman Angus McCall. 'I thought what my dad would say if I died before I've even had a chance to brass anyone up.'

'I couldn't understand why I was taking such a fucking long time to die,' said Lance Corporal Billy Finn. 'And then I realized I was still alive.'

Rifleman Jamie Dermott had believed that he was dying, too. He remembered how he had stretched out his arms as the blast hit him as though he was stretching out for Agnieszka and the baby.

Even the men who weren't in the blast and weren't actively thinking about what had happened to Riflemen Nelson and Buckle felt the knowledge of it lodged inside them. And anyone who had seen their bodies flying through the air knew he would not forget it, even if he never talked about it again to anyone. Today's contact had been a warning of what was to come.

Jamie Dermott leaned back against the wheel of the Vector and closed his eyes. He was thinking that even Dave, who had years of training and experience and had seen two tours of Iraq, had probably fired more rounds today than in all of his previous contacts put together. Well, they had joined up to fight. They had trained to fight. And now that's what they were going to do. No one would admit that the suddenness and ferocity of today's contact had been a shock. But it had.

Jamie reached surreptitiously for a picture of his wife and baby. He liked to look at it during odd moments when Wiltshire began to seem far away. He liked to remind himself that there was another world, less barren than this one.

He glanced at his watch. Four thirty in Afghanistan. Midday at home. Agnieszka would be in the kitchen now, maybe moving smoothly around Luke's high chair on her long, long legs, spoon in hand, singing softly under her breath. For the next six months, she would be there and he would be here. Six months. Luke would change a lot by the time he got back. Jamie would have experiences which he couldn't imagine now and which he would probably remember for the rest of his life. He sighed and looked around at the FOB, a bleak collection of isocontainers and tents and mud buildings that would become home.

1 Platoon lit cigarettes and found a tap and refilled their Camelbaks and water bottles and drank deeply. In a movement that had already become so instinctive they didn't even think about it, they ran their fingers round the top of the bottle to wipe off the sand before they swigged from it. The water was warm. A few people organized a brew.

Jamie wasn't hungry but he could work out where the cookhouse must be from the activity of A Company, now emerging from their tents and heading to the centre of the FOB. Lance Corporal Finn and Rifleman Bilaal worked it out too.

'Fancy some scoff?' Finn said. Mal nodded. Corporal Sol Kasanita, their section commander, was looking away. They slipped behind the Vectors and around the back of some mud buildings.

The other men were watching A Company.

'They're big blokes . . .'

'Marines,' Sol Kasanita said.

'I thought they looked like boot necks,' said Angus.

Even Dave, touring the base, was taken aback by how much bigger and older and tougher the outgoing A Company looked than his own men. He glanced back at his platoon, lounging around, smoking and gulping tea by the vehicles, looking skinny even in body armour. And they looked younger still because they were clean-shaven new arrivals while the commandos hadn't shaved for weeks and their uniforms were shabby and worn.

The outgoing company sergeant major, who was showing them around, indicated the cookhouse. Dave glanced inside. Among the hulks of A Company were two noticeably smaller men.

17

'Lance Corporal Finn and Rifleman Bilaal get out of there NOW,' Dave roared.

'But, Sarge, we were only—'

'Out! You're on boil-in-the-bag until A Company goes. *Now get back to the wagons!*'

It was always the same. Whenever there was food, you'd always find soldiers doing their own strike op on the cookhouse.

Mal and Finn went back to the group, persuading two members of A Company to accompany them.

'Thank fuck you're just the advance party. If they'd sent the whole shitload there wouldn't be room to breathe here,' said the men from A Company.

'The rest are coming in by air when you go,' Finn said.

One of the men pointed at a ginger-haired rifleman from 2 Section. 'Careful, mate. We've had some big mortars incoming lately and two of them landed right where you're standing!'

The lad skipped rapidly to one side to a chorus of laughter.

'Come on, bruv,' said Mal, offering the marines cigarettes. 'Tell us a bit about the place. Can we use that gym over there?'

He pointed at treadmills, exercise bikes and other equipment arranged in two neat lines, gleaming in the afternoon sun.

One of the commandos took a cigarette. 'That's the civilian area. The contractors live in the isoboxes.'

The gym was surrounded on two sides by isoboxes which looked as if a big crane had lifted them off the back of a ship straight into the heart of the desert. They were arranged in an L-shape with the spine of the L turned sulkily against the rest of the camp.

'The contractors have got air conditioning.' There was no mistaking his disgust.

'They haven't found a way to air-condition the gym yet.' He drew on his cigarette. 'Since it's in the open air. But it's just a matter of time.'

'Is that gym just for the civilians, then?' Finn asked.

'We can use it too. So long as we don't disturb them.'

'Oh, yeah,' his companion said. 'No disturbing the civilians. No whistling at Emily. Unless she whistles at you first.'

Mal swallowed hard. 'Who's Emily?'

The marine took a long, slow drag and rolled his eyes. His mate licked his lips.

'What can we say about Emmers?' They shrugged theatrically.

'Well, let's just say she's hot . . .' said the smoker.

'Very hot.'

'In fact, she's a sex grenade.'

'Waiting to explode. Any fucking second.'

Finn grinned and sucked on the end of his roll-up. 'Maybe it's not going to be too bad here after all.'

The marine finished his cigarette and threw it to the ground. 'Oh, it's bad. But Emmers has a way to make you feel better. Know what I mean?'

The lads knew what he meant.

'Senzhiri? Sin City more like.' The marines turned back to the cookhouse. 'Just listen for Emmers's whistle and you'll see what we mean.'

1 Platoon looked a lot more cheerful now.

'I'm glad to hear the British Army is beginning to recognize our needs . . .' Finn tried to inhale the last of his roll-up.

Sol shook his head. 'They're winding you up, Finny.'

'She's here doing civilian work,' Jamie said. 'Not to entertain the troops.'

There was a yell from Company Sergeant Major Kila for the prisoners to be unloaded. He handed two pairs of blacked-out goggles to the 3 Section guards and the detainees were led away across the FOB, stumbling sometimes, hands tied in front of them.

Their appearance caused a sensation. People moving to the cookhouse stopped in their tracks. Everyone stared. A few came over to ask for the story.

'I've been here six months and I've never seen a choggie close-up until now . . .'

'I've never seen one at all . . .'

'So you're the cook and you don't get out of the kitchen?' Angus McCall said.

'No, mate, I've been on patrol almost every fucking day. You can get brassed up by ragheads but you just don't see them.'

The whole platoon stared at him. 'You never see the flipflops? Ever?'

19

'A choggie boot up a tree or a shadow behind a hedge, that's the closest you fucking get.'

'And they clear up their dead so fast you hardly even see a fucking body.'

The platoon talked about today's ambush and Jamie watched A Company's faces as they listened. These men were tired. Numb. They looked as though if they'd wounded an insurgent carrying an RPG, they might not have bothered to search for him down a side street.

'You're ready to go home, mate,' he said to the commando standing nearest.

The man nodded.

'I don't want to waste my time decompressing in Cyprus. I just want to get back.'

That was how Jamie felt right now when he thought about Agnieszka. And he'd only just arrived.

They started the vehicles and the pressure cookers and opened their boil-in-the-bags. After eating they sat around in the evening sun. The heat was still merciless although it was almost night and barely summer.

'What's it going to be like in a couple of months?'

'How're we going to carry forty, sixty, eighty pounds of kit in this?'

They had another brew and smoked and farted while they waited for Dave to call them.

At last he did.

'Prayers. In that building over there.'

The men stared at a small, low shed with sagging roof and ancient mud walls. It looked a thousand years old.

'The Cowshed,' Dave said. 'They say you can still smell the shit.'

Sitting on the floor of the Cowshed, packed in tightly with the rest of the platoon and their Bergens, Jamie thought he could detect the smell of long-departed goat. Or was it just the whiff of rancid soldier in a tight space?

He watched the new boss with curiosity. Second Lieutenant Weeks was standing at the front, clearing his throat and looking nervous. Jamie felt sorry for him. Fresh out of Sandhurst, he'd only met his men for the first time a few days ago at Bastion. He'd faced a fire fight on the way here and two men were already down. It hadn't been a good start. Thank God he had Dave for his platoon sergeant.

Dave was waiting for all three sections of the platoon to file in. He was rocking impatiently onto his toes and then back on his heels. 'Get a move on, you lot,' he barked, glaring at the last men in.

'There's no room with all this kit on the floor, Sarge,' someone protested.

'Then make fucking room.'

Jamie watched Dave counting the men. The Officer Commanding of the outgoing company had expressed admiration for the way they'd taken two detainees but he knew Dave would happily have traded them for Steve Buckle and Jordan Nelson.

Before everyone was seated, Dave began.

'We had a tough time getting here, lads. We'll give you news of Steve and Jordan as soon as we get it. Most of us didn't think we'd be firing that many rounds so soon but you responded well. I was proud of you, and pleased to see your training pay off.

'Unfortunately, because of the contact, A Company can't get away today after all and the rest of our company can't get in. The handover has been postponed until tomorrow and that makes the FOB a tad overcrowded tonight. We just have to keep out of the way until they go. So it's boil-in-the-bag until A Company's out of here.'

There was a groan. Jamie imagined how A Company must be feeling. Bags packed, ready to go, minds on home and still stuck at base.

Dave moved aside for the boss. Gordon Weeks tried to step into the space Dave had left him. But without Dave's energy and certainty to fill it, that space was suddenly immense.

'Er . . . thank you, Sergeant . . . er . . . that is indeed the case. Welcome to FOB Senzhiri. Popularly known, I gather, as FOB Sin City. Er, because of the crowding situation, I suggest that we sleep around the Vectors tonight, or until A Company has vacated. Now. Er . . . Um . . .'

Dave's face remained expressionless. But Jamie could guess what he was thinking. Weeks just didn't know how to speak to his men.

21

He'd already tried at Bastion and had been a mumbling wreck. He wasn't doing much better today.

'Er . . . well . . .' The young officer's face reddened as he floundered. The men began to look at Dave for help. Boss Weeks seized this idea.

'Er, um . . . I think perhaps we'll start with Sergeant Henley's, um, health and safety information,' he said at last.

'OK, lads,' Dave said. 'The first thing I want to say is about washing. There are civilian contractors here and the boss is going to talk to you about them. But remember this. Those civilians get to shower every day; you don't. That's the way it is. I don't want to hear anyone whingeing about it. You take showers every other day at most, and for no longer than three minutes, or there won't be enough water. I'm only going to shave every three or four days. No one should shave more than that.

'You've all got sun block: use it. You've all got water: drink it. Lots of it, more than you think you need. Aim for nine litres a day and definitely not less than six. When we're going out on a short patrol, take at least three. Fill your Camelbaks and take bottles too. It's fucking hot today and it's going to get hotter. Out there in fifty degrees with a lot of kit you could die if you don't drink. So drink.

'Get out of your boots whenever you can. I don't want to catch any lazy bastards who can't be bothered to take off their boots before they go to sleep. That is very, very stupid. Get the air to your toes on every possible occasion. You've got foot powder: use it. Your heels crack, you'll be miserable and no one's going to be sympathetic.

'Your hands could also crack in this heat and when you use gun oil those cracks are going to hurt. A lot. You've got cream. No one will think you're stupid if you use it. They'll think you're stupid if you don't.'

No one shuffled or stared unseeingly or had that distant look in his eyes which meant he was thinking about food or home or sex. Everyone in the Cowshed was alert and listening to every word. Jamie saw the boss looking at Dave with respect and amazement. He was studying his sergeant's technique. Jamie could have explained to him that there was no technique. Dave was just a man other men listened to.

'Right,' Dave said. 'The boss is going to tell you about Sin City.'
Gordon Weeks coughed.

'The sergeant has mentioned the, er, civilians. What you really need to remember is that FOB Senzhiri is not just here for military reasons but strategic reasons also. There is a multinational contractor team working from the base on an oil and gas project and they must be treated with respect. Now, er, I understand relations between the soldiers here at the base and the contractors have sometimes been, er, strained in the past but, remember, the civilians are not your enemy. They are French, American, er—'

'Sir, did you say something about a civilian called Emily who's French?' Finn called. 'We can't hear too well at the back!'

There was a rustle of anticipation at the mention of Emily's name. The boss looked confused.

Dave was quick. 'No, Lance Corporal, clean out your ears. He said the civilians are not your enemy and some of them are French. There is no civilian called Emily. Now shut up.'

'Oh,' said the boss. 'But there is. I've just met her. She seems very nice.'

There was more rustling and suppressed laughter.

'Was she, by any chance, whistling, sir?'

'Shut up,' Dave growled. 'We'll take questions at the end.'

'Anyway,' the boss went on, 'the point is that the civilians must not feel harassed or annoyed by us in any way. Please don't speak to them or attempt to strike up a conversation unless they speak to you first. Remember that we are here to protect them and that's our first task. Their exploration work, er, necessitates frequent field trips and it is our duty to ensure they can, er, carry out their work safely and successfully.'

Jamie thought: Just tell us not to piss off the civilians. He hoped Dave would run over all the points again afterwards.

'The contractors have access to alcohol. We, of course, are dry. Apparently problems have arisen when civilians have invited soldiers to, er, partake, er, with them.'

The men exchanged glances. No need to ask which civilian liked to booze with the lads. It had to be Emily.

'The rule is, even when offered drink, please don't take it. However, one bonus, well, a few bonuses, we can thank the

23

contractors for, are the gym, er, the covered toilets to spare their blushes and, er, the catering staff. We have, er, Mr Taregue Masud in charge of the cookhouse who I understand has been something of a catering legend since the Falklands.' The boss turned to Dave. 'Do you know him, Sergeant?'

'Yes, sir, from Iraq. A very good cook.'

'Er, let me, er, remind you that, while protecting civilian operations is our prime objective, I should perhaps reiterate that we are also here to reinforce the pressing demands of our NATO commitment.'

The men looked at Dave as though Boss Weeks was speaking another language and Dave was his interpreter. Dave remained expressionless. The young officer cleared his throat again. It was hot in the Cowshed and his cheeks were round and red. He looks younger than me, Jamie thought.

'Ahem. The people of Afghanistan are not our enemies. Despite the unpleasant welcome we received in the town this afternoon, most are glad of our presence. Er, without us they would be over-run by the Taliban, many of whom come from faraway countries, do not speak their language and wish to dominate and suppress them.

'Um . . . er . . . the people of Afghanistan want peace and by holding back the Taliban we can support their elected government and bring stability to their country. But the Taliban are driven by religious fervour and hatred of the West, they observe no rules and, er . . . er . . . they are formidable opponents.

'I have been asked to remind you of an unfortunate statistic that we should bear in mind throughout our work here.'

He took a deep breath.

'One man in ten will go home in a body bag or badly injured. One in ten.'

For the first time, Boss Weeks stopped staring over the heads of the men he commanded. He looked directly into their eyes. His gaze slid from face to face, row to row. All eyes were upon him. Everyone was still. There was silence.

'There are about thirty men in this room now,' said the boss. 'Which means it is highly likely that three of us won't be going home.'

The boss remained silent. As the silence continued, his words penetrated more deeply. Faces reddened. Men fiddled with their boot laces. They avoided looking at each other. They stopped thinking: It won't be me. They began to think: Don't let it be me. They stared at the ground. They couldn't look at each other knowing that three of them would die here, wondering: which three?

Chapter Four

BOSS WEEKS HEADED STRAIGHT FOR THE MUD-WALLED ROOM WHERE the detainees were being questioned.

Just before he entered, he was halted by a scream, a horrible, animal sound. What could Iain Kila be doing to the Afghans? Gordon Weeks barely knew the Company Sergeant Major. The man had been polite when they had first met at Bastion but he had made it clear that, as the veteran of countless contacts, he regarded Weeks as just another in a long line of young, inexperienced and uninteresting officers.

Inside, the boss was surprised to find that Kila was nowhere near the two Afghans. The CSM stood silently, hands on hips, in a shadowy corner with the CSM of A Company. At a battered table in the centre sat the blue-robed prisoner, his wrists still tied in front of him.

Far from being terrorized by big men, he was being questioned by two small women. One was speaking to the detainee in a soft voice. The other was watching silently. Second Lieutenant Gordon Weeks understood instantly, instinctively, without thinking about it, the way he didn't have to think before firing back at the enemy, that this silent woman was beautiful. He had to stare at her. There was no choice.

She was leaning against the edge of the table. He could tell that her figure was slim and well shaped beneath her body armour. She was brown-skinned, large-eyed, dark-haired. Her cheeks slanted, her jawline was sharp. Weeks thought she must be used to every

26

man at the base staring at her all the time but, when she became aware of his gaze, she turned to him. Their eyes met. Her look was icy and it said that she found his stare intrusive. He felt his face redden. He looked away from her at once.

The seated woman had fair hair and sharp features. She wore a Royal Military Police badge. She was pretty enough too, but in a more ordinary way. She glanced up at him. But the flow and rhythm of her words to the detainee did not falter.

CSM Kila came over.

'What are they saying?' Weeks asked in an undertone.

'Fuck knows,' Kila said.

'Aren't these women supposed to interpret for you while you conduct the interrogation?'

Kila glared at him. 'They act as interpreters. But Jean's Royal Military Police, Asma's Intelligence Corps.'

'Was it the detainee who screamed?'

'Yeah. But nobody hurt him.'

'Then why . . . ?'

'They're headfucking him,' Kila said.

Weeks tried not to show how much he disliked the man's language and the aggressive way he used it.

'How long have these women been here?'

'Long enough for the CSM from A Company to know they're hot shit. You noticed Asma, sir. Admiring her Intelligence?'

Weeks avoided his meaningful glance.

The atmosphere around the table was electric. Asma leaned over the man and joined in the questioning. Weeks strained to hear her voice. It was without harshness. The women passed words back and forth like skilled footballers passing the ball. He wondered what they were saying. They spent a lot of time agreeing with each other, that much was obvious. The gentleness of their tone was eerie because the effect of their words was dramatic. The detainee responded as though to a series of blows.

Suddenly the man cried out and started to talk. At first he muttered, looking down at his feet. Then his voice grew stronger.

He was thin and his bones protruded. His face was clouded by anger and resentment.

'What's he saying?' Kila asked.

'Just a minute.' Asma broke into English. 'Give us a bit of bleeding time. We're getting there.'

She obviously was English. She had some sort of accent, maybe London. Disappointingly rough, thought Weeks. Although she didn't look it.

The detainee sighed and said something and the women backed away. Asma looked at her watch. She pointed to something and the man turned his chair to get a closer look. Weeks tried to see what she had shown him, without success. He looked at Iain Kila for guidance.

'Saying his prayers. He got disoriented by the blindfold so she had to tell him which way to Mecca.'

Nobody took their eyes off the prisoner as he prayed.

'Looking good.' The other CSM walked over to them. 'Looking very good.'

'So what the hell is going on?' Kila asked.

'We've passed the first stage,' Jean said. She had a Scottish accent.

'Which is?' Weeks asked.

'I'm visiting my relatives and I just got caught up in the firing, I don't know anything about it.'

'So what's he saying now?' Kila asked.

'He's telling us about Taliban activities in this area. But he's not telling us exactly where.'

'The OC wants it all.'

'He'll have it. Don't forget, we haven't even started on the other one yet.'

Weeks listened to her soft Scots accent and wondered how she had learned fluent Pashtu.

'Um . . . doesn't the detainee have a serious leg injury?'

'Not that serious.' Kila's tone was defensive.

'But he was hit!' Weeks said.

The woman paused. 'Skimmed. Not hit. And he's received medical attention.' Her voice was stiff, as though the officer had made an accusation.

She moved back to the table and spoke quietly to her colleague. Asma kept her back to Weeks and continued to ignore him. When the prisoner had finished praying, she invited him to return to the table. She started to talk. Her tone was coaxing.

Suddenly the man's voice rose. He began to shout. He jumped to his feet and roared hoarsely at the beautiful, dark woman. His arms struggled against his plasticuffs. His face thickened with anger.

Asma produced a pistol, so quickly that Weeks hardly saw her. She darted to the prisoner and held it against his head. The man froze. His speech was halted mid-sentence. His eyes stared straight ahead. The room was silent. Jean moved up to his other side and began to whisper in his ear as Asma slid the safety off the pistol. The man heard it. He still didn't move. Jean carried on whispering.

The detainee swallowed. He sank back down into his chair. And began to talk. The women took it in turns to ask him questions. Boss Weeks recognized the same question more than once. The pistol did not move from his head.

'What's he saying?' Kila was almost beside himself with impatience. But the two women ignored him.

Gordon Weeks was shocked. He waited for Asma to put away the pistol. It remained firmly pressed against the prisoner's temple.

'Isn't this a bit . . . unethical?'

Kila turned to look him full in the face for the first time. He seemed to have trouble focusing, as if the young officer was so insignificant that he was barely visible to the naked eye.

'This man's got information. We want it.' His lips hardly moved.

For a few moments, Weeks did not reply. He found his mouth was dry. 'Carrying a pistol in an interview, let alone threatening with it, is contrary to all rules of tactical questioning.'

Asma heard him. She gave him a steady glare before turning back to the detainee.

'We're not at Sandhurst now. This is the real world. Sir.'

A few minutes later the boss left the tent. He had a sick feeling in his stomach, like the time he'd stumbled across the school bullies at work on a young kid. He'd tried to intervene then. But he said nothing now.

Darkness had fallen. He found his way over to the cookhouse where some of the A Company officers were still eating. He only wanted a cup of tea but the plump little man by the sink who was clattering pans and shouting at his cooks insisted on resurrecting some old lasagne, an operation which caused a fresh outburst of clattering. The soldiers had to yell their

29

conversation over the pans and the TV, which was tuned to *Flaunt*.

The cook had to be the Bangladeshi whom Dave had praised earlier. When the lasagne arrived it was good, but Weeks could eat little. His mind kept filling with disjointed pictures of the day's events. He had done well enough at Sandhurst, but now, having faced the reality of battle for the first time, he was asking himself if he really wanted to be in the army at all.

On the screen, a woman writhed seductively. Weeks didn't notice her. He didn't join in the officers' chat. He went to find his platoon. They were cleaning their weapons or slumped against the vehicles listening to their iPods or showing each other footage of today's contact. A few already had their heads down, body armour for pillows, rifles on their webbing away from the sand, helmets over rifles. That must be the way the platoon sergeant had taught them. Dave Henley seemed to have a firm hold over the men and to keep them in good order.

'Well, sir,' Dave said, 'would you like the good news first?'

'Good news?' Weeks echoed listlessly. The best news he could imagine right now was that they were all going home.

'We've been told to expect three new men as soon as possible.' The platoon was already under strength, even without today's losses.

'How soon is that?'

'If we're very lucky, within the week. There'll be an experienced machine-gunner for 2 Section. In 1 Section, Jamie Dermott will replace Jordan Nelson on the GPMG and two new lads are on their way. That's the good news. The bad news is that they're both straight out of Catterick.'

'Oh dear . . .' Weeks's brow furrowed. 'It seems you'll be surrounded by beginners.'

'We soon knock sprogs into shape,' Dave said cheerfully.

It was impossible not to like this sergeant. Weeks knew that he was leaning heavily on him.

Billy Finn was sitting nearby. 'Excuse me, but can I ask if you're a betting man, sir?'

'No, Finny,' Dave growled.

But Weeks heard himself say: 'I have been known to show a passing interest in the two thirty at Chepstow, Lance Corporal.'

Finn jumped to his feet. 'I'm taking bets on the new bloke in 2 Section. Five to four on says he's ginger.'

One of the first things Weeks had noticed when he met his men last Thursday was the unusually high number of red-haired men in 2 Section.

'Come on, sir. You give me five dollars and you get nine back, that's including your stake, if he turns out to be a ginger pisswizard.'

'How did you arrive at those odds?'

Finn gave him a cheeky smile. 'I used to be a bookie's runner, sir. I was offering eleven to ten on but there weren't many takers.'

'And how many men in 2 Section already have ginger hair?'

'They've only got seven lads at the moment and five of them are pisswizards of one shade or another.'

'Yeah,' Mal agreed. '2 Section's a freak show.'

'They can't take their helmets off or aerial surveillance think we're under enemy fire,' Jamie said.

Finn's eyes sparkled. 'A fiver at five to four on says the eighth bloke's a ginge, sir.'

'I'd rather bet on him not being ginger.'

'I can do that, sir. Would you like me to calculate the odds for you?'

Dave groaned.

'No, I'll give you a fiver at five to four on.'

'Yessir!' said Finn, jumping up and producing a wallet to receive the boss's money. He gave Dave a wide grin.

'How many dollars have you taken, Finny?' Dave said.

'A bookie never tells. Let's just say most of the lads in the platoon like a flutter and these are very generous odds.'

'You sure you've got the money to pay out if you lose?'

'Trust Billy Finn!' Finn cheerfully pocketed the fiver.

Dave offered Weeks a brew and the pair of them sat down a little away from the others, talking quietly into the Afghan night.

'No further news of the casualties?'

Weeks shook his head sadly. He hardly knew the injured men but Dave was sure he felt their loss acutely. Dave had been hearing Steve's screams inside his head. He'd listened to men screaming in agony before. Sometimes he heard it again months later when he

31

was far away. In his sleep, or without warning in the back of his head late at night when he was driving on the motorway. As though there was a casualty lying on his rear seat.

The boss yawned. Dave yawned too. Around them men were falling asleep. Dave felt ready for some kip himself. He'd just phoned home, talking first to little Vicky and then to Jen. It had been the usual chatty stuff. Gradually the Wiltshire camp with its wide, wet streets and its rows of houses and his own living room had formed again in his mind. But when he put down the phone it had all vanished in the hot Afghan air.

Chapter Five

JENNY KNEW SOMETHING HAD HAPPENED. DAVE WASN'T ALLOWED TO say anything about anything on the army phone but she could still tell that he was keeping something from her.

He'd used up every one of his thirty allocated minutes. He and little Vicky had cooed idiotically at each other for at least ten of them. The strange gaps, the overlaps, the complications that always occurred when there was a two-second delay on the patchy line never mattered to Vicky. It only mattered when two adults had things to say to each other.

Jenny had told him all the small stuff from home. Everyone said this was the right way to talk to your man when he was away and over the last few years she'd been given plenty of opportunities to perfect her technique. So it was a quick reference to the broken gutter before moving swiftly on to what the nursery had said about Vicky being ahead of her age, the date the hospital was going to scan the baby, her mum inviting his mum over . . . she sometimes listened to her own voice, wittering on, and wondered what he was thinking. Did it mean anything when people were trying to kill you in an alien land that the gutter on a house in Wiltshire was leaking? They both had to pretend it did. But today he wasn't pretending as well as usual.

She put the phone down with that all too familiar feeling. Loss. Regret. Disappointment. The knowledge that all the important things had not been said. Phone calls were a brief interlude in her life and his. And then they went away and lived in their separate worlds, waiting always for the next disappointing call.

She picked up Vicky, who seemed to share her sadness. They stood at the window. A grey day was melting into a grey evening. The street was wet. Irregular patches in the pavement were filled with water. The houses looked ugly. Sometimes, when the lights were on in the living rooms and the TVs flickered, she felt cosy on a dark evening. Not tonight.

Headlamps travelled slowly up the street. As the car passed Jenny could see it was Agnieszka Dermott's old Vauxhall with Luke in the back. Where had she been? Agnieszka never shared the details of her life with the other women. Within a day of the men leaving for Afghanistan the wives at the camp had got together in each other's houses. Even if they hadn't said anything in particular there was a sort of strength in knowing that everyone felt the same way. But Agnieszka hadn't joined in.

Jenny and Vicky stood at the window so long that night fell and the glass began to throw their own reflections back at them. Jenny saw herself, tall, blonde, angular, Vicky sitting on her hip with one leg stretching across the bump of the baby.

More headlamps. A car drew up outside Leanne Buckle's place. And in that moment, Jenny knew what Dave hadn't been telling her.

There was an endless pause before a man got out. He was carrying a briefcase. Jenny recognized him at once. The Families Officer. That could only mean one thing. Jenny felt her throat constrict and tears press behind her eyes. She tried not to cry for Vicky's sake then saw with relief that the child had fallen asleep.

So she let her tears spill as the Families Officer walked up the front path to Leanne's door. She watched him ring the bell. Leanne's bell didn't work and when nothing happened after a few minutes he had to knock. Leanne answered, carrying a twin, legs hanging. The other one was probably behind her somewhere, bawling, the way they did when Leanne only picked one of them up.

Jenny couldn't see Leanne's face but, before the man even had time to speak, it was clear she had guessed why he was there. Her hand went up to her head as if she was warding off a physical blow. Her body swayed. The man stepped inside and the door closed behind them.

34

Jenny's face was wet with tears. It hurt too much to think about it. She tried not to think.

The phone rang again. She grabbed it before the noise could wake Vicky. Her whole left side ached now where she had stood too still holding the child for too long. She sank onto the sofa without letting go of Vicky, and put the phone to her ear.

'Oh, Jen, there's some bad news . . .' Worry could not remove the warmth from Adi Kasanita's voice. Jenny loved Adi. She had exchanged another life in a sunnier world for rain and tax credits which never stretched far enough, and yet she was always cheerful, always kind. She never joined in the gossip and ignored the petty rivalries. And when she detected an undercurrent of anger or unhappiness, she confronted it without flinching. If we wives were soldiers, Jenny thought, I'd want Adi to be my sergeant.

'Something must have happened to Steve Buckle,' Jenny whispered. She didn't dare to speak because she might wake Vicky. No, that wasn't true. She didn't dare to speak in case her voice cracked and she started to cry.

'You looking across the road?' Adi lived about five doors away.

'The Families Officer's just gone in.'

'Jen, I knew you'd be really upset so I'm ringing to tell you that he's not dead.'

How did Adi always know everything? She just did. But she never told unless there was a good reason.

Jenny swallowed.

'How bad is it?'

'Lost a leg.'

'Oh, Christ, oh, shit . . .' Jenny tried not to swear in front of Adi but she couldn't always help it. Adi and Sol Kasanita were Christians. They never talked about it, Jenny didn't ask.

'Lost a leg and a lot of blood but they think he'll survive.'

'Is anyone else hurt?'

'That new lad in 1 Section, Jordan Nelson, he's got some bad burns. I don't know him. He was in Germany and he's not been here long.'

'I don't either. Is he married?'

'No, lives in the barracks.'

'Are they flying home?'

'Jordan Nelson will soon be on his way to Selly Oak. But they can't fly Steve out until he's stabilized. They say his condition's critical.'

Jenny swallowed again. Critical. The word sounded like the crack of a whip.

'What are we going to do about Leanne?'

'You take my kids, they're practically asleep anyway. I'll go over to her when the Families Officer's finished.'

Jenny felt relieved. Always ready to listen to anyone's problems, right now she felt unable to deal with a hysterical Leanne. She just wanted to go to bed.

'Are you sure?'

'Get your mattresses down and I'll be over in half an hour.'

'OK . . .' Jenny felt so tired she could hardly stand up. 'OK, Adi. You take care of Leanne tonight; I'll go to her tomorrow.'

'There is something you can do . . .'

'What?'

'Phone Agnieszka.'

Before he left, Dave had particularly asked Jenny to look out for Jamie Dermott's wife. Jenny liked Jamie a lot and knew he was worried about her. She was Polish, alone with a child who seemed to be handicapped and without family here except her snotty and unhelpful in-laws. But looking after a woman who wouldn't join in anything had proved difficult. Jenny had asked her round and offered to baby-sit. But the one time she had come over and Jenny had tried to introduce her to everyone, Agnieszka had wrapped her long and beautiful legs around the bar stool in the kitchen and said little. She'd looked as though she wished she was somewhere else, with someone else.

'Can I call her tomorrow? She's only just got home, I saw her.'

'Oh, sure. You sound so tired; you get all the kids into bed and then you go yourself, honey. We only need to make certain she hears the truth from us first and not some horrible rumour.'

Jenny put Vicky to bed and pulled out a couple of mattresses onto the little girl's floor for the Kasanita kids. She stood looking at her daughter's sweet, sleeping face. The rounded jaw, the pink cheeks, the wisps of hair curling around her forehead.

'Don't marry a soldier,' Jenny whispered to her. 'Whatever you do, don't marry a soldier.'

She wished she hadn't. She wanted to be Dave's wife, but not an army wife. It was just too much. The intensity of living with all the other army families, the knowledge that their burdens were your burdens, the dull ache at the emptiness on the other side of the double bed where Dave should be lying. And beneath it all, the fear. The fear when you woke up and when you weren't even thinking about it and when you were asleep. It wasn't a surprise when there was a knock on the door one damp, dark afternoon and the Families Officer was standing on the step. Because in your heart you were expecting it all the time.

She decided now that she must persuade Dave to leave the army, and soon. Before there was a knock at her door.

Chapter Six

DAVE ROLLED HIS SLEEPING BAG OVER AND LOOKED AT THE SKY. The mountains, many kilometres away, were glowing a thousand shades of red and purple in the dawn. Everyone back in the UK calls this place Theatre, thought Dave. We are In Theatre. It is the Theatre of War. But no one ever tells you that the scenery's bloody marvellous.

He lay still, watching the light change and the mountain colours lose their depth. He was thinking about Jordan Nelson, how his little brothers and worried mother would be sitting miserably under the strip-lighting of a hospital canteen while surgeons picked shrapnel out of his organs.

He got up and stretched. A Company and the civilians had first call on the washing area, the toilets, the cookhouse. He could see them moving around at the heart of the FOB. As soon as he could, he would try to find out if there had been any news on Steve or Jordan overnight.

But first, compulsively, he counted bodies. Twenty-six.

He stretched again and yawned. He looked up. And saw a vapour trail, bright orange against the blue sky. It was moving at speed and there was a smell of sulphur in the air. A rocket. It was going to land in the FOB before he could even shout a warning.

'Incoming!' he yelled, as it hit the ground with a thud deep enough to jolt his heart and enough noise to obliterate his voice. There was a small firework display at the heart of the camp that would have been spectacular if hadn't been so deadly. But no one was near the rocket's landing site. The closest building was the Cowshed and its thick walls stood up to the impact.

The sentries in the sangars were already firing. Civilians in shirt sleeves and body armour who had been eating breakfast were rapidly retreating to the mud-walled safe area at the heart of the camp. And A Company were leaping into action all over Sin City. Some were dressed and ready to go, others were leaving their tents with their boots on the wrong feet, grabbing their weapons, pulling on their helmets, but they all knew where they were going and what they were doing.

Battle-hardened, Dave thought enviously, as he tried to organize his own comatose men. Compared with A Company, they were like headless chickens.

'Get your body armour on!' he yelled as lads jumped to their feet and, forgetting they were still inside their sleeping bags, tumbled to the ground. Two men laid claim to one pile of webbing and started arguing.

'For Chrissake, shitheads!' Dave shouted. 'Helmets, boots, body armour but get out of your sleeping bags first. Then straight to your fucking positions.'

He might as well have been telling them to go straight to the moon, although they had all been given their stand-to positions in case of attack by the boss yesterday.

The air smelled of cordite. Another RPG landed almost exactly where the first had. And 1 Platoon were still at the Vectors messing with their boot laces.

By the time everyone was in the place with their weapons, the order to stand down was being shouted.

'You were a fat lot of fucking use, tossers,' Dave overheard A Company muttering. 'Better sharpen up a bit.'

Dave's lads looked boyish and confused as they made safe their weapons, gathered up magazines and straightened their bodies. The Officer Commanding A Company appeared, checking out the damage with his second i/c. A sandbagged area of the FOB had been badly hit.

'We'll leave R Company to sort that,' the outgoing OC told Boss Weeks cheerfully.

39

Nobody wanted the contact to prevent A Company from going. The FOB was too crowded. CSM Kila had to break up a fight between one of the ginger lads in 2 Section who had sneaked into the cookhouse and an A Company Royal Engineer who had called the infantry platoon a bunch of ginger mingers. Finally, to everyone's relief, it was announced that A Company would be leaving at 1600 hours.

1 Platoon spent a sweaty day filling sandbags and remaking walls.

'Been swimming, mate?' a passing A Company engineer asked Billy Finn. The Lance Corporal wore only a pair of shorts and sandals. His wiry body was running with sweat. His face was bright red from his exertions and because he had failed to use any sun block.

He tried to reply but his mouth was so dry he had to take a swig of water first.

'You'll get used to the heat,' the engineer said.

'Since you're used to it already, fancy lending a hand?' Finn croaked.

The engineer shook his head. 'If I had a quid for every sandbag I've filled, I'd be a fucking millionaire.' He was going home. He couldn't wipe the grin off his face. 'My body's here, mate, but in my mind I'm already cuddled up with a nice curvy bird.'

At 1545, when people were already starting to imagine they heard the distant thud of Chinooks, A Company vacated their tents. Dave's platoon rushed in and grabbed their cots and started to hang up their posters.

'Oh, Christ . . .' Angus McCall watched Mal attaching a picture to the tent rails by his cot. 'I thought she was all mine.'

He held up an identical photograph.

'She was waiting for me in *Nuts*,' Mal said. 'Your girl must be her twin sister.'

The air was thick with the thunder of helicopter rotors and suddenly the rest of R Company were streaming into the base.

Dave didn't greet them. His first words were: 'Brought the mail bag?'

They'd been away from the UK for well over a week now,

training in the comparative luxury of Camp Bastion before leaving for Sin City. He knew that, consciously or unconsciously, everyone was waiting for their letters. It was important to distribute them as rapidly as possible.

When he went over to the sangars to where Sol and Angus were on stag, he saw two bottles of urine and a condom beneath the tower.

'I reckon the condom must be something to do with Emily, Sarge,' Angus said.

Sol Kasanita laughed. 'The marines had a lot of women supporting: medics and psych ops and Intelligence,' he said. 'Emily isn't the only woman in Helmand Province.'

'What is all this shit about Emily?' Dave asked.

'Emily's the number two civilian here. Their number one is that old guy who wanders around, Martyn someone. And Emily's his side-kick. The marines have a name for her.'

'Let me guess.'

'The sex grenade.'

'Uh-huh.'

'Now,' Sol said, 'according to the marines, when she needs a man she just whistles.'

'And one bloke isn't enough, Sarge! Sometimes she needs a whole platoon!' Angus added.

'I can't wait to meet her.'

'If she exists,' Sol said.

The air was still now. From up here the town seemed to have grown out of the ground. Its walls were the same colour as the surrounding desert. Suddenly, hauntingly, the call to prayer crept across the sand towards them.

'Not him again,' groaned Angus. 'He never stops wailing.'

'It's Friday,' Dave said.

Angus looked blank.

'Holy Day. Like Sunday used to be in England before we found out PC World was more fun than "All Things Bright And Beautiful".'

Sol didn't catch his eye. Dave remembered that the Fijian was a practising Christian. He never mentioned it, but Dave had seen the Bible by his cot and back in Wiltshire he'd seen Sol, Adi and the kids all bundled into their rusty old car in their best clothes on Sunday mornings.

About an hour after the Chinooks, the convoy of Vectors finally set off, carrying the last of A Company back to Bastion. They roared past the sangar sending up choking clouds of powdery dust, which hung in the air long after the vehicles had disappeared between the town and the mountains.

'Goodbye and good luck,' Angus McCall muttered insincerely. At lunchtime he'd got into a heated argument with two men from A Company, insisting that Manchester United led the Premier League in 2005. Later, Dave had told him quietly: 'You were wrong. It was Chelsea. They were defending champions and they won it again.'

Angus had looked sheepish. 'I remembered that halfway through. But I wasn't going to give in to the bastards.'

That night, he booked some phone time with his father. He said: 'I hate marines.'

'A lot of them are big, strong, brave men,' his dad said. 'The sort of man you should be, Angus.'

Angus immediately regretted the argument in the cookhouse and thought that he'd probably never be that sort of man, like a marine, like his dad. If he was, he'd have backed down from the Premier League argument and admitted he was wrong.

'Did you know any marines?'

'Course I did. Marines, Paras and . . .' John McCall dropped his voice. 'SF.'

There was always something in the knowing way his dad talked about Special Forces which made Angus sure his dad had been in the SAS. He knew that John McCall had fought with distinction in the Falklands, although the medals themselves had been stolen many years ago.

His parents were divorced and since early childhood he'd spent every Saturday afternoon with his father. From the moment that John McCall turned the sign around in his newsagent's so that the door read 'OPEN' from the inside and 'CLOSED' from the outside, Saturdays were war stories, war films, war games. And whenever his dad talked about the SAS, Angus knew that he would apply for

Selection himself one day. Even though he was sure he could never be good enough to get in.

'So!' said John McCall resuming his normal tone. 'Was the journey to the base OK?'

'Had a contact.'

If he'd told his mum that, she would have panicked. But he could hear the shrug in his dad's voice. 'Oh, well, start as you mean to go on.'

'Now we're two men down in my section.'

'Two men down already? What's the matter with them?'

'One lost a leg, the other had burns.'

'Dear oh fucking dear. They didn't last five minutes, did they? Where are they now?'

'I had to carry my mate who lost a leg to the helicopter. They were flown to Bastion. Soon as they're stable they'll be back to Selly Oak.'

'Helicopter!' scoffed John McCall. His accent was still strong although he had left Scotland years ago. 'A helicopter! Sitting there waiting, was it? On the TV they're always saying you boys haven't got enough helis. Turns out they're on hand twenty-four seven. Fuck me, warfare's changed.'

Angus felt himself deflate. Of course his dad was right. All that fear and excitement he'd felt during today's contact had been sheer cowardice. Because there was always air support waiting to bail you out.

'I was scared,' he admitted. 'Until a Harrier came in to sort them out.'

'There you are! You knew a big machine would come and save you! Och, you lads have got it good. I mean . . .'

But now the line was breaking up. There had been a two-second delay which meant the men kept talking over each other. Angus lapsed into silence. He wasn't sure he should have told his father anything about the contact over the satellite phone. John McCall's voice came and went in his ear.

'I have to finish now, Dad,' he shouted. 'I have to ring Mum on this card.'

But his father didn't hear.

'Air support . . . Harrier . . . Goose Green . . . weather conditions . . .'

43

Angus finally hung up.

'All right, mate?' Corporal Curtis from 3 Section was next in line for the phone.

'Yeah.' From the day Angus had joined up, conversations with his father had left him feeling flat. He'd thought his father would be ecstatic at his enlistment but he'd received the news quietly. Then, during the passing-out parade at Catterick, Angus had stumbled over his own big feet. It was something he'd never forgive himself for. He'd immediately, anxiously, looked into the crowd, to the place where he knew his divorced parents were sitting together in hostile silence. He'd been in time to catch the look of contempt on his father's face.

That night, the base came under attack again. 1 Platoon advance party knew where to go and what to do this time. As the rest of the company floundered they slid easily into their positions while the new arrivals dithered.

The contact was brief. It consisted of one badly aimed grenade, which almost missed the base completely, and ten minutes of light arms fire.

'You were a fat lot of fucking useless tossers,' Finn said to the newcomers.

'Better sharpen up a bit,' Jamie added.

It was a while before they had a chance to do so. There were few contacts on patrols through the town or the desert. Attacks on the base were minimal. Each day a small party of contractors, escorted by 3 Platoon, left and came back reporting no threats. And there were no sightings of Emily around the civilian area.

'Because she doesn't exist,' Sol said. 'That's why.'

'Ever thought the marines were winding you up?' Jamie said.

Lunch had been sausage, egg and chips, Finn's favourite. He pushed his empty plate away and leaned back in his chair. 'I'm absolutely sure that Emily is in those isoboxes. She just doesn't come out much.'

'Well, why doesn't she come to the cookhouse with the others?'

The civilians were becoming a familiar sight in the cookhouse. They generally sat together in one corner with their food and their cans of beer. Their boss, Martyn Robertson, and a few of the others mixed with the soldiers. But most looked as if they'd prefer to have their own cookhouse in their own quarter of the camp.

'Miss Emily work very hard, she mostly take her meals in isobox,' said a cook, who happened to overhear them. 'I take her meal over now.'

Mal, Angus and Finn looked enviously at the lad. He was small and brown-skinned.

'I go now. You go if you want.' He held out a tray.

'Go where?'

'You ask questions! You take Miss Emily lunch and you find out answer!'

The lad handed Finn the tray.

'Thank you!' said Finn, balancing it expertly on the tips of his fingers. 'Miss Emily, here I come . . .'

Mal and Angus leaped up to join him.

'Oh no you don't,' Finn said.

Mal's expression was deadly serious. 'We'll need to form a cordon.'

'I'm the second i/c of your section and you're staying here. That's an order, McCall.' Finn swept out, tray held aloft.

The boss came into the cookhouse in time to see Finn waltzing away with the tray. Jamie noticed him smile rapidly at the dark-skinned woman from Intelligence, who was sitting alone. The woman did not smile back.

'Where's Finn going with that tray?' Weeks asked as he sat down.

Jamie grinned. 'Undercover.'

The boss looked concerned.

'I hope he's not going to make a nuisance of himself.'

Finn still had not reappeared when the others went back to their base duties.

'We're out on patrol at 1500 hours,' Sol said. 'And there's going to be big trouble if Finny's not back.'

'He's probably just helping Emily sync her iPod,' Jamie said. But neither of them was now so sure that Emily the sex grenade was just a joke.

Finn did reappear by the vehicles at precisely 1445, adjusting his clothes and grinning broadly. He winked at Angus and some of the other lads.

'Whoops, I seem to have forgotten something!' He bent ostentatiously to tie his bootlaces.

Sol put his hands on his hips.

Finn straightened, beaming and stretching lazily. 'She just wouldn't let me go! Fuck me, I could use a cigarette . . .'

'Shut up and get into the wagon, you lazy bastard,' Dave said.

Once the convoy was under way, Finn's PRR went into meltdown.

'Sorry, lads,' Finn said. 'Can't say too much. Ongoing mission . . .'

'Is she hot?'

'Rocket-propelled, mate. So hot she's on fire.'

'In your dreams, Finny.' Jamie shook his head.

'You were right about one thing, Jamie. She's no grenade. She's heavy fucking artillery.'

'Lance Corporal Finn,' Dave snapped, 'if you don't can this crap and start looking pretty fucking sharp you're going to experience some heavy fucking artillery from me.'

PRR went silent.

Chapter Seven

DAVE'S HEAD FELT LIKE A WAR ZONE. HE KNEW HE'D FAILED TO follow his own instructions and drink enough water today. He'd spent the morning shovelling admin shit and drawing up rotas. By lunchtime the names and numbers looked like he was squinting at them through a heat haze, the ops room was an oven and he was dripping with sweat just leaning against the wall under a large piece of paper on which someone had written: *Living The Dream???* And now here was Finn boasting about having sex with one of the civilians. However bad your headache, Billy Finn was guaranteed to make it worse.

Dave had to stay alert.

The Helmand River snaked through the centre of the Green Zone like an artery. They drove past orchards crisscrossed by irrigation ditches, collections of houses that were almost villages, lonely compounds with goats outside them, small towns walled like fortresses, fields, woodland, high crops, jungle.

The two women interpreters had wrung information out of the detainees about a Taliban stronghold. The detainees couldn't or wouldn't pinpoint the compound, but they'd said enough to confirm the outgoing Officer Commanding's suspicions.

So now the convoy was putting his theory to the test. Dave wasn't pleased that they'd been sent with less than a full platoon. He'd told CSM Kila he didn't feel at all happy about crossing this part of the Green Zone with so few men. Kila had agreed but Major Willingham had refused to revise his plans.

'Don't get out,' Kila said. 'You've not got the manpower. Whatever happens, just keep going.'

'Why can't we take more men and do a proper foot patrol?'

'Too busy guarding the FOB and protecting Topaz fucking Zero and his mates.'

Topaz Zero was Martyn Robertson's call sign. Whenever Kila referred to him, he swore. So did most of the officers. Dave had even overheard Major Willingham muttering incantations under his breath which might have included the words Topaz fucking Zero.

'He should care a bit more about men's lives and a bit less about his precious fucking oil,' Kila said.

Everyone on board the vehicles was bad-tempered. Sitting in a scalding hot metal box for two hours was no one's idea of fun, and they knew the chances of getting out in that two hours were slim. They took it in turns to go on top with Jamie, who'd replaced Steve Buckle on the GPMG.

The attack was sudden and intense. There were trees on either side of them, and poppy fields beyond. The poppies were taller than a man. They grew so thickly that, even from the air, Dave knew it was virtually impossible to catch sight of anyone moving through the crop. Muzzle flashes sparked up from all sides. The men on top of the vehicles returned rapid fire without any sense of the precise location of their targets.

Dave watched tracer rounds whiz past from his seat at the front of the lead Vector. He longed to debus and give the choggies a proper fire fight. Speeding through like this felt too much like running away. But the boss followed orders and kept the convoy going.

The river carved its way through the foliage ahead of them. The water gleamed in the sunlight. The landscape opened up on either side of it, filling their perspective with light and space. Then they returned once more to the dense, sunken world of interwoven shadows and raking gunfire.

Someone yelled into their mic: 'Oh, fuck it, *no!*'

It sounded like Sol Kasanita. Sol almost never swore.

'Man down . . .'

Man down. The words Dave dreaded. The words that echoed in his worst nightmares.

'*Sol?*'

He couldn't hide his anguish. Sol Kasanita, built like a rock, solid as a rock, dependable as rock. For an instant Dave stared into a gaping hole where that rock should be.

Laughter rang in his ear.

'It's all right, Sarge!' Jamie said.

'He was just getting his head down!'

Mal's voice. And more laughter in the background.

'Stop fucking about and get someone else up on top!' Dave roared, embarrassed by his sudden rush of emotion. 'What's going on with you bunch of dickheads? On second thoughts, don't tell me. Just get on with your jobs. And if I ever hear anyone fucking about with Man Down again I'll personally remove their balls.'

He could see a network of compounds in the distance. The detainees had said that fighters from Iran, Pakistan and the Gulf all trained somewhere close by. But there were also civilians: women, children, old people.

The open, arid desert was visible again now. The firing finally petered out as they reached the edge of the Green Zone. Dave kept his eyes fixed on the track ahead of him. The intensity of this attack certainly supported the OC's theory about the location of the Taliban stronghold. He'd want a strike op next.

A few hundred metres ahead, a goat strolled out from a cluster of trees.

The driver kept on going. And so did the goat. It ambled along the track towards them.

'Go firm,' Dave said. 'I don't fancy goat in my rations.'

The driver stopped.

'What's up?' asked the lads in the back.

'Goat hitchhiking,' Dave said into the mic. An old man ran out of the trees further along the track, waving a stick and shouting.

The goat, which had been impervious to the roaring line of Vectors, started at the sight of the stick or the old boy's spindly legs and cantered towards Dave's wagon, head back and eyes rolling.

Suddenly there was a massive fireball in front of them instead of a goat. The windscreen filled with dust. There was a second ear-splitting explosion. The Vector rocked and then vibrated like a dog shaking water from its coat.

'*What the fuck* . . . ?'

A chorus of voices in his ears.

But in the front of the Vector there was silence. Dave and his driver contemplated their near escape. Two lives down, Dave thought. The first time, Steve took the hit. Now the goat. How many can I have left?

'Fucking hell,' the driver said eventually.

'Big one,' Dave said.

'Yeah . . . but I don't get it. A goat couldn't set off an anti-tank mine.'

'Anti-personnel stacked onto an anti-tank, I reckon. Or two.' Dave's throat was thick with dust. 'Apparently the Taliban like to do a bit of stacking.'

'Good thing you told me to stop,' the driver said.

'I thought I was being kind to a dumb animal.'

Their eyes scanned the track, gouged and pitted from the explosion.

'No sign of the old geezer with the knobbly knees and the stick,' Dave said.

'He'll be hiding in those trees somewhere.'

'He won't have been close enough to the blast to get hurt.' But Dave wasn't completely sure about that.

The boss came on the radio and Dave described what had happened.

'Where's the old man?'

Dave rolled his eyes at the driver. 'He was a good two hundred metres away.' He didn't want to stop and look for him.

'We'll have to make sure he's not hurt,' the boss said.

'They planted the IED, not us.' Dave didn't bother to hide his irritation. 'Maybe his grandson put it there and forgot to tell him. Or maybe he planted it himself and hadn't told the goat . . .'

But he already knew the boss well enough to guess what would come next.

'He's a local farmer and, um, probably has nothing to do with the, er, insurgents. He may not even speak their language. He could be a casualty and we, um, have a duty of care to him if he's, er, hurt.'

Dave sighed. You could count on Boss Weeks to take the moral high ground.

'Right,' he said unenthusiastically. 'Dismount 1 and 2 Sections. Sol Kasanita, you bring 1 Section up here to me, Baker bring 2 Section. Corporal Curtis and 3 Section stay here and cover.'

He could hear the men moving reluctantly. It had been a long, hot drive and sausages at the cookhouse in Sin City seemed like a much better idea.

'Move!' Dave barked. 'Let's get it over with.'

'Bit of a problem here, Sarge.' Sol sounded embarrassed.

'Oh yeah?'

'Finn won't let me go.'

Dave thought of the exploding goat. He was going to explode himself if his men kept on like this.

'Listen, lads . . . !'

'He can't walk,' Finn explained cheerfully. 'He's going to get into trouble out there.'

'I can manage,' Sol said.

'You fucking can't,' said Finn.

'Did you say he can't walk?' Dave repeated slowly.

'Fell down from the top,' Sol admitted. His voice was miserable.

'Twisted his ankle,' Jamie said.

'Maybe broken it,' Finn added.

'It is not fucking broken!' yelled Sol and there was a momentary silence as everyone remembered again that Sol never swore.

Dave said: 'Try to find a more heroic way to die, Sol. OK, you stay there. I'll have Finn with the rest of 1 Section. Get moving. Come on, 2 Section, where are you?'

He got out and the men joined him. He didn't press the mic button; he didn't want the boss to hear what he was about to say next.

'All we're doing is keeping the boss happy now, lads. Just go up the track looking for a wounded civilian, then through the trees, and we'll work our way back herringbone. Don't take too much time or trouble over it. Finn leads with 1 Section, Baker follows with 2 Section and, as Sol's out, I'll go behind.'

Finn's watchfulness was so acute that it was almost a sixth sense. When he was around, it was hard to make anyone else point man.

'What are we looking for, Sarge?' Jamie asked.

51

'An old geezer. Dead or wounded. He's got a beard . . .' He turned to the driver. 'He did have a beard, didn't he?'

'They've all got fucking beards.'

'OK, beard and knobbly knees. Last seen holding a stick. The boss is worried that he may have gone the same way as his goat.'

'I'll look for the beard, you look for the knees,' Jamie told Angus.

'Get your sling clip undone, for Chrissake, Bilaal,' Dave said to Mal. 'And two hands on your weapon!'

'Oh, yeah, sorry, Sarge.'

Mal wasn't thick or lazy. Far from it. The sling clip would limit his firing arc and Mal knew that but he just wasn't thinking. Not enough about soldiering, anyway. He thought about women all day and all night. He was probably standing there fantasizing about Emily the sex grenade right now. But if you could just get him to concentrate, he was good.

They moved forward up the track, along the line of trees, up to the site of the explosion. They stared in silence at the scorched earth and shredded foliage.

'There but for the grace of God . . .'

'Could be a few bits of barbecued goat . . .' Jamie prodded the ground with his foot.

'Let's hope it's not barbecued beard.' Dave led them to the place where the old man had emerged onto the track. They peered between the trees. The soil was sandy, the canopy thick with tangled leaves.

Finn plunged in and the others followed.

'OK, swing left and back to the vehicles,' Dave said. 'If he's lying wounded, we should find him.'

It felt like another world in here. Cooler. The shade from the overhead leaves was green.

Just ahead of Dave and to his right, Angus suddenly stopped. Dave stopped too. It took a moment for him to realize why. Their stillness made the woods seem unnaturally quiet. The trees came to an abrupt end. Ahead of them, walking casually across an open field, along the top of one of the drainage ditches, were four insurgents.

Their weapons were slung carelessly over their shoulders. Their sergeant really should have bollocked them big-time. Two were carrying belts of ammo. They must have been firing at us a few minutes ago, and now the contact's over here they are, walking home in pairs, talking and laughing. Just like us after a contact, Dave thought, experiencing a strange sense of fellowship with the enemy even as he raised his weapon to kill them.

He muttered into the mic but did not look around for the others. He took the safety off and watched the insurgents drop, one by one, into the ditch. It was so easy and so quick that he was hardly aware of the sound of his own rifle. He thought someone else, a bit further up the herringbone, had fired too, although he wasn't sure.

He reported back quickly and then silently moved forward, telling Angus, Jamie and Mal, who were nearest, to come too while the others covered from the woods.

The field felt uncomfortably exposed. Dave became aware that something was nagging at him. Angus McCall had seen the enemy first but instead of taking immediate action, he'd frozen. It was the shock and rigidity in McCall's imposing frame which had alerted Dave to the enemy presence. It should have been the sight of Angus raising his weapon. He made a mental note to deal with the problem later.

'Four enemy dead, now searching,' he muttered into his mic.

The men were lying in the drainage ditch, their hair tangled with the undergrowth, their bodies crumpled.

'You take the two at the back,' Dave instructed Angus.

He jumped down into the ditch. The water was thigh-high and smelled rancid. Some of it splashed onto his face. It soaked rapidly through his clothes.

One of his dead men was still holding a weapon; the other had dropped his on the bank. Dave took both AK47s and pushed them right out of reach. Jamie swept them up.

Angus scrambled down to the other two bodies further along the channel.

'Got an evidence bag?'

'No,' Angus said miserably. 'Didn't think I'd need it.'

Dave groaned. 'Got anything at all to put stuff in?'

'Well . . . my Camelbak, I s'pose.'

Dave was just about to yell at him when Mal dragged a couple of evidence bags from his belt kit. 'Here's some.'

Dave pulled at the first body. He was surprised by how light it was. This man was a lot thinner than any British soldier, Dave thought, as he pressed his knee into the bony back and turned the corpse over.

'Clear.'

Jamie Dermott: cool, efficient, focused. Dave liked to work with a man he could rely on.

He began a systematic search from the head down. When he reached the feet he found they were bare. He looked in the water and the bank for shoes. There were none. He felt the man's feet. Still warm. And the soles were hard and leathery as sandals. These were habitually bare feet. The man had been barefoot with an AK47.

He turned the body over. Man? He was scarcely more than a boy.

He extracted a mobile phone from his pockets and folded papers and some beads which looked as though they might have religious significance. There was a laminated ID card, too, with a photo and indecipherable script. Dave didn't waste a second examining it. The sound of their rounds would certainly draw the enemy and it was just a matter of time before they came under fire again.

The second insurgent had been dragged down into the ditch by the weight of his ammo belt. As Dave pulled up the soaking body, he heard Angus.

'He moved! Christ, he's fucking alive!'

Dave stared along the ditch. 'Get his weapon away!'

Angus had failed to clear the weapons before starting his search. Mal moved rapidly from the bank to swipe the AK47 out of arm's reach.

'Get on with it!' Dave said.

'I lifted him and he moved!' Angus had dropped the body back into the ditch and was now staring at it, his face horrified. The man was covered in blood and showed no apparent signs of life.

'*Get on with it!*'

Angus did not move.

Mal raised his SA80 and fired twice at the man's chest. Blood appeared like a fast-blooming flower. The weapon's report was followed by silence.

Angus remained motionless.

'*Now search him!*'

Dave's roar finally seemed to wake Angus from his dream. He grabbed the body and started to search it correctly but his face remained blank.

Dave watched. His men had done this often enough in training, but searching a real body methodically and professionally – without thinking destructive thoughts about how the man had a mother and maybe a wife and small kids and a bunch of mates he'd been to school with all waiting for him to come home – was something else again.

He heard a nearby volley of fire. Their own shots had certainly drawn the enemy, who must now have found the convoy. He wondered how long it would take them to discover that a small group from the Vectors was in an exposed field with the bodies of four of their fighters. And all because of an old geezer with knobbly knees.

His second body was bigger and stronger. The man wore more serious kit, solid sandals, and had a Pakistani passport in his pocket. This was not a local, but a professional Taliban fighter.

He slipped the passport and personal effects into his evidence bag and, when Angus had finished, they climbed out of the ditch and ran back to the cover of the woods.

'Firing from all sides.' Boss Weeks's voice crackled in Dave's ear. The column of men advanced slowly and quietly through the trees. Dave told the convoy to move forward for them. They remained hidden as they waited for its slow advance. Dave saw the thin, anxious faces of his men, looking for the enemy on all sides. Angus looked up.

'Fucking hell, Sarge . . .'

Almost directly above them was a foot. The foot was attached to a thin, brown leg. The leg was attached to a man and the man was attached to a weapon. The weapon was trained on the path of the oncoming convoy.

They understood the man's stillness with one glance. From the rigid position of his head, his neck frozen like a frightened animal's, they knew that he was unable to disengage his weapon from the branches to aim it at them. He'd turned to stone in the hope they wouldn't look up.

'McCall, step back to fire,' Dave said. 'So you get something a bit more useful than his arse.'

Angus had frozen when he had a clear view of four insurgents crossing a field. He'd frozen when he found one of them wasn't dead. Now Dave wanted to give him another chance but he saw the lad's face was rigid with alarm. He'd experienced enough death for one day.

Finn said: 'I'll do it.'

He stepped back.

The Taliban sniper looked down at them, knowing what was going to happen. Dave stared up into his brown eyes. The man looked back at him and started to speak. He didn't cry or yell and he showed no fear. He spoke in a strange, soft way, without plead-ing. It was affecting, more affecting than any cry or shout could have been.

There was a flash and the report of a weapon. The man slumped forward.

'Sorry, mate,' Dave said quietly.

A mobile phone fell from the man's clothes and Jamie caught it neatly. The convoy drew level with them and, under fire, they piled into the back of the first two Vectors.

'Let's go.'

Dave thought about the man in the tree, whose pleas for his life he'd ignored. Technically, it was a legitimate killing: the man's weapon had been trained on the convoy. He told himself that the man wouldn't have spared him if their positions had been reversed. All the same, he found himself wishing he had brought him in as a prisoner. He didn't feel uncomfortable about the insurgent Mal had shot in the ditch, even though he was aware that this might be harder to explain under the Rules of Engagement.

Finn said: 'That's the first time I've killed someone.'

'Me too,' Mal said.

'All right with it?' Sol looked up at them as he nursed his ankle.

'Yup,' Finn said. ''Course. That's what we're here for.' But his face was hollowed and drawn.

'It did feel well weird.' Mal sounded uncertain.

Angus said nothing. He examined his feet, his cheeks hot and red, as the convoy sped out of the Green Zone.

Chapter Eight

BOSS WEEKS COLLECTED HIS MEAL IN THE COOKHOUSE THAT EVENING and, without giving himself a chance to think about it, joined the two female interpreters. His heart started beating faster and his senses were suddenly extra alert, symptoms he now associated with enemy contact.

The women, who'd been talking intently to each other, looked up without welcome when he sat down.

'*As salaam alai kum*,' Weeks said awkwardly.

'What?' Jean stared at him.

He tried to smile back. He didn't dare look at Asma.

'*As salaam alai kum*,' he repeated, more clearly this time. His food suddenly looked less appetizing.

'Oh-oh,' Asma said. 'We've got another Captain Boyle here.'

'Captain Boyle?'

'He was with A Company.'

'A marine?'

'Engineer. He had this book: *Speak Pashtu in Six Weeks*,' Asma said. 'He used it like a car instruction manual.'

Weeks permitted himself to look at her, but only briefly. She really was stunning. Those large, almond-shaped eyes and slanting cheek bones. Why wasn't every man in the place writing her poems and offering to clean her weapon?

'*Kur-see*,' he said, pointing to the chair. '*War!*' He pointed to the entrance. '*Meez.*' He tapped the table.

'Oh Christ.' Asma rolled her enormous eyes.

Jean started to giggle.

'How long have you been learning it?'

'For months.' Weeks gave a gesture of helplessness. 'I still can't complete a sentence.'

'Most people give up when they get to the sentence structure.'

'The alphabet alone makes me feel like coming out with a white flag. How did you two crack it?'

They both looked as though they'd answered this question a thousand times before.

'I was in Kabul as a kid,' Jean said. 'My parents were aid workers out here until I was twelve. Asma came to the UK at about the same age.'

Asma nodded. 'My parents managed to slip through the Soviet net and, well, it's a long story but we ended up in London. My mother never did learn much English. So I've been translating for her for most of my life.'

'Your family's Pashtun?'

'Yes. We lived in Kandahar province.'

'Do you remember it?'

'Of course.'

'So does this feel at all like home?'

She smiled sadly and shook her head.

'An FOB doesn't feel like home. Even after a month.'

'How does your family feel about . . . ?'

'Me doing this job?' She looked even sadder and studied the table in front of her. She held an empty water glass in her long, slim fingers. She turned it around and around.

'I don't have any contact with them,' she said. 'I married a man who wasn't Pashtu, wasn't even a Moslem. So they don't consider me a member of the family any more.'

Weeks felt a rush of emotion. She was married. But his disappointment didn't overcome his compassion. To be exiled from any family must be hard, and the Pashtuns were a proud and close-knit people.

Jean was watching him closely. 'It's worse than that. She's ended up with no husband *and* no family.'

'Wouldn't your family take you back when . . . when . . . ?'

'When I divorced?' Asma shook her head. 'When you get to

58

understand the Afghan people a little better, you'll know there can only be one answer to that question.'

He looked down awkwardly at his meal.

'Eat up!' Jean said cheerfully. 'I hear you've had one helluva day. You went out on a routine patrol and ended up with five Afghan bodies on your hands.'

'We had a very . . . interesting . . . patrol,' he said carefully.

'You might need to go over the RoE with your men. From what I've heard, there are some questions to be answered.'

'We've discussed the matter fully and I'm satisfied that the Rules of Engagement were observed.' He'd been aware of a certain amount of hesitation on Dave's part in the debriefing, but had decided not to pursue it.

'I think Major Willingham will want to satisfy himself too,' Jean said. Her smile was both bright and determined.

Weeks felt his jaw muscles clench. He'd watched these two contravene every rule in the tactical questioning book. And now they were suggesting his men had ignored the RoE. He felt his face redden further. He cursed this stupid habit. He cursed his entire blood supply.

'Obviously, the police don't get involved unless the OC is worried. But this is a small base and I've offered the major my help if he wants to look into it,' said Jean.

Weeks tried to suppress his anger. He was aware that she was still watching him intently. He was also aware of the steady and un-nerving gaze of the beautiful Asma.

'My men only narrowly avoided being blown up by a double landmine. A goat took the blast instead. They were confirming that there had been no civilian casualties when they encountered the enemy. They faced the stark choice of firing or being fired upon.'

Jean raised an eyebrow. 'Are you sure you've been told all the details?'

Weeks thought about that. Well, no, of course he couldn't be sure that he'd heard the whole story. But he wasn't going to admit that. 'Their actions were entirely justifiable.' He hoped he was right.

Dave had taken Sol a meal and been told that his best corporal had a twisted ankle and had to keep the weight off it for at least a week, maybe two.

'Isn't there anything you can do?' he asked the departing medic. The man turned and shrugged. 'Shoot him?'

'Good idea.'

'Sorry,' Sol said miserably. 'I'm really sorry.'

'How the hell did it happen?' Dave asked. 'If it had been Finny or anyone else I'd know they were pissing about. But you . . .'

'I was on top. I was firing. Then I shifted my weight around and . . . well I stumbled and the next thing I knew I was falling.'

The Fijian was built like a brick shithouse. He'd fallen on Dave during an impromptu football game and Dave still had the bruises.

'Not the lads below playing some stupid fucking trick on you?'

Sol shook his head. 'They wouldn't do that.'

'Not if you were under fire, I guess. I suppose we're lucky you didn't shoot yourself as you fell.'

'Yeah,' Sol said. 'I'm trying to tell myself how lucky I am. Heard any news of Steve or Jordan?'

'Jordan's OK at Selly Oak. All they can say about Steve is that he's stabilizing. Hasn't stabilized enough for me to speak to him, though.'

Sol sighed. 'So until my ankle gets better, Finn will be section commander?'

'He'll have to step up when we're out on patrol. But I'm pissed off with him.'

'All this stuff about Emily?'

'Yeah. I don't remember anything about shagging the contractors in the camp orders, do you?'

'It's just a wind-up. And when you're out there and you need Finn to be good, he's always good.'

'Under pressure he's good. The rest of the time he's all mouth.'

'You can't step anyone over him.'

'I know.'

'So it'll be Finn to command and Jamie as second i/c?'

'Yup.'

Sol placed his empty plate on the ground beside him, lay back on his cot and shut his eyes.

'What happened to Angus today? The lads have been ripping into him. Mal's his best mate, but he's been tearing Angry apart.'

Who needs sergeants, Dave thought, when you had mates to

60

keep you in order? 'I don't know what's going on with that lad,' he said. 'I intend to find out now.'

Angus McCall was eating by himself while Mal and the others were on the other side of the cookhouse. He was watching the TV intently. Although he must have been aware that someone was sitting down next to him, he didn't look up.

'Anything you want to talk about, Angry?' From the way McCall hunched his oversized body, Dave knew that the lad had seen him enter the cookhouse and was bracing himself for what came next.

'Nah . . .'

They both watched the screen. Impossibly beautiful women in gauzy dresses followed a man through London's meaner streets solely because of the way his underarms smelled.

Dave glanced across the room at Mal, self-proclaimed babe magnet. Mal wasn't watching the TV. He was locked in discussion with Finn. Jamie was laughing at them. Dave could tell from the way that Mal and Finn were squaring their shoulders and puffing out their chests that the talk was about women in general. Or maybe the elusive sex grenade in particular.

'You're not sitting with your mates tonight. Have they been taking the piss?'

Angus said nothing. He watched the women in their gauzy dresses.

'You had a bit of trouble out there today . . .'

Angus still didn't respond. His cheeks looked like they were weighing down his face.

'It's strange, arriving in theatre. One minute you're at home buying a few beers in Tesco and the next minute you're in 'Stan being asked to kill a man.'

Angus nodded and continued to stare at the screen.

'I can't make you slot someone. If your conscience says you shouldn't, then don't,' Dave said. 'And I'll try to respect you for it.'

Angus shook his head. 'It's just because I thought he was dead and he started moving. It's just because I wasn't expecting it.'

'You have the right to say: No, Sarge, let's try to save his life.'

'That would be fucking daft.' Angus looked at Dave for the first time. 'We'd only just shot him.'

'I agree with you there, Angry. But the fact is, we were operating at the edge of the RoE and some people would say we should have carried him to a medic there and then.'

'Fucking daft.' Angus turned back to the TV. 'What's the point in firing at someone if you make them better afterwards? Makes it all a stupid fucking game.'

'If he's wounded, some people would say we should have brought him back for treatment . . .'

'That's shit.'

Dave watched the TV. A game show. A contestant was being offered the chance of winning fabulous amounts of money if he chose the right coloured box. The man's face ballooned as he tried to make a decision. The audience shouted advice. They shouted louder and louder. Red! Blue! Green!

'And then there was the bloke up the tree.'

'I was going to do it!' Angus looked distressed now. 'I was just going to do it and you changed your mind and told Finn instead!'

Dave smiled. 'Pissed you off, did I?'

'Fucking right you did! I was going to do it!'

'That's another one where the RoE get a bit murky,' said Dave. 'Because in my heart of hearts I knew he was jammed there and so was his weapon and he wasn't in much of a position to fire on anyone. And I was just beginning to think that maybe we'd take him in for questioning. But I didn't think it fast enough and Finn fired.'

'I was going to slot him . . .'

'You need to get a grip on yourself, Angry. You could find your-self in a situation where it's kill or be killed. And hesitation won't help you then.'

'I was just slow today!' Angus protested. 'That's all.'

'You've never killed a man, have you?'

Angus shook his head unhappily. 'There wasn't a lot of action in Iraq when I got there.'

'Nothing to be ashamed of. I know men who've been through their entire careers without firing their weapon except in training. A lot were never operational.'

'My dad was operational.'

'Oh, yeah, Falklands wasn't it?' Dave said, as though he didn't know already. As though he hadn't heard a thousand times. Finny had sometimes threatened to slot Angus if he talked about his dad one more time and even Angry's best mate Mal seemed to have some sympathy for that idea. But Dave knew that Angus measured everyone against McCall Senior.

'My dad had to kill Argentinians. He said he didn't feel anything at the time. But later it can get to you.'

'Yeah, it can get to you later. If you let it. But if you remember that we're professional soldiers and we're doing a job here and our job is to deal with the choggies before they can deal with us, that makes it easier. We're just doing our job.'

They watched as the man on the screen chose the red box. They waited to see if he'd become a millionaire. After a long pause it was revealed that he hadn't. The green box had been the right one. The man started to cry. His wife, who had been shouting at him to open the green box, came on stage and started to cry too. The game show host started to cry.

'I'm OK with killing.' Angus looked at Dave again. 'Next time I'll do it.'

'OK.' Dave nodded. 'You'll get a lot of chances to prove yourself.'

'I will,' Angus said. 'I'll prove myself, Sarge.'

In his heart, Dave wasn't convinced. The RoE were grey and confusing but something else was holding Angry back. Dave had thought about keeping him on camp duties for a few days. He decided to let him stay with the others for now.

Dave looked across the room. Finn was talking to a group of contractors. Dave saw with dismay that they were getting out their wallets. They were young oil engineers with large salaries, which made them prime targets for Finn. Dave strode over to issue Finny with a stern warning, but he was too late. The group were already putting away their wallets and dispersing.

Chapter Nine

JAMIE'S TEXT SAID HE HAD BEEN MADE ACTING SECTION 2 I/C. WHAT did that mean? If Agnieszka saw one of the other wives and they forced her into conversation as usual then she would find a way to ask them about a 2 i/c.

She didn't have anywhere to go today but she put Luke into the car because something had now gone wrong with the TV. Maybe she had hit the wrong button, maybe the set was really broken or maybe, maybe, maybe a thousand things but the result was the same: no TV. And she relied on TV to calm Luke down and send him off to sleep.

It calmed her down too. She liked the programmes where people went to auctions with their old junk. She liked to see their faces as the bidding went up and up. Yesterday there had been a new game show and she had watched a man almost win a million pounds. At the last minute he had chosen the wrong box and he had cried. Agnieszka had cried with him. A million pounds would turn the world from black and white to colour. A million pounds would make the bumpy road smooth.

The man had chosen the wrong box because he had not listened to his wife, who was shouting the right answer from the audience. Now they would have to drive home and carry on their unchanging lives together knowing that maybe their dreams would never come true.

Agnieszka found herself driving towards the city. There was a cathedral and in the quaint streets surrounding it were many small, understated shops. But Agnieszka preferred the superstore on the outskirts. It was a cathedral of sorts, because you felt calm and peaceful when you walked up its wide aisles.

She hummed along to the warm, soft music as she passed the stationery and art materials. The goods on the shelves were a riot of colour like indoor flower beds. Luke was sleeping deeply and she could look at the shelves undisturbed.

Agnieszka made her way to the TV department and wandered between the sets, even though she could not afford to buy one. She read the cards carefully which described the special features of each set.

'Hello, Mrs Dermott.'

She looked up. A man was grinning at her. For a moment she didn't recognize him, just knew she felt pleased to see him.

'Darrel Gregg from the garage,' he reminded her. But by then she had remembered. She smiled.

'Buying a TV?'

'I already have TV but it broken.'

Darrel's face fell. He was reflecting her own face back at her, she realized. The corners of his mouth turned down and his eyes looked sad.

'Let's get this straight. Last week it was your car . . .'

She tried to turn up the corners of her mouth to see if his corners would turn up too.

'. . . and this week it's the TV.'

'Also dishwasher. That breaks even before car! Also gutter!'

He gave her such an immense smile that she smiled back. He had a row of even white teeth which seemed to fill his face with smile. Then he began to laugh.

She started to laugh too. 'My husband go and whole house fall down!' It seemed ridiculous now. It was so absurd that all you could do was laugh at it.

'I hope at least the car's running all right.'

She nodded, still smiling.

'Car is perfect. Like new car.'

He looked pleased. 'Glad we were able to help. Now what about your lad's hospital appointment? You got up the motorway and everything was OK?'

'Well . . .' She felt her face cloud again. You could laugh about broken TVs, dishwashers, cars, gutters. But you couldn't laugh about a baby who needed fixing.

His face clouded too. 'Not OK, then?'

Now she felt tears stinging at her eyes. She knew she must not speak or they would come flooding out of her. It was something you could do in private but never in public, certainly not with some man at the superstore. She glanced at Luke, sleeping peacefully in his buggy, his face round and his eyelashes long. He looked just like any normal baby. But he wasn't.

The man was watching her with concern. His eyes wrinkled at the edges when he smiled and then if he stopped smiling the wrinkles were still there. He was old, she thought. He might even be thirty.

'Mrs Dermott . . . I . . . look, what's your first name?'

She blinked at him. Her eyes felt wet. Damn. Damn!

'Agnieszka,' she said in a voice so small that he asked her to repeat it several times.

Finally he repeated it himself: 'Agnieszka!' He made it sound like a sneeze.

She felt herself smiling. 'Agnieszka!'

'Bless you! But I'll never be able to say that. I'll just call you Aggie. So listen, Aggie, got a few minutes to come to the café with me? I'd like to buy you a coffee and hear all about this beautiful boy of yours.' He gestured towards the sleeping baby.

She nodded and they went up the escalator together, Darrel steering the buggy expertly up the moving stairs.

She sat down and he reappeared a few minutes later with a tray.

He put a coffee cup down in front of her. 'And crisps in case you feel salty. And a muffin in case you feel sweet.' She didn't move, just rocked the buggy back and forth while he unloaded the tray. It felt good to sit still and let someone else look after her.

'OK,' he said, 'tell me about your little boy.'

So she told him about Luke's fits. The trip to the hospital yesterday had been inconclusive. She hadn't even discussed it with Jamie yet. She was waiting for his next call, when she would try to explain what the doctor had said, even though she hadn't understood most of it and the link would disappear for whole sentences at a time.

'Has he had a scan?'

'He will have scan, doctor said.' She had understood that much, anyway.

'Did he say what's causing the fits?'

'He say it hard to know because Luke so young, we wait a few months to be know anything.'

'Well, did he give any idea what it might be?'

Agnieszka shrugged. At this point the doctor had lost her. His language had become complicated and she had suspected he was being evasive.

'Luke's still a young baby, Aggie, and, let's face it, arriving into this world can be a bit of a shock. Some children take a while to adjust.'

Agnieszka looked at him with admiration. He spoke so firmly and with such knowledge that he sounded like a doctor, he sounded the way the doctor at the hospital should have sounded. 'I like that I understand every word you say.'

'But your English is fantastic!'

'No. But you very clear.'

'Right then, here's something to be clear about. We have to sort out this broken TV of yours or you'll end up with a new one you don't need.'

'I don't have money for new TV. I don't know why I come here today, honest.' She was glad she had, though. The coffee tasted good. It had a layer of thick milk on top and beneath, despite the two tiny sachets of sugar she had added, was the bitterness she loved.

'Does it start when you switch it on?' He was sounding like a doctor again.

'It start but I don't get good channel or good picture.'

'Cable, digital or terrestrial?'

She didn't know.

'I can sometimes sort that kind of thing out. I'm not a professional, mind. But would you like me to have a look?'

She was so surprised that she upset her coffee. Embarrassed, she mopped it up with a series of increasingly brown, soggy napkins. Then he insisted on getting her another coffee.

While he was gone, she caught sight of a pregnant woman marching through the supermarket section of the store beyond the café. A toddler sat at the front of her trolley, feet dangling. The woman seemed to be in a hurry, not in a dream the way Agnieszka had been through most of her pregnancy.

A second later she realized that it was Jenny Henley with little Vicky. Agnieszka willed Jenny not to turn. But of course she did. She'd passed something she wanted so she stopped and swung the trolley around and there was a moment when she faced Agnieszka directly. Agnieszka's heart sank. She hoped Jenny would just wave and keep going.

It took Jenny a moment to recognize her neighbour. Instinct told her to smile, wave and keep on shopping. She was due back at Leanne Buckle's with the groceries in time to make lunch for everyone because all Leanne could do was cuddle the twins and twist a wet tissue around in her fingers until she had some more news of Steve.

But Jenny liked Jamie a lot and she remembered how Dave had specially asked her to look out for Agnieszka. She remembered the woman's isolation. And when Jenny had phoned with the news about Steve, Agnieszka had almost burst into tears. She decided to push her trolley over to the Polish girl for a quick, friendly hello.

'I'm rushing!' she said apologetically as she approached. 'I wish I could sit down and have a drink with you, Agnieszka.'

'Oh, I'm all right,' Agnieszka said sweetly. Her smile was shy and she looked down at the ground.

'Steve's still stable,' Jenny said, as though Agnieszka had asked about him. Because she ought to have asked, Jenny thought. 'But they must have given him a lot of morphine or something because no one's spoken to him. I know Dave hasn't. And Leanne's just waiting by the phone.'

'I very, very sorry for Leanne.' Agnieszka spoke with such sincerity that Jenny forgave her for not asking.

Agnieszka was looking at Vicky now.

'How are you, little darling?' she asked, her expression suddenly radiant. Vicky responded immediately to that smile. Who could fail to? Jenny thought. When Agnieszka smiled her apparent dissatisfaction melted away and her whole face was transformed. She really was beautiful. She made Jenny, who longed to find time for the hairdresser, feel dowdy. The baby kicked her heartily and she stroked her stomach as Vicky prattled on to Agnieszka.

'You're welcome to drop by any time,' Jenny told her. 'I wish you would. I hate the first month or two after Dave goes. I get so fed up. Bring Luke over and we'll have a cup of coffee.'

The invitation was delivered warmly but it was received with nothing more than her usual polite nod.

'Must get moving.' Jenny swung the trolley around. 'It's terrible if Leanne's twins get hungry and they both start crying at once!'

Vicky and Agnieszka waved passionately to each other. At the place where the café melted into the superstore, Vicky said: 'Mummy, who's that man?'

Jenny turned in time to see a man approach Agnieszka with a cup in his hand. Jenny watched as the two exchanged smiles.

'I don't know, sweetheart,' she said. Had he been lingering with Agnieszka's coffee on the outskirts of their conversation so that Jenny didn't see him? She felt her face reddening. She didn't know why.

Chapter Ten

AT SENZHIRI FORWARD OPERATING BASE, NOTHING MOVED IN THE baking afternoon heat. The contractors were out with 2 Platoon. 3 Platoon was on patrol in the nearby town. 1 Platoon was on base duties. They'd been away a month now, three weeks of it here at Senzhiri. Time and the heat had dulled their yearning for home.

Mal had finished cleaning his weapon and fallen asleep on his cot. It was night time and his mother was writing someone a letter. The kitchen smelled of her home-cooked spicy food and his father's cigarettes. Mal was running through, on his way out as usual. His mother gave him a sweet, weary smile as he left.

He went to a club. His clothes were right, he smelled good and he felt lucky. The music throbbed inside him like his own heartbeat. He was watching a girl dancing and she was looking back at him as she moved. Her name was Emily and she was hot, hot, hot . . .

'Move, you lazy bastard!' a voice roared in his ear.

He opened his eyes. No hot babe. Just Sergeant Dave Henley, hands on hips, standing over him.

'And if you're going to get your head down, get your boots off! How many times do I have to tell you?'

Mal scrambled off his cot. The dream was over but the beat of the music thudded on inside his head.

'Chinook's here, you should be unloading with the others.'

Mal blinked. So that wasn't a bass line. It was rotor blades.

He stumbled out of the tent, still half asleep. The dream refused to go away. He was partly in Afghanistan and partly inside his dream in England. He remembered his mother's face, her tired smile. The thud of the helicopter's blades seemed to cut into him. They cut through to a vein and tapped directly into a homesickness he had felt on first arriving but had not known was still there.

But a Chinook meant supplies and supplies meant mail and there would certainly be a letter from his mother. That must have been what she had been writing in his dream. He'd dreamed the letter and now it would arrive. Also, he'd met a couple of girls just before deployment and both relationships had reached that red-hot stage where the girls wanted more. So they might write too. With luck, they might even have included pictures. With a lot of luck, they wouldn't be wearing any clothes.

His step quickened as the Chinook blades slowed and men emerged from different tents and buildings around the camp.

Finn was there already.

'Oh yes oh yes!' he said. 'Our new toys have arrived!'

Angus was standing over a wooden crate. Mal took the other end and Finn went with them to the Company Quartermaster.

'So what's in here?' Mal asked.

'I reckon it's the new shotguns,' Finn said.

The platoon had trained on Salisbury Plain with the new Benelli M4 shotguns but when they had arrived in Afghanistan they had found the first consignment was behind them.

'If it's the new shotguns,' Mal said, 'why aren't there more of them?'

'Because there are more coming. Or so they say.'

'I've heard that one before,' Mal said.

'Why are you lot hanging around?' The CQMS glared at them. 'Not got anything better to do?'

'Just interested to know what's in the crate, Colour,' Finn said.

'Well you can fuck off because I'm not telling you.'

Angus started to argue but Finn and Mal pulled him back to the Chinook.

'No point getting nasty with the colour boy,' Mal said.

'You want to get nasty, Mr Angry, you could try killing the Taliban some time,' Finn said.

'Kill them?' Mal cried. '*Kill them?* Why would he do that when he could just stand in a fucking ditch and stare at them instead?'

Angus reddened. No one ever noticed your best moments; they just picked up on your mistakes and failures and kept throwing them back at you. And Mal was the worst. Angus thought his mate should understand and maybe even tell the others to fuck off but Mal seemed to feel Angus had let him down personally.

Nobody took much notice of the new lads on the Chinook when the bulging mail bag emerged. Dave sent them to find a cot while the letters were distributed.

Finn had learned not to expect blueys, but he hung around in the hope that someone, maybe one of his babymothers, might have written for once. He watched his mates opening their letters and, for a few minutes, he saw them all go home. They read their mail and they weren't here in Afghanistan any more. Finn thought that, if the Taliban knew what they were doing, this was the moment they should choose to attack.

Angus had a bluey from his mother. It didn't say much but, still, it was a letter. Angry hoped his father might remember how much the post mattered when he was far from home, but his old man seldom wrote.

Jamie had a whole stack, as usual. His entire family were enthusiastic letter-writers but he tore open Agnieszka's envelope first. She'd sent pictures and a poem she'd read in a Polish magazine. Her English translation was almost incomprehensible but Jamie liked it all the more for that.

Sol hobbled up and found a thick envelope full of drawings from the kids.

Dave had a long bluey from Jenny. He glanced at a few lines halfway down the page before unfolding it. '. . . how much you think of us, if you ever get time to think about us out there, because sometimes you don't even call once a week and I . . .'

He decided to read it later. Included was a card from Vicky which he pulled out at once: she'd dipped her toes in bright paints and treated him to a vibrant, fire-coloured footprint. He imagined Jen pressing the little foot onto the card and Vicky squealing. He tried to imagine their faces. But he couldn't.

Mal opened his post eagerly. There was just one from his mum in her shaky writing, half capitals, half small letters. He watched while the blueys were distributed in case there was more for him.

Nothing. He sighed. He wanted a woman, one he knew or one he didn't. This Emily woman, the elusive civilian who kept herself so hidden here at the base, she was the only hope.

It took a while for people to notice the new lads hanging around by the empty cots and to realize who they were.

'Which section are you in?'

The two younger lads, one black, the other small and fair, said they were in 1 Section. But all eyes were fixed on the third newcomer.

'Are you in 2 Section?'

'Yeah. 1 Platoon. I'm Ryan Connor. Moved over from D Company. They sent me because I'm a gimpyman.'

'Yes!' yelled everyone who had taken a bet with Finn. 'Yes!' Rifleman Connor was strawberry blond.

'No, no, no!' cried Finn. 'We said ginger. This man's no pisswizard.'

'He is fucking ginger.'

'Come on, mate, you're beat, he's pure pisswizard!'

'He is not!'

Finn started to pull Rifleman Connor out of the tent into the sunlight. Connor was a tall, gangly man with uneven skin and scars on his face. He allowed himself to be dragged for a few paces before he grabbed Finn by his shoulders and swung him around.

'What the fuck do you think you're doing?'

Finn looked at Connor's face for the first time and saw the street there.

'Sorry, mate, very sorry.' He offered his hand. 'Billy Finn, 1 Section second i/c.'

Rifleman Connor looked at him uncertainly. Then he shook hands.

'Basically,' continued Finn, 'these guys are trying to screw me out of a lot of money because of the colour of your hair.'

'What's the colour of my hair got to do with anything?'

'Just walk into the light, mate, and I'll explain.'

Connor stepped out into the burning sunlight. He was taller than most of the men around him.

'Just crouch down a minute, bruv, so we can all see the top of your head.'

'Is this a joke?' Connor still wasn't sure whether to be angry or amused. 'I mean, I didn't expect to get to the FOB and have everyone running their fingers through my hair.'

'It's more red in some parts than others.'

'He's definitely a pisswizard.'

'He's ginger, totally ginger, here on the side.'

'Bollocks,' Finny kept yelling. 'This man is blond.'

'This man is a ginger pisswizard. I got my fiver down at five to four on, Finny! You owe us money.'

Finn caught sight of the reddest of the 2 Section redheads. 'Oy, Broom, get over here and put your head right next to Connor's.'

'I'm not snuggling up to no man,' Broom protested but Finn had him now in an iron grip.

'Crouch down here and shut up.'

Broom was small enough to push around. He squatted shoulder to shoulder with Connor, still protesting.

'Now, lads. Broom . . .' Finn announced triumphantly, 'is a pisswizard.'

There was silence as everyone contemplated the two heads.

Broom said to Connor, 'You're probably thinking this is one of them weird initiation rituals.'

'I'm thinking someone's taking the piss,' Connor said.

'Thank you, lads, for your patience,' Finn said.

'It's running out,' Connor warned ominously.

'Side by side,' Finn went on, 'you can see that this is red.'

He pulled a tuft of Broom's hair.

At that moment, Sol limped past, looking for 1 Section's new recruits. They were standing at the edge of the group.

'You're out on patrol,' he told Finn. 'Now.'

'Corporal Kasanita! Let Sol decide.'

Sol glowered at them. His ankle was hurting and the medic was still refusing to let him do anything but light duties and he hated to miss another patrol.

'I'm not deciding anything,' he said. 'Finn, you're acting section commander. So you shouldn't expect me to get your men to the vehicles on time.'

'Shit!' Finn looked at his watch.

'You should have them ready over there right now.'

'OK, OK, but just tell us something, Sol. Is this man's hair red or not?'

Sol barely glanced at Rifleman Connor. 'Not really,' he said.

Finn's face broke into a broad grin.

Sol ignored the howls of protest. 'Adam Bacon and Jack Binns? You're in 1 Section, 1 Platoon and I'm your section commander, Sol Kasanita.' He held out his hand.

He thought how young these two kids looked. The black one could not take his eyes off the furore behind them, where the row over Rifleman Connor's hair threatened to turn nasty. Sol saw Dave striding purposefully out of the ops room.

'Come over to the cookhouse and we can talk away from these idiots,' Sol said. 'The sergeant's going to sort them out.'

Even from the cookhouse it was clear that the redhead debate was turning into a fight. As they sat down, Sol heard Dave's voice booming over the chaos. Then there was silence.

'That's our platoon sergeant. He's put a stop to their nonsense,' Sol said. 'Dave Henley. He's the best. He takes good care of us. He'll be having a word with you soon.'

The recruits nodded nervously. The sound of Dave bawling out the lads had not been reassuring. It was followed almost immediately by the sound of everyone rushing to get ready for the patrol.

'They're going out now,' Sol said. 'I'd be with them if I hadn't twisted my ankle. Next time, you'll go too. With Lance Corporal Finn as your acting platoon commander.'

They nodded glumly. They already knew who Finn was.

'When will your ankle be better?' Binns asked hopefully.

'Oh, a few days more.'

'Then you'll be back in charge again?'

Sol nodded.

Bacon said: 'Does it matter what colour the bloke's hair is?'

'Only if you've put some money on it. Finn was running a book. He's always running a book. If there were two flies crawling up the wall, Finn would take a bet from you on the first to get to the top.'

The recruits grimaced.

'The lads don't often argue like that,' Sol said. 'We're usually very good mates. We have to be. Our lives depend on it.'

He paused.

'So, how long you two been in for?'

'I only joined before Christmas, me,' Rifleman Bacon said.

'Me too,' Jack Binns said. 'I'm working in Currys and we're having a one-day special September sale and I'm getting really fed up and I think, right. So in my lunch hour I go over to Army Recruitment and I sign up. Just like that.'

Sol gave his wide, lazy smile.

'Currys' sale in autumn. Theatre in summer. Not sure which is worse.'

The engines were roaring now. The platoons were leaving the base. Leaving without Sol, yet again. He tried not to listen.

Binns said he came from Dorset. 'See, nothing ever happens there.'

'How about you?' Sol asked Adam Bacon. 'Much happening where you're from?'

'Yeah, there's a lot happens in Wolverhampton. Sometimes too much.'

'So you came here for a bit of quiet?'

Bacon smiled.

'My mum thinks it's safer in Afghanistan than round my manor. But it's the wrong time for me, maybe. I like to rap, see. And it's all just started taking off and then it's all over because I'm away training to Catterick.'

Sol smiled back at him.

'There's a lot of lads like rap here. They'll want to hear what you got.'

Bacon grinned. He didn't want to admit that his greatest hope was not that he'd go home alive but that he'd get a chance to rap for his new mates.

Sol heard the sound of the convoy fading into the distance. Soon it would be nothing more than a silent dust cloud making its way towards the Green Zone.

Mal had been selected to use the new shotgun: he was obviously delighted but Sol would have liked to keep an eye on him. He didn't believe that Finn gripped 1 Section fiercely enough. One man down and Sol knew he would blame himself and his stupid ankle for ever. Dave had told him he'd stay alongside them. But Sol knew Dave already had enough to do.

'OK.' Sol turned back to Bacon and Binns. 'Let me tell you some of the things you lads need to remember if you're going to stay safe. I'll start with foot powder . . .'

Chapter Eleven

MAL SAT WITH THE BENELLI M4 SHOTGUN ON HIS LAP, CRADLING IT lovingly as the Vector bumped its way across the desert.

'Yes!' he'd said, punching the air, when Dave told him he'd be the first to use the new weapon. 'Let's hope we get into close combat so I can use it!'

'Yeah, let's hope so.' Dave had rolled his eyes. 'Never mind the rest of us.'

Dave was still annoyed with Finn for leading the platoon into a punch-up. Since the new gunner from 2 Section had hair which might or might not be red, Dave had declared the betting void and told Finn to give everyone their money back.

'I don't want any more bets,' he'd said to Finn. 'You're a fucking soldier, not a bookie, and you've made the whole platoon late for a serious operation.'

They were clearing a river crossing today. The OC had intelligence that the Taliban was planning to take control of it. Almost the entire company was involved and the civilians had been told they were confined to base with minimal staffing. Martyn Robertson had objected strongly but the OC had overruled him, explaining that if the Taliban took this crossing then getting the oil exploration team across the river would be almost impossible.

They dismounted and left the track on foot. At first it was a relief to plunge beneath the canopy. Mal moved ahead with the shotgun. The only downside was that he was expected to carry his SA80 as well. The heavy rifle was like an old friend who'd overstayed his welcome. Until they came under distant fire, when he reorganized himself to use his SA80 and the shotgun felt like a gatecrasher at the party.

The other sections of 1 Platoon advanced towards the firing on their right flank. Dave heard the new gunner giving it some with the gimpy. Poor bloke. Off a Chinook into a crowd of lads all staring at his hair like farmers at a sheep auction, then straight onto patrol before he'd drawn breath. But his fire was effective. The combination of Jamie with his GPMG on one side and Rifleman Connor with his on the other brought silence. Dave guessed the enemy had moved. The incoming rounds had been more of a warning than a threat.

1 Platoon moved forward to the river, 1 Section on the left flank. They emerged from the trees and crossed an irrigation ditch into a field of high crops.

Although it was early the sun showed them no mercy. Clouds of pollen were released by the plants, its pungent odour magnified by the heat.

'Christ, do they make their animals eat this shit?'

'It's giving me a headache.'

'I feel ready to get me head down . . .'

'Stick some in your pocket for later and you'll be fucking glad you did,' Finn said.

Dave's eyes narrowed. He looked closely at the exotic plant. Each leaf consisted of delicate fingers, like a hand in a lace glove.

'Is it what I think it is?'

His question was met with smothered laughter but no one replied. The plant certainly wasn't a poppy: they had passed a field of these further back, their pods closed tightly like tiny purses. There were brown slits down the side of each pod where the resin had been extracted.

It must be cannabis.

'Anyone caught trying to sneak this weed out of here's in big trouble,' Dave snarled. 'Did you hear me, Finn?'

'Yessir,' Finn said cheerfully. 'I never touch it these days.'

'Oh, come on, Sarge. Can't we pick the pretty flowers?'

'Who was that?' Dave didn't recognize the voice. It sounded drunk. Had someone already managed to help himself to this stuff?

Could you consume it straight off the plant? A man who preferred a pint, Dave suddenly regretted that he hadn't learned more on the warm summer evenings in the south London streets where he was brought up. They'd sometimes been hazy with its distinctive smoke. The smell in the field was far stronger and its acrid notes more jarring.

Nobody answered Dave's question. His head was throbbing badly. He wanted to close his eyes to shut out the bright sunlight. Unlike most of the fields around here, this one was enormous. They stumbled on without ever seeming to reach the other side. The clouds of pollen grew denser and the stench more pungent.

When they finally reached the irrigation channel they found they were far more scattered than anyone had realized. In the dense cannabis forest everyone had thought his mates were close. Dave had believed he was bringing up the rear but now he discovered he was near the front.

Finn instructed everyone to group and go firm. They dodged back into cover and waited for further orders.

They sat down with relief, shading themselves from the flying pollen and beating sunlight. They gulped down water.

Jamie couldn't stop sneezing.

'You all right?' Dave asked.

'Must be the sodding pollen,' Jamie said. 'It doesn't normally get to me.'

Finn wiped his eyes. 'This stuff can really make you feel bad.'

Angus's face was pale. 'It's making me want to puke.'

'Me too,' Mal said. He put both his weapons down. He hoped there wouldn't be any close combat now. He didn't feel ready or able to move to the front and respond.

The firing was closer but sporadic. Dave could hear Major Willingham directing operations. They waited. There were still no orders for them. Finally, after almost half an hour, Boss Weeks told 1 Platoon to prepare to move closer to the river. Dave looked around 1 Section, slumped in the cannabis plants. He hoped the others were more prepared than this lot and that the stags were still alert.

They moved to the corner of the field but were told to wait again. They sat down once more, swearing as pollen clouds billowed around them. Some of the lads closed their eyes. Dave suspected a few had fallen asleep. He was fighting against doing so himself. If he just closed his eyes and relaxed his body, he knew sleep's warm embrace would close around him . . . He tried to hide further from the sun, amongst the stems of the cannabis plants, and the movement released yet more pollen.

The firing sounded increasingly far off and unthreatening, and the lads rested their weapons against the plant stems.

'You seen Emily lately, mate?' Mal asked Finn drowsily.

'This morning,' Finn said. 'Went over to the gym and I heard this whistle. So I turned around . . . phwoar!'

Mal gave a little moan. 'You going to share her?'

'S'pose I'll have to,' Finn said. 'I'm fucking exhausted.'

'If you don't fucking shut up about Emily . . .' But Dave was too hot and tired to think of a suitable threat.

The sun moved lazily across the sky but its intensity did not ease. Dave closed his eyes. He said to himself: I won't let myself sleep. I'll just rest a moment . . .

Then the boss's voice, clear and precise, was right in his ear. Dave sat bolt upright. Oh, fuck. Had he been asleep?

Finn gave him a grin and a meaningful wink.

Dave swallowed. He felt sick now. Boss Weeks's voice said that there was a compound, not currently visible, about four hundred metres away at the riverside. 1 and 2 Sections should move down the irrigation channel to clear it, with 3 Section covering.

'Keep everyone else out of the cannabis field,' Dave warned the boss. 'It makes you feel weird.'

'Sergeant, are you slurring your speech?'

'Course not, sir!' Dave said as crisply as he could.

There were protests from the commanders of 2 and 3 Sections, who liked the sound of a cannabis crop.

'No,' Dave said. 'You want to stay alert.'

'OK, lads, we're moving,' Finn said.

The section began to stir. Getting up with so much weight on was always hard. Now it felt impossible. Their heads hurt like a bad hangover.

Finn and Jamie struggled to their feet and then pulled up each man in turn. They began to move down the irrigation channel towards the compound. Dave noticed men stumbling. He felt

81

irritated and angry and didn't really know why. Then Mal gave him a reason by stopping dead in his tracks. Angus collided with him and the two nearly fell over.

'What are you shitheads doing?'

Mal said something to Angus and the two of them stood motionless.

Dave yelled: 'Get on with it.'

'I can't,' Mal said.

'Why not?'

There was the sound of a big, angry insect by his ear. Rounds, and now more rounds, swarming like bees. The section made its first fast move of the day and ducked into the ditch. Dave looked at the line of men taking cover.

A round pinged off his helmet. More rounds bounced on the ground around them or plopped into the water. There was another ping on his helmet. He felt like a slot machine in a crowded arcade. He crouched further beneath the banks of the channel.

They were ready to fire back but it was almost impossible to see where. Jamie followed the sound and gave the enemy repeated bursts with the gimpy. Angus suddenly stood up during the brief silence that followed.

'For fuck's sake!' Dave yelled.

But now Angus was barging past him and back along the ditch.

'What the fuck are you doing?'

Angus was retracing their steps. He hunched his huge body as he ran but he was still dangerously overexposed.

'No, no, don't do it!' Mal's plea fell on deaf ears. Angus was gone, a huge, lumbering, mud-covered animal, drawing enemy fire.

'Get the fuck back here you fucking, fucking wanker!' Dave yelled.

Angus didn't reply. Dave looked at Mal for an explanation. Mal was suddenly very busy with his SA80, firing at nothing in particular. Then Dave realized what was missing. The shotgun.

'Christ, he hasn't gone back for the Benelli!'

Mal wouldn't look at him and Dave knew he was right.

Dave stared up the drainage channel but Angus was already out of sight. He had reached the cannabis field and was threading his way into it.

'If the choggies have got there already they'll have booby-trapped it!' Dave yelled into the radio. 'McCall, don't touch that shotgun and get back here! Get back NOW!'

'The choggies can't have moved in on our last position yet!' Mal said.

'What about the one before that?' Dave saw Mal's face freeze as he tried to remember whether he'd left the shotgun at the first or second place they'd stopped.

'McCall, leave the fucking shotgun,' Dave roared again. 'Stay where you are and we'll come for you.'

Jamie's voice: 'Strange movement in that line of trees. I think the Talis are firing from up in the branches.'

Dave turned to Mal. 'Did you have it when we stopped the second time?'

Mal's miserable expression was the only answer Dave needed.

Jamie let the gimpy do its work. A weapon fell from one tree but a body didn't follow. The answering fire began to lessen.

Drowsiness, sickness and headaches were peeling away from them now. Dave's head began to clear. Angus was fucking around in the stuff that had fucked them up in the first place. *I'll kill him* . . . Then he realized the Taliban was likely to save him the trouble.

With a sinking heart, he knew the lost shotgun was going to jeopardize the whole operation. The only safe way to go back for it was with the help and cover of all three sections and EOD to check for booby traps before they touched it. He knew it never would have happened if Sol had been here.

3 Section had moved round and were firing along the treeline as well now.

'1 Section, move forward,' the boss told them. Finn set off at the front. All Dave's instincts propelled him forward. But then those instincts were overridden by the knowledge that Angus was completely alone behind them and to leave him or the shotgun was unthinkable.

'Hold firm!' he said reluctantly.

'Move forward,' the boss said.

'We've got a problem at the back.'

'What problem?'

Mal's face turned towards him, blanched despite the sun, his brown eyes sunken.

Dave sighed. 'ECM not working.'

'1 Section, hold firm,' the boss instructed. Electronic Counter Measures was the only protection they had against walking into a remote-controlled mine, so no one was going to make them go forward without it.

They were still under sporadic fire, but Finn kept looking their way. Dave knew it wouldn't take him long to notice Angus's absence.

'Did we leave Angry behind?' Finn suddenly blurted into the mic.

'No.' Dave was still wondering what to do. If the rifle was at the corner of the field there was a chance Angus could get back with it alive. If it was still at their earlier position, then he would have to ask for support from the whole platoon.

'Is everything OK there?' the boss asked.

'Just what is going on, Sergeant?' Major Willingham's tone was crisp and indignant. 'Have you got a man down?'

'No, sir.'

'ECM problem,' the boss said helpfully.

'Well, hurry up.' The major sounded irritable. And Dave knew him well enough to be sure that the gap between an irritable OC and an angry OC was very narrow.

The silence stretched. Dave thought he could hear Major Willingham breathing like an angry bull into his mic. Ahead of them the other platoons were engaged in some intense fighting. Even the newest recruit must feel himself pulled towards the action; they were pinned in a ditch by their own incompetence instead. Dave wished the enemy would open fire and give them an excuse to hold firm but of course the Taliban weren't there when you needed them.

'Look, what's going on?' the OC roared at last. 'I want 1 Platoon to move forward. Surely you've sorted out your ECM problem by now!'

'Er . . .' The boss couldn't conceal his nervousness. 'How long will it be, Sergeant?'

'Any moment now.' Dave's gaze was fixed on the cannabis field, his heart sinking.

'Shit, Sarge,' Mal said bleakly.

'We'll have to go back for him.'

Finn ran down the ditch towards them. Dave told him what had happened and watched as Finn's eyes darkened.

'The fucking idiot!'

Dave recognized the fury of his own first reaction. He knew that worry came next.

'At least we're not under fire now . . .' Mal said.

'Angry's got everyone confused!' Finn said. 'Even the fucking flipflops.'

'Or maybe they've moved,' Dave said. 'Either to reinforce the centre or into the field to look for him.'

In the silence that followed, Finn's face rearranged itself, as Dave had known it would, into shock. Whatever happened, even if it meant botching today's whole operation, they could not allow a man to fall into the hands of the enemy.

'For fuck's sake!' the major exploded in Dave's ear. 'This is ridiculous. I need you forward. Now!'

To Dave's relief, the Taliban machine guns kicked off.

'Under intense fire,' Boss Weeks reported quickly. He obviously knew that Dave had a bigger problem than an ECM gremlin. 'We can't move forward yet.'

'If you'd moved when I told you to then you'd be there by now,' the major yelled.

The tension on the net was palpable. Dave's eyes were fixed on the field, but there was still no sign of Angry.

'I'll have to tell them what's happened,' Dave said. He felt hollow. He felt sick. This was a massive and embarrassing failure for his platoon. 'Sir—'

'Look!' Mal shouted.

A puff of something that looked like smoke but must have been pollen was rising from the edge of the cannabis field. Angus had stepped out of it and was running towards them, still bent double. He was carrying his rifle and the shotgun. His presence drew a volley of fire which Jamie on one side and gunners from 2 and 3 Sections soon silenced.

'Yes?' the major said wearily. 'What is it you're trying to tell me, Sergeant? I have a feeling that you're about to cock up today's action.'

'Not at all, sir,' Dave said. 'The ECM's working now and we're ready to move forward.'

'Well thank Christ for that!'

When he reached them, Angus handed the shotgun across Dave to his mate.

'Listen, Angry, thanks . . .' Mal said weakly. 'You shouldn't have—'

'You fucking shithead!' Finn shouted.

'No time for that here,' Dave thundered. 'I'll deal with you two when we get back. Now just get on with the fucking job.'

The section made its way along the ditch towards the compound.

Chapter Twelve

DAVE DIALLED HOME ON THE SATELLITE PHONE. WHEN IT connected he listened to the ringing tone without hearing it. His head was ringing already from the bollocking he'd just given Riflemen McCall and Bilaal.

Mal shouldn't have left the shotgun. But Dave knew he'd been overcome by the cannabis plants. For Chrissake, he'd fallen asleep himself.

But there was no such excuse for Angry McCall's dash to save the shotgun. It was so insane that, deep inside, Dave couldn't help admiring the lad's bravery and commitment to a friend. Especially since that friend had recently been merciless in his criticism of Angry's own mistakes.

Dave had threatened to send Angus home, threatened anything he could think of, and the huge lad had hung his head and bitten his lower lip in silence.

'You said you were going to prove yourself,' Dave reminded him. 'And you will. But today you didn't. I'm putting you on shit duties for a week.'

He was just about to dismiss the lad when McCall said: 'Sarge?'

Dave waited, hands on hips.

'Sarge, I did it because I thought it was what my dad would have done.' He looked up briefly, then back at the ground.

Dave sighed. 'You've got to learn to be your own man—'

The phone's insistent ringing snapped him back into the present. It was going on too long. Jenny should be at home because Vicky would be in bed. So why wasn't she answering? The ringing gave him a hollow feeling. Had there been an emergency? No, he would have been told.

This sound of the unanswered phone was a sound more empty than silence. He forgot Mal and Angry and with each ring his mind and heart were pulled a little closer to home. He was tugged back to England, to Wiltshire, to the camp, to his street, to his house and to Jenny, Vicky and their unborn baby. The journey made him tired and tense. He had reached that point in his absence when it was better not to think about them too much. And now he had gone all the way back for Jenny. And she wasn't there.

Dave held the phone to his ear even though the ringing had stopped. He was standing behind the place where soldiers washed their socks in the CQMS's green bowls, behind the showers, behind the civilian area. Nobody was washing now but he could see a few socks and shirts and pairs of underwear hanging limp and forgotten in the Afghan darkness. This was the most private place he could get a signal to ring Jenny. He'd wanted to tell her he loved her. He'd meant to explain that the reason he didn't phone more was that he tried not to think about her too much. Because too many home thoughts could make life here unbearable. He'd wanted to say all that. But she wasn't there.

Jenny had put Vicky to bed. She was so tired she'd gone to bed herself soon afterwards. At first the ringing phone was a ringing phone in her dreams, reinforcing her sleep instead of disturbing it.

Finally she was jolted awake. Her heart pounded. The telephone. And it must be the middle of the night. A night sound more ominous than silence. Maybe it was bad news. She tried to roll over to reach the receiver but she did not like to roll onto her pregnant belly. She had to shuffle to the edge of the bed instead.

Just as she grabbed the receiver, the ringing stopped.

'Dave?' she said. Even though she knew he'd gone. 'Dave?'

She heard her own voice in the empty room, talking to no one. She closed her eyes and turned on the light and when she opened her eyes the bedroom filled up the dark with familiar things. Which didn't mean it wasn't still dark really. One switch of the light and it would be there again.

She dialled 1471. We do not have the caller's number. It had certainly been Dave. She'd missed his call. She felt an acute sense of loss. She'd missed his call. She started to cry. She'd missed his call. God knows when he might get his hands on the satellite phone to ring again. There were times when he barely rang once in ten days and now she'd missed his call.

And it would have been a close, intimate, night-time call when they might have said the things they were supposed to say, instead of the breezy daytime calls interspersed by shouting and chuckling from Vicky. She would have been able to tell him how she wanted him, no, needed him, to leave the army.

She felt the heat of her tears as they ran down her face and onto the pillow.

She hoped he'd call again. She lay awake, waiting. It seemed to her now that she'd spent the whole of her married life waiting for the phone and the reassuring sound of Dave's voice. It also seemed to her that the other wives received more calls when the lads were away than she did. Leanne often got two calls in a week. So did Adi. At this thought, her tears flowed faster.

Try again, Dave! she thought, and she thought it so hard that maybe he would read her mind from the other side of the world.

Chapter Thirteen

DAVE DECIDED TO TRY AGAIN, JUST IN CASE JEN HAD BEEN SLOW picking up. But a voice interrupted him.

'Er, Sarge . . . you finished, then? It's just . . . it's my bird's birthday and . . .'

You were never alone in an FOB. There was no privacy anywhere. He saw Rifleman Broom from 2 Section hovering awkwardly at the edge of the light.

'Here you are, mate.' Dave handed over the phone.

He strode back to the tent he shared with the sergeant major and the other platoon sergeants.

Sitting on his cot he joined in the talk about the day's success. By the time the company had left the area all resistance had been silenced and Major Willingham was confident that they'd foiled any Taliban hopes of taking the river crossing. And they'd done it without air support.

'So we won it for a day,' Dave said. 'How do we know they won't be back tomorrow?'

The others shrugged. It was a question most of them preferred not to ask.

'What was all that crap on the radio when you couldn't move forward?' asked Sergeant Barnes of 3 Platoon.

Dave groaned and told them how Angus had gone back for Mal's shotgun.

'I take it you've bollocked them both,' Sergeant Somers of 2 Platoon said.

'Yep.'

'Why the hell did he do it?'

'He screwed up on a foot patrol early on and he's been trying to make up for it ever since. But that's not the reason he gave me.'

'What reason did he give, then?'

'He said it's what his dad would have done.'

Everyone groaned. There was no one in the company who hadn't heard Angus McCall talking about his war hero father.

'Actually,' CSM Kila said, 'I don't blame McCall.'

All faces turned to him.

'He was wrong, of course, and you had to bollock him. But all he did was use Taliban tactics against the Taliban. Unlike us, the choggies don't move around in fucking great platoons with enough hardware to sink a ship. They don't have men out there carrying eighty pounds of equipment. They run around in their sandals with a rifle slung over one shoulder and maybe a mobile phone, and one of them can halt seventy-five British soldiers just by planting a booby trap in the right place.'

Some agreed they could fight better in smaller, lighter units, like the Taliban. Others preferred the safety of a large company.

'But,' Iain Kila said, 'the real difference between the way we fight and the way the Taliban fight is down to RoE.'

Everyone looked at Dave.

Kila said: 'They aren't going to let you get away with that bloke in the ditch.'

Dave had been questioned twice about the man Mal had shot.

'That pretty monkey is still insisting to the OC that you ordered Bilaal to kill a wounded man. She wants you investigated,' Kila warned.

Dave looked around the tent. 'Would anyone here have casevaced out a bloke you'd shot and were body-searching for dead? If he was barely showing signs of life? And if carrying him back to the convoy would put your own men's lives at risk? Would anyone here really have done that?'

Everyone shook their head except Sergeant Somers. The ensuing discussion was lively. Dave had meant to get back to the satellite phone and give Jenny one last try but when the talk at last petered out he fell asleep instead.

Chapter Fourteen

SERGEANT JEAN PATTERSON OF THE ROYAL MILITARY POLICE SHARED a room with Asma at the base. As soon as they had met each other they had both known it would be one of those friendships that would long outlast their time at Sin City. Today they were interpreting at a *shura* requested by local tribal elders.

'We're working with that blond platoon commander,' Jean said in her soft Scottish lilt as they approached the convoy that was going to take them into the town. 'And he can't keep his eyes off you.'

'Which one? They're all blond.'

'The one whose men need to pay a bit more attention to the RoE.'

'Oh, whatsisname who's learning Pashtu. You nearly made him cry the other night when you were going on about that bloke in the ditch.'

Jean grinned. 'His name's Gordon Weeks. And he wouldn't turn down a few Pashtu lessons from you in private.'

'I don't teach Pashtu,' Asma said. 'And especially not to him. He's the geezer who was moaning about the way we interrogated the detainees and he really pissed me off.'

They arrived at the convoy of waiting vehicles and were met by a smiling Gordon Weeks.

'*As salaam alai kum,*' he said enthusiastically.

'Morning!' said Jean, her voice friendly. Asma did not dignify his Pashtu with a reply.

They climbed on board the Vector. The Officer Commanding

appeared with a Royal Engineer and the civilian oilman, Martyn Robertson.

When everyone was ready, the boss gave the signal and the convoy set off.

'Now remember,' Major Willingham said as they rumbled through the desert. 'The tribesmen have invited us to this meeting and that is a very good sign. They want to hear exactly what you're doing, Martyn, and you need to impress on them the benefits your work can bring to the area. But don't let's miss a chance for information-gathering.' He glanced at Asma. 'Any intelligence will be very welcome. Especially if they can help us pinpoint the exact location of that Taliban compound.'

The headman's house was extensive. The entire complex, house and yard, was bounded by high, thick walls. Shady trees were visible over the top. It was a tantalizing sight from the hot, dusty world outside.

'OK, dismount,' Dave said. His soldiers positioned themselves around the walls.

Only one armed soldier was going into the meeting. Dave had chosen Jamie. He was to adopt an alert but non-threatening stance near the door.

Major Willingham and his team got out of the wagon. The boss held the door open for the two women. Dave didn't miss the officer's glance at the attractive girl from the Intelligence Corps, or the way she swept past him without looking at him or thanking him. Jamie followed the group closely.

Inside, Jean and Asma sat down on the carpet. As usual, just being here felt wrong. They knew that, for the Afghans in the room, their role in the men's discussions was barely tolerable. Women where they shouldn't be. Women negotiating with men. Women in trousers.

Asma lowered her eyes as she sat down and hid her legs. She had grown up hating *burqas* and all they stood for. Symbols of Islamic oppression. But whenever she sat on a carpet in her combat gear with the smell of sweet tea wafting around her, all she wanted was a *burqa*. She suspected covering yourself from head to toe in shapeless folds and creases gave you a kind of escape, even a kind of protection – not just from men, but from yourself.

93

Boss Weeks sat down next to her.

'*As salaam alai kum*,' he said to their hosts. Asma raised her eyebrows, Major Willingham stared at him, but the Afghans smiled and responded with a similar greeting.

'Been learning the lingo, eh? Well at least they understood you.' Martyn Robertson lowered himself creakily on Asma's other side. 'Had a guy called Boyle in the last company who kept trying to speak the lingo and the locals never understood a word he said!'

The head tribesman went through the usual welcome procedures but Asma felt he chose his words with unusual grace and sensitivity. As Jean translated Asma could not resist murmuring to the boss: 'The way this man's talking: he's a cut above a lot of the others we meet.'

The man introduced his two sons, who also sat cross-legged on the carpet. There were other, older men alongside them who weren't introduced. Standing at the edges of the room, leaning silently against the rugs that hung on the walls, were more men, most of them young, some still boys. And by the doors stood a tall rifleman. He balanced his weight evenly on both feet. From time to time Jean glanced at him. She never once saw him move.

Asma took over the interpretation. Major Willingham made a short speech which sounded as though he had learned it off by heart. He said that NATO was committed to supporting the democratically elected government of Afghanistan, and that the Afghan people should decide their own future and not let the Taliban tell them what to do. The Taliban were using and attacking civilians while Britain was committed to helping the Afghans create a stable, peaceful country which was true to its Islamic principles. Britain would fight extremism and do everything possible to help Afghanistan's reconstruction and development.

Asma had translated similar speeches often before. This time, however, she found herself embellishing it a little. Afghanistan was a great country, she added, and it was time for such a country to take its rightful place on the world stage, something it could never do if the Taliban was in control. She glanced at Jean as she spoke. Jean raised an eyebrow. Asma wanted to giggle, until she saw the effect of her words on the Afghans present and knew she had said the right thing.

The elder son started to speak, thanking Major Willingham for his generous and noble words. Jean translated this with precision and the officer, who had no idea of Asma's embroidery, looked startled.

The son now turned to Martyn.

'I understand that you are in our area to look for precious oil and gas reserves. Please tell us more about this.'

Martyn grinned. His brown face was as wrinkled as the rock formations that fascinated him.

'Well, we've found something interesting. I'm sure there are reserves here, but that isn't enough. It has to be possible to extract the oil.'

'And what would that mean for our area?'

'A natural resource always means one thing: greater wealth and jobs.' Martyn glanced at Major Willingham.

'And that would lead to greater stability,' the OC added.

'If drilling starts here – and it would only start with the full agreement of the Afghan people – then my company would certainly be making a substantial investment in this area,' Martyn said.

The elder son smiled politely. 'I have spent time in Saudi Arabia.'

Jean saw both the major and Boss Weeks lean forward with interest. She knew what they were thinking. How had this son of a tribesman travelled so far if not with the support of some outside group?

The son continued. 'Are you suggesting we might have oil reserves like theirs?'

Martyn laughed. 'I can't promise to turn Helmand Province into Saudi. But there could be enough oil to make a difference around here. Where there's oil and gas, roads follow and better housing, better sanitation, improved health care . . . all the things you and your government want.'

'When did you visit Saudi?' Boss Weeks asked.

Asma could tell he badly wanted to know the answer but was trying not to sound too keen. She added a note of polite restraint as she translated the question.

'I studied at university there before returning to my homeland.

95

With my qualifications I could have stayed in Saudi Arabia or travelled anywhere in the world, but I wanted to come back to my home and work for the good of my people.'

Asma looked hard at Boss Weeks, willing him to make an appropriately cordial response.

He said lamely: 'That was jolly good of you.'

'Your action shows great commitment and love for your people and they must surely benefit greatly,' she said. The son looked pleased. Jean nodded her approval. The two women often despaired at the diplomatic incompetence of the officers.

They discussed the needs of the village and what the British Army could realistically supply. They talked about electrical generators and wells and walls around the school yard. Two old men in spotless robes brought everyone more tea. They offered a plate of round, flat savoury bread. Asma took a piece. The very smell of it, the way it sat in her hand, reminded her of her mother's kitchen.

The elder son took this opportunity to speak directly to Asma. He had piercing blue eyes and sharp features. The younger son looked plumper-faced and spoilt.

'May I ask how you, a woman of fine Afghan features and good Pashtun breeding, came to speak both our language and English so perfectly?'

Asma looked down at the carpet, studying its tiny loops and intricate colours. She knew it could take a woman a year or more to make a carpet like this.

'My family left Afghanistan when I was young,' she said. 'And of course we spoke Pashtu at home. I spoke English at school.'

She thought of that home. A grey flat made of grey concrete in a grey block under grey skies. Did it ever stop raining over their patch of east London? Was it ever anything but grey?

Impulsively she told him: 'Now I have returned to Afghanistan I do not understand why my father took us away.'

He looked pleased by this.

'Where is your tribal homeland?' he asked. But Asma knew better than to answer this question. Tribal complications ran deep and vengeance and anger could leap across generations and geography. They could even cross this boiling plain and somehow arrive in a wet, grey concrete flat in London.

'I should not come to your house and talk about myself,' she said shyly, 'when there is so much to discuss about the future of this area.'

The man nodded. 'Nevertheless, your position is an interesting one. Do you see yourself as Afghan? As English? As Pashtun?'

'What's he saying?' Boss Weeks asked.

'He's talking about the school wall,' she lied. To the tribesman she said: 'Allah chose to offer my family refuge in Britain during difficult times and for that I thank Allah and Britain.'

It was a reply she had prepared long ago for any Pashtun who asked her that difficult question. But none had before now.

'And do you really believe,' the son pursued, 'that by working for the British Army you are working in the best interests of the Pashtun people? There is a lot of work to be done here but an army which comes to fight can't do that work. Or is it that after living so long in England you don't care about the Pashtun people?'

His words were confrontational but his tone was gentle.

Her cheeks began to burn.

'What did he say?' Boss Weeks was getting more impatient.

At last she said: 'He asked if the British Army would really be prepared to build a wall around the school.'

'He seems to be speaking to you about this wall with some intensity . . .'

She shrugged.

They debated the likelihood of a mortar attack on the school and whether a wall would really help prevent this. They learned that only a few weeks ago women and girls had been killed at a village school not far away.

'I hope it was rebuilt,' the engineer said. 'In the UK we support the education of women.'

Asma thought of her own education in east London. That had been grey too. She had gone to the same grey, concrete place as hundreds of other teenagers in grey uniforms and the last thing on anybody's mind had been their education. The idea that women and girls might die for the right to this education would have seemed amazing there.

Jean and Major Willingham were now locked in a discussion

with the head tribesman which brought all other conversation around the carpet to a halt.

'What's he saying?' Weeks hissed.

'They're discussing the Taliban,' Asma said.

The tribesman said they had heard about a training base near the Helmand River. He named an area. Asma recognized the name at once from her interrogation of the two detainees.

'In fact,' said the tribesman, 'we have reason to believe that our brothers in this area are sheltering many fighters. And we must remember that our brothers may not have been given a choice.'

'And the focus of this activity? Exactly where is it?' the major demanded.

Jean translated this as: 'Some indication of the exact location would be extremely interesting and helpful to our understanding of this situation, if you would be kind enough to share this information.'

The tribesman looked at his elder son.

'Asad?'

Asad said he wasn't sure exactly which compound it was. He once again named the area.

'Could you be more precise?' Major Willingham urged.

But Asad shook his head.

'We would very much like to welcome you here again. By then we will perhaps have found the answer for you.'

Asma had a feeling that he wanted to discuss with his family whether to disclose the compound's location, but the OC looked pleased enough.

'That would be extremely helpful.'

Asma translated: 'We thank you for your generosity and understand that you have the interests of Afghanistan and its future and those of the Pashtun people at heart.'

The tribesmen smiled and the meeting ended amicably. It seemed to Asma that the good-looking soldier, in his position by the door, had remained motionless throughout. She saw him, very quietly and unobtrusively, radio the men outside. She watched Jean grin at him as she passed and his face broke into a smile in return.

When they emerged into the sunlight the Vectors were waiting.

Soldiers appeared as though they had materialized from cracks in the dry walls and climbed aboard.

'No doubt about it. Someone fancies you,' Jean muttered to Asma.

'He's got really amazing eyes. They're so blue I had to keep looking at the carpet in case they burned a hole in me.'

Jean gave her a sideways glance. 'His eyes look an ordinary sort of grey to me.'

Asma looked confused.

'I'm not talking about that tribesman, for heaven's sake,' Jean said.

Asma blinked.

'Duh. I mean Second Lieutenant Weeks. He just couldn't stop staring at you. And when you were chatting away to Ol' Blue Eyes he was getting really agitated.'

'Don't talk daft!'

'I swear it.'

'What about you then? You kept looking at someone all through the meeting.'

'Did I? Who?'

'That soldier over by the door.'

Jean giggled.

'*And* you gave him a sexy smile on the way out. *And* you were looking at him in the cookhouse the other night, too.'

'Well . . . he's nice to look at . . .'

'Are you blushing? I reckon you are!'

'I reckon I might be too . . .'

They did their best to look serious again when the officers climbed in beside them.

'Well,' Major Willingham said as the Vectors set off through the dust. 'Do we trust them? Or are they just trying to use the British Army to fight some local feud against whoever lives in that compound?'

The engineer pulled a face.

'Whatever their motive, it's not greed. They're not asking for the earth, just a school wall.'

'But that elder son. He's educated. He's spent a few years in Saudi; he could so easily have come under the influence of . . .'

Boss Weeks nodded: 'I think his history's highly suspicious. I found that man highly suspicious. I mean, possibly dangerous.' Then he coloured and added: 'Although of course I'm not used to dealing with these people.'

'Well let's ask someone who is,' the major said. 'What did our interpreters make of them?'

Jean said: 'If Asad was Saudi-educated he will have come back with new ideas. That may be good, because he can handle concepts like oil exploration. And it may be bad.'

'There's a danger,' Asma continued, 'that he'll have come back *wahabi* – that is, with no respect for the old tribal customs. If you're *wahabi* then you regard a lot of the local practices as no more than superstition. So when Arab fighters, and other insurgents, get here and stamp all over the local traditions and run amok with their weapons, he might think that's cool. Or he might think he's promoting Pashtun interests.'

'Very interesting,' Major Willingham said. 'I saw you having a conversation with the son. How dangerous do you think he is?'

Jean watched her carefully. They all waited for Asma's answer.

'Well,' she said at last, 'my instinct is quite strong on this one. I think we should trust this family.'

Chapter Fifteen

'YOU'VE GOT SOME CALLS TO MAKE.'

Dave had been summoned over to the ops room. *Jenny* . . . His stomach lurched. *Something's happened to her.*

'Is it my wife, sir?'

'No, nothing like that. It's about the two men you lost. Rifleman Jordan is doing well in Selly Oak but he's made repeated requests to talk to you about the incident. And Rifleman Buckle . . .'

'Yes?' Was the 2 i/c preparing him for bad news? His enquiries about Steve had always met with the same noncommittal response. Now Dave felt his heart thump.

The 2 i/c said: 'Rifleman Buckle would also like a word with you.'

'So he's well enough to talk now!' Dave's heart was still pumping hard but it was feeding relief to all the tiny, faraway capillaries that had drained as he braced himself for the worst.

He was handed the phone and, after being passed along a chain of medical personnel, he heard a voice he recognized.

'Dave, is that you, mate?'

The voice was airless, as though its owner was wearing too tight a uniform. But it was unmistakably Steve Buckle.

'Good to hear you, mate! I've been asking to speak to you every day but they wouldn't let me.'

'Not fucking surprised,' Steve said. 'They didn't want your language upsetting me, you old heap of shit.'

Dave laughed not because it was funny but because no dying

man could speak that way and it meant Steve was going to live. Beneath his laugh, though, he felt uneasy. He'd been mates with Steve, but, even as a mate, Steve had never called his platoon sergeant a heap of shit.

'How are you?' Dave asked.

'Terrible.'

'All over?'

'All over, mate. Broken a bunch of ribs and an arm and I've got a shitload of bruising and I'm every colour of the rainbow.'

'Is that all?'

'Isn't that enough?'

Dave proceeded cautiously. 'You've been lying there a long time for a bloke who's only got bruising.'

'Bit of shrapnel in the arm, broken rib . . . let's see, was there something else?'

Dave felt his lungs tighten, then his gut.

'How's the leg?' he asked.

'My legs are all right, mate.'

'Does your head hurt?'

'Yep.'

So that was why no one had been allowed to speak to Steve.

'Only because I need a beer,' Steve added. 'What sort of country is this, where no one can drink a beer?'

'Well, what country is it?' Dave asked. 'Go on, you tell me.'

'Can't remember the name . . .'

'Can you think straight?'

'Since when could I think straight?'

'Do you remember anything about the accident?'

'The last thing I remember we had our stuff ready and we were getting in the Vector to go somewhere . . .'

Steve's voice petered out.

'Who was in the Vector with you?'

'Everyone!'

'Name them if you can, Steve. Go on. Name all the lads in 1 Section.'

Dave hoped his questions weren't causing Steve anguish but he had to know. He had to know if the IED had blown away a piece of Steve Buckle's mind.

'Well. There's you . . .'

'I'm not in 1 Section, am I?'

'Aren't you?'

'Not really. What do I do?'

'Ummm . . . who am I talking to?'

Oh shit.

'I'm Dave. Your sergeant. So you'd better look sharpish.'

'Oh, yeah. Dave. Yeah.'

'Now tell me what's wrong with you apart from shrapnel in your arm and bruising.'

'Um . . . I keep falling asleep.'

'That's the morphine.'

'I'm falling asleep now. The doc's here, want to speak to him?'

'Yeah, all right, Steve. Listen, you need a lot of rest so just relax. That's an order. Have you spoken to Leanne yet?'

But Steve wasn't there any more.

Dave was aware that people in the ops room had been listening to him. Major Willingham was at a desk nearby and so was the 2 i/c. The OC's laptop blinked and people seemed to be on the radio or working on documents or shuffling papers around but it was all a pretence. The note of alarm he could not edit from his voice had somehow placed the ops room on alert.

He avoided everyone's eye. A new, crisp voice crackled on the phone now.

'Rob Webb speaking. I'm the doctor monitoring Rifleman Buckle.'

'Dave Henley, Buckle's platoon sergeant. So is it the morphine or has he got head injuries?'

'Probably still traumatized. It's hard for us to do detailed assessments here: we just have to get him well enough to ship him off to England, but we've had a bit of trouble stabilizing him.'

'He started off sounding like Steve . . . and then I realized he wasn't really there.'

'Sometimes he is. For brief periods. That's why we're still hoping his head injuries won't cause a long-term problem.'

'Does he actually know he's lost a leg?'

The doctor's reply, when it came, was careful. 'Well, he has been told.'

'Has he taken it in?'

'His nervous system's telling him it's still there and it hurts a lot. He's chosen not to look.'

'Christ . . . Has he spoken to his wife?'

'Actually, that's what I wanted to ask you. Now you've talked to him, what do you think?'

'Well . . .' Dave said. 'I know Leanne's desperate to be in touch. But if she hears him like that then it could make things worse. Has he asked to phone her?'

'He hasn't remembered he's married yet. But he remembered you were his sergeant.'

'Christ.'

'That's soldiers for you. He asked to speak to you by name. I heard him forget who you were towards the end of the conversation, but he certainly knew at the beginning.'

'I don't reckon he should speak to Leanne.'

'He's good for thirty seconds, maybe.'

'But he's not going to say any of the things Leanne will want to hear.' *When do any of us say the things they want to hear?*

'OK, maybe we'll wait a bit longer.'

'I'll tell her we've spoken but morphine got in the way. How's his leg?'

The doctor paused again.

'Well . . . it's a bad injury and we're still fighting to keep things under control. And if this call had taken place earlier in the day he'd have been a lot more lucid.'

When the call ended Dave sat staring into space. People were looking at him, waiting for him to say something, but he surrounded himself instead with a ring of silence.

'Do I conclude,' asked the OC eventually, 'that Rifleman Buckle isn't doing so well?'

Dave remembered how Steve Buckle was one of the quickest, funniest lads in the platoon. Just when Billy Finn thought he'd had the last word, Steve would always come back with a killer punch line.

'He's making a physical recovery. It's just he doesn't sound much like the Steve I used to know,' Dave said quietly.

'Early days,' the major said.

Dave's call to Jordan Nelson was a picnic by comparison. The machine-gunner could remember almost everything up until the moment of the blast.

'Did you see me, Sarge? Did you watch me flying?'

'Poetry in motion, mate,' Dave assured him.

'I haven't looked in the mirror yet. I expect I look like Tutan-fucking-khamun. And they won't take the bandages off for weeks.'

He paused. 'How's Steve?'

'Stable,' Dave heard himself saying.

The constant use of this word since Steve's accident had pissed him off big-time, but now he understood. You could take refuge in the sheer dependability of a word like stable. Without really thinking what it might mean.

Chapter Sixteen

VICKY WENT TO NURSERY FOR TWO HOURS ON A WEDNESDAY AND Jenny had a list as long as her arm of things to do in that two hours. But she had no sooner got home in the empty car and begun to tackle her chores than the doorbell rang.

She sighed. It might be Leanne, armed with a twin on each side, saying she needed to talk. She had to talk to someone, poor love, since they still hadn't let her talk to Steve.

But it was Agnieszka. Luke was in his pushchair throwing his arms up and down in that strange way of his and Agnieszka stood there, white-faced, tight-jeaned, barely smiling. Jenny felt resentful until she reminded herself that, in the superstore, she had actually invited her.

'Come in!' she said. 'And just don't look at the mess.'

'I don't see any mess,' said Agnieszka. Although there was plenty.

Agnieszka left the buggy on the doorstep and carried Luke into the house. She sat stiffly, holding Luke, while Jenny made coffee. She didn't want any herself. The very smell of it revolted her at this stage of her pregnancy.

'We've got some baby toys Luke might like to play with . . .'

Jenny dragged herself upstairs to the box under Vicky's bed. She selected so many toys that she could not see the steps properly when she came back down and three from the bottom she tripped. She lurched forward, losing her balance, pulled by gravity and her own unaccustomed bodyweight towards the floor. She saved herself by grabbing the banister just in time. The toys thudded down the stairs as she swung there. She felt so much like a big baboon that she wanted to cry and laugh at the same time.

Carefully she disengaged herself from the rail and her feet found the ground. She picked up the toys and went back into the living room where Agnieszka was drinking her coffee. Luke did not need the baby toys. He was lying on the sofa across his mother, falling asleep.

'Have you heard from Jamie?' Jenny asked brightly as she sat down.

'He try to phone every day.' Agnieszka could have no idea of the minefield she was crossing.

'Every day!' Jenny attempted to keep her voice even. Her heart was still thumping from her near-fall on the stairs; Agnieszka's words made it beat harder still. 'How does he manage to call so often?'

'He not always manage. Sometimes three whole days without one word. But he buy other men's minutes.'

The thought that Dave might sell his minutes so that other men could call their wives made Jenny feel as though her body was made up of thin tubes, all of them hollow. Then, just as quickly as they had hollowed, the tubes filled with anger. But she remembered that, as sergeant, Dave would not be playing the system. Her anger abated. He would not sell his minutes. Although her Dave would certainly give them away to a man in need. She felt another surge of anger. He would give them away, forgetting that his own wife had needs too.

'That your father?' Agnieszka, pinned to the sofa by the sleeping Luke, gestured to a picture.

Jenny put aside her thoughts of phone minutes and heaved herself up to fetch it from the shelf. She grabbed a wedding picture too.

'Yep, this is my dad.' She handed the first frame to Agnieszka. 'He died when I was ten. This is the only good photo I have of him.'

Agnieszka studied the picture carefully. 'Where live your mother?'

'My mum lives in south London, about a mile from Dave's mum. Isn't that strange? They've become mates since we introduced them. Although Dave and I grew up in the same area we didn't know each other then. And we went to different schools.'

'So how you meet?'

'Windsurfing.' Jenny laughed. 'I moved down to the south coast with a boyfriend and when we split up I stayed there because I was enjoying the windsurfing so much and I had quite a nice job. And one day Dave showed up. We met wearing wetsuits! Then we arranged to meet with our clothes on and we didn't recognize each other. But one thing led to another . . .' She held out the wedding photo.

Agnieszka took it. 'You look beautiful.'

Jenny smiled. She knew she did look good in that picture. Tall, slim, her hair swept back and her makeup perfect but, most of all, she looked genuinely full of joy. And Dave wasn't one of those awkward grooms. He looked like a man who had found the right woman and knew it.

'You marry in London?'

'No, here.'

'Dave already in army when you meet?'

Jenny was still smiling. It was good to remember those times. The first tentative dates, the feeling that she had met someone really special, then the knowledge that he was not just special but significant for her and finally the understanding that she wanted him to stay significant for ever. There had only ever been one problem. The bloody army.

Her smile faded.

'Yeah. It was the only thing I didn't like about him.'

Except that all the things which made him a good sergeant also happened to make him an attractive man. He was tough and fair, compassionate without being soft, reliably strong and a man who could take responsibility. Jenny loved him for all those things. So did the army.

'Why you not like army?' asked Agnieszka. 'Lots of men looking for work but our boys got safe jobs.'

'Safe?' Jenny gave an empty smile. 'Safe? Try telling Leanne that.'

'Yeah, yeah, but you know what I mean. We got somewhere to live, we got our house.'

Jenny glanced around her. Actually, there were days when she hated the small, nondescript box with its magnolia walls. She occasionally had inspired ideas about turning it into something

108

more. But she was always defeated by the cost or the practicalities or the endless regulations.

'If you just see some apartments in Poland . . .' Agnieszka said quietly. 'If you just see some places where people live and think they very lucky. Then maybe you understand this not such a bad place.'

Jenny felt ashamed. Agnieszka, of course, was right. If you compared it to a lot of other homes in the world, or in the UK, then of course army housing was good. Only when you compared it to your friends' houses did you feel despair at the mould, the flooding, the malfunctioning drains, the insipid design and the sameness of it all.

She asked Agnieszka about herself and how she had met Jamie and Agnieszka told her Jamie had been a university student working in a hotel during the vacation and she had been a barmaid at the same hotel. She had done nothing to dissuade Jamie from walking out on his education and joining the army: she could see it was what he really wanted. But his parents had associated her arrival in his life with his decision to leave university. They had tried desperately to persuade him to wait until he had a degree so that at least he could go to Sandhurst. But Jamie had not wanted to be an officer.

'So they blamed you?'

'Yes, they blame me. They live in big house. They invite us for weekend and make me sleep in another room from Jamie. They say: Agnieszka, try to make him change his mind! And I say: Mr, Mrs Dermott, his mind made and Jamie very stubborn. After this they don't like me. Not before wedding, not at wedding, not after wedding.'

'They must love Luke . . .'

Agnieszka shook her head.

'Luke disappoint them very much.'

They both looked at Luke. There was a sweetness about him which Jenny loved but something was not right, you could see it even as he slept. The shape of his head or the way it lay at such a strange angle, as though he was trying to escape from himself.

'What does the doctor say?'

Agnieszka's face had closed itself into a discontented pout as she talked about her in-laws. As she talked about Luke's doctors, the pout didn't disappear.

'Tests, tests, more tests and then they say it too early to tell.'

'I'm sorry,' Jenny said gently. 'It'll be easier for you when you have a diagnosis. When you know what's wrong, you'll know what to do.'

She felt her own baby kicking and longed for the day she could cradle him in her arms and know he was safe and well. She held her bump with the same tenderness with which she would soon be holding the baby.

'I just want to know!' said Agnieszka and there were tears in her voice.

Jenny felt her own throat constrict. How often, she thought, does Agnieszka cry alone? How often do we all? She remembered the sight of Agnieszka, alone, in the café. In a sudden rush of affection, Jenny said: 'Listen, next time you feel like a cup of tea at the super-store, tell me and I'll come with you.'

Agnieszka's face lit up. 'Thank you.'

And then Jenny remembered that Agnieszka hadn't, in fact, been alone. She'd been with a man. A thought crossed her mind. It was fleeting but it left a small bruise behind. Had Agnieszka come today for some sort of reassurance that Jenny hadn't seen the man: was it this reassurance which had triggered that radiant smile?

Luke was waking up now.

He opened his eyes and looked around and in an instant stepped from sleep's quiet bliss into an outpouring of misery. His mouth opened so wide it seemed to be swallowing up his face. He could barely breathe he was yelling so hard. The room was filled with his roar. His arms and legs waved.

Agnieszka had placed the photos on the arm of the sofa. Jenny tried but failed to leap up in time to rescue them from Luke's flail-ing hands. By the time she had lumbered over, it was too late. They fell to the floor, smashing against each other. Jenny's father's smile was jammed against his daughter's wedding. Splinters of glass lay across the carpet. One frame was dented.

As Jenny bent to rescue the pictures, she saw that her father's forehead had been cut. She stared at the gash, half expecting it to bleed.

It was impossible to say or do anything while the storm went on. She looked at Agnieszka, sitting passive and expressionless in the

110

face of Luke's fury, waiting for it to end. How could a mother watch so silently and do nothing to calm him? Jenny told herself that Agnieszka had probably tried many times. But still she had to resist the urge to pick up the baby herself.

Agnieszka saw the broken pictures but made no attempt to apologize. She seemed unmoved by the damage to the only picture of Jenny's father.

Jenny looked anxiously at the clock.

'I have to pick Vicky up from nursery!' she called over the noise. 'Do you want to stay here?'

Agnieszka was rooted to the spot while Luke screamed. She said she'd leave when she could. She'd pull the door shut behind her.

'Mind the glass on the floor!' Jenny left Agnieszka on the sofa with the roaring baby, a small pile of glass splinters at her side, the broken photos on the sideboard. She tried not to think of all the things she had promised herself she'd do this morning.

When she returned from the nursery, Agnieszka and Luke had gone.

Vicky was being difficult because she was hungry. Jenny normally had her lunch ready when she got home but today, instead, there had been Agnieszka. She turned on the TV for the little girl and tried to make her promise not to go near the splintered glass. But, when she put her head around the door, Vicky was dancing on the carpet barefoot. Jenny began to pick up the glass by hand and then by vacuum and while she did so Vicky's lunch burned dry.

As the smell of charred beef burger leaked into the living room, Jenny rushed back to the kitchen leaving the vacuum on to keep Vicky, who was frightened of it, away from the glass.

She threw the lunch in the bin and was starting again, the noise of the TV competing with the vacuum in the living room, when the phone rang. Her first instinct was to let it ring. But it might be Dave. She picked it up.

'Hello . . .' His voice was far, far away.

She wanted to cry.

'Dave!'

'Are you OK?' He sounded so distant.

111

'Look, talk to Vicky for a minute,' she said. 'Her lunch just burned and there's glass all over the floor. Talk to Vicks while I sort it out.'

She heard his silence echoing back at her. In that silence was the space between England and Afghanistan. Seas and landmasses. Plains and mountains.

'Oh!' she said, dismayed.

'Vicky?'

'No. No, this is still Jenny. Saying I miss you. And I wish you rang more often and didn't give other men your phone minutes. And I wish you rang me in the night when it's quiet and we can talk properly.'

'I don't give other men my fucking minutes,' he said. 'And when I ring you in the night you don't fucking answer.'

'You're not talking to one of your men now,' she snapped. 'Can't you stop being a sergeant and start being a husband for just a few minutes a week?'

Suddenly the line became clearer and she heard his sigh. Was it resignation? Or regret that he had called at all?

'Oh, Christ,' she said. 'I'm sorry. Dave, I'm sorry. I don't want this kind of phone call. I was with Leanne most of yesterday and so the house is a tip and then Agnieszka came round this morning the minute I'd dropped Vicks off at nursery so I didn't get anything done. And Luke smashed the photos from the living room and the one of Dad got cut and Vicks is hungry but there's glass all over the floor and I burned her dinner and . . . and I know you don't want to hear all this. You don't have to sound patient with me because I *know* how boring it all is compared with killing the Taliban. And I *know* you're wishing you hadn't made this call. I *know* the reason you hardly ever ring is that, when you do, all you hear is this stuff . . .' She glanced at Vicky and closed the kitchen door, dropping her voice. 'You don't have to say it because I already fucking *know*, Dave.'

Dave said: 'Jen, I do love you.'

'What?'

'Nothing.'

'What did you say?'

She had heard. She just needed to hear it again.

'Jen, I love you. I don't give other men my minutes. The reason I don't phone you more often is that I try not to think about you because when I do I want you and miss you. OK? Do you *know* that too?'

She started to cry.

'How are you feeling?'

'A bit uptight.' She sniffed.

'You don't say!'

'Like when air support comes along and drops a bomb on something but it doesn't actually go off? But you're all sitting in your trucks thinking it might any minute?'

'Oh, like that. Yeah, that's uptight. How's the baby?'

'Kicking a lot. And I'm enormous and no one can believe I've still got so long to go.'

'So did Agnieszka come round just so Luke could smash our photos?'

'She came round to make sure I hadn't seen her with some bloke at the superstore. But I had.'

'What bloke?'

'I don't know who he is. She was having a coffee with him and she didn't want me to see.'

'You're not saying she's messing about with someone?'

'I don't know. I might just be thinking that sort of thing because I'm uptight.'

'Is Agnieszka the type to mess about?'

'Not really. But then everyone's the type when they're lost and lonely.'

'Except you.'

'No one's going to try messing around with a woman whose belly's bigger than a house. So you're safe for the time being.'

'Stay pregnant until I get home.'

'No thanks. I'd explode.'

'Jamie's devoted to Agnieszka,' Dave said quietly.

'Yeah, he rings her all the time.'

'Hasn't stopped her cheating on him, though.'

'She might not be. Except that . . .' Her voice trailed away.

'What? Except what? The line went dead.'

'That wasn't the line, it was me. I'm probably wrong. But when

113

I was driving back from nursery with Vicky, I thought I saw him.'

'Who?'

'The bloke who was in the café with her.'

'Well, where was he this time?'

'In a car. So I might be wrong. An old red Volvo. But it was driving towards her house. And now it's parked outside.'

Dave groaned.

'I hope you haven't told anyone.'

'Not about the car. I did mention seeing her in the café . . .'

'Oh-oh.'

Jenny sank down into one of the kitchen chairs. Her legs ached. She had been focusing so hard on the call that she had been standing up throughout and now a great tiredness washed over her.

'I've only told Adi.'

'OK. Adi's watertight. What about Leanne?'

'I didn't tell her because she can't think about anything except Steve. If they'd just let her talk to him . . . she's really falling to pieces and if she could hear him it would make a big difference.'

'I used to think Leanne was unbreakable,' he said.

He wasn't wrong. Leanne Buckle didn't put up with any nonsense from Steve or anyone. If you were angry about something you'd go and see Leanne and she'd feel angry for you. When Jenny had been pregnant with Vicky and Dave had been away, Leanne had taken up Jenny's fight with a shop over a faulty TV set and won it. This new, lost tearful Leanne scared Jenny a bit; she was so different from the old Leanne.

'Even the strongest woman would have trouble coping right now. She just sits by the phone waiting to hear if Steve's going to live or die. She's scared to go out in case there's news.'

'We can't afford for Leanne or you or anyone back home to fall to pieces,' said Dave. 'You're part of the army. More than you know. If you fall, we fall.'

'I don't want to be part of the army,' said Jenny. 'I don't want you to be either.'

'What?'

'I hate it. I want you to leave.'

'No.'

'It's driving me crazy, not knowing if you're safe. Not hearing from you.'

'Jen . . . I'll try to phone more often, all right?'

'It's not about phoning. It's about leaving. I'm serious, Dave. I think you should come out of the army and live in the real world with me and Vicky and the baby.'

'This isn't the time to discuss it.'

'When is the time?'

'When I get back. When you're not pregnant and uptight.'

She took a deep breath.

'I'm serious and I'm not going to shut up, Dave. I want to talk about it.'

'OK, we will, only not now because there are too many people around.'

She didn't want to argue with him.

'Promise? Because I won't let it go.'

'Promise. And, listen, Jen, don't fall apart like Leanne.'

She gathered her strength. 'I'm not falling anywhere. Except asleep sometimes.'

She thought she could hear him smiling at the other end. But his voice was serious. 'Don't say anything to anyone about Agnieszka messing about. This is important. I don't want Jamie hearing any rumours. So whatever you're thinking, make sure you keep it to yourself.'

'And what about you men? Aren't there women at the base? Suppose rumours reach us about you?'

'There are two women. One's Royal Military Police so we don't talk to her. The other's Intelligence Corps so she doesn't talk to us.'

'I heard about another.'

'There aren't any more.'

'Her name's Emily.'

Dave laughed out loud.

'How did you hear about Emily?'

'People talk. There are wives who don't like the sound of her.'

'Well, the only lad ever to clap eyes on Emily is Billy Finn. And he's keeping her all to himself.'

Chapter Seventeen

MARTYN ROBERTSON WANDERED OVER TO THE 1 SECTION LADS IN THE cookhouse and introduced himself.

'Thanks for covering us at the *shura*.' He held out his hand and shook each of theirs solemnly, then sat down with them.

'We were doing our job,' Dave said. 'No thanks necessary.'

'Well, I felt safe with you. Which one was in the room with us? You?' The American looked at Jamie.

'Yeah,' Jamie said.

'And what did you think of that meeting?'

Jamie'd mostly been alert to the body language, but he'd found himself listening anyway and having a few private thoughts of his own. He'd noticed the way the boss kept staring at that pretty, Intelligence Corps woman. And he'd decided that the tribesman's son with the blue eyes was probably a nasty dude beneath all those warm words.

'Nothing, sir, it's not my job to think anything.'

'Don't sir me, call me Marty!'

It was impossible to know how old he was. As old as the hills, thought Dave. The man's face was gnarled, its skin cracked and lined; it reminded him of the mountains around here.

'Where you from in America, then?' Finn asked. 'I'm always meaning to go there.'

Dave raised his eyebrows but said nothing.

'Texas. I was brought up living, breathing and thinking oil,' said Marty. When he smiled his face broke into canyons.

116

'Where are you boys from?'

'London,' Dave said. *But probably not the London you know. Not your London of hotels and bridges and tourist restaurants.*

'Gloucestershire,' said Jamie. 'I grew up living, breathing and thinking cheese.'

Martyn tried to repeat Gloucestershire without much success.

'So you Brits got your Worcestershire Sauce and your Gloucestershire cheese,' he said affectionately, mispronouncing both counties. 'And how about you, young man?'

'How about what?' Finn said.

'Where're you from?'

Finn shrugged. His deep brown eyes were always searching, always alert, like a bird's. 'Everywhere,' he said at last.

'Oh, c'mon, you must have been born somewhere?'

'In a caravan. Going nowhere.'

'You were born in a trailer?'

'I'm trailer park trash.' Finn flashed a dazzling smile. 'I mean, without the park bit. 'Cos we never park anywhere for long.'

'Your family was always on the move?'

'Yup. I'm what's called a pikey back home.'

Finn rolled up his sleeve to reveal a tattoo. *Pikey. Just nick it.* Martyn looked confused.

Dave explained. '*Nike. Just do it.* It's an ad that appealed to Lance Corporal Finn's subtle sense of humour.'

'One of the things pikeys like to do is bet,' Finn said. 'Are you a betting man by any chance, Marty?'

Dave and Jamie groaned.

'Ignore him,' Dave advised the American but Martyn was nodding enthusiastically.

'What's your name?' he asked Finn.

'He's called Finn,' Jamie said.

'As in Huckleberry?'

'No,' Jamie said. 'As in shark.'

'Well, Huckleberry Finn,' Marty said, 'as a matter of fact I've had a bit of success in casinos. My idea of a good vacation is Vegas and a lot of blackjack.'

'Great! Show me how to play and we'll have a game some time!'

'Oh no you won't,' Dave said. 'Finny, you've been banned from betting in this FOB.'

Finn looked ready to protest but Martyn had turned to Mal.

'Where you from? I took a peek when you were guarding those prisoners and thought you looked just like one of them.'

'No relation, honest,' Mal said. 'My tribe's in Manchester.'

'Your parents are from Yemen, aren't they, Mal?' Dave said.

'It wasn't called Yemen when they lived there. I forget what it was called.'

'Could you find it on a map?' Martyn asked.

'You must be joking. But I couldn't find Manchester, either.'

'I guess you're Moslem, though?' Martyn persisted.

Mal shrugged awkwardly. 'I'm not anything really.'

'A babe magnet,' Finn reminded him.

Mal smiled. 'Oh, yeah. Babes. That's my religion.'

'But you must have—'

Jamie glanced over Martyn's shoulder. 'Who's that?'

They all turned.

Dave said: 'That's someone who just went out to the High Street to pick up a bit of shopping . . .'

'. . . and woke up in an FOB in Afghanistan,' Jamie finished.

A substantial woman with a Sainsbury's shopping bag was standing at the food counter. She was obviously just on her way back from the supermarket because the contents of the bag bulged a bit. A head scarf was knotted severely under her chin, wisps of white hair visible beneath it. She wore a grey suit with knee-length skirt stretched tightly over her ample frame. Her shoes were solid.

'Or maybe,' Jamie said, 'there's a Sainsbury's in town and no one told us.'

Martyn smiled. 'That's my colleague, Professor Emily Fullerton.'

There was a pause.

'Emily?' Dave's eyes narrowed. 'Did you say Emily?'

'*That's* Emily!' Jamie said.

'*That's Emily!*' Mal cried.

Every face turned towards Finn, who, despite trying to look nonchalant, couldn't stop himself grinning.

'Oh, yeah!' he said as though he'd just noticed her. 'That's Emily.'

They watched as the woman withdrew the contents of her

shopping bag. She handed a package carefully to the chef, Taregue Masud, who beamed at her.

'She needs him to put some samples in his freezer,' Martyn said.

Finn was chuckling.

'Oh, *man*!' Mal couldn't hide his dismay. 'You're never shagging *her* on hot afternoons!'

'You all fell for it! I had you all over! I had every single man in the platoon after that old bird!'

'Not me,' Jamie said.

'Nor me,' Dave said. 'Or Sol.'

'Whenever I told you I was with Emily, I was in a sangar getting my head down for an hour.'

'You shithead!' Mal's expression was tragic.

'I knew it wasn't true,' Jamie said.

'Will someone tell me what I'm missing?' Martyn asked.

Dave coughed. 'Well, the marines started this rumour. And Finn's been doing his best to spread it . . .'

'They said there's a lady in the isoboxes called Emily who's a bit of a . . . er . . .'

'Sex grenade,' Finn said helpfully.

Martyn burst out laughing.

'Well, maybe Emily is a sex grenade,' he said. 'Never judge a book by its cover.'

'What's she doing here?' Dave asked.

Martyn rolled his eyes. 'I've had her imposed on me by the company. I can smell oil at a thousand paces, but that's not good enough for the company. They have to send an academic out to sit in an air-conditioned box all day and analyse my results and argue with me.'

Dave grinned. 'You're the best of mates, then.'

'I fight with her every day.'

'She an engineer?'

'A geophysicist. And if she started the sex grenade stuff with me, I'd run a mile.'

Emily was issuing instructions to Masud, who was nodding vigorously. 'Yes, madam. Yes. Yes, madam.'

'Where's her body armour?' Dave asked.

Marty pulled a face. 'She doesn't always wear it. You can

try giving Emily orders. But even Nick Willingham's given up.'

'Well, Finny,' Jamie said. 'I just hope you don't get lynched.'

'I had the whole platoon hot for Emily!' Finn still hadn't stopped chuckling.

'I want to cut you,' Mal said.

'It was just a joke,' Finn said.

'Angus'll want to cut you too. So will all of 2 Section.'

'And just wait till you get back home,' Dave said. 'Jenny told me half Wiltshire knows about Emily the sex grenade and some of the wives are getting really pissed off.'

Finn rubbed his hands.

They watched Emily march out of the cookhouse. And then, simultaneously, they all started to laugh.

When the others got up to go, Finn remained seated. 'How about we play some blackjack?' he asked Martyn in an undertone.

Dave swung around, fixing him with a meaningful stare.

'I mean, for matchsticks or something. Not money of course.' The oilman launched into an explanation of the game as the others left the cookhouse.

'We might as well let them get on and fleece each other,' Dave said wearily.

'The Yank seems a nice enough guy,' Jamie said.

'Topaz fucking Zero tries to go sniffing out oil wherever he wants, whenever he wants and expects us to do the security without any consultation. The marines got fed up with him and now the OC can't keep him under control either. He may be nice,' Dave said, 'but you'll see, he's trouble.'

Chapter Eighteen

THE SUN GREW STRONGER DAILY. IN WILTSHIRE THE WOMEN changed into their summer clothes and lay in their back gardens whenever they could, soaking up the light and heat as though it was a rare commodity they had to hoard. In Afghanistan temperatures soared up to 50 degrees and men sheltered from it.

'Is it that much hotter?' the lads asked. 'It's always been hot.'

'It's bloody hot but you're used to it now,' Dave told them.

He'd watched his men grow leaner and stronger as they muscled up carrying heavy kit in blinding heat day after day. Some even seemed to grow taller. And they were more proficient. Dave had to impose fewer and fewer of his on-the-spot penalties, like shit duties or press-ups, for lapses at kit inspection.

Everyone was falling into the routine of base life and their thoughts of England were fading like old snapshots. Their feelings of longing, loss and love still welled up at unexpected moments then mysteriously subsided. Every man experienced this. No one spoke about it. The new arrivals were no longer getting a hard time just because they were new. And the casualties they had replaced, Buckle and Nelson, were seldom talked about now. Until word came through that Steve Buckle was flying back to the UK at last.

Dave phoned Leanne as soon as he heard.

'Remember,' he warned her, 'they'll have dosed him up with extra morphine for the flight so he won't be himself.'

'But why haven't they let me speak to him yet?' Leanne demanded. 'They keep saying soon, soon.'

He was relieved at her anger. It was more like the old Leanne than the anxious, tearful woman he'd been hearing lately. He had one of those sudden and unexpected bursts of homesickness. He was remembering Leanne, plump, loud and funny, sitting in the garden with Steve one summer's day. They'd been pretending to argue and after a few beers the argument had turned into a comedy act. No aspect of married life was too private to escape their slick one-liners. Dave hoped it wouldn't be long before they were con-cocting some good jokes about prosthetic limbs.

'Can't he talk, Dave? I mean, has he lost the power of speech?' Leanne asked, her voice cracking and a sob breaking through. The good jokes began to seem a long way off.

'I've already told you, Leanne, he can talk but he doesn't always make sense. Probably because of the morphine.'

'Probably! Dave, is my Steve brain-damaged? Are they sending me back some sort of fucking vegetable?'

'No. But he took the full force of a big blast. He has to recover from the shock.'

He tried to distract her by asking about the arrangements that had been made for her in Birmingham.

'We've been given an army flat for a week. My mum's meeting me there. She'll take care of the boys for me and I'll mostly go in by myself.'

Dave could tell that inside her head she had walked into Selly Oak hospital and experienced her reunion with Steve at his bedside many times. He wondered what it would be like when it finally happened.

Leanne and Jenny stood by the car in front of Leanne's house. Everything was loaded for the trip to Birmingham. The car was so full of high chairs, travel cots, toys, a pair of sit-on scooters, packs of nappies and suitcases that there was hardly room for the driver. The two small passengers peered from their seats at the back, still and quiet as though they knew something important was happening.

Leanne seemed reluctant to drive away.

'I'm scared,' she said.

Jenny was learning not to be surprised by the new Leanne. If the old Leanne knew what fear was, she never would have admitted to it.

'What sort of scared?' Jenny asked. 'First date scared? Walking down a dark street and someone's following you scared?'

Leanne drew on her cigarette. She had started smoking again. She did not want the twins to see her so she leaned out of windows or rushed into the garden or hid in the car to smoke. Now, she was leaning against the bonnet with her back to them, as though they wouldn't notice the smoke if they couldn't see the cigarette.

'Horror movie scared. Like, when someone goes up the creaky stairs and opens a door and you don't know what's behind it? But you know it's something awful?'

Jenny looked at Leanne's large, unhappy face. Leanne had put on weight. Since Steve's accident, she could not stop eating. She reported how her sleepless nights were punctuated by frequent trips downstairs to the fridge. She had always been large but the new Leanne did not joke about it or constantly announce to the world that she would be starting a new diet tomorrow.

'Is your mum meeting you at the hospital?'

'At the flat. If she can find it. God knows how she'll manage to drive through Birmingham, she even gets lost in camp.'

There was almost no cigarette left but Leanne seemed to want to smoke it anyway.

'I'd better get going.' She did not move. 'Before the boys start yelling.'

Jenny put her arms around Leanne. There felt like an ocean of belly between them both.

'Wish I was big for the same reason you are,' said Leanne.

Jenny pulled back in surprise.

'Do you want another one? You always said the twins were more than enough!'

Tears were gleaming at the edges of Leanne's eyes. She sniffed.

''Course I want one. Now I know I can't have one.'

'Why not?' Jenny asked.

Leanne sniffed again. 'How much of him got blown away, Jen? Did it stop at his leg?'

Jenny shook her head. 'Oh, c'mon. If he'd lost his private parts they would have told you!'

'It might all be there, but will any of it work? Now they've cut his nerves and blood vessels and things? And what sort of a marriage are we going to have if he can't . . . ? And even if he can, I'm not sure I'll want to. With a bloke who's got a stump for a leg.'

'You'll want to because he's your Steve and you love him and he's gorgeous, leg or no leg.' Jenny's voice was firm.

Leanne looked at her doubtfully.

'Know what you're doing, Leanne? You're in the horror movie, walking up the creaky stairs and trying to imagine all the things behind the door. That's how horror movies work. You scare yourself imagining things that aren't even there.'

'Yeah.' Leanne had turned to face the car, its outsize load and the waiting twins. 'Yeah, well by tonight I'll know, won't I?'

'Ring me,' said Jenny. 'Just ring me and tell me. I'll listen.'

Leanne sniffed again. She squeezed Jenny's arm but did not look at her. Jenny knew she was trying not to cry. Leanne climbed in and slammed the door. Her face, behind the wheel, was pale and puffy.

She wound down the window.

'I've waited to see him so long . . . and now I don't want to go,' she said, her voice turning squeaky at the end.

'Go,' Jenny commanded her. 'You'll feel better once you're on your way.'

Vicky, who had been occupied picking daisies from a strip of lawn outside Leanne's house, came and took her mother's hand. The pair of them waved as the car drove slowly down the road towards the entrance of the camp.

Chapter Nineteen

DESPITE A SERIES OF MINOR STRIKE OPS, INTELLIGENCE AND aerial surveillance, it was impossible to pinpoint the location of the Taliban training centre. Regular skirmishes with the enemy had not led to another contact as serious as the one that had greeted their arrival. The river crossing had been the focus of most of the fighting, and occasionally the base itself.

'We mustn't get lax; we should guard the oil-exploration team even more carefully,' Major Willingham announced. 'The Taliban are probably hoping that by staying away from the contractors, our protection will slacken.'

The civilians themselves did nothing to make the soldiers' job easier and the OC devised increasingly complex strategies to fool the enemy. It was Boss Weeks's job to explain the strategies to his platoon. Dave dreaded these explanations. The platoon commander was increasingly good on the ground, particularly under fire, but he was still shit at giving orders.

As the men filed into the Cowshed, he kept clearing his throat. Ahem. Ahem.

Dave counted the lads in. Twenty-three, twenty-four soldiers plus support. All here and gradually getting their arses on the ground, while the boss shifted nervously from one foot to the other. Ahem. Ahem.

Dave tried not to gag on the lingering aroma of unshowered men working in spiralling temperatures combined with the whiff of long-departed goat. He wondered what would happen to the

Cowshed when the troops eventually left and the base was dismantled. Probably, like the other mud-walled buildings, it would stand here for centuries more, patched up and used once again to house a family and their stock. From recent house assaults in the Green Zone he had learned that animals and humans mixed easily in the indoor/outdoor world of Afghan compounds. In fact, he suspected that the animals had more freedom than the women.

By the time the last two men arrived, Boss Weeks was clearing his throat almost continuously.

'Right,' Dave said. 'Sit down, shut up. In a minute the boss is going to deliver. First I want to tell you about Buckle and Nelson. Jordan's at home with his family and expected to make a full recovery although he had severe burns so he'll be no oil painting. Steve Buckle's a lot better and he left for the UK yesterday. He should be installed in a comfortable bed in Selly Oak and he'll see his family again today.

'Next I want to bring you up to speed on the Rules of Engagement.'

Dave glanced at Weeks. He wanted to forget the wounded Taliban fighter in the ditch, but the boss had warned him that the OC still intended to question him about it.

'Every so often we all need a reminder about the RoE. So here it is. We're operating under Card Alpha. That means we can only engage the enemy if we know they're enemy and we only know that if they're armed. There are a lot of grey areas. Like if you believe your life is in danger, maybe from a suicide bomber, no one's going to blame you for taking action. But if we remember the basic rule we should be OK. Right?'

The platoon looked back at him. A few people nodded.

'Over to you, sir.'

The boss cleared his throat before he began.

'Now our . . . er . . . American, er, friends have decided that there is a new, er, necessity for them to concentrate their exploration activities in one, er, specific area, and indeed some of you may have noticed that, er, this has, er, indeed been the case.'

For Chrissake, thought Dave. The boss sounded as though he'd come from another planet. A good officer, and Dave had worked with a few, had the common touch. A good officer knew how to adjust his language – and occasionally even his accent – for the men. But Boss Weeks was incapable of any adjustment at all. He had so many plums in his mouth he was practically choking.

'The contractors will be guarded by, er, 3 Platoon and 1 Platoon will be acting as decoys. So it has been decided that we are to send out, er, the first decoy at, er, first light. The second will leave thirty minutes later and the third thirty minutes after that. While those who are travelling direct to the destination site, will, er, be 3 Platoon leaving thirty minutes after that . . .'

Weeks turned to the map Dave had pinned to the wall. He looked about vaguely for a pointer. Dave handed him a stick.

'Er . . . 1 Section will set off west, cross the river here, swing north and then east to go around the . . . er . . . er . . . Early Rocks after crossing the river . . . er . . . here.' He tapped the map. 'You may recognize that this is the river crossing we cleared recently. 1 Section is not just a, er, decoy but a patrol establishing our continuing presence by the river crossing. 1 Section will carry out the, er, useful function of ascertaining that our recent attempts to keep the Taliban from this area remain successful.

'Thirty minutes later, 2 Section will travel due north, then turn east and then travel south along the main highway where the Americans are extremely active and where we don't, er, anticipate too many problems. One hour after the departure of 1 Section, er, 3 Section will go directly south and then travel back north on the highway. And thirty minutes later, er, 3 Platoon will leave with the civilians. They will proceed due east and then, er, north towards the, er, er, Early Rocks . . .'

Dave groaned inwardly. All the boss needed to do was give them a general picture and then tell each section precisely what they were doing, where and when. The lads didn't need a strategy meeting and they didn't need a load of waffle. Dave shut his eyes while the platoon commander floundered on.

'. . . and so in that way,' Boss Weeks finally concluded, 'the enemy is liable to be, er, thoroughly confused.'

The Cowshed was silent.

'Well they're not the only ones, sir,' someone said from the back of the room.

There was a murmur of agreement. The boss swallowed hard.

Dave didn't need to open his eyes to know who'd spoken out. He glared directly at Finn but it was too late. Finn's dark eyes were shining.

'So, sir, 1 Section goes west and then up around the, er, er, Early Rocks, 2 Section goes north, 3 Section goes south and the civvies are going due, er, east then north with 3 Platoon, are they, then, sir?'

'Er . . .' the boss began.

'Yes, Lance Corporal,' Dave growled, 'that's what you've been told.'

'Correct, yes, that's . . . er . . . correct . . .' Boss Weeks said.

'I think the decoy teams should be out first and last and the civvies heading straight to the oil site should go out second,' Finn said.

'Yeah,' Mal said. 'If the flipflops are watching they're less likely to target the second team.'

'Much more likely to follow the last one,' Angus said sagely.

'If the aim is to protect the civvies then they should be right in the middle of things, not at the tail end,' Finn said.

Next to them sat the two new lads, Bacon and Binns, now universally known as Streaky and Binman. Dave knew Finn had taken the two lads under his wing and right now the pair, who knew no better, were nodding vigorously in his support.

Muttering broke out all over the Cowshed as the boss floundered in response to Finn's suggestion.

Dave waited. Order was gradually slipping from the boss's control and he wanted to give the young officer a chance to wrestle it back. He glimpsed Jamie Dermott sitting silently at the back, his face a deep shade of red as the boss lost the meeting.

Gordon Weeks's eyes bulged and he swallowed again and for a moment he did not speak or move. Then he started to explain things once more to the closest group while the noise grew louder around him.

Dave decided that it had all gone far enough.

'Right!' he roared. 'Wind your necks in!'

There was instant silence.

'This has been decided and we're not interested in hearing what you think about it. Order of march is: 1 Section, 2 Section,

3 Section out first as decoys, then 3 Platoon takes off with the contractors. Got it? Now we'll show you where you're going and when and you can shut up and listen because we're not saying it a third time.'

Dave proceeded to give the orders.

'Thank you, Sergeant.' Boss Weeks looked around. 'Any questions?' He was obviously hoping there weren't.

Finn opened his mouth. One look from Dave and he shut it again.

'Sir, are there enough medics for each section?' Jamie asked.

'Good question,' said the boss. 'The strategy we've devised for the civilians is stretching all our resources. The remaining medic will be with 1 Section because they're going through the Green Zone.'

'I'll also be with 1 Section and so will the boss,' Dave said. '1 Section is crossing the river at a hot point. We've cleared it once and the Taliban have given every indication they're keen to take it back so God knows what we'll find there. But thanks to the demands of Topaz fucking Zero we're so undermanned that we won't be able to do anything about it except report back.'

'Does 1 Section get the WMIKs?' another lad asked.

'Always nice to have the fire power,' Dave said.

'Very nice,' agreed the boss. 'That's why the civilians get the WMIKs.'

'Will 1 Section get a shotgun?' Mal asked.

'So you can try giving it to the Taliban again?' someone called.

'A shotgun would be nice, too,' Dave said.

'Very nice,' the boss agreed. 'That's why the civilian escorts get the shotguns. I don't believe we get a mortar man either.'

Finn made himself heard above the noise of disbelief. 'So there's just one medic, then, for 1 Section? That's all the support we get because the civilians have got the rest? Even though we're going through the Green Zone?'

'That's right, Lance Corporal,' Dave said firmly.

'Do we get a driver?'

'Nothing to drive, we're not getting any vehicles!' said Corporal Baker from 2 Section.

'Apart from drivers, obviously, the only personnel the civilians can spare are two engineers, a signaller and an interpreter,' the boss said.

'And a fat lot of fucking use they are,' Dave said, 'when all we can do is keep moving.'

There were no more questions.

'Good, well then, rehearsals will be at 1930,' the boss said. 'Synchronize watches. In one minute it will be 1635 . . .'

Everyone looked at their watches in silence. The minute passed slowly.

'It will be 1635 in ten seconds. Five, four, three, two, one. Mark one, two, three, done.'

Boss Weeks left, looking relieved.

Nobody moved. They knew what was coming next. As soon as the commander was out of earshot, Dave started.

'Right, shitheads, I don't ever want to hear that fucking backchat again. Not ever. Anyone who gives lip in this platoon gets gripped by me. And you know I'm not nice. Because lip in the FOB is soon going to turn into lip the other side of the hesco and if shitheads don't do what they're told out there then there's only one fucking outcome. And that's more casualties. Got it?

'Since some of you have got such short memories, I'm going to remind you what we told you before deploying to Afghanistan and what we told you when we got here. One in ten of you goes home in a body bag or fucked up for life. And it's going to be a fucking sight more than that if you don't work in a team. Look around you. Look at the lad sitting next to you. He might not go home. He's looking at you. You might not go home. Think about it before you try to be funny next time. Because corpses can't laugh.

'So wind your necks in and get on with your jobs. I want to see some teamwork. And let's hope I'm not phoning the hospital at Bastion to see how you are after tomorrow.'

He was angry. But it was hard to be very angry after the men had been given such a bad set of orders.

They trooped out in silence. Some exchanged glances. Some, like Jamie Dermott, still looked embarrassed. Others, like Sol Kasanita, just looked unhappy.

'You can stay behind,' Dave said as Finn passed him. Finn studied the ground. Dave waited until the room was empty.

'Time for you and me to have a little talk, Billy Finn . . .'

Face reddening, Finn continued to stare at the footmarks the men had left in the Cowshed's dust. For once, he made no attempt to respond. When he was finally dismissed he left slowly, the setting sun throwing a long, faltering shadow before him.

Dave found Boss Weeks alone in the ops room.

'I was piss poor, wasn't I?' the platoon commander said. 'I just don't seem to be getting any better at it.'

Dave smiled. In spite of everything, he couldn't help liking Boss Weeks.

'If you don't mind me saying so, sir, it's a bad idea to involve the lads in the full strategic picture. Each man needs to know what he's doing, but if you give him too much detail he gets confused. And if you explain everything to everyone, they think they have the right to contribute. Or the cocky ones do, anyway.'

'I knew that. But it's the same every time. I open my mouth and it all goes out of the window.'

'I've dealt with Lance Corporal Finn,' Dave said. 'I can guarantee you won't have a problem with him again.'

'Has he often challenged orders in the past?'

'He's a bright lad and a very good soldier. But he never stops talking and he's still got a lot more to learn.'

Boss Weeks looked down at the ground. 'He's not the only one,' he said quietly.

Chapter Twenty

THE FLAT WAS ONE SPECIALLY RESERVED FOR FAMILIES VISITING wounded men at Selly Oak hospital. It was lovely, at least it had been before Leanne filled it up with all their stuff. There was no lift and she had made many journeys carrying baby paraphernalia up and down the stairs, the twins screaming and trying to follow her each time she left them for the next load.

There was no sign of her mother. Because she was lost. Of course. And probably too flustered to use her mobile.

Leanne looked at her watch again and again, aware that visiting time had begun and that Steve was waiting for her. Maybe she should just go, and take the twins. But everyone had told her not to do that. She would be unable to have the conversation with Steve she had waited such a long time for. And the hospital couldn't really want children on these wards, not for long.

The old Leanne would have blustered her way in. But now she didn't have the confidence. Steve had lost a leg and God knew what else, while she had lost some other things that probably didn't even have a name. Bits of herself. The bits that usually didn't worry and thought they could cope with any crisis. She had always been good in a crisis. But this wasn't a crisis. This was the rest of her life.

At last she heard the sound of her mother's car outside.

Leanne jumped up with a twin under each arm and ran down the stairs.

'Nana! It's Nana!' she told them. That tone of anticipation again, intended to whip kids up into a frenzy of excitement. The same tone everyone used when telling the twins they would soon see Daddy again. Except that the boys were only eighteen months old and might already have forgotten who Daddy was. They probably thought he was some sort of chocolate bar they'd get if they were good.

Leanne's mother sat behind the wheel, her face red, her hair dishevelled.

'What a journey!' she said to Leanne before greeting the boys.

Leanne put down the twins and crossed her arms. 'You got lost. Just like I said you would.'

'Well the signs aren't clear enough. They don't tell you anything!'

As her mother heaved herself out of the car, Leanne glanced at her scalp. Her mum's roots were showing and a lot of them were grey now.

The boys ambushed their grandmother. She picked one up but the effort made her breathless. The other pounded with his fists at her skirt.

'Oh, Leanne, I'll have to sit down for a while before you leave me with them,' she said. For a moment, Leanne hated her. She hated her mother for getting older. One day she would be too old to help at all.

'But visiting time's going to end soon, Mum.'

'They'll have to let you in anyway, Leanne. If they try to keep you out they'll have me to answer to.'

Leanne recognized in her mother the firm, confident woman she herself used to be.

They went up the stairs and Leanne's mother admired the flat and Leanne made her a cup of tea and saw to her amazement that her own hand was shaking as she put the sugar in.

'You not having a cuppa?' asked her mother.

'Mum, I really want to get to the hospital. And I have to walk there because of the parking.' Leanne never walked anywhere if she could help it.

Her mother pursed her lips.

'Switch on the telly!' Leanne suggested, switching it on herself.

She fetched her handbag. Its familiar, shapeless bulges felt reassuring, like an old friend.

'I must go, Mum. You'll be all right.'

Her mother put down her tea with a pained expression. Both the twins ran to Leanne and hung onto her.

'I'm going to visit Daddy now,' she told them. She wanted to say something nice. *You can see Daddy for a very little while tomorrow. I'm going to give him a big hug from you. I'll be back soon bringing lots of love from Daddy. Nana's so pleased to have you all to herself.* But no words came out. The twins mobbed her and she had to squeeze out of the door silently, their cries pursuing her all the way down the stairs.

Outside, the sun shone. Leanne sweated as she walked. It felt weird not to be dragging a twin on either side, as though a part of her body was missing. But it was Steve who was missing the body part, not her. She tried to prepare herself. She was seeing Steve again and that did make her heart beat faster because she loved him and missed him. But then, she was seeing a different Steve. A Steve who had been thrown in the air and come down another Steve.

She reached the hospital and stood outside for a moment to force back down something that kept trying to push its way up inside her body. Was it vomit? Or just an enormous sob? She struggled to control herself and, when she felt numb enough, stepped through the door.

She was directed to his ward. Now she walked slowly through it, looking for Steve. She knew she wouldn't recognize his body, so she only looked at faces. Every bed contained a man with some part of his body bandaged. The wounded. Men who had photos of themselves smiling under the hot Afghan sun wearing camouflage and body armour and helmets, carrying Bergens and a lot of kit. Looking big and whole. They would never look that way again.

There was a whiteboard behind a desk with a list of names. *Buckle 313.*

It must be a bed number. She walked on. No, it was a room number. She found 313. Outside was another board. You could see where the names of previous patients had been rubbed out underneath. Steve's name was scrawled in purple over them.

The door was open. She went in. The man in the bed was sitting up. There were sheets pulled across him haphazardly as though he didn't care whether he was covered or not. His eyes were open but he didn't look at her when she entered the room. Her heart gave a jump. It was Steve, definitely, recognizably Steve. He looked just exactly the same! What had she expected? That he had turned into some kind of a monster?

'Sweetheart!' she said.

And suddenly, for the first time since the Families Officer had called that evening, it didn't matter that this was Steve minus a leg. He was here and he was alive. She took his hand and kissed his face and tears fell down her cheeks. They were tears of relief and of joy. For Chrissake. Why had she been so scared? Nervous about seeing Steve, her Steve! She could not stop kissing him and she could not stop crying.

It took a few moments for her to realize he was not kissing her in return.

Leanne pulled her head away from his. Her face ached with smiling. She hadn't smiled since his accident. Not at the boys, not at her friends, not at her mother who had driven all the way from a small Northamptonshire town today just to help out. She had created a world without happiness for everyone around her and it must have been terrible but it would be OK now. Steve was back, he was all right and they would be happy again.

They looked at each other. Steve grinned sheepishly at her, as though he was ashamed of causing her tears. She smiled back. Her tears kept falling. Steve didn't like women crying. If she had cried in the past he had shown impatience or made a joke of it. She waited for a joke now. He remained silent, still smiling. Was he embarrassed? He reached out and wiped her wet face with his finger.

'Oh, Steve, I love you. Oh, thank God you're back,' she said. If only the tears would stop. She kept touching his face. It was unmarked. He had shaved recently and the skin was smooth. His smile did not falter. Yes, he was pleased to see her.

She leaned close to him. She whispered: 'Speak to me, Steve!'

He said: 'What do you want me to say?'

I love you, I've missed you, it's so good to see you, I've been lying in hospital at Bastion thinking about you, are you OK, where are the kids, what's been happening at home . . .?

'Isn't there anything you want to say to me, then?' she asked. She had sat down on the bed now but her face was no longer close to his.

He shrugged.

'I'd like to know how the lads are getting on.'

'Which lads?'

Let him mean the twins. Please let him mean the twins and not . . .

'1 Platoon. Are they all OK?'

She swallowed.

'Yeah. So far as I know. I spoke to Dave Henley and he didn't say there were problems, we haven't heard about any casualties. Except the lad who was hurt with you: Jordan someone.'

'How is he?' asked Steve, showing the first sign of real interest.

'He's got these bad burns but he'll be OK. He's gone home to his mum for a while, I think.'

Steve nodded. His eyes slid off around the room.

'Are you looking for something? Is there anything you want?' she asked.

'No.'

His hand was held in hers. She loosened her grip as she realized he wasn't looking for anything. He just didn't want to look at her.

'Steve . . .' she said. His eyes swivelled back to her.

'Can you remember my name, love?'

There was great sadness in his face. She realized it'd been there all the time, even when he'd smiled at her. She just hadn't chosen to see it before. He closed his eyes as though he didn't want to see her reaction to his next words. His voice was quiet.

He said: 'I'm not sure who you are.'

Chapter Twenty-one

SO HE HAD GIVEN ORDERS ONCE MORE AND GIVEN THEM BADLY. Thank God the sergeant had bailed him out yet again. Gordon Weeks went to the cookhouse and ate alone.

He was toying with his shepherd's pie when someone put their plate down directly opposite him. He looked up and saw that it was Asma. This was so astonishing that for a moment he did not speak.

'Hallo!' he said at last.

'Forgotten your Pashtu?'

'Well, I think I might be losing it. But there wasn't much in the first place.'

'What's up?' she said. 'I've never seen anyone look so miserable.'

Her big almond eyes looked levelly at him. She half smiled. He had never seen her smile fully, let alone laugh, not even with her friend the policewoman. He looked away. She was too beautiful to stare at for long. And perhaps a little bit too sad.

The FOB was a strange place, he decided. He'd been to boarding school and then university and he'd mixed almost exclusively in his own social circle all his life, even at Sandhurst. In the UK he'd have acknowledged this girl's beauty but kept her at arm's length. She had a strong London accent which, when she had translated at the *shura*, had kept emerging coarsely from under her Pashtu, and spoke of a landscape he didn't really understand.

But here at the FOB, things were different. Many of the officers were from similar backgrounds to himself, Major Willingham included. However, the personnel he found himself respecting most,

137

like Dave, were from a completely different world, one he had previously barely acknowledged. Asma too – and yet he found her the most attractive woman he had ever met. And she was sitting opposite him now, inviting him to confide in her.

'Sometimes,' he said slowly, 'the gap between where I am as an officer and where I want to be seems a little daunting.'

'You haven't been doing it for five minutes,' she said gently. 'When did you pass out of Sandhurst?'

'Just before I came here.'

'There you are then!'

He tried not to notice the way she held her knife and fork. 'I think I manage pretty well in theatre. I've been trained for that. But when I'm here at the base doing everyday things, trying to communicate . . . I've just given the men orders for tomorrow and . . . well I've never been much of a public speaker. If it wasn't for the sergeant yelling at them, I'd lose control.'

'But you're OK when you're out there fighting?'

He nodded. 'So far.' He felt himself blushing again.

'Better to be that way round. I'm on patrol with you tomorrow and I'd rather be with a platoon commander who can lead against the Taliban than someone who knows how to deliver an after-dinner speech.'

'I wish I could do both,' he said quietly.

'I'll bet, when you stand in front of the boys, you're too busy thinking about all the differences between you and them. See what I mean?'

He shook his head. She was mesmerizing. It was hard to listen to a word she said when he just wanted to study her lovely face. The skin on her cheeks was supernaturally smooth and soft. Did women in FOBs get up in the morning and put on their makeup? Or did she just look this way without even trying?'

'See, you're different,' she continued. 'You can't imagine their lives back home, and they can't imagine yours. No way. But when you're fighting, you're united. There aren't any differences; it's you against the enemy. So it's easier to communicate then, innit?'

He thought about this and decided she was right. He was just about to tell her so when her friend Jean sat down beside them.

Weeks gritted his teeth. Not just because he was enjoying these uninterrupted moments with Asma but because he'd begun to dislike the policewoman. He knew his men avoided the RMPs like the plague. Boss Weeks had been brought up to believe only those with something to hide avoided the police, and he had nothing to hide. Yet he'd also found himself avoiding the sharp-faced, sharp-eyed Jean.

She smiled at him. '*As salaam alai kum.*'

'Good evening,' he replied.

'I've had an informal chat with the Officer Commanding about that incident in the Green Zone . . .'

Weeks looked at her gloomily. 'Which incident? There have been so many.'

For the first time he saw Asma laugh. He wasn't sure why. But he watched with pleasure as her face changed shape, broadening to reveal a row of even teeth. He loved to hear the giggle bubbling up from inside her like a spring. From that moment, it became his private mission to make her laugh again. It was a challenging mission. He knew he was seldom funny.

Jean Patterson did not laugh.

'The only incident I'm aware of took place some weeks ago when your men opened fire on a group of Taliban fighters. While their bodies were being searched, one turned out not to be dead. We'll never know the extent of his injuries because he was then shot at point blank range.'

'He was perceived to be dangerous. He was reaching for his weapon.'

'The weapon should have been removed during the routine search. And apparently another soldier did remove it at once.'

'He was killed because he was a threat,' Weeks insisted.

'No. He was killed because the sergeant ordered it. The soldier who was searching the insurgent quite rightly hesitated. But another soldier followed the sergeant's order and shot the man.'

Weeks never physically brawled and seldom got into verbal arguments but he recognized the surge of adrenalin that was suddenly pumping through his body as fighting adrenalin.

He leaned forward. 'Jean . . . may I call you Jean?'

'Certainly, Gordon.'

'Jean. The sergeant saw that his men were in danger because they

139

were in intimate contact with a member of the Taliban. That man may have been feigning death while perfectly healthy. What would you have done under the circumstances?'

Jean leaned forward too. 'Gordon. Since the man was lying wounded in a ditch, I'd have treated him as a casualty.'

'Jean. He was a Taliban fighter. There can be no question about that, he was fully armed. Of course he had to be dealt with like any other armed insurgent.'

'He may have been an insurgent but he was also a member of the human race. He—'

'Jean—'

'Gordon!'

Weeks was aware of the delightful Asma laughing at them both. He did not allow himself the pleasure of looking at her. He supposed they were comical, but he was so angry now he did not care.

Jean raised her voice. 'The man was no longer armed and he was wounded. He required medical treatment.'

'How do you know? My men certainly fired on him, and his comrades were certainly killed. But he might have been unhurt and feigning death. It is, after all, a common enemy tactic.'

'Your men have all described him as wounded.'

'My men aren't doctors and are not trained to spot the difference between someone who is wounded and someone who is pretending. And do you know what order, precisely, the sergeant gave to shoot him?'

Jean nodded confidently. 'He said: "Get on with it." '

'I'm not familiar with that order. Are you?'

Jean sighed.

'In fact,' the boss went on, pressing home his advantage, 'I don't remember ever hearing that order before. I don't think I learned it at Sandhurst. So I'm surprised you recognize those words as an order to kill.'

Jean leaned back in her seat. There were red circles in her white cheeks.

'His men knew what he meant.'

'Have you asked Dave Henley what he meant?'

'Sergeant Henley has a reputation,' Jean said. 'He's considered a very tough and no-nonsense sort of sergeant who might not tolerate legitimate hesitation on human rights grounds by one of his soldiers.'

'Sergeant Henley is considered an outstanding NCO precisely because he's tough and no-nonsense,' Weeks snapped, 'and this is the best protection for his men after body armour.' Her accusation made his heart pump faster, dispersing anger through his body. 'He has a humane and compassionate side which does him great credit. Before you make any assumptions or accusations you should ask him what he meant by those words.'

'It isn't appropriate for me to ask him because this is not yet a formal investigation. But I'm not going to let this one get swept under the carpet. I expect someone in his unit to question him very closely.'

'And so we will,' Weeks said. He believed he'd won this skirmish and it was therefore better to stop the battle.

He glanced over at Asma at last. Incredibly, for a few minutes he had actually forgotten she was there. Now he felt happy to see her again, as though she had just walked in. He remembered that she had said she would be out on patrol with him tomorrow. When he looked more closely, he was surprised at the expression on her face. It was something like admiration.

Chapter Twenty-two

'NOW THEN, THIS SHOULD DO IT . . .' DARREL CROUCHED DOWN beside the television. 'And if it doesn't, I've got another idea.'

Agnieszka set his coffee on the table and then knelt down to watch him. The baby lay on the floor nearby. Luke liked that. He liked just lying there, staring up at the ceiling, rearranging himself from time to time. When the atmosphere was tranquil he became tranquil too.

'How you know what to do?' Agnieszka stared at the nest of wires and the way he flicked through the buttons and settings on the machine.

He looked up and gave her a quick grin. His eye was caught by a picture behind her, the large one at the back of the room. Jamie was in uniform and smiling, his eyes shining as he looked over the camera as though a mountain was looming right there behind the photographer and he was about to climb it. Agnieszka loved that picture. Steve Buckle had taken it when the platoon was training in Kenya. She had enlarged it and then bought a nice frame.

Darrel gazed at the photo for a few moments longer than politeness demanded. Then he turned back to his wires and answered her question.

'I've always been good with this sort of stuff. When I was a kid I used to take things apart to see how they worked. And my dad always made me put them back together again myself, he wouldn't help me. Sometimes I hated him. But it meant I learned a lot.'

She watched him work. Now she knew his face better she could see that he was handsome. The first time she had met him she had liked his smile but found him ordinary enough. Since then the tapering lines of his face had pleased her more and more.

It occurred to her now that she could draw those clean lines. On impulse she fetched her sketch pad. It was at the back of a cupboard where, despite Jamie's encouragement, she barely looked at it these days. She settled on the sofa sketching his dark features as he bent over in concentration. He was older than Jamie and that made his lines deeper and stronger. Jamie was certainly good-looking but his face still had youthful curves which reminded you of the boy he'd been until a few years ago. Whereas Darrel was more of a man.

Luke, on the rug, murmured sometimes to himself. Otherwise the room was quiet except for the scratching of her pencil strokes. Darrel did not know she was drawing him until he looked up. He stared at the pad.

'Show me!'

'When it finished. You please continue.'

'But I have finished. Look.'

He retreated to the armchair where Jamie usually sat, pressed some buttons on the remote and the TV sprang into life, its picture clear. He turned down the sound and then zapped through the silent channels to prove that he could.

Agnieszka was delighted. She watched the pictures rushing past with a smile on her face. That game show was here again, the one where you watched the faces of people who had won a million, or won it and then lost it all. And then that channel was gone, replaced by leopards on a wildlife programme which gave way to a splinter of a soap opera with sulking, angry faces, which was rapidly replaced by a serious newscaster who turned suddenly into a football match. The whole world, in its infinite variety, was galloping past as Darrel zapped his way through the channels. Agnieszka thought: That's how my life feels. As if the whole wide, colourful world out there rushes by while I sit here alone in Wiltshire.

The picture disappeared altogether and Darrel turned to her.

'Oh, Darrel, that very clever what you done!'

'You can tell me I'm clever if it's still working next week.' He looked pleased. 'I'll phone you to check. Now let's see what you're drawing.'

She sighed. 'I only start five minutes ago . . .'

But he was delighted with her sketch. He looked carefully at every line and then held it at arm's length. He told her how good it was until she went pink with pleasure.

'Please, take this home with you. Maybe your wife like it also.'

She'd seen his wedding ring, of course. She'd noticed it the first time she met him at the garage. They'd met at the superstore, then he'd come to the house to diagnose the problem with the TV and she'd given him a cup of tea and they'd talked. He'd said she needed some gadget and now here he was installing it. That was three, no four meetings. And he'd never once mentioned his wife. Today was Saturday. Didn't she ask him where he went? This thought filled Agnieszka with apprehension. She wasn't sure why.

'My wife won't like this picture.' He smiled at her. 'Because it looks just like me.'

Agnieszka blinked at him.

'I'm separated.'

'Long time ago?'

'No.'

'Since when?'

'Since I had that cup of coffee with you.'

'But that was only . . .'

'A month ago.'

'You just separate!'

'Listen, Aggie, these things don't happen overnight. Everything's wrong and you put up with it and think this is just the way things are. But everyone's unhappy. And sooner or later you have to admit it to yourself. And do something about it.'

Agnieszka felt her heart beating faster but she did not know why. Anyway, whatever her heart was doing, her head needed time to go through this slowly and methodically.

'So one day, the day of superstore coffee, you say: *Enough!* And you leave your wife?'

'Sort of.'

'Not exactly?'

'My wife was in the store that day and she saw us.'

Agnieszka leaned back on the sofa, her head tilted, and looked at the ceiling. She didn't know where else to look. Her long, slim neck swept up to her jawline, her chin jutted towards the roof. Darrel watched her. Agnieszka rolled her eyes.

'Oh God, God, everyone was in superstore that day. Was it half-price special offer day, maybe?'

Darrel smiled.

'You, me, my wife . . . who else was there? Oh yes, your neighbour with the little girl.'

'The sergeant's wife. She didn't see you.'

'I made sure of that. But I didn't realize my wife was around as well. And she saw us talking.'

'So marriage ends?' Agnieszka stared at him now, her blue eyes very round. 'Marriage ends because you take coffee with me?'

'It was ending anyway, Aggie. Coffee just finished it off.'

'But she must understand we only take coffee!'

Darrel shook his head.

'She saw me talking to you. Like I really wanted to hear what you had to say? Like I found you interesting? And she said it was years since I talked to her that way. And she was right.'

'And marriage *ends*?' Agnieszka was leaning forward. She was whispering. Just saying the words felt sinful enough. 'Marriage *ends* because of way you talk to me?'

He shrugged. He did not look sad, contrite, hurt or anything a man at the end of his marriage might look.

'After many years?'

'Eight.'

She shook her head as though she was trying to shake it clear.

'Because of *coffee*? With *me*?'

'Because it had already ended years ago. So all it took was one coffee to finish it off completely.'

'So now what you do?'

'I've moved out. I'm staying with my mother, for the time being. Until I can get myself sorted. Gillian and the kids have stayed at home.'

'You have kids?'

'Three.'

'Three!'

He laughed at her amazement.

'Well, it's not so unusual in this country. How many do people in Poland have? Ten?'

'Usual to stop with one. Sometimes a long, long time before two. And three not very ordinary.'

But it wasn't the number of children itself which amazed her. It was the nonchalance with which he could end the marriage that supported so many. It gave her an uncomfortable feeling: unease with her own role in this. How could meeting a man in a shop and having a coffee with him result in such a thing? Had the wife, watching unnoticed, detected an interest in Agnieszka which Agnieszka had been unaware of? Or had she been aware of his interest but chosen to ignore it because she wanted her TV repaired? The thought made her curl up on the sofa. It made her feel unclean.

Darrel said quietly: 'It's not your fault.'

But she did not uncurl. So she had unwittingly ended this man's marriage. It wasn't her fault. But did that leave her with some responsibilities towards him?

She heard him get up. What was he doing now? Crossing the room? She did not uncurl to see. She shut her eyes and ears and said Aves to herself to keep them shut. Then she remembered. She should pay him for repairing the television, for the gadget he had bought. If she didn't pay him then there was an implication of friendship. Or obligation.

She jumped up. The room was empty except for Luke, now asleep on the floor, his mouth open and his hands up as though he was under arrest. Her sketch lay on the sofa.

She ran to the door but she was too late. His car was just pulling away.

Chapter Twenty-three

THE MAIL ARRIVED MINUTES BEFORE 1 SECTION LEFT FOR ITS PATROL and the boss delayed by ten minutes so that the men could read it before they jumped on the Vectors.

Dave got a letter from his mother, a letter from Jenny and, ominously, a letter from Jenny's mother too. He started the one from Jenny, then left them on his cot and went to count the men into the vehicles.

'We're a decoy, so don't let's delude ourselves we're a fire team,' he reminded them.

Sol was standing at his side.

'Just help me with my English, would you?' he muttered. 'What's the difference between a decoy and a sitting duck?'

Dave rolled his eyes.

'You don't need any help with your English,' he said. 'Today there is no difference.'

Sol's ankle had healed and Dave had been relieved to have him back commanding 1 Section.

He turned to the lads jumping on board the Vectors right now. Streaky Bacon and Jack Binns were still battle virgins. They'd been on patrol and escorted contractors and been caught in sporadic, low-key fire fights but they had not yet been involved in anything more serious. Although they insisted that they were ready and eager to do so, neither had fired a shot.

'You're not going out for a fucking picnic!' Dave barked at Streaky. 'Sling your weapon, sprog, and get two hands on it.'

147

Binns, climbing in behind Streaky, undid his sling clip rapidly before Dave could see. He looked sheepish when he saw Sol watching him.

Dave jumped in beside the driver of the first vehicle as it pulled away. The boss sat with Asma at the front of the second.

As they rumbled across the desert Dave felt on edge. His eyes scanned every ripple in the landscape. Ever since that goat had exploded so spectacularly right in front of him, he'd been forced to accept that IEDs had become impossible to spot. Before then he had tried to persuade himself that, if he was alert enough, he couldn't be caught on the wrong end of an explosion.

Nevertheless, he kept his eyes peeled for a pile of stones or recently disturbed earth which might hint at something beneath the surface. He stared hard at a young man watching the convoy from his motorbike whose mobile phone could be a detonator.

It was common knowledge that the Taliban were stepping up their use of IEDs. Their explosives were getting bigger and better and the capacity of the Vectors to withstand their blasts was now in question because most of their armour was on top rather than underneath. Since 1 Platoon had arrived in Sin City, news had filtered in regularly of British soldiers elsewhere in Helmand Province who had been killed or injured by mines. There were anti-personnel mines and anti-tank mines and, if you managed to avoid all these, there were always the Soviet-era legacy mines.

As they crossed the featureless desert they passed the first train of camels Dave had seen here. It was a biblical sight, the line of humped backs and long necks making slow and rhythmic progress across the sand.

'Could be two thousand years ago,' the driver said.

'Except for the IEDs.'

'This route has been cleared.'

'Cleared last week doesn't mean it's still clear today.'

'You're not your usual self, Sarge. Having a bad day?'

'I'm pissed off with being sent out undermanned. There's just not enough of us. And one's a woman and two are sprogs. The civilians are forcing us to spread ourselves too thin. So we're a decoy and we're supposed to keep going but the Taliban don't know that. To them we're just the enemy.'

'Well maybe we'll have a nice quiet ride today,' the driver said cheerfully.

'You don't sound your usual self either,' Dave said. The driver was famous for his gloomy predictions.

'I've got mail in my cot. One from the missus and one from my bird. What more can a man ask for?'

'Let's hope you don't meet your maker today, then, or everything you've got will get sent straight back to your missus unless I remember to pull it out first.'

The man's face clouded.

'Fuck it, I never thought of that.' Then his expression brightened again. 'But she can't nag if I'm dead, can she?'

The incoming fire began the moment they arrived in the Green Zone.

'Keep going,' said the boss. The men on top cover returned fire.

They passed the point where the platoon had dismounted last time they were here. They passed the cannabis field. Dave thought he could smell it and when a roar went up from the lads in the back ('We know where we are! Too fucking right we do! Got everything you came with, Mal?'), he was sure he could smell it. They drove towards the river crossing and the firing suddenly and mysteriously stopped.

'I don't like this,' said Dave. 'Go slow.'

'If we keep our heads down and get moving we'll be through it in no time.' The driver was a lot less happy than he'd been ten minutes ago.

'Oh, yeah? We're supposed to have cleared this area. But they started firing the minute we got here. They're telling us they're back. Slow down so I can keep a sharp look-out.'

The driver slowed. There was still no firing.

'The fuckers are behind us, so let's just take a run at it,' the driver said.

'No. Slow down more.'

The driver barely slowed at all.

'Slower!' Dave yelled, his eyes fixed on the track ahead. He could see it start to rise about two hundred metres in front of them where the track became a bridge over the mighty Helmand River. He could smell the pollen of cannabis and other plants mixed in with the hot dust. Big, floppy leaves tapped gently against the side of the vehicle as they passed. Dave's senses were so alert they seemed to be screaming at him. He did not blink and his eyes were dry with the effort of scanning the dusty track.

He thought: If I was a guerrilla fighter I'd let the army believe they'd cleared this crossing. Then I'd go back. I'd put an IED just before the bridge. I'd make sure no other traffic passed and pedestrians were kept away. An army convoy would come along and it would seem quiet here. The front of the convoy would be blown up. Everyone would stop. Then I'd ambush the rest from behind. So they'd be trapped . . .

Until now there had been a lot of detritus floating around in his mind: fragments of last night's dream, the knowledge of Jenny's letter on his cot, the information that his knee was hurting for no reason, the worry that Steve Buckle might never recover his mind, a curt warning from Major Willingham that he would have to interview Dave about the death of one wounded insurgent in a ditch. All those thoughts stopped now. The sudden certainty that the Taliban would have planted an IED in their path and in a place where it would cause most chaos sliced cleanly through all the other voices in his ear.

'*Stop!*' he yelled as they approached the bridge.

The driver responded to the volume and urgency of Dave's instruction by slamming on the brakes. Behind them, they could hear the second vehicle screeching to a halt too, and the third behind that.

'What's going on?' the boss demanded.

Dave didn't reply. The Vector stood still, ticking in the heat, smelling of fuel, clouds of dust circling around it. The firing which had met their arrival in the Green Zone had stopped. Everything had stopped. There were no kids gathering in a cluster to stare at them, no old men in the nearby fields holding their aching backs as they straightened, no small cars bulging with big Afghan families travelling in the other direction. There was only silence.

Dave wondered if he should feel stupid. He had just halted a patrol which had orders to keep moving. He had done so on a hunch. He had no evidence for his suspicions.

The driver was looking at him. 'You all right, Sarge?'

Dave stared ahead. It seemed to him that, between their stopping place and the rise where the bridge began, the dirt of the track lacked the patina of daily use.

He reported: 'Suspicious ground at vulnerable point ahead.'

He looked hard at the track. If anyone was waiting to press a button at the other end of a command wire or a mobile phone, their only vantage point would be just inside the jungle on either side of them. There was visibility from nowhere else. He sent men down to search through the greenery. While they did so he leaned forward and stared at the track.

'I think I see something ahead,' Dave said. 'Have the engineers got mine detection equipment?'

There was a groan from the engineers.

'I take it that means no?' Dave listened to the sound of his own voice. It sounded rough, as though he was still bumping along the rutty track.

'No, we've got it, Sarge. Only we don't have 4Cs any more.'

'And?'

'We've got an Ebinger but we're not certain how to use it; we haven't been trained on them yet.'

'I'm sure the combined brains of 1 Section can help you work that out,' Dave said. 'Quickly.'

The men came back to the Vectors having found no trace of anyone close enough to both see and detonate a device. Dave began to have doubts. Then he heard the boss.

'Our interpreter has just picked up some enemy chatter which indicates there could be an IED . . .'

'Got the detectors sorted?' Dave demanded. 'Come on! We're sitting ducks here! Just because no one's firing at us doesn't mean they've all gone home for a nice cup of tea.'

The engineers dismounted and Dave sent men to cover them on the ground. The engineers stood arguing over how the machine worked but at last one of them put in an earpiece and began sweeping his way slowly forward.

Dave watched him. He had a sudden memory of a beach on the south coast of England soon after he had met Jenny. The first time they'd spent the night together, they'd gone down to the sea before dawn and watched the sun come up across the ocean. They'd lain close, tired but relaxed, on sand which retained the coolness of the night. Then, suddenly, they were surrounded. Old men with metal detectors were sweeping the beach at first light for treasure.

Dave sighed and turned from the memory. It had no place in this hot, hostile world.

The engineers advanced slowly along the track. About five paces before the bridge, they stopped. The first passed the machine and earpiece to the second. He nodded. They began to dig with the machine, brushing the sand gently from side to side.

'Got something?' Dave was hot and tense. Were they being watched? Or were the enemy firing positions right behind the Vectors, waiting to prevent their escape?

After a few more minutes, the engineers shook their heads. 'Just an old bolt buried in the track.'

'Can we come back now?' asked the younger engineer.

'Nope,' Dave said.

'There's probably a hundred old bolts between here and the bridge. They probably dropped them when they built it.'

'Move ahead with caution,' Dave said. 'The bolt might have been dropped. Or it might have been planted there.'

The engineers shrugged. It didn't seem so surprising to them that an old bolt was buried in the track. But Dave had heard enough stories in Bastion to know that the Taliban could make men lazy with false readings so that by the time they reached the big one they were completely unprepared.

After a few more paces, he saw that the engineers had detected something else.

'Another fucking bolt,' they muttered, looking around anxiously.

'Careful, careful!' Dave knew they felt vulnerable out there, despite the cover. He could see that they were digging less cautiously now, with the perfunctory attitude of men ordered to do an unnecessary job.

The boss said: 'Our interpreter is picking up a lot of chatter from the enemy. She thinks they're close.'

'I'll bet they are,' Dave said.

Suddenly one of the engineers stopped. He pulled the other over to look and they both peered down into the hole. There was a pause and then, simultaneously, they turned back to the Vectors. Dave couldn't see their expressions, but something about the angle of their heads and the tension in their bodies told him all he needed to know.

'OK, get back in the vehicles. Now!'

He reported to the boss: 'They've found the IED ahead.'

'We'll need EOD to clear it,' the boss said.

'We'll need to get out,' Dave said. 'Before the Talis trap us here.'

But it was already too late.

The engineers were nearing the Vectors when the first shots bounced around the vehicles. The men ran the last few paces and jumped aboard as the ambush kicked off. The enemy weapons, including first machine guns and then RPGs, started almost simultaneously. They had been in position. They had been watching. They had been waiting for this order.

The weight of fire was so intense that it would not be safe to drive through it. The boss reported briefly while the drivers realigned the Vectors in a defensive position. Dave only wished they'd stopped further back. He guessed they'd be fighting here for a while and there were better places to do that than under a hundred metres from an IED waiting to explode.

Chapter Twenty-four

INSIDE THE VECTORS, THE MEN LOOKED AT EACH OTHER AND HELD their weapons closer as the noise erupted around them and they were thrown around by the vehicles' frantic manoeuvres.

Streaky Bacon thought at first it was raining outside. Then he wondered if maybe someone was throwing money at them. Finally he realized it was raining rounds. Without warning he felt waves of nausea running through his body. He caught sight of Binns's face, blanched white, and he realized that Binman felt like throwing up too.

So this was it. A real fire fight against a real enemy. Streaky had played Call of Duty 4 often and well; he'd impressed his instructors at Catterick and if anyone had asked him what he was looking forward to in Afghanistan apart from rapping he would have said fighting.

Since arriving he'd been on patrol and he'd heard the other lads' stories and knew that men at other FOBs had been under fire daily. He'd been disappointed that so far he'd seen very little action. But now they were being ambushed by a real enemy whose object was to kill them. There was no screen between himself and the action and at the end of this game a dead man didn't get up to fight again.

The Vectors found their defensive positions and stood still. The engines were switched off. The firing intensified and, without the engines to mask it, the sound was more frightening. Binns and Bacon exchanged wide-eyed looks. They tried without success to hide their terror.

The machine-gunners were operating at warp speed overhead.

'Section! Rapid fire!' Sol said and their rate of fire doubled. The enemy responded in kind.

Streaky saw Binman's eyes widen still further. There were dark circles beneath them and below the dark circles Binman's skin was so white it looked like a mask.

Streaky would have liked to put his fingers in his ears but he closed his eyes instead. He could hear the thud of the enemy weapons. On top of one Vector was a GPMG and on the other were two minimis and if you closed your eyes and concentrated there was both a rhythm and a beat to the weapons. Streaky reached into his pouch for the stub of a pencil he always carried around with him and the creased piece of paper he wrapped around it and he tried to find some good flow.

> *fire liar cry die, retire to a nice quiet . . .*
> *head dead sweat*
> *scared . . .*

What rhymed with *scared*? Did anything rhyme with *scared*?

There was a massive crash and a flash that leaped out of nowhere and for a crazy moment Streaky thought they had been struck by lightning. Then he heard Dave's voice in his ear. It sounded strangely cool and distant inside Streaky's hot, sweaty head, as if Dave was directing operations from some beachside bar a huge distance away: 'Get out and get down.'

'What happened?' Another disembodied voice.

'RPG hit a corner of the truck and bounced,' someone said.

'Everyone all right?'

'Get out, *now*!' Sol yelled.

And then men were piling out of the Vectors, their bodies crouching, slinking around the truck while all around them the orchestra of fire played in the theatre of war.

Streaky, waves of nausea running up and down his body, got behind the Vector and ducked.

Scared . . . unprepared!

That was it. Streaky felt for his pencil. Yes!

I'm scared, I'm unprepared man, for what may lie ahead
man . . .

He sat down in the dirt and watched rounds bouncing all around the vehicle. It looked as if the ground was cracking. Overhead, the trees were cracking.

'Fucking hell,' Binman shouted.

'Wish you stayed at Curry's now?' Streaky hoped he sounded ice cool but he knew his voice had emerged high and splintered like a kid's.

They crouched down amid the flash and crack and thud of the battle.

Rapid fire, I'm not scared,
No I'm a liar, I'm unprepared
I want to cry, I start to sweat
Mama, I'm still a child inside my head,
Don't want to show it, don't want you to know it,
But if I shut my eyes I see me dead . . .

'Get some fire down!' Sol shouted.

Streaky looked up from under his helmet, trying to think of a rhyme for *dead . . . bed, said, fed, dread . . .*

'What do you think you've got rifles for, to hang on the fucking Christmas tree?' Finn yelled. '*Use them!*'

Streaky realized he and Binman were the only ones not firing.

He shuffled to the side of the Vector and looked out. He could see rounds flying down the track. One pinged off the Vector and then against his helmet like someone trying to wake him.

He ducked behind the vehicle again, pulled his rifle into position and looked through the sights. He was crouching too low to aim at anything except a snake. Reluctantly he got up onto one knee. Binman, at his side, did the same. A round ricocheted off the ground in front of them. Trying to ignore it, his finger shaking, Streaky released the safety.

The first time he fired he had no idea where the round went or where it landed. His hand would not stop shaking. He fired again. What was he aiming at? He was staring through the sights. But there was nothing to see.

He dodged back behind the Vector. He felt as though he had been exposed out there for an hour. Binman was still behind him. This was Binns's chance to move forward and take up the firing position Streaky had vacated but he didn't. His face was a ghastly white, like a vampire in a horror movie.

Since Binman was frozen to the spot, Streaky kept his head down, pointed the SA80 up the track behind them and fired intensively. When his shoulder began to hurt he paused. And then he fired some more. He felt his body relax a little. Inexplicably, he wanted to giggle. This wasn't so difficult. Since the Taliban was invisible, you could aim anywhere and there was a chance of hitting one of them. He heard laughter and realized it was his own. He fired faster and faster to the sound of his own laughter.

'Slow it down, for Chrissake,' someone shouted, maybe Dave. Streaky paused and looked around. It was a relief to stop firing. Had he really been laughing? He saw that the men with the most firepower and the best positions were high up on the vehicles. But they were also the most exposed.

A shout came from Jamie on top. Streaky and Dave both turned in time to see him stagger.

'Shit, come and help,' Dave shouted to Streaky, scrambling to his feet and diving inside the vehicle. Streaky followed him. They found Jamie already there, his body doubled, hanging onto the side.

'Sit down,' Dave ordered. 'What happened?'

Streaky helped Jamie down. Gasping for breath, Jamie managed to say: 'A bloke standing over me with a fucking great sledge-hammer brought it down right on my back . . .'

His face drained. He closed his eyes. He was going to pass out. Or was he going to die? Streaky felt sick.

Dave shook Jamie awake, looking desperate, as though he thought Jamie wouldn't wake up if he lost consciousness.

'You've been hit,' he said. His voice was strangled and urgent. Streaky looked at his sergeant and saw shock carved into every crevice. Dave was already old: probably in his late twenties, Streaky thought. But now he seemed ten years older even than that.

Streaky watched Dave's face cave in a little as he searched for the wound. He knew that, as far as a sergeant can be close to one of his men, Dave was good mates with Jamie. Personally Streaky found Jamie a strange geezer. He was posh and apparently he had been to college and he obviously should have been an officer but for some reason he had wanted to be one of the lads instead. Streaky had meant to ask him why, when the moment was right. Now it seemed he might never have a chance.

Jamie wordlessly pointed to the place and Dave gently readjusted Jamie's position so they could reach the wound without twisting his body. Dave's face was frightening Streaky Bacon now. He needed his sergeant to be hard. Invincible. And instead Dave was showing signs of shock because his mate was hurt, just like anyone else.

Dave glanced at Streaky.

'Don't just sit there staring, get the fucking medic!' he snapped. But the medic was already climbing into the Vector. Streaky was the first to see the deep tear at the bottom of Jamie's body armour. He pointed to it. Dave swallowed.

The medic pushed Streaky aside.

'OK, I've got him,' he said. He was trying to release Dave back out there again. But Streaky could see that Dave, although he was certainly needed outside, did not want to leave Jamie.

'Get someone on the gimpy!' Jamie said weakly, his eyes closed. 'They're closing in on us, I could see it from on top.'

'It's too exposed up there, everyone has to come down,' Dave said, and he gave the order.

The medic took off Jamie's armour and pouches and webbing, handing them to Streaky who put them down carefully, almost reverently. When the medic crouched to examine Jamie's back they could all see the massive swelling appearing on the right side.

'You've been hit.'

'I know that.'

'You're a lucky boy. I think it was a high-calibre round. I'd say it's a 7.62mm.'

'He'd be dead if one of them hit him,' Dave said, his face still a caricature.

'I've heard of them bouncing off,' the medic said. 'The ceramic plates inside this body armour are amazing.'

'Maybe I am dead,' Jamie said weakly. 'And you're all dead too.'

'Not me,' Streaky said. 'I'm still here—'

There was a huge crash outside the Vector.

He added: 'I think.'

'So we're all dead and something the bishop forgot to tell us about heaven is that it's one long fire fight with the Taliban,' Dave said.

'You're winded and a bit shocked and you're going to have one helluva bruise. But you're alive,' the medic told Jamie.

'You could have fooled me,' he said.

'And,' the medic added, 'you're a lucky man. A few centimetres higher and it would have been right through your neck.'

'Just stay sitting down quietly,' Dave told him.

'Well, if I'm alive I'm OK to get back on the gun so give me my kit.'

'Oh, no, you're not OK,' the medic said.

Dave was already carrying the GPMG down and setting it up on the ground outside.

'Get a belt loaded,' he yelled at Streaky, a command which was causing Streaky some panic when Jamie staggered out of the Vector. His exposed body drew a burst of fire. He didn't so much duck as fall behind the gimpy.

'You probably should sit inside, mate,' Dave said gruffly.

'Don't talk shit.' Jamie sorted out the belt for Streaky and edged Dave away from the machine gun. Dave watched him for a moment then the boss arrived at their side.

'When the fuck is the air support arriving?' Dave asked. 'Because we'll soon be standing here with nothing to throw at them but bottles of water.'

'We'll have to slow our rate of fire to make it last longer,' Weeks said.

'They'll notice and move in.'

'They're already moving in,' the boss shouted back, over the whoosh of an incoming RPG. 'If we get really low then we might have to try blowing up the IED and exiting forward over the bridge.'

'No!' Dave shouted back. 'They'll have left an IED on the other side too.'

Binman appeared from behind the Vector to help Jamie with the machine gun and Streaky returned to the fire fight with renewed energy.

'Slow your rate of fire!' Sol ordered him a few minutes later. Streaky nodded and paused and then forgot. Now the machine gun was back at work he tried to keep his rifle firing almost as fast, which was impossible of course, but made him feel more effective. He paused at last, his weapon burning in his hands. He looked around. So where exactly were the flipflops?

He watched enemy rounds bouncing like hailstones, threshing the leaves and dust into something like fine confetti. He searched for muzzle flashes. He listened. He decided the flipflops must be everywhere. He swallowed. They were heavily outnumbered. And if they weren't surrounded yet, they soon would be.

As the fight intensified, Streaky saw the boss push the woman interpreter into the back of the Vector. She obviously didn't want to go but she climbed inside and Streaky glimpsed the medic in there with her. Everyone else, including Dave, including the signaller, including the boss, was outside firing back at the ambush.

Mal vacated a prominent firing position to refill magazines and Streaky stepped into it. He swallowed, raised his weapon, released the safety and started to fire once more. When he stopped, he watched a round bounce along the track in front of him and estimated that it had come from a tree only about fifty metres away. Fifty metres! He fired at the high branches of the tree. No body fell but, all the same, it felt good to have something to fire at. He fired again and again and again to make sure.

On every patrol so far, Streaky had submitted to a sense of help-lessness. He didn't think about what he did. He followed orders. He didn't know where he was, in what direction they were driving, how far from the base they were or what the reason for their mission might be, even if the boss had tried to explain it. He just expected other people to tell him what to do.

Now, with his hands hot from his weapon, the smoky, sulphuric smell of the battle filling his nostrils and its noise all around him, his senses were heightened and so was his understanding. He understood that the enemy was to the rear and on two flanks. If they succeeded in moving forward of the convoy then the Vectors would be totally surrounded. That was a thought so uncomfortable it was enough to induce streams of sweat all of its own, separate from the sweat induced by carrying a lot of kit in sweltering heat, separate from the sweat of the battle itself.

I'm weaker in emotion than in arms and fire aim
The smoke I'm inhaling isn't keeping my mind sane,
It feels like rehydration's a better soldier's game . . .

On Streaky's left, Angus was firing rapidly. Streaky tried to copy him. He fired round after round after round. You could lose yourself in firing. It was as though you ceased to exist and your body became a part of your weapon. It was good to think of yourself as a weapon. It made you feel invulnerable. It made you feel like a killing machine.

When at last he paused there was a rap forming in his head.

We're pinned down
It's a sin to frown, I wish I could grin but it's grim in this town
No houses no streets no shops and no women
Just choking on the smoke and no joking I need water,
water water water . . .

What rhymed with water?

There was the sodium glare and the crash of an RPG, so powerful it made Streaky duck. With his head down, words inserted themselves into his brain.

Water . . . daughter, sorter, halter . . . no good, none of them, not one of them was any good.

The grenade had missed the Vectors and was landing on the track in front of them. There was a pause. Everyone, including the enemy, was waiting to see if it had hit the IED.

'Cover!' Dave roared.

But the grenade fell short and firing resumed.

'We're short of ammo,' Dave told everyone. 'Watch and fire. Watch and fire. Conserve ammo.'

Streaky didn't hear him.

Water, transporter

Good rhyme.

Water, mortar

Yes! Even better!

Water, slaughter!

The best! Despite the battle all around him, Streaky smiled.

Nearby, the boss was asking over the radio when the air support was coming. It sounded as though they were giving him the brush-off because the fragments of his reply Streaky could catch were: '. . . outnumbered . . . supplies . . . seriously overexposed . . .'

There was a pause.

'And when *will* it be available?' the boss demanded.

Binman's face appeared, chalk white and smelling of vomit.

'Shit,' he said to Streaky.

'Listen, bruv,' Streaky said, 'I was going to sick up and then I started firing and I felt a lot better when I had something to do and now I'm loving it. I just keep on firing, that's what I do.'

But Binns rolled his eyes in his white, white face and did not speak. The medic climbed out of a Vector to take his arm.

'Come on, sprog,' he said to Binman. 'You're in shock. And I'm not surprised. Your sarge says you've never done this before. It's what they call a baptism of fire.'

Binns was getting into the Vector just as the woman interpreter jumped out.

Streaky sneaked around the side of the Vector to fire more rounds, very quickly. He began to feel confident despite the knowledge that nothing they had done, not the constant rattle of their machine guns or the full force of their small arms, lessened the enemy's strength. In fact, the Taliban firing positions were getting closer. They seemed to be moving in around the sides of the Vectors now so that even crouching behind the vehicles you could feel exposed.

Nausea gripped Streaky again. If the flipflops slipped forward of the Vectors, 1 Section would be completely surrounded. He knew there was an IED up there. He hoped it was enough to keep the Taliban back. Involuntarily he glanced towards it and saw a shadow flicker through the distant undergrowth. Streaky came from the vertical world of high-rise flats in Wolverhampton and he was alert to any horizontals. Here was something the wrong shape moving swiftly through the woods. He readjusted his position to see it better.

Someone next to him was raising their weapon too. It was the woman interpreter, with her SA80. She had seen the shadow and was taking aim. Suddenly anxious to beat her, Streaky fired again and again, as fast as he could. The shadow fell.

'We'll never know,' said the woman, 'which of us did that.'

Since she had only fired a few rounds, Streaky thought it was certainly him. But he smiled at her anyway. She smiled back.

'What are you doing?' the boss thundered behind them.

'Using our weapons,' said the woman. 'We saw the enemy trying to sneak forward.'

'Just slotted a flipflop!' Streaky said gleefully.

For some reason the boss didn't seem to share his excitement. 'Get over the other side, will you, and slow down the ammo rate,' he snapped.

Streaky could hear the conversation as he went. The boss said: 'Asma, I asked you to stay in the Vector. The OC prefers women not to engage in frontline fighting.'

And the woman was saying: 'Frontline? Where the fuck is that? They're all around us!'

Streaky ran across to the back of the other Vector. He glanced behind him at the woman and saw the boss trying to persuade her to return to the wagon. Then he slipped into a firing position and started again. He let round after round rip into the nearby trees and undergrowth. If there was any living thing there, it must soon be dead.

What rhymed with *enemy*? Absolutely nothing. It was impossible to find a word in the English language that rhymed with *enemy*.

He saw an RPG flying high overhead. He stepped behind the Vector, watching the grenade's bright, graceful arc. It had a sort of beauty. Dave saw it too. He knew, from its height and its trajectory, exactly where it was going to land. He shouted: 'Cover!'

Some firing continued but everyone who'd seen the RPG sailing towards the river, including the enemy, stopped and waited. And then came the explosion.

Streaky felt the heat of the blast wave and the force of its punch in his chest. He was blown against the side of the Vector. The ground rocked, the world rocked and, when he looked up, the sky was rocking too. It was breaking into a thousand tiny pieces and falling on their heads. Some men were flung to the ground, others threw themselves there. A few grabbed the Vectors for security, but the Vectors were rocking with the shock too.

Streaky was on his stomach, helmet down.

Enemy . . . destiny! Yes! It wasn't perfect but it would do. The two words worked well together. *Enemy, destiny*, yes.

Branches, leaves and plants were still flying through the air, smoke rose upwards in a steady column from the riverside, and it felt like minutes before the world began to steady itself. Even the enemy was quiet.

The silence that followed the blast brought with it a small window of calm. And then the firing started again and most of 1 Section understood at once that the enemy had used the distraction to move still further forward.

Dave shouted: 'Fix bayonets!'

Streaky's heart sank. Bayonets were what you used when the enemy was just a few metres away. Bayonets were what you plunged into people's bodies while you looked into their eyes. He fumbled with his, trying to imagine what it would be like to run at a man and shove a bayonet into his chest. He thought he might not be able to do that.

He tried to scramble to his feet, fighting against the weight on his back which kept dragging him back down. Finn, who had managed to remain standing through the blast, grabbed his hand to help him. Streaky saw the boss helping the woman to her feet. The blast had thrown the boss on top of her. Or perhaps he had thrown himself there to protect her.

'We now have a way out,' the boss said to Dave, his voice full of dust.

'No,' Dave said.

164

'There's a bit of a crater but we can get round it and over the bridge!' Weeks insisted.

'No!' Dave repeated. 'There'll be more.'

'More what?'

'IEDs. On the far side of the bridge.'

'The enemy is now extremely close. I mean, I think there are some only twenty metres away,' the boss said. Dave didn't reply. He kept on firing. Streaky did the same. But a few minutes later, he heard Dave and the boss arguing again. It seemed they had been told an Apache was arriving and the boss wanted to put down smoke now.

'No!' Dave said.

'The pilots will need it,' the boss insisted.

'Too soon!' Dave said.

'But surely we—'

Dave interrupted him. 'No, no, no! If we put smoke down now we'll just get a load more incoming. I don't have time to explain!'

The urgency in his voice made Streaky increase his rate of fire.

'How many times,' the boss roared in his ear, 'do I have to tell you we're running out of ammo? Use less, for Chrissake!'

'Oh yeah . . .' Streaky slowed his rate a fraction.

At the sound of a rhythmic, distant thudding, he felt relief flood through his body. It was almost over. He'd been both surrounded and outnumbered in an ambush and it was almost over at last.

Enemy fire was ceasing a little. 1 Section immediately eased their firing too. The bonds that had glued them to their weapons began to loosen.

'I've never been so fucking happy to hear a rotor blade,' Finn said, his voice filtered through dust.

'OK, now smoke,' the boss said, glancing at Dave.

'Wait . . .' Dave said. 'Mini flares are a lot better.'

Sol explained: 'Smoke hangs around for too long.'

'It gives every Tom, Dick and Harry Taliban our position,' Dave said. 'Just make sure you've got the pilot's attention . . .'

When the helicopter was chopping up the air overhead, they sent up a flare.

Remaining alert to catch any fleeing insurgents, the men watched the massive metal bird begin its hunt from the sky. Two scrambling, anxious figures jumped from trees that were only ten metres from the Vectors.

'Too fucking close,' Dave said.

Before they could run, Angus McCall took aim without hesitation and killed one. Mal took the other. Angus could not resist turning to catch Dave's eye. Dave nodded at him. Whatever had held Angus back before had evaporated in this fight for his life.

'We were lucky. They didn't have many RPGs and they weren't very handy with them,' Dave said. 'If they'd had mortar we wouldn't have stood a chance.'

'And if we'd had mortar it would have helped,' the boss said quietly.

'An HMG would have been good, too.' Dave went over to Jamie. 'I wish you'd sit down, mate.'

'I'm all right,' Jamie insisted.

'You don't look all right; your face is a weird colour.'

The medic appeared. 'We'll have to get you to Bastion. We need to check for internal injuries.'

'You can forget that,' Jamie said. 'No one's taking me away from my mates for no good reason.'

Sol said: 'I really don't want to lose you, but you have to be checked out. You know the score.'

Jamie sighed. 'Listen,' he said to the medic. 'I'm OK. I'll let you know if I'm not OK.'

The medic shook his head. 'We'll have to give you a proper examination back at the FOB, then.'

'OK,' said Jamie, 'but I'm not going anywhere. Unless it's in a body bag. And someone else can carry the machine gun back on top for me now.'

Angus heard this and picked it up at once.

Before following him on board the Vector, Jamie said: 'You have to admire the flipflops. They don't give up, do they? They must have known that air support would come sooner or later and try to finish them off. But they didn't stop.'

The boss said: 'They don't care if they die. That's the most frightening thing about them.'

Asma nodded. 'We've been fighting for our lives. But they've been fighting for Allah.'

'If you don't mind me saying so,' – Finn turned to her with admiration – 'I never would have expected a lady to get a grip in a fire fight like that.'

Asma raised an eyebrow. 'I'm no lady,' she said. 'I'm from Hackney.'

Finn laughed and held out his hand.

'That explains everything.'

They were still shaking hands when the boss appeared.

'Please stay alert, Finn,' he said briskly. 'The second AH is arriving shortly and insurgents may flee too close for the Apache to fire at them.'

Dave turned to Asma. 'Well done. Nice one.'

She looked pleased and glanced at the boss. He turned away.

The second helicopter arrived and they sent up another flare. One Apache put down fire along the treeline. The other flew over the adjacent fields, targeting leakers as they ran away from the scene.

The soldiers watched for any who tried to seek protection from the helicopter by lying close by. It was a relief to be still at last and not to feel hot metal burning their hands. Streaky knew he'd thought of some good lines during the fire fight and was now scribbling furiously, although he'd already forgotten some of them.

Binman, colour returning to his cheeks, crawled from the Vector with the medic to see the Apaches hunt the insurgents from the sky. The boss and Asma stood side by side, watching.

Dave sat down and leaned his back against a wheel of the vehicle and closed his eyes. He drank some water and waited as the Apaches did their work.

About half an hour ago he had reached for some gun oil and found Jenny's letter in the pouch next to it. He had thought he had left it with the other mail, since bringing anything personal out of the base was strictly forbidden in case of capture. He must have stuffed it in the pouch without thinking. But, now it was here, he wanted to read it.

With his eyes shut, he tried to pretend for a moment that today had just been a training exercise on Salisbury Plain. He tried to imagine that he'd be home this evening to find Vicky in her high chair and Jen manoeuvring her belly around the little kitchen. But

167

the image had the unreality of a dream. For an ugly moment the woman with the belly was a figment of his imagination. She was nothing to do with him. She barely existed.

Alarmed by this, he reached into his pouch for her letter.

Dear Dave,

If my writing looks funny it's because I have to stretch over the bump to get the pen on the paper because there's no way the bump will fit under the table any more. This baby's big but it's a lot quieter than Vicky was. Sometimes I panic that it's not kicking. I nearly drove up to the hospital for them to check today, it was so quiet down inside my belly. And just when I was thinking about getting in the car, kick, kick. Hey, Mum, it's me. So I think this baby's going to be a laid-back sort of person. I mean, like you, Dave. Not always running around in circles like me.

Dave read the words but they did not penetrate. He knew that this was a letter from his wife, whom he loved, about the baby, whom he also loved although it wasn't even born yet. But there was a disconnect between this world of bumps and kicking and kitchen tables and this world that was Afghanistan.

Well I've been good and I haven't told anyone about the man who's hanging around A. That's not a secret code. I just can't spell her name. I went round to her house a little while ago because she dropped Luke's mug in the park. But I didn't knock because the red Volvo was outside. Then I phoned her later and she said that the repair man had just left. Not sure what he was repairing.

Dave glanced over at Jamie. He was back up on top now with the machine gun, watching the Apache's high-precision operation intently. His face looked a deathly white and battered and bruised as though the round had bounced off his cheeks. When it seemed that the helicopter had found an insurgent hiding at the edges of the track, Jamie got ready to fire if the man tried to escape by running towards them, but the Apache pilot fired first.

Here was a man, thought Dave, whose heart and soul was concentrated in the work he'd been trained for. He must be in a lot of pain right now but his commitment was undiminished. Agnieszka's antics with some bloke in Wiltshire could never hurt Jamie the soldier. But she could destroy Jamie the man, who was made of marshmallow.

Dave, I didn't really want to write about what A's up to. I wanted to write about us. It's much easier to write it than to say it.

I can't go on like this. I'm pregnant and I need you here. I don't mean I need you to help with things, even though I do. I mean I need you here. And you're not. And so long as you're in the army you never will be. I can just about cope with the fact that you won't be there when the baby's born. Just about. But it's knowing you can't get home if you're needed, that's one of the worst things.

Worse even than that is knowing you might never come home. You can't imagine what it's like. You don't know how awful it is to think there's a possibility this baby will never know its father and Vicky won't remember you except from pictures. And that's another thing. I wish I had a really nice recent picture of you instead of wedding pictures and quick snaps. Because that's what you are for me at the moment, a man in a wedding album and in lots of snaps but not a man who's here. And I love you and I want you to be here.

So I want you to leave the army, Dave. I want you to really think about what matters in your life and understand what the army is doing to us. Think about what I've said, darling, and please would you . . .

Her neat writing continued over the page. Dave closed his eyes. He was in Helmand Province, Afghanistan, and that other world in Wiltshire could not influence events here or influence him. It was something that happened concurrently but separately. The camp there, with its wives and children, was a treacherous sea of emotions waiting to drown him. Here, life was clear and straightforward. You were under fire. Your life was under threat. You fired back.

He stuffed the letter back in his pouch. He hadn't meant to bring it anyway.

Soon afterwards they were cleared to exit the area. Technical officers and support were coming to check for further devices. But 1 Section could go home to Sin City.

Dave sometimes saw the cases of enemy rounds at the base of trees as they rumbled past. Once he saw a sandal. He wondered if its owner was sitting dead in the branches but he couldn't be bothered to stop the Vector to look.

'Tell me something,' the driver said as they bumped back along the track. 'How the fuck did you know there was an IED there?'

Dave yawned. 'The interpreter said something about it.'

'Yeah, but that was after you'd told me to stop. You'd already said there was one ahead. But I couldn't see the fucker for love nor money.'

'The surface of the track didn't look right.'

'I don't know how you saw that. I thought you'd gone AWOL for a minute. You were sweating like a pig.'

'Who isn't sweating like a pig? But OK, I'll admit it was a guess. I'd have felt pretty fucking stupid if I'd been wrong.'

'You weren't wrong, though. From now on I'm going to make sure I'm always driving you.'

Chapter Twenty-five

1 SECTION HADN'T BEEN ABLE TO SHOWER SINCE RETURNING TO Sin City. There was no water. So they'd kicked off their boots and changed into shorts and flipflops and were lounging on their cots or cleaning their weapons when there was the deafening crash of a mortar.

'Stand to! Stand to!'

Everyone groaned.

Jamie sat up, shirtless. He'd been showing off his spectacular high-calibre bruise. Binns, who was taking pictures of it from different angles, put down his camera. Finn rolled over. Angus and Mal closed their eyes as if that would make the mortar attack go away. Streaky Bacon looked alarmed and then swigged more water as though someone was going to confiscate it.

'Come on, lads,' Sol yelled. 'Stand to!'

'Maybe there won't be any more now . . .'

Mal's words were drowned by the sound of AK47s.

The men responded like sleepwalkers.

'Get up, get going, get out there,' Sol shouted. 'Helmets! Boots!'

There was another ground-shaking crash and the men accelerated a little. But not much. Angus put his boots on the wrong feet, Binns couldn't find his helmet. Jamie winced as he pulled on body armour. Streaky, who'd been cleaning his weapon, tried to put it back together again but found nothing would fit.

'Lucky for us 2 Platoon are on the .50 cals tonight.' If the heavy machine guns were always sited in the same place, the enemy soon worked out their arcs of fire. So every contact the .50 cals had to be moved.

'We've already spent three hours fighting today,' Finn grumbled.

'Three hours?' Bacon said. 'Three hours!'

He could remember every moment of today's battle. He'd remember it for ever. But it seemed to last seconds rather than hours.

'Oh, right,' Sol said. 'I'll go and explain that to the Taliban and ask if they'll come back tomorrow, then. *Get out there!*'

The men ran to their firing positions at a loping pace and returned fire half-heartedly. Dave watched Binns. He was trying hard; he knew he had a lot to make up for. The others had teased him and Sol had talked to him but Dave knew he would have to grip the lad. Binns obviously knew that too; he'd been avoiding him.

'You shouldn't be here,' Dave said to Jamie. 'You should be lying down. You heard what the medic said.'

He'd advised him again to go to Bastion for a proper check-up, but without success.

'I'm fine,' Jamie insisted.

The one man who remained focused and kept firing was Angus. Straight after today's ambush, Dave had noticed the subtle changes in the lad's demeanour. Angus held himself differently. His face was sharper and he moved with a new confidence. Dave recognized this sudden maturity. Kill a man and age a year, he thought to himself.

The fighting stopped as suddenly as it had started. Everyone waited for a renewed attack. Men stayed in position but they relaxed. Angus got down into some cover and lit a cigarette.

'You were good today, McCall,' Dave said. He knew Angus would understand his previous failures had been forgiven. Even though it was dark, he could see the big lad blush in response. He thought he saw Angus's tattoos blush as well. To his relief, Angry did not use the occasion to mention his father.

No one trusted the silence but when it continued the men gradually stood down.

Thirty minutes later, in 1 Section's tent, Dave found Jamie fast asleep. 'Thank God for that.'

Binns and Bacon were sitting on their cots with their boots on.

'The medic gave him a mountain of pain relief and he was out like a light,' Binns said.

'Good,' Dave said. 'Now boots off, you two, if you're getting your heads down.'

The two lads immediately sat bolt upright.

'Or if you're not getting your heads down you should get over to the cookhouse with the others.'

'Not hungry,' Bacon said.

Binns could not meet Dave's eye.

'Eat anyway. And drink. I've got a lot to say to you about your performance today during the ambush, Bacon, and the first thing is that you didn't drink enough.'

'I know.' Streaky nodded. 'I just didn't think of it.'

'It's easy to forget, especially when you're fighting. But in those temperatures, by the time you realize, it's often too late.'

He turned to Binns.

'What have you got to say for yourself, lad?'

Binns looked wretched. He stared at the ground and fiddled with a corner of his sleeping bag liner. Dave noticed a framed picture which Binns had evidently been looking at and shoved beneath the cot at his arrival. A pretty girl smiled out from it. She was sensibly dressed and her hair was neatly brushed. A girl-next-door type, the sort who worked in a building society.

'Sorry, Sarge,' he muttered.

'Listen, Binns, I blame myself for not gripping you earlier. It was one hell of an ambush and I was so fucking busy I couldn't get on top of you and neither could Sol. Normally I would have noticed earlier and I would have made you pull yourself together.'

'I couldn't help it, Sarge.'

'You could. It didn't happen during the mortar attack this evening, did it?'

'No. I felt a bit safer here at the base with three platoons firing back.'

'An ambush is a tough call for your first fire fight but I don't want any excuses. You fucked up badly today and you've got a lot of ground to make up now.'

Binns looked as though he was going to cry. But Dave knew he had to be merciless, for Binns's sake and everyone else's. He was

173

glad the boy's mother, or the sweet-faced girlfriend, couldn't see him.

'We were in the shit today. We weren't just fighting for ourselves but each other, and we were fighting hard. No one could stand over you, our hands were full. And you were a dead weight. You were sitting in the Vector or puking at the back and relying on us to take care of you. That's not team playing, is it?'

'No, Sarge.'

'You've had the training, Binns. Now put it into practice. We're not going to carry you, so pull your weight or get out of this platoon.'

Binns nodded. He still could not look Dave in the eye.

'OK, Binns, go eat. And don't be surprised if all the lads tear you apart for what happened today. You'll have to work hard to make them forget it.'

Jack Binns sloped off, head hanging.

'By the way,' Dave called after him. The lad paused and turned. 'You're on shit duty for a week.'

'Yes, Sarge,' Binman said.

Dave watched him go. Over in his cot, Jamie turned over, snored for a moment and then fell silent. Dave sat down on Binns's cot and turned to Streaky Bacon. 'And how do you think you did today?'

'Did some good rap,' Bacon grinned.

'You did *what*?'

Streaky's smile wavered.

'Got some good flow. Good rhymes and raps in my head while I was fighting,' he said. 'I'm a rapper, see.'

Dave, who ten minutes ago had felt tired and in need of food, felt the sudden rush of energy that anger brings.

'A *rapper*!' he said, jumping to his feet. 'Did you say you're a *rapper*?'

Bacon wished for a moment he'd never heard of hip hop.

'Well . . .' he said, 'I try to do a bit of rap, see, and—'

'No, no, no!' said Dave, the strength of his own fury surprising him. 'You're a *soldier*! You didn't come to Helmand Province to rap about it. You didn't do all that training and travel all this way to sit there under fire thinking that *IED* rhymes with *ABC* or *I can't see* or *fly with me*!'

174

He did not miss Bacon's look of fleeting admiration for these fast rhymes. But the admiration was rapidly replaced by trepidation as Dave went on.

'You're a soldier, Bacon. That means you're here to fight not fuck about giving it MC Bacon. While we were saving your bacon, Bacon, you sat on your arse working out that *yes I can* and *kill that man* rhymes with *Taliban*. Is that fucking fair?'

Bacon said nothing. His deep brown eyes shifted from side to side.

'I've asked you a question,' Dave said. 'Now answer it. Is it fair for you to sit writing rap while your mates fight for their lives and yours?'

There was a pause.

'No,' Bacon said.

'No WHAT?'

'No, Sarge.'

Dave sighed and sat back down.

'OK. You wrote some fucking good rap today. Apart from that triumph, how else did you do?'

Bacon rolled his eyes upwards and straightened his body.

'Well, Sarge, I think I did OK.'

'What makes you think that?'

'I got some rounds down.'

'Well, yes, you're a soldier, that's what you're paid to do.'

'And I think I killed at least one man.'

'Oh, yeah?'

'I saw him fall. Only . . . the woman just may have shot him because she fired too.'

'Where was he?'

'They were everywhere except on one side and, understand see, Sarge, I thought if they ran forward we'd be completely surrounded, and that didn't make me feel good so I was watching. And when he ran forward I got him.'

Dave nodded.

'Good thinking, Bacon. How many rounds before you shot him?'

'Well, I don't know. A lot . . .'

'You had rounds left for him, did you?'

'Well, yes, I did, Sarge.'

'How many rounds did you have left at the end of the ambush?'

'Altogether, Sarge?'

'Yep. Bandolier, magazines, how many altogether?'

'Well, I counted. Twenty.'

'Twenty.'

'Yes, Sarge.'

'Christ. Well, that tells me a few things. First, you were firing too much, too quickly. You were told to slow it but you couldn't stop, could you?'

'Well, Sarge, I thought—'

'It was an ambush. We were under siege conditions and we'd been told to wait a long time for air support because we needed an Apache. There was no point a Harrier dropping a five-hundred-pound bomb or we'd all have been blown to Paradise. We had to wait for a fucking Apache to do some targeting because the choggies had closed in on us. If the Apache had taken another twenty minutes, we'd have been out of ammo. Because a sprog like you was just throwing it down.'

'I didn't throw it, Sarge.'

'Well did you know what you were firing at?'

'No one could see the flipflops, Sarge.'

'You should have stopped and looked at the other men. Did you watch Angus, for instance?'

Streaky shook his head.

'If you had, you'd have noticed that he was thinking before he fired. When the rounds closed in he assessed where the Taliban firing points were. He didn't just poke his weapon out from behind the Vector and send as much fire up the track as fast as he could. He didn't try to turn an SA80 into a machine gun, Bacon.'

Streaky hung his head.

'Well, I killed one guy,' he said stubbornly.

'Maybe one of the fifty rounds you threw at him did hit him. Or maybe the woman sergeant from the Intelligence Corps got him in three. We'll never know. But I do know that I saw you refilling your magazines when you'd used up all your ammo.'

Bacon blinked at him.

'What should you do, Bacon?' asked Dave. 'When you're using

up ammo fast, when should you refill? Should you wait until it's all gone, then refill?'

'Erm . . .'

'When three magazines are empty, change. Wait for a quiet period or pull back for a few minutes and change. Don't wait until you're clean out. Because you never, ever, ever want to find yourself out there with a weapon and no ammo.'

'Oh, yeah,' Bacon said. 'We did that in training.'

'Glad your training didn't desert you completely. But in training guys sit behind you and remind you. This was a real fire fight with a real enemy and we were all too fucking busy to sit behind you. And if we'd been overrun and you'd ended up defending yourself, you wouldn't have had the ammo to do it with. Now let me ask you another. What did you do with your empty magazines?'

Streaky grimaced.

Dave told him the answer: 'You dropped them on the ground. And let other people pick them up for you. Like your mum goes into your bedroom and picks your clothes up off the floor. But you're not at home, now, Bacon, your mum's not here to clear up after you and you pick up your own fucking magazines, got it?'

'Yes, Sarge.'

'So let's run over those points again, Bacon. One: drink more. I don't want to see you coming home to base with a half-full Camelbak again. Two: fire less. Don't waste ammo, choose your target. And don't wait until you're clean out to get more. Three: clear up your own fucking magazines.'

Bacon hung his head and nodded.

'I have to tell you this to make a good soldier of you.' Dave's tone softened. 'That way you stay safe. And so do your mates.'

Bacon didn't look up.

'You're on shit jobs with Binns for a week. Now get something to eat.'

Bacon stood up. His face was sullen and angry. His rolling, swaggering walk had a touch of insolence about it. This lad did not take criticism well, even necessary and practical criticism. But it crossed Dave's mind that he had gripped Streaky Bacon a bit hard tonight. Maybe he should have congratulated him on killing one Taliban fighter and for keeping his nerve in an unnerving first ambush, especially when his mate was falling to pieces.

'Poor bastard, it was his first time.'

Dave had forgotten he was not alone. He turned towards Jamie but whatever snippets of the conversation he'd heard, it seemed he had fallen back into a medicated sleep again.

'Shut up, Dermott, or I'll have you casevaced,' he said affectionately, thinking that Jamie was right and he was wrong but there was almost no one else in the platoon who was allowed to tell him so.

He got up. He didn't regret a word he'd said to Streaky. But he was beginning to regret the words he hadn't said.

CSM Kila sat with Dave and the other platoon sergeants in the cookhouse. Sergeant Barnes of 3 Platoon had spent the day with the civilians.

'That fucking woman professor . . .'

'What! Emily? The sex grenade? Ventured out of her isobox?'

'Emily. The pain in the arse. Ventured all over the fucking shop. And if you thought Martyn Robertson was difficult, you try working with her. She wants to go where she likes when she likes and sod everyone else. Picks up her shopping bag and marches off as if she's just on her way to market and doesn't want to miss a bargain.'

'Apparently,' Kila said, 'she has one of the finest geophysical brains in England.'

'Yeah, well, the finest geophysical brain in England could get splattered all over Helmand if she doesn't use it more. I said: "Professor, have you noticed that we soldiers generally move around in platoons? That's about thirty soldiers, Professor. Well that's to keep us safe. If you wander off like that then you could become an enemy target, Professor."'

'What did she say?'

'She says: "I have no enemies, Corporal." I say: "Professor, I am in fact a sergeant." She says: "Army ranks are of no interest to me because I am not fighting a war. I am carrying out an analysis of Afghanistan's natural resources."'

'Fucking hell,' Dave said.

'Fucking hell,' the other sergeants agreed.

'The finest geophysical brain in England and not one ounce of common sense,' Dave said.

He told the others about today's ambush.

'And this evening my head's caning and so's everyone else's, the medic gave us all something. It's got to be because we were so close to the explosion.'

'You were bloody nearly *in* the fucking explosion,' Sergeant Somers of 2 Platoon said.

'We should never have been sent on that route without manpower. They had us pinned down and we didn't have the men or the fire to keep them back much longer.'

Kila promised he'd talk to Major Willingham again about unnecessary risks.

When the other two sergeants had gone, Kila leaned forward and said quietly: 'There's a rumour going round about you, Dave.'

Dave raised his eyebrows and tried to think what that rumour could be.

'That you're leaving the army.'

Dave stared at him. The CSM stared right back.

'Where the hell did you hear that?'

'From Wiltshire.'

'*Wiltshire!*' Then Dave realized. 'Oh, someone's been talking to Jenny. But what the hell has she been saying?'

'She told Steve Buckle's wife who told someone who told someone who told ... well, I don't know who. Anyway, people are talking about it.'

Dave felt angry with Jenny. She had started a rumour which had clearly slipped beyond the circle of gossiping wives to the NCOs. It couldn't have come to Iain Kila through his wife because, although he'd already had three, he didn't have one at the moment.

'Jenny's thinking of me leaving the army,' Dave said. 'I'm not.'

Kila looked sympathetic. 'They all go through that one.'

'Well the baby's due soon. And Jenny spends a lot of time with Leanne Buckle ...'

'How's Steve, then?'

'Haven't heard yet. Leanne's with him in Selly Oak. What happened to Steve certainly scared Jen, though. She's only started this stuff about leaving the army since Steve's accident.'

Kila shrugged. 'You were a soldier when you married her, weren't you?

'Yeah. She knew what she was letting herself in for. But when I remind her about that she says it makes no difference. And today I got this long letter begging me to leave. And there's a letter from her mother I haven't even opened which probably says the same thing.'

'Just ignore it.'

'You don't know Jen. She's like a dog with a bone once she gets an idea into her head.' Actually, Jenny's determination was one of the things Dave loved about her. Unless she was determined to make him do something.

'Then string her along. Aren't you doing a degree course through the army?'

Dave laughed. The classes he'd attended and the coursework he'd finished seemed far away and trivial, like a game he used to play.

'Engineering,' he said. 'I work on it when we're not operational or away training. So that's not very often.'

'Well,' Kila said, 'when do you expect to finish?'

'It'll take years and years at this rate.'

'So tell her you'll leave when you've got your degree.'

Dave chuckled. 'Good idea, Iain! She'll have to agree it'll improve my job prospects.'

Kila grinned back. 'Women. You just need to know how to handle them.'

'Not much chance here for you to practise your handling skills.'

Kila's grin broadened meaningfully. Dave squinted at him.

'Well I knew the boss was after the Intelligence Corps bird but I didn't think you . . .'

'I'm not interested in that iceberg. Or Professor Sex Grenade. That only leaves one.'

'Not the monkey!'

Kila leaned forward and spoke quietly. 'There's a limit to how far I can go here at the base of course. But between you and me, I wouldn't say no to a bit of monkey business.'

Chapter Twenty-six

BOSS WEEKS WAS EXHAUSTED. THE DAY'S ADRENALIN HAD DRAINED out of him, leaving him feeling like a hollow shell. He had taken something for the thumping headache from the bomb's blast wave and was too tired now even to look at the pictures of the ambush that kept playing inside his head. He only knew one thing. He wanted to be with Asma. The ambush had been a terrifying, intense experience. She had shared it. Even if they didn't talk about it, he wanted to be near her.

In the wagon she had mentioned she liked to walk around the perimeter after dark, looking at the stars. So now he was walking the perimeter, hoping. He passed other people. But none of them was Asma.

He saw a firefly. Then he realized it was the red tip of a cigarette, lighting up as the smoker pulled on it. And finally he saw that the smoker was Asma.

Gordon Weeks was so pleased that he tried not to be disgusted by the cigarette.

She smiled sheepishly.

'OK, I didn't happen to mention that my little night-walking habit was connected to my little smoking habit. But I only have three a day. One in the morning, one at lunchtime if I can and one walking around the hesco at night. That's not so bad, is it?'

He was thinking of a reply when she went on.

'Look, most people would've smoked a whole fucking packet after what happened today. But this is only my third, I swear.'

He could not imagine feeling this way in the UK about a girl who smoked. In fact, he couldn't think of any girl he knew who smoked.

'Does Jean smoke too?' Whenever he saw Asma in the cookhouse or around the camp, Jean was always there. He looked over his shoulder for her now.

'No, she disapproves just like you do,' said Asma.

'Did I say I disapprove?'

She laughed then. How had he done it? He had made her laugh without trying at all. When he tried he was lucky to get a half-smile out of her.

'Well, you do, don't you?'

'Er . . . er . . .' And it gave him great pleasure to hear her laugh again.

'I thought so,' she said, drawing on her cigarette. 'I'm trying to give up. But an FOB where everyone smokes may not be the right place. Although Jean says there's never a right place to give up.'

'You seem very good friends with Jean.'

'Yup,' she said, throwing down her cigarette stub and stamping on it fiercely. They were in the darkest part of the camp now and, although their eyes were accustomed to the night, they could barely see each other. But Weeks could sense her. He could sense the warmth of her body. As well as, regrettably, the smell of the extinguished cigarette.

'Listen, it's obvious you're not keen on Jean. But you don't know her.'

He was silent.

'She takes her job seriously and she gets pissed off here. We both do. We're used as interpreters at this FOB but we're trained to do a lot more. Jean's Royal Military Police. That's what she joined up to do. She didn't join up to interpret for engineers who want to talk about fucking wall-building.'

'But,' said Weeks, 'without her interpretation the school wall would never get built.'

'She thinks it's a waste of her skills because a local Afghan interpreter could handle it. And you want to know something, Gordon? She's right.'

'What about you? Do you feel your skills are wasted?'

'I could be doing a lot more at Bastion. Listening to intelligence, helping piece it altogether, getting something useful done.'

'So why have you both been sent here?' asked Weeks.

'Because of the civilians. It's part of the contract that top-level interpreters are on hand for them.'

'Top level, eh?'

They had completed a circuit now and their faces picked up the light from some of the brighter tents and reflected it. She was ridiculously beautiful. He could not understand how she could stroll around the hesco without a line of panting men behind her. Except that she was so skilled at freezing people out. The only man he'd seen her respond to warmly was the tribesman at the *shura*, the one with the moviestar looks. When he thought of the way Asma had talked to that man he felt a stab of something which might have been anger. Although it was probably jealousy.

She was smiling now. 'Yeah, top level, that's us. Which means we speak Pashtu and our English is a lot better than the locals'.' She giggled, adding: 'Innit?'

So she had detected how irritating he found *innit*. Weeks smiled too.

They walked on towards the darkness. Overhead the Afghan night was a canopy of stars. The constellations were the same as at home, of course, but they stood out less here because they were saturated by thousands more.

'Oooh, it's so fucking beautiful!' said Asma.

Weeks thought that her English may be better than the locals' but it still left a lot to be desired.

He took a deep breath.

'Is that why your friend Jean gets so hot under the collar about one half-dead Taliban fighter in a ditch? Because she's looking for police work?'

'Well,' said Asma, 'yeah. But she's right. You should keep gripping your blokes about the RoE.'

'But she's gripping an exceptionally good sergeant. It does nothing for morale when someone so respected gets a public dressing-down.'

'That geezer they shot would probably still be alive today if, say, 2 Platoon had found him. Sergeant Somers is a bit different from Sergeant Henley.'

Since arriving in Afghanistan everything the boss thought he knew or understood had been challenged. But in this strange, new world, there had been one rock-solid certainty. And that was Dave Henley. Of course, he was the boss and Dave was the sergeant. But they both knew that Dave was in charge. Dave handled the men when he could not. And thanks to him they had escaped serious harm on more than one occasion. Weeks had felt the foundations of his world crack in a few places but he could not allow any cracks in the foundation that was Dave.

He said stiffly: 'Over the weeks I have known him I have learned to respect him and trust his judgement totally.'

'He just might be a bit weak on the RoE,' said Asma.

'He is both an exceptional sergeant and a good man,' the boss insisted. 'The Rules of Engagement are very hard for soldiers on the ground to apply when their lives are in danger during a contact. We tell them this isn't a war. But it's difficult for them to understand why we're here.'

'So why are we here?'

He stopped walking in surprise.

'To support the reconstruction of Afghanistan by encouraging democracy and keeping the Taliban at bay.'

She swung round to look at him in the dark.

'If you learn Pashtu for the rest of your life,' she said, 'you'll never do more than talk bollocks in two languages. You'll never, ever understand this place and neither will any of the fucking politicians who sent us here.'

'But . . . well . . . then . . . what are you doing? Working with the British Army?'

She hung her head.

'I don't know sometimes.'

He waited for her to speak. His heart was thumping. What was she trying to tell him? That she was a security risk?

'I'm going to have another cigarette,' she announced rebelliously.

'So that would be four today?'

'Yeah.'

She lit up and held the cigarette lightly between her long fingers and began to walk again, inhaling deeply.

184

'Asma,' he said, when they were in the dark part of the camp once more. 'What are you saying to me?'

'The ambush today . . .'

'It was quite a contact.'

'I was scared.'

'So was I,' he admitted.

'Gordon, I think I killed a bloke.' Her voice was small.

'Are you sure?'

'No. That black kid in your platoon was firing at him too but he was all over the place. I think my round brought the geezer down.'

'You didn't have to fire at all. If you remember, I told you that—'

'Oh, give over, Gordon.'

She was right. Give over, Gordon. Here she was, confiding in him, and all he could do was remind her of the rules.

'Actually,' he said, more quietly, 'I'm almost certain I killed someone today, too. And it was the first time for me as well. Since we were fighting for our lives I didn't think about it then. I have since, though.'

'You get back to base and think: I killed the enemy. But all I can think is: shit! I killed my Moslem brother.'

This relationship was getting more complicated every time he spoke to her. Not just a smoker. Not just from Hackney. Not just a lot of *innit*. Not just a girl who swore like a trooper. But also a Moslem.

He said awkwardly: 'So . . . are you a practising Moslem?'

'I was brought up Moslem, of course. Then we came to England and the longer we stayed here the more it sort of peeled off. Like paint. And when I left my family I thought I'd peeled it away completely. The army wanted me because of my Pashtu and I never even thought twice about why. Not till we went to that *shura* . . .'

It hadn't been the *shura* that reminded Asma of her Moslem roots, he thought. It was that man with the startling blue eyes. He'd talked to her intensely in Pashtu. She'd claimed they were discussing the school wall but Weeks had been sure they were having a much more significant conversation. Because why would the school wall have made her blush?

'So,' he said. 'You were radicalized at the *shura*.'

She laughed.

'Now you're going too far, Gordon. Radicalized, for God's sake! They weren't pro-Taliban. But they were pro-Afghanistan and probably they support the idea of a new country called Pashtunistan. Either way, they were asking themselves what we're doing on their soil.'

'What exactly did the tribesman say?'

'It's nothing anyone said. It's just the way they think. I recognized it because the dad was a bit like my dad. See, it's complicated being Pashtun. There's all the hospitality and the right words and the pride and honour. But if anyone gets it wrong, you've got to get angry, and it's really fucking awful anger. After that you've got no choice, revenge is next, whether you want to or not. The *shura* took me right back to all that.'

The passion in her face and voice fascinated him. He just wanted to watch her but he made himself reply.

'That's very interesting, Asma. But what do their complications have to do with us? They don't want the Taliban here and neither do we. It's simple.'

'No, no, Gordon, you don't understand, that's the fucking problem. If we're going to fight here, we need a straightforward reason. Good guys and bad guys. But when I talked to the tribesmen I remembered how Pashtuns aren't straightforward. We can't just come here thinking we'll slot our world into theirs. It won't work. Can't you see that?'

'I can see it would give you doubts about your work here.'

'I can live with doubts,' she said, reaching for her pack of cigarettes, taking one out, tapping it on the lid and then slowly putting it away again. 'I'm happy to think I'm out here saving soldiers' lives when I listen to the enemy on their cellphones. I'm pleased to turn into a fucking diplomat at meetings with the locals. That's all sweet, Gordon, I like it. But when I actually kill a bloke, then doubts start buzzing around inside my head.'

He reached for her hand in the dark. She looked around at him in such surprise that he squeezed her fingers and rapidly let go. But he felt as though the imprint of her hand remained in his. He could still feel its warmth and fragility as he said: 'I understand what you're saying, Asma, and I respect it.'

Chapter Twenty-seven

JENNY'S GARDEN WAS FILLED WITH MOTHERS AND CHILDREN. Adi's idea was that everyone should get together. They could have gone to the park. But Jenny, whose house was on a bend in the road and so had a larger plot than most, had offered her garden instead so that they could use the paddling pool.

She was regretting it now. It had taken hours to put blankets and cushions and toys all over the lawn, to drag out the paddling pool and fill it and to lay out food in the kitchen with paper plates. And now she was running around with mugs of tea and cups of juice.

The other mothers sat on the blankets and chatted. There was Adi and all her children, Agnieszka and Luke, Leanne with the twins, Sharon Kirk and Rosie McKinley whose husbands were in 2 Section and who had five red-haired kids between them, a couple of 3 Platoon wives . . . the door bell rang again. It was Tiff Curtis, whose husband was commander of 3 Section.

'Sorry I'm late, Jenny, we do Shake and Shout on a Tuesday.' Her little girl clung to her arm.

'I do Shake and Shout all day every day,' Jenny said cheerfully, leading them through to the garden, trying not to notice the way Tiff, as she passed the living room, gave it one of those appraising stares. There were only so many things you could do with a married quarters living room but everyone always wanted to see anyway.

'You're huge, when are you due?'

'Another six weeks.'

As soon as Tiff's little girl saw so many other children, she put her thumb in her mouth.

'Oooh, look at the paddling pool!' Tiff said. 'And all the toys!'

The little girl immediately hid behind her mother.

Adi called a welcome and Jenny returned to the kitchen to finish making more tea. Tiff sat down on the blanket with the other mothers and put her daughter on her lap.

Jenny washed mugs and wished someone would give her a hand. Agnieszka was the only mother who was not busy with small children. She could have offered to help. Luke, who seemed to have two states of being, asleep and screaming, was thankfully asleep. So Agnieszka was doing nothing. She sat on the blanket, leaning on one arm, her long legs stretched out to the side like a mermaid.

Her face turned dutifully to the others as they talked but she did not join in and Jenny could see she was not listening. She was day-dreaming. Jenny remembered the broken photo frame. Her father's damaged photo and the wedding picture were now lying flat on the shelf instead of on display the way they should be. She felt doubly resentful.

At that moment, a mobile rang. It made everyone jump. Agnieszka dug rapidly in her shorts pockets. When she found the phone she held it close to her. She tapped a few keys and then turned away to read it.

She's anxious, Jenny thought. In case someone sees it. Because it's from him.

When her phone rang, Agnieszka caught herself hoping it was Darrel. She turned away from the stares of the other mothers, just in case it was.

Her long fingernails made tiny clattering noises on the keys as she unlocked the phone. For a couple of weeks it had buzzed with Darrel's short, funny messages. Or sometimes he spoke to her, telling her he'd found some part for the broken dishwasher, and then, if Luke was asleep, they would talk about other things, too. On a few occasions they had talked for more than an hour. If Luke was angry or having a fit or hungry, then Darrel didn't try to distract Agnieszka. But he always called her back later. He seemed to understand how hard it was to manage a child like Luke by your-self without another adult to speak to.

Contact with Darrel had stopped abruptly after their last meeting. She missed him. She sometimes rewrote their final conversation in her head. In this version, Darrel didn't leave. He sat down on the edge of the sofa and talked to her sweetly and softly about how he felt. He explained how he respected the fact that she was married and then he said he hoped they could be friends. He took her hand and smiled at her.

Agnieszka knew this daydream was dangerous. Because she loved Jamie. So why did she like to pretend another man was sitting on the edge of the sofa talking about his feelings for her?

Turning now so that no one could see the phone or her face, she read the message. It wasn't from Darrel. It was from Jamie. These days, when the phone at home rang, it was almost always Jamie. She knew he made strenuous efforts to call her and that most wives did not hear so often from their men. But sometimes it was hard to know what to say. He couldn't talk much about what he was doing. And when he asked about her, she usually said: 'All just the same. Nothing ever happen.'

But Jamie also texted her in secret.

The men had handed in their mobiles at Bastion on their arrival in Afghanistan. Jamie had done so, but he had kept a second, secret phone. It was an old one of Agnieszka's and she had given it to him the night before he left. He had watched her slip it into his Bergen.

At first he'd fished it straight out.

'Niez, if I'm found with it I'll be in big trouble.'

Agnieszka had thought about this and then said: 'Listen, darling, just hide it. And if they find you say your wife leave it in kit and you don't even know it there.'

'But mobiles are banned for a reason. The Taliban can pick up the signal. And they can use it in all sorts of ways. It could compromise everyone's safety.'

'Huh!' said Agnieszka, wrinkling her nose. 'When you are in base, just text to tell wife you love her. Taliban cannot read English and they not interested in love. So, no compromise, everyone happy.'

He had frowned but he hadn't removed the phone. She'd thought he wouldn't use it, but he had. Just the occasional little message, like the one about becoming acting section 2 i/c. Well even

Agnieszka couldn't understand that, so she doubted the Taliban would. Or he texted to tell her how much he loved her and missed her and was thinking of her. And why would the Taliban care about that?

While the other women talked and the children splashed and Luke slept, Agnieszka read the message.

Hit by high-calibre round thought i was dead. Uuu and only u were in my head. It bounced off armour and I'm fine. Xxxxx J

At the first sentence she almost let out a small shriek. She composed herself. She glanced up. No one was looking. They were too busy with their children and their chatter. She read the message again and again. She tried to remember exactly what he meant by a high-calibre round. Was it a huge bullet? She wondered if she could somehow slip the question into the conversation without anyone guessing it was related to the text message. It was vital no one guessed Jamie had a secret mobile.

She looked up once more and this time she realized someone was watching her. Jenny, making tea in the kitchen. The last person who should know about the text was the sergeant's wife. Agnieszka put the phone back into her pocket.

When she brought the tea out, Jenny said pleasantly: 'Everything all right, Agnieszka?'

'Everything good. I just hope Luke don't wake up because he often wake up very angry.'

Jenny smiled.

'We'll help you if he does.'

Jenny's smile was thin and tired, Agnieszka thought. She looked as though she was ready to have the baby tomorrow. Agnieszka decided that Jenny had a lot on her mind and was certainly not interested in texts and probably hadn't even been watching her after all.

Leanne was talking about Steve. He was still at Selly Oak. She had stayed a week and was due to visit him again after surgeons had carried out a small operation on his stump. Then he would go to Headley Court for a new leg and rehabilitation.

'He might even come home for the weekend between hospital and Headley Court!' She looked pleased.

'That's great, Leanne!' said the other women brightly.

'There was a welfare officer from BLESMA who had a long talk with me and told me all the things he'll be able to do when he's got his new leg. It's amazing, the technology now . . .'

'Yeah, some blokes have even gone back to frontline fighting,' said Rosie.

'That'll be Steve!' Jenny said.

Leanne pulled a face. 'Not if I can help it.'

Tiff leaned forward and said quietly: 'It's been a terrible time for you, Leanne. We've all been thinking about you a lot.'

Leanne hesitated. 'The worst was when he was at Bastion so long and they wouldn't let me speak to him. Thank heavens for Dave.'

Jenny, swooping to remove someone's mug of tea from a child's reach, was surprised.

'He rang me a few times to make sure I was OK. He was really kind. He spoke to Steve once and then he phoned me straightaway.'

Leanne had not mentioned this before. Neither had Dave. Jenny smiled and tried to look as if she knew.

'He was trying to explain that Steve was on so much morphine he didn't know what time of day it was and I'd be really upset hearing him like that.' She swallowed. 'He made me feel a lot better. It was so good of you, Jen, to let him use your minutes on me.'

Jenny straightened up, an empty mug in her hand, her smile rigid.

'So how was he, Leanne, when you saw him in the hospital?' someone else asked.

'Well . . .' Leanne's face creased a little and she swallowed again. 'Just to see him alive . . .' Her voice cracked, suddenly and without warning. 'They didn't let me speak to him before I saw him . . . and if you can't see them or hear them or touch them, you don't really believe it, do you?'

The others watched as her face folded in on itself and tears ran down her cheeks. Her body shook with sobs. Sharon Kirk put a hand over hers.

'Oh, Leanne, we know how you must feel,' Rosie McKinley said.

The children fell quiet. They watched soberly with big eyes as sobs shook Leanne's generous frame. Tiff Curtis's daughter sucked her thumb with renewed passion. A few of the mothers felt hot, wet tears running down their own cheeks. Children who were old enough ran to push the tears away.

'Why are you crying?' they demanded with a mixture of curiosity and fear.

'Because Leanne's sad and we're feeling sad for her,' Sharon Kirk explained.

Jenny stooped awkwardly to put an arm around Leanne. Gravity and the weight of her belly pulled her to the ground. She settled at Leanne's side and held her friend as she cried.

'Oh, God, sorry, everyone, sorry . . .' Leanne dabbed at her eyes. She looked down at Jenny's belly, protruding absurdly between them both. 'Sorry, Bump,' she added and some people laughed too loudly because it was a relief to laugh.

Rosie passed Leanne a tissue and she slapped it against her face as though she was scolding herself.

'You don't have to say sorry.' Adi had been hands-on at the paddling pool and was now, as usual, drawn to the emotional centre of the gathering. 'We all understand, honey, we're all feeling what you're feeling.'

'You lot understand better than anyone. But you can't really understand until it happens to you and I hope to God it doesn't.'

There was a silence. Leanne had voiced what everyone was thinking. Don't let it happen to us.

'See,' Leanne said, 'he's not really the Steve who went away. He's only just beginning to understand that he's lost a leg. For a long time he wouldn't believe it, Dave said. And there was the shock from the blast . . . his brain sort of came unwired . . .'

'But what happened at the hospital?' Tiff asked.

'Well, he recognized me in the end. But at first he wasn't sure who I was and that was awful. Then after a day or two of just sitting there and chatting, he remembered and then he was almost normal. Except there was this . . . sadness. He was all turned in on himself. He wasn't really interested in us . . .' Her voice almost failed her and she whispered the rest. 'It was ages before they let me take the kids in. He was pleased to see them. Sort of. But before that he didn't ask about them at all . . .'

Tears spilled down her cheeks. Her big round face was wet now. Her mouth twisted itself into strange shapes.

She whispered: 'He's alive . . . but it's like a bit of him really did die out there . . .'

Jenny wanted to cry but she swallowed, trying to strengthen herself deep inside and all the way up her throat, so that her voice came out sounding calm. 'Oh, Leanne, it's all a question of time. He's been traumatized.'

'And,' Rosie said, 'seeing you and the boys was probably very emotional for him.'

'He didn't seem very emotional about us!' Leanne was wailing now.

'But you know how our lads don't let themselves show it,' Adi said. 'When they get emotional, they don't know what to do with it. Not like us, we can have a good cry.'

'He didn't seem emotional,' Leanne sobbed. 'He seemed as if he didn't care a lot.'

There was a silence on the blanket, broken only by Leanne's lunges for breath. In the paddling pool, children shrieked and splashed. Mothers eyed them without hearing them.

'Did he tell you he love you?' Agnieszka asked. Everyone turned to her in surprise. She'd been silent until now.

Leanne looked as though someone had hit her in the face. She winced in pain and her voice, when it emerged, was a high-pitched wail. 'Noooooooo! He didn't say that! He acted like I wasn't part of his life! Like his life was out there fighting with the lads and now it was over.'

And she broke down again.

Jenny cried too this time. Vicky came over and cuddled up close to Jenny and Leanne and the big, big bump, and she cried as well.

'How am I going to manage?' Leanne cried. 'What's going to happen? He's not Steve any more. He's this stranger with one leg!'

All the mothers cried and then the babies started and a few more of the toddlers. Only Agnieszka sat watching them all, biting her lip, dry-eyed.

Chapter Twenty-eight

1 SECTION HAD FINISHED EATING BUT REMAINED GLUED TO THEIR table watching a TV news item about Afghanistan. Since the Taliban were stepping up their use of IEDs, or roadside bombs as the reporter called them, politicians were calling on the Prime Minister to send the troops more helicopters.

Angus McCall gave the screen two thumbs-up. 'That's it, that's what we need for IEDs. We need to fly over the fuckers.'

Finn said: 'Yeah, but we've still got to get out there on foot patrol. We need wagons the bastards can't blow up.'

'Well, my dad says that—'

'Aaaargh!' Finn cried. 'What does he know about the Taliban?'

Angus grew red in the face. 'My dad knows about fighting!'

'Your dad never fought out here, did he? Everything's different here! And it's just a matter of time before Terry Taliban starts taking down our air support.'

'My dad says that Black Hawks are—'

Finn pulled a face and stuffed his fingers in his ears. 'I am so fucking sick sick sick of hearing what your dad says about everything!'

'Because he knows what he's talking about! He was in the Jedi!' Angus reddened still more then. Not with anger but because he hadn't meant to say that. His dad had never actually claimed to be in the SAS. But he'd implied it. When Angus had asked him out-right once, John McCall had said: 'Lad, I can't talk about that. Not everyone tells every detail of what they've done. We don't all go and

194

write fucking books about our achievements. For some of us, just knowing what we did, and our mates knowing what we did, that's enough.'

So that meant he was in the SF then. Angus knew it. But if his father hadn't told anyone in all these years, he was sure he shouldn't have blurted it out in the cookhouse.

The head chef's sudden appearance prevented Finn from taking the discussion further. Taregue Masud was one of the more popular men at the base. But he ruled his kitchen so tyrannically that he was known as the Regimental Sergeant Major. The lads soon learned not to get in his way, not unless they wanted to buy the RSM's bootleg DVDs or T-shirts he'd had printed with SIN CITY across them in camouflage colours.

He stood over Dave holding a large parcel wrapped in a black plastic bag.

'Evening, Taregue,' Dave said. 'That was an award-winning steak pie tonight.'

But the chef was not in the mood for pleasantries. 'What the bloody, bloody hell is this thing doing in my third freezer?'

He slammed the black plastic bag down on the table.

'Well, I couldn't exactly say . . .'

The RSM was about to explode. The cookhouse fell silent as he untied his apron, peeled it from his polyester shirt and threw it to one of his kitchen staff. There were cheers and whistles but the line-up of young assistants looked too nervous to join in. They knew what was coming.

The RSM put his hands on his hips. Suddenly no one was eating any more, or talking or watching TV, despite the fact that it was Arsenal v. Chelsea. Taregue Masud had run army kitchens all over the world and generations of soldiers had learned that when the apron came off fireworks always followed.

'I am informed by my staff – and my staff are very reliable – that you and your men have been keeping this item in my freezer. Now just take a look please, Sergeant, and tell me what it is.'

Dave lifted the plastic bag up and weighed it in both hands with an expression of extreme seriousness.

'From the temperature and the general rigidity of the item, I'd say it's frozen goods.'

'And what is it? What is this frozen goods?' Masud loomed dangerously over him.

Dave turned to Streaky and smiled. Streaky was alarmed enough to look right back at him for the first time in a while. 'I believe Streaky Bacon can help us here.'

The RSM's eyes narrowed. He'd sold Streaky a Sin City T-shirt only that morning.

'Aha! So it was you who placed this in my freezer! And may I ask exactly when?'

Streaky raised his eyebrows and rounded his eyes and was about to protest when he remembered how nobody ever believed his denials. Except sometimes his mum.

He took the black plastic bag reluctantly in his hands and appeared to weigh it, just as Dave had. It felt like a slab of frozen meat.

'Open, please!' the RSM cried.

The cookhouse was deathly silent now. Someone had turned off the TV. Everyone watched Streaky. He pulled at the tie. Tiny splinters of ice scattered as he opened it. He carefully withdrew the contents.

The piece of meat was wrapped in DPM. At one end was a badly butchered mess of frozen blood. At the other, Streaky saw a foot. A human foot. The toenails were a shade of blue. The heel was pink. The ankle, which disappeared into the trouser leg, was encrusted with small icy hairs. Rifleman Bacon shrieked and threw the leg onto the table.

The cookhouse was in an uproar. The lads were laughing or shouting and the RSM was jabbering in Bengali. To prove that he had just been surprised, not scared, Streaky forced himself to laugh along with everyone else. He picked up the leg gingerly and held it up. People stared in fascination. Taregue hopped angrily from one foot to the other. Streaky couldn't hear a word he was saying, but knew it had to do with a human leg not being a nice thing to find in your third freezer.

'Thank you, Streaky,' Dave said as the noise died down. 'If we weren't dry here, I'd buy you a drink.'

Streaky glared at him.

'But what are you going to do about this alarming thing? Are you

196

expecting to leave a human leg with some sort of medicinal powder around the toes inside my freezer? Because if you are really thinking that then let me tell you—'

Dave signalled for the RSM to calm down. 'The leg belongs to one of our lads who's now back in Selly Oak. When I next speak to him I'll ask him what he wants us to do with it.'

'We could get it stuffed for him,' suggested Mal.

'Look good on his mantelpiece,' said Angus.

'Or hanging in the fucking National Gallery. Frame it and Steve's leg could sell for millions,' agreed Finn.

The chef rolled his eyes. 'This is disgusting. I am not housing a human foot in my freezer with its leg attached. It is not worth millions to me.'

Streaky put the leg quietly back in the bag. He was still embarrassed that he had looked scared in front of everyone. He would lose face for that. There were already people here not showing him respect because he was new and now Dave, fucking Sergeant Dave who was always on his back, had made things worse.

Dave was watching him. He turned away from the din to Streaky.

'All right, mate?'

'Man, why you fucking do that to me?' asked Streaky. 'You got no respect.'

In the circumstances, Dave didn't think he would insist on Sarge.

'It's all right,' he said kindly. 'You did all right.' But he could see Streaky disappearing inside himself, his face sullen, head down.

'Suck it up, mate,' Dave told him.

Streaky glared at the ground.

'Well then, rap your way out of it,' Dave suggested.

Streaky did not look up. 'What, man?'

'You said you could rap. You told me you've been thinking hard about your raps. Well then, let's hear you.'

Streaky shrugged. He watched as the cooks opened negotiations with the soldiers. Somehow a complicated deal was being struck which involved freezer space for the leg until Steve decided what he wanted to do with it, a consignment of Sin City T-shirts for the whole platoon and some bootleg DVDs.

The leg was finally carried back to the freezer, upright like a flag.

People were beginning to drift away or gather around the football match.

Streaky stood up, his heart beating fast.

'You planning to rap?' Binns asked, recognizing the look.

Streaky nodded.

'I been thinking about it . . .' He climbed up on the table.

'Oh, yeah!' said Binns. 'I'll beatbox.'

They had done this routine at Catterick more times than they could count. Binns knew he was a sprog when it came to fighting but when it came to beatboxing, he was confident. At last here was one thing he could do well and he wanted to show it.

He climbed up on the table beside Streaky and put his fingers to his lips and made a series of such extraordinary sounds that everyone stopped what they were doing and turned to the sprogs.

'Hey, listen to Binman!' said someone. A few people began to clap to the rhythm. Once it was established, Streaky joined in.

> You get hot in Sin City, you get tired in Sin City
> You got a lot on your plate when you live in Sin City.
> Brother you get hungry here in Sin City,
> Brother, you get hungry, so what do they do?
> Brother, of course they offer you stew.
> They offer you stew but take my advice.
> Don't start to chew, just you think about it twice.

Everyone was swaying now or pointing to the rhythm. Binman, red-faced, was a one-man drum kit.

'Get off that table!' howled the RSM from the back of the cookhouse. Streaky and Binman could hear him but they took no notice and neither did anyone else. The whole cookhouse was enjoying the beatbox and waiting for the rest of the rap.

> Take my advice when they offer you stew
> Oh soldier just you think twice before you chew,
> Get a knife, cut a slice of that belly of pork
> 'Cos it could be marinated Buckle you got there on your fork.
> His left leg was wrapped up in deep refrigeration,
> And Buckle leg and carrots are not the best combination.

People were laughing now as they clapped. Binman's face was an unhealthy shade of red but he was still beatboxing. The RSM was advancing with a roar: 'Just get down off my table, please.' But even his assistants weren't listening to him and a couple of lads reached out to prevent him closing on the rappers.

If the carrots are too crunchy then just you consider this,
That could be Steve Buckle's toes you chewing with your chips.
I'm telling you man, the cooks in Sin City never run out of
    meat,
I'm telling you man, they got freezers full of soldiers' feet.
We the British Army, we don't feed no Taliban,
We keep British arms and legs just for the British man,
We don't put no tasty morsels on the Taliban shelf,
Our lads get blown up, we gonna eat them ourself.

Streaky had run out of breath and run out of words. He was amazed he'd got that far. He'd thought each line was the last and then more flow had arrived from somewhere in the back of his head.

During the applause that followed he looked back at the smiling faces. They were telling him this was a good rap. He had earned back some respect. Even the officers had enjoyed it, and the civilians were nodding approval.

Streaky searched for Dave's face. For a moment he couldn't see him. Then he found him standing in the corner, arms folded. Dave nodded. Streaky smiled back.

Someone came up and tapped Dave on the shoulder. It was an officer who had just slipped into the tent. He hadn't heard the rap and he wasn't responding to the atmosphere. He had a serious expression on his face and he was muttering something to Dave.

Chapter Twenty-nine

DAVE FOLLOWED THE 2 I/C OUT OF THE COOKHOUSE INTO THE DARK night.

'What's all the hilarity about?' He was leading Dave towards the ops room.

'A couple of the lads are rapping.' Dave would've gone on to talk about Steve's frozen leg if the 2 i/c didn't look so grave. He guessed he had been called to the OC for some reason. It could be the insurgent they'd shot in the ditch. CSM Kila was always warning there would be an inquiry. Maybe his interview was tonight.

'Well, I'm sorry to interrupt,' the officer said. 'There's an urgent message for you.'

Jenny. Dave's stomach lurched.

'It's from Selly Oak.'

His stomach lurched again. Steve Buckle. The whole cookhouse had just been in uproar over Steve's leg. And now . . .

'What's happened, sir?'

'That's not clear. But his doctor has recommended that you phone him.'

The OC was in the tent under a desk light, surrounded by papers. He greeted Dave but carried on working. There were half-opened packets of custard creams on the tables and on the 2 i/c's desk a crumbling fruit cake that people had obviously been picking at.

Dave would have preferred to use the satellite phone in some private place instead of the ops room phone within earshot of officers, signaller and company clerk, but the 2 i/c was already waving the handset at him with a number to dial. The man who answered sounded uncertain. Dave asked to speak to Rifleman Steve Buckle and after a pause the man said: 'That's me.'

'I didn't recognize you, mate! It's Dave, Dave Henley. How are you?'

'Thank Christ.' The voice sounded stronger, but it still wasn't completely Steve. 'Shit, I need to talk to you.'

'Good to hear you're in the UK at last!'

'Tell me how everyone is! Please! What's happening out there?'

Since this was the ops room phone, Dave spoke more freely than he could on the satellite. 'A lot of the time it's quiet. But we were caught in one fuck of an ambush . . .'

'What happened?'

There was a note of longing in Steve's voice. Dave guessed that knowing his mates were fighting without him was hard. He gave Steve the detailed description of the ambush he knew he wanted.

'If AH had got there much later, we'd have had it. There was one of the bastards already just ten metres away from us and our ammo wouldn't have lasted another fifteen minutes, even at a very slow rate of fire,' he concluded.

Steve was silent.

'Steve?'

Silence.

'Steve?'

Nothing.

'Has the line gone dead, mate, or did my bedtime story lull you off to sleep?' Except it was a summer's afternoon in England.

No response. And then there was a strange, strangled sound. Was Steve choking? He sounded in pain. Maybe his leg was hurting a lot.

'Shit, I wish I was there!'

Then Dave knew that Steve was struggling to control his tears.

'Fuck, fuck, fuck, Dave, what the hell am I doing in fucking Birmingham when I should be there with you knocking the shit out of the Taliban? There's blokes wandering around this hospital in dishdash! I mean, the hats, the robes, the beards, they say they're here visiting their sick relatives! And I want to kill them. And the nurse says: no, Steve, they're British citizens.'

Dave cleared his throat.

'We're not fighting every Moslem, Steve, you know that. We're not fighting everyone in dishdash. We're just fighting the Taliban.'

'I wish I was there with you. I'd give anything.'

Dave was thinking Steve had already given enough when Steve moved closer to the phone and half whispered: 'Listen . . . I've got something to tell you.'

Dave waited. He could hear Steve gathering his strength at the other end and when the words came they were breathless.

'I've lost a leg!'

'Oh. Yeah. I know that, mate.'

'How do you know?'

Dave thought of the black plastic bag Masud had dumped on the cookhouse table in front of him not thirty minutes ago. He thought of Streaky's rap. Christ. Had someone really suggested to the whole cookhouse that they get the leg stuffed? Or hang it in the National Gallery? Why had they all been treating Steve's leg like the funniest thing since *Borat*? Was it because they all knew the truth was so fucking awful? He felt his face growing red.

'Er . . . well . . . I've seen it.'

'You've seen my leg?'

'I mean, I saw your leg getting blown off.'

'Fucking hell. You saw it. So what happened? People keep asking me and I'm fucked if I can remember.'

Dave described the ambush on their arrival here. It seemed such a long time ago now that it already felt like a dream.

'So you went down with a stoppage . . .' repeated Steve.

'. . . and you took my place on top, mate. Yeah. And that's when it happened. If you're thinking that it could have been me . . . well, you're right.'

There was a long pause.

'Fuck me,' said Steve very slowly.

Dave did not know what to say. Finally he spoke into Steve's silence. 'I don't know why it was you and not me. I've asked myself that a lot of times.'

'Yeah . . . yeah . . .'

'When are they giving you a new leg?'

'What?' Steve wasn't listening.

'Your new leg. When do you get it?'

'Oh, soon. They have to do a bit of an operation on the stump but not much. Then I go to Headley Court and join the British Paralympics team.'

'And you've seen Leanne and the boys?'

'Yeah, yeah.' His voice was flat.

'How are they?'

'Well, they've all still got two fucking legs so compared with me they're all right.'

'Come on, Steve, it's hard for them as well.'

'Some bloke's coming round to see about adapting the house.'

'What sort of adaptations?'

'For a disabled person.' His tone was bitter. Of course his tone was bitter.

Dave said: 'Mate, I'm not going to give you all that shit about blokes with no legs who climb mountains and win races and—'

'Yeah, yeah, yeah, I know. Dave, listen. There was this para who lost a leg and they gave him a new one and he went back out to Afghanistan. Someone said he got back out on the same tour! Think there's a chance I can do that?'

No!

'Yes!'

'Really?' Steve's voice became loud and excited, more like the old Steve.

I'm leading him up the garden path. He has to accept life won't be the same with one leg. Or does he? Or could he really get back to the frontline? What's the right thing to do?

'Well, I mean, it depends how good you are on your new pin. You might not be able to do everything we do . . . or anyway, not on this tour . . . but anything's possible.'

Dave had heard about that para who rejoined his mates. He just wasn't sure the bloke really existed.

'I want to do exactly what you and the lads do. Prosthetic–' Steve stumbled over the word. It took a couple of tries before he could say it smoothly. 'Prosthetic legs are amazing now, you can do anything, you can carry kit and fight . . . I have to get back out there with the lads, Dave. That's all I want. If I know I'm going back, then I can stand Selly Oak, Leanne crying all over me, all the crap.'

'Well, that's something to aim for.'

Steve's response was robust.

'I'll show you, mate. They're not fobbing me off with a desk job. I'll be out there for your next ambush.'

Dave finished the call wishing someone would tell him the right way to handle Steve. He wondered if anyone had told Leanne. He thanked the officers and went outside to see if by any chance the satellite phone was free so that he could call her. Rifleman Ben Broom from 2 Section was just sneaking off with it.

'Did you book that phone?' asked Dave.

'Yes, Sarge.'

'How many hours a week do you spend talking to her, Broom?'

'I like to keep an eye on my bird, Sarge. If I don't keep calling her, she might fly.'

'You and Jamie Dermott are never off the fucking phone.'

'Funny you should say that, he's booked in after me.'

But all those calls were not enough to keep Agnieszka from flying, thought Dave. He went to the list to book himself in for some phone time with Leanne but the schedule worked one week in advance and few slots were available. Men were getting up in the middle of the night to speak to their loved ones. Dave saw a space tomorrow morning but it was no good: from 0700 1 Platoon was out all day. Because, for the first time, they were on civilian escort duty.

Chapter Thirty

THE CONTRACTORS WERE LATE, AS USUAL. WAITING TO LEAVE SIN City with them were all three sections of 1 Platoon plus support staff including engineers, signallers, medics, the Company Sergeant Major and Jean Patterson as interpreter. The hardware was the usual light weapons and machine guns in the Vectors, two WMIKs, one with a .50 cal heavy machine gun and a gimpy, the second with a 40mm grenade machine gun and gimpy.

'Fuck it, do the civvies get a whole mortar platoon as well?' asked Finn as they waited by the vehicles. 'And how about an A10 fly-past?'

Angus lit a cigarette. 'Ever have the feeling civilian lives are more important than ours?'

Jamie said: 'Yeah, but we joined up and they didn't. Anyway, when they're protected, we're protected.'

Dave was striding past for some more ammunition. 'Fucking right. I think we're in for an easy day, lads.'

They were sitting with their backs against the Vectors. Sol's shadow suddenly fell across them.

'OK, 1 Section, there's a hold-up so let's do a few checks while we wait. Bacon, your weapon isn't clean, sort it out when you get back.'

'I cleaned it last night!'

'Well, clean it again. Angry, sorry to hear you broke your wrist.'
'But I didn't!'

'Then unhook your sling and get your arm out of it. Mal, don't forget the shotgun.'

Mal rolled his eyes. No patrol left the gates without someone reminding him about the shotgun.

Sol was frowning at Jack Binns.

'You don't look right . . . get up.'

Binns tried to do this but the weight he was carrying pulled him back. Sol took an arm and tugged him to his feet, then looked him up and down.

'What is going on with your kit, Binman?'

'Don't feel right.'

'If your webbing's on wrong, everything's wrong. Let's take a look. Get your pouches off.'

Binns began to struggle with his Camelbak and his pouches. He handed them to Jamie, who was sitting nearby.

'I've been having a bit of trouble getting things in the right place . . .'

Sol shook his head. 'Have you been like this since you got here?'

'It used to be all right . . .'

'So, Binns, how much are you eating?'

'Dunno.'

'I reckon you've lost a lot of weight. I see you in the cookhouse but I've never thought to check how much food's on your plate.'

Streaky Bacon spoke up.

'Sometimes Binman doesn't eat nothing at all.'

Sol looked at Binns for an explanation. Binns stared at the ground.

'It's too fucking hot to eat and I'm too fucking knackered carrying all this kit around.'

'What about your rations when you're out?'

'They don't taste nice. That boil-in-the-bag chicken stuff just makes me want to puke. I always give it to Angry.'

Sol turned to Angry who looked defensive.

'Yeah, well I like it.'

'Don't eat the sprog's rations!' said Sol. 'You can swap but you can't eat his or he'll die of starvation.'

'But I get hungry! And he doesn't want it!'

Sol ignored him.

'The Lancashire hotpot's good,' he told Binns. 'Try finding someone who'll swap you a chicken for a hotpot. And they're bringing in a lot of new flavours now.'

Binns looked unconvinced.

'He's a vegetarian, that's the problem,' said Bacon. Binns shot his mate an angry glance.

Finn hooted.

'Fond of little furry animals, are you? Well, so am I! Served up with brown sauce.'

'I just don't eat meat,' said Binns. 'I wouldn't call myself vegetarian.'

'There's some no-meat meals,' said Sol. 'We'll have to sort you out. Why didn't you tell us before?'

Binn glared at the ground. 'I'm not gay.'

Sol looked around dangerously at the others. 'Does anyone here think gay men don't eat meat?'

'No, Sol.'

Sol glanced at the isoboxes to see if there was any sign of the civilians. They were already half an hour late.

'Give your meal bag to Mal and he'll get it changed if there's time.'

'The colour won't give you any new meals. They're all his own personal property. He buys them with his own fucking money,' said Finn.

Binns searched through his pouches for the bag and handed it to Mal, who headed off to the CQMS.

'And don't you nick it! Change it for a vegetarian one!' Sol yelled after him.

'I did try and eat the meat. Only it made me puke,' said Binns miserably.

'Listen, man, no one's going to make you eat pukey stuff, but you got to eat something. You're worrying me. This is a harsh climate and we're doing a hard job and you've got to take care of yourself. You drinking enough?'

'Yeah. My Camelbak's full.'

'Good. Show me your pouches.'

'You mean . . . open them?'

'Yep. You show it for kit inspection. But now I want to see where you keep it. Where's your ammo?'

'Here.'

'On your right hip, good. Make sure the rounds are facing away. What else is in there?'

'Nothing.'

'Where's the rest of your ammo?'

'In my day sack.'

'What good is it there?'

'I can get it out when I need it.'

'No, Binman, you don't want to scrabble around in your day sack under fire. You need to be reaching into the pouch on your belt. What have you got in your left pouch?'

Binns opened it and pulled out a toilet roll.

'Try throwing that at Terry Taliban, he's never seen it before,' said Finn.

Angus said: 'Yeah, he'll be scared shitless.'

'Toilet roll should be somewhere out of the way,' said Sol. 'Keep the rest of your ammo in your left pouch and a bit of gun oil there too.'

'Er . . . I've got gun oil here somewhere . . .' Binns was frantically opening and closing pouches.

'No good. You have to be able to put your hand on it when you need it. That's why I keep mine in my front left. Where's your bayonet?'

'In my day sack.'

'How's it going to help you there, Binman?'

'Well, it's on the side so I can reach in and . . .'

'It goes on your webbing! Frog edge on, tie it in with something. There's no point having a weapon if it's not to hand. Last time I checked you had everything in the right place!'

'It all went wrong when I started losing weight and nothing fit me any more.'

'Right, open that pouch for me . . . let's take a look. Hexi, water, peanuts, picture of pretty girl, OK. Where's your morphine?'

'Left map pocket,' responded Binns automatically.

'Good. Okay, let's get your kit on so it fits.'

The lads watched.

'That webbing wouldn't even go around Angry's arm,' Finn said.

'Wouldn't even go around my dick,' Angus said.

'Dream on,' Jamie said.

'Take no notice of them and try this,' Sol told Binman. When Binns nodded, Sol passed him his pouches to hang on it, working his way carefully from the back round to his hips.

Mal appeared holding a meal pack.

'Pepper risotto with cheese. The colour said he's got an impressive array of vegetarian dishes produced to the highest standard and he looks forward to sharing them with you and hearing your comments.'

'The colour boy said that?' asked Sol, astonished.

'Nope,' said Mal, flopping down on the ground with the others. 'He said: look through this box, find one of your gay meals and then fuck off, nancy boy.'

'Ah, that sounds more like him.'

Angus was shuffling about, smoking impatiently. 'If an entire platoon of men and support and a fucking convoy of vehicles can be ready to go at 0700 hours, why can't Martyn Robertson get himself out of his isobox on time?'

'I could have stayed in my cot a bit longer,' said Mal, who was always last to get up.

'Which wagon are the contractors in?' asked Jamie.

'See that one up there with the cushions, the air-conditioning, the reclining seats, the bar and the satellite TV?' said Finn.

At that moment the civilians appeared. Martyn was surrounded by a cluster of young engineers, but marching determinedly ahead of the group, handbag over her shoulder and a bulging shopping bag in each arm, was Emily.

'Oh no!' said Sol, who had heard all about Emily's last outing.

'That's why they're late, they're bringing a woman,' said the lads, pulling each other up. 'Because ol' Emily's been getting sexed up in front of her mirror.'

The vehicles started and men began jumping aboard. The boss greeted them and gallantly helped Emily into the civilians' wagon before jumping into the front himself.

CSM Kila, throwing Dave a crafty look, opened the door at the front of the second Vector, where Jean was seated.

'Mind if I join you?'

She gave him a faint grin and he leaped aboard as the convoy moved off.

'Funny the way the civilians hardly ever get attacked,' he remarked, settling himself next to her.

'Because the Afghans want this oil and gas project to go ahead.'

'But what do a bunch of flipflops know about oil and gas?'

Jean pursed her lips. 'At the *shura* the town headman was friendly and showed a real interest in the exploration.'

Kila thought for a moment.

'Listen, diplomacy isn't my strong point. I'm a soldier and I just say what I think.'

'And you think . . . ?'

'Well . . .' He looked at her. 'I think that you are very beautiful.'

Jean began to colour. He watched as a pink glow, turning to red, rose from her neck up to her cheeks. She glanced involuntarily at the driver, hoping he hadn't overheard.

'Sorry, sorry,' said Kila hastily. Although he didn't look sorry. 'Got distracted for a moment there. What I meant to say is that I think the town headman may not be so friendly.'

'You weren't even at the *shura*.' Her voice was cool.

'If he can call off the Taliban because he likes the oil exploration project then he's got to be Taliban himself. At a high level. Otherwise they'd just tell him to fuck off. Oh!' He looked shocked at himself. 'Excuse my language!'

Jean reddened but said nothing. Instead she pursed her lips again and indicated that she had picked up something on the radio which required her intense concentration. Kila smiled.

Their destination was a parched place at the foot of hills which were themselves at the foot of mountains so that layer upon layer of rock towered above them on one side. On the other the desert was so hot and flat that when the men dismounted it was like stepping into a giant frying pan. Heat radiated up as if it came from the centre of the earth.

The contractors debussed.

'You want to watch this little lot,' said Kila to Dave. 'When you've got your engineering degree you might be back here doing a bit of oil exploration yourself.'

'As a civvie?' said Dave. 'Guarded by 1 Platoon? No way, you can kiss my swingers.'

Kila lit a cigarette, waved the match out and threw it away. It bounced a few times on the thin, hard desert floor.

'Jean reckons the Taliban aren't targeting the civvies because they're keen on some oil revenue.'

'How are you getting on with the monkey, then?' asked Dave. 'I've seen you with her in the cookhouse.'

Kila looked sly and drew on his cigarette. 'I'm finessing her.'

They heard the sound of raised voices: Martyn's deep and slow, Emily's fast and high-pitched. They were taking it in turns to grab a site map and jab their fingers at it. The boss was attempting to broker peace.

'He should just bang their fucking heads together,' said Iain Kila.

Dave smiled. 'Finessing is definitely your strong point, Iain.'

The work started. The young engineers carried a black box where they were instructed, mostly by Emily, and everyone was ordered to switch off machines and engines and be silent whenever it was in place and the engineers were taking readings.

Angus started a dirtiest joke competition and soon everyone was joining in. Raucous laughter swept across the desert. Men in 2 Section not on look-out or covering the contractors challenged 3 Section to a poker game, which also became noisy. The sun moved slowly in the sky. People munched their way through their ration packs.

Mal, Angry and Streaky had a meal but Binns, pale and puffy-faced, did not open his bag.

'What's up, buddy?' asked Martyn as he passed.

'He's right off his rations,' said Angus.

'I'm not surprised, they look like crap and they smell like crap,' said Martyn. Binman looked grateful.

'He's going to puke,' Streaky said knowledgeably. 'His face always goes puffy first.'

Martyn said: 'Wait here.'

He came back with a bag of sandwiches.

'We get ours made for us by the chef and they're good. Go on, try one.'

'What's in them?' asked Binns miserably.

'Egg and mayonnaise, stuff like that.'

Binman, with great reluctance, bit the corner of one sandwich. His face brightened and he ate some more. Martyn's face broke into a smile as Binns began to tear pieces off the sandwich hungrily.

Angry watched with disgust. 'You've spoilt him now. He'll never eat his ration pack.'

211

Martyn turned to glare at Angus.

'This kid just needs to eat, it doesn't matter what. He looks half starved.'

'That's because Angry always eats his rations,' said Mal.

'Makes sense. I'm hungry, he's not.'

Martyn glared at Angus, shaking his head.

'Just clean up your act, son. He's your buddy, you should take better care of him.'

Angus's large, round face turned bright red. He looked as though he wanted to reply but he said nothing.

Martyn turned back to Binns. 'Finish it up, I don't want it. I have to get back to Enemy now or she'll make my life hell.'

He strode off across the sand.

'Fucking nosy American know-all,' said Angus McCall, as soon as he was out of earshot.

'Oh, come on, he's a nice old guy,' said Mal.

Binns nodded, his mouth full.

'He's an American shitbag,' said Angry. 'They all think they know everything. Binman has to eat rations like the rest of us.'

But the sandwich had fortified Binns and now he was opening his risotto. After the first slow taste he began to spoon it into his mouth enthusiastically. Sol, on stag, swung around in time to see this and gave him a thumbs-up.

Jamie was watching the contractors.

'What the hell are they doing?' he asked Dave. They had built a wooden pier and were now bending over this and its accompanying paraphernalia.

'Could be preliminary passive seismic measurements,' said Dave knowledgeably.

'So they're measuring earthquakes?'

'If it's a seismometer they're supposed to make some sort of noise, like an explosion, so they can measure the sound that comes back. Maybe it's a gravimeter . . . I dunno, Jamie.'

Watched over by machine guns and surrounded by WMIKs, Vectors, soldiers, poker and dirty jokes, it soon became clear that Emily was agitated. She and Martyn frequently raised their voices. On one occasion she marched up to Weeks.

212

'Mr Weeks,' she said angrily. 'Would you please ask your men to be quiet!'

The boss passed on the instruction, along with a warning about the nature of the jokes. There was silence for a while. Then the talk and laughter started again.

Emily, her large face red with the exertion of working in the sun, confronted Weeks again.

'Mr Weeks!' she said. 'Not only are your men creating un-necessary noise but so are your machines.'

'What machines, Professor?' asked the boss. 'You told us to switch everything off and we did.'

Martyn appeared at Emily's side.

'They say their machines aren't on!' Emily told him.

He rolled his eyes. 'Emily means your radios.'

'You want us to switch off our radios?' said Boss Weeks. 'We can't possibly do that.'

'Oh, for heaven's sake,' Emily said irritably. 'No wonder our equipment isn't performing! It's picking up your frequencies.'

'But in the, er, er, event of a-a-a-attack we'd be powerless to communicate!'

'In the event of attack there would be far too much noise for us to continue working anyway!' Emily evidently regarded enemy attacks as nothing more than an inconvenience. 'So you would be welcome to turn the radios back on.'

'I'm s-sorry, but no,' said the boss.

'But if you keep your radios on then you will invalidate all of our work!'

'No.'

'Mr Weeks, I insist.'

'It's Second Lieutenant Weeks, actually,' he told her.

'I have little respect for military rankings or protocol,' she said. 'And I realize that every time you come out with us you are hoping to fire your guns and shower any passing Afghan with bullets but I have no interest in your war games and I must ask you to cooperate.'

'I can't switch off the radios,' said Weeks.

'But you will invalidate our work!'

'I'm s-s-sorry. But it would be too dangerous to switch off.'

'Then our work here today must be at an end.'

'All right. Back at the base we can agree with the OC how to deal with this problem in future,' Weeks concurred.

'If only they had sent a more senior officer, he might have been able to make a decision here and now!'

'No, er, er, officer, however senior, would agree to switch off the radios.'

Dave and CSM Kila were watching.

'I didn't know he had it in him,' said Kila.

'He's come a long way. Still can't give a good set of orders, though.'

Kila said: 'Think we ought to give him a bit of support?'

'He's coping. And if he can cope with her he can cope with anything the Taliban throws at us.'

'I am here making a major contribution to the development of Afghanistan, Officer,' Emily was saying. 'I understood you were here for the same purpose. Now I find another perfect example of how the needs of those engaged in the peaceful activity of reconstruction have been ignored yet again in favour of war, war.'

'The radios are needed for your p-p-protection.' Weeks's face was beetroot red. 'There's nothing warmongering about maintaining radio contact.'

'I'm sorry to say that since I have been at the base my views have been confirmed that the British Army is a warmongering force. The best that can be said is that it keeps some very aggressive young men off the streets of the UK.'

The lads who were listening looked at each other.

'Does she mean us?' they muttered.

'Unfortunately,' continued Emily, 'the poor Afghans are on the receiving end of this aggression.'

She instructed the waiting engineers to return with the gravimeter while Martyn shrugged helplessly at Weeks. The boss ordered the men to pack up.

'Congratulations, sir,' Dave said.

'Fucking well done, sir,' agreed Kila. The boss blinked in surprise, since Kila had never called him sir as if he meant it. 'That was one hell of a handbagging.'

Weeks was still red-faced. He did not reply. He was thinking that if standing up to Emily won him this much respect, he wished Asma had been here to see it.

As the convoy prepared to leave, Martyn Robertson climbed into the front of the Vector with Weeks.

'There's no way I'm travelling at the back with Enemy, she'll be moaning all the way.'

Their route took them across the empty dustbowl of the desert, around the strange shapes of the Early Rocks which jutted eerily from the flat landscape. Gordon Weeks studied their distant outlines.

'I'd sure like to visit that place,' Martyn said. 'It's a weird formation. Natural although it looks manmade.'

'Reminds me of Stonehenge,' Weeks said.

'Those rocks are so big they'd make Stonehenge look like it was made out of pebbles. You can't tell the size of them when there's nothing near to compare them with.'

At that moment a shabby, dusty car, driven by a man but full of women passengers, their brightly coloured headwear flapping from the open windows, cut across the desert. As it neared the rocks the massive outlines towered over the car as if it was a tiny toy.

'Pilgrims,' explained Martyn. 'The place is some kind of holy shrine, that's why we aren't allowed to go there.'

Weeks made a mental note to ask Asma about the Early Rocks.

After this landmark the desert was featureless, apart from the occasional town or village, until the straight lines of FOB Senzhiri were visible in the distance. Usually they could expect some enemy fire if they approached to the east past a small, hilly zone but today they continued unhindered.

It was strange, thought Weeks, the way no one took a potshot at them when the civilian wagon was in the convoy. Without the civilians, they were guaranteed at least some token firing.

Martyn was evidently thinking the same thing.

'They sure leave us alone these days,' he said. 'Must have finally understood that there's nothing to gain from getting in our way.'

Weeks was silent. He feared Martyn was wrong.

Chapter Thirty-one

JEAN AND ASMA LAY ON THEIR COTS IN BODY ARMOUR AND HELMETS listening to almost incessant firing. They shared a room in one of the safer areas of the base. Reinforced with concrete, it nestled inside thick Afghan mud walls.

Jean said: 'I'm sure the enemy waits for the contractors to leave the base before they start this.'

'But only a couple of the contractors went out today,' Asma said. 'Martyn's still here because he's coming to the *shura*.'

'Well, the Taliban don't know how many are in the civvies' Vector.'

At that moment their beds were shaken by a particularly loud explosion. Small, powdery pieces of wall scattered over them.

'Toenail time,' said Jean.

Asma nodded and reached for her makeup bag. They always painted their toenails during intense fire on the grounds that military morticians probably wouldn't bother with toenails before their corpses were carried through Wootton Bassett.

Jean was pulling off her boots.

'Not much chance we'll get out for the *shura* now.'

'It'll be all over by then.' Asma chucked a tiny bright red bottle over to Jean's bed and shook a similar pink one herself.

'Is your mate Gordon Weeks coming again?' asked Jean.

'No,' said Asma. 'We've got a different platoon today.'

'Shame. That rifleman from 1 Platoon who stood by the door last time is really nice.'

'There'll probably be another nice rifleman today for you to smile at.'

'Well I like that one. Got chatting to him about skiing in the cookhouse. It's amazing how thinking about snow can make you feel cooler in these temperatures.'

Asma was placing a piece of foam between her toes. 'That's an achievement. You chatting with a rifleman. Considering how they all hate monkeys.' Now she had begun to follow the line of her nails slowly and carefully with the tiny brush.

'Well, when he'd got over that one he was all right. His name's Jamie. I worked for one season in Val d'Isère and he used to go every year with his family and it turns out we were there at the same time.'

Asma looked up from her toes at Jean for a moment and raised her eyebrows comically.

'Skiing with his family every year? And he's a *rifleman*?'

Jean pulled a face. 'And he's *married*.' She opened the red bottle. 'But he's all right.'

They both concentrated on their nails, pausing only briefly when another explosion shook their cots.

'Do you think Iain Kila's all right too?' asked Asma.

'Yuck!' Jean stopped painting and sank inside her body armour like a tortoise. 'Yuck, yuck, yuck, yuck, yuck.'

'He likes you,' Asma said.

'He's scary. Imagine him in a narrow alley on a dark night when he's had a few.'

'All these big hard men are softies underneath. They just need a good woman to help them show their feelings.'

Jean guffawed. 'And the last good woman was called Trudi.'

'Did he tell you that?'

'Nope. Her name's tattooed on his arm.'

Asma changed feet. 'Well, at least he's got an Underslung Grenade Launcher tattooed on his other arm.'

'Are you kidding?'

'How cool is that?'

'You are kidding!'

'Yes,' giggled Asma. 'But he's the sort who would.'

Jean giggled too.

'I think you like him,' said Asma.

'I do not.'

'You're always talking to him.'

'That's because every other soldier avoids me. Apart from Jamie. They all think I'm trying to arrest them.'

Asma had finished her toenails. She screwed the brush back into the bottle and then tipped the contents of her makeup bag onto her cot. She bent over, sifting through everything, so that tiny bottles fell against one another with soft clinking noises. She said: 'Well, you did make a big fuss about that guy they shot in the ditch.'

Jean was only starting on her second foot now. 'The OC's promised he'll investigate and write a report. I know they want to sweep it under the carpet but I'm not going to let them. The fact is, they filled a wounded man with bullets.'

'Course he was wounded. They shot him.'

'It's uncivilized,' insisted Jean. 'Soldiers storm compounds and see people living cheek by jowl with their animals and wandering around in flipflops. So they decide the Afghans are a bunch of savages. They should look at their own behaviour sometimes.'

'Keep going with that one and you'll drop a popular sergeant in the shit.'

'It's good to remind people about the RoE,' said Jean. 'Keeps their baser instincts under control.'

'OK, but don't expect them to like you for it.' Asma was applying mascara now, holding a little mirror up with the other hand.

'Well, Iain Kila still likes me. I wouldn't talk RoE to him, though.'

Jean finished her toenails and sat up and watched her friend's dexterity with the mascara. 'Are you putting on your face to impress that tribesman you fancy at the *shura*?'

Asma giggled. 'I wouldn't say *fancy*. But he's a very attractive man. And he makes Afghanistan seem a very attractive place.'

'In other words, you fancy him.'

Asma giggled again and shifted the mascara brush over to the other eye. 'Think I could be his fourth wife?'

'You'd get a bit bored stuck at home all day with the other three.'

'No, I wouldn't, because I'd be busy having at least ten kids.'

'So that's something about Afghanistan you don't find so attractive, then?'

'If my mum and dad hadn't got out, I'd certainly have six kids by now and another on the way. So I'm glad I'm English. But Afghanistan's always going to have a pull over me.'

'It's that tribesman who's pulled.' Jean got up, found her camera and took a picture of Asma in helmet and body armour holding her mirror and mascara.

'Don't you dare put that on Facebook,' said Asma, blinking rapidly. 'How do I look? Need a bit of eyeliner?'

Jean turned away. 'If you're trying to look good for some tribesman then I'm not giving you any advice.'

'Well, Gordon Weeks might be in the cookhouse.'

'He needs no encouragement. Never stops staring at you.'

'He held my hand a while ago.'

'Is that all?'

'There's nothing much going on between me and Gordon Weeks. We're just two saddos stuck in an FOB in the middle of nowhere.'

'There is something going on and you know it.'

They'd grown so accustomed to the firing that the lengthening silences had become more startling than any explosion. The changing pace of the battle was as familiar to them as music and they knew it was time now to put the nail polish away.

Asma stuffed the makeup bag into her day sack, untied her hair and began running a brush through the ends without taking off her helmet. Only then did she look up at Jean.

'Listen, Gordon's so bloody shy he can't even kiss me, let alone go further. He acts like I'm going to break if he touches me.'

'That's sort of nice in a way,' said Jean.

Asma paused, the brush in mid-air.

'It is sort of nice. No one ever treated me like I'm fragile before.'

'That's respect.'

'Yeah, well, I like respect but I could handle a snog as well.'

'You could throw your arms around him and get on with some serious snogging and hope he enjoys it.'

Asma laughed. 'He'd be so shocked he'd jump right over the hesco like a fucking kangaroo.'

There was the deep rumble of an aircraft approaching low overhead.

'Great! Air support. Just when it's ending anyway,' said Jean.

'Sounds like an A10. Brace yourself . . .'

A few minutes later came the crash. The ground shook. More debris fell on their cots.

'Must have dropped it on that hilly bit up the road. At last. That's always their main firing position,' said Jean.

'Nah, too close to town,' said Asma. 'That's why it's always their main firing position.'

They listened. Apart from the groan of the departing aircraft, there was silence. It was broken by one defiant enemy round. This was greeted by machine-gun fire from the base. More silence. Another round. Another reply. And then nothing.

'Those guys would delay dying for five minutes just to fire one more time,' said Jean.

Asma pulled off her helmet, shook her long, dark hair loose and brushed it from the roots down.

'What do you expect? They're Pashtun. So do you think the cookhouse will be operating yet? I'm hungry.'

Jean said: 'Listen, I want to say something. This bloke we're seeing this afternoon . . .'

'They're all blokes. Which one?'

'The blue-eyed tribesman who's got you putting on your mascara.'

'Asad, I think his name is, innit. Short for Asadullah.' Asma put away her brush.

Jean looked serious. 'Iain Kila said something.'

'What?'

'I said the civilians weren't coming under fire because the locals like the idea of oil and gas income. And I told him how Asad and his family wanted to hear about it at the last *shura*.'

'And?'

'And he said: then Asad must be Taliban. Otherwise he couldn't call them off.'

They were leaving their room now. Outside the sun was bright. The smell of cordite lingered in the air. There were clouds of dust circling as though there had been a sudden storm. As they crossed to the cookhouse men began returning from their firing positions. Sergeant Somers was shouting at one of his lads. Asma stopped.

'No, Jean. Asad told us there's a compound in the Green Zone which is swarming with insurgents. We've got more intelligence which says he's right. And he's going to tell us which compound. He wouldn't do that if he was Taliban, would he?'

'I don't know, Asma. Those guys are complicated.'

'I really think he wants us to help him get the Taliban off his territory.'

Jean grinned at her.

'Like you said, you're a saddo stuck in an FOB in the middle of nowhere. And you fancy him. So I don't trust your judgement.'

The 2 i/c, carrying a mug of tea, came out of the ops room, saw them and raised a hand to stop them.

'There's a very slight change of plan for this afternoon. The Professor will be coming to the *shura*.'

Jean remembered the last time she had been out with Emily.

'Oh no!'

'Sorry. We tried to talk her out of it.'

Asma said: 'Does she realize she'll be sitting cross-legged on a carpet?'

'And she'll have to cover up,' added Jean. 'Her knee-length skirts won't do.'

The 2 i/c looked embarrassed. 'I didn't think of discussing her wardrobe. I'll leave that to you girls.'

'You want us to go and tell her?' demanded Asma.

The 2 i/c nodded sheepishly.

'You're all scared of her!' said Asma. The 2 i/c nodded again.

Chapter Thirty-two

THERE WAS A SMALL CLUSTER OF PEOPLE OUTSIDE LEANNE'S HOUSE. Across the door was a banner saying WELCOME HOME HERO! Several children carried signs: OUR HERO STEVE. The twins wore outsize badges saying: YES HE'S OUR DAD! The welfare officer and a group of uniformed men from the rear party stood talking in quiet voices separately from the women and children.

Leanne clicked shut her mobile. 'He's coming!'

Her voice had gone squeaky again. Adi Kasanita was standing closest to her.

'He's coming, he's coming!' she boomed, so that everyone could hear. People stopped talking and straightened, the signs were held aloft and, as a small army car drove slowly up the road, there was cheering.

Leanne's heart beat so loudly that she could hardly hear the cheers. A twin was wrapped around each leg, waiting, and all she could think for one stupid moment as Steve's face became visible through the windscreen was: what happens if one of the kids tries to grab his leg? And finds it's not there? Because she had tried to explain but they were just too young to understand. They were too young to understand what was happening right now. They were too young to understand that the man who had just arrived was their dad.

When he got out of the car Steve's face was white but he was smiling. The driver ran around and tried to help him. The small crowd stayed back and Leanne went to help too.

222

Steve's smile slipped.

'I can fucking do it myself,' he growled.

She felt something inside her curl up as though it had been singed by a hot fire. She fixed her smile and kissed him on the cheek. 'Sweetheart, welcome back.'

She would have liked him to take her in his arms and kiss her passionately the way he did after a long time away. Right here in front of everyone. But he was reaching for his crutch.

He moved unsteadily down the path to renewed cheering, Leanne behind him, the driver hovering close by. Everyone smiled and spoke to him as he passed. He grinned back without focusing on anyone. Rosie McKinley started singing 'For He's a Jolly Good Fellow!' Everyone joined in.

'He wouldn't use the wheelchair,' the driver was explaining. 'Wouldn't even let me put it in the car.'

Jenny was holding the boys' hands now, as well as Vicky's. They made no attempt to run to their father but looked up at him with big eyes. Leanne grabbed them.

'Don't you dare cry,' she muttered to Jenny, who was biting her lip. She began to drag the twins reluctantly along behind. A glance around at Agnieszka and Adi and Rosie and Sharon and all the other women whose husbands were in Afghanistan told Leanne that every one of them was close to tears. They all wanted their men home too. But not like this.

Steve entered the house under the banner and made his way to the living room where Leanne had laid out some food. There were balloons in all the corners, huge bunches of them, and red, white and blue paper bunting around the wall which a group of mothers had made at playgroup.

Leanne could see that Steve was relieved to sit down in a chair. His face was twisted with pain. She hadn't been sure the big welcome was a good idea but her friends had wanted to do it. Now that she saw his strained smile she knew it had been a mistake.

The boys were sneaking closer to their father. One of them grabbed his good leg. Then . . . oh no! He had swiped at his father's other trouser leg, found it empty, and was now examining it with disbelief. Steve laughed, a deep belly laugh, a Steve laugh, and the tension in the room suddenly dissolved.

'You won't find a lot in there, mate!'

Everyone laughed at this and the boys ran around giggling wildly, picking up their father's empty trouser leg, hooting and putting it down again.

The adults clustered around Steve with questions. The room became noisy. Leanne buzzed about with sandwiches and crisps and drinks. She watched Steve out of the corner of her eye. He had always liked being the centre of attention. You could often hear his voice above everyone else's at a party. She listened now. He was talking to Jenny Henley.

'Dave had a stoppage and he went down to sort it out and I got on top and that's when it happened . . .'

Leanne saw Jenny's face turn white.

'Yeah,' Steve continued loudly, 'a few seconds' difference would have meant it was him and not me. Dave must be one of the few blokes in the British Army to be saved by equipment malfunction . . .'

Jenny said something and Steve shrugged.

'He certainly owes me a bloody drink . . .'

Leanne knew that Steve had replaced Dave on top of the vehicle just fifteen seconds before the bomb blast. Because of those fifteen seconds, Jenny had been comforting her for weeks instead of the other way round. She had struggled with this knowledge quietly in the night and sometimes, for a few minutes, she'd even hated Jenny. But not enough to tell her. And now Steve had not hesitated to blurt it out.

His voice was booming across the room again.

'When I get to Headley Court on Monday morning they'll start fitting me up for a leg socket. As soon as that's right I can try out some new legs. Then I just have to pass a fitness test and I can get straight back out there!'

And in answer to another question: 'Yes, there's a chance I can make it back out to the FOB before this tour ends . . .'

Leanne didn't take time to think. She found herself striding across the room.

'You're kidding!' she said, smiling broadly as though he had just cracked a very funny joke.

'No, darling, I've already told you.'

224

'I thought you must be kidding!'

'Leanne. I've trained to fight. I've lived to fight. There's nothing else I can do.'

'The army's full of interesting jobs, you don't have to serve in the frontline . . .' She heard herself. She sounded aggressive. This wasn't the time and it wasn't the place but she couldn't stop.

'What do you want me to do? Go and work for the quarter-master handing equipment out to other blokes?'

The party noise was dampening a little now. People were stopping their conversations to listen.

'Well, that's better than going back out to get the other leg blown off so we have to go through it all again!' she replied loudly. There were two Leannes in the room, the Leanne who was so tense and angry she couldn't stop herself shouting. And a small, calm, quiet Leanne who knew the welcome party was on the brink of disaster and could do nothing to save the situation.

'You can do anything, Steve!' said a warm voice behind her. 'If you say you can get back out to that frontline, then I believe you will!'

Steve looked past his hurt wife to the smiling face of Adi Kasanita.

'Thanks, Ads. I'm glad someone believes in me.'

'Honey, everyone believes in you,' she said sweetly. 'Leanne too. She's so sure you'll do it that she's scared to death, poor girl!'

Adi put an arm around Leanne and some people laughed and joined in and one of the officers said there was a para who had gone straight back out to Afghanistan with a new leg. After a while the voices and the children and the balloons made it seem like a normal party again.

Leanne didn't want it to end. Whenever anyone said they had to go she persuaded them to stay a little longer. The officers were the first to drift off, then all the other men in uniform said they had to get back to their offices, and finally the mothers said: 'You two need some quiet time alone together.'

Leanne wanted to shout: 'No, we don't!'

But Jenny and Adi took the boys and suddenly the house was still, more still than it had been for months. Even at night when Leanne lay sleepless in her bed, it wasn't this still.

Steve sat with his head back in the chair and his eyes closed. Leanne busied herself with the clearing up. Finally he spoke.

'That was a load of shit.'

She froze, a stack of dirty cups in her hand.

'You could say thank you.'

'What have I got to thank you for? Signs saying I'm a hero? Well, I didn't even get to the fucking base. I was only in Afghanistan five minutes. I'm no fucking hero. My mates are out there fighting, they're the heroes.'

'So that's why you want to go back,' she said bitterly.

'Yeah. I want to go back. Get over it. I want to go back.'

His crutch was leaning against the chair and he reached for it. He was going to stand up. She moved forward to help and was still moving when she realized that he had picked up the crutch to throw it at her. It hurtled with force across the room. She dodged. It hit the side of her body and bounced off onto the buffet table. With a crash it landed on a pile of plates.

She stared at the mess of food, broken crockery and crutch and then turned to Steve, her hip throbbing with pain.

'Why did you do that, Steve?'

But he had closed his eyes and did not reply.

Chapter Thirty-three

'YES,' SAID EMILY, GUARDING THE ENTRANCE OF HER ISOBOX SO THAT Asma and Jean could not see past her to its interior. 'I am indeed coming to the *shura*. I shall be very interested to learn from the local people how it is to live under British military occupation.'

'Good!' said Jean cheerfully. 'We're here to help you prepare.'

Emily raised her eyebrows. Asma thought she looked like a bird that wanted to peck you. Her nose was beaky and her alert eyes were very round.

'And what preparation is necessary?'

Asma explained that they would all be sitting on a carpet.

Emily shrugged.

'I daresay I shall be a little uncomfortable but I will manage.'

'So, if you don't mind me asking, what exactly will you be wearing?' asked Jean.

Emily looked affronted.

'I have no plans to change.'

They glanced politely at her sleeveless blouse and sensible skirt. Her clothes struggled to contain her ample frame.

'I'm sorry, but you really need a loose, long-sleeved top to cover your arms. And you must cover your legs.'

Asma added: 'We wear combat trousers and that's all wrong but at least they're baggy and they hide us. You can't go in showing your legs, Professor.'

Emily's strong, clever face frightened her. The confidence her intelligence gave the professor was like body armour. It meant

227

Emily had views she was so sure about she wasn't scared to express them. It meant Emily did not care about her appearance and had no interest in what others thought of her.

'You certainly couldn't show your young legs but I doubt they will take much notice of an old woman like me,' Emily said airily.

Both Jean and Asma rushed to correct her and Emily weakened.

'Well, we'd better have a look at my clothes then. Don't stand there letting the heat in.'

She stepped aside. After the fierce light outside the isobox seemed gloomy. They could see piles of papers and two computer screens which apparently Emily had been using simultaneously. A bed was pressed against one wall and it was also covered in papers. But the most amazing thing about the office was its temperature. Asma and Jean closed their eyes and felt the delicious and unaccustomed pleasure of air-conditioning.

Emily was flicking through clothes on a small hanging rail jammed in beside a computer.

'I have a long-sleeved blouse. But I don't have a long skirt. And I'm certainly not wearing that ridiculous camouflage stuff. I have no wish to make myself look like a bush.'

Asma did not want to open her eyes and reply. She just wanted to feel the cool air soothing her.

Jean said: 'Surely you have something that will cover your legs.'

Emily blinked. 'Why should I? I am not a Moslem.'

'Trousers?'

'Certainly not.'

'Nightie?'

'No.'

Asma opened her eyes with an effort.

'Do you wear pyjamas?'

'Well, I do have pyjamas but if you think I'm—'

'You could wear them under a skirt. That'd be better than nothing.'

Jean agreed. 'It won't look so different from the clothes Afghan women wear.'

Emily put her hands on her broad hips.

'I am not going out in my pyjamas.'

'You don't understand,' said Jean. 'To the Afghans this is about your body and not your clothes. They don't care what you wear as long as you cover up. We can only visit them if we show proper respect. Asma and I always cover our bodies and we drape a scarf over our heads when we go to *shuras*.'

Asma added: 'We're out there and we're women, that's bad enough for the locals. Uncovered women are just like: *no!*'

'That view is of course unacceptable to me.'

'Professor, we're in Afghanistan, we've got to respect Afghan traditions.'

Emily raised her eyebrows and looked birdlike again. She leaned forward to peck.

'I can't see how arriving with troops and bombs to kill Afghans is respecting their traditions. However, this obviously matters to you both very much and you know the country and its people. So if you insist, I'll wear my pyjamas under my skirt. Although I shall feel rather silly.'

Jean and Asma were ready and waiting with the military escort before the civilians emerged.

'I'm telling you now so you don't laugh. Emily will be wearing pyjamas,' said Jean. 'She's got nothing else to cover her legs.'

Sergeant Somers of 2 Platoon and his commander instantly guffawed.

'That's what you mustn't do!' Asma told them.

The OC looked around the group fiercely.

'The girls are right. It is very important that *no one laughs*.'

Emily arrived wearing pink pyjamas, a grey skirt, a pink blouse and pink headscarf knotted under her chin as well as full body armour and the OC was the first to burst out laughing. Despite glares from Asma and Jean, he was closely followed by the engineer and the 2 i/c. Martyn grinned from ear to ear and 2 Platoon muttered jokes to one another and staggered about stifling laughter. A few took pictures.

'Get on the wagons!' their sergeant growled at them. And then immediately clamped his hand over his mouth.

'At least all the colours match,' Asma told Emily kindly.

'And we take our body armour off before we go in,' Jean said. 'You'll feel more comfortable without it.'

'I'm delighted to have brightened up everyone's day,' said Emily grumpily.

'It's all in the interests of building strong local relationships.' The OC handed her up into the Vector.

'Local relations would be much improved if you didn't spend so much time peppering them with bullets,' retorted Emily. Martyn rolled his eyes at the OC and then climbed up behind her.

When they reached the tribesmen's house they were once again welcomed warmly by Asad, his father and brother. In the background hovered a large group of men and boys. Nobody here seemed to find Emily's pyjamas funny.

As they sat down, Asad caught Asma's eye and smiled. He was every bit as attractive as she remembered him. He was tall, much taller than most Afghans. His features were strong. And his blue eyes in that brown face were startling.

'It is a great pleasure to welcome you to our home again,' he said warmly.

She smiled back, dropped her eyes and told him how honoured the party was to attend the house and meet his family once more. Of course, the officers were supposed to present the greetings and she was supposed to translate them. But you could wait for ever for soldiers to do charm.

Emily lowered herself onto the carpet with difficulty and clearly did not enjoy crossing her legs. She was introduced and her role explained and the tribesmen listened politely then turned to Martyn with their questions.

'Is your search for Helmand's natural resources proving successful?' Asad asked him.

Martyn said: 'Yes, we've had some very interesting results.'

'Is oil everywhere in this region? Or just in one place?'

Emily did not intend to be ignored. Before Martyn could answer she said: 'We are concentrating our activities in the area we believe to be most productive.'

Asad's father nodded and turned back to Martyn: 'And how can you know from looking at the earth that there is oil and gas beneath it?'

Martyn smiled. 'I've been an oilman all my life. I just know, I can feel it, I can almost smell it.' He glanced at Emily. 'Although some people need persuading about my hunches.'

Emily looked at Martyn coldly and then said to the tribesmen, 'Naturally our exploration is scientific and our suppositions should be data-based. We carry out an initial rough analysis of the terrain by looking at its predominant geological eras. After preliminary exercises which help us pinpoint where the most likely compression has occurred we do a detailed analysis by, among other less accurate methods, taking seismic readings from the rock.'

Asma and Jean looked at each other in despair.

'I can't translate that,' said Jean.

Asma attempted it and the tribesmen nodded as though they'd understood. Asad asked Asma: 'Who did you say this woman is?'

Asma explained again that Emily was an eminent professor who knew more about geophysics than anyone else in the UK.

'So we can be sure, then, that the site is a true one?' asked Asad.

Asma translated this and Emily nodded vigorously. 'Certainly!' She glanced at Martyn. 'I do not make mistakes.'

Martyn grimaced.

Major Willingham was impatient. He said: 'Last time we were here you mentioned that you believed there was a Taliban training centre nearby.'

Asad's father nodded.

'We do believe that. We believe people are coming from all over the world to train at that centre. Some of them even come from England!'

The OC ignored this. He asked: 'What effect are the Taliban having on this area?'

'We live in fear. They arrive at our homes and demand hospitality, they eat our food, take our animals and steal from our shops. They even bring drugs into our households,' said Asad's father passionately.

'So you would like the area cleared of them?'

'Yes. We would like them to go back to their own countries and leave us to our Afghan traditions.'

'Then why don't you fight them yourselves?' demanded Emily.

'We are powerless in the face of their international strength.'

'You said you would tell us exactly where the Taliban training ground is. If you do so, we can help you clear this area of their influence,' said the major. He was trying to appear relaxed, thought Asma, but a slight breathlessness in his voice gave away the importance of the question.

'We have discussed this among ourselves and we can tell you exactly,' said the father.

Asad said something to one of the boys hanging around at the side of the room. The boy ran off and, while they waited for his return, hot, sweet tea was served by old men.

Emily tried to take advantage of the break to stretch out her legs but Jean stopped her at once.

'Don't put your legs forward!'

'Why ever not?'

'It just isn't OK.'

Asma's face was reddening for Emily. 'You can stand up, but you can't stretch out.'

The boy returned with a map and everybody pored over it. Martyn was quick to find the Early Rocks.

'Can you tell me anything about that place?'

'It is a very holy shrine,' said Asad's father. 'A great Sufi poet lived at the rocks and when he needed water he drew water from the ground and there has been water ever since.'

'And,' added Asad, 'women believe that drinking this water will give them a boy child. In the past it was a very popular location on holy days. But people today realize that these old shrines are more like superstitions than anything the Prophet would have approved. So no one goes there much now.'

'Of course you know it,' said Asad's father, 'because it is near your oil site.'

Martyn and Emily looked surprised.

'But how do you know where the oil site is?' demanded Emily. 'Has Martyn told you?'

The men smiled and the younger brother, who had remained silent until now, laughed out loud.

'This is our world,' said Asad. 'We know everything.'

'What is it called?' she asked.

'The place you visit so often with your box?'

Asad's finger rapidly moved across the flat desert to settle at the edge of a mass of contour lines. He had pinpointed the site exactly. The OC and the 2 i/c exchanged glances.

'It has no name,' said Asad's father.

'We should give it one, since it is a place of some significance. What will you call it, Father?'

The older man thought for a moment, stroking his beard. Then he said: 'Allah is bountiful.'

There was a murmur of assent from all around the room before Asma could translate.

'Allah is bountiful? That's the name they've given it?' asked Martyn. 'Maybe it works in Pashtu but it doesn't do a lot for me in English.'

'I think what they're saying,' said the 2 i/c, 'is that they regard the oil and gas site as Helmand's winning lottery ticket.'

'They would be quite right,' added Emily.

'They probably feel that Allah doesn't leave a lot to chance,' said Asma quietly. 'And I'm sure they disapprove of lotteries.'

'I get where they're coming from,' said Martyn. 'What they're trying to call the place is Jackpot.'

'Jackpot,' echoed the OC with approval.

'Jackpot!' said the 2 i/c.

'OK,' said Martyn, 'I'm sold on that. Jackpot it is.'

During this conversation Asad had been talking intently with his father. Although it was clear, from the way Emily and Martyn kept rearranging themselves uncomfortably on the carpet, that the visitors were ready to go, the father now spoke to them all. Jean translated.

'We would like to extend an invitation to everyone here today. My daughter is to be married next month. We would be very honoured if you would consider joining our family and friends for the wedding celebrations.'

The invitation was received in shocked silence. Even Emily and Martyn looked to the OC for a reply.

'Um, well, actually, we'd love to, really, but we honestly couldn't . . . I mean, we wouldn't be able to . . . '

He looked helplessly at Jean who looked at Asma.

'You should be flattered,' she said. She was blushing. 'I doubt anyone else in the British Army has been honoured this way.'

'I'd certainly love to go,' stated Emily.

233

Asma said: 'Sir, it would be an amazing chance to win hearts and minds locally.'

But the OC shook his head.

'You know as well as I do that it could be a trap.'

Asma stared back at him, her dark eyes wide, feeling offence on the tribesmen's behalf.

The major said: 'I'm sorry, but it just wouldn't be safe. And, realistically, how could we come without huge protection? Which would be quite inappropriate at a wedding.'

Emily opened her mouth to argue but Jean was already replying.

'Jean's saying that you really want to accept. But you'd be in trouble for contravening current security procedures,' Asma explained quietly to the OC. 'She's saying you're honoured ... you're sad that our rules prevent it ... you appreciate this warm gesture of friendship.'

The major nodded. 'Very good,' he said. 'Very creative. I can leave it to you girls to say the right thing.'

The news was received with apparent disappointment by Asad's family. Asma was glad that Jean was the interpreter inflicting this disappointment.

Driving home, the OC said: 'I must admit, their invitation seemed genuine enough and I felt bad turning it down.'

'An Afghan wedding would have been a most interesting experience,' agreed Emily.

'And,' said the 2 i/c regretfully, 'Afghan feasts are apparently delicious.'

Asma sat quietly thinking how much she would have enjoyed the wedding. When she was a teenager her family had been invited to the occasional Afghan celebration in London but she had known that these affairs were no more than pale imitations and adaptations of weddings in Afghanistan.

Suddenly Martyn spoke: 'I don't trust those guys.'

Everyone turned to him.

'You think the invitation was a trap?' asked the OC.

'Well listen, I just hated the way he could put his finger right on the map at Jackpot. And he even described the gravimeter. Which means they've been watching us and we didn't know it.'

The OC did not miss his chance.

'Perhaps now you understand that the level of protection we offer you is necessary.'

He glanced at Emily. She sighed.

'Merely watching us indicates only that they are curious.'

Martyn folded his arms defiantly.

'Yeah, well don't forget the guy's Saudi connections. I don't trust any of them, least of all that son.'

Asma and Jean exchanged glances but remained silent.

The OC said: 'Well, the main thing is they gave us the information we went for. Now we've got the detail on the Taliban's activities in the area, we can take the appropriate action.'

Chapter Thirty-four

A STRIKE OP ON THE TALIBAN COMPOUND WAS SOON ANNOUNCED. It was too big for R Company to handle alone so another company was flying in from Bastion to help.

'Who are they?' asked Dave.

CSM Kila said: 'Paras. And most of them have been out here before. So they know what they're doing.'

'So it'll be their op,' said Dave. 'And we'll be supporting them.'

Kila shrugged. 'Don't worry, there'll be enough action to go round.'

The oil exploration programme went on hold while R Company went operational. For once, Emily and Martyn were united. They wanted to get on with their job and there was a public argument in the cookhouse.

'You're here for us!' Martyn didn't shout but his voice was raised. 'You're supposed to put our work first. And now you're telling us we're on hold while you go fighting.'

The OC was tight-lipped. 'Let me explain *again*. With such a major Taliban installation so close to this FOB, you soon won't be able to continue with your work unless we take action.'

'They've given us no trouble so far!' retorted Emily. 'Although they have no doubt felt the need to defend themselves from your attacks.'

The OC gritted his teeth.

'Our intelligence is that there are now many insurgents in this area. They seem to have a direct route from here to various centres of the narcotics trade where they are in frequent contact with troops from our other bases. So this action is necessary for everyone's safety, not just yours.'

1 Platoon gathered in the Cowshed for prayers. Boss Weeks said they would drive to the Green Zone and form part of an outer cordon with the rest of R Company. The Paras and their support would arrive in three Chinooks which would drop them inside the cordon, close to the compound. There would be two Apaches and two A10s on hand at all times. The outer cordon would aim to close in and join the fighting.

'Tomorrow's operation could turn into a very major and decisive battle. It will demand focus, professionalism and bravery. I want you to know that I am completely confident of the ability of every man in this platoon to perform under extreme pressure.'

Dave, standing at the front next to the boss, arms folded, noted that the boss had just spoken without an um or an er. He was saying what the men needed to hear. And incredibly, for the first time, they were all listening to him.

He stole a glance at Weeks's now grizzled face. His fair hair hung around his ears and that boyish, round-cheeked look had been replaced with sharper, more robust lines.

'This operation is a major offensive. It's the first time we have been in theatre with another company. And not just any company, but Paras.'

'That's why they get to take the compound while we hang around on the outside, then,' said Ryan Connor from 2 Section. 'Because they're Paras.'

'The Paras get all the fucking fun,' said a couple of lads from 3 Section, and all their mates agreed with them loudly.

Dave said, 'You lot don't own this bit of Helmand.'

'I think you should be very pleased that we've got such experienced soldiers alongside us,' the boss said.

'We're not going to see much of the action, though, are we, if we're stuck in the outer cordon?' called Mal.

Dave put his hands on his hips. 'Got a short-term memory problem, shitheads? We're catching fleeing insurgents and closing in on the compound to support the Paras. That's action.'

The boss added quietly: 'The last ambush 1 Section was involved in might be considered enough action for some people, Mal. We were extremely lucky to escape serious injury.' He glanced at Jamie.

'And let's keep it that way,' said Dave. 'I don't want any sloppiness because you think the Paras are going to take the brunt of the contact for you. Just stay sharp.'

R Company was due to leave the base at 0400. The base was already so busy at 0300 that there was an empty phone slot. It had been booked solidly since the operation was announced and Dave, as usual, had been too late for a place. He hadn't spoken to Jenny for a week. Or even two.

He knew he should stop sorting ammo and grab the phone. His mind was on today's operation and he did not really want to realign his thoughts with the small domestic world of Wiltshire. The call would be affectionate, but it would have to be brief.

When he held the battered handset at last, it felt rare and precious. Not because it could connect him to Wiltshire, but because it was something every man wanted.

He dialled Jenny's number. He was determined that he wouldn't spend ten minutes apologizing for not phoning before. As the number rang he felt the usual fear that she wouldn't answer and the usual relief when she picked up.

'Jen!'

But the voice he heard was not Jenny's.

'Dave, is that you?'

It was his mother-in-law. Not a good sign.

'Trish! Where's Jenny?'

'She's across the road at her friend's, whatsername.'

'Leanne?'

'Leanne. Is that the one who had something happen to her husband?'

'He got sent home.'

'Not in a coffin, I hope?'

Typical Trish. Salt of the earth, always there to help in a crisis and guaranteed never to look on the bright side. Ever since they first knew Dave was coming to Afghanistan she had been darkly hinting at the inevitability of his demise, until Jenny had begged her to stop.

'Not in a coffin, but not in one piece,' he conceded.

'Well, there you are, then. And they've sent him somewhere else now.'

This was Trish's I-told-you-so voice. It was entirely predictable and always entirely justified because nothing bad could happen which Trish hadn't already anticipated. Some people had hobbies. Trish spent her leisure hours concocting disasters.

'I think he's gone to Headley Court. Trish, is everything all right with Jenny?'

'No. She's not good, I'm afraid. She's been told she needs a lot of rest . . . oh, here she is now. Do you want to speak to her?'

He gritted his teeth.

'Well, yes please, Trish.'

'All right, I'll let you two talk. But, Dave, I must say something. Jenny's had too much to cope with alone here, and now it's beginning to show. Who knows what effect this is all having on the baby? We may not know for years but these things always come out in the end.'

He rolled his eyes as the prophet of doom droned on.

'You need to reconsider your position, Dave. You're out there fighting a war no one agrees with or understands while your family's here without you. Think about it, Dave. There. That's all I've got to say.'

'OK, Trish, I'll give that some thought.'

Trish handed over the phone and he was alone with Jenny. There was a pause and then they both guffawed.

'Christ, your mum doesn't change, does she?' said Dave.

'I don't know what I'd do without her.'

'What's up, love? What's happened?'

'I've been feeling weird for a while . . .'

'You didn't tell me.'

Ooops. Stupid. How could she tell him if he didn't phone? He braced himself for her to point this out but she evidently decided not to.

'Well, I'm just about to have a baby, it's normal to feel weird. But for the last couple of weeks I've been getting a bit spaced out and my ankles were so swollen I could hardly move. Then my hands started to swell too and I just felt dreadful. The midwife said my blood pressure was too high. I've got to have complete rest.

239

If I don't get back to normal in a week, I have to go to hospital.'

'But what will they do there?'

'I don't know. Monitor me, I suppose.'

'Oh, Christ. Is the baby OK?'

'Yes. The worst case scenario is that they'll have to induce me a bit early.'

'Induce!'

'Dave, don't worry.'

'Early!'

'Not very. We'll manage, love. Your mum's coming to help next week so I know I'll have a laugh then.'

Jenny and Dave's mother were good mates. Dave just wished he could feel the same way about her mother.

'How's Vicky?'

'Fine! Everything's fine.'

But he knew everything wasn't fine. And he knew he was powerless to do anything.

'I miss you. I worry about you,' he said. He kept his voice even so he didn't betray his anguish.

'Well, don't. I'm OK and it's my job to do the worrying around here.'

'If you were OK your mum wouldn't be there.'

'All I do is lie around getting bigger. And Mum gets smaller. She's lost three pounds.'

'How's Leanne? How's Steve?'

'Well, you can worry about them if you want something to worry about. He's been horrible to her. Really angry. Seems to want any excuse to shout at her. As though she planted the bloody IED.'

'I thought he was at Headley Court now.'

'They're giving him at least two legs, maybe more. One for every occasion. But he's still horrible to Leanne. He's on an anger management course or something now.'

Dave was aware that around him the base was buzzing with activity. His own men were gathering by the wagons already and sharing cigarettes. The air was thick with anticipation.

'Jen, shit, I'm really sorry, I've got to go . . .'

He rushed the rest of the call and then put down the phone feeling dissatisfied. He hadn't been able to tell her that in less than an

240

hour he would be leaving for a big operation. And she had apparently decided not to nag about him leaving the army, at least for now. So they had talked about Steve and Leanne. As usual, there had been more unsaid than said between them. It was better not to phone at all.

He walked briskly back to the ammo.

1 Platoon was outside and ready by the wagons at 0330. The world was still dark but light threatened. You could see the red line of dawn waiting to disperse far away in the east.

The men had checked and re-checked their kit and now they sat quietly. There was little conversation. They were thinking about the day ahead and the possibilities it would offer, for both bravery and for death.

Sol looked 1 Section up and down. As usual, he stopped by Jack Binns. He made it his business to keep an eye on this lad and just yesterday had discovered that his heels were cracked. He spoke sharply, breaking the group's silence.

'Did you remember to put that cream on, Binman?'

'Yeah, but they don't hurt much.'

'That's because I gripped you in time.'

Mal said: 'They'll hurt when you've been on your feet all day, Binman. I let my heels get cracked and every step was like treading on fucking knives.'

'Is that why you lost the shotgun?' asked Finn. 'Because your heels hurt?'

'Fuck off,' said Mal, lighting a cigarette and handing Finn one.

'All right, Mr Angry?' Finn asked Angus, who was sitting leaning on his Bergen with his eyes closed. 'Want one of Mal's ciggies?'

Angus did not open his eyes. 'Nah.'

Sol had been watching Angus too.

'What's up with you?'

'Nothing.'

'Had anything to eat this morning?'

'Nah.'

'Not scared of a fight, are you?' asked Finn.

'Course not. I just don't want to fuck up in front of the Paras.'

Sol's face creased into a frown. 'Who cares about the Paras?'

'I do.'

'Thinking of doing P Company, Angry?' asked Mal. 'Is that what it is? Scared you'll let yourself down?'

Angus opened his eyes. 'I'm not good enough to do P Company.'

'Bollocks,' said Mal.

'You're the right size. Toms are mostly gorilla-shaped people,' said Jamie.

'Toms are mostly gorillas,' said Finn. 'Forget the people bit.'

'You've got to think you're God's gift to the British Army,' said Sol. 'Or you can't join the Paras.'

Finn drew on his cigarette: 'I thought of doing P Company.'

'Why don't you, then?' Binman asked.

'Because he'd miss us,' said Mal.

'What's the point? Just so I can wear a red beret and jump out of aeroplanes? I thought: Finn, you already have enough women chasing you, so forget it.'

'You said your old man was in the Jedi, right?' said Bacon to Angus, who had closed his eyes again now. Angus did not reply. But Streaky continued.

'Well, why join the Paras? Why don't you follow in your dad's footsteps and go straight for the Jedi?'

'Selection,' said Finn. 'Now that really is a killer. Have a go at joining the Jedi, Mr Angry.'

'I wouldn't be good enough.'

'Your dad could give you a few tips about Selection,' said Mal.

'He never talks about it.'

Jamie said: 'Are you sure he was in the Regiment?'

Finn narrowed his eyes. '*In* the Regiment? *In* it? Angry's dad fucking *ran* it. And I mean he almost couldn't find the time because he was so busy walking on water. He walked right across the fucking South Atlantic and single-handedly took back the Falkland Islands.'

Angus jumped up, like a sleeping animal suddenly woken, and grabbed Finn.

Sol roared: 'Get off him, McCall, NOW!'

'Don't you insult my dad, you fucking diddicoy, you fucking piece of thieving shit from a caravan, you fucking . . .'

Two people grabbed Finn's right arm just before the knuckles came into contact with Angus's face. Four people dragged Angus away.

Dave appeared.

'What the hell is going on here?'

'This piece of shit insulted my dad!' yelled Angus.

'For Chrissake, McCall, anyone who doesn't get insulted by Billy Finn isn't worth knowing.'

Finn's eyes were narrowed but between the lids they glittered dangerously. His face had thinned with fury.

'Show a bit of respect,' said Sol, letting go of Finn's arm. 'And you, Angry. Save your fighting for the Taliban.'

The pair melted back into the group, shoulders still squared.

It was almost 0400. Sol took Finn and Angus aside as the others climbed into the Vectors.

'A section with its own fight is no good at fighting the Taliban. Put it behind you. Both of you. Now. And I don't mean: snarl at each other across the wagon. I mean put it right behind you so you can fight alongside each other as mates.'

They both nodded at Sol and then at each other. It wasn't much but it was enough. They jumped on board and sat at opposite ends of the wagon.

Asma had climbed up beside the boss at the front and this had put Gordon Weeks in a very good mood despite the day that lay ahead. He had barely slept but now he felt wide awake and alert.

'I hope you won't have to fire one at the Taliban this time,' he said. 'They won't be more lenient on you because you're a woman.'

Asma sighed and yawned. 'You don't understand the Taliban.'

'Does anyone? Do you?'

'It's not like being in the army. It's not one bloody great organization. It's a bunch of smaller groups all arguing among themselves. A few are fundamentalists, most aren't. Some are part of a big machine, some aren't. Some people hedge their bets and join because they think the Taliban will be here for ever and the British will go. Or they join because they're made to. Or paid to. Or because they're angry at civilian deaths. Or because they think the British are bad for the opium crop . . .'

Her voice disappeared inside another yawn and she closed her eyes. Weeks sneaked a long look at her. She was beautiful in the early morning, too, but it was a different beauty from the Asma who smoked under the stars every evening. In this light she looked more fragile. He started to imagine waking up next to her and then remembered abruptly that he was supposed to be discussing the Taliban.

'Today the enemy isn't disaffected local farmers. We know that a lot of the men in the compound are committed international fighters who want to control Afghanistan.'

She shrugged. 'We'll never eradicate the Taliban or drive them out.'

'Are you telling me we can't win today?'

'What's to win? All this fighting won't bring peace. But I'm sure we'll clear the compound and kill a lot of them.'

Too soon they reached the edge of the Green Zone. The boss told his platoon to debus and then jumped out himself. Asma was to be driven forward behind the inner cordon fighting and he smiled at her before he slammed the door.

'Be careful today,' he said softly.

Chapter Thirty-five

DAVE STOOD COUNTING THE MEN BY EACH VECTOR AS THEY JUMPED out into the dawn.

'Two hands on your weapon, McKinley!

'For Chrissake, Gayle, how many times do I have to tell you to unhook your sling clip?

'Do your pouches up, Bacon! Get a grip.

'Two hands on your weapon, Mara! Get a grip.

'Sling clip, Broom. Get a grip.

'I hope there's water in that fucking Camelbak, Binns.

'Two hands on your weapon, you. And you! Get your finger out of your arse.

'Switch on, O'Sullivan, your pouches are a mess, sort yourself out.'

Maybe he should count the number of times he told lads to get two hands on their weapon and, when he reached a million, leave the army the way Jenny wanted him to. *Jenny.* He watched the section commanders lead their men off and then followed them into the orchard. *Jenny.* He hadn't told her he loved her. He had just talked about Steve and Leanne, his mind on his ammo. And then he had put the phone down with a sense of loss.

They proceeded in silence, waiting for the enemy to know they were there, waiting for the first shots. Within five minutes, the shots came, peppering the silence. But they sounded far enough to the right to allow the men to continue without changing direction. No one fired. They continued to stumble into the half-dark along a field's edge, against the cover of a treeline, listening for the next shots.

After a long pause there was more firing. It was still to their right and this time it was much closer. 2 Platoon reported that they would take cover and open fire.

Dave and the boss had a brief conversation and decided to keep going. As the shots got louder, Dave wondered if they were moving towards the enemy or the enemy was closing in on them.

'We'd better take cover,' he told the boss as they emerged from the field and reached some crumbling walls, pink with age. Previous fighting, perhaps with the Russians or maybe more recently, had turned this building, whatever it had once been, into a ruin. You could see the holes of previous explosions.

The lads seized the chance to get down with their weapons and fire back. There had been rumours about today's operation long before it was confirmed. It was a relief to end the long period of anticipation by firing at last.

'Keep something back for later, lads,' Dave said.

He looked along the ruined walls at his men. Angus and Finn were so intent on their jobs that their argument was forgotten. Streaky and Mal were focused too but they were both giggling insanely. Men sometimes heard laughter in contacts but they seldom guessed it was coming out of their own mouths. Just nerves, thought Dave, as the first contact of the many they expected today kicked off.

'Tell your boys to slow their rate of fire,' he told Sol, 'or we'll be low on ammo before we get to the big fight.'

In the distance was the unmistakable thump of helicopters. Chinooks. Bringing Paras. At the sound, enemy fire eased. 1 Platoon seized the chance to advance.

Corporal Baker, the commander of 2 Section, asked to take his men further out than originally agreed. He had identified an enemy position and wanted to outflank them.

Boss Weeks agreed to this. 3 Section, which was nearest to the target compound, pressed forward with 1 Section to join the Paras, who could be heard landing now. The helicopters were attracting not just light arms and heavier machine-gun fire but RPGs as well. As if the Taliban had been expecting them.

Apaches must be guarding the Chinooks: Dave could hear their chain guns putting down some 40mm cannon rounds to help the Paras get out. From the deeper thud of the Chinook rotor blades Dave estimated that they were on the ground for less than thirty seconds, just long enough for platoons of Paras to stream out of the back. And then they took off into their own dust. They flew right over Dave's head towards the desert, an Apache hovering high on either side. He knew the Chinooks were scheduled to return to base while the Apaches were staying around for this operation but the sound of the disappearing rotor blades left a deadly silence. It was broken only by distant fire.

Maybe the enemy had moved now, converging on the newly arrived Paras. Which would trap them nicely in the cordon. Except that Dave knew better than to underestimate the Taliban.

They crossed a ditch and then a field of dried-out poppies, their pods cracking and dry stalks breaking as the men passed. The fighting continued but it still seemed far away. 1 Platoon was wrapped up in a local silence which was broken suddenly by the sound of an explosion nearby. A loud, dull thump. Dave barely had time to recognize it before the screaming started. He could hear it in his earpiece, a hideous backing to the voice of 2 Section's Corporal Baker reporting, breathless with horror, that there was a man down. And he could hear it in his other ear, more faintly but for real: deep, primal roars of pain just a few hundred metres away.

'Fuck, it sounded like a mine . . .' Dave was saying as he turned towards the explosion, his heart sounding louder in his ear than the far-off contact.

He was point man now: the boss had pulled 1 and 3 Sections around behind him. He moved rapidly, stumbling sometimes, once nearly falling into a ditch, his Bergen banging on his back. All the time he was getting garbled reports in his ear from Corporal Baker that they were under mortar attack. Then someone else was shouting: 'Keep back!' In the confusion, it became clear that the man screaming was Broom.

Dave was breathless now but he kept running, following a drainage ditch half-filled with dirty water. His mind was focused on getting to his men but he could not help remembering a dark Afghan night and Ben Broom stealing away with the satellite phone: '*I like to keep an eye on my bird, Sarge. If I don't keep calling her, she might fly . . .*'

Dave, his breath short and his heart thudding, reached 2 Section just in time to see the second explosion. He saw the smoke go up with bits of debris inside it. Shrapnel. Or – and he tried to keep his mind from going there but the thought kept coming anyway – the body parts of a victim. He could hear more screams of agony.

'Another man down.' Shock had leached all expression from Corporal Baker's voice.

Another voice, the boss's: 'Are you under mortar fire, Baker?'

'Don't know. It could be mortars . . .'

Dave was still gasping for breath. 'It's a fucking minefield!'

The men were clustered at the edge of a large weed-infested clearing in the woods. It might once have been a field but no one had farmed it for a long time.

'Freeze!' ordered Dave. 'Everyone freeze! And don't anyone try to get near the casualties, however much they scream.'

The boss organized 1 Section and 3 Section to cover the clearing as Dave reached the group. Most were at the side of the field and those who were close enough now leaped to the edge. Lying about fifteen metres into the clearing was the body of Rifleman Ryan Connor. About five metres beyond him was Ben Broom. They were both screaming, shouting, roaring for help, which no one could bring them.

'Don't anyone go near!' yelled Dave as he saw their mates wavering, faces contorted with agony for their friends. Two had frozen in positions halfway towards them. They looked ready to try to bolt the rest of the way.

'Kirk, O'Sullivan, stop!' shouted Dave. 'I said freeze! Don't move a foot, don't move a fucking inch.'

He worked his way through the trees around the edge of the field, over dense undergrowth.

'My leg, my leg, I've lost my fucking leg, I looked down and my fucking, fucking leg was gone!' shrieked Broom.

'Help, God help me, holy Jesus,' screamed Connor in a voice that sounded full of Afghan earth.

2 Section stood at the edge of the clearing, watching hopelessly and helplessly, longing to run to their mates, faces blanched. A few

tried to call encouragement to their friends but their voices were robbed of strength and depth so they sounded like a voicemail message.

Dave looked at the casualties and saw that Broom had certainly lost his lower leg and maybe an arm. Blood was pouring from his body. Connor was surrounded by blood too, but it was hard to see from here where he had been damaged.

'Mine strike. Two tango one casualties. Out,' the boss reported.

Dave could guess what had happened but he let Corporal Baker tell him anyway: 'Ben was cutting across the field and suddenly, bang! He was lying there screaming so Ryan ran over to him and, bang! I thought it was a mortar attack. I didn't stop Ryan because I thought it was a mortar . . .'

Dave said: 'It'll be a legacy minefield. Soviet. The Russians picked a spot and scattered them everywhere. That's why this place isn't cultivated, the locals all know about them.'

'I've lost a fucking leg, my fucking leg's gone, my leg, my leg, my leg . . . fuck it, fuck it . . .' shouted Ben Broom.

'Can you get some morphine into yourselves?' called Dave but neither Broom nor Connor could hear him over their own roars of pain.

'*Heeeelp*, fucking *heeeelp*, I'm dying . . .' screamed Ryan Connor.

The men, faces ashen, waited for Dave to tell them what to do.

'Chinook's coming,' came the boss's voice.

'No room for it to land here,' said Corporal Curtis of 3 Section.

'The Chinook can't land in a minefield,' snapped Dave. 'And let's hope it's got a very long winch. Because the downdraught could set the whole fucking field off.'

The boss said: 'There aren't any winches on the Chinooks.'

'What! Someone nicked them all?'

'They had a design fault. So they all got packed off back to the UK and the replacements haven't arrived yet.' The boss's voice was small and miserable.

'Well, what good to us is a fucking Chinook without a winch?' demanded Dave.

'We've asked the Americans for a Black Hawk.'

'Will that have a winch?'

'Yes.'

'How long will it take?'

'They're waiting for clearance now.'

'*How long?*' It was unbearable to hear the agony of the men in the minefield. You just wanted them to stop. And you knew that if they did it would be worse.

'The Americans can't operate without high-level clearance.'

'Oh, fuck, do we have to wait for the President of the United States to find time to OK it?' yelled Dave.

'We're doing our best.' The boss did not sound defensive. He sounded deflated. 'We're going to locate the nearest helicopter landing site for a MERT team, because getting the casualties out and away to a Chinook may be quicker than waiting for the Americans.'

Getting the casualties out may be quicker.

'Fuuuuuuuuuuuck!' roared Broom. He looked as though he was floating on an island of blood. He was only fifteen metres away and he was as unreachable as a man a thousand miles offshore. He would die from his blood loss unless help reached him soon.

Knowing his voice had to be both strong and severe to check Broom's yells, Dave bellowed: 'Stop shouting and start helping yourself, Broom.'

Broom fell abruptly silent.

'There's a bloody mess around your right leg so get your morphine out and shove it in at the top of your left. Come on, go for it! Now!'

Broom began to fiddle with his pouches.

'Get on with it!' bawled Dave mercilessly. 'It's in your left thigh pocket. Do it! Do it now! What about you, Connor?'

Connor responded with an awful cry. It was both the whimper of a small child and the roar of a large, injured animal that knows it is about to die, but it was not the cry of a man.

Dave tried the same tone on him. Connor, however, was past responding to commands.

'Shit, shit, what can we do?' Corporal Baker's face was ashen. His tone picked up the misery of the injured.

Dave looked around him at the nearest men. Shocked faces, shaking hands, a few tears.

'2 Section doesn't look safe for this job.'

1 Section, covering the field, were closest.

'I'm looking for mine-clearance men in 1 Section. I'll take you, Dermott . . .'

He sent Mara from 2 Section to replace Jamie's position.

'Me, Sarge!' Angus was already leaving his position in anticipation. Dave sighed.

'All right, McCall. But just stay behind Jamie.' He was sending another man up to replace Angus when Finn shouted: 'That should be me, Sarge.'

Angus turned to glare at him.

'I'm not taking a section commander or a 2 i/c.'

'But Angry's too big and clumsy!'

Dave ignored him. 'Jamie, you start over here and work your way towards Connor. McCall behind you. Then I need two men to start from over there and work towards Broom. I'll have you, Binman. And Mal follows.'

The men he had chosen blinked at him as if they had just woken up.

'Right, Dermott and McCall here, Binns and Bilaal there. Bergens off, bayonets ready, GET GOING.'

The men began to struggle out of their Bergens.

'Make sure you've got water, man behind must have a stretcher, carry only what you need, something to eat but not much. Of course, trauma kit. Give them some extra field dressings, someone. OK, then down on your belt buckles and it's *look, feel, prod* with your bayonets before you move forward. Remember that one? *Look, feel, prod.* Got mine markers? Got mine tape?'

They were taking off their pouches now, rummaging through them at the same time for mine tape, grabbing their bayonets. Binns looked skinnier and skinnier as the pouches came off. Finn moved in to help him.

The two front men got into position and eased down onto their stomachs at the edge of the minefield.

'Gently! DON'T HURRY!' roared Dave. 'Or you'll be lying there too.'

At a double moan from both casualties Jamie and Binman from their separate positions began to scrape urgently at the surface of the soil with their bayonets.

251

'GENTLY! This is your new-born baby. It's a bag of fucking eggs. It's a MINE and it's going to explode!'

'They're coming,' lads called to the casualties. 'They'll soon be getting you out of there.'

Broom was moaning more quietly now he had a shot of morphine inside him. Connor had fallen ominously silent.

'Ryan's still breathing,' shouted Kirk. 'I can see that.'

Kirk and O'Sullivan were the two members of 2 Section who had been stuck in the minefield when Dave had ordered them to freeze.

'If I go forward on my stomach from here,' called Kirk. 'I can get to Ryan faster than Dermott and McCall.'

'No,' shouted Dave. 'I want you two back safely, not bumping around the casualties in your Bergens in a minefield.'

Kirk started to argue.

'Shut the fuck up and tell me what you can see from there,' ordered Dave. 'How much leg has Broom lost?'

'About half. Maybe a bit more.'

'Connor?'

'Dunno. Can't see what's wrong with him.'

'Shrapnel, maybe. But he's got two legs, two arms?'

'I think so, Sarge, but there's so much blood . . . he could be missing a foot.'

'All right, Kirk. Now, you and O'Sullivan get your bayonets out, mine markers ready.' They reached carefully for their bayonets, wobbling dangerously because they could not move their feet.

'Sarge, I don't have mine markers,' called O'Sullivan miserably.

No matter how many times you did kit inspection, no matter how often you reminded men, they were guaranteed not to have the vital bit of kit when they needed it.

'Why the fuck not, O'Sullivan?'

'Erm . . . I used them for something else . . .'

'What else can you do with mine markers? For Chrissake?'

O'Sullivan stood helplessly in the minefield, his face gawping.

'Oh don't bother to tell me now. Got anything else you could use?'

'There's markers here, Sarge,' said McKinley. 'Can I try throwing them over to him?'

'Can you *fuck*! We're trying to get him out alive, shithead.'

'Use your peanuts!' shouted Corporal Baker to O'Sullivan.

'His peanuts? His *peanuts*?'

'Yeah, Sarge. O'Sullivan buys up the peanuts from everyone else's rations, he loves them, his Bergen's full of bags.'

'We need something that will stick in the ground.'

'He could anchor them with stones. Run a bit of mine tape between them.'

'It's better than nothing.' Dave shouted to O'Sullivan: 'Got your mine tape?'

'Yes, Sarge.'

'Right then, you two. Remember, no hurry. Go slow and live. Now crouch down. Take a look at the ground all around you and then feel it with your fingers. That includes the ground between your feet. Go behind you, go in front, go to the side. Then use your bayonet to prod. Do that until you've got a box around you big enough to lie in. So after that it's down on your belt buckles, sort yourselves out and start moving this way. SLOWLY.'

There was an urgent voice at his side.

'Sarge, I could start this end and make a path towards—'

'No, McKinley. I've already got eight men out there. I don't want to lose a ninth.'

On the radio the boss's voice said: 'I've been trying to get EOD but they're all tied up. Thought an engineer with mine-detecting equipment would help but we haven't managed to extract them yet . . . there should be some on their way soon . . .'

'Yeah,' said Dave. 'Yeah. Soon. OK.'

No helicopter, no winch, no mine detectors and no fucking EOD. Just two men bleeding to death and six more in danger.

'The casualties seem to have gone rather quiet,' said the boss.

'Yeah.'

Dave was tired of shouting. He was tired of talking. He was wet with sweat. And he felt powerless. The screams and moans of the wounded had worn him down, as though he had been the one screaming and moaning. Now that the men he had sent were out there doing their jobs, their lives were in their own hands.

His eyes swept across the minefield. The two casualties, baking in their own blood like cookies under the strengthening morning sun. Jamie, making painfully slow progress on his belly across the field, the large shape of McCall behind him. 1 Platoon, stretched out around the clearing, many backs to the action, searching the woodland for enemy movement. A collection of drawn, anxious faces, chiefly those of the shocked 2 Section, fixed on the two rescue teams. And, most surprisingly, the small, skinny shape of Jack Binns, followed by Mal, ootching with skilful speed towards the body of Ben Broom.

Chapter Thirty-six

WHEN BINMAN HAD HEARD HIS OWN NAME, STANDING IN THE woods watching the casualties' blood pump into the soil, he'd thought Dave was gripping him. Because, as usual, he must be doing something wrong. It took a few moments to realize that he'd been selected to clear a mine path to the casualties.

As he struggled to find his tape he thought to himself that he must have been chosen because Dave wouldn't mind losing him. Then he remembered that Jamie Dermott had also been chosen, and Dave would certainly mind losing Jamie. Only then did it occur to him that Dave had picked him to do this work because he might be good at it. And Mal, who was much quicker and better at everything, had been told to follow him! Mal was a fantastic medic but until they got to the casualties he could do nothing more than follow on his belly, maybe widening the mine path a bit, because, incredibly, Binns had been put at the front.

By the time Binns was on his knees at the edge of the woodland, liberated from his Bergen, bayonet in hand, he felt lightheaded. He had been selected to do the most difficult job. Along with good-at-everything hot-shit soldier Jamie Dermott. It was incredible.

His best mate, Streaky Bacon, clasped his shoulder.

'Good luck, Binman. I'm going to write a rap about this . . .'

The seriousness of Streaky's face reminded Binns of the danger ahead. So did one of the casualties, who gave a sudden, sharp scream of pain.

Binns didn't know Ben Broom well. But he knew he had to save his life. And if he failed, his failure would stay with him for ever. He closed his eyes and thought about what he had to do.

Look, feel, prod. Go. He worked vigorously on his knees and was soon able to move forward onto his belly, until Dave gripped him for it.

'Slower, Binns, for Chrissake!'

Binman soon decided to keep the bayonet for prodding and use his fingers to feel the ground. It was weird to scrape his hands across the rough Afghan soil. He had helped his grandfather in his allotment at home in Dorset where the soil was nothing like this: it was dark and friable and always damp beneath the surface. This soil had been roasting in the cruel sun for years. There was no moisture. It felt thin and lifeless.

The earth was gritty beneath his palms. He swept aside handfuls and let them fall gently. He dug his fingers into it until his nails were packed solid.

He heard Dave instructing O'Sullivan and Kirk to do the same.

'Sarge,' shouted O'Sullivan, 'can I pull these weeds up? It'll be easier to feel the soil.'

'No!' Dave roared back. 'We don't know how deep the root system goes.'

Binns had already worked that one out. So far he hadn't encountered many weeds but he worked carefully around them when he did.

It took hours and hours to move one inch. It took for ever. Binns concentrated so hard on his hands and the soil beneath them that days might have passed. The rest of his body didn't exist. He had turned into sharp eyes and gentle hands. Every time one of the wounded let out a cry, he felt himself speeding up.

'Ignore everything except your work, especially ignore the casualties!' shouted Dave. 'Don't hurry. Are you hurrying, Binman?'

Binns shook his head but did not speak. He was squeezing the point of his bayonet into earth his fingers had loosened, and then easing his body forward a bit more. Then a bit more. And then a bit more.

He heard Mal behind him.

'He's working fast, Sarge, but he's being well careful.'

To Binman, Mal said: 'You're doing a fucking good job. I just hope the Taliban don't move this way. Because I'm feeling exposed out here.'

Binman heard Mal's words but he was working patiently now on a particularly resistant mound of earth. He scraped at it very, very gently. The earth did not want to move. Was it caked to something solid beneath? He tried a new tactic.

'What the fuck are you doing?' asked Mal.

'Blowing,' said Binns.

'Oh. Thought you were just dripping your sweat on it.'

Binman became aware how hot he was. His helmet was a metal oven and his head baked inside it. His body was manoeuvring under a hot blanket.

'Binns, have you had any water yet?' bellowed Dave from the side of the clearing. He sounded further away now, but the casualties looked no closer.

'He hasn't, Sarge!' shouted Mal.

'Drink!' ordered Dave. 'Get your tube in your mouth and pause.'

Binman was blowing harder now on the resistant earth. This time it turned to dust and puffed up into his face. His eyes filled with grit. He shut them and kept blowing. When all the loose earth had gone he found himself staring down a steep indent. Just visible at the bottom was something hard and probably metallic. He stopped. For the first time since he had started this long, slow journey on his belly, he was still.

'Use your Camelbak,' Mal said.

Binns did not move.

'Oy! You going to puke?'

Binns lay still, waves of heat rising from the hot soil around him.

'Water!' Mal prompted him. 'Now!'

Jack Binns tried to speak. But the inside of his mouth was coated with dry soil. His throat was dry. His eyes were dry. The only water was his own sweat, dripping down his face and off his chin.

'Eh?' demanded Mal.

'Something might be there.'

Mal said: 'Might be. That's enough for me, mate!'

Binns looked up then and managed to find the delivery tube of his Camelbak. He sucked on it long and hard. The water was almost cool and it cleaned out his mouth and as it trickled down his throat he realized he had been concentrating too hard to notice his deep, deep thirst. The joy of the water was so intense that he did not know how long Mal and Dave had been shouting at him.

'Back! Go back!'

'I'm not going back.'

'You have to fucking go back to go round it,' Mal said, grabbing hold of his feet and dragging him.

'I don't want to go back!' said Binns. But he was powerless as Mal pulled him a metre back along the path he had so neatly marked.

Binns sat up then to get a better view of the mine and how he should go around it. He saw the bodies of the wounded ahead. He had felt as though he was making no progress at all but now he realized he was a little over halfway to Broom. One of Broom's legs disappeared into a pool of blood. Flies were gathering around it in swarms.

Binns remembered the golden hour. You had to get your casualties to Bastion inside the golden hour. How many hours had he already been here carving this route with his hands? And now he had lost one metre of the few he had gained.

Broom lay still. He was so quiet he might be dead.

'He's still breathing,' said Mal.

'Go left, Binman,' shouted voices. A few said: 'Try right!' Jack Binns thought of his mother's living room, how he and his mother and brother would watch TV game shows, shouting at the contestants what they should do.

Another voice cut through the others.

'Binns! Cut left and you'll link up with the path O'Sullivan cleared. Unfortunately it's marked out in peanuts. You can eat them if you like, as long as you mark it properly.'

It was the boss. Binman swung his body to the left. The brief break had reminded him how hot he was and how dangerous the work. His heart thudded as he rounded the mine. Suppose it was enormous? Suppose he hadn't swung wide enough? If it exploded under him his innards would be ripped out. There would be a few moments when you knew you were dying. He shut his eyes. Yes, for a couple of seconds, you'd know it was happening. He would feel pain and sadness and loss because he was leaving it all behind. He'd think of his mother and Ally. Then it would all be over. Death would be a sort of blackness where nothing ever happened and he wouldn't know or care. Ally would cry at his funeral and then marry someone else and have kids and grow old and he wouldn't see any of it. Because he wouldn't be there. He wouldn't exist.

He felt sick. His hands became less systematic and then they stopped.

'Binman!' Mal sounded worried. 'I know you're going to sick up. I know it.'

Binns could not tell him that he was suddenly, halfway between a casualty and the edge of a minefield, paralysed by fear. Out of the corner of his eye was the distant line of Jamie's Camelbak, with Angus's following. They were heading towards Connor at a snail's pace. Jamie paused and put his head up to drink. He looked over at Binman. His face was filthy. You could see sweat lines running through the dirt even from here. They exchanged distant glances.

'How are you moving so fucking fast, Binman?' shouted Jamie.

Binman summoned all his energy. 'Hands. And blowing.'

'Blowing. Good idea.'

Jamie lowered his body back down, his face distorted in pain. Binns remembered how this man had taken a machine gun round and just carried on working as though nothing had happened. He watched as Jamie disappeared behind some weeds. The field was full of bodies. The casualties were on their backs. And on their bellies, inching in their different directions, inching towards possible death, were Jamie, Angry, O'Sullivan and Kirk.

'Binman!' hissed Mal. 'Don't fuck up. You're doing a great job. Don't fuck up now, mate.'

Slowly, Jack Binns took his bayonet and pushed it into some soft ground ahead of him which his hands had already massaged. Nothing happened. There was no explosion. He was still alive. Heartened, he began his fast, concentrated work again.

'Sarge!' shouted Mal. 'How did you know Binman would be so good at this?'

Binns turned briefly to glance at Dave, who was standing at the edge of the minefield. You could see his helplessness. He could yell, warn, cajole. But the situation was outside his control. His face was red with the heat, the effort of yelling instructions and the extreme tension. He had even forgotten, Binns noted, before turning back to his worm's eye view of the dry earth, to take off his Bergen. Next to him stood the boss. His face was anguished.

'I watched his fingers when he was beatboxing with Streaky,' Dave called back. 'In another life, that lad would have been a concert pianist.'

Binns heard them talking about him but paid no attention. He felt as though he was inside his own hands as he scraped and prodded. He stabbed another little mine marker into the ground and crawled forward again. Mal was right behind him but he seemed a thousand miles away.

'Oh fuck, oh fuck, oh, get me out of here!' moaned Broom suddenly. The old blood was drying in the sun, new blood was still flowing, his wounds were sizzling and the swarm of flies around him was growing.

'We're nearly there!' said Mal. 'Go firm, Broom!' As if Broom was thinking of making a run for it.

'Tell Kylie I love her,' said Broom.

'You'll soon be telling her yourself, mate!'

Suddenly Connor spoke: 'It's OK . . .'

'Hello, hello, I thought you were unconscious, Ryan!' said Mal.

Connor was lying still, staring up at the sky as if it was drawing him to it. He sounded calm. 'It's OK, lads. Just leave me to die. I just want to die.'

'Fuck that,' said Mal. 'Don't go dying on us, mate.'

Angus, behind Jamie, roared: 'Fuck that, Connor, we're nearly there and we're not buggering about in all this dirt for nothing.'

'Did you get morphine in you, Ryan?' asked Jamie suspiciously, but Connor did not reply.

All four of the rescuers were closing in on the casualties now and they could have a conversation without shouting.

From the edges of the field, 2 Section was yelling.

'Didn't see him take morphine, don't think he did.'

'Come on, Ryan, don't fucking give in now, mate!'

'The boys are nearly there!'

'And if they get blown up, there's a helicopter with a winch on its way!'

'Get your morphine in, Ryan. Go on, get your morphine in!'

'No,' shouted Dave. 'If he's in and out of consciousness, he shouldn't take morphine now. Is he losing consciousness?'

Mal turned and nodded. He was close enough to see that Ryan Connor was in no state to join in this discussion. He lay, without moving, his eyes open, staring at the sky. 'It's his arm, Sarge. Still there, but not pretty.'

'Mine!' yelled Jamie suddenly.

He had frozen in his position on the ground.

'Well, I mean, it could be a big stone. Or it could—'

'Divert!' Dave called. 'Divert right.'

Angus, who had been working on widening Jamie's path, sat up and glared.

'It only might be! If it's a stone, we're wasting time diverting for fucking hours.'

The boss yelled: 'And then you'll have the rest of your life to think about how you took a short cut and lost your leg!'

Dave put his hands on his hips and his face reddened still more as he roared: 'Plus let me tell you something about these Soviet mines, Angry . . . they weren't all designed to kill a man. A lot were designed to take away what matters most. Which for some of us is our bollocks.'

There was a shocked silence. Every face turned towards the casualties. Angry stopped arguing and dragged Jamie back and Jamie continued working his way forward at a wider angle.

Binns was aware of all this as though it was a TV programme other people were watching. He was working his way through a weedy area now and the dry weeds smelled pungent. It was harder to feel the soil. He cut some down to ground level with his bayonet, being careful not to disturb the roots. But he was close to Ben Broom, close enough to see his boots through the undergrowth.

The crack of fire took him by surprise. For a moment he thought a mine had exploded. Then he realized that he had focused so hard on mines that he had forgotten that other threat: the ragheads. Maybe everyone had. He dared to take just one quick look around before he got his head down. There were rounds tearing up the ground all around him. Dust rose, weeds flew, earth shook.

From the lads at the side of the field there was a rapid, angry and intense response.

Mal, behind, said: 'Fuck it, this could set one of them off . . .'

His voice was scared. Binns felt nausea rising up through his body. He was lying in a minefield. A round could hit him. A round could set off a mine. His hands could detonate a mine. The danger was immense. Death almost certain. So he might as well get on with his work. It was better than lying here doing nothing.

He did not raise his head but laid his chin on the gritty soil, placed his hands ahead of him and took some comfort from the familiar feel of the dirt as he ran his fingers over its surface.

'Fucking hell, Binman!' Mal's voice was high-pitched, as if someone was strangling him. 'I felt something bouncing off my body armour.'

Binman escaped from his own nausea, the agony of the wounded and the terror of Mal by slipping inside his own hands. *Look, feel, prod.*

'Fucking bastards!' the lads were yelling at the Taliban as they fired. 'We fucking hate you for that!'

One round did set off an explosion. Binns was aware of it as a massive flash and plume of smoke in the corner of his eye. He did not stop. He did not want to think about it. If anyone was hurt there were plenty of others to deal with them. *Look, feel, prod.*

The firing ceased as suddenly as it had begun.

'Thank Christ for that,' said Mal. 'I just hope Ben or Connor didn't take any of it.'

Binns continued to work. He was aware that men on the side of the field were busy, moving around, but he didn't look up. He could feel his closeness to Broom now. He had gained speed when he had briefly taken over O'Sullivan's mine path, checking the ground with his fingers and replacing the peanuts with markers. Mal was eating the peanuts and was on his fifth packet.

'Don't rush it at the end!' roared Dave.

'You there already?' called Jamie, looking up.

'Binman's going for the land speed record,' Mal told him.

Binns's heart beat harder. This had been the longest, slowest, hottest fifteen metres of his life. And he was nearly there. His hands sifted soil faster, his bayonet poked energetically.

'Not too fast, mate,' said Mal behind him.

And then it happened again. Another strange clod of earth,

clinging, lumpen, reluctant to move. Like an arrow pointing downwards to draw his attention to something. This time Binns didn't blow on it, not even lightly. He knew.

'What's up?' asked Mal.

'Another one.'

He heard his own voice, faint and hoarse like an old man who'd smoked all his life.

'Oh, fuck it. We're nearly there. And it's right by Broom. How are we going to get him out with that in the way?'

Binns felt defeated. He put his face down in the dirt for the first time, feeling it crunch and crumble beneath his cheeks. He closed his eyes. He felt far from home. And home wasn't even England right now. It was twelve metres away with his mate, Streaky Bacon, and all the others.

Mal was up on his knees surveying the scene.

'OK, you'll have to go left again. Then we'll go in around Ryan's side and it might help getting Ryan out too.'

Binns was a mine-clearing machine. Mal dragged him backwards and he started looking, feeling and prodding to the left before Mal had let go of his legs.

'What's up? What you doing?' shouted Dave.

Mal knelt and explained. He turned to the others watching at the side of the field.

'What about that explosion?'

'We're OK. But it ripped a tree to shreds like lettuce, that's all,' shouted Streaky.

It took for ever to arrive at Broom. Crawling around the last mine was the longest, slowest part of the longest, slowest journey.

'You're doing well, Jamie's nowhere near Connor yet,' said Mal.

'It's not a race,' said Binns.

But they were there and Broom was still alive, although his eyes were closed and his breathing shallow. Mal began to move into position.

'Stop!' yelled Dave. 'Just be careful. You must clear the position all around the casualty before you treat him. You must do that!'

Binns and Mal could hardly stop the forward momentum of their bodies towards Broom. Dave had to yell at them three times to prevent them touching him. So Binman began to worm his way around the wounded soldier, around the blood, around the buzzing swarms of flies and around the landmine that was lying painfully close by. Mal taped it off. He was kneeling with his tourniquet and dressings at the ready, waiting to pounce on Broom's trauma kit as soon as they were clear.

He talked nonsense in a soothing voice.

'Two minutes, mate, just two minutes . . . and the man you have to thank for our speedy arrival today is one Binman, now better known as Snakeman because he crawled all the way here on his fucking belly. He was chosen for the job because he's got the smallest belly in the whole platoon. You should have seen him slithering up the minefield . . .'

Broom did not respond.

'OK,' said Binns at last, and Mal moved in to the bloody mess where Broom's leg should have been.

Binman sat still for a moment and watched Mal in action. Despite his haste, Mal's movements were smooth and experienced. He used the tourniquet with strength and wrapped dressings with a rapid professionalism. He ignored the flies swarming all around him.

The nausea that always seemed to be waiting inside Binns swept up through his body to his throat again.

'Write on his forehead that he's had his morphine, will you?' said Mal. Without looking up, he added: 'And if you puke all over the casualty, I'll cut you, Binman. I mean it.'

Binns swallowed and said shakily: 'Come on, Ben, wake up, mate. We're going to get you out of here now . . .'

There was no time for Binns to be sick because Mal had shaken out the stretcher. Broom looked small and light without his kit but when they lifted him Binns thought his arms would fall out of their sockets.

'He doesn't look this heavy!'

'Deadweight,' replied Mal shortly.

'But he's not dead!'

'Doesn't matter. Still a deadweight.'

Binns tried to take Broom's Bergen but Mal rescued him and handed him Broom's weapon instead, a rifle with UGL. They lifted the stretcher carefully and carried it gingerly around the taped mine.

Afterwards, Binns remembered the journey back down the path with the stretcher in slow motion. It could only have taken a few minutes. But with Broom's weight breaking his arms, the heat suddenly blinding and the flies following them, it felt like an hour.

Many hands were waiting at the side of the woods for the stretcher. Kirk and O'Sullivan, covered in dirt, were the first to grab it as soon as it was clear of the minefield.

'Fucking good job, you two. Fucking fantastic work, Binman.'

Gasping for breath, Binman was clapped on the back by Dave. He blushed and nodded. He looked for Streaky who was covering across the minefield. Streaky gave him a big smile of approval and a thumbs-up.

The boss was there, talking on the radio.

'We've decided to get this casualty off now,' he told Dave, 'and bring the Chinook back for Connor.'

'How far away is the HLS?'

'Five minutes,' said the boss. 'Let's get Broom moving there now.'

'What happened to the Black Hawk?' asked Dave.

The boss gave a snort of humourless laughter.

'How many men can I have to cover the stretcher team?'

'Take 2 Section, they're not doing much good here.'

Binman watched Jamie and Angus at work. They had just found another mine and were diverting once more.

Dave said quietly: 'Binman, relax now. Just sit down and drink!'

But he was too late. Binman was already walking back up the cleared mine path.

Dave yelled at him to come back but Binman knew he had to continue his work because in the time Jamie could work his way around this mine, Binns was sure he could connect his own path to Connor.

He lay down in the place Broom had lain, avoiding the huge bloodstain, now feasted on by flies. He started his work again. This time his hands hurt. He realized they were blistered. It was worse than cracked heels but he could ignore the pain if he concentrated. He rubbed his palms over the soil with a touch that now felt light and experienced, the way Mal had been with the dressings.

He realized someone was behind him.

'Don't rush, mate.' It was Mal. He had ignored Dave's warning and come back too. Binns suddenly felt happy. He did not know why. 'Just get your water tube in your mouth. And don't listen to Sarge doing his nut down there.'

Binns silently, doggedly, worked his way towards Connor. There was a lot of shrapnel from the two exploded mines here, glass and bits of metal. He twice cut his hands and Mal yelped in pain as he knelt on something sharp. But nothing could stop Binman now. As the unmoving shape of Ryan Connor got closer, he speeded up.

'Fuck it, I can't see him breathing,' said Mal.

Angus had his hands on his hips. 'Hey! You're going to get to him first!'

Jamie barely looked up. He was working like Binns, face close to the dirt, hands just in front of his face, bayonet used only for the final prods before he advanced. He said: 'We could all be too late.'

Dave had stopped yelling at Binman and Mal for returning to the minefield and wanted to know the state of the casualty.

'If he's alive it'll be mouth to mouth as soon as we get there,' called Mal grimly. 'He's in shreds. I mean, his arm. Down to the bone. And there's a lot of shrapnel just below his body armour . . . Not sure about his foot . . .'

'Clear the position before you touch him! Remember!'

But Binman had already begun his slow shuffle around Ryan on his belt buckles. He was almost all the way round and Mal was ready with equipment when Binman's long, thin fingers felt the strange thickening of the soil which told him something lay beneath. He was a few inches from Ryan Connor's shoulder.

He stopped.

'Oh fuck!' said Mal. 'Tell me no!'

'Maybe.' He blew very gently on the earth and saw buried metal.

'Don't mess with maybe,' said Jamie from ground level. He was close to them now.

'We could clear a wider position over your side,' said Binns. 'Then we can pull him over away from this mine.'

Jamie had reached Connor's feet. Binns circled back around his head. He and Jamie worked towards each other, widening the cleared area around the unmoving body when simultaneously they both found something. Two more mines, within a metre of each other. They stopped. They knew this must be the heart of the minefield.

'What a load of shite,' said Jamie. 'We can't move him this way. Or that way.'

'If I have to do mouth to mouth I could just about kneel over there . . .' said Mal. He reached across from his safe spot and found Ryan Connor's wrist. He felt a very faint pulse.

'He's alive!' he shouted down the field. 'Just!'

'You're not doing anything to him six inches away from an un-exploded mine, mate,' said Jamie. 'All we can do is get him onto a stretcher and out of here. Even that's going to be fucking dangerous.'

'There isn't room for four people,' said Binman. He was staring at the bloody mess which was Ryan Connor's body. He remembered how Ryan had flown out from Bastion with him and Streaky and how they had arrived in the FOB and everyone had been looking at the colour of Connor's hair for some reason Binman had never discovered. Ryan's hair didn't look so red now that it was surrounded by the surreal red of his own blood.

'There's not even room for two,' said Jamie. 'Especially if one of them's Angus.'

'I can pick Connor up by myself,' said Angus.

'Yeah, gorilla, but can you pick him up without putting any weight on the ground there, or here, or here?'

'Yeah, I can do it,' said Angus.

'You can't,' Binns told him. 'We didn't come all this way for you and Connor to get blown up.' He spoke as though he had travelled a hundred miles.

Jamie said: 'Two of us can probably do it. We lift him straight out of this area and onto a stretcher over there.'

Binman knew one thing. He would not be lifting Connor.

'I'll take his Bergen,' he said. He was starting to shake. Four men and a casualty were standing or lying within a metre of three mines they knew about and maybe more they didn't. He felt as though all his nerve endings were shredded, like the tree Streaky said had turned into lettuce. Maybe he'd used up all his good luck and there was none left for the near impossible extraction of Ryan Connor.

'We'll have to lift him with his kit on, too fiddly to get it off here,' said Jamie.

Mal and Jamie discussed which of them would help Angus pick up Connor. Finally they agreed that Jamie was in a better position.

Mal took Connor's gimpy. Binman followed him back along the mine path.

Binman was aware of all the faces looking at him from the woods as he neared. Embarrassingly, inexplicably, he wanted to cry. But their eyes were drawn away from him. Now that Binns and Bilaal had cleared, Jamie and Angus were attempting to lift the heavy body of Connor and remove it with surgical precision.

'What the hell is going on?' Dave asked Mal as soon as he and Binman reached the edge of the field.

'Three mines. Two on one side and the other by his left shoulder. No room to get his Bergen off, no room for a stretcher. So they're lifting him out and—'

'No!' yelled Dave up the minefield. 'Christ, no, no, no! Are you fucking crazy? Stop right now!'

Binman had just stepped into the woods when the flash of an explosion, bright enough for him to see it without turning around, lit up the world.

Chapter Thirty-seven

WHEN THE PHONE RANG, JENNY GRABBED IT INSTINCTIVELY AND clasped it to her ear. She moved instantly from a dream to awake. She recognized the thickness of the dark in the room: it was the middle of the night. The house was still. There was only one person who would ring at her at this hour.

'Dave? Dave!'

'Jenny. Is Agnieszka.'

There was a pause while the name registered. Agnieszka almost never called. At any time. Let alone the middle of the night.

'Agnieszka! Christ, what's happened?'

She heard a sob at the end of the phone. Then Agnieszka replied. But her English had disintegrated. She spoke too loudly, with the emphasis on the wrong words, the vowel sounds muddled.

'What, Agnieszka? What? I can't understand you . . .'

'Something not nice happen!'

'But . . . what?'

'I get text message from I don't know who.'

'From a stranger?'

'Yes.'

Jenny was relieved that the problem was so trivial. Then she began to feel angry. Agnieszka had woken her up at . . . she glanced at the clock . . . 2 a.m. To tell her about some text message.

'Well, take no notice, there are shedloads of crazy people out there, Agnieszka. They send random messages to strangers.'

'No, no, no. This one know me.'

'Oh. So what does it say?'

'It say . . .' Agnieszka started to cry. Her words were choked by tears. Jenny had to ask her to read it three times. Finally on the fourth try, she understood.

'It say: Jamie is dead.'

Jenny was shocked into silence. Her head was filled by the sound of Agnieszka's sobs.

'Christ,' she said at last. 'You've no idea who sent this? Did it come from . . . how could it have come from . . . well, none of our boys at the FOB have mobiles, do they?'

Agnieszka was wailing now. Eventually Jenny understood her words.

'It come from Jamie's number!'

Jenny pulled her swollen body upright on the bed so she could concentrate more easily. She bent her legs and the bump banged against them.

'Jamie's phone? Did he leave it behind in the UK?'

'No!'

'But if he took it to Afghanistan he would have handed it in at Bastion. Everyone does.'

Only a high-pitched wail could escape through Agnieszka's tears. Finally she spoke.

'Jenny, don't tell Dave. Please, please don't tell Dave. Don't tell anyone. Promise.'

She sighed into the darkness. 'All right.'

'Jamie give in his phone with other boys. But he have another, I give Jamie another little phone. My old one, to keep private. Sometimes he text me.'

Jenny felt her body tense.

'So . . . Jamie's been texting you.'

'Listen, he not text army secrets. Just stuff for me, private words.'

Probably every wife in the camp hated the confiscation of their husband's mobile in Afghanistan. Maybe some had argued. Probably a few had suggested taking a secret phone. But the men all knew that using a mobile in that hostile world was opening yourself and your mates up to the Taliban. And surely any wife would have thought her husband's safety was more important than getting a few text messages? Except Agnieszka.

'He never say what they doing or where or anything like that. Just personal things.'

So maybe I'm an idiot, Jenny thought. Maybe all the other wives had given their husbands a secret phone and maybe they all received secret, loving texts. All except the sergeant's wife. Who barely got a call in two weeks, and then it was so rushed it was meaningless. Even though the sergeant's wife was about to have a baby.

But Agnieszka was crying enough for both of them, with huge sobs. Jenny knew what it was like when the sobs felt bigger than you were.

She said: 'So . . . what do you think has happened?'

'I scared maybe Taliban take Jamie. And maybe kill him. And take mobile and use to text me.' Her words ended on a wail of despair.

'OK,' said Jenny briskly. Her brain, which had not been making its usual quick connections recently, suddenly became an ordered, logical entity again, like one of Vicky's toys where everything snaps into place.

'Does he really carry the mobile around with him? When he leaves the FOB?'

'I think he leave at base . . . except maybe they go on operation for a few days.'

'Well Dave rang me a few hours ago. Which would be early morning in Afghanistan . . .'

'He say they leave base?'

'Well of course not, Agnieszka, he doesn't say that kind of thing. And there's no way Dave could have phoned and sounded normal if anything had happened to Jamie.'

But there had been a sense of bustle and urgency in the phone call which suggested they were going somewhere. Now she looked back, the call felt like something which had been slotted in because he might not have another chance to ring her again soon. She bit her lip.

'Maybe they leave base and something terrible happen . . .'

Jenny thought hard. 'Look, I'll try Adi. If anything's happened she'll know, she always knows everything.'

'But,' breathed Agnieszka, 'you not tell! About secret mobile!'

'No. But I can't call her for a few hours. She gets up early, I'll ring after seven.'

'After seven o'clock!'

Agnieszka sounded stricken.

'Well, I can't call her at two in the morning!'

'But . . . Jamie!'

Jenny sighed. She imagined her own panic if she had received such a message about Dave.

'OK, OK, I'll phone her now.'

'What will you say?'

'I'm not sure yet. I'll call you back.'

'You don't mention secret mobile?'

'No, no.'

It was a while before Adi answered the phone. Her voice was clogged by sleep. For a few moments she did not understand who was calling her.

'Oh, Jenny, Jenny, I was having such a dream. I was in Fiji . . . Honey, is it the baby? Is it coming? Do you need me?'

'No, it's nothing to do with the baby. Adi, I feel terrible calling you in the night . . .'

'Listen, I know you would only call me at this time with a problem so tell Adi what it is.'

Her voice was settling down into its usual rhythms. It was losing its sleep rust.

'There is a problem. But it's not mine. Adi, have you heard from Sol lately?'

'Not for a few days, darling. And I don't think many people heard yesterday because they closed the phones for a while.'

'Oh, God!'

The phones were shut down for a death or serious casualty. If anyone in any FOB anywhere was killed, the men couldn't call out until relatives had been informed.

'Something could have happened on the other side of Helmand, our boys wouldn't even know about it.'

'Dave rang me at about ten thirty.'

'So they reopened the phones. Did he say why they closed them?'

'No . . . nothing.'

'He called you and everything's all right?'

272

'I think everything was all right then. They might have been leaving the base.'

'Honey, I don't understand, what's going on with you?'

'Agnieszka's worried about Jamie.'

There was a silence.

'She rang you in the night to tell you?'

'She rang me in a terrible state. She thinks he's dead.'

'But why?'

Jenny wavered. She was about to lie to her friend. And it wasn't even her own lie. It was Agnieszka's lie. She felt resentful. Why should she keep Agnieszka's secrets? Then she remembered why: because she had promised she would.

'It's some kind of special day for them, an anniversary or something, and he swore he'd phone. And he didn't.'

'But she can't expect him to keep a promise like that, it's impossible. The phones could be broken or he might be busy or outside the FOB . . .'

'She's so upset.'

Adi began to sound annoyed: 'And she's got you upset too, and for no good reason. Why isn't she ringing the Welfare people with her worries instead of someone who's about to have a baby? Or better still, don't ring anyone. She should just wait.'

'You're right. But it's not very nice waiting for bad news.'

'It's not very nice getting bad news. But she hasn't.'

'No.'

'Tell her to stop worrying.'

'OK, Adi.'

'Listen, honey, we could all lie alone in our beds worrying all night and phoning our friends so they worry too. But we don't let ourselves. Do we?'

Adi was right, as usual. There were a lot of things you dared not let yourself think about. And you certainly wouldn't let your friends start thinking those things either.

'OK. Thanks, Adi. Sorry I woke you.'

'And don't you worry now, not about nothing! You get rest like the doctor said.'

Jenny rang Agnieszka back. The line was engaged. Who was Agnieszka calling now? She waited and redialled. Still busy. Her eyes closed. A huge weariness engulfed her. Maybe Agnieszka's phone was engaged because Jamie was calling at last. Or maybe she was talking to Welfare. Or to that man. Jenny had promised Dave she would tell no one about the man she'd seen with Agnieszka. And now she had promised Agnieszka that she would tell no one, not even Dave, about the illicit mobile. Also, she had lied to Adi. Her life was beginning to feel full of secrets and they weren't even her secrets, they were Agnieszka's.

Agnieszka waited for Jenny to phone back. The minutes ticked past. Was Jenny still talking to Adi? Was she phoning other people? Had she fallen asleep?

Her anxiety was like a massive machine waiting to run her over. Her nerves throbbed as she listened to the silence, listened for a car stopping outside. Then the doorbell. Then the Families Officer. Standing on the doorstep with news that would crush her like a great juggernaut.

Jamie dead. Jamie not there any more. Jamie's body in a big, dark bag and then a wooden box, buried in the cold ground. Jamie icy and unfeeling, Jamie without love or warmth or life inside him. Jamie unable to put his arms around her or hold Luke. Had all his absences been a way of preparing her for this final, awful absence? She wanted to howl with pain, howl like a wolf.

Still no phone, no car. The silence assumed huge proportions of its own as she waited for it to end. It seemed to get bigger as it went on and on, like a sound getting louder. Except it was silence. She was almost grateful when Luke started to whine. She went in to him. His cot was on wheels. She rocked it over a bump in the rug she had made by stuffing towels under it and he went back to sleep. The unbearable silence resumed.

If only there was someone. But there was only Jamie and he was out there. Last night there had been a TV programme about the Arctic and how it was melting. Instead of being shocked by this, Agnieszka had been horrified by its kilometres of white emptiness. The wasteland had reminded her of her own life. A polar bear floating on a small iceberg through freezing seas, far from other polar bears or any life at all, had made her weep with sad recognition.

Then she had an idea.

She reached for the phone.

After a few rings, a sleepy voice answered.

'Yes?'

'Hello . . .' She spoke quietly.

The voice was surprised. It was uncertain. And it was wide awake.

'Hello?'

'Who is this?'

But she could tell he knew who it was. He was just scared to hope he was right.

'It me.'

'Aggie?'

'Yes.'

'Aggie!'

Surprise. Pleasure. Then a realization that this was around 2 a.m.

'Aggie, are you all right?'

'Help me, Darrel. You always fix everything. So now I ask for help.'

'Aggie, I'll fix anything I can. What's happened?'

'Oh, God, something so awful I can't stand it.'

'Tell me.'

'I sorry to ring in night.'

'Well, I wasn't busy. I was only sleeping.'

'I don't know what to do . . .'

'Tell me, Aggie.'

It was a relief to tell him. The call to Jenny had been awkward, full of guilt and confession. And she had sensed Jenny's disapproval. Now she was talking to someone who really cared about her, who could share her concern and understand it.

'Listen, when my husband go to Afghanistan he take a secret little telephone . . .'

She finished the story, her throat catching on the words *Jamie is dead.*

'Darrel? You still there?'

'Yes, Aggie. I'm thinking. The problem is that you need to find out whether the message could be true. Without telling anyone where it came from.'

'Darrel, that exactly right. Exactly. You understand.'

This was different from the hysteria of her call to Jenny. This was a more quiet desperation.

'OK, is there some sort of place you army wives go for help? Supposing something happened to Luke and you had to contact your husband urgently . . . ?'

'I go to Families Officer.'

'You've got a choice, Ags. Either you sweat it out and wait. Because if he's really dead they'll come and tell you soon enough. Or you go to this Families Officer and say you got a text, you don't know who from or where from, it was anonymous. You say you immediately erased it from your phone but it's been worrying you ever since.'

Darrel was right. Either she waited or she contacted the Families Officer with every detail of the story except the one she didn't want him to hear.

'But, for what it's worth . . . well, I don't think your husband's dead. It sounds to me like some of his mates have found his mobile and they're trying to teach him a lesson.'

'No one teach such nasty lesson.'

'There are enough nasty people around. I don't think he's dead.'

She felt as though someone had put their arms around her in a warm embrace. Darrel, who fixed things, was fixing this.

'Ags, can you contact this person, this Families Officer, in the middle of the night?'

'Um . . . maybe there's a number. But maybe I don't contact. Maybe I wait until morning.'

'Can you stand it?'

'Yes. In morning I go to office.'

'That's my suggestion.'

'Oh, Darrel, talk to me a little while.'

She didn't want to put the phone down and hear the silence again.

'No, you talk to me, Aggie. Go on. Tell me what you've been doing since we last met. Any more drawing?'

She snuggled down under the duvet and talked. It felt intimate. Her voice became soft. He even made her laugh. There were whole minutes at a time when she was able to forget the big, black abyss that had opened up in her life tonight. They talked for two hours and at the end of their talk she was so tired that she slept.

Chapter Thirty-eight

DAVE SCREAMED AT JAMIE AND ANGUS NOT TO LIFT THE CASUALTY BUT it was already too late. He could see that Jamie, standing at Connor's head, had taken the weight and was amazed by it. People always were. You could double a man's weight when he was injured or dead. And then there was his Bergen too. Bad enough without fucking mines every six inches.

He could barely watch Jamie's attempts not to stagger. Mal had marked the path more clearly with tape and once the body was up the pair had to exit in a straight line and then swing sharply to the left on a tight arc to reach the stretcher.

They had laid it out in the safe area which had been cleared around Broom. Even from here you could see a black mass of something there which might be leg or it might be flies or maybe both.

Jamie stayed firm, but until he could get his arms more securely under Connor's shoulders, his body was bent at a weird angle to compensate for his poor grip.

Dave's hand was on his forehead as he watched, as though he had received a blow to the head or was trying to ward one off. There was a tense silence all around the clearing. Binns and Mal were just stepping off the minefield and into the woods, Binns looking wretched. And, suddenly, the enemy opened fire.

Two shots from an AK47 ripped into the silence, cracking open the tension like an eggshell. Within a moment Finn's gimpy was chattering back, and so were at least ten rifles. Streaky was sure he saw the shadow of a man in the distant trees fall. He saw it because the field and the trees and the weeds and the lone figures at the centre of the clearing lit up suddenly like a stage.

The explosions were a series of lightning strikes ripping out of the ground and across the field. Everyone felt the hot breath on their faces. The men from 3 Section along the more distant edges received the explosions like a large fist punching them, a few felt the patter of shrapnel on their helmets or the searing rip of it on their exposed skin. Others received the debris of stones and branches as the trees that protected them were torn. And in the centre of the field the two soldiers, their casualty hanging between them, were turned to stone.

The two watched as one mine detonated and set off another and they waited helplessly for the string of explosions to reach them. No one, not even Dave, could do anything but watch as shrapnel was thrown into the air and plumes of black smoke shot up. It was a volcano and they were powerless against its might.

The first detonation had been at the far end of the field but, as each mine set off those around it, the explosions moved closer. The rational side of Dave had so far counted five explosions, but there had probably been more than ten mines involved. And then, when the end of the field was a smoking, burning, dusty hell, the detonation stopped.

Everyone waited for the next explosion. They were motionless, as though even breathing too heavily could detonate a mine. And then, in silence, Jamie and Angus began to continue their pains-taking extraction towards the stretcher. It took a moment for Dave to see that Angus's arm was bright red.

'Christ, what's happened to you, McCall?' he yelled.

Angus did not respond. Neither he nor Jamie looked up. They were near the stretcher now and the safe area.

'He's been hit . . .' said Mal, walking back up the mine path again to where Angus and Jamie were settling Connor on the stretcher.

Dave knew it was useless to stop him. The boss tried, without success.

'Mr Angry . . .' Mal said from a distance. There was no room for a third person inside the tape.

'Fuck off.'

'You're wounded.'

278

Angus was shaking. 'Just fuck off, Mal.'

'We can get his Bergen off now. You can take it,' said Jamie.

He was shaking too.

'Angus, for Chrissake let me see the arm.'

'No.'

Blood was dripping from it now. Part of the sleeve was missing.

'Morphine!' said Mal.

'Not fucking likely,' said Angus. 'I don't want to go back to Bastion.'

'Let me carry Connor, then. You're a danger to everyone like that,' said Mal. And, amazingly, Angry moved aside for him and then stumbled off, carrying Connor's Bergen, down the track.

Mal immediately bent over Connor.

'Well?' bawled Dave.

'Still alive!'

'Don't do medic stuff, the Chinook's landing soon,' yelled Dave. Wait for a Black Hawk and you could wait until Christmas.

'It's landing in five minutes!' called the boss.

Mal and Jamie picked up the stretcher and began the slow, hot, march down the field for the last time.

'Angry's taken a hit there,' Mal said to Jamie.

'So have I.'

'You what?'

'I've been hit.'

'Where?'

'Ribs. I'm OK. It bounced off my body armour, just like last time. But I can feel it. Just like last time.'

'Holy shit,' said Mal.

'It's OK. It was probably only an AK47 this time,' said Jamie. But his voice sounded weak and the second he was relieved of the stretcher by 2 Section he sat down on the hard woodland floor and put his head in his hands.

Angus's arm was already being treated.

'Looks as if you've been in a knife fight,' said McKinley.

'Did I take a round?' asked Angus.

'I think you took shrapnel but it's too full of shit to tell now.'

Blood was seeping through faster than McKinley could dress the wound.

279

'I won't do more because you'll be on a Chinook in a few minutes.'

'I won't!' roared Angus.

'You will, McCall,' said Dave.

'Sarge . . .'

'McCall, you're going,' said the boss.

'But the medics here can see to me, sir!'

'They're up at the front nearer the fighting.'

'I am not going nowhere, I'm staying with my mates. And don't try giving me fucking morphine when I'm not looking,' muttered Angus.

'Wouldn't dream of it, mate,' said McKinley.

'By the way, McCall,' said Dave. 'Fucking well done, mate.'

The platoon was starting to move towards the helicopter landing site. The men who had gone with Broom led the way.

Corporal Baker had wanted to carry Connor's stretcher. He stumbled along tearfully with the bloody and near-lifeless rifleman.

'Need an extra hand that end, Aaron?' asked Sol kindly. He felt bad enough but he knew how much worse he would be feeling if his section had been the one caught in the minefield. He remembered how Aaron Baker had radioed excitedly to say he wanted to outflank the flipflops. Now he would spend the rest of his life wishing he hadn't.

'I can do it,' said Aaron Baker.

Jamie was walking slowly towards the back of the section with Binns. They did not speak but they were bound together by the enormity of their experience on the minefield.

'Dermott, you all right?' asked Dave.

'I'm OK. I think I'm just bruised.'

Dave surveyed the filthy faces and bodies of Jamie and Binman.

'That was good work under a lot of pressure, you two,' he said. 'Very good, both of you. Well done, Binns.'

Jamie nodded and glanced at Binman and then smiled at him. There was both exhaustion and triumph on his dirty face. The sprog had finally done something right.

They reached the field where the Chinook was due to land. So did everyone else. CSM Kila, medics, EOD, engineers and 2 Platoon were all assembling.

'Too fucking late,' Dave told them. 'It's all over.'

He and Iain Kila pulled the wounded off to one side with the medics. As well as Connor and Angus there were three members of 3 Section with shrapnel wounds, plus Jamie with bruising from a round as well as seriously cut hands. Binns was surprised to find that the skin all over his own palms was sliced as though by razors. As soon as he saw them, they started to hurt.

Connor was loaded first while the boss and CSM Kila argued with Angus.

'I do not need to go anywhere!' Angus was yelling.

'You won't be able to fight. You'll just be a liability if we have to stretcher you out later,' said the boss.

'I can fight!' roared Angus.

CSM Kila's face turned into a mask of anger.

'Get on the fucking Chinook,' he said. 'You've got a deep wound there and in the time you've wasted arguing, Ryan Connor could be fucking dying.'

Angus grimaced and climbed on board the helicopter.

'Anyone else?' roared Kila.

'This shrapnel wound should go, what about you, Jamie?'

'I feel fine.'

'OK, we can cope with everything else here,' said the medic, shoving a bloodied face from 3 Section forward.

The helicopter took off instantly. Everyone watched it go. There was silence as its rotors disappeared into the distance.

'Right,' said Dave to the others. 'Let's get on with what we came here to do.'

Some lads looked surprised. A few had forgotten they were supposed to be supporting the Paras.

'To be honest, there isn't much left to do,' said Boss Weeks. 'The Paras have just about completed the op. The Taliban put up some big opposition at the start and then fled. We're picking them up in the area but there hasn't been much more than a few skirmishes.'

'I thought that place was a choggie training school,' said Dave.

The boss shrugged.

'They didn't make much attempt to defend it. In fact, it was empty except for goats and women and old folk. So either we were misinformed or they knew we were coming.'

'Oh, shit, we've missed the action,' groaned a few people. 'We've been stuck out here all day.'

'We had enough action,' said Dave.

'And we've only been stuck for an hour,' said the boss.

Even Dave couldn't believe that.

'An hour? It felt like . . .'

The boss looked at his watch.

'It took you just one hour to get those two men off the minefield. An amazing achievement, which has saved their lives.'

'Fucking incredible,' said CSM Kila. 'You should be proud of this platoon.'

'I'll be honest,' said Dave. 'It was the worst hour of my life.'

Chapter Thirty-nine

THE WIVES, THE REAR PARTY, THE SUPPORT STAFF, EVERYONE IN THE camp was talking about casualties in 1 Platoon. Something had happened in Afghanistan while England slept and rumours ran around the barracks and the houses, along the telephone lines and through cyberspace.

Jenny was sure she knew the truth because Adi had phoned her first thing to tell her.

'Something did happen last night, Agnieszka was right about that. But Jamie's OK.'

'Who, then?'

'Two lads, Ben Broom and Ryan Connor. In our platoon but not in Sol's section.'

'I don't know them.'

'Broom has a girlfriend who works at the day nursery.'

'Kylie! Her boyfriend's in Dave's platoon and his name's Ben!'

'Well apparently he's going to survive. But the other one is touch and go. There are more injuries but they're patching them up at Bastion.'

Jenny was surprised to find Kylie at work today when she took Vicky in. She was a pretty, noisy girl who usually wore bright colours and bright lipstick.

'They crossed a minefield,' she said. 'Ben's going to live. But he's lost his leg below the knee.'

Vicky squirmed in Jenny's arms, the baby kicked and Jenny felt ready to cry.

'Kylie, I'm really sorry.'

'It isn't such a big relationship for me, you know,' said Kylie. 'But now he's injured everyone thinks I'll stick by him. I suppose I have to for a while. His parents are wailing all over me like I'm their daughter-in-law. But it probably wouldn't have lasted long anyway.'

'You've got to lead your own life,' Jenny heard herself saying as she put Vicky down. Kylie leaned closer.

'And I'll tell you something else. I might not even be able to look at it. I mean, the place where the leg was.' She pulled a disgusted face. 'That kind of thing grosses me out.'

'You should talk to Leanne Buckle,' said Jenny.

'But she's married to Steve. I'm not even living with Ben and we haven't been going out that long.'

When she got back from the nursery, Trish made Jenny sit down with a cup of tea in front of the television.

'Oh, Mum, I never watch daytime TV, I don't have time.'

'Feet up!' said Trish. 'You look as if you haven't had a wink of sleep for two days.'

This was almost true. At first the programme, a chat show, made her feel relaxed and sleepy. But memories of last night intruded. Who had sent that text message to Agnieszka? She had rung Agnieszka again this morning. Adi had already called her with the news and when Jenny rang Agnieszka had been in a hurry. She certainly had not wanted to talk about the message.

Jenny was sure it had come from the Taliban. Dave had explained before he left that the enemy intercepted signals and then sent their own messages. It hadn't meant anything then but now Jenny understood. The Taliban had picked up Jamie's loving texts to Agnieszka and calculated how they could hurt her. Coincidentally, they had sent their own text when Jamie really was in danger. But the sender didn't know that. He was a man far away who had never met Agnieszka but knew only one thing about her: that he hated her because she was loved by a British soldier. He hated her enough to send a message that would cause alarm and misery. And the faceless man had achieved his aim. The Taliban had penetrated Agnieszka's house, then Jenny's and then Adi's in a new, shocking, personal way.

'I have to go out,' she told her mother.

'Why?'

'There's someone round the corner I must talk to.'

'Just relax, for heaven's sake.'

'I can't relax until I've spoken to her.'

'Until you've put your feet up, you're not going anywhere, my girl,' said Trish sternly. Jenny felt fifteen again. She giggled.

'I'm not going clubbing to eye up Leroy Tanner,' she said.

Trish looked knowing. 'I always said that boy would end up in jail and I was right, wasn't I? I can't think what you saw him in.'

Jenny knew exactly what she had seen in Leroy Tanner but, eight months' pregnant with her second child, this wasn't the time to think about it.

She got up, slowly.

'I'm only going around the corner, Mum, and I'll only be five minutes.'

Before Trish could argue, the phone rang and Jenny, who was passing it, picked up the receiver.

'Hi,' said a distant, weary voice. 'Hi, darling.'

'Dave!'

'Managed to get the phone again.'

'You only rang last night!'

'Well, it was this morning for me and I was in a hurry. And I didn't tell you that I love you.'

She could hear tiredness and pain in his voice.

'I love you too. And I know about the minefield. Everyone in camp knows. Ben Broom and Ryan Connor, right?'

'I can't talk about it.' He sounded more vulnerable than she had ever heard him. 'Jen, I miss you.' She realized that she could not imagine, know or even understand what crossing a minefield meant. The gulf between them had nothing to do with miles. It was a gulf of understanding. And Dave knew it too.

'Sweetheart . . .'

'I can't talk about it, Jen.'

'I know. Is Jamie OK?'

'Yes, but he's definitely used up another life. Why?'

'Agnieszka was worried.'

'Why?'

'Oh, she didn't hear from him when she expected to, that's all.'
Another lie. And this time to Dave.

'Jamie was bruised. Couple more lads went to Bastion with
shrapnel wounds but they're OK. They'll all be back in a few
days.'

Jenny told him what Ben Broom's girlfriend had said. Dave
thought grimly of Broom, holding the satellite phone: *I have to
keep phoning my bird, Sarge, or she might fly.* Nothing had made
her fly faster than a missing leg.

'How does Leanne feel about Steve's leg?' he asked. 'Does she
think it's disgusting too?'

'She's getting used to it. She was scared they'd never have sex
again.'

'And have they?'

'I doubt it. He's only been home for that one weekend and he
slept downstairs and was a real shit to her. She was so miserable
that a BLESMA welfare officer came to see her.'

'Steve wouldn't play the victim and let her run around him, eh?
I'll give her a call.'

'With your minutes?' asked Jenny swiftly.

'What?'

'How many of your phone minutes have you used up calling
Leanne?'

'Don't you want me to phone Leanne? Because I won't if you
don't. I just—'

'Oh, love, of course I want you to phone her. I'm so bloody glad
I'm married to a bloke who does that sort of thing. I just feel as
though you don't care how many of our minutes you give to other
people. They're precious to me. And you act like they don't mean
anything to you.'

'They're not just our minutes. I call my mum too!' Although not
very often.

'OK, fine, they're your minutes and you can do what you like
with them,' she snapped.

So here we go again. She couldn't stop herself. She wanted him
to call more often but what did he get when he phoned? Sniper fire.

'Come on, Jen,' he said softly.

'I miss you so much!' Her voice began to dissolve. 'And I meant everything I said about you leaving the army. I wish you'd give it some serious thought.'

'I have. And I've decided I should wait until I've got my degree. I'll be a lot more employable then.'

'How long will that take?'

'Ummm . . . well as soon as I get back I'll step up my hours.'

'What's the soonest you could finish?'

'Another few years, probably . . .'

'Dave! I can't wait that long.'

'Those years will flash by. With two young children your hands will be so full that—'

'They'll flash by without you! That's the point! I want to bring up two young children with you, not with a voice on the phone who's always away training or fighting or crossing minefields!'

'When we get back from this tour, I might be at home for two whole years.'

'I've heard that one before.'

'Jenny. Love. I don't need this pressure. Not now. I didn't ring you because I want another battle.'

The tone of his voice said that all day, every day he had to be strong. He had to watch his men, correct them, guide them and protect them, he had to make decisions that were fair but firm and the greater the danger, the fiercer the contact, the harder the pressure, then the stronger he had to be. He couldn't afford to weaken. Ever. Even when he was watching eight of his men in a minefield.

Jenny heard his tone and her anger evaporated.

'Oh, darling. I'm sorry. I just want you out of there. I don't want to add to the pressure.'

'I'm already under a lot, Jen.'

She was quick. 'Are you in some kind of trouble?'

'Maybe.'

'Because you let your men cross a minefield?'

He was indignant. 'No! For fuck's sake!'

'Well, why, then?'

'Because of something that happened long before today. Soon after we arrived.'

'Did anyone die?'

287

'Not any of our men.'

'You mean . . . a Tali died?'

'Yup.'

'And you're in trouble?'

'They're interviewing me about it this evening. I thought they might wait a bit. Since some of us have had a bad day. But they can't.'

'Oh, Dave! Because you killed the enemy!'

'Yup.'

'That's ridiculous!'

'I think so.'

'Whatever you did, I know it was right.' Her anger was redirected now, away from him and onto the army.

'Thanks, love.'

'I'll bet the Taliban don't start accusing each other of killing the enemy. I'll bet they wouldn't hesitate to kill you under any circumstances.'

'That's why it's fucking ludicrous.'

'But . . .' She was thinking now. 'Maybe they'll throw you out of the army for this. That would make the decision for you!'

'Don't say that, Jen. You don't want me court-martialled, do you?'

It was unbearable to hear him so hurt.

'Christ, no,' she said truthfully. 'They won't, will they?'

'They could.'

When the call was over she felt bereft. She loved him. But he had so much to deal with that she could not ask him to share her burdens too. He loved her. And she was on her own.

Chapter Forty

AGNIESZKA WAS WOKEN BY LUKE AND THE PHONE AT THE SAME
time. She had been in such a deep sleep that for a moment she
wasn't sure which to grab.

'Hallo?'

'Agnieszka, it's Adi. I'll be quick, I can hear Luke calling for you.
I rang because Jenny said you were worried. Well, something did
happen in the night. Everyone's talking about it. I think our boys
found some landmines or something. There are casualties but
nothing serious in 1 Section.'

'Jamie all right?'

'Fine. So stop worrying.'

But she already done that. Somehow Darrel had managed to
persuade her that everything was all right.

Agnieszka looked at the time and started to hurry. She had
agreed to meet Darrel for coffee this morning and first she had to
sort out Luke and herself, then put on her makeup. Darrel had
wanted to take her for lunch, he said, but he couldn't get away
from the garage then so he would sneak out for a coffee instead.

It was one of Luke's angry, spiky mornings, when he responded
to even her lightest touch as though her hands were covered with
barbed wire. Finally, with relief, she left him to cry so that she could
get ready. She peered in the mirror at her tired face then reached for
her makeup bag. She might not be able to repair the dishwasher,
TV, car or gutter but she could certainly fix her face.

Of course, there was no reason she needed to look especially good for Darrel. But the pots and brushes and tubes and pads of colour pleased her. Making up was a form of painting. She used shading to make subtle contours pronounced and with the right brushwork around her eyes they could look huge.

She glanced at her watch. She was going to be late. You couldn't hurry makeup.

The phone rang and her steady hand, applying eyeliner, wobbled. She swore in Polish, reminded herself to Hail Mary, hesitated. And then answered.

'Morning, Agnieszka, it's Jenny.'

If only she hadn't picked up the phone. If only she hadn't called Jenny last night. She dealt with her as quickly as she could and then got back to her eyeliner. She was going to be late and Darrel only had thirty minutes.

The phone rang again. She glanced anxiously at her watch. She almost didn't answer.

'Hello?'

'It's me, Niez.'

'Jamie!' She was both pleased and apprehensive. She hoped it wasn't going to be one of those long calls.

'I . . . I've been hit again.'

'Hit? Who hit you?'

'Taliban. Fired at me. It bounced off. I'm just bruised.'

'It bounce off!'

'Off my body armour.'

'Oh, God, Jamie.' She remembered the Hail Mary she had just promised to do. And now, for a bullet bouncing off body armour, she would offer many more.

'It's OK, Niez. I'm OK. There's just a few moments after it first happens when it seems like you're going to die. That's when I thought about you and Luke. Everything around me got sort of brighter. It was strange. The trees and the earth and people's blood, whatever you're looking at gets really intense. So did the smells. Maybe that was because I thought I was leaving it all behind. And I wanted you to be in my mind when I died so I thought about your face and it was so, so beautiful . . .'

She had never heard him talk like this before.

'Jamie . . . you a little bit shocked?'

'The medic says I'm fine.'

She wanted to ask him about the phone message, demand to know who might have found the cellphone and used it to text her so cruelly. But these satellite calls were monitored. The army actually listened when husbands phoned their wives. She could say nothing.

'It happened before. I got hit before. And it was worse because it was a machine-gun round. It hit my back, just below the neck. I was on top, looking into some woods. After I felt it, I waited to die and the trees were amazing. Beautiful. I can't explain it. I'm not explaining it very well, am I, Niez?'

She felt frantic. This was turning into one of Jamie's long, thoughtful calls. Sometimes he talked and talked and she stopped trying to understand him and just let his voice wash over her.

But there was no time now. Holding the phone with her left hand, she was trying to apply mascara with her right. If she left any later than this there was almost no point in going: Darrel's break would be over.

'You explain very well, darling. You sure you OK? Everyone there think you OK?'

'Babe, I don't talk to the other lads this way. Or they'd probably think I'm barking. But you understand – don't you, Niez?'

'I think so, darling.'

'You always understand me. That's one reason I love you so much.'

She took a deep breath. 'Darling, I have my hair cut today.'

'Oh, no! Why? Don't do that!'

'Just a trim. You won't see any different when you get back.'

'All right. A centimetre, no more.'

'Darling, I have to go now, to hairdresser.'

'Oh.' Resignation, disappointment, maybe some pain. Because he had been speaking to her from his heart when she had been worrying about her hair appointment. 'I could tell you were in a bit of a hurry.'

She said as many Hail Marys in the car as she could between the camp and the city. But she knew that for what she had just done to Jamie she could never say enough.

When they arrived it turned out to be market day. Stalls and people with shopping bags covered the central parking area. She found another car park and then another. Full. And people were queuing for spaces.

Finally she phoned Darrel. She was so exasperated with the traffic, the people, the screams from the back seat that she wanted to cry herself, except that it would ruin her makeup.

'We'll have coffee at the White Lion. You can park there, at the back. See you in ten minutes.'

Darrel really could fix anything.

But when she got to the White Lion, Luke was still screaming. His face was red and wet, his huge mouth bawled. She rocked the buggy helplessly. You couldn't take a screaming baby into a quiet hotel. Everything, including Jamie's call and Luke's shrieks, the traffic and the market stalls, was conspiring to sabotage her meeting with Darrel.

'All right?' said Darrel, squeezing between two cars to reach her. He was as casual as if they had last seen each other yesterday, instead of when they had rowed, weeks ago.

She smiled at him. She wanted to stare. In her thoughts there had been a handsome, lean-faced man. Here was someone much more ordinary, wearing a shirt she did not particularly like. What was she doing here, by this hotel in this city with this man? She tried to fit the stranger who stood grinning before her into the frame her memory had woven for him.

He gave her a light kiss on the cheek.

'I can't come inside when Luke does screaming.'

'Can I pick him up?'

Agnieszka shook her head.

'Sometimes it make him worse.'

'Can I try?'

She shrugged.

Darrel reached into the buggy and with expert fingers undid the safety harness. Because he had three children of his own, she thought.

He lifted Luke out and the child arched his back and bellowed, his face a violent beetroot colour. It was impossible to talk with that noise, impossible to think. Darrel walked around the car park, Luke over his shoulder howling with rage.

Quite quickly there was a change. Agnieszka could see how the child's body lost its rigidity and he began to curl into Darrel's shoulder. He continued to scream but she heard that the fight had gone out of him.

Now Darrel was nestling Luke into the crook of his arm, the child's back pressed against the dislikeable shirt, his feet dangling. From this safe, high place, Luke stopped crying instantly and stared at the world.

'How you do it? How you do that?' demanded Agnieszka. Luke was looking around with wide eyes.

'It'll give us some peace for a while. Let's go in and grab a coffee while we can.'

'But he not asleep!' Agnieszka never went anywhere if Luke was awake.

'Well, he might enjoy a cup of coffee,' said Darrel. 'Come on.'

They sat in big armchairs by a sunny window where they could watch the passers-by, Luke still in the crook of Darrel's arm. When he showed signs of restlessness, Darrel fished in his pocket for his keys and Luke touched them quietly as though they were something rare and interesting.

'There's something I could get him which should keep him amused for a while. I'll drop it in tonight on my way home,' he said. She smiled at him. So now he was going to fix Luke as well.

'He don't do like this with me,' she said sadly.

'What? Relax?'

'No, he always shouting. Until he shout himself to sleep.'

'Are you relaxed now, Aggie?'

'Yes.' She smiled.

'There you are then. So's Luke.'

He reached carefully for his coffee.

'So your husband's alive and well. Did you find out who sent the text?'

She frowned. 'I don't know. Maybe I never know. Darrel, you not back with your wife?'

'No.'

'You see her?'

'Well, we sort of got back together. For about a week. It was a stupid mistake so I'm at my mum's again.'

She found herself blushing. She did not know why.

'Agnieszka, I knew you were married when I met you.'

She remembered telling him that at the garage. He had said: where's your car? And she had misunderstood and said: Afghanistan. And they had laughed.

'I like being with you anyway. You're married but your husband's away. And your family's in Poland. And you need help sometimes. And I like helping you. Is that OK?'

She nodded. She looked at Luke, who had fallen asleep on Darrel's lap, still clutching his keys. 'Yes. It's OK.'

'Is it OK to go out sometimes? Even though you're married?'

She swallowed.

'Yes. It's OK.'

She knew Jamie wouldn't like it. But Jamie wasn't in Wiltshire trying to cope with Luke and broken things and hospital appointments and awful text messages. Jamie was in Afghanistan. And Darrel was here.

Chapter Forty-one

DAVE STROLLED AROUND THE PERIMETER OF SIN CITY. DARK HAD already fallen. In fifteen minutes he was due to go to the OC's tent to be interviewed about an insurgent who had died in a ditch months ago. The event seemed distant now, like something in his childhood.

He breathed deeply, tilted his head and stared above him. He was in the habit of looking at the dazzling Afghan skies whenever he could. The same stars must be hanging over Wiltshire but here the air was so clear that there was real depth of vision and you could see thousands, millions more stars.

He thought about the Taliban fighters, sitting in their compounds, smoking and talking and looking up at the same night sky. They had been staring at this incredible overhead display all their lives. It was, for them, a part of being at home, like the intense summer heat, the poppies, the mountains and the dust storms.

He passed the boss with the woman from Intelligence. The woman was smoking, Gordon Weeks was talking. Dave could understand how, after such a day, the boss would want to spend some time with this woman if he liked her. Weeks was so intent on what he was saying that he didn't even see Dave.

'Want one, Sarge?' asked some lads from 2 Section who were also walking the perimeter in a small group, unusually silent. Their faces shone out of the dark when they lit their cigarettes.

'All right,' said Dave.

'But, Sarge,' came McKinley's voice. 'You don't smoke.'

'I do tonight,' Dave told him, inhaling deeply.

'Any news on Ben or Ryan, Sarge?'

'Ben's doing better than Ryan. Although Ben took more shrapnel than we realized.'

'What about Ryan's arm, Sarge?'

'Unfortunately they've had to take it off below the elbow.'

The lads looked as though he had punched them.

'Is he going to make it?' asked McKinley quietly. 'He lost a lot of blood.'

'I don't know. He might not.'

'How about the others?'

'They took a lump of shrapnel out of Angus McCall's arm. Kev Swift from 3 Section had shrapnel too. But they'll be back in a couple of days.'

Dave strolled on. He was aware that his hand was shaking slightly as he smoked. He moved the cigarette into the other hand. That shook, too. He hated this involuntary movement and tried to still it but the tremor would not go away. He yawned. He wished he could just go to sleep. The stress of the day had left his body wrung out.

Sol, going back from the cookhouse after dinner with the lads, saw Dave smoking. He had never seen that before. Should he go and speak to him, or would Dave rather be alone before his difficult interview? He decided the sergeant looked as though he wanted to be alone.

Sol followed the boys back to the tent. They were hovering in the entrance. Finn put his finger to his lips as Sol approached.

Inside, someone was sitting alone on his cot talking to himself. Jamie Dermott.

'*Hop, Frog, hop! Your mummy's waiting and your daddy's looking for you! Hop across the big, wide pond!*'

'They put him on pain relief for the bullet bruise,' muttered Streaky. 'Maybe the medic gave him too much.'

'*How can I cross a pond as big and wide as that, Frog asked Snail?*'

Finn's eyes were glittering.

'*But Snail didn't know. He asked Fish. But Fish didn't know.*

Finally Frog asked the Great Crested Newt. And the Great Crested Newt said: hop, Frog, hop, that's what frogs do!'

Finn, with a delighted smile, balanced on one foot, arms out, and began to hop over to Jamie's cot. Mal followed him.

'Hop! Hop!'

Bacon wasn't far behind, yelling: '*Hip-hop!*'

'*Because,*' added Binns, hopping after them badly with his bandaged hands waving, '*that's what frogs do!*'

Sol stood still, his arms crossed, watching and shaking his head. They had spent the morning in a minefield. Two men in their platoon had been very seriously wounded. And now they were jumping around like kids.

Jamie scowled as the ragged line of men hopped towards him. Mal squeaked: '*Great Crested Newt, how can I cross the pond?*'

Finn replied, in a deep voice: '*I am the wise Great Crested Newt and I say: Hop, hop, you little green bastard, that's what fucking frogs do!*'

Mal squeaked: '*Oh, Snail, how can I cross the great wide pond?*'

Finn was breathless now.

'*You're nothing but a little green slimeball so go drown yourself.*'

'*Oh, Fish, how can I . . .*'

Sol shook his head again. Jamie stood up without smiling.

'Fuck off, shitheads. I was recording a story for my kid so he won't forget my voice. And you've ruined it.'

They stopped hopping.

'Now I'll have to record the whole thing again and it's about the fifth time of trying because there's never any peace around here.'

Sol walked into the tent.

'Lads, leave him alone. He's been crawling around mines and he's cut and bruised from a round. Give him some space.'

'Oh, shit, man, we could help you,' said Bacon.

'The only way you can help me is by letting me get on with it.'

'No, man,' insisted Streaky. 'We can do the sounds. Just you have a listen to Binman . . .'

Binns did a frog noise.

'That's quite good,' Jamie conceded.

'Here's a great crested newt . . .'

Jamie laughed. So did the others.

'See, your kid will really enjoy it with us in the background. Where's the story book?' asked Bacon.

'There isn't one.' Jamie showed them some scrunched pieces of paper. 'I'm writing it myself.'

'Ooooh, yeah!' said Bacon enthusiastically. 'This is going to be a 1 Section production. Tell me what happens to that frog!'

Jamie tried to smooth out the scrunched-up paper. He looked embarrassed. 'Well, I haven't worked it all out yet. But basically a bird carries him in its beak all the way across the world and he has to get back to his mum and dad.'

'Aaaaaaaaah,' said Mal and Angus, who were cleaning their weapons now.

'And he has to keep asking the way. He crosses the desert and a big pond and he has to climb a mountain . . .'

'I can do the wind on the mountain. *Whhhhhhhhhh.* How's that?' asked Bacon.

'Here's the frog crossing the pond,' said Binman. '*Plop. Plop. Plop.*'

Finn said: 'It's from you to your kid, right? So the frog comes under enemy fire. And a round hits him but he's wearing his frog armour and it bounces off . . .'

Binns did the rounds bouncing off.

'*Ker-ping!*' said Bacon.

Then they did machine guns and a bit of mortar.

'OK, OK, I get it,' said Jamie before they could get carried away. 'I'll write it and you can help me record it.'

'You been doing this ever since we got to Sin City?' asked Sol.

'No. I thought of it when I got hit by that round. And then after the minefield today I knew I had to do it for Luke. In case . . .' His voice trailed away.

'In case anything happens to you,' said Streaky.

Jamie nodded.

'You'll soon have time to record all the stories you want,' said Finn casually. 'We're going on a little holiday.'

'Oh, yeah?' said Sol.

'I reckon we could do with a break. After what happened today. Look at Binman, all pale and thin because he's spent the day nipping in and out of unexploded mines.'

298

'I'm always pale and thin,' said Binns miserably.

Sol said: 'I don't know about any breaks.'

'Ah. But you don't play blackjack with my mate Marty.'

Finn and Martyn Robertson had become friends over a pack of cards.

'The OC is pissed off with the civvies for always going to the same place every day . . .'

'Where we went with Emily?' asked Mal.

'Jackpot, Marty calls it. Well the Engineers are going to build a whole new camp there. A temporary one. We're going for a week while the civvies measure up their oil field.'

Sol looked suspicious.

'First I've heard of it.'

'Just you wait, the boss will be announcing it soon. We're going to Jackpot where there's nothing to do all day but tell frog stories and get our heads down while the civvies mess about with their black boxes.'

Sol still looked sceptical.

Finn grinned at him. 'We need some R&R. So I'm looking forward to it, lads.'

Sol decided to catch Dave and ask if he knew anything about a temporary camp at Jackpot. He thought Finn might be right but he didn't think his 2 i/c should be first with the news. He got as far as the entrance to the tent when he looked at his watch and realized that Dave would be going into his interview with the OC now.

Chapter Forty-two

JENNY PADDED OVER TO AGNIESZKA'S HOUSE THREE TIMES BUT DID NOT find her at home. She decided to try again in the evening when Vicky was in bed. Trish was irritated.

'What do you have to tell her that's so important?'

'Just something a bit awkward.'

'What's wrong with the phone, then?'

'Her English goes to pieces on the phone.'

Trish shook her head.

'You be careful,' she said. 'Take your mobile so you can call me if anything happens.'

'For heaven's sake, Mum. If anything happens you'll hear me yelling I'll be so close.'

It had rained earlier and the warm evening air felt refreshing. Jenny breathed deeply. In another month her life would be changed again. There would be a tiny new demanding person in the centre of her world alongside Vicky.

She felt relaxed. Now that Trish was here, her hands and ankles weren't so swollen and she felt well again. She strolled around the corner. Some older children were still playing at the rec. The grass had been mown and she inhaled its sweet smell. A man with a big grey dog passed her and smiled. She could hear the soothing summer coo of a wood pigeon.

Ever since she'd known she was pregnant she had been sure of one thing: Dave wouldn't be in Wiltshire for the birth. They'd both thought deployment was inevitable. She'd braced herself for the date and when they were given it she was prepared for the knowledge that she would give birth alone. So she'd shrugged.

'Oh, well, there's no way round it.'

He'd been miserable: 'Shouldn't have married a soldier, Jen. An accountant would have been a nice, safe option.'

She'd kissed his unhappy face to say it was all right and that she could cope without him.

But now the baby wasn't far away. The days would still be fine but there would be a nip in the air every morning and spiders' webs in the garden. And she could no longer pretend it didn't matter that Dave wasn't here for her. Because it did.

She rang Agnieszka's bell. After a long time the door opened cautiously and a section of Agnieszka's face appeared through the crack.

'Hi, it's only me!' The door was on a chain. 'It's me! Jenny!'

At this point the chain should have clinked off the hook and the door should have swung open. But it didn't.

'Agnieszka, is this a bad time?'

'Is very difficult because I busy with Luke.'

'There's something I have to say to you,' Jenny said. 'It will only take a minute. It's important.'

'Yes?'

Agnieszka still did not open the door.

'It's a bit difficult to say it on the step . . .'

'What? I don't understand, Jenny.'

Jenny shifted her weight from one foot to the other impatiently. She felt dizzy suddenly.

'Can't I come in for a minute?'

Agnieszka took the chain off and opened the door only far enough for Jenny to step onto the mat. But she did not move aside to allow her visitor in further.

'Jenny, house is big, big mess, I am very embarrassed,' she said. And she did look embarrassed. Her eyes were big and her face was red. She was holding a toy, a set of big plastic keys, the sort that lit up and played music if the child pressed them.

'I'm not staying,' said Jenny, her eyes flicking past Agnieszka to the living room. She could see no sign of the mess. Not that she cared.

'Listen, I've been thinking about that text message. There's a good reason the lads can't use their phones in Afghanistan. It's because the signals get intercepted and used by the Taliban. And I think that's what happened to you, Agnieszka. That shitty message came from the Taliban. To upset you and frighten you.'

Agnieszka looked shocked.

'From *Taliban*?' she echoed. 'No, it just silly joke.'

'I think it came from the enemy. They have the technology to read all Jamie's messages to you, it's not hard. That's why our boys can't use their mobiles out there.'

Agnieszka bit her lip.

'I don't like to think Taliban send me a message.'

'Me neither. And I'm feeling really bad now. Because you've asked me to keep it a secret from Dave and I don't like keeping secrets from him.'

Agnieszka looked terrified.

'It's OK. I gave you my word I won't tell him. And I won't. But for everyone's sake, I want you to promise that you'll ask Jamie to stop using it.'

'Stop using mobile?'

'Yes. It's too dangerous for everyone.'

'But how he text me?'

'On the army satellite phone, like everyone else.'

'Huh, he used to buy lot of minutes but these other men also buy them so Jamie don't get so many.'

Jenny began to feel angry. She had a prickling sensation under her skin. She knew her face was reddening.

'We all have to manage on thirty minutes a week! How do you think the rest of us feel?'

Agnieszka's even face assumed that dissatisfied, sulky expression Jenny had seen before.

'You must stop using the mobile,' Jenny repeated. 'Or I'll have to tell him.'

'So you tell Dave after all!'

Jenny's head was spinning.

'Only if you don't stop. And now you know the Taliban can intercept signals, surely you want to stop! It's dangerous, Agnieszka, it could be dangerous to you, too.'

Agnieszka's face drooped into a dissatisfied pout. 'I don't see how it dangerous for Jamie to text me from base. He don't send text about operations.'

'They've got your number, Agnieszka. They know you're a British Army wife. They could even locate you in the UK. Isn't that a bit scary?'

Agnieszka did not look scared. She looked sulky. Jenny had promised Dave that she would try to like this woman. She was certainly trying. But it was hard. Her head began to ache.

'And how I tell him? Because army monitor talk on satellite phone, they hear if I ask him to stop with mobile.'

'You'll have to find a way to do it. With hints and things.'

Agnieszka looked annoyed.

'Please, Agnieszka, don't ask me to have secrets from Dave.'

'OK. OK. I tell Jamie not to use it.'

'Thanks very much. I know it's hard for you. But it's hard for all of us.'

Agnieszka opened the door a little wider to indicate that Jenny should go now. She looked, thought Jenny as she stepped outside and the door shut swiftly behind her, as though she had agreed to do an enormous favour.

Jenny did not notice the smell of the newly mown grass any more. She felt angry. If anyone was entitled to texts and extra minutes with her husband it should surely be a woman about to have a baby in his absence. She decided to walk around the block. Because despite everyone's insistence that she sit around resting to keep her blood pressure down, she had found that walking was more relaxing than watching TV and drinking endless cups of tea with Trish.

And why had Agnieszka been so determined to leave her standing on the doorstep? She had clearly not wanted her there at all. Jenny walked faster, her belly preceding her like a big, round wheelbarrow. Her head was spinning and throbbing now. She walked in time with the pain.

It was only when she passed an old red Volvo parked at the end of a quiet side street that she realized. First she recognized the Volvo, then she remembered whose car it was. So that was why Agnieszka had not wanted her to come inside the house. That was why she was so impatient to get Jenny out of the door. Because that man was there.

Chapter Forty-three

'COME ON IN, SERGEANT HENLEY.' MAJOR WILLINGHAM'S TONE WAS friendly. He was with the 2 i/c, CSM Kila and Gordon Weeks. The 2 i/c was making mugs of tea as usual. Iain Kila called him, in private, the Brew Bitch.

'Before we get down to business, I'd like to congratulate you both, Gordon and Dave, on the way you and your men dealt with that horrific incident today. You must be very proud of everyone, not least the four men who risked their lives saving the casualties.'

'If there'd only been helicopters with winches available no one would have had to risk their life,' said the boss firmly. Dave was pleased. The boss was beginning to grasp the fact that the best way of fighting against the enemy was fighting for your men against the big machine of the British Army.

'I agree with that and the point has been very strongly made,' said the OC.

'Any update on the condition of Connor or Broom, sir?' asked Dave.

'I spoke to Bastion an hour ago. They just say they're stable. Which could mean anything.'

CSM Kila added: 'But we've had three calls from Angus McCall to ask what's going on here.'

Dave smiled.

'Scared he'll miss some action.'

Iain Kila said: 'His dad has good cause to be proud of what that lad did today.'

'His dad?' asked the OC.

'His father was in the Regiment,' the boss explained.

Iain Kila raised his eyebrows. 'Says Angus.'

The major smiled. 'If everyone who claims to have been in the Regiment was telling the truth then Hereford would be the size of Canada.'

He sprawled back in his chair, legs stretched out. On his desk was an open cake tin, its contents half eaten, probably sent by a relative or big-hearted member of the public.

'Now then, I'm sorry to question you about an old incident, Sergeant Henley, when you've had such a shit day. But I promised to get a report in about it and now they say they need it by first thing tomorrow. As you know, we've got this Royal Military Policewoman here at the base. As well as the woman from the Intelligence Corps. It's all a bit of bad luck really: the pair of them are only here because they're fluent in Pashtu—'

'But, sir, they're good value,' Iain Kila said. 'They were good news with the detainees.'

'And their monitoring of the Taliban radios has been fantastic when we're operational,' added the boss.

'Oh, they do a fine job both interpreting and diplomatically: we were even invited to the tribesmen's wedding, as you know, and I'm sure that was something to do with the charm of our interpreters. But the fact is, the RMP won't stick to her interpreter role, she insists on doing monkey work even when we really don't want her to.'

Dave glanced at the boss. He looked tense.

'She's got a bee in her bonnet about the Green Zone patrol when you dropped five Talis. I can stave off a full investigation if I say the right things in my report now. You know which incident I'm talking about?'

'Yes, sir. After the goat set off the IED for us.'

'Which makes me wonder if we shouldn't have goats trotting in front of our patrols all the time. Like miners had canaries. Anyway, can I ask you to think back and take me through exactly what happened after the goat was blown up? And please understand that this is a relaxed and informal discussion.'

Suddenly it didn't feel relaxed or informal. The OC sat up straight to take notes. The tent was silent.

Dave told how, after the IED had detonated, he and 1 Section had walked up the track looking for the old man who had been herding the goat. He described the appearance of the four Taliban fighters, apparently going home and unaware of their presence. He said that both he and Jamie had fired at them and all four had dropped.

'Now let's get this straight. You were searching the dead men, all of whom were in a ditch, when McCall shouted out that one of the bodies was still alive. And you said . . . ?'

'I think I said: get on with it.'

'*Get on with it*,' echoed the major, giving the words great significance. 'Can you remember what exactly you meant by that?'

'Well, I knew that our fire would certainly draw enemy fire. It was just a question of when they could locate us. And we were a small, vulnerable group out there in the field. So we needed to move quickly.'

The major scribbled on his pad, nodding.

'But what did you want him to get on with?'

Dave paused and glanced at Boss Weeks.

'Isn't the interpretation of his words by his men more important than what he actually meant?' suggested the boss.

'Fair point, Gordon. *Get on with it*. The men could have understood that to mean: remove his weapon and examine his injuries so that we can casevac him if necessary. Do you think they understood you to mean that, Sergeant Henley?'

Dave looked thoughtful. He glanced at the CSM who nodded slightly.

'Maybe,' he said cautiously.

'I think the RMP here at the base suspects you might have meant: get on and shoot him,' said the OC nonchalantly.

Iain Kila said: 'Well, that's not how the rifleman searching the body understood it, because he didn't shoot.'

'Rifleman Bilaal shot him,' said Dave. 'But I think he was already dead.'

'How do you know? Did you see the wound or the blood?'

'I saw blood. But I knew it mostly because I'd shot him myself.'

The major smiled.

'You know you're a good shot?'

'Good enough to hit a lad when he's that close. I'd seen him fall into the ditch. He had no body armour – it would be amazing if he could survive, and survive well enough to act dead. So when McCall said he was moving, I thought that it could be a death twitch. I've seen that before.'

'There was absolutely no doubt in your mind that the man was dead or very close to dead?'

'I thought this was a dead body twitching. If there had been any movement at all. But the rifleman who was searching him had been in his first real contact. He was showing signs of shock. In that state he could have imagined the body was moving. So I was more worried about him than the insurgent. What I wanted was for the rifleman to stop imagining things, pull himself together and get on with the body search.'

'This was McCall?'

'He froze when we shot the insurgents, although he was at the front and the first to see them. He had another chance a few minutes later and he blew that too. He's OK now, fighting very well, and he distinguished himself on the minefield today. But like a lot of lads, he fell apart the first time he was asked to face the enemy.'

CSM Kila nodded. So did Gordon Weeks. The major sat back in his chair with a satisfied smile and the 2 i/c approached with the teapot and his Brew Bitch smile: 'Would anyone like a top-up?'

'But, Dave,' Weeks said, 'the OC might have to explain why Rifleman Bilaal then shot this dead body.'

'Mal thought the bloke was dead too,' said Dave. 'I've talked to him about it. But he's McCall's best mate and he could see him falling apart. He threw down a few rounds just to reassure Angus.'

The OC sipped cheerfully at his tea.

'Good! I think I have enough there to keep the monkeys off our backs. The Rules of Engagement are misty in places and it's too easy for people sitting in offices to tell men in the heat of battle how they should have behaved. I hope you'll hear no more about it now, Dave.'

Dave had been worried about this interview and he knew that the outcome should have been a relief. But after today's bloodbath on the minefield, this investigation into a dead insurgent, although correct and required by law, seemed absurd.

Chapter Forty-four

BILLY FINN TURNED OUT TO BE RIGHT. ABOUT A WEEK LATER AN announcement was made that, as soon as the engineers had finished building the temporary base at Jackpot, 1 and 2 Platoons would be moving there for a week with the civilians. Patrols continued but oil exploration work was halted in the meantime.

A Chinook arrived, kicking up a spiral of fine dust which reached high into the air like a storm. The back was opened and out came three men in flipflops, shorts and T-shirts. The lads stared at them. They were carrying kit but the most noticeable item was an old tin teapot dangling on a string from a Bergen. They were talking and laughing as if they had just arrived at their holiday destination and couldn't wait to get their towels out by the pool before any Germans did.

'Who the hell are they?' men asked each other. But not for long because the mail bags had been unloaded. People pounced on their blueys and took them to their cot or some other private corner to read them, like dogs dragging away bones to maul in private. As usual, Finn, who had nothing, watched other people reading their letters.

'All right, mate?' he asked Mal.

'Yeah,' said Mal. 'Why?'

'You don't look too happy.'

'I'm good.'

'Women trouble? One of your babes found a bloke with better wheels?'

'I told you, I'm blowing everything I earn here on a beamer when I get back, and I mean an M3. Women are going to be gagging for a ride with me, there are no better wheels.'

Finn said in an undertone. 'Listen. There's a rumour going around that the blokes who arrived on the Chinook are SF.'

Mal laughed out loud.

'Yeah, they look like big hard killing machines.'

'Well, who do you think they are?'

'Bunch of tossers.'

Later, in the cookhouse, the lads were having a brew while Streaky gave them his minefield rap. He had been writing it in his head when he covered the rescue operation. It had taken the edge off his anxiety for Binman but now, a week later, it didn't sound so special. The others listened impassively right to the end:

> ... *It was a Russian who's dead now who laid that mine then*
> *fled,*
> *The Russian didn't guess it would take a British leg,*
> *A Russian soldier left two British boys for dead*
> *And the ragheads laughed and fired while Connor bled and*
> *bled.*

Binns immediately said it was good. Sol agreed with him.

'Didn't like the stuff at the beginning about the Paras,' said Finn.

'You just try finding a good rhyme for Paratrooper,' said Streaky sulkily.

'*Angry snooper*,' said Jamie.

'*Mini Cooper*,' said Mal.

'*Let's play snooker*,' said someone.

They all looked up. It was Martyn Robertson, who was sitting down next to them with a cup of coffee.

'You want a game of snooker?' asked Angus, hopefully. He'd been allowed back to the FOB with his bandaged arm only if he stayed on Light Duties for two weeks. And playing snooker sounded like a good Light Duty.

'I prefer pool myself,' said Martyn patiently. 'But the point is, Angus, *Let's play snooker* rhymes with *Paratrooper*.'

'Oh, yeah,' said Angry. He reddened. Why did Topaz fucking Zero

310

always put him down? Then Martyn surprised him by flinging an arm across his shoulders.

'You're a good kid,' he said. 'We can't play pool but you're very welcome to join in with the blackjack.'

'Don't mind if I do,' said Angus, mollified.

'So, guys,' said Martyn, 'who's seen the Green Berets? Or whatever you call them in Britain.'

1 Section sat up straight.

'That would be the SAS: Special Forces, Jedi, Blades,' said Finn, with a meaningful look at Mal.

'I've seen three geezers in flipflops,' said Streaky.

'Yup, they're here on some special operation.'

'The Regiment!' said Angus. 'Here!' He tried to hide his excitement in case anyone laughed at him. 'I mean . . . those guys with the fucking teapot?'

'They look like new oil engineers,' Binman said.

Martyn frowned. 'Oil engineers have better taste in shirts.'

'But . . . I'm bigger than they are!' said Angus. The Jedi. SF were here at Sin City.

'They might be hard, though,' Jamie said.

Binns shook his head. 'Seem a bit ordinary to me.'

'How do you know this, Martyn?' Sol asked. Martyn just looked mysterious.

Before the Chinook could take off again, the base came under fire. This invariably happened with the arrival or departure of a Chinook. The insurgents knew about the vulnerabilities of the old machines: an RPG in the right place could do a lot of damage. The contact was sufficient to delay the helicopter's departure. Although AH support was requested, all the Apaches were busy so the occupants of Sin City threw themselves into putting down the attack. It took at least an hour and in that time not one of the SAS men was seen.

'You'd think the cream of the British Army would give us a hand,' Finn said when they were finally told to stand down.

'Maybe they're busy sorting out weapons and making plans and stuff,' Angus said. 'For their special operation.'

'Or maybe,' said Mal, 'they're lazy bastards.'

'Bet they get paid shitloads of money, too,' added Binman.

'Think they'll let us cabbie their weapons?' asked Angus.

Mal said: 'Oh wow. They have the best shit in the world.'

'One thing's for sure, mate, the Regiment don't leave their weapons lying in dope fields,' said Jamie.

'Fuck off,' said Mal amiably.

'They're in the Cowshed. Reckon we can go and talk to them, Sol?' asked Finn.

Sol shrugged. 'I suppose they can only tell you to go away.'

Angus, Mal and Finn found the men having a brew with their feet up apparently oblivious to the fact that the base had been under attack. They looked like ordinary soldiers, perhaps a bit older, on R&R.

'Didn't you want to fight?' asked Finn.

One of them was reading a dog-eared paperback. He looked up.

'No way. I joined the Regiment to get away from all that army shit.' And he went back to reading his book.

'So can we have a butchers at your weapons?' Finn persisted.

One of the other men got up and fetched a weapon for them. It was long and thin and mean.

'You can have a butchers but not a cabbie,' he said, passing it to Finn.

'Oh, shit!' said Angus who was always badgering Dave to send him on a proper sniper course. He was already the team's sharp-shooter. 'Is that the . . . could it be the . . .'

'The L115A3.'

'Holy shit, how long have you been using it for?'

'Not long. It's replaced the L96A1 now.'

Angus was like a kid who had just broken into a toyshop. 'Fuck me, how many rounds will it do?'

'Five.'

'And what's the range?' Finn was holding it up and looking through the sights.

'Well, it'll do two kilometres. But closer is better because I'm not sure the sights are as good as the weapon.'

'So you're all in different places, then?' asked Mal.

'Yeah, we've got a button here, right by the trigger, see, and when we get a good sight picture we press it and the signal goes to the liaison officer. When he's got three lights on, he'll tell us to fire. Or maybe just two lights. One isn't enough.'

312

'Fucking hell,' said Mal. Angus was speechless.

Finn handed the rifle to Mal. He said: 'That is high precision. One man two kilometres away.'

'We're targeting some kind of a family party,' said the SAS man. 'So we've got to be accurate. Don't want any kids running up to their dad at the wrong moment.'

'Holy shit,' breathed Angus. 'What a life. You just fly in, slot this guy and fly out again.'

'We fly in and we hope we slot him,' said the SAS man. 'It doesn't always happen that way.'

'Bet you never make mistakes,' Angus said to him.

'Oh yes he does,' chorused the other SAS men, refilling the teapot.

But Angus ignored them because he did not want to believe the Special Forces ever made mistakes.

Mal was looking through the sights.

'I'd give anything for a day with one of these in Wythenshawe. It would be just the job there.'

'Who do you want to top in Wythenshawe, mate?' Finn asked. But instead of answering, Mal passed the rifle to Angus, who was waiting with arms outstretched. He held it carefully, aiming at some faraway target beyond the hesco.

'How long have you been in the Regiment?'

'Five years. I was in the Tigers before that.'

'Ever come across the names of blokes who used to be in the Jedi?' asked Angus shyly, handing the rifle back.

'Well, yeah. Mostly on the front of books. You only get in if you've got a degree in Creative Writing.'

His mates laughed but Angus was serious.

'Ever hear John McCall mentioned?'

The man and his colleagues exchanged thoughtful looks. 'McCall . . . McCall . . .'

'That's his dad,' explained Mal. 'His name's Angus McCall.'

'Well we're probably not old enough to have known your dad,' said the man. 'And I can't say I've heard the name.'

Angus tried to hide his disappointment.

'But I don't know the names of everyone who's ever been in the Regiment. Now you'd better fuck off while we get prepped up.'

That evening, Angus sneaked back to the Cowshed. There was no

313

sign of the men or their weapons. The paperbacks were lying on the floor along with the tin teapot. He had personally been on stag and had anyway kept an eye out for the men. They had just evaporated into thin air. He knew that, more than anything, he wanted to be one of them.

Chapter Forty-five

JAMIE RECORDED THE NEXT PART OF HIS FROG STORY FOR LUKE. By now almost everybody in 1 Section was providing sound effects or background music.

'*And so the little frog began his journey towards the deep, deep river. First he had to cross the Green Zone . . .*'

'*Ribbit, ribbit*,' said Binns.

'*It was full of ditches and trees and fields growing fruit and flowers. The little frog wanted to stop and look at the flowers and maybe have a bite to eat but he knew he had to keep on hopping . . .*'

'*Ribbit, ribbit.*'

Streaky and Finn provided a musical accompaniment.

'*And so the little frog hopped towards the place where he knew his mum and dad were waiting for him and would wait for ever if they had to. Just one more mountain to cross and he would be there.*'

'Splaaaat! That's the sound of a 500-pound bomb falling out of an A10 on top of the fucking frog! You're making me puke!' roared Angus from his cot.

'Aw c'mon, Mr Angry,' said Streaky. 'His babymother will play it to his little boy every night.'

'I'm going to the cookhouse, I can't stand it any more,' said Angus.

'I have to stop now anyway. I've got a call booked to Niez,' said Jamie.

'Is that the end?' asked Binns.

'There's a bit more. I want to finish it before we go to Jackpot in case I get slotted there.'

'We'll finish it for you if you do,' said Streaky.

'Yeah,' said Binns. 'Just leave the mic and the rest of the story by your cot.'

'It wouldn't be the same,' said Jamie. 'But thanks anyway.'

He went out and hung around near the phones. He could no longer text Agnieszka: she had made him promise not to although she hadn't explained exactly why.

He dialled the number and it rang and rang. No reply. And he might not get another chance to phone before they left. Answer. Answer! He couldn't explain, even to himself, why he needed her to be there. He just knew that, if she wasn't, there was nothing.

Then, just when he had given up, she picked up the phone.

'Niez, where have you been? It's been ringing and ringing!'

She sounded distant.

'Asleep.'

'But it's not night time in England!'

'No, darling. I tired today.'

'Why, Niez?'

'Well, I just tired, I don't know why. Raining weather. Luke has two fits this morning. So now he sleeps and I sleep.'

'What have you been doing?'

'Nothing.'

Jamie felt desperate.

'Talk to me, darling.'

'What you want me to talk about?'

Some of the men found that words failed them after a few months in Afghanistan when it was time to make a weekly call to their loved ones. They detached from their families and communicated less as they became immersed in this other world. But that wasn't true for Jamie. The worse things became, the more Jamie needed Agnieszka. He had rung her twice since the minefield a week ago. He needed her and she knew that and she supplied him with loving words, small stories, sweet chatter. But today she seemed unable to do so.

'Tell me what you did last night. Or today . . .'

'Watched TV.'

'Don't you go out?'

'Yes, I walk. I like to walk now if weather good in the evening. They cut grass and it smell good. Or I listen to birds. But today it rain so I was a prisoner.'

'Niez, I'll ask my mother to phone you and invite you . . .'

'If she does not invite me herself I don't go.' Agnieszka's voice conveyed a mixture of hurt, boredom and anger. 'She does not ring me.'

They both knew that Jamie's mother was so saturated in disapproval – disapproval of Agnieszka, of Luke's undiagnosed condition, of Jamie's army rank – that she preferred not to pick up the phone.

'Where do you walk?' he asked her.

'All around. Everywhere. I getting very fit, this is my aim in this summer weather, to get a little bit fit.'

'You're already fit, darling. I miss you so much. And I might not be able to phone for almost a week.'

'Why?'

'I can't tell you that. How's Luke?'

'He fits today. But sometimes I think he relax a bit more, cry a little less. He like me to pick him up more too.'

Jamie had worried quietly to himself about the way Agnieszka took care of Luke's physical needs so attentively but seemed to take no real pleasure in him. That was probably because he cried such a lot. While Jamie was happy to feel Luke's sleepy little head tucked into his shoulder, Agnieszka never seemed to share his delight in the child's love and helplessness.

'That's good,' he said. 'That's very good.'

'Yeah, he give me a bit of a smile sometimes.'

'Oh, Niez, that's fantastic.' He felt relieved and at the same time deprived. Luke was going to stop crying and start smiling and he wasn't there to receive those smiles.

'I'm recording a story for him. About a frog. The lads are doing background noises and I think he'll enjoy it.'

'Jamie, I don't think Luke old enough for understand stories.'

'He doesn't have to understand it. Yet. He just has to hear my voice and know it's his dad.'

317

'Well, OK, we can try.' She sounded unimpressed. But then she hadn't heard the story yet.

He sensed she wanted to get away, that she wished the call would end. She probably had nothing else to say and there was nothing he was allowed to tell her.

'I miss you and love you,' he said.

'Yeah, Jamie, me too. Luke too. We think of you, OK?'

Was her voice fractionally more dismissive than usual? It was rising to indicate the end of the conversation. Maybe she had another hair appointment. He told her he loved her again and hung up.

He was left feeling empty. He always felt empty when she had gone. But this was something more. It was instinct. The instinct told him his calls to her did not matter as much as they used to. They mattered less because he had now been away so long that the landscape was re-forming without him. The thought was unbearable. He was losing importance. The contour map was changing.

Dave was next for the phone. Jamie looked desolate as he handed it over. He always looked miserable when he'd finished talking to his wife but this was something more.

'What's up, mate?'

'Nothing.'

Dave studied him closely.

'Everything all right at home?' He hoped that Agnieszka hadn't told Jamie there was another man. He hoped there wasn't another man. But if there was, Jamie didn't need to know about it when he was here, far away, unable to do anything.

'No, fine. Luke's starting to smile.'

'That's good news, then.'

'Yeah, yeah I know. I just wish I could see it.'

'Not much longer,' Dave said. 'Couple more months then we're home.'

'How's Jenny? Blood pressure OK now?'

'I'm about to find out. But I'm sure she'll have it under control.'

Trish answered the phone.

'Thank God you've rung at last,' she said. 'Jennifer's just gone into hospital.'

'Oh no.'

'They're monitoring her.'

'Oh, Christ.'

'It's all right, Dave, it's the best place for her. I could see by look-ing at her she wasn't right and I was worried anything could happen at home here.'

'What's going to happen in hospital?'

'She's got pre-eclampsia. It's very serious, for her and the baby. So if her blood pressure goes up much more, they'll have to induce.'

The silence was so long that Trish thought he hadn't heard and she repeated the news, slowly and clearly as though speaking to someone who knew very little English.

Dave was irritated. 'It's OK. I can hear you. If they induce will you be with her? During the birth? Because Adi Kasanita said that she'd—'

'I'll be there. Even though you know very well you should be the one, not me.'

'Don't start, Trish. Please.'

'I'm sure you don't want to hear it and there's never a right time to say it so I'm going to get it off my chest now, Dave.'

She took a deep breath. The satellite phone clicked into the crystal clarity it only attained very occasionally and never when you wanted it to. Dave braced himself.

'There comes a time in everyone's life when their family must come first. You've got a daughter and you'll soon have another child and you've got to start treating them right. They're more important than the British Army, for heaven's sake. You're out there fighting some stupid war for people who're nothing to do with us for no reason anyone can understand. When you should be home with Jennifer. She needs you and you're not here.'

She drew breath and he braced himself for her next blast wave. It was like seeing a bomb fall and waiting for it to go off. 'She's the most loyal wife you could find, Dave, but she's sick of it. I expect she's been too nice to tell you that.'

No, thought Dave, she's told me. She's even put it in writing.

'I know there are women around here who can't take it. Watching the news, hearing about another death. Wondering if it's their man. There's a lad from across the road lost his leg, you know.

319

And another just lost his arm, that's what people are saying.'

'I do know.'

'Well it's too much for some girls always waiting for that sort of news. They look around them and then they find other fellas who know how to treat them. And Jennifer's a good-looking girl, Dave.' Trish's voice was thick with dire warning.

'That's one thing Jen wouldn't do,' said Dave confidently. 'Like you said, she's a loyal wife.'

'I'm not saying she wants to. I'm not saying she doesn't love you. I'm saying you're driving her to it. Now think about that, Dave. Just think about it.'

'OK, Trish, I will think about it. But the fact is that the skills I've picked up in the army don't translate well to the outside world. I mean, they aren't valued. I don't know what I could do out there.'

'I should have thought you could do security work. There's so much crime now that security guards are getting more and more important.'

Dave tried to imagine himself on night duty at a building site, sitting in a wooden box with an electric heater and a TV, plodding around the site at regular intervals. He tried to imagine himself doing any of the things mates who'd come out had done: one was a chimney sweep, one had spent years trying to get a job and now did youth work, one had become a bus driver. He shook his head involuntarily.

'Can I phone Jen at the hospital?'

'You can try. She's not allowed a mobile but you can try her ward. I doubt you'll have much luck.'

Trish gave him the number and he talked to Vicky for a few minutes and then tried the hospital. But he was cut off when his call was transferred to the ward. He tried again and this time he was put through but no one answered. He tried once more but the phone rang on the ward and then went dead. The midwives were probably all dealing with emergencies, he thought. He just hoped Jenny wasn't one of them.

Chapter Forty-six

IN THE AFTERNOON 1 PLATOON WAS SENT OUT ON A ROUTINE patrol. Nobody knew why the boss suddenly ordered the Vectors to slow down as they approached three bearded Afghans in dusty clothes at the roadside. He ordered a door to be opened and, without the convoy even stopping, the three men jumped in and the wagons continued.

Asma was at the front of the second vehicle with the boss, listening to the radio.

'What the hell is going on?' she asked him.

He shrugged but did not explain. Although she would have to know, sooner or later.

'Those weren't the SAS guys?'

He sighed. 'Yes.'

'I must say they looked bloody authentic.'

'Not a sniper rifle in sight.'

'I wonder what they were doing out here all night and all day?'

'Waiting for a big event to start.'

'A big event? It's not a holy day.'

'A family event.'

'Did they top someone at a family gathering? That's brave.'

The boss said nothing and the convoy rumbled on. He thought he had escaped. But in a few minutes she turned to him again.

'What kind of family gathering?' she asked suspiciously.

He looked at her but did not reply.

'A wedding?'

He nodded. Asma's face began to redden. But when she spoke her voice was icy.

'Please, Gordon. Tell me it wasn't the wedding we were invited to.'

He looked embarrassed.

'Well, I wasn't invited. You were.'

Asma was silent. He waited for the explosion.

'You're Intelligence Corps. I assumed you knew who the target was,' he said.

'The SAS don't tell every low-down ant in Intelligence what they're doing.'

She had been staring listlessly at the road ahead but now she turned to look directly at Weeks again.

'So who was the target?'

He braced himself. It was better to get it over with. 'Asad.'

'No!' It was more of a cry than a protest.

'Asma, I know you won't want to believe this. But Asad was a very high-up Taliban commander. If today's op went according to plan, the snipers have just killed him.'

'No!'

'I'm sorry. I know how much you liked him.'

Weeks had received the news about the operation yesterday and his first thought had been for Asma. The tribesman stood for something that mattered a lot to her. If Asad was a rival, Weeks took no pleasure in the knowledge that his rival would be wiped out.

Her face was all strong bones and big brown eyes now.

'Liking him didn't come into it!' she said, her face showing this was untrue. Liking had certainly come into it. 'I trusted him!'

'I'm sorry,' said Weeks. 'You made a mistake. He was a Taliban commander. But so high up he was rarely called upon to fight.'

Asma shook her head with incomprehension. 'I can't believe it! His father spoke against the Taliban!'

'It's not so unusual for a father to have one son in the Afghan National Army and another in the Taliban. You told me that yourself. You told me that Afghans like to hedge their bets when it comes to taking sides. You said that, after so many years of war, they have to. But Asad was in more deeply than that. He was committed to the cause.'

Asma looked away from him at the dust clouds billowing on all sides of the Vector. He could hardly bear the unhappiness on her face. He stopped short of pointing out what might have happened if the OC had accepted the wedding invitation.

Neither of them said a word as they re-entered the base. When the wagon stopped and the driver got out, Weeks turned to her.

'Asma, don't be upset . . .'

He was shocked to see that she was fighting tears.

'I'm not fucking upset,' she spat.

'It's a war. We have Rules of Engagement and international laws governing our behaviour but it's basically a dirty game and you can't trust anyone.'

'You don't understand! Someone who knows nothing about this country and its people thinks he had the right to judge Asad and find him guilty. And today those bastards put him to death! What fucking right do they have to decide who he is and what he thinks?'

'They have the right to decide he's dangerous and that he puts a lot of other lives at risk.'

'I hope they know what the fuck they're doing! Because if they're anything like you, with your posh farmhouse and your polo and your private school, they don't have a fucking clue! You don't even know anything about England. Let alone Afghanistan!'

Weeks did not reply. Asma did not get out. So they continued to sit in the hot Vector watching the men debus. Dave was running around with ammo. The drivers were sharing cigarettes in the shade. Weeks could not remember being more miserable. His wretchedness felt as though it penetrated to his bone marrow. Somehow, together, he and Asma had managed to develop an intimacy despite all the differences between them. And she had just ended all that.

He wondered which gap was wider: the eighty miles between his family's farmhouse and the flat in Hackney where she had been brought up? Or the gulf between England and Afghanistan? The distances seemed so great that they were insurmountable.

She sighed into the silence. He wished she would speak. Apologize, unsay it, reach for his hand. He glanced at her and saw from her deep brown eyes that she would do none of these.

'You fucking idiots don't understand. You talk about the Enemy. But sometimes the Enemy is the Future.'

'What does that mean?'

'His beliefs were too complicated for you fucking morons to understand. He was no fundamentalist but he certainly had principles. If he was fighting for something it was probably Pashtunistan. What makes a bunch of fucking wankers think it's OK to top anyone who believes in a cause? Maybe what he believed in had some value. Shit, I hate you all.'

'All who?'

'All you wankers who think you know. Well, now you'll pay for being so fucking sure. We went into their house and accepted their hospitality and now we've shot their son. At a family wedding, for fuck's sake. It's OK for the SAS, sneaking in and out of here and then going off to kill someone else. We've got to stay here and face it when they take their revenge.'

'Now you're being dramatic.' He heard his own voice, how his vowels had been honed in farmhouses and on polo ponies. He understood how it must irritate her. 'The point of the Regiment's op is that it didn't look like any British Army operation the locals would recognize. The intention was to make them think a rival tribe had carried out the killing.'

She rolled her eyes.

'They're not stupid.'

She was getting out of the wagon now.

'Gordon, I've already explained the Afghan code of honour to you. Now just you wait and see what happens.'

She slammed the door.

Chapter Forty-seven

IN THE COOKHOUSE, FINN AND MARTYN ROBERTSON WERE TEACHING
Angus to play blackjack. Dave always kept an eagle eye on these
games but so far he had been unable to detect stakes that were anything higher than matchsticks.

'I bet you earn a lot of matchsticks in a week, working for an oil
company,' said Finn as they waited for Angus to decide whether to
draw another card.

'More matchsticks than you could ever imagine, Huckleberry.
But there's not a lot of chance to spend it here.'

'What do you do with it then?'

'I got houses, I got ex-wives, that's where most of it goes. But I've
enjoyed our blackjack, and when I get out of here I think I might
just take me to Vegas for a weekend.'

'We do a thing called decompression when our tour ends. We all
go to Cyprus to get drunk.'

'Well, I'll need a lot of decompression in Las Vegas after all these
months with Emily the Enemy. I just wish she wasn't coming to
Jackpot tomorrow.'

'But you're a lucky bastard,' said Finn. 'Money to blow in Vegas.
Any chance of a job when I come out of the army?'

Martyn smiled wearily.

'I get asked that every week.'

'Not by people as clever as me, Marty.'

'Maybe not ... Come on, Angry, or we'll have to set a time
limit.'

'All right, then,' said Angus. 'Give me another card.'

Martyn dealt him a card. Angus looked at the face value and thumped his cards down in disgust.

'Whooooar, that's me out! Bust again!'

Finn picked up the hand and looked at it.

'You need to think a bit more, mate. If you'd stuck at what you had you'd probably have been quids in.'

'He thinks way too much. It took him five minutes to go bust when others could have gone bust in five seconds,' said Martyn.

Angry got up.

'Well, that's me out of matchsticks. It's a stupid game, anyway.'

Martyn raised his eyebrows but said nothing and at that moment Taregue Masud arrived with a cloth to wipe the tables.

'Excuse me, sir, I now ask you for permission to make this table very nice and clean for your game, sir.' A demanding monster with his men, he had been instructed to treat the civilians with great respect.

'Don't make it damp or the cards will get wet,' Martyn told him.

'No, sir, they won't get wet because I will use this towel, sir, to dry the table.'

Angus was leaving. 'I'm going to get my head down now because we're off early tomorrow. So if Jamie Dermott's recording that fucking hopping frog shit in our tent . . .' He could be heard grumbling all the way across the cookhouse.

'That young man needs to get over himself,' said Martyn.

'He's not called Mr Angry for nothing.'

'He's just like his father,' said Masud. 'Yes, oh yes, his father was just exactly the same. His name's McCall, I believe?'

Finn stared at Masud as the man dried the table with unnecessary zeal, his face frowning with concentration.

'You know his father?'

Masud paused.

'I knew that boy when he walked in here the first day and I've spent these months, many long months, racking my brains to know how I know him. Finally one day I realized. He looks just like his father and his father worked for me in the Falklands. John McCall, I think his name was, yes I'm sure it was John McCall.'

Finn leaned forward, his face all acute angles and his eyes narrow.

'His dad worked for *you*?'

'John McCall was one of my cooks. We had a tent in a field, gracious knows how many ration packs, not one ounce of fresh food and we had to open all the ration packs and cook for hundreds of men every day. It was a difficult time, an exceptionally difficult time, to tell you the truth, probably worse than Iraq. Because it was very, very cold and we are talking about very, very hungry men.'

Finn said: 'His dad was a *cook*?'

Masud nodded extravagantly.

'Oh yes, oh yes. We were Army Catering Corps in those days. Then we were the Royal Logistic Corps and then soon after that I was a private company. Doing the same thing for the same boys but as a private company. Well, I ask you, how strange is the world?'

But Finn did not answer this question. He had one of his own.

'So John McCall was a cook in the Army Catering Corps?'

'Oh yes, certainly. He was guaranteed to serve your sausages with a scowl, that was John McCall.'

A huge grin spread across Finn's face.

'So Angry's dad was ACC. Not SAS. Did anyone ever go from being an army cook to fighting in the elite special forces?'

Masud laughed. 'I don't believe that is very possible. To tell you the truth, I think John McCall was just a very grumpy cook, actually, and it seems to me his son is rather similar.'

He wandered off to wipe down another table, chuckling to himself.

'SAS. ACC!' Even Martyn had heard references to Angus's dad in the cookhouse. 'Well, I can see how you could get those two mixed up. Leave out the Cs. Add a few Ss. Yes, I can see how Angus might think his pa was in the SAS.'

Finn started to laugh. He flung down his cards and his whole body shook with laughter.

'He was a fucking cook! I don't believe it! What a Walt!'

Martyn was laughing too, now.

'I mean,' said Finn, 'Mr Angry's dad wasn't just in the Regiment. He was a war hero who won back the Falklands single-handed!

And you should have seen Angry with those SAS snipers! "Do you remember my father, do you recognize his name . . . ?" '

'So is the father lying? Or the son?'

'Definitely, definitely the father. Angry believes every fucking word. You should see him when we're out there fighting. Doing things that are so brave they're insane. And then he goes all solemn and says: "It's what my dad would have done." For fuck's sake! What his Dad would have done is turn the sausages over in the pan!'

Martyn laughed again.

'I guess you're not going to let him hear the end of this.'

Finn's face pulled itself back into something like its normal shape and he looked serious for a moment.

'Nah,' he said. 'Nah, I'm not going to tell him. Angry drives me insane with his dad talk. But he's built his whole life on the back of his dad's lies. I couldn't take it all away from him.'

Across the cookhouse, Asma was eating alone because Jean was saying goodbye to Iain Kila. Her friend arrived breathlessly and grabbed the last meal.

'Won't you see him in the morning?' asked Asma.

'They're leaving at 0400. So I kissed him goodbye. In a sangar.'

Asma raised her eyebrows.

'Just a minute. Last time I asked you if you liked him you said yuck, yuck, yuck.'

Jean blushed. 'Well, I still think he's a bit yuck. But they're going away to this flimsy camp made out of barbed wire for a whole week. And right after we've shot the local warlord. So I thought I should kiss him in case he doesn't come back.'

Asma shrugged and said nothing.

'You're not saying goodbye to Gordon, then?'

'Nope.'

'He came in here earlier. He was looking around for you, I'm sure.'

Asma stabbed her food with her fork.

'He can look all he likes. I'm still fucking angry with him.'

Jean caught her eye.

'Asma. You're angry with the British Army for shooting your

bonny blue-eyed boy and you're taking it out on Gordon. And why on earth did you have to bring farmhouses and polo into it?'

Asma put down her fork and sighed.

'I shouldn't have said that. I really had a go at him just because he's posh. So I expect he thinks I'm jealous.'

'Are you?'

'I wouldn't want his big house and all his fields and horses. What would I do with them? I can't even imagine going home and meeting his mum. For drinks in the drawing room. I just couldn't do it, Jean.'

'You're prejudiced,' said Jean.

'I am not.'

'Has he invited you home to meet his mum?'

'Well . . . yes.'

'Asma, you're a sad cow. He's got over his prejudice. You just can't get over yours.'

But Asma shook her head.

'I don't buy into their crap. I don't buy into who they are or how they think. I know he was a bit *wahabi* and probably a Pashtun nationalist and you thought it was suspicious the way he rubbished the local shrine, but you can say what you like about Asad, he probably had more in common with me than Gordon does.'

In the night, when she woke up and heard the first men up preparing for their departure, Asma felt a small twinge of guilt and regret. She turned over. She tried to go back to sleep.

Then she remembered that Asad was dead and she felt a renewed surge of anger. Someone who had never met him and didn't understand his cause had ordered his death and the SAS had appeared from nowhere and shot him and had now evaporated back to Hereford.

Probably the suspicious officers, Gordon Weeks among them, would offer a different interpretation but she knew that, in the meetings with Asad, human relationships nurtured on the carpet over cups of sweet tea had triumphed briefly over weapons. And what had they done? Shot him.

She had not been inside a mosque for many years and she looked on Islam with the cold distance of a divorcee. She was a member of the British Army. No one had coerced her into joining. But the

British Army had killed Asad. For the second time on this tour she had the uncomfortable feeling that she had personally shot her Moslem brother.

She did not open her eyes but lay in bed listening for the sound of the departing convoy.

Chapter Forty-eight

DAVE DID NOT SLEEP. HE MANAGED TO GET HIS HANDS ON THE satellite phone when it was still only ten thirty at night in the UK.

Sure that the hospital would have sent Jenny home by now, he dialled his own number first.

'Nope. Still there.' Trish sounded sleepy. 'And she's getting a bit miserable on that hospital food. I took her in something tasty tonight to tickle her appetite but she's gone right off everything.'

'That's what she did towards the end when she was pregnant with Vicky,' said Dave. But Trish, as always, knew better.

'She had a good diet throughout that pregnancy. No, Dave, I'm afraid that something's very wrong if Jennifer's off her food like this.'

Knowing that Trish would not be happy unless something was very wrong somewhere, Dave rang the hospital. This time he got through to the ward.

'We don't normally give the phone to patients after four in the afternoon,' said the nurse. 'This is extremely late to call.'

'But I'm her husband.'

'Most husbands get here during visiting hours.'

She sounded prim and disapproving.

'I'm not most husbands. I'm on the other side of the world. I'm in Afghanistan and I'd like to talk to my wife.'

'Can't you phone during our normal hours?'

'Well,' said Dave, 'I suppose I could try having a word with the Taliban to arrange a little ceasefire during your visiting times . . .'

'All right, all right,' said the nurse. 'But please try to respect hospital rules in future.'

Dave gritted his teeth and waited a long time. Finally a small, sad voice he hardly recognized came on the line.

'Daaaaave!'

Oh, shit, she was crying.

'Stop crying,' he said. When soldiers cried, as they occasionally, unaccountably and ashamedly did while fighting, his policy was to grip them immediately. Stop crying, he would say in a brisk voice, get yourself together, focus and do a professional job out there.

But with Jenny he couldn't even manage the brisk tone. And the other stuff, about focusing and being professional, didn't really apply. He stood out under the Afghan stars, the phone pressed to his ear, listening to a woman crying in Wiltshire. The base and his mates and the lads suddenly weren't here. Just the stars and the sound of Jenny's sobs.

'Jen, tell me how you're feeling,' he said at last.

Her sobs eased a bit.

'Fucking awful. I told them to induce me just to get it over with but they thought I could go a little bit longer and every bit longer I go on is better for the baby.'

'But you're important too.'

'Jenny isn't here any more. She's been replaced by a big swollen-up monster who can't move her feet or her hands and whose head's going to explode any minute.'

'Oh, shit, I wish I was with you.' He had a horrible feeling that was all he ever said to her these days.

She was crying again now: 'And there was a story on the news tonight about some soldiers who shot some poor little Afghan children and . . .' Pause for sobs. 'It wasn't you, was it?'

'No, love. We give them sweets.'

'Oh. That's OK then.'

'They probably got shot because some poor little Taliban fighters were using them as human shields.'

But she was crying again now.

'Look, I can't help it, Dave. People get emotional before they have babies. And I know you hate it when I'm like this and I know you want me to be strong and sensible and make it all right that you're away but just now it's not all right, Dave, it's *not, not, not fucking all right*!'

Dave suspected that Jenny was sharing this one not just with him but with Nurse Prim and an entire ward of large-bellied women, all nodding in agreement.

'You've got to leave the army! You've got to. Because it's bloody awful being looked after by your mum like all the girls who don't know who the father is. The family men should be here with their families.'

'Stop, Jen. You know I love you and you know I want to be there. But I can't. And I have to go away for a few days. So I won't be able to phone. I feel terrible about it. You know what this is doing to me.'

'You! You! What do you think it's doing to me? You never even ring!'

'I do but they don't pick up the phone on your ward or they pick up and then cut me off. I do my best.'

Like shattered glass, she was breaking into sobs again.

'Oh, Christ,' said Dave. 'If thinking about someone can help and caring about someone can help, then that's what I'm doing, OK? Thinking about you and loving you and Vicky and the baby and caring about you. But I won't be able to call you. So please, please try to calm down and relax just for me so you don't have pre-eclampsia any more and you can go home. Don't for God's sake have the baby when I can't even speak to you.'

Now she was inconsolable. He held the phone away from his ear while she cried and cried. His Jenny, his strong, determined Jenny, was awash with hormones and at the mercy of her blood pressure. She had turned into this shouting, sobbing wreck.

'Can I talk to the doctor? Or even that nurse?' he asked her. But she could not hear him over her tears.

When the call ended he thought of putting in a request for compassionate leave. It might even be granted. But that would mean deserting his men out here, and deserting them just before a dangerous five-day operation. It would be like a snake shedding a skin. He didn't want to do it.

'Er . . . Sarge . . .' said a small voice.

Dave opened his eyes. He realized he had been gripping the

phone as though it was about to run away. He saw Mal standing there, waiting for him.

'Sorry, Bilaal,' he said. 'You want the phone?'

'Nah, Swift's next . . .'

Mal gestured into the well of darkness where Swift stood, barely perceptible.

'Here,' said Dave. 'I've finished now.'

'Thanks, Sarge,' said Swift, taking the phone and stealing off into the night with it. Everyone had a favoured private phone spot, somewhere the signal was strong enough and he could fool himself he was alone. Then at the end of the call there would invariably be someone waiting silently to take it. You could never be alone in an FOB.

Dave expected Mal to evaporate just as Swift had, but instead he stayed nearby.

'What's up with you, Mal?' asked Dave. '1 Section don't even have to get up yet. Can't you sleep?'

'No,' said Mal.

Dave felt weary. Right now he needed to walk through the quiet night and think about Jenny and instead he would have to talk to Bilaal.

'Want to help me carry ammo and talk?'

'Yeah, great, Sarge, good.' Mal sounded nervous. He was a skinny lad with a lot of nervous energy. Whenever a battle was starting Dave could hear Mal clearing his throat over and over again. He often giggled as he fired. And if he had told Mal either of these things he would be amazed.

Dave wondered if Mal was going to start talking about some woman problem. Whenever 1 Section stopped for a brew, Mal would be talking about women. He was obsessed, as though he had only just discovered their existence.

'Sarge, you know I'm a Moslem?'

Dave was so surprised that he stopped. This was already not sounding like the kind of conversation you have loading ammunition. 'Well . . . yes. But I don't see you dropping down on your knees every time you hear the call to prayer.'

'I was brought up Moslem. We were never, you know, devout. But I've always been on a Friday.'

'To the mosque?'

'Well, yeah, but, I mean, I'm normal too. After the mosque, I go out clubbing.'

'Normal means lots of different things to lots of different people.' Dave was curious to know where this conversation was leading. He realized he preferred to talk to one of his men about something that was bothering him than think about his phone call to Jenny. Because no matter how important what was going on at home, it was so far away that you could always find something much nearer to eclipse it.

'This Moslem thing, I sort of hide it, know what I mean?' asked Mal, offering Dave a cigarette and lighting one himself.

For a moment Mal's face, brown and lean, wrapped around his cigarette, was illuminated. Then he inhaled and there was only the red tip at the end, glowing in the dark.

'So you feel you have to hide it?' asked Dave.

'Yeah. Because we're fighting a bunch of ragheads, right? And I don't want people thinking I'm one of them. And anyway, I'm not. I'm not like them.'

'No. Because they're trying to take over this country and we're trying to stop them,' said Dave.

'Yeah, that's it. All I've got in common is I know a bit of the Quran. And we look a bit the same.'

'So what's up then, Mal? Any of the lads got a problem with you being a Moslem?'

'No, no, nothing like that. It's at home, Sarge.'

'At home?'

'See, there are a lot of Moslems where we live and they see me drinking and clubbing and chasing women and they don't think nothing about it. But then they hear I'm out in Afghanistan fighting other Moslems. And they don't like that.'

'This isn't a war against Islam.'

'Well, the way they see it, Islam's got a war against the infidel. And I'm fighting on the wrong side, see.'

Dave was asking himself why Mal was telling him this now, just before their departure.

'Are you worried your family could suffer because you're out here?'

'They already are suffering, Sarge. See, they haven't been telling

335

me because they didn't want to worry me but then my sister sent a bluey the other day. And I want to go home and sort the bastards out. I want to sort them out a lot more than I want to see off the Taliban.'

'What exactly's happened?'

'My sisters get spat at in the street. My brothers drive these taxis, see, and someone keeps trying to torch them. And my mum and dad were just sitting down to a nice meal and some fucking bastard put a flaming rag through the letterbox. They soaked it in petrol and set light to it and then stuffed it into my mum's hallway that she's kept so nice all these years.'

'Shit,' said Dave. 'That's a criminal offence. I hope they called the police.'

'The police have done fuck all! They take notes and they don't do nothing. They told my dad they don't want to inflame community tensions. Inflame. That's the word they used. And what my dad should have said was: then the community needs to stop inflaming my fucking hallway. But my dad's not like that, he'll just nod his head when people treat him like shit.'

Dave thought for a moment.

'I'm sorry, Mal. This is terrible.'

'And it's all my fucking fault, innit? It's my fault for joining up.'

'No!'

'And my brothers know who's doing it. People I was at school with, who used to be my friends, they're the ones!'

It was easy to imagine Mal in the school playground, demanding justice against aggressors, attacking them furiously, standing his ground in his nervous, excited way.

'Sarge, I want to go home and sort this one out.'

'You what?'

'I want to go home. If the police won't see to those fucking bastards, I'll have to see to them myself.' Mal's eyes were glittering in the dark.

'Now just a minute . . .'

'See, I'm the youngest in my family. I've got all these brothers and sisters and they're much older than me, and they get attacked, they keep their heads down. They're like that Taliban dude we shot. Sitting up in the tree with his weapon wedged there, keeping very quiet hoping we wouldn't notice his fucking legs dangling in front of our faces? That's my family! Keep quiet and it'll go away. But we shot that geezer, didn't we? Keeping quiet doesn't do anything! My family don't know you have to fight people.'

Mal drew breath and Dave was able to interrupt him at last.

'You came here to fight people. You're fighting the Taliban in a professional way as part of a disciplined army sent here by a democratic government—'

But Mal would not let him continue.

'Back home in Wythenshawe, no one knows those words, Sarge! They don't know about democratic and disciplined and—'

'You joined the army to fight and that's what you do out here and that's what you're paid for. You're not paid to take your fights home to Wythenshawe.'

'Sarge, if I didn't go to Jackpot today, I could maybe just go home for a week instead, maybe bring my R&R forward and—'

'And make matters worse there? Mal, I can refer this one up the chain if you want me to. And they might say yes. But it would be a mistake. And they wouldn't say yes before we take off in the wagons this morning.'

'But maybe if you ask them now, it could all be agreed by the time we get back.'

'I will if you want. But take my advice and don't do it. Your family's older and wiser than you and they're dealing with it. You're here and your job is to be a soldier.'

'But if I just had a week I could—'

'We all have troubles we'd like to fly home and sort out. But we have to concentrate on doing our job.'

He could not see Mal's face clearly.

'It's terrible what's happening to your family. But you can't do anything from Afghanistan and that's probably a good thing. If you go back and get into a fight, it won't help your family and it won't help you.'

'I dunno,' said Mal.

'You'll have to come to Jackpot, it's too late to change that.'

Mal was silent for a long time.

'Think about it. Let me know if you want me to kick it upstairs.

But if you take my advice you'll let your family handle it back at home and you'll do what you came here for.'

Dave heard his voice, strong and sure. He should take his own advice. Only a few minutes ago he'd been considering asking for permission to fly home himself. His thoughts reverted to Jenny again. She had probably already calmed down from that angry, emotional phone call and by now she would be regretting it. So her blood pressure would fall. So she wouldn't have pre-eclampsia any more. And then everything would be OK.

Chapter Forty-nine

EVERYONE, EXCEPT MARTYN, EMILY AND THE ENGINEERS, HATED Jackpot on arrival. One glance at the flimsy defences made the soldiers uneasy.

'This'll be good in a mortar attack,' they said miserably.

The sangars were solid enough, built up on hesco, but the rest of the perimeter was trench and wire with, in places, sandbag protection. The civilian zone was marked by a low wall of sandbags but they, too, had to use the exposed oil drums for toilets. Except for Emily. She had a small, private area with sheeting around it.

'Can't I use that too?' demanded Martyn.

'No,' said Emily. 'This is the Ladies.'

'I don't want to take a crap in front of everyone in this camp,' Martyn complained to the OC.

'You'll have to,' said Major Willingham, 'unless Emily agrees to share it.'

Otherwise the camp consisted only of a collection of tents and the perimeter wire.

Martyn studied the wire.

'Nick,' he said to the OC. 'Think we could move it about twenty feet to the right? Seems to me that part of our exploration area is just outside the fence.'

The OC said, in a voice that was many degrees lower than the ambient air temperature: 'No, Martyn.'

Martyn burst out laughing.

'Just kiddin' you, Nick!'

The OC did not smile.

The camp sat at the base of the hills which swept up to the huge, looming purple mountains. The hills were to the north and so gave it no protection from the desert sun, which was even more merciless here than at the FOB. A constant hot wind created dust devils, tiny tornados that span purposefully across the desert, through the wire and straight into the camp. In the distance, the Early Rocks rose out of the flat plain like weird and lonely skyscrapers.

The wind distributed the sand everywhere. It got into people's clothes, their tea, their ration packs, their boots, their ears.

Dave and Sgt Somers of 2 Platoon did not keep their men on boil-in-the-bag; they had resolved that every day they would boost morale by cooking something from the ration packs. Dave liked to think he could turn virtually any ration pack into a presentable meal: he'd trained as a cook when he first left school, before he'd been seduced by the army recruitment ads. And he had persuaded Masud to let him take some fresh food and a few spices from the kitchen to Jackpot.

But the men's reaction to his first concoction was unenthusiastic.

'Delicious, Sarge,' they said, digging their plastic spoons into his stew. 'Tastes of sand.'

'Oh shit,' said Dave.

'No, Sarge,' said Finn. 'Sand. That's better than shit.'

'I can sense that you've attempted to include a subtle blend of herbs and spices,' Boss Weeks told Dave. 'But I'm sorry to tell you that the predominant taste is definitely sand.'

'If we had to stay here and eat sand for a long time,' said the OC, who had heard Dave was a good cook and so was eating with 1 Platoon, 'our teeth would be ground down to almost nothing. That's precisely what happened to the Native Americans. Ancient skulls show that, by the end of their lives, desert dwellers had no teeth left.'

The men looked at him miserably.

'We could just swallow without chewing,' suggested Jamie. 'That way we'd fuck up our intestines but we'd keep our teeth.'

Dave laughed at that. It was relieved laughter because this was the first time he'd heard Jamie speak since they'd left Sin City. He walked around looking so miserable that his eyebrows were knitted together. It could only be something to do with Agnieszka.

The soldiers were soon bored. All they could do was keep watch and stare in disbelief at the wild enthusiasm of the engineers for this desolate and empty place. Even Emily stalked around the camp in her sensible shoes, rubbing her hands and smiling happily.

'I told you. This is R&R for us, while the civvies do a bit of work for once,' said Finn, dealing another hand of cards to a group of lads from 2 Platoon, who he assured Dave just played for cigarettes.

Angus preferred to be busy. He volunteered for any job going, helped the engineers carry their kit and did other people's stag for them while they slept or played cards.

He stood up in the tower surveying the endless flatness of the desert. He liked to stare at the Early Rocks in the distance; they looked like something that had been there since the beginning of time. He also kept an eye on the antics of the civilians. They'd brought a lot of equipment in separate wagons, including some kind of drill.

'They're never drilling for fucking oil already!' he said to Streaky, who was on stag with him.

Streaky yawned. He was not interested in the oil exploration. 'I am so fucking bored. At least back at Sin City there was a bit of to-ing and fro-ing and stuff in the town to look at. I even got to like that geezer calling from his tower every five minutes.'

'Moslems have to stop what they're doing and pray about twenty times a day,' said Angry knowledgeably. 'That geezer's telling them to get down the mosque.'

Streaky yawned again. 'I used to think he was a noisy bastard but at least he kept me awake.'

'Don't you write rap in your head when you're on stag?'

'I'm so bored I can't even write nothing,' said Streaky. 'I just want to go back to the FOB. And so does everyone else. I never seen so many miserable soldiers. There's the boss was fighting hammer and tongs in the wagon with that Intelligence woman and now he's gone sad, there's Dave worried because his missus is having a baby, there's Jamie in a strop about something. Even Mal's not his normal self.'

'I'm my normal self,' said Angry.

'Me too. And Binman. I reckon it's because we've been out here a long time but we've still got a couple of months to go.'

Angus said: 'I could do another six months. I don't want to go home.'

Beneath, the contractors were burying something that looked like a bolt. They had drilled a hole and buried three so far. Emily and Martyn argued about the exact location of each hole. The last bolt had been buried and then, after a heated argument, dug up again.

'Streaky . . .'

'Yeah.'

'I saw something move over there.'

Streaky looked. 'Emily?'

'No! Up in the hills.'

They both stared at the rugged and scarred landscape. Where they rose out of the flat sand, near the perimeter fence, there were prickly, moisture-starved bushes that looked as hostile as the desert itself. Huge boulders, which geological eons ago might have cascaded down from the mountains, lay like pebbles on the hillside.

'Where?'

'See Three Boulders? See Red Bush? In between.'

Streaky creased up his eyes to peer at the landmarks.

'I can't see anything. Nothing's going to fucking move in this heat.'

'I saw a shadow or something!'

Streaky stared and stared.

'You imagined it. Everything looks as though it's wiggling about a bit in the heat.'

Angus was stubborn.

'I saw something . . .'

'Well, nip down to the boys at the entrance and tell them to get on the radio,' said Streaky, yawning. 'And I'll keep looking.'

Angus ran down to the men from 2 Platoon on stag. They looked anxious and immediately radioed the tent that had been set up as an ops room. Angus ran back up to Streaky.

'Seen anything else?'

'Nope.'

'Have you been looking? Just to the left of Red Bush?'

'I've been looking but there's nothing out there.'

Word was now spreading around the camp. A few people came out of their tents with their weapons. Everyone was staring towards the hillside. Even the contractors realized that something was up and stopped work. The OC emerged, pen in hand, hands on hips. Dave came up to the sangar.

'What did you see, McCall?'

Angry began to feel embarrassed.

'I don't know, Sarge. Just movement.'

'What sort of movement?'

'I don't know.'

'Did you see anything, Bacon?'

'Nope. And I've been looking.'

Angus described again where he had seen the movement and Dave stood still watching for some minutes.

'It was probably the wind,' he said at last. 'Look.'

He gestured out across the desert behind them to the Early Rocks where a sandstorm was visible. A hot breeze had begun to bluster against their helmets and throw sand onto their faces. It was approaching.

People went back to their tents and closed them up against the sandstorm. Only the contractors worked on.

'Can't you stop until the storm is over?' asked the OC.

Martyn looked astonished.

'Why would we do that? We're just getting to the exciting bit.'

The OC did not share his excitement. 'Which is?'

'Dynamite!'

Even Emily looked pleased.

'For many years now, for environmental reasons, dynamite has been rarely used. But because we are working under exceptional conditions here we have been given permission.'

Martyn grinned happily. He did not seem to notice the sand in his hair, teeth and ears. He wore sunglasses but it was probably in his eyes too.

'In my view, dynamite's always been the best. See, we send a charge down into the shot hole over here . . .'

'It will be over there,' corrected Emily.

'And the geophones we've planted will give us seismic readings.

343

Now, if we've got them in the right place and if Emily can get her signal and imaging processing right . . .'

'It will give us a sort of picture of what lies beneath the surface,' finished Emily excitedly. She walked off to the group of waiting engineers. When she was out of earshot Martyn leaned towards Major Willingham.

'Which we don't need because when you've been in this game as long as me you know from the aerial photos, some elementary surveying and the gravity readings exactly what's under there. But I'd hate to put these guys out of a job.'

There was another radio message from the sentries.

'Excuse me,' said the major. 'We have a keen rifleman who's insisting once again that he can see something moving in the hills.'

'Which keen rifleman?'

'McCall.'

Martyn smiled. 'Angus. He's too darn keen. Probably just wants something to do.'

Anyone prepared to brave the sandstorm came out to look at the hills. But there was noticeably less interest this time.

'Where was it?' Dave asked Angus patiently.

'Same place!'

'Did you see it, Streaky?'

'Nope.'

'It must have been something big if you saw it in a fucking blizzard.'

The hot wind lashed their faces and threw handfuls of sand at them. The sky was turning orange.

'Yeah, it was something flapping. Like, in England it would be washing on the line. But here it's probably someone's clothes.'

Dave watched the hills.

'Angry,' he said at last. 'Either it's gone or you're imagining things. Now you two get down off this tower and send Jamie Dermott up. We'll finish your stag for you.'

Streaky looked grateful but Angus said, as he climbed down: 'I definitely saw something, Sarge.'

Jamie arrived.

'Thanks, Sarge. Stag in a sandstorm is every soldier's dream.'

'They only had another ten minutes to go and McCall kept seeing things.'

'He just wants something to happen.'

Dave told Jamie where Angus claimed to have seen movement but now there was so much sand you could barely see the hills at all.

'I wanted to talk to you, Jamie,' said Dave. 'Anything up?'

Jamie did not look at him.

'No.'

'Don't piss about with me. You don't have to tell me but I wish you would. I'm getting sick of seeing you slope about like a sore prick at a stag party. What's happened?'

Jamie shuffled round so his back was to the wind. Dave waited. Jamie's lean face looked dark. It wasn't the tan and it wasn't the facial hair or even the sand. His face was shadowed the way rooms get dark when you close the curtains and shut the doors.

'Is it Agnieszka?'

Jamie swung to look at him.

'What have you heard about her?'

Dave tried to appear startled by this question. He shrugged innocently. 'Jenny's in hospital so I'm not getting any gossip. Have people been telling you things?'

Jamie sighed.

'No. But Niez's changed. She's sort of . . . cut herself off from me.'

'Why would she do that?'

'She might just be pissed off with me being away. Seriously pissed off. Or she might have met someone else. Or both.'

'Got any evidence?'

'Not really. It's just the way . . . Well, she used to be really pleased to hear from me. You could tell by the end of the call she felt better about everything. And now it doesn't make any difference when I ring. That's how it feels.'

There must be rumours flying around camp, Dave thought, about Agnieszka and this bloke. And the rumours must have reached Jamie.

'We have to trust our wives,' he said. 'Because that's all we can do.'

345

'Yeah,' said Jamie miserably. 'Yeah.'

'I wish I could ask Jen to go over and talk to her . . .'

Jamie looked embarrassed. 'Your problems are worse than mine. Jenny's ill and she's having a baby and you can't even phone her.'

'Know how I cope with that one?' asked Dave. 'I don't think about it. I could worry about Jen all day but what's the point? There's nothing I can do and worrying about it'll mean I can't do my job properly here. That's what a professional soldier has to do, mate, and you're a professional soldier. He has to leave home behind.'

Jamie gave the ghost of a smile. 'It'd be easier to leave home behind if we had a bit more to do here. I mean, I can understand why Angry keeps seeing flipflops under every boulder. At least that'd mean there's a chance of some action.'

They finished the duty in silence. Dave was thinking that, despite his claim, he hadn't managed to cut Jenny out of his thoughts. At any random moment in the day, no matter how busy he was, he would suddenly hear, as though in a dream, their last phone call, punctuated by her sobs. At night he tried not to give in to the panic he felt because he was in the middle of the desert, unreachable, while Jenny and the baby lay in hospital in a life-threatening state.

When they came down from the tower, Dave was about to busy himself with his next sand stew when the OC called him over. Boss Weeks was already there, smiling. Dave hadn't seen him smile since his pretty friend from Intelligence had sat at the front of the Vector bawling him out.

'Good news,' announced the major. 'I've had word from Bastion that Broom and Connor were stable enough to leave Afghanistan yesterday. They'll be landing shortly in the UK.'

Dave smiled too.

'They wouldn't have sent them on stretchers if they thought they could hang on and send them in body bags!' he said.

'Exactly!' The OC was beaming. 'There are so many long faces around here that I'm hoping it'll cheer everyone up.'

Chapter Fifty

BEN BROOM HALF OPENED HIS EYES. THERE WAS A STRONG POSSIBILITY that he was dead. He did not try to remember the event that had led to his death but images floated through his mind. A blue, blue sky, the colour burned away to one side by the white heat of a massive sun. His mates shouting to him but never coming near him.

There were other, darker images, of people standing over him and talking to him. But he didn't know any of these people. They weren't in his platoon or in his family. No one he loved was there. So death was full of strangers.

A stranger was standing over him now.

Broom thought that probably the dead didn't speak to each other but he decided to try anyway. He was surprised by the sound that emerged, of a wheezing, clanking old motor.

'Come again?' said the man.

'Am I dead?' repeated Broom.

'Nah. You're not dead. This isn't heaven. And I'm no angel.'

Broom stared at the man and gradually he felt his life and his past taking shape inside him. He had been blown up in a minefield and taken here to Bastion where the surgeon had told him he'd lost the lower part of his leg. He felt sad as the weightlessness of not-knowing left him and was replaced by the burden of this knowledge.

'Funny, you look like a bloke I used to know.'

'Who would that be then, Ben?'

'He was in our platoon. But he got casevaced back to England.'

The man grinned. 'You don't say.'

'His name was Steve.'

'That's a coincidence, then,' said the man. 'My name's Steve.'

'Steve . . . Buckle.'

'Fucking incredible! The same! That's my name too!'

Broom blinked. He raised his eyebrows so they disappeared somewhere under the cover of his bright red hair.

'Hello, Steve.'

'Hello, mate.'

'So . . . did they fly you back out? To pick up your leg from the cookhouse?'

'My leg! In the cookhouse! Now you're really talking crap, mate. They've had you drugged up to the eyeballs. They didn't fly me back to Afghanistan, they flew you back to England.'

Broom looked at him trustingly.

'Where am I then, Steve?'

'Selly Oak. Just look at the telly and you'll know you're in England.'

Broom did not move but his eyes swivelled to the screen. Two glittering bodies, strangely linked, cavorted in unison across a lit stage.

'I was watching it while I waited for you to wake up,' said Steve. 'And know what I was thinking? Could I be the first amputee on *Strictly*?'

Broom's eyes moved from the TV, with its swirling, complete human beings, to Steve Buckle.

'Must be Saturday then.'

'You've got it, Ben! I'm at Headley Court now but they brought me up here for a long weekend to see the docs and to see you and a bloke called Ryan Connor who took over a gimpy after I got blown out of the platoon.'

'Ryan's really been poorly,' said Broom.

'Yeah, right. Not like you, Ben, you picture of good health, you.'

'The bottom half of my leg got blown off by a landmine. Fuck me, Steve, am I going to be explaining that to people for the rest of my life?'

'Yeah. See, it's not, like, a temporary thing.'

Broom felt his eyes go wet. He had lost a leg. He had lost it for ever.

Steve Buckle sat down.

'Go on then, cry. I fucking cried, mate.'

Broom's arm was bandaged and so was part of his face. He was lying flat and had no idea how to move. He lay crying quietly until Steve placed a tissue in his good hand. This was a revelation. Broom had forgotten he had a good arm. Very slowly he closed his fingers on the tissue, bent his elbow and aimed the tissue at his nose.

'Well done, mate,' said Steve.

'Oh, fuck it,' said Broom. 'What's going to happen now? What's happening with my bird?'

'Your mum's outside with the bloke from BLESMA. He's getting her prepared to see you without your leg.'

'What about Kylie?'

'Dunno,' said Steve dully. He had heard about Kylie from Leanne.

'Is she out there?'

'Dunno, mate.'

'Shit, what will I do now? What can I do without my leg?'

'Well, it took me a long time to understand this, or maybe a long time to believe it. But you can do pretty much everything. And it'll be easier for you than me because I've got a short stump and it's a fucker for fitting a socket. Yours came off below the knee. That's much easier.'

'I won't be good enough for the Paralympics. I won't be good enough for anything. I won't be good enough for my bird. Buckle, why did I have to be in that minefield? There are a hundred and twenty men in R Company, I don't see why it had to be me.'

Steve switched off the TV.

'At least you admit it. I spent more than a month telling everyone my leg was still there. I could feel it, see. Can you feel yours?'

Broom looked thoughtful.

'I can't feel anything at all. I'm sort of numb. I hope I don't pee in the bed.'

'You're on a catheter, probably. And you can't feel anything because of the pain relief. But you will.'

Broom stared at him.

'Does yours still hurt?'

349

'Yeah. And I mean it's sometimes excruciating. That's where there's no leg any more. Explain that if you can. The doc can't.'

'Can you walk yet, Buckle?'

'Just wedge yourself up on your good elbow and watch me. I'm not very good yet because we're having trouble with my socket.'

Broom, with a supreme effort, raised himself a couple of inches from the bed and leaned on his elbow. Steve Buckle, a big, tall man and one of the platoon's dominant personalities, shuffled, very slowly, with intense concentration, along the side of the bed. He did not speak until he had sat down breathlessly on the chair.

'See? I mostly use a crutch but I'll be throwing it away soon. I'm getting a leg for running, maybe a couple of them. And there'll be a leg for walking. Then I could have a very smart leg which looks like the other one. A leg for the shower . . . probably even more legs than that. But I've got to learn to walk first.'

'You'd turn into a fucking spider if you tried to use them all at once.'

'You'll have that too, Broom. You'll have a leg for every occasion. We'll start feeling sorry for those poor buggers with only the two.'

Broom remained propped on his elbow but closed his eyes.

'Buckle, you didn't look ready for *Strictly* just then.'

'Listen, mate. I don't know about dancing but I do know about fighting. And Afghanistan is the best fucking fight for years. I'm getting used to the idea that I'm missing this tour but I'll tell you something: I'm not going to miss the next one.'

Broom kept his eyes shut.

'Get real.'

'You feel that way now because you're still at the beginning. You're at the bit where you think your life's over. But it's not. It's all a big challenge but challenges are what we joined up for, mate. And I'm going to get back to the frontline. That's my biggest challenge yet.'

'You're married,' said Broom. 'Got kids?'

'Twins. Boys. They're not two years old yet. I'm going to be out-running them until they're at least twenty-one.'

'What about your wife then?'

'What about her?'

'Does she fancy you any more?'

'Dunno.'

'Haven't you seen her then?'

'She visits me in Headley Court. Just a few hours at a time.'

His tone was indifferent. Broom looked at his big face and saw he was angry.

'So, how is she with it?' he persisted.

'With what?'

'You having one leg.'

Steve shrugged.

'She pisses me off, to tell you the truth. It's the way she looks at me. All sympathy. *Sit there. Let me do that. How are you feeling?* Dabbing her eyes when she thinks I won't see. I want to clock her one. I went home for the weekend between Selly Oak and Headley Court. Big mistake. I ended up chucking my crutch at her.'

Broom was silent, thinking that Steve Buckle could be a scary sort of bloke.

'It's not her fault, mate. Why are you so pissed off with her?'

'Dunno. She's overweight. Doesn't take care of herself. Sits around doing nothing in front of the telly. Then she comes in looking all sorry for me and I think: I could live without you easier than I can live without my leg. And other times I think: why've you got two legs? You hardly use them.'

Broom eased himself off his elbow and lay back down.

'I do get really angry,' Steve said. 'You will too.'

Ben Broom was assaulted by fear after fear. They came sneaking up on him like a series of ambushes.

'Will I have to leave the army?'

'Shouldn't think so.'

'What will I do?'

'What do you want to do?'

'Same as before.'

Steve got up.

'Then do it.'

'My bird might not fancy me any more.'

'So find one who does.'

Steve started to leave the room. He used a crutch this time, moving forward with comparative ease.

Broom felt desperate. He didn't want to be left alone.

'When will they make me look at it?' he called.

Steve was near the door now.

'What? Your stump?'

Stump. The word was horrible. Broom nodded and swallowed.

'Not until you're ready. They know what they're doing.'

'When are you coming back?'

'When I've seen Ryan Connor and after your mum's been and your bird if she's here. And if either of them starts crying all over you, just tell them to fuck off. I mean it. Don't put up with their shit. You're soon going to be skiing better than they ever could.'

Ben Broom started reorganizing his face. It took a bit of effort. The muscles felt tired before he'd even started to practise a smile. But by the time his mother walked in with the welfare officer, red-haired, freckled and too tearful to speak, he was ready for her.

'Hi, Mum! Great to see you. For Chrissake, there's no need to cry because I'll be learning to ski soon . . .'

Chapter Fifty-one

'I'M GETTING FED UP WITH CLEANING WEAPONS ALL THE TIME AND never using them,' said Sol.

They had just eaten another sand sandwich. The civilians were busy. Angus had disappeared on stag again.

Binns said: 'I'm wishing the Taliban would attack us just to give us something to do.'

'Write a rap about Jackpot, Streaky,' Finn said to Bacon. 'We'll help. It'll give us something to do.'

'You can't write a rap about nothing happening,' said Streaky. 'Rap's rough and angry. Not bored and sleepy.'

'It's another game of cards then, lads,' said Finn, reaching for the pack.

Jamie groaned.

Mal closed his eyes.

'OK, guys, we've finished with the dynamite for now.'

Martyn had appeared in a cloud of fine dust.

'That's a shame,' said Finn. 'It was the only interesting thing going on around here.'

Everyone had wanted to set the dynamite off but Emily had shaken her head and wagged her finger.

'This is a radio-controlled explosion and human error could have a catastrophic effect on our results.'

'What happens now, Martyn?' asked Jamie.

Binns looked up hopefully.

'If you've finished with the dynamite, can we go back to Sin City?'

'Emily has to collate the results from all the seismometers. When she's put them together in the lab –' Martyn gestured to one of the Vectors – 'they should give us a complete picture. But if the images are wrong then we'll have to adjust them and repeat the experiment. So we can't go anywhere until she gives us the all-clear.'

'What are you going to do, then?' demanded Finn. 'While Emily's in her lab?'

'Play blackjack with you,' said Martyn, sitting down on an upturned crate.

The sandstorm had ended a couple of days ago but the camp was still covered with its sand. Even the playing cards retained a gritty residue.

Dave came out of the ops room holding a radio.

'McCall thinks he's seen some movement in the hills again,' he said.

Everyone groaned.

'Right, we'll have a few more pairs of eyes over there,' said Sol. 'Mal, Binman, Streaky, go for it.'

'But last time he said that we called out aerial surveillance and they didn't find anything!' moaned Binns.

'Yeah,' said Dave, 'but there was a sandstorm so the eye in the sky might have made a mistake.'

'Certainly,' agreed the OC, emerging behind him. 'And we shouldn't get complacent.'

But the men came back reporting there was nothing to see.

'Maybe,' said the boss to Dave, 'Angus should spend less time in the tower.'

'Well, let him finish his stag,' said Dave. 'He's down in ten minutes anyway.'

When a lad from 3 Section had replaced him, Angus climbed down from the tower to find Martyn sitting in the shade of the sangar.

'Hey, Angry, come talk to me.'

'What? Now?'

'Yeah. I'm sort of interested in this movement you keep seeing.'

Angus was already red from the heat and now he reddened still more.

'No one believes me.'

'Well, describe it, can you?'

Angus was surprised, but he sat down and got out a cigarette. He offered Martyn one and looked relieved when he didn't accept.

'Well, it's like a shadow. When the sandstorm was starting and I could hardly see the hills, that time it looked like it could have been a person. But the other times it's been like when you see a cloud shadow. Which sort of appears and then disappears when the sun goes in . . .'

'What do you think it is?'

Encouraged by his interest, Angus said: 'At first I thought maybe it was the shadow of an aircraft. Some sort of aerial surveillance. But I don't think so. I don't know what it is.'

'An animal?'

Angus shrugged.

'You want it to be Taliban. Right?'

Angus flicked his ash down. 'Well . . .'

'Because you want some action. Right?'

'That's what I signed up for.'

'You've already shown one helluva lot of courage. I've heard about some of the things you've done. Your dad must be proud of you.'

Angus looked at the ground.

'Not really. See, my dad was in the Regiment. So he did some amazing things himself. Especially in the Falklands war.'

'This is really none of my business . . . but can I say something?'

Angus watched Martyn's corrugated face curiously.

'Supposing I told you that you've already done much more than your dad ever did? Supposing I said that you don't have to keep trying to impress him, being a hero, looking for action. Because he never was in the Special Forces. Would that be a relief?'

Angus's eyes had grown suddenly bulbous. His cheeks were bright red. His cigarette was turning to ash.

'What do you mean?'

'I've grown to like you, Angry. I used to think you were a big thug but since then I've seen that you're a good guy underneath all that noise. That's why I'm telling you this.'

Angus seemed to swell in the heat.

'Your dad wasn't the hero you think.'

'What?'

'I'll tell you something. It's going to upset you at first. And then, in a little while, you'll begin to feel good about it.'

Chapter Fifty-two

JENNY LAY IN BED STARING AT THE DOCTOR. HE WAS YOUNG, brown-skinned, very busy and ordinary in every way. Except that his head kept erupting into bright stars.

'Feeling terrible?' he asked.

'Yes.'

'We can't let you go on with blood pressure like this. We've tried everything to get it under control but it's moving the wrong way. So I'm afraid we'll have to induce you.'

The doctor had no idea, Jenny thought, that now his head was spinning round and round like a horror movie.

'I just want it to stop now.' She meant his head, her sickness, the pain, the swelling, the whole horrible pregnancy. She wanted to swap it for a baby.

'It's not doing the baby any good either. So we'll go for some oxytocin now and we'll see how dilated you are in an hour.'

'OK.'

The nurse nodded and the doctor began to leave.

'Oh!' He turned. 'It may be quite quick once it starts, so I should get your partner here as soon as possible.'

'Ha!' said Jenny. It was a cross between a laugh and a cry. 'Ha!'

The nurse muttered something to the doctor.

'Afghanistan?' Jenny heard him say. 'Well, I don't think he's going to get back in time.'

Jenny wanted to shout: *Get back in time! He won't even know about it until next week!*

The midwife bustled in and started messing around with drips.

'Do you want to phone your birthing partner?'

Jenny called Trish who did her best not to appear flustered.

'Right. OK. I'll get Vicks over to your friend's house.'

'Mum. You don't have to do this. If you take Adi's children, she'll come.'

'Of course I want to be there!'

'Are you sure?'

Jenny found herself wishing that Dave's mum was staying again and could be her birth partner instead of Trish, who would approach the entire process anticipating that it could and probably would go wrong.

'Well, I think so . . .'

'Listen, just dial the number I left by the phone and talk to Adi. I don't care who comes.'

She felt too sick to argue. The nurse was taking her blood pressure and frowning.

'This had better work quickly . . .'

'Or what?' asked Jenny.

The nurse didn't answer but she continued to frown.

Jenny closed her eyes.

'Oh, Dave, Dave, Dave. You are such a fucking bastard.'

'I beg your pardon!' said the nurse.

'My husband. Should be here.'

'Your blood pressure would be just as high. Actually, it drops on some women the minute their husband walks out of the room. Now the best thing you can do for yourself and Baby is close your eyes, breathe slowly and relax.'

Jenny tried to close her eyes, breathe slowly and relax. But her heart was beating ludicrously, as if there was something big and scary in the room. And maybe there was. Her own loneliness. Dave's absence. The knowledge that she was bringing a child into the world and it would be a long time before he even knew about it. She felt hot water fall from her eyes, as though whatever was driving up her blood pressure was squeezing out her tears too.

Later, someone came in. Another nurse, another blood pressure check. She kept her eyes clamped shut. But whoever was here did not take her blood pressure. They were standing in the room silently, watching her.

'Who is it?' she asked.

'It no one really,' said a small voice.

'Agnieszka!'

'Oh my God, Jenny, I come at wrong time. I bring you flowers! I thought you ill in hospital. Then they say this is birthing room. I didn't know you have baby right now!'

Jenny opened her eyes and smiled.

'Agnieszka, give me a hug. I've never been so pleased to see anyone.'

Agnieszka leaned close in her squeaking leather jacket and jangling earrings.

'But you have baby now, this minute!'

'Not yet, they've only just induced me. Will you stay with me a while? Where's Luke?'

Agnieszka put the flowers on a shelf.

'Friend waits with him in car park.'

Jenny had never seen Agnieszka with a friend. Except that man.

'You'd better not stay too long then,' she said.

'Oh, Jenny, you have baby all alone?'

'My mum or Adi or someone should get here soon . . .'

'I stay till they arrive.'

She felt ridiculously grateful. She suddenly loved Agnieszka, for the way she stood so shyly, put the flowers where Jenny couldn't see them and then picked up her hand and squeezed it tight.

'God, it awful that Dave can't phone. I think our boys are now far away from base because I have no telephone call for days.'

'Yeah. They're out of contact for a while.'

Jenny bit her lip and fought tears. Agnieszka did the same but less successfully.

'These men! They say they love us. Then they leave us to have baby alone!'

Jenny thought of how Agnieszka struggled daily to deal with Luke's fits and his anger. 'And then they leave us to bring them up alone.'

Agnieszka nodded sadly.

'Dishwasher break. Gutter water run down wall. Drain blocked so bath full for hours. Things fall down. Buggy squeak. And where are men? In Afghanistan.'

They smiled at each other. Then Jenny watched Agnieszka's face dissolve into shooting stars.

'Why baby come so early?'

'My blood pressure's gone bananas. It's called pre-eclampsia.'

'I know this thing. I was nurse in Poland.'

'You're a nurse!' Jenny realized that she didn't know Agnieszka at all. They had never talked about her life in Poland, as if she hadn't really existed before she came to England.

'I come here so I never finish training. Sometimes I think that, if Jamie here to help, I continue training in England. But how is this possible with Jamie away?'

'OK,' said the midwife, bustling in with a file. 'Is this your birthing partner?'

'No, I stay until partner arrive,' said Agnieszka.

'Sorry, you'll have to go now,' the midwife told her. 'We can't have people coming in and out.'

Agnieszka looked pale and distraught as she hugged Jenny.

'Good luck,' she whispered as she left.

'Right.' The midwife was brisk. 'I have to take your blood pressure and we hope it's dropped. Then I'll check your dilation and we hope it's increased.'

'Supposing it's the other way around?'

'Then it's a C-section I'm afraid.'

'I don't want a Caesarean!'

The midwife took her blood pressure and pulled a face.

'You've got to do what's right for you and Baby. Which means you may not have a choice. I'll call the doctor now and I think he'll say he wants you in theatre right away. To be perfectly honest, I think they're ready for you in there.'

Jenny burst into tears.

'It's not the end of the world,' said the midwife. 'A lot of women ask for them.'

'But there's no one here with me!'

The midwife smiled.

'Only an obstetrician, an anaesthetist, a midwife, God knows how many theatre staff and two paediatricians. You can't be lonely in a crowd like that.'

But they're all strangers, thought Jenny.

After a mumbled conversation at the door the doctor nodded to a porter and Jenny was swept off along a hospital corridor towards the operating theatre.

Chapter Fifty-three

ANGUS AND FINN WERE ON STAG TOGETHER AGAIN.

'Just one more day here,' said Finn. 'Topaz Zero has promised we can go back to Sin City as soon as Emily's results are right, and they're almost right.'

'Great,' Angus said, without enthusiasm.

'They can't keep us here any longer because Marty needs a crap. He's not going to use the oil drums out in the open like everyone else. And Emily won't let him use her toilet.'

'He hasn't had a crap all week?'

'Nope. His bowels are probably silted up with sand.'

It was morning. The Early Rocks were at their clearest, lit up from the east. And the desert didn't look so flat when the sun was at this angle, lighting its contours. Across the camp the hills were mysterious with morning shadows.

'He had a talk with me,' said Angry suddenly.

'Topaz Zero? About his bowels?'

'No, Finn. About my dad.'

Finn had been scanning the hillside to discourage Angus from seeing things there. But now he swung round to look at his mate. 'Your dad?'

Angus did not meet his gaze.

'You know all about it. You're the only one who does.'

Finn turned back to the hillside.

'All about what?' he asked cautiously.

362

'Finny, stop pissing about. Masud told you and Martyn about my dad.'

'And Martyn's told you. What a fucking shit! Why did he do that?'

'You didn't tell anyone else?'

'No, Angry. Fuck it, I didn't even tell you!'

'Why not? We've come to blows before now over my dad.'

'Because he's your hero. I wasn't going to take that away from you.'

Finn looked at Angus and saw the pinched look of sleepless nights and disappointments.

'Masud might not be right, Angry.'

Angus's face twisted. 'That my dad was a cook, nothing more? I believe him.'

'Why?'

'Well . . . things.'

'Like what?'

'Like, I never saw my dad's medals and he always said they'd been stolen. I thought it was weird that he never tried to get them back. And . . . he told me a load of shit which didn't sound right. But I tried not to fucking notice.'

Finn took a deep breath.

'Going to have it out with him?'

'I've been lying in my cot at night thinking about killing him.'

Finn said: 'I want to kill Martyn. Why did he have to tell you?'

'First off I hated him for it. But now I think he was right when he said I was living under my dad's shadow. He said I should crawl out from behind it. See, I kept thinking I was seeing movement over by those boulders. And that was because I was looking extra hard. Because I wanted to be extra sharp.'

'What's going on down there?' asked Finn suddenly.

They looked across the camp. There was a small commotion. Sergeant Dave Henley seemed to be at the centre of it.

The OC called Dave over to his poncho. Here at Jackpot with its heat and inactivity and civilians moving freely among them, there was a new informality. The major was wearing body armour with shorts and flipflops. There were papers spread all over his sleeping bag and the day was so airless they didn't even flutter.

The major said: 'I've got some news for you.'

Jenny. Dave felt his body turn to stone. Everything inside it that had been moving, the blood running, the cells growing, stopped for a moment.

The major's tone was hesitant. It must be bad news.

'Congratulations, Dave. You are the father of a new baby girl.' The OC's face broke into an enormous smile. Dave took a breath in but could not breathe out again until he knew more.

'And Jenny? Is she all right?'

'The baby was delivered by Caesarean section because of some kind of emergency. But she's doing well now.'

The news knocked Dave from behind. His knees almost went from under him. He reached out and held onto a tent pole. A baby girl. And Jenny was fine. Something was banging away behind his eyes. Shit, it was tears. Tears of relief and tears of joy. He turned away from the major in embarrassment while he fought with himself to contain his feelings.

Major Willingham coughed.

'I wish we had more information. I wish you were able to speak to her. I understand you knew that she's been very ill and this week must have been hell for you, Dave, unable to communicate. Like a true professional, you gave no indication.'

Where did all this emotion come from? It appeared so suddenly, and with such a fucking intensity, that it must have been contained somewhere inside him waiting to explode. When the wagon had blown up at the beginning of their tour, he had felt like a rag doll thrown across it. Now he was a powerless rag doll again. But this blast came from inside him.

The major said carefully: 'When my children were born, I probably cried more than they did.'

Permission to cry. Well, Dave didn't want it. He was not going to give in to tears in front of the OC. He closed his eyes and thought of Jenny, lying in bed with a tiny baby lying on top of her, the way she had been with Vicky. He thought how much he loved her and Vicky and the new baby. The little girl had a passport to his love, an automatic right of entry, and he didn't need to see her to know that. She was his baby and Jenny's, and a new birth brought with it the joy of hope and possibility. It didn't matter where in the world you were, that joy was the same. And now all the worry was over because everyone was safe.

'I gather there is an email on its way with pictures which I will show you as soon as we get back to base,' said the major, stepping forward to shake his hand vigorously. 'Congratulations. Warm congratulations.'

Dave managed to speak, although there was a thick crust around his voice. 'Thank you, sir.'

'It's very hard for you, not having access to a phone. As soon as we get back . . .'

'Yes, sir.'

Dave wandered off into the camp, dazed. A number of people had seen the OC shaking his hand.

'Everything all right?' asked Iain Kila. 'Got some news?'

Dave nodded and told him. He managed to keep his voice on a railway track, straight and strong, so it couldn't be shunted by emotion. Kila pumped his hand and Dave was startled to see that the big, hard man had damp eyes.

'Congratulations,' said Kila. 'Looking forward to buying you a drink when we get to Cyprus.'

'Shit, I'm really happy for you, Sarge,' said Jamie, and Dave could see he meant it.

As the news spread, Dave received many congratulations and promises of drinks. He was surprised how affected some people were by the news, particularly those who were already fathers.

He answered the same questions over and over again.

'Pre-eclampsia, it's something to do with blood pressure.'

'Don't know how much she weighs.'

'Yeah, I bet Vicky's all over her.'

'Dunno what we're going to call her.'

'Jenny's mum was supposed to be there. I hope she was.'

Nobody said it. Nobody said: 'You should have been there too.'

When he came down from the tower, Finn was particularly happy with the news.

'I'm certainly buying you a drink. Didn't like to tell you this, Sarge, but I was offering eleven to ten on that it was a boy.'

Dave frowned but felt too happy to bollock him.

'How many lads had a punt on that?' he asked.

Finn grinned.

'The whole fucking platoon.'

Chapter Fifty-four

DARREL TOOK AGNIESZKA AND LUKE TO THE BEACH. THEY MET AT THE supermarket and transferred a mountain of baby equipment from her car to his. Finally they transferred Luke himself.

'You need a break,' said Darrel as they headed south to the coast. She had been upset after Jenny had given birth in an operating theatre without Dave or her mother or even Adi to hold her hand.

'I should have stayed with her. But she was expecting her mother to come. And Luke . . .'

'You did the right thing, Aggie,' Darrel assured her.

Agnieszka had continued to look miserable.

'No. Dave in operating theatre is right thing.'

But heading south for the coast was making Agnieszka feel more light-hearted and relaxed. They were having an Indian summer and the air sparkled in the sun.

They parked on the clifftop and by now Luke was awake and beginning to look angry.

'I think he a little bit hungry,' said Agnieszka, worrying that they would not get down to the sand before he had started to express his hunger in the earsplitting way he expressed all his needs.

'OK, well, let's feed him now,' said Darrel. 'Where's the milk, where's the food?'

She pointed to a bag and he lifted it out. With the other hand he unstrapped Luke. He carried everything to a sheltered seat overlooking the sea, sat down and proceeded to feed the surprised baby.

Agnieszka stood watching. He held the child so tenderly in his arms. It moved her. It was the same with Jamie. She knew Jamie was now machine-gunner for his section and she had seen pictures of him in the past with an immense, dark weapon of crafted metal. She knew it was his job to kill people. Then he came home and held his baby with the same hands that had worked the killing machine and his gentleness never failed to touch her.

She looked across the blue bay to the strange white rocks that stuck out of the water at the land's edge like teeth.

Darrel was saying: 'There you are then, mate. Enjoying that? OK, let's wipe your mouth and have another go. Good, isn't it?'

She swung round.

'Why you so nice to my baby?'

'Because,' Darrel said, 'he's your baby.'

He handed the contented bundle that was Luke to Agnieszka.

'He needs a hug from you.'

Agnieszka felt doubtful about this. She had found the baby buggy with its sheepskin lining far more to Luke's taste than any hug from her. Holding him when he screamed had never been a successful strategy. But she took him now. She looked down at his relaxed, satisfied face. He almost smiled. She began to rock him from side to side. He fixed his big, blue eyes on her and now he did smile. She smiled back.

'How often do you do that?' asked Darrel.

'He not usually like it.'

She'd tried cuddling him and rocking him when he was born but nothing she did had been right for him. He'd glared at her with an angry pout and loudly, continually, endlessly expressed his dissatisfaction. And so he had become a nappy that needed changing, an open mouth that needed feeding, a loud scream that only walking, walking and more walking could silence, an angry, demanding little emperor who had to be placated and rocked to sleep. Then he was a patient, with his fits, his hospital visits and his doctors. But he was almost never a baby who needed cuddling.

She said: 'He so calm it must be sea air.'

Darrel agreed, and told her to carry him down to the beach while he followed with the stuff.

So she carried Luke down the zigzag path, past sweet-smelling flowers, and he kept his eyes fixed on her all the way, except for the occasions when his focus slid to the blue sky and puffball clouds or the sharp outline of agaves on the cliff. He was asleep by the time they reached the beach.

'Oh, I thought to change his nappy,' said Agnieszka.

'Leave him, he's peaceful,' Darrel told her as they found a spot on the sand to make their own and laid out the towels and set up the sunshade over Luke. Agnieszka placed him carefully beneath it and he did not wake.

She was embarrassed to take off her clothes and reveal her body in its bikini. She fussed around the baby and the bags until Darrel had changed into his swimsuit under a towel.

'I'm going for a swim,' he told her and she watched him walk towards the sea, lean and strong.

Quickly she took off her own clothes and adjusted her bikini. Then she lay down under the warm blanket of the sun, feeling its rays bless her and kiss her, basking in its generosity. It was different from the sun Jamie was always sheltering from in Afghanistan. The English sun was kind. She closed her eyes and felt its light and heat on her eyelids.

Everything was all right when Darrel was around. He had been a good friend to her lately. He had said that they would be friends, no more, and the friendship had made life more pleasant. She was happy. Luke was happy. Darrel was happy. It was a simple structure and its simplicity gave it strength.

She became aware of a shadow falling over her. She opened her eyes. Darrel was standing nearby, looking at her.

'Asleep?' he asked.

'No.'

He lay down beside her and it was like the tide coming in: she could sense his presence straight out of the sea, wet and cool.

She opened her eyes. He was lying close to her.

'You are beautiful,' he said.

She told him: 'Please don't say this.'

He kissed her. Not a long kiss, or a hungry one. His lips were salty. She pulled away and lay back in the sand and closed her eyes. She tried to imagine Jamie's face. But it was a blur. Jamie was an absence. And Darrel was here, he was now.

He said: 'Aggie . . . when we get back tonight, I don't want to drop you off by your car and drive away.'

She kept her eyes closed.

'Aggie . . . look at me.'

She opened her eyes. He was leaning over her. The sun had already found his cheeks and forehead. He looked healthy and full of fresh air.

'Aggie. I want to come home with you tonight. I don't want to leave you outside a bloody supermarket.'

She felt relaxed and happy. She certainly did not want the day to end with Darrel driving off while Luke screamed. And she did not want to go home alone to the blocked drain and the dingy house. Jamie was away somewhere and would not ring. Luke would have a fit. It was unbearable.

'Well, Aggie?'

She said: 'I want you to come home, Darrel. I do. But . . .'

'We'll go to your place, then. And see how we feel.' He rolled to one side. He had been shielding her face from the sun and now it smothered her again. 'No pressure, Ags. I just want to make this a perfect day.'

Chapter Fifty-five

JAMIE AND DAVE WERE ON STAG. THE CAMP WAS QUIET. ONLY THE air moved a little, descending slowly down the hillside. When it reached Dave's cheeks it felt like hot breath. He watched a piece of litter, lying inside the wire fence below them. It didn't even flutter.

He looked out across the plain and then back to the hills. Nothing moved. He looked inside the camp. Nothing. He knew Emily was in her lab. There was no sign of any other civilian at work. The soldiers who weren't on duty were under their ponchos, asleep. He glanced over at the major's poncho. The soles of two feet were visible beneath it.

'Thank God we're going home tomorrow,' said Dave, realizing he had just called Sin City home. But compared to this God-forsaken piece of nowhere it was full of comforts. The cookhouse, with tables to eat at. A phone to call Jenny from. The chance of seeing pictures of the baby on the OC's computer. Even the Colour Boy's bowls seemed like a luxury if they had some cool, clear water in them for a good wash. But most of all he wanted to speak to Jenny.

There were strange, unpredictable moments, just standing here on stag or sitting in the ops room, when he got what felt like an actual physical ache in his heart for Jenny. He always meant to tell her about those aches next time he spoke to her. Although he never did.

'You're definitely first in line for the phone when we get back,' said Jamie, as though he could read Dave's mind.

'Yeah. For once I won't be waiting.'

'And I want to get the phone after you. I really want to talk to Agnieszka.'

'Going to try to sort things out?'

'Yeah. I'm hoping we've just got our wires crossed. Or she was just having a bad day last time we spoke.'

'You'll probably find that everything's all right,' said Dave. 'It's easy to read too much into a short conversation when you're this far apart.'

'But after six months, she'll have changed. And so will I. So will Luke.'

'Yeah. Nothing's ever exactly the same. You have to work hard to find your place in the family again.'

'It'll be different for you at home.'

Involuntarily, Dave smiled.

'Two kids. It's going to take a bit of getting used to.'

The silence returned. The half-hearted breeze gave up and stopped completely. Nothing moved at all in the intense heat. Even Jamie, at Dave's side, was as still as a reptile. Was there life somewhere in that vast expanse of sand? Small mammals, bugs? Maybe they burrowed down deep where the earth was cooler and went to sleep until last light.

It would be easy to fall asleep on stag in this heat and have the piss taken out of you for ever. Except that suddenly Dave felt wide awake. His back straightened. His senses strained.

Jamie looked at him.

'What's up?'

'There's something happening.'

Jamie looked around at the camp with its hardware and soft tents. The flat desert plain was so still that even the dust lay pinned to the ground by the sun. The Early Rocks rose like statues. And on the other side of the camp were the hills and then the purple shadows of the mountains.

'Can't see anything.'

'Over there.'

Dave's back was stiff now and his face alert.

'But it's so quiet and—'

'It's the wrong sort of quiet.'

Jamie put his head on one side and Dave knew he was considering whether it was possible that his trusted sergeant had finally cracked.

'Don't look at me like that. Look at the hills. Look across the camp to Three Boulders and then right and down some. Now stare.'

There was a long pause.

'I'm staring. And I'm not seeing anything.'

'Keep looking at the shadows. They seem still but they're not. They're moving. Very, very slowly.'

Jamie watched.

Dave said: 'I only saw it when my eyes started to glaze over a bit.'

'What are your eyes, fucking infra-red?' There was admiration in Jamie's voice and Dave knew that he could see it too now.

'Doesn't look right, does it?' Dave said.

'It's like watching a ship going over the horizon. You think it's still, then it disappears and you realize it was going all the time.'

Neither man moved. Their eyes were fixed across the camp to the side of the hill.

'I reckon Angry McCall might have been right,' Dave said. 'I reckon there's someone—'

But he was silenced by an extraordinary sight. A small, hunched figure in shirt sleeves and body armour but without a helmet was walking outside the perimeter wire towards the hillside.

Chapter Fifty-six

AGNIESZKA AND DARREL DROVE UP FROM THE COAST, ACROSS moorland and forest, through the centre of the city and finally towards the rolling countryside where the camp was situated. And all the time, Agnieszka was asking herself what she wanted to happen next.

When the time came to turn into the supermarket where they had left her car, Darrel did not turn. He did not look at Agnieszka or ask her if she wanted to change her mind, he just drove on past the supermarket towards her house.

Luke was quiet. Agnieszka did not speak. She was frightened now. What was she doing? Did she still love Jamie? You didn't just switch off love. Thinking of him caused a strange, twisting feeling like a corkscrew buried inside her chest. She loved him but his absence was immense. Gradually he was becoming a ghost, a vapour, a shadow, as though one day he would disappear altogether.

She glanced at Darrel. His face and body were more than the light and shadow of memory. But if he went home tonight then he would just be a memory too.

Her heart beat faster as they entered the camp. She felt sick.

As they neared the house she saw, at the end of the street, a dark-skinned woman surrounded by small children. Adi Kasanita. Trailing home from the rec with her kids before bedtime on a summery evening. Adi's walk was slow and relaxed. She swung her hips as she pushed the buggy with one hand and held a toddler with the other. The older children were playing some sort of game at her side, surging around her like water. Adi was talking to them and laughing. She looked content with her uncomplicated life.

Agnieszka watched her and knew that Adi had got it right. Yes, Adi, relaxed and smiling with her kids on a warm evening, was the way it was supposed to be. The day by the sea, her car hidden at the supermarket, their furtive kisses on the beach, it hadn't really been wonderful. It had been complex and furtive.

She stole another quick glance at Darrel. For a moment she hated him. He made her feel so good that she had chosen not to notice that he was a huge, threatening storm gathering over peaceful waters. But she knew it really. That was why her heart thudded and her head spun with nausea.

'Darrel. Don't come in. You can't come in.'

He looked across at her in surprise.

'What?'

'I very sorry. I want that you drive back to supermarket for my car.'

'Ags, you're scared. You don't have to be scared.'

'Don't come to house, Darrel, it very dangerous for me.'

'Listen—'

'No, please! Please don't come home now.'

He sighed and passed her house without even slowing. At the end of the street they turned.

'What changed your mind?'

'I very sorry, Darrel.'

'Was it that woman with the kids you were looking at? Is she a friend of yours?'

'Yes.'

'I thought you said you don't have any friends here.'

Agnieszka closed her eyes. It was true that Adi wasn't really a friend. She was one of a group of women who had invited Agnieszka into their circle often enough, and Agnieszka had chosen to remain outside their orbit. She had thought it was boring, stifling and small-minded. Now it looked warm and attractive. It looked safe. But if Darrel came home with her she would be stepping far, far from its protection.

He said: 'If you're worried what your friends think, I could come back later, maybe. When it's night.'

'No.'

'I'll make sure no one sees me.'

She shook her head vigorously.

'No, Darrel. Please. It wrong to do this.'

She waited for his reaction. For a minute his face darkened and he looked angry. Then she saw him wrench a smile from somewhere.

'OK, Ags. We've had a good day. We won't ruin it now. We'll stay friends,' he said.

'Yes,' she said. 'We are friends, just friends, Darrel.'

At the sound of her own sureness, her nausea evaporated and she felt the relief, all through her body to her nerve endings, of a narrow escape.

Chapter Fifty-seven

'FUCKING HELL!' SAID DAVE.

He and Jamie stared in silence for a moment at the sight of Martyn Robertson crossing the desert, alone, unarmed and unguarded. His walk was shambling in the heat. He leaned slightly to the left as if he'd grown that way over the years. He was crossing the flat area around the base and now reached a spot where the hills began. That spot was directly to the right and down from Three Boulders.

Dave's body was already swelling and his face expanding as he filled himself with breath to yell.

'Staaaand tooooo!'

Before his words could bounce back at him from the hillside he was leaping down from the sangar.

'Keep shouting,' he told Jamie. *Stand to, stand to, stand to,* whispered the desert to the camp and the hills to the desert.

Heads started to appear under ponchos. Jamie could see Dave running towards the sentries at the main entrance. He looked up into the hills. Martyn was still visible, scrambling over the layers of pink rock now, towards the suspect shadows. He had heard the shout, glanced over his shoulder and evidently chosen to ignore it. He continued climbing. Jamie waited to wave at him, but Martyn did not turn again.

'Staaaaaand tooooooooo!' Jamie roared.

Now more men were emerging from ponchos, stumbling in untied boots, cramming on their helmets, looking around them bewildered.

'Staaaaaaaaand tooooooooo!' Jamie yelled into the echo of his last shout.

Dave had reached the sentries.

'What the fuck is that idiot doing out there?'

The lad looked scared.

'It was all quiet and he said he needed a crap. Wanted a bit of privacy.'

'Fucking dickhead!' Dave grabbed the lad's radio.

'It was all quiet,' the other sentry repeated defensively.

'What's going on?' Major Willingham's voice over the radio.

'Topaz Zero's out there and so's the Taliban,' Dave told him.

'Out there! Outside the fence!' the officer roared. 'What's Martyn doing?'

'Said he wanted a crap in privacy but he's walked right into the choggies. Look to Three Boulders, right and down a bit . . .'

The major had his binoculars out but by now Martyn had gone. He had completely evaporated. Dave wanted to believe he was crouching down enjoying his privacy somewhere but he knew it was too late. It had been too late five minutes ago. They had lost Martyn Robertson. Their primary task here, the focus of all their efforts, had been to protect the contractors. And they had lost their key man. He had walked into the arms of the Taliban.

'Get two vehicles out there NOW, and fucking get him back,' the major roared. Within seconds Dave was up in a Vector with the driver, eight men and another wagon behind him, but the pit in his stomach told him they were wasting their time.

They were barely out of the gate when the firing began. The Vectors headed straight towards it. Behind them, inside the barbed-wire fence, their own firing team were already in trenches, a line of helmets and weapons looking strangely neat inside the dust clouds. On the other side, hidden somewhere in the pink-purple rock of the hillside, were the enemy. And Martyn. Dave thought he could make out his footprints in the sand.

Men were starting to pile out of the wagons into the dust and clatter of machine guns and AK47s. Dave saw an RPG sailing grace-fully in the direction of Emily's lab.

He did not have time to see where it exploded, or whether it had exploded at all, because the OC, recognizing the enemy's superior fire power and the vulnerability of the vehicles, had ordered the men back inside. The drivers roared straight on around the perimeter and in through the entrance.

'That's just about the fastest lap I've ever done,' Dave's driver said. Dave looked across to Emily's Vector. She was standing at the door, her arms crossed. Her engineers were lying face down on the desert's sandy floor, their bodies half under the wagons, as they had been told to do in case of attack. One was remonstrating with her, trying to persuade her to lie down but she remained defiantly standing, glaring at the Taliban.

'Get down!' he yelled at her. 'We've lost one civilian, we don't want to lose another.'

She turned to him now and, even from this distance, he could see not confrontation but shock and bewilderment on her face.

'Get down!' he repeated. She slowly lowered her body, hanging onto the side of the Vector.

But he knew the firing wouldn't last long. The Taliban had their hostage. While most were putting down fire, some would be spiriting Martyn away. If they hadn't already killed him.

Sure enough, the firing eased rapidly and then stopped.

Dave listened as the OC, standing with one hand on his hip, spoke into his radio. 'Contact initiated when Topaz Zero decided to go for a crap outside the base. Vehicles sent to retrieve him. Enemy then engaged us with RPGs. By the time we got to assistance of Topaz Zero we had lost him. I repeat, we have lost Topaz Zero. Unknown dead or alive. Assume taken hostage. Over.'

The voice from HQ was crisp and formal. 'Roger. Topaz Zero has been taken hostage. Wait. Out.'

The major kept a few men back to guard the camp and civilians and sent the rest out to scour the hillside. While he requested Apaches to help with the search he stood helplessly staring at the spot where Martyn had disappeared, as though he would mysteriously reappear.

1 Platoon ran across the desert to the hills. Outside the wire the expanse felt bigger and the heat fiercer. And the hillside itself was different when you were climbing across its face. The boulders were not big, round shapes but massive, dark obstacles. Hostile bushes tried to hold you back, small, sharp rocks slid treacherously away beneath your feet.

'Fucking hell, Sarge,' said Bacon. 'It's steeper than it looks.'

'If we had our Bergens on, we'd never get anywhere,' said Binns. His wiry body coped well with the climb when he had no weight on his back.

'Stop kicking fucking rocks down here,' roared a red-faced Angus, from further down the hill. He was carrying ammo.

'Can't fucking help it,' called Finn. 'They just slide out from under our feet.'

Dave halted and turned to where he thought he had seen the shadows. Breathlessly he spoke on PRR. 'Can you hear me, Jamie?'

The sangar looked far away. Jamie held up a hand.

'Are we anywhere near the place we saw them?'

'Nope, you're way out.'

Angus arrived and flopped down on a rock next to Dave, gasping loudly for breath.

'We can't be!' said Dave. 'We're down and to the right of Three Boulders!'

'You're too far down and you're hardly right at all.'

'Fucking hell.'

They sighed and carried on across the sizzling face of the hill, sweating and silent, too shocked by what had happened even to moan.

A shout went up from the boss.

'They were here! They left ammo!' He held up some spent cases.

'Yeah, you're in the right sort of area now,' Jamie told them.

'They've made quite a nest around these bushes,' reported the boss. 'The ground's all flattened out. There's a bit of food and a couple of rags . . . they were here a long time.'

'I knew it,' said Angus. 'I fucking knew it. They've been there for days. I saw them.'

No one looked at him.

'You were right, Angry,' said Jamie on PRR.

'Shit, McCall, I wish we'd taken more notice of you,' said Dave. 'Fuck it.'

'Pity Martyn didn't believe you,' said Finn quietly.

Angus and Finn looked at each other for a long moment.

'Nah,' Angus said. 'Nah, the poor bastard thought he was doing the right thing.'

'Er . . . Sarge . . .'

Dave turned to Binns.

'What'll they do to Topaz Zero?'

CSM Kila stumbled up to them before Dave could answer.

'I'll tell you what they'll do to Topaz Zero!' They waited while he tried to catch his breath.

'I s'pose they'll kill him,' said Streaky.

'Oh, they'll kill him,' agreed Kila. 'And they'll put it online for everyone to see. So they'll make sure they behead him or skin him alive or disembowel him or something really entertaining.'

There was a silence. It was broken by the distant throb of helicopters.

Boss Weeks, who was further around the hillside, stooped by a bush.

'Here too! Another nest.' He held up a sandal. The sole was worn away. 'They even made a path . . .'

He ordered 2 Section to accompany him and they stumbled off, scrambling on loose rocks, hanging onto boulders, swearing at the bushes as they tried to follow the path the insurgents had made. Dave thought how quickly and stealthily the Taliban hiding there must have moved along these paths. It was easy to dismiss them as primitive but their thin brown bodies were lightly clothed and burdened only by a weapon, which made them the fittest fighting force for the terrain.

The voices of 2 Section grew faint. On the radio the boss said: 'There's so many paths it's like a giant wasp's nest. They must have been swarming here.'

The Apaches were close now. They flew low and began hunting over the hillside. Dave watched with a sense of hopelessness.

'What were the flipflops waiting for? The right moment to attack?' he wondered out loud. 'Were they planning a big ambush?'

Iain Kila shrugged.

'They certainly changed their plans fast, then. Because they never dreamed a fucking civvy would walk right over to them and offer himself as a hostage. They must have thought Allah was rewarding them for good behaviour.'

'Shit,' said Dave, imagining Martyn in the hands of tribesmen and feeling a sudden rush of affection for him.

'I've got no sympathy,' said Kila. 'He knew he shouldn't leave the camp. From the moment we got to Sin City, the fucking civvies have been behaving like they're above the fighting. It's: "I'm a civvy and it's nothing to do with me." ' He imitated the civvies in a high, simpering voice. 'Well, the Taliban don't think that way. To them we're *all* fucking enemy and now Topaz Zero knows it.'

Chapter Fifty-eight

'HELLO, MOTHER. HELLO, BABY.'

Jenny opened her eyes.

'You were asleep.'

'Leanne, hi. I wasn't asleep, I just fed her and closed my eyes for a minute.'

'How's the world's most adorable little girl?'

Jenny smiled. 'Adorable. Very quiet and content.'

'I didn't bring Vicky.'

'Is she OK?'

'Having a great time with two nanas fighting over her.'

'Where are the twins?'

'Dave's mum took them with Vicky to the rec. She'll be in to see you later.'

'They said I could stay a day or two longer. Or I could go home. Think I'm naughty for staying?'

Leanne lowered her body onto the bedside.

'I think you'd be naughty not to.'

'If it wasn't for Vicks I could move in here.'

Jenny felt Leanne's weight tip the bed dangerously. Leanne was getting bigger and bigger. She noticed how flesh was gradually swallowing the features of her friend's face.

'I'll take a picture or two and email them to Dave,' Leanne said. 'Then when he gets back to the FOB he'll have a whole collection.'

'Does anyone know when they get back?'

'Nope, but when they do the first thing that's going to happen is Dave'll phone you.'

Jenny felt a waterfall feeling inside her chest. She was getting used to the feeling, which was nothing to do with her milk coming in. It was the familiar sensation of sadness sweeping through her body. Because a baby had been born and the baby's dad probably didn't even know.

'Watched the news?' asked Leanne cautiously, and now there was another sensation in Jenny's body, the one where everything curled itself up into a ball. This was fear. The TV news, with its sketchy reports of dead soldiers, no names or details, always generated anxiety. Which was why she tried not to watch it in the hospital.

Leanne saw her face and said quickly: 'No one's dead.'

But Jenny could not relax until she knew. She waited, her body stiff with tension.

'Something's happened and Adi thinks it happened to our lads.'

The baby rearranged herself in her cot. Leanne paused. Both women turned to watch silently until the tiny body was still again.

'The Taliban have taken a hostage. A civilian oil worker. Adi thinks 1 Platoon were supposed to be guarding him.'

Jenny groaned.

'Dave's in trouble then?'

'Maybe.'

The news didn't seem to bother Leanne much. She was looking in her big, shapeless handbag for something. Why should she care if 1 Platoon was in trouble? thought Jenny. Steve was at Headley Court and Leanne had enough troubles of her own.

'How is he?' she asked.

'Who?' Leanne had the contents of the handbag out on the bed now. Along with the notebook, chewing gum, chocolate wrappers, makeup, tissues, old receipts and the keys with the SpongeBob SquarePants keyring, were balls of Play Doh and a toy car.

'Your Steve.'

Leanne found her phone and threw everything else back into the handbag.

'Say cheeeeese . . .' She held the phone up at arm's length.

'Wait!' Jenny began to rearrange her hair. Then she smiled at the lens, remembering that she was smiling for Dave. She tried to make her eyes talk. *I love you, I miss you, why aren't you here?*

Leanne clicked and then took a few of the sleeping baby.

'So?' demanded Jenny.

'So what?'

'You don't want to tell me, do you? About Steve? When you went up to Headley Court yesterday?'

Leanne sat back down on the bed heavily and Jenny felt it tip again.

'It was fucking awful.'

'His leg, you mean?'

'His attitude. He keeps saying really shitty things. About my weight. Like I'm totally unfanciable.'

'Steve probably feels totally unfanciable with only one leg,' Jenny said softly. 'But he's pushing it off onto you.'

'Well, if he wants a sex life he's not going the right way about it.'

'You've got a really strong marriage, you two. I know you can get over this one.'

'We used to have a really strong marriage. Now there's me, him and his fucking injury. Who was it said that marriages get a bit crowded when there's three of you?'

'I bet he was pleased to see you, though?'

Leanne's face began to look rubbery. Jenny knew what was coming next. Tears. 'Jen, I don't want him to come back. I want him to stay at Headley bloody Court for ever.'

'Oh, Leanne, you don't mean that.'

'I do! He was a right bastard. Nice for five minutes but he had the TV on and he didn't turn it off when we came in. Then one of the boys walked in front of the screen. And that was it. He was yelling and screaming and shouting. Using really bad language. Ethan didn't know what he'd done, poor little love.'

Jenny guessed that Leanne had already cried today. She looked full of pain as though she hadn't cried enough and now she wanted to cry some more.

'Was he ever like this before?' she asked.

'Well, you knew him, Jen.'

'Not behind closed doors I didn't. Was he ever horrible when you were all at home together?'

'He was no saint. He had no patience. He'd snap. He had his limits and I learned not to go near them. But this isn't snapping, Jen. I swear he wants to hit us. You should see his face. One minute he's chatting away, the next he's all twisted up with anger.'

'Maybe he only lets it go when you're around because he knows he can with you. Because he loves you and trusts you.'

Tears fell down Leanne's cheeks. She said: 'If this is love, I don't need it.'

'How are you around him?' asked Jenny.

Leanne shrugged, and the flesh that lined her neck and shoulders hugged itself.

'A bit scared if you want the truth. In case he starts throwing things again.'

'Were you always a bit scared of him? I used to think he had a temper.'

'Fuck it, Jen, he's always had a temper but he never used to talk to me like this. He used to show me some respect. Even if he doesn't love me any more, he could still do that, couldn't he?'

Jenny nodded. Leanne sniffed.

'What are you thinking?' asked Leanne, fishing a tissue from the big handbag.

'Nothing.'

'I know you, Jenny Henley. I know you're thinking something.'

The baby suddenly jumped in her sleep and threw her arms into the air as though a current ran through her. But she did not wake.

'I'm asking myself,' said Jenny carefully, 'why you can't stand up to Steve the way you used to.'

Leanne's big face disappeared behind the tissue.

'Um . . .'

'Why?' demanded Jenny. 'Because he's lost a leg?'

Leanne said: 'He used to be a big, hard soldier and now he's this angry man with one leg who wants to be a soldier. Telling himself he'll be able to carry kit and run about with a gimpy and fight on the front line. It's so sad, Jen . . .' She started to cry again and now the baby was waking up, waving her arms and making small, guttural noises.

'Pass her to me, would you? It really hurts my stitches to lean over there.'

Leanne did not stop crying as she struggled to her feet and picked up the tiny girl very gently. Her tears dripped onto the baby, who opened her eyes in surprise.

'Oops,' said Leanne, handing the little pink bundle to Jenny. 'Sorry, gorgeous.'

'What are you trying to do, baptize her?' The baby effortlessly aligned herself against Jenny's body and then began to feed.

'I get fed up with crying,' said Leanne, through sobs. 'I'm so fucking bored with it.'

'Maybe Steve's getting fed up with it too. Maybe if you were a bit more like you used to be, then he'd be more like his old self too.'

Leanne took some deep breaths, and when her voice was almost under control, she squeaked: 'How was that, Jen? I can't remember. How was I?'

'You were a tough cookie and you didn't take any nonsense from Steve and you could drink him under the table if you wanted to, and the Buckles were just about the funniest, most popular couple in the whole camp. Probably in the whole of Wiltshire.'

Leanne blinked at her.

'Us?'

'You. And if Steve ever gave you shit, that's just what he got back.'

Leanne sat up a bit straighter, her face thoughtful.

'So,' Jenny asked, 'why did you change?'

'Well . . . I think it was all that time they kept him at Bastion, when I didn't know how he was. I got sort of destroyed by worry . . .' Leanne was twisting her tissue tightly around her fingers and it was disintegrating.

'You can stop worrying now. He's all right.' Jenny remembered something Dave had said on the phone, something about Steve getting irritated because Leanne wanted to treat him like a victim. 'He's not just all right, he's got a goal and he's going for it. Why aren't you supporting him?'

'Because I don't want him back out in Afghanistan.'

'He wouldn't be happy sitting in an office. That's not Steve. He never was that way and he's not going to change just because his body's different. C'mon, Leanne, wake up and smell the coffee.'

Leanne stared at her.

'What should I do?'

'Try being yourself. If he liked wimps he would have married one.'

When Jenny looked at Leanne's face she wondered if she'd gone too far. A few minutes later, Leanne got up to leave.

'Have I upset you?'

'No, no, of course not.'

But she had. She could tell from Leanne's voice. She could tell from the way her footsteps disappeared down the hospital corridor, loud and angry.

Jenny felt sadness sweeping through her. That waterfall feeling again. She looked down at the baby, who was lying peacefully in her arms, watching her face steadily.

'She hardly noticed you, did she?' Jenny said to her tiny daughter. 'Too many problems to think about you. And you know why? Because she married a soldier. So don't do it, Baby.'

Chapter Fifty-nine

THE PLATOONS STAYED IN THE CAMP AN EXTRA TWENTY-FOUR hours, searching ceaselessly but hopelessly for Martyn on the hillside. Then the order finally came to return to Sin City.

The men looked back before they jumped into the wagons. A few gazed at the hillside for a moment, as if Martyn might suddenly emerge from behind a bush shouting: 'Wait for me! I was only having a crap!' Most just took a quick glance around at the desert they had scarred with their wire, trenches and sandbags.

'We leaving all our wire and stuff here for the Taliban to help themselves?' asked Mal.

'The engineers are coming to take the camp down,' the boss told him. 'I'm glad we don't have to.'

'Goodbye, fucking Jackpot,' Finn said. The name seemed stupid now. It was a strutting name. It reminded you of the way Martyn swaggered around the camp with his misplaced, brash confidence.

'*Jackpot, shithole, lost spot, dead loss* . . .' Bacon muttered under his breath.

The journey back was oppressive. It was not only the heat that kept the men still in their seats but their sense of failure. They had agreed often enough in the last twenty-four hours that Martyn never should have gone outside the wire like that. But, inside, every man took some responsibility for what had happened, and the higher his rank the worse he felt. Major Willingham, Dave thought, looked ten years older than when they had arrived here.

The men on top watched as the huge jagged teeth protruding

389

from the earth became the Early Rocks. A carload full of pilgrims, mostly women in bright headscarves, was crossing the desert towards the shrine. And then they were gone too and the empty desert rolled on and on before them.

When the convoy arrived back at the FOB it was getting dark. The doors of the wagons opened and Emily was first out, followed by the engineers. Saying nothing, their faces still pinched with shock, they quietly trooped off towards their isoboxes.

The men jumped out, grateful for the silence, the stillness and the evening air, but they were immediately surrounded by the rest of the company, eager for an account of Martyn's kidnap.

Boss Weeks opened the door at the front of the wagon but he did not dismount. He looked hopefully for Asma among the faces surrounding the Vectors. Jean and Iain Kila were already locked in conversation. But Asma was nowhere to be seen. His eyes searched the base for her. No Asma, but he could see evidence of the news they'd received that Sin City had come under heavy attack today. There was damage everywhere. Sandbags were ragged. A sangar had collapsed in one corner. He hoped Asma was safe. Even if she wasn't speaking to him.

He heard the 2 i/c greeting Major Willingham.

'So, sir, do you think there's any chance we'll get Topaz Zero back?'

Weeks listened intently to the OC's answer.

'No, I don't. God, what a fucking catastrophe. Nothing happened to us and then everything happened in five minutes. So my career's pretty much a T4.'

He was aware that someone was standing in the Vector's open doorway. He glanced down. Asma! He could not stop himself smiling broadly.

Weeks jumped out and she smiled back.

'I'm sorry you've had such a hard time,' she said.

'Asma, I want to apologize.'

'You don't have anything to apologize for, Gordon.'

'I didn't really listen to you, but I've had all week to think about what you said. And yesterday proved you right. I'm sure Martyn's kidnapping was cold, calculated revenge. As cold and calculating as the way we took out their man.'

'But we heard he walked right up to them! They didn't plan that bit.'

'They were certainly planning something. There was evidence that they'd been watching us and perhaps gathering in numbers ready for some kind of ambush.'

'Shit, Gordon, I want to say I'm sorry too. I'm sorry about all the shit I gave you. I've been feeling fucking awful about it.'

'Don't apologize for being right,' he said. They smiled at each other again, more awkwardly this time.

'When I saw the mess and no sign of you . . .' Weeks gestured around at the damaged base '. . . I was worried that you'd been injured.'

'Yeah, well, we had an interesting time today. Even Jean had to get out there with a weapon and she could barely remember which end to fire from. The second i/c was just about to ask the cook to get on the .50 when it all stopped.'

Weeks laughed at the thought of the pan-wielding Masud behind such a heavy weapon.

'Taking Martyn has turned the local Taliban into a bunch of cocky bastards,' Asma said. 'The way they were gloating on their mobiles. I just wanted to tell them all to fuck off. Anyway, we can expect a lot more attacks like that now.'

The men sorted out the ammo and the wagons and then began to cluster in the cookhouse. Dave tried to call Jenny but the phones had been taken out of action while relatives were informed of a fatality at another base.

He went to the ops room and found it a hive of activity. Most of the officers were there and Iain Kila was passing around steaming mugs.

'Second i/c's too busy to make a brew!' he explained. 'I never thought I'd see the day.'

'What's going on?'

'All hell's let loose over Topaz Zero. He's an international news story now.'

'So the OC isn't going to remember that he told me I could get online as soon as we were back to look at the new baby . . .'

Kila, who could carry four mugs of tea at once, plonked them down without finesse and went straight over to the 2 i/c. After a hurried conversation in undertones, the officer got up.

'Congratulations, Sergeant. But don't be too long, will you? I'm waiting for an urgent email from the Foreign Office.'

Dave went straight to his inbox and found that Leanne Buckle had sent three sets of pictures. The earliest email said:

Weighed in at 7lbs 9oz, so just as well she didn't go to term or she'd probably have been a ten-pounder. Completely gorgeous. You are a lucky bastard, Dave Henley. Love, Leanne.

He clicked on the first picture and caught his breath when it filled the screen. There was Jenny, looking tired, her cheeks red and her hair pulled back from her face, but it was her smile that made his eyes dampen. He knew that Jenny had been smiling at the camera just for him. She had the exhausted exuberance of a new mother and that tiny, sleeping bundle she was holding up was his daughter. He bit his lip.

In the next picture Vicky was standing at Jenny's bedside, peering at the tiny red-faced figure. Both the baby and Vicky surveyed each other solemnly. The scene was lit by Jenny's smile again.

The most recent set showed the baby asleep and Jenny trying to rearrange her hair. He stared hard. This was Jenny less than twenty-four hours ago. It was the closest he had been to her since leaving the UK. Her smile spoke to him. It said: *I love you, I miss you, why aren't you here?* He swallowed.

'Very nice,' said the OC, appearing behind him. 'Now let's see the baby.'

Dave clicked on the picture of Vicky and her new sister.

'Good heavens, they both look just like you!' said the OC.

Dave grinned, pleased.

'Now, if you don't mind, Martyn's capture is causing a political storm . . . But the phones are no longer minimized. I haven't told the other men yet so that you can be the first.'

Everyone in the cookhouse was watching Martyn on TV. A black-and-white picture of him had suddenly appeared behind the newsreader. In it he was looking a few years younger and had a bit more hair, smiling happily as though he had just won at blackjack. The graphic said HOSTAGE CRISIS.

The reporter looked serious: 'Mr Robertson, an oilman of many years' experience, has been actively engaged in an exploration project that experts believe will make a major contribution to the development of Afghanistan. NATO governments, particularly the US and the UK, hope that if the exploration is successful it could offer Afghanistan an alternative income to narcotics. Diplomats are working round the clock behind the scenes to secure his return . . .'

'Diplomats!' scoffed Boss Weeks. 'What diplomatic relations does the British government have with the Taliban?'

Kila shook his head. 'Poor bastard. Poor fucking bastard.'

'What are they doing about it apart from talking?' demanded Mal. 'Why aren't they looking all over Helmand Province?'

Finn said: 'The odds are getting longer every minute.'

The others stared at him.

'What odds?'

'You mean, the odds on Martyn coming back alive?' asked Jamie.

Finn looked around swiftly for Dave. He was not in the cook-house.

'Yes, lads, I'm offering Burlington Bertie on Martyn's safe return. The odds'll be a lot longer tomorrow so now's the time for a punt.'

He was met with blank faces.

'Burlington Bertie. That's a hundred to thirty. Who's up for it?'

Dave took the phone to his favourite private corner near the washing place. For once it was deserted.

It took a while to get through to the hospital. He hoped Nurse Prim wouldn't answer again but he recognized her voice at once. Evidently she recognized him too.

'Is that the husband who's in Afghanistan?' she asked beadily.

'Yeah. Can I talk to my wife?'

'It's taken you a long time to phone. She'll be going home any day,' said the nurse.

'Well, we're so busy playing cards and watching the grass grow that I just couldn't be bothered before.'

'Now, now, there's no need for sarcasm.'

He could hear her carrying the phone through the ward.

'We were all very shocked to hear that British soldiers have killed

393

some Afghan children,' she said reproachfully, as if Dave had personally been out spraying bullets into kids.

'Not guilty,' he pleaded.

He could hear the cries of babies. His heart thudded. Babies. And one of them was his.

'Hi, love,' said Jenny.

He swallowed.

'Dave? Are you there, love? Oh, don't say we've lost the line!'

'I'm here, Jen.'

'Hi, darling!'

'I couldn't phone before.' Bad start. Defensive.

'Don't worry, you're here now.' She sounded relaxed.

'Is it all OK? I mean, you're OK, the baby's OK, tell me everything's all right.' Too anxious.

'Calm down, everything's fine. It all happened quickly in the end. There wasn't even time to do it properly with groans and contractions and things. They just had to get her out so I had a Caesarean. It's goodbye bikinis, but who cares?'

'How are you, Jen?'

'Fine. I'm taking painkillers. But I've felt so much better since she was born. All the swelling's gone, the dizziness has gone. I've turned into a gentle old cow, giving milk and more milk.'

'And the baby?'

'A bit surprised to find herself out in the real world so suddenly.'

'Wasn't ready for deployment?'

'She responded well to the alert. Now she's happy as Larry. Likes to be held and cuddled and she's drinking a lot.'

'Trish was there?'

'For the birth? Well, sort of.'

'Only sort of?'

'She was there when I came out of the operating theatre.'

'Oh, shit, shit, you were alone.'

'Nope. There were doctors and nurses everywhere making a big fuss of me. And then Mum was waiting outside. And then your mum arrived.'

'Are they both staying at our house?'

'Yeah, spoiling Vicky rotten.'

'I've only just seen the pictures.'

'Isn't she gorgeous?'

'Yeah,' said Dave. 'Yeah. She's gorgeous. So are you. All I want now is to get home.'

'Still think the army's where you want to be?' Jenny asked.

'That was a cheap shot.'

She laughed. 'Just answer the question!'

'At this moment,' he admitted, 'I'm not so sure.'

When the call ended he turned and saw a silent figure, hanging back in the shadows.

'Jamie Dermott, I should have guessed,' he said, holding out the phone.

'I haven't booked it. But I guessed they weren't minimized any more . . .'

'Go on. Phone her. Get it sorted out,' said Dave.

Jamie was already dialling. He asked how Jenny was but Dave could tell he wasn't listening to the answer.

About ten minutes later, when Dave was wandering around the base, squinting in the dark at the damage caused by today's attack, Jamie caught up with him.

'Well?' Dave was running his hands over a wall of sandbags and wondering if the engineers would say they should rebuild the whole bloody thing. He looked up. Jamie was smiling.

'Everything's fine! She was all over me!'

Dave grinned back at him in the dark. 'I told you it was only a misunderstanding. Six days with no contact and she's gagging to talk to you. It just proves you've been phoning her too often, mate.'

Chapter Sixty

THE HOSTAGE CRISIS CHANGED EVERYTHING AT SIN CITY. SUDDENLY THE base was the focus of interest – from the international community as well as the Taliban. The major announced that the civilians were to be evacuated. They would be replaced in the isoboxes by top army, Foreign Office and Intelligence personnel.

A line-up of officers waited to receive the VIPs. The base came under frequent attack now and the Chinook was greeted by a volley of fire. Two Apaches hovered on either side, firing back.

Some of the arrivals climbed out looking terrified. A few wore city suits under their body armour. The OC greeted them and the 2 i/c led them away. The OC remained with the small group of soldiers who had assembled to say goodbye to the civilians, departing on the same Chinook.

Emily was tearful.

'Martyn and I did nothing but argue. But I think we did like each other really,' she sobbed, as she shook hands with the men.

Finn raised his eyebrows and said nothing.

'Don't talk about Martyn in the past tense,' said the OC. 'We may get him back yet.'

Emily clearly did not believe him.

She prepared to board the Chinook, handbag glued to her shoulder, bag of papers in her other arm and an engineer carrying her suitcase.

'Goodbye, my dears,' she said to Asma and Jean. 'I appreciate how well you prepared me for the *shura*. It rates as one of my most fascinating experiences and the young tribesman was a most interesting cultural encounter.'

They did not dare to tell her that the young tribesman had been shot by Special Forces and this action had probably prompted Martyn's kidnap.

She shook hands with the OC and his officers. 'Thank you. Thank you for guarding us so well. I owe you all an apology. I have spent the last months telling you that your precautions were unnecessary. I will regret, to the end of my days, that I encouraged Martyn to treat this protection with such disdain. I have made it clear to anyone who will listen that his kidnap is not your fault.'

The OC smiled ruefully. 'Thanks, Emily. But that may not be enough to save my career.'

The Chinook took off, as it had landed, under fire and accompanied by Apaches.

'I liked her in the end,' Asma told Gordon Weeks.

'Emily?' he said in surprise. 'You and she are very different.'

'You mean, she's brainy and I'm pretty.'

'I suppose I do mean that . . .' He caught himself in time. 'Although you're brainy too, of course.'

She laughed. 'Not bloody quick enough, Gordon. But what I like about Emily is, she knows who she is and what she believes and she sticks to it. She doesn't care what anyone else thinks of her.'

The helicopters had disappeared. The enemy had stopped firing, although a few enthusiastic lads up in the sangars seemed keen to provoke a bit more of a fight. Jean had been called to the ops room. And, without discussing it, the boss and Asma were wandering towards the cookhouse for a brew. They had started to snatch a few minutes together whenever they could and Weeks suspected that these short meetings were becoming the high point of his day. He even found himself feeling agitated if he didn't see her for a long time, as though she was a drug he depended on.

'But you have beliefs which you stick to, surely,' said the boss now. He was fascinated by her background and returned to the subject as often as she let him.

'Christ, Gordon, you're always prodding and poking. Look, I left Islam behind. I left my family behind. I left my husband behind. It doesn't all add up to a lot of sticking power.'

'Maybe it just means you can't do things by halves,' said Weeks, pouring her a brew. She cupped her hands around the mug as though they were back in England and it was cold outside.

'When I got married I knew that meant I was leaving my family and leaving Islam. It all seemed far behind me. Until I came here.'

'So you've found your roots again.'

'Oh, you do talk a lot of crap. I've found my fucking DNA. That doesn't mean I want to rush down the mosque with my shoes off praising Allah. It just means I'm a bit more interesting than someone who's always lived in one country with one family speaking one language in one way.' She did not meet his eye.

'Like me,' he said. She still did not look at him. 'So you don't find me very interesting. You know nothing about what it's like to be me in my world, but you've decided it's all farmhouses and polo ponies and therefore not interesting. Maybe you should find out a bit more before you dismiss it.'

He saw her wince a little. He wasn't really offended. He was just challenging her because he had learned that she liked that.

She stood up, smiling. 'Oh, fuck off, Gordon Weeks!' she said cheerfully. But she was blushing. He studied the way her skin darkened, from the neck upwards. It was lovely.

'See you later. I have to get over to the ops room now or Jean'll kill me.'

He watched her go, carrying her mug of tea carelessly. He wished he could show her his world. The big old farmhouse, the horses in their rugs running their muzzles across frosty winter grassland, the log fire, the warm kitchen, the draughty bedrooms, that place on the dining-room wall where his parents had marked the heights of their growing children. He tried to imagine Asma there, but it was impossible. Not because she came from Hackney but because she seemed to belong to the swelling heat of the Afghan desert.

The soldiers saw little of the new personnel at the base but the OC, who now shared his ops room with at least fifteen people, was more visible. He frequently stood outside the ops-room door, looking hot and miserable.

Asma and Jean spent all day in there listening to radios with more senior Intelligence officers. If they slipped out to have a meal with Kila or Weeks they were invariably called back. Cooks ran in and out with loaded trays. The 2 i/c appeared only when dashing to the cookhouse to replenish his supply of teabags.

'They eat a lot of scoff and drink a lot of brews,' said Finn. 'But what are they doing about Martyn? For fuck's sake, why aren't we out there tearing into every Terry Taliban in Helmand?'

After four days Dave herded 1 Platoon into the Cowshed and the boss told them there was to be a clearance operation on the tribesmen's house where the *shuras* had been held. According to intelligence, Martyn had actually been kept there for twenty-four hours. He had been moved on now but their job was to round up for questioning any insurgents who remained and to look for signs of Martyn's occupation.

'What's the point in finding signs of Martyn after he's gone?' asked Mal.

The boss shrugged.

'It's too much to hope that there will be signs of *where* he's gone. Probably the object is to feed the international press corps with something to keep Martyn at the top of the news agenda.'

As their convoy rolled into town every man quietly hoped that Martyn would be found at the compound. He had been Topaz fucking Zero, before: mostly irritating, sometimes entertaining and finally liked. Now, in his absence and with his new status as helpless victim, he was loved.

They found the streets deserted. The bazaar was without buyers or sellers. The new school wall was in place but behind it the classrooms were empty.

'Bad sign,' said Dave to the driver. And within five minutes the convoy was met by machine-gun fire. Rounds ricocheted around the narrow streets, bouncing off the mud walls until the soldiers were forced to dismount, take cover and find firing positions.

Sol was trying Bacon as GPMG man for this patrol and Binns was feeding the ammo and looking for targets. The pair of them were excited and nervous to use the gimpy out on an operation for the first time.

'Just ask me if you need help,' said Jamie, who had given up the gimpy to them reluctantly.

'Cheeky bastard dude down there!' said Binman, pointing

to a figure taking stock of their position from a far doorway.

'I see him!' said Streaky. He trained the sights on the space the figure had just vacated. When the insurgent stepped out again, weapon raised, he was instantly felled by a hail of fire.

'Cool, Streaky, that was cool!' Binns found himself laughing. He didn't think it was funny but he was laughing all the same. Bacon giggled too. They became so hysterical they were barely able to fire.

'For fuck's sake, you two,' said Angus. And then his voice cracked and he gave a rumble of laughter. He continued to laugh as he fired.

'What's so funny, Streaks?' giggled Binns.

'Binman, I just don't know!'

But they could not stop.

'Pull yourselves together and get on with the job,' Sol told them harshly. 'Or I'll hand the gimpy back to Jamie.' Men were always laughing as they fired. It looked like a kind of mania and Sol hated it.

The platoons were splitting into sections now to get through the maze of narrow streets and approach the compound from the positions they had agreed. The town was a labyrinth of alleyways and high mud walls.

'Stay together, 1 Section,' Sol warned as they struck off into a side street. 'This place is a rabbit warren.'

Over PRR Dave said: 'Fix bayonets.'

All members of his platoon, wherever they were, did so. You could do this mechanically, without emotion, like Angus. Or you could do it, like Jack Binns, with apprehension, knowing that this was a close-quarters measure and that it might mean you'd find yourself within arm's length of the Taliban.

'Don't worry,' Mal said. 'No one ever really uses their bayonet, not in the last hundred years. It's just to make you feel better.'

'You're all right,' said Binman. 'You've got the shotgun.'

'Have you, Mal? Sure you didn't put it down somewhere?' voices shouted.

'Get moving and stay alert,' Boss Weeks told them sharply as he followed them down the alley.

The soldiers felt vulnerable making their way through the twists and turns. Rooftops and windows gave the enemy any number of good firing positions and shots could be heard from all over the town. They advanced cautiously, Sol leading.

When Finn, near the back, saw movement on a roof he stopped suddenly. Behind him Boss Weeks froze and behind him the signaller.

'Don't fire,' the boss instructed.

Finn who had been prepared to lay down a few rounds to warn anyone armed up there that he was ready for them, grudgingly put the safety back on the minimi. They waited. Ahead of them, the rest of the patrol waited too. No one liked standing still here. The men looked around them constantly, like birds. Finn's attention was fixed on the roof. Slowly, a head edged out. And then another. Dark-haired, brown-skinned, big-eyed, it was two small boys, eager to see the soldiers pass.

'Shit,' said Finn. Jamie took a bag of sweets out of one of his pouches and threw it up to them. The boys caught the bag delightedly. But instead of eating the sweets they began to use them to bombard the men below.

Jamie laughed but Finn was angry. He shouted: 'Little bastards!'

'We know what they want to be when they grow up,' said the boss. Finn caught one of the sweets and stuck it defiantly in his mouth as the section moved on.

There was firing nearby and the boss heard on the radio that this was 2 Section, who were accompanied by Dave. One insurgent had been killed. Two more had fled.

Sol rounded a corner and almost walked into a man running towards him, looking over his shoulder. In a split second Sol took in his presence and the weapon he was carrying, a Kalashnikov PKM.

Sol knew, without actually having time to think it, that he had to be quicker than this man or his deadly weapon could slaughter the entire section. He did not give himself the luxury of hesitation. He darted forward. The insurgent turned to find himself eyeball to eyeball with Sol's wide, dark face. Sol had time to watch the man's features scatter into a mixture of surprise and horror before plunging the bayonet into his chest. The insurgent staggered and Sol pulled out the bayonet.

'I've got him,' said a voice from behind. 'Get down, Sol.'

Blood spurting from his chest, the man was still attempting to raise his weapon. Sol dropped onto the dusty ground and Mal fired the shotgun. The man fell.

The rest of the section rounded the corner and halted when they saw the corpse. Blood was blossoming in widening circles all over his torso. His eyes were open but clouding rapidly.

Sol stared at him and at the man's blood on his bayonet. 1 Section crowded around him.

Binns turned a shocked face to Mal. 'I thought you said no one had done that for a hundred years!'

Streaky asked: 'Was it hard to get it in him, Sol?'

'It was much easier than you'd think. And I've always worried a bit about getting it out but it extracts really easy, too.'

Another man, carrying an AK47, emerged through a doorway down the alley. Seeing them, he turned to run.

Mal raised the shotgun again. Its report echoed around and around the high walled alley. Everyone waited for the man to fall. He took his few last paces running from life to death. He turned into a ghost as he moved: his momentum remained forward as his body crumpled.

The boss was describing the dead men over the radio to Dave, who confirmed they were the pair who had escaped from 2 Section. 'At last the fucking shotgun's come in useful!' said Mal happily.

The boss was watching Sol.

'All right?' he asked.

'Yeah, course,' said Sol, wiping the insurgent's blood off the bayonet by scraping it across the man's body. He turned to Angus, the sharp shooter for the section.

'Don't s'pose you've got the pistol?' he asked hopefully. Dave had told Angry to bring his SA80 and not his sniper rifle today, which usually meant that he had left the pistol behind as well.

'Yeah, I did stick it in,' said Angus. Sol's face lit up. The boss smiled.

'Well done, mate,' said Mal. 'That'll save Sol getting his bayonet dirty again.'

Angus handed over the pistol. But Sol's bayonet remained fixed. Then he led them on, past the two bodies, through the tiny, winding streets. When they arrived at the compound where Asad's family had lived, everyone recognized it. But the only welcome today was the chatter of AK47s.

Chapter Sixty-one

2 PLATOON WAS ALREADY IN CONTACT. THE ENEMY WAS NOT EXPECTING attack on another flank: a few were lying along the top of walls. When they realized that there were soldiers on both sides they evaporated, but not before Binns had killed one of them with his rifle.

'Shit, oh, shit,' said Binns when he saw the body of a Taliban fighter roll off a wall and fall to the street. 'Shit, was that me?'

Jamie looked at him hard because Binns had been involved in numerous fire fights over the last few months.

'So have you been missing them until now, Binman?'

Binns coloured.

'I never was sure before that it was me.'

'Go!' roared the boss behind them, aware that they had a good opportunity to advance if the enemy was reorganizing.

Covered by 2 Section, 1 Section ran forward to the shelter of an adjoining wall while engineers laid a bar-mine.

'You've been inside, boss, you know the layout here,' said Finn while they waited.

'I know the layout of the rooms nearest the door,' agreed Boss Weeks. 'I'm not sure how helpful that is.'

As rapid fire continued on the other side of the compound, the engineers retreated and a small hole appeared in the massive walls.

'We're attacking at state red,' the boss reminded them.

Sol took a grenade from his pouch and threw it into the room and Mal pulled him back by his webbing. There was a pause followed by a roar, then smoke, dust and shrapnel. Mal scrambled in behind it with the shotgun. There was no sign of anyone in the room, alive or dead. He put down thirteen rounds and then sank onto one knee and let Jamie, immediately behind, fire over him.

The others piled in through the hole and, behind them, the boss and then 2 Section. They spread out, moving from room to room, double tapping into every corner. They were outflanking the enemy now, who were still fighting 2 Platoon across the compound. The Taliban, recognizing their poor position, threw down machine-gun fire in no particular direction before melting into the walls.

Jack Binns found himself at a doorway and approached it gingerly. How did you know what would be waiting in there for you? A bunch of grandmas having a cup of tea, deaf to the fighting like so many Afghan civilians? Or a wild fundamentalist with a grenade? Each called for a completely different response.

He burst in through the door, twisting to see all around it at once, wanting to fire but not daring to, at least not until he knew for sure about the grandmas.

The room was empty, to his relief. Suddenly a man jumped through a doorway on the other side. He was carrying a machine gun and behind him were more dark figures.

Jack Binns looked into the thin, bearded face of a Taliban fighter. He stared into the man's startled eyes. He wanted to run away. All his instincts, every reflex, told him to remove himself from this danger. If he had still been standing, hesitating, at the doorway, then he would have done exactly that, but he was so far inside the room he'd be shot from behind if he ran. In a fraction of a second he knew he had to kill this man and kill him instantly, or he would die.

It seemed to Binns that minutes passed between the appearance of the insurgent and the sound of his own weapon firing. And in that time he did not remove his eyes from those of his opponent. The communication was so intense that he felt he had been talking to his opponent instead of killing him. He watched as blood emerged across the front of the man's clothes.

He continued to fire: when the first man fell he left the second without cover. He looked into another set of brown eyes and, as he watched their owner stagger, a cool, rational compartment in his mind told him that a stoppage in his rifle would mean the end of his life now.

He fired more as that same rational part of his mind warned him that the two men behind were not only ready for him but ready together. Fuck! He couldn't shoot them both at once!

Binns told himself calmly that he was about to die but he might as well keep firing. To his astonishment, both men fell at the same moment. One shouted something. It sounded like: 'Oh, Mum, I'm sorry!' Binns assumed it was some Pashtu phrase that sounded like English.

A voice in his ear said: 'Good, Binman, very good.'

It was Finn.

Jack Binns wanted to ask Finn how long he had been there but he couldn't speak.

'You got three out of four!'

Finn threw a few more rounds into the bodies to make sure they were dead and then stepped over them. 'You needed me for the fourth, though. Glad I got the English bastard.'

Binns felt sweat drip down his face and neck and run in rivers along his backbone. The last body lay across the doorway. He knew that he could not touch it or step over it. Finn pushed it aside with his foot.

'Did you catch the Brummie accent? I'm glad I killed him, the fucking heap of traitor shit.'

Binns was starting to shake now. He stared at the bodies scattered across the floor, the faces of the men who only minutes earlier had been alive with all their thoughts, feelings, complexities and inner secrets. He had taken that away from them now, there was nothing left.

'Get yourself together, Binman,' Finn said sharply. 'Come on. So you've killed a few blokes, we've got a lot more to do here.'

Binns didn't move.

Someone came in behind him. Binns jumped nervously and turned to fire again.

'Hey, don't shoot me!' Sol was surveying the bodies. 'You've done some good work, Binman.'

Jack Binns wanted to say: I couldn't run away or I'd have been killed; that's the only reason I did it. But he remained silent.

'This fucker's English,' Finn told Sol. 'Can you believe it? I mean, I could have been at school with him.'

'Thought you didn't spend a lot of time at school, Finny.'

Sol bent down and searched the bag that had been slung across the man's shoulder. He pulled out a mobile phone, a Pakistani passport and a British passport.

'Someone's going to be very interested in that,' Finn said.

But Sol was already moving on.

'Let's go. They're bringing in more men.'

'Think my mate Martyn's still here?' asked Finn hopefully.

'We won't know if we don't look.'

Sol pushed Binns roughly ahead of him.

'Stay focused,' he ordered. 'Stay on the job.'

Binns stumbled forward wordlessly.

On the other side of the compound, the firing eased and stopped.

They haven't gone, thought Mal. They're drawing breath.

'There are still Taliban inside this compound somewhere,' said the boss. 'Unless there are tunnels.'

To Mal the place suddenly seemed immense and complicated, full of corners and staircases and dark places like somewhere in a dream. At home he played computer games but this was not like those games. This was full of the sights and smells of recent occupation. A warm teapot. A cushion with an indentation where someone had been sitting. Empty cartridges. A pair of sandals by a doorway, neatly arranged.

Jamie sensed Mal's hesitation.

'We'll work this side together,' he said. Jamie was quick, quiet and methodical. He made Mal feel calm as they entered rooms stealthily, checked briefly for civilians and then attacked the nothingness with a rapid burst of fire.

Finn and the boss were moving forward too. When the boss recognized the doorway to the room where he had sat around the carpet exchanging warm pleasantries with this family, he felt a deep blush start in his chest and creep up his body to cover his face. How had it ended like this? Finn bounced ahead of him into the room and was ready to put down a burst of 5.56mm when he halted abruptly.

406

'Shit, boss,' he said.

There was the carpet Weeks recognized on the floor, the smell of sweet tea and another smell, an aromatic spice. There were the rugs on the walls. And huddled against them, a small group of civilians.

Gordon Weeks looked at the women and registered their fear. Their eyes were wide and a child hid its face against its mother. Next to them an old man stared at him. Was there accusation in those eyes? Weeks recognized the man. He had handed around tea and warm, flat bread at the meeting. He had stooped and smiled politely. Who was he? A grandfather? A servant? Suddenly Weeks was ashamed of his lack of knowledge of Afghan culture. Why hadn't he asked Asma more, studied more?

He felt his blush deepening. His hosts, or one of them, might have proved to be a prominent Taliban leader but Weeks could not forget that he had been a guest here once and he was no longer behaving like a guest.

The boss greeted the old man in Pashtu and the man bowed his head but did not reply. And that was another thing, the boss thought. Why hadn't he persevered with learning Pashtu?

He said in clear, slow, precise English: 'Please stay in this room and you will be safe. There are Taliban in the house and we are trying to remove them. We are looking for information about the hostage. Then we will go and you can resume your lives.'

He knew the man could not understand. He just hoped his tone was reassuring. But the old man continued to stare at him with accusation in his eyes and Weeks guessed that he was being held responsible for the death of Asad.

'I didn't kill him,' he said to the man, who stared back un-comprehendingly. 'I didn't trust him but I certainly didn't kill him.'

It was ludicrous, but it was better than saying nothing. To his surprise, the man listened and then got up creakily. He traipsed off down the open hallway. The boss understood that he was intended to follow. He warned the lads not to fire.

The old man led him past walls covered with rugs and matting to the shady courtyard where no doubt the men of the house sat and talked under leaves in the daytime and stars at night. The boss remembered that this was not a theatre of war for the people who lived their simple lives here but a home that might be full of memories.

The morning sun was already caning the soldiers in their heavy kit but the courtyard felt cool, as though it was air-conditioned. The leaves created green shade and there was a large stone bowl of water and a few lemon trees, branches weighed down with fruit.

The man led them to a tiny mud-walled enclosure in one corner that might be a dog kennel. There was no dog now but evidently until recently there had been a very big animal here because its turd burned hot in the sun and a large chain was attached to one wall of the doghouse. The places where the chain had been dragged across the ground had been rubbed bare of vegetation and had turned to dust as fine as talcum powder.

The man gestured and said something.

Angus and Finn were behind Weeks.

'Maybe he wants to sell you a dog,' suggested Finn.

'Cover me, I'm looking inside,' Angus told them, sinking onto his hands and knees and crawling into the kennel. Its door was already open but he pushed it open further. Inside it was dark and smelly. He crawled in. There was nothing, except a mattress on the ground.

'Holy shit! Holy fucking shit!'

But there was no time to show the boss what he had found because they were in contact again. Evidently the insurgents had regrouped. There were tracers whizzing in both directions. The men dived for cover. It took a moment for them to realize that no one was firing at them. The fight was going on over their heads across the courtyard and neither side had registered their presence among the trees.

The boss advised the old man to get down. The man ignored him and returned to the house, walking past the rounds as though he was invisible.

'The doghouse is good cover,' the boss said reluctantly. He crawled in, followed by Angus and Mal.

'See that?' said Angus, his huge body concertinaed into the small space. 'He was here! Martyn was here!'

Gordon Weeks twisted round and saw the word MARTYN was scratched into the wall. He could not hide his excitement. Finn was so pleased he kept fingering the name.

'Shit, he was here! Shit, we're hot on his trail!'

The boss gave a sit rep over the radio and then the news about Topaz Zero's signature.

Angus and Finn were in their firing positions, lying in the dog's doorway now. Finn nodded to the turd.

'Glad to see Marty finally had that crap.'

'The shit's old. He left at least a day ago,' said Angus.

'But at least he's still alive!' said the boss from behind them.

Angus grinned. 'We're going to find the old bastard. We might even get to him before they cut off his bollocks!'

'He liked you,' said Finn. 'All that shit about your dad . . . He pissed me off big-time for telling you but he did it because he liked you.'

'Know what I was thinking when he told me?' Angus said. 'I was wishing that Martyn Robertson *was* my fucking dad.'

'That's why you want to rescue him,' said Finn. 'If the Taliban got their hands on your real dad you wouldn't give jack-shit.'

'Nah, I'd buy them a pint,' said Angus. 'But I'm bloody sure we'll get Martyn back.'

'We all are,' agreed the boss. 'Especially now we're hot on his trail.' Angus started firing but Finn paused to think. 'I may have to shorten my odds. I've been offering Burlington Bertie on Marty being found alive but I could go bankrupt on that. If you're interested in a flutter, boss, it'll have to be fifteen to eight now.'

'Didn't Dave Henley stop you taking bets?' asked the boss, watching tracers cross the courtyard like fireflies.

'What he don't know about he can't grieve over.'

'And is it right to turn Martyn's misery into a bookie's opportunity?'

'Boss, trust me. When we get Martyn out alive his first question's going to be: Finny, what odds did you have on me?'

'Stoppage,' said Angus, falling back. 'Get on with it, Finny.'

Finn shuffled forward.

'You're doing well, Angry, with that fiver you gave me at a hundred to thirty. That's looking like a very good punt now.'

Angus said: 'Don't you ever fucking shuddup? Look, there's a bloke on the roof there.'

Finn fired and the man teetered along the edge and then, as though in slow motion, fell, arms first, into the courtyard.

'This is a shit-hot position. We see it all and no one sees us. From now on, everywhere we go, I'm heading straight for the fucking doghouse.'

The battle was easing. Some well-aimed mortars from 2 Platoon produced a massive dust cloud and then silence. 2 Platoon began to advance through the compound.

'Just go firm, 1 Platoon,' said the OC. 'We don't want a blue on blue.'

Angus, Finn and the boss waited. Finn sorted out his ammo.

'I miss Marty, because he's the only real betting man in the place. No one else risks more than a fiver.'

'No one else earns enough,' said Angus.

'Officers do,' said Finn pointedly.

The boss sighed. 'Oh all right, Finny. I'll do a tenner at fifteen to eight if you don't tell Dave Henley. But I'm just going to make bloody sure we find Martyn so I get my money back.'

Chapter Sixty-two

STEVE DIDN'T ARGUE WHEN LEANNE ANNOUNCED THAT SHE WANTED him to come home from Headley Court for a day. Since everything he did and said felt hurtful now, she took his failure to put up a fight as indifference.

'For heaven's sake,' said Jenny. 'You've turned into one of those things in rock pools at the seaside that close up when you touch them. They even close up when they feel your shadow.'

'Sea urchins?'

'No . . . I've forgotten. My brain can't remember more than the time of the next feed. Anyway, I'm trying to say, stop being so touchy. Steve's happy to spend a day at home. You're happy he's coming. Act happy. The old Leanne would have been laughing and joking all the way down the M3.'

Jenny was changing the baby's nappy. Vicky and the twins were watching TV. Leanne, who was folding washing for her friend, paused thoughtfully.

'What did the old Leanne do if Steve went all silent on her?'

'I expect he did it all the time and she didn't even notice because she was too busy being a stand-up comedian.'

'I don't do funny any more.'

'Well, start again.'

Leanne sighed. 'I'm going to ask Kylie at nursery if she'll take the boys for the whole day.'

'Oh, Leanne, I wish I could help . . .' Jenny gestured around the

411

room. It was strewn with discarded clothes, pink toys and dirty washing. 'Now Mum's gone, it's chaos here.'

'The boys'll be fine with Kylie.'

'She split up with her boyfriend. Ben. The one who lost a leg. People are saying nasty things about her for not sticking by him.'

'Not me,' said Leanne quietly. 'I don't blame her.'

She was nervous when she arrived at Headley Court to pick up Steve. She half expected to find that he had forgotten or wasn't ready, and as she parked she prepared herself to get upset. She sat in the car in a disabled parking place near the guardhouse, chewing her lip. It was a windy autumn day. Each gust buffeted the car and threw rain against it. She jumped when her phone rang.

'Anemones!' said Jenny's crisp voice.

'You what?'

'Sea anemones. They're the things that pull in all their petals if they see your shadow because they think everything wants to hurt them. That's what you mustn't be, Leanne.'

'So how am I supposed to be again? Just remind me, Jen.'

'Big, noisy, happy, loving, lots of fun, very funny. In other words, just yourself.'

'Christ. I can still do big. But that's about all.'

'Oh, and sexy.'

Leanne swallowed again.

'At the moment we're two people who don't fancy each other.'

'You can change all that.'

'Jen . . . listen. I told you I saw his leg. What's left of it. His stump. I told you I saw it in hospital. But I sort of didn't because it was still bandaged. I haven't really seen it yet.'

Jenny sighed.

'You'll have to see it some time.'

'Yeah.' Leanne's voice was very small.

'Just brace yourself and tell him he's still gorgeous and don't start looking sorry for him. And if he tries giving you shit, don't burst into tears, for God's sake.'

'Right.'

'Just put your arms around him and tell him he'd better watch out or you'll rip off the other leg.'

Leanne guffawed.

'Christ, Jen. I'm not such a good actress.'

'Leanne, today you're going to win an Oscar.'

Leanne closed her eyes and took some deep breaths. She started to get out of the car and then paused. She hammered out a quick text: *'I'm coming in to get you. So you better watch out.'*

Agnieszka watched the rain. The wind was throwing it against the window. It was just a matter of time before she heard the familiar sound of water pouring from the leaking gutter.

She could see the road, dark as a long, cold river. A car passed, moving slowly, its lights on although it was morning, its windscreen wipers waving from side to side. Luke started crying. She did not turn away from the window.

'That how I feel, Luke. Just like you,' she told him.

Someone walked along the pavement, body doubled against the wind, towing a child along in hat, coat and scarf. The child was crying and objecting but its mother was pulling it along anyway.

The car that had passed stopped now. It was parking outside. She saw it was a sports car but she watched it without interest. A man got out. Darrel! She felt her heart miss a beat. Then she was annoyed with herself. Most of all, she was annoyed with her heart.

Steve switched on the TV as soon as they were in the living room. Leanne switched it off.

'What d'you think you're doing?' he demanded.

'I can't seduce a man while he's watching daytime TV – he might get me confused with one of those antiques auction shows and try to flog me for a fiver.'

He looked at her without smiling and raised his eyebrows.

'So that's why you brought me all the way down here and got the kids out for the day.'

She sat beside him on the sofa and took his hand. He was still her big, handsome husband. She used to feel proud, walking around shopping centres or taking the kids places with him. She often saw other women glance twice at Steve. And his face hadn't changed. It was the expression on it that was different.

'Nah. It's because I've always wanted a disabled parking badge and I need you to sign the forms.'

413

He didn't smile. 'I don't need a fucking blue badge, and you didn't need to sweet-talk the guardhouse into giving you a disabled space today.'

'So you've got a souvenir replica of the Eiffel Tower instead of a leg and you like to show it off. Why should that stop me getting the best parking place at Tesco?'

She saw his face re-form itself into angry lines.

'I am not driving a car with a fucking blue badge.'

'Shut up, Steve, and take your clothes off.'

'What?'

'Don't have a problem undressing, do you? After all, you're not disabled.'

He looked at her with apprehension. She moved closer to him and began to kiss his face, especially around his ears, like she used to. She felt him relax a little. She kissed him on the mouth and he responded. She began to feel triumphant. Then he pulled away.

'Leanne . . .'

Oh-oh. She tried to kiss his mouth to stop him talking. She could feel him giving in to her. Then he pulled away again.

'Leanne, listen . . .'

She looked at him. His eyes were large and soft now. They had lost that cross, bulging look and the angry lines around his mouth had disappeared.

He said: 'You've never looked at my stump.'

'You've never shown me.'

'I put my socket and leg on when you come up to Headley Court. But when you're not there, I lounge around without it.'

'Why don't you lounge around without it when I'm there?'

'Because you don't want to see it.'

He was right. But she was not going to admit that.

'Because you hide it from me,' she said.

He swallowed.

'Want to see it, then?'

'Well, I've already been to the Eiffel Tower. Got the T-shirt. So show me something I haven't seen.'

He swallowed again.

'You want to do it . . . here?'

'We could go down to the rec. But tongues would wag, Steve.'

She began to kiss him again and this time he gave in.

'OK,' he said at last. 'Here goes.'

He took off his trousers. She stared at the join between the socket and the metal leg. She had seen that before: Steve and most of the other lads with metal legs walked around at Selly Oak and Headley Court in shorts. Only the older amputees covered up and tried to make the prosthetics look like real legs, she had noticed.

Her heart began to beat faster. She remembered Jenny telling her that today she had to win an Oscar. It was essential not to show fear, disgust or horror. She concentrated hard on looking relaxed. She thought she was succeeding. But when she tried to smile she found she was unable to.

Steve took the leg off the socket. He made several attempts to lean it against the sofa. She did not help him. It began to slide to the floor. She did not catch it. The leg landed with a thud. Then she watched as he released the socket at the top of his leg. Already his movements were practised and fluent. She reached out and very gently stroked his forearms as his hands worked. She tried not to pay any attention to the part of her that felt dizzy with fear at what she was about to see. She reminded herself that this was Steve. She wanted him to know that he was still her Steve.

And, suddenly, there it was. Steve's stump. It grew out of his groin and was recognizably a human body part. The surgeons had rounded it off nicely: it was covered with tight flesh like the rest of him as though it had always been that way. What had she expected? A dripping mess of hanging wires like a fire in an electrical show-room? So, after all that, his stump wasn't an ugly, scary deformity. It was Steve.

She knew he was watching her. And it was easy to smile. Very slowly, she reached out and touched it. Yes, it even felt like Steve. Even more slowly, because her bulk, as usual these days, got in the way, she leaned forward and kissed it. Gently, and lovingly.

Steve watched her. She looked up at him from his small fraction of a leg and smiled.

Agnieszka ran to open the door quickly so no one would see him. She didn't want to smile at him but she could not stop herself.

'Darrel!'

'I don't start work until one today. So I thought I'd stop by and show you my new wheels.'

'You get new car?'

'Yeah, came into the garage last week. A part-ex. It's a Mazda MR2, not very new but some old bloke had it for years and didn't drive anywhere. It's even still got its original tyres!'

He talked about the handling, the acceleration, and something about cylinders. She nodded and tried to look as though she understood, the way she did when Jamie talked about weapons.

'I see from window!'

She went back to the living room and peered out at the car.

He followed her. 'I was going to take you for a ride in it. But it's just not the weather today.'

'We go when sun shines again. Darrel, this very nice car. This beautiful car.'

And it was. He looked pleased.

'Er . . . Shouldn't you . . . ?' He hesitated. 'So, what's upset Luke?'

She realized, for the first time since he had started, that Luke was still crying.

'He always begin when doorbell ring,' she said, going to his pushchair and unstrapping him before she remembered that she had answered the door before Darrel had rung.

Darrel held out his hands as if Luke was an old friend.

'How are you doing, mate? Want a hug with Darrel?'

She handed Luke over and gradually, walking slowly around the room and chatting in a calm voice, Darrel worked his magic. She watched as Luke turned into a quiet, soft, pliable baby.

Darrel said, softly: 'Aggie, I've got something to tell you.'

'Something more than new car?'

'Yeah, something else. I'm going away for a while.'

She felt her body stiffen. She looked up at him.

'My boss has a garage back in his home town. And it's not doing very well. He wants me to spend a few weeks sorting it out.'

There was a long silence.

'Where this garage?' she asked at last.

'Great Yarmouth. East. The other side of London. Not far from Poland.'

'You not come back for a few weeks?'

His face drooped.

'I'll try. But the place is in a right mess. I'd rather get the job done and finished . . .'

'When you go?'

'Today.'

'Oh!'

She turned away from him, back to the window. It sounded as though someone was throwing gravel at the glass. But it was just the rain.

'Look at me, Aggie.'

She did not want to face him. She felt desolate. Desolation was a long, flat field, covered with snow. The field had been there when her father died. And when she had first arrived in England. She had cried herself to sleep each night for a whole month at the hotel where she worked. The field was there every time Jamie went away, every time Luke went to the hospital. And now here it was again. That blanket of snow over frozen earth in a field in a frozen world far from anywhere.

'Ags? Come here.'

She walked over to him obediently and he put his free arm around her. He managed to kiss her, although he was still holding Luke with the other arm.

'Aggie, it's not for long and I'll ring you often,' he said softly.

He stroked her hair and the repetitive movement was soothing.

'I want to take care of you. I wish you hadn't sent me away the other day, after the beach.'

She closed her eyes. She leaned against him. It was one thing to look at Adi Kasanita on a summery evening laughing with her brood of healthy kids and think that was how life ought to be. And another to send away your only friend when you were stuck alone in a small house with a sick child on a rainy day. She was sure now that she did not want Darrel to go.

'Will you miss me?' he asked.

She nodded. She was frozen.

'I have to get to work,' he said softly. 'I'll be back soon, Ags. Take care of yourself.'

He carefully settled Luke into the corner of the sofa and this time the baby did not object. Darrel bent over Agnieszka. When she didn't turn her face up to him he kissed her on the forehead.

She stood at the window watching the beautiful car drive away. She did not permit herself to feel anything.

She switched on the TV. The screen was filled with British soldiers. They were wearing desert camouflage and streaming out of the back of a Chinook. This must be Afghanistan. Her heart missed a beat.

'A new development,' said the anchorman, 'in the unfolding Afghan hostage crisis.'

Afterwards, Steve held Leanne so tightly that it crossed her mind he was trying to kill her. It was a moment before she realized he was trying not to cry. The thought that this big man had been moved to tears by having sex with his wife brought tears to her own eyes.

'You can cry if you want, sweetheart,' she said. 'I am.'

As soon as she had spoken, his entire body was shaken by the immense sob that followed. He held her as he cried and cried. When she looked at his face she saw the pain there. The pain of the leg he had lost, the pain of the new reality, the pain of all the hopes and possibilities that had been exploded in a few seconds under the hot Afghan sun. She cried too, as though she could carry some of his pain and save him some tears.

'Life's going to be different now, love,' she said at last, passing him a third wad of tissues. 'But that doesn't mean it's going to be worse.'

He nodded and put an arm around her. 'I still love you. I don't always show it but I do.'

She smiled.

'And,' he added, 'thank God I can still do it.'

'Oh, you can still do it all right.'

When she stood up to go and make them a sandwich she realized that she felt relaxed for the first time in months. If she fell asleep now she would sleep for the rest of the day and the whole of the night. Instead of waking up and tossing and turning for hours and then sneaking down to the fridge as though it was her secret lover.

'Turn on the TV, sweetheart, it's time for the news,' said Steve. He sounded like his old self again.

418

She switched on and went into the kitchen. She didn't feel hungry! She decided to go without a sandwich and just make one for Steve. She was reaching for the bread when she heard shouting.

'Bloody fucking stupid bitch!'

She ran back to the living room.

'You left the zapper over there, fat cow! Look, there's something about the lads and I can't reach the zapper to turn it up!'

He was roaring. His eyes were bulging with fury, his face was angry black lines.

She rushed to the zapper and dropped it.

'For fuck's sake!' he screamed. She picked it up and hastily turned up the volume. His eyes blazed as he turned away from her. He was intent on the screen.

Leanne sat very still. She watched the newsreader without listening.

'. . . now made a ransom demand for the safe return of the American hostage, oil exploration expert Martyn Robertson. The Foreign Office has refused to comment on reports that his kidnappers are demanding as much as thirty million dollars, as well as the release of a number of Taliban detainees.

'Martyn Robertson was kidnapped by insurgents in Helmand Province while under the care of a British Army escort. The army has issued a statement saying that every effort was made to keep Mr Robertson safe but members of his family are calling for a full inquiry into how the Taliban slipped through the army's security net.

'The kidnappers are rumoured to have set a two-week limit for the delivery of the ransom. They are unlikely to let the hostage live past that deadline.'

The picture changed, the story changed, a different reporter appeared on the screen. Steve and Leanne continued to watch, mute and motionless, from separate chairs.

Chapter Sixty-three

THE MEN WERE CLUSTERED AROUND THE TV IN THE COOKHOUSE. Martyn Robertson was the first news story. There was a shocked silence as the newsreader announced the ransom demand and execution threat.

A grainy video was shown of Martyn looking miserable. He said he was being well treated and he read out a prepared text about the evils of imperialist powers in Afghanistan.

The watching men searched the background for clues to Martyn's whereabouts but behind him was only a mud wall that could be anywhere in Helmand Province, anywhere in Afghanistan. The report cut to politicians from both sides of the Atlantic talking about their determination to free the hostage without giving in to terrorist demands.

'That's a load of crap,' said Swift from 3 Section. 'We should be driving around this area ripping the shit out of every Taliban bastard for miles around.'

'Can't we just go through the whole town looking for him?' asked Aaron Baker. 'He's probably in someone's cupboard.'

'Why aren't we *doing* something to find Martyn?' people shouted.

'And what good are fucking diplomats?' asked Mal.

The OC was in the cookhouse with the men. He looked tired. 'Secretary of State Clinton is making a surprise visit to Kabul. While she's here, she's going to talk to the Afghan President about Martyn.'

His words were met by silence. Finally CSM Kila said: 'With respect, sir, that'll do fuck all to help.'

Major Willingham was doleful.

'I know.'

'Can't we find him? Can't we go and fight with the fuckers?' men said. 'We've got to get to him before the bastards slice his head off.'

But the OC held his hands up to indicate his helplessness in the world of politicians and diplomats.

After dark, Asma escaped from the ops room to have a cigarette and join Gordon Weeks for a walk around the perimeter. Foreign Office staff, walking with their heads tilted back so they could see the amazing Afghan stars, kept bumping into them.

'They get paid danger money to come to an FOB,' said Asma. 'It's a fortune. But the first sign of any incoming and they're into the bunker and down on the ground.'

Weeks stepped around a stumbling man in a smart suit and body armour.

'Their greatest risk is falling and breaking a leg while they stargaze.'

She giggled.

'God it is so fucking good to get out of the ops room! It's stuffy and smelly and horrible. And so are all the officers.'

Weeks decided she had just paid him a compliment without even knowing it. Suddenly he felt happy. Happy to be with Asma, under a spectacular night sky, hearing her laugh.

Without thinking he reached out and drew her to him. Their body armour bumped. He smelled the hint of perfume and the odour of cigarette. Her arms were bare and the softness of her skin excited him. Then his courage failed. He kissed her on the cheek and released her.

'What was that for?' She was laughing at him.

'I don't know what came over me,' he said. 'I hope you don't mind.'

She laughed again and then they walked on in silence.

'So,' he began awkwardly. 'Are you sitting there with your head-phones on just listening all day?'

'Yup. Except when someone nicks me headphones.'

'Is it ever interesting?'

'It's enough to make me take up fucking knitting. I mean, why do we look at the radio when we're listening to it?'

'But are you getting anywhere?'

'Well, it's frustrating. I knew Martyn and I feel this sense of urgency, especially now we've only got two weeks. But there are guys in there who are treating it like just another bloody day's work. It's more about politics than about finding him.'

'But do you hear anything on the radio that may lead us to him? The men all want to get out there and search.'

'Hmmm. Depends how you interpret what they say.'

'Because the Taliban speak in code?'

'Their codes aren't very complicated. But they chatter a lot about nothing. So it's hard to tell what's crap and what matters. There was a lot of stuff about a holy place today so the colonel's convinced they're hiding him in a mosque.'

'Well, they might be.'

'Or they might just have been talking about mosques. Because Moslems do.'

'Any idea which mosque?'

She laughed again.

'No. So if your blokes want something to do, they could search them all.'

Chapter Sixty-four

'FOLLOWING AN INTELLIGENCE BREAKTHROUGH WHICH SUGGESTS THAT Martyn is being held in a mosque, the colonel has decided that every mosque within a one-hundred-kilometre range of this base is to be cleared and searched tomorrow morning,' announced the boss.

'So what will we do *after* lunch?' asked Jamie Dermott.

Gordon Weeks said: 'It is important to clear as many mosques simultaneously as possible and clearly this base doesn't have the manpower. So troops from other bases will be taking part and other companies are being flown in to help.'

'How many are we doing?' asked Angus.

'There are three mosques in the town by the base and each platoon will clear one. You will, of course, behave respectfully and politely. To you it may feel like any building to be searched: to a Moslem a mosque is a very holy place.'

Dave involuntarily glanced at Mal. He was staring at the ground, his face red.

'Don't they have to leave their shoes outside? Well, I'm not taking my fucking boots off,' said Angus.

'You can keep your boots on,' said Dave, rolling his eyes.

The boss continued: 'There is to be no shouting or swearing in the mosque. And, although we will have to enter with our weapons, we must avoid firing them unnecessarily. It's a green entry so strictly, strictly no grenades. Plus total respect for any religious objects like the Quran, please.'

'On training they told us that the Taliban store weapons in mosques,' said Bacon. 'Where's their respect, then?'

'They not only store weapons but they frequently fire from mosques. But that's no reason for us to do the same.'

'So how can Martyn Robertson be held in a mosque if it's a public place?' asked O'Sullivan.

'Good question. Either the Taliban has to ensure the silence of an entire community, which is possible. Or he'll be kept in a cupboard, room or underground area around the mosque. In short, we don't know.'

'Will there be many people inside? Saying prayers and things?' asked Binman.

'The operation has been deliberately timed to avoid the five Moslem prayer times. But there may well be people inside the mosque and we will have to indicate to them, very politely, that they should step aside while we search the place.'

'Right, lads,' said Dave. 'We'll show you a map of the town and the mosque so you all know what you're doing. Concentrate. Stay alert. Use your eyes and your heads. We're undermanned, we all need each other and we're doing a vital job tomorrow. We're going to try to find Martyn alive. I don't have to tell you what happens to him if we fuck up.'

As they approached the town the next day they saw with relief that the place was busy. It was market day. The narrow streets throbbed with people, cattle and goats. The smell of sewage met the smell of spice. Women, their faces covered, their bags bulging, stepped around steaming animal dung. Stalls groaned beneath the weight of their produce, sellers shouted for buyers, bright fabrics were draped psychedelically on top of one another.

To the soldiers the bustle could only mean one thing: no Taliban.

1 Platoon split from the rest of the convoy to go around the outskirts of the town. The men would be dropped at a point nearest their allocated mosque and had been told to make their way towards it rapidly.

Everything went according to plan at first. No one tried to stop them and the locals ignored the presence of armed soldiers in their midst.

424

'So . . . er . . . where is the mosque?' asked Mal, who was point man.

'What do you mean?' demanded Sol.

'Well, according to the map, it's here,' said the boss.

'Where?'

They were lingering in a side alley now. Dave, at the rear, said: 'Get moving, we're supposed to take the place by surprise.'

'Get moving where?' asked Mal. 'I don't see a mosque.'

Everyone looked around them.

'Shit, shit, shit,' said Dave. 'They could have Martyn gagged, bound and out by now. Half the town knows we're here.'

'Can't we ask the way to the mosque?' suggested Bacon.

'How's your Pashtu then, Streaky?' Finn said.

The boss, staring at the map, shook his head: 'I don't understand. This is supposed to be the right place . . .'

'What's the problem? This is the fucking mosque, look!' Binman was pointing to a tannoy above the door of the low, squat building on their right.

Mal took a step back to stare at it.

'That's never a mosque! In England mosques don't look like this. No one would go if they did.'

'It's just an ordinary house . . .' said Finn.

Sol said: 'Ordinary houses don't have loudspeakers to call people to prayer. In you go, Mal.'

'No minaret, no arches, nothing written on the outside, nothing,' muttered Mal mutinously. 'How was I to know?'

'In you go, mate,' said Sol.

Mal paused.

'Go on!' roared Dave from the back.

Angus finally pushed in front of him and the others followed.

Dave asked Mal, 'What's the problem?'

'I haven't washed my hands and face.'

'What?'

'I didn't think I cared. But we're supposed to wash before praying. I don't usually go in a mosque without . . .'

'Listen, mate,' said Dave, 'you can stay outside with 2 Section if you like. I'm sorry, I should have thought.'

'Fuck that,' said Mal, and he stepped into the mosque.

Inside it was almost dark. After a few moments their eyes began to adjust. As the interior materialized they quickly spread out. There were just a few men, kneeling on the mats provided, who looked up in shock at them. Light filtered in through small, high windows. There were arches overhead and at the back some cupboards and a couple of rooms. Without saying a word, the soldiers quickly and quietly searched the place.

An old man came up to remonstrate. He was holding a book, bound in threadbare fabric which looked very old. Angus did not see the man and, after searching a cupboard, swung round to find him there. As he turned, his day sack knocked the book out of the man's hand. It lay sprawling, face up, on the matting. The man stared at the book as though it was alight, and then he looked into Angus's face and shouted in Pashtu.

'Really, McCall. Can't you be a bit more careful?' snapped the boss.

Angus turned red and looked at the old man with embarrassment. 'Sorry, mate, it was a mistake,' he said.

The man continued to shout.

'He's saying: you big, clumsy twat,' said Binman as he passed.

'Sounds like my dad,' muttered Angus.

He bent to pick up the book but the man shouted louder.

Angus paused, unsure what to do.

Mal was watching.

'He's saying get your filthy, infidel hands off the Holy Book.'

Angus stood up again and the man picked up the book himself with the greatest reverence and started to dust it down, apparently apologizing to it.

'I've fucking had enough of this,' said Angus. He went to the door but bumped into a man carrying a sack on his way in. The man stopped and stared at Angus in horror.

'Christ, everyone's looking at me like I'm fucking Dracula today!'

The man put down the sack and backed out of the door.

'It's yer fangs,' said Finn.

Angus stepped out after the man to where the other two sections of the platoon were covering. The man stared at the soldiers as though seeing them for the first time. He turned and ran.

The soldiers were all outside the mosque now. Dave looked at Angus for an explanation.

'Saw me and scarpered,' said Angus.

'We should have stopped him. I bet he didn't just do that because you're ugly.'

But by now Finn was looking in the sack.

'Fucking hell!'

The men crowded round.

'Opium?'

'Weed?'

'There are two . . . Well, they're round and they look like . . .'

He reached into the sack.

'Careful,' said Dave. 'Be very, very careful.'

Finn pulled out a mortar round. The men instinctively backed away.

Dave took the bag gingerly and pulled out the other round. It was partially wrapped in brown paper but it was clearly the twin of the first and attached to it were battery and wire.

'So that was going to be a roadside bomb for us,' said Boss Weeks. 'Nice of him to hand it over.'

'I wish you'd told us to stop that geezer,' Dave said. 'We'll never catch him now.'

Finn's voice was higher than usual.

'I wish I wasn't standing here holding this fucking thing.'

'We'll put them down very, very gently . . .'

'What, here?'

'No!' Sol pointed down the alleyway. 'Over there where it's a bit wider. It'll be easier for us to cover.'

Finn and Dave carried their bombs carefully, their tread slow, their bodies stiff. The boss walked ahead.

'No, down here, it gets wider still.'

Finn looked miserable.

'Well, why not walk all the way back to the fucking base with them and see if they blow up on the way?'

'Just ten more metres,' coaxed Sol.

They set the mortar rounds down in the dusty alleyway and the boss radioed for someone to deal with them.

The men waited.

427

'Well, this is going to help us find Martyn, innit?' they said. 'Sitting here in a fucking alleyway.'

After three hours EOD arrived to dismantle the mortars.

'They would have been enough to see off a lot of men,' the bomb disposal expert said cheerfully. 'Shame you let the bastard walk away.'

Back at Sin City it emerged that today's operation had annoyed the locals in some parts of the area. Troops had been in contact, others had been stoned by angry crowds. In a few mosques, caches of weapons had been found. But there was still no sign of Martyn.

Chapter Sixty-five

SIN CITY WAS TURNING INTO A MEDIA CIRCUS. A PLANE-LOAD OF journalists was to be flown in so they could record their pieces to camera from the FOB.

The OC sat in the cookhouse running his hands through his hair.

'As if we haven't anything better to do! We're expected to spend our time protecting journalists who like putting on body armour for the camera. Apparently one has already asked us if we can lob a few grenades in the background. Another wants us to go linear across a poppy field so they can film us from the air with him in the middle position. And a third has put in a request for everyone at the base to go to their positions and fire as though we're under attack. But only when there's no enemy around.'

'How is that going to find Martyn?' roared the men. 'We're running out of time!'

'Can't we say no, sir?' asked Dave. 'On the grounds that we're soldiers and not film extras?'

The OC rolled his eyes.

'The government thinks this crisis is good for the war. The threat to Martyn's life is mobilizing British public opinion. As far as they're concerned, the more journalists the better.'

At that moment Martyn's face appeared on the TV screen and the noisy cookhouse was instantly silent. The anchorman explained that the hostage still had not been located and his kidnappers were still refusing to negotiate. There was one week to go until his execution and an appeal for his release had been made by a close friend and colleague.

A cheer went up in the room when Emily appeared.

'Martyn is a man who was working in Afghanistan because of his interest in and compassion for the Afghan people. He holds them in the highest regard and his work was designed to help their economy and improve their standard of living. I therefore appeal to his kidnappers to recognize him as a friend and supporter and to treat him as an honoured guest.'

'If Martyn sees Emily,' said Angus, 'he'll beg the Taliban to finish him off.'

Finn said: 'The Sex Grenade's talking bollocks. Martyn didn't give a shit about the Afghan people. He was paid a fucking fortune and he's got shitloads of ex-wives to support. That's why he was here.'

'Think Emily's appeal will make any difference, sir?' asked the commander of 2 Platoon.

The OC pulled a face.

'We have just seven days and I'm not sure the diplomats can achieve anything in that time.'

'But we can!' said the men. 'We could search a lot of houses in seven days! Let's get out there and fight!'

The OC shook his head helplessly.

'I'm powerless to authorize any house searches. Or fights. The colonel's here and he's working with the Foreign Office. It's right over our heads, boys.'

But the journalists' visit was abruptly cancelled. Suddenly there were rumours that intelligence had located Martyn. The company would go operational as soon as the SAS arrived.

Although the OC would not deny or confirm the rumours, commanders quietly told their men to prepare for a major operation. But as the deadline for Martyn's release approached, nothing happened.

The men waited. Much of their talk was about Martyn but many of their thoughts were about home. One month left here. Some people had barely dared allow themselves to think about their loved ones before now. Involuntarily, as they stood over the green bowls washing in an inch of water, the possibility of a warm bath began to occur to them. Or a long shower. When they sat in the cookhouse with mugs of tea they thought about pub gardens and cold beer.

Jamie phoned Agnieszka.

'Just a few more weeks! A few more weeks!' he said.

'That wonderful.' Her voice was flat. She was trying to summon enthusiasm but she was not successful. When Jamie had called her after a week at Jackpot she had been warm and loving. But since then he had felt her detaching again and going into some cold, quiet orbit of her own. Each call ended with a sense that she was further away.

'I don't get it,' Jamie told Dave. 'Is there some other bloke? Is it that I mean less and less the longer I'm away? Or is she sort of . . . depressed?'

'One more month,' Dave reminded him. 'Then you can put everything right again.'

'Yeah,' said Jamie. The mail had arrived and there had been nothing from Agnieszka.

Dave saw Mal also looking miserable after the blueys were handed out.

'One more month,' he said. 'Then you can get back to Wythenshawe and sort things out.'

Mal shook his head.

'Nah, you were right, Sarge. My family wants me to keep away. They say I'll only make things worse. So I s'pose I'll stay in barracks and they'll come down to see me.'

'It's not nice to feel you can't go home,' said Dave. He wasn't sure Mal was capable of staying away and keeping out of a fight.

'What's the matter with everyone?' he asked Sol. 'We've got one month to go and no one's getting excited.'

'It's because of Martyn. And it's because some people remember that home isn't always so nice when you get there.'

Dave was surprised. 'You don't feel that way, Sol, do you?'

'Listen, I can't wait to see Adi and the kids. I just can't wait. But there's always this strange period when I first get back. I sort of don't know what to do with myself. Because Adi's so used to doing everything and she doesn't know how to make room for me. Know what I mean?'

'Yeah. Jenny's always different when I get back. I mean, she's always changed the way we do things and she expects me just to know it.'

Sol looked worried.

'We've waited and waited to see each other. But then I get there and I just have to keep out of Adi's way so I don't go upsetting her.'

'Everything's going to be different in our house anyway because of the new baby.'

'So have you agreed on a name?' asked Sol cautiously. 'Adi said it would probably be Lisa.'

'Lisa. Oh, no. Don't say Jen's back to that one.'

'It's a nice name.'

'It's the name of an auntie who died or something. And I don't like it. I hope she hasn't registered the baby as Lisa.' Going away for six months relieved you of a lot of responsibility. And that meant you sacrificed some of your rights. But Dave thought that helping to decide your baby's name shouldn't be one of them.

'What do you want to call her, then?' asked Sol.

'One of the old-fashioned names like Ruby or Sophie. I used to like Emily but I've gone off that . . .'

'What does Jenny say?'

'She says: no way.'

In the cookhouse, over a brew, in the back of the wagons, in the toilets and around the cots, voices could be heard at any time: 'What the fuck is happening? Where are the fucking Jedi, if that's what we're waiting for? When is this operation?'

With three days to go until the deadline, tension became acute. Action in the ops room was frantic. But action in the ops room never seemed to translate into action on the ground. Finally, a Chinook arrived.

About twelve men ambled out of it, tin teapots hanging from their Bergens. They wore flipflops, shorts and tasteless shirts.

'Yes!' said Angus, punching the air. 'It's them!'

'Looks like the cream of the British Army, teapots at the ready,' said Jamie.

'And just when I was thinking of lengthening my odds again,' Finn said.

Dave called 1 Platoon into the Cowshed for prayers.

'We've been very patient,' the boss told them. 'At last, this is what we've been waiting for. We're going to rescue Martyn.'

He explained that they would be leaving the base early to-morrow. The SAS would be in the wagons with them, dressed in camouflage to look like the rest of the lads. R Company would help them take the site and the SAS would find the hostage.

'Right. Synchronize watches. In one minute it will be—'

The lads looked at each other.

'Er, sir,' said Dave. 'You've forgotten the prayers.'

The boss looked back at him and blinked.

'That's it. That's all there is.'

'But . . . where we are going?' asked Dave.

The Cowshed was suddenly still. No one moved a muscle.

'I don't know. We haven't been told.'

'Well, is it a very large compound? Is there any kind of internal map . . . ?'

The boss shrugged.

'I don't know. It could be the size of Buckingham Palace or it could be a shepherd's hut.'

There was a silence. Dave looked at the lads and every face stared back at him.

'Just take all the weapons you can carry,' he said. 'In case it's Buckingham Palace.'

The boss coughed. 'One more thing. It has been very hard for the British to retain this operation. The Americans wanted to take it over and run it in their own way with their own forces. We don't agree with their approach and feel it could be detrimental to our relationship with the Afghans. So we're doing it, and we're doing it our way with, apart from the Regiment, only the men we happen to have here on the ground: bussing in reinforcements is the kind of manoeuvre that might alarm the kidnappers. I need hardly tell you, then, that if things go wrong there will be a lot of international mud-slinging. Not just this company's reputation but the reputation of the British Army is at stake.'

1 Platoon agreed in the cookhouse afterwards that they didn't care about the reputation of the company or the British Army. They just wanted to find Martyn.

As before any major operation, everyone wanted to use the

phone. Twice that evening it was double-booked and fights broke out. Jamie, who had been waiting patiently for his turn, saw that it was not going to come. He walked briskly around the perimeter a few times, trying to walk his worries about Agnieszka out of his system. He faced battle fearlessly. Only his wife could induce this sense of panic.

Finally he went back to his cot. Binns and Bacon were there, just leaving for the cookhouse.

'Hey, Jamie, we forgot to finish your story. About the frog!' They did a few frog impressions to remind him.

'Ribbit, ribbit!'

'Yeah,' said Jamie, without smiling. 'I know. I was never in the mood.'

'Let's finish it now,' they said.

Jamie shook his head.

'No point. I'll be seeing Luke in a few more weeks.'

He was delving in his day sack for something.

Binns and Streaky shrugged helplessly at each other.

'Woman trouble,' muttered Streaky as they left. As soon as they were gone, Jamie pulled out the cellphone Agnieszka had given him. He had to communicate with her somehow. He had to tell her how much he loved her. And to make sure she knew that, however bad she was feeling, he would soon be there for her.

He switched it on, glancing constantly towards the door as it found the signal. He was about to start his message when the phone told him he had a message waiting. This surprised him. Agnieszka didn't want him to use this mobile any more for some reason, so it was strange that she had used it herself.

He opened the message.

It said: '*I love another man now.*'

He read it again.

It still said: '*I love another man now.*'

He read it again and then again. The message was written in ice. It was freezing his hand. It was freezing his body. It was freezing his heart. If someone walked in he knew that he would be powerless to switch off the phone and to hide it. Afterwards he found the phone in the day sack. But he could not remember putting it away.

I love another man now.

434

Chapter Sixty-six

JENNY DROPPED VICKY OFF AT NURSERY AND THEN PUT THE BABY IN HER pram. She was trying to get herself back into shape before Dave came home and had just been given her post-op all-clear. On the days Vicky went to nursery, Jenny aimed to walk three miles a day, and walk quickly.

She liked the crisp autumn air. She liked the way the camp was sleepy on weekday mornings when all the kids were at school. She liked the way the sun shone now: brightly but not oppressively.

The fastest route to the countryside was past Agnieszka's house and she glanced at the windows and thought she saw the Polish girl's face there. She waved, but Agnieszka was gone.

Jenny felt uncomfortable. She should have asked Agnieszka to bring Luke in his buggy on this crisp, clear day: she was one of the few mothers who would enjoy a fast, invigorating walk. But she admitted guiltily to herself that she did not want to share her walk with her.

Agnieszka had visited Jenny just once since she came out of hospital and had seemed even more withdrawn than usual.

'Are you OK?' Jenny had asked her. Agnieszka replied with one of those tight little half-smiles. You never knew what she was thinking.

Jenny had spoken to Adi about it. 'Does she ever see anyone or go out?'

'Oh, yes, I see her around with the buggy,' Adi had replied. 'And, you know, you're too busy to take care of Agnieszka. We're all too busy.'

Adi had been unusually brisk. Jenny wondered if it was because she had also seen Agnieszka with that man. Well, if Agnieszka was having an affair, it certainly wasn't making her any happier.

The last houses in the camp were the officers', large with big gardens and huge, leafy old trees outside them. And then she was in the countryside. It wasn't wild countryside. It was shared between farmers and tank drivers so the fields of sheep were criss-crossed by warnings, signs and tank guidance posts.

She walked hard and fast. There was no one around today until, when she was just about to turn for home, a runner approached her. He was moving quickly and as he neared she noticed the sweat dripping from his face before she saw that his left leg was made of metal.

'Steve!'

He slowed, recognized her, then stopped a few metres past her. At first he couldn't talk. He bent over, puffing and sweating.

'Hi, Jenny. I got back last night and thought I'd . . .' His voice disappeared inside his own breath.

'Well, just take your time,' she said. 'I mean . . . I saw this bloke haring along but I never guessed it was you!'

'I'm out of breath because I'm out of condition,' he puffed. 'Nothing to do with the leg.'

He stood upright then walked over to the pram and peered in.

'She's growing. Looks a bit like her dad, though, and that can't be good. Got a name for her yet?'

Jenny said firmly: 'Not until Dave's home.' She was trying not to peer at the strange, streamlined metal contraption that grew out of Steve's shorts. 'It's amazing you're running already!'

'Go on, Jen, stare at it. Everyone wants to.'

She blushed. 'It looks strong.'

'Has to be, the hell it's going to get from me.'

They grinned at each other.

'It's nice you're home for the lads getting back,' she said.

'Well, with any luck I'll be fit enough to run with them.'

'That's why I'm out today, too. I'm trying to get my figure back before Dave comes home.'

'You never lost it, Jen. Unlike some people who never had it.'

She knew who he meant. For a moment she wanted to ignore this but she could not leave her friend undefended.

'Leanne put on a lot of weight after your accident, Steve. Eating was her way of coping.'

His face changed. She watched the muscles in it rearrange themselves. Usually so big and open, he was darkening suddenly. He looked angry. He gritted his teeth and his jaw sharpened. He was even a bit scary, she thought. He had never looked that way before.

'Yeah, well, it was a while ago now and she's had plenty of chance to lose that weight again. But she won't lose it sitting in front of the TV.'

'It's been hard for her . . .'

'You think it hasn't been hard for me? The easiest thing in the world is to sit around and be a couch potato but there's no way I'm giving in to it. She shouldn't either.'

'I know you've been to hell and back, Steve. I really admire you for having the grit to start running. And because you're determined to fight again. But Leanne's been in bits. You've got some goals: get walking, get running, get back out with the other lads. Her life fell apart and it hasn't been so straightforward putting it back together.'

He looked thoughtful.

'Goals is a good word, Jen. If we give Leanne some goals that might help her . . .'

She decided to steer the conversation away from Leanne.

'Steve, how are you going to feel when the others get back?'

His face changed again. Suddenly all the tight, angry lines loosened and he looked less sure of himself.

'I'd sort of like to be there when the bus gets into the square. So would Ben Broom. Ryan Connor's not ready for that yet.'

'Oh, Steve, that's a fantastic idea. They'll be so pleased to see you. I know it would mean a lot to Dave.'

'But he'll be looking for you. Everyone will be with their family. The lads' stuff is over for a while when we first come home.'

'You don't think Dave's going to walk straight past you!'

'Maybe it's not the right time.'

'But . . . how will you feel? Seeing them all get off the bus?'

437

Steve swallowed. Jenny watched him again. She did not remember that his face had ever had this mobility before. She had no recollection of the way emotions passed across it like clouds. Perhaps he'd just been better at hiding them. Now he looked vulnerable. His eyes were crinkling and his mouth was twisting unhappily. He looked as though he might cry.

'Steve?'

'I'm not sure I can handle it. Because I missed the whole fucking tour. And they've had all these experiences. They'll have been changed by what happened. Even if they tell me everything, I didn't go through it with them. I wasn't there. So I don't feel as though I know them like before.'

Jenny's eyes dropped from Steve's anguished face to the pram where the baby slept peacefully under her white blanket.

'Steve . . . I know what you mean. Because I feel exactly the same way.'

They walked back to the camp together. When they passed the rec, they paused for a parking car.

'Mazda MR2, very nice,' said Steve. 'I've always fancied one of them myself.'

A man got out of it and walked up the road.

'Who's he?' asked Steve.

'I don't know,' said Jenny. But she was sure she recognized him.

Agnieszka had seen Jenny walking and noted the way she stepped out cheerfully in the autumn sunshine. She had decided to do the same. But just putting on Luke's coat had resulted in such howling protests that she almost gave up. He was still protesting now while she put on her own. Next there was the tedious ritual of pushing and pulling a large buggy through a small hallway. Was it worth it? Was it worth even trying to leave the house?

The bell rang. Probably Jenny, already coming back from her walk. Agnieszka didn't want to speak to Jenny or anyone else but she opened the door, sighing and pulling the buggy out of the way.

'Hi, Aggie.'

Her heart leaped. It soared. It was suddenly attached to a balloon, which was gaining altitude at an absurd rate. Her heart was light as a feather because it was shedding weight as it flew. The atmosphere up here was thin, her head was dizzy.

'Ags?'

When she still could not speak he stepped inside. The door clicked shut behind him. He wrapped his arms around her and kissed her and she felt herself, without hesitation, return the kiss.

'Have you missed me?' he asked.

She closed her eyes. She couldn't explain to him that it had been snowing since he left, a cold, frozen winter world.

'It's OK,' he said. 'I'm back now, Ags.'

Chapter Sixty-seven

THE LADS WERE QUIET WHEN THE CONVOY LEFT THE NEXT DAY. Nobody wanted to screw up in front of the SAS men and the wagons were peppered with them.

Dave, in the front, expected them to go into the Green Zone. He had thought it very likely Martyn was held in one of the maze of compounds near the river. But instead they swung towards the desert. His heart sank as he realized they were heading back towards Jackpot. So they were returning to the camp. He'd hoped it would be dismantled by now. They were in the dusty bowl of the desert that led to Jackpot when the convoy suddenly swung left.

'Christ!' said Dave. 'We're not going to a compound. Or the camp. We're going to the Early Rocks.'

As they drew closer he began to understand how massive the rocks were. They had looked like stark, strange shapes jutting from the desert sands in the distance but close-up they were more complex. There must be water, because bushes and small trees sprouted all around. And running around the base of the rocks was a ring of earthworks at least two metres high. So the mysterious shrine was a natural fortress.

The massive rocks towered over them as they reached the entrance to the shrine. Built around one rock as though it had grown out of the sand was a tiny gatehouse. The wagons slowed as they reached it and threw out some of the SAS men. The wagons speeded up again and the boss passed on the orders: 'In sixty seconds we will have the rock circle very loosely surrounded. You will dismount and close in on the circle, scrambling over the bank at the base of the rocks. We don't know exactly what we'll find inside except probably underground tunnels and, we hope, Topaz Zero. Your job is to suppress the enemy so that our colleagues can locate him. The enemy will be positioning now. So take advantage of their confusion to debus fast and close in rapidly on the rocks.'

Dave said at once: 'Fix bayonets, lads.'

The drivers were told to stop one hundred metres from the rocks.

'Go closer!' Dave ordered his driver.

'But the boss said—'

'Closer! You can move back when we're all out.'

The driver screamed towards the rocks and stopped about sixty metres away.

'Everybody out, go, go, go!' Sol yelled at 1 Section.

The men began to rush towards the rock circle. The weight of their kit was oppressive. It bounced on their backs and their pouches rattled on their bodies. Binns, the lightweight, had been fast as a school kid. Now he was a lumbering animal, staggering and doubled over as he ran.

'I wish I could take this fucking shit off and really run!' he shouted to Streaky. But Streaky could not hear him over his own heaving breath.

Angus was still back at the wagon. In addition to his normal rifle, pistol, kit and ammo he had mortars and the sniper rifle too. By the time he had staggered down from the bus the others were halfway across the open ground. He knew he was carrying too much weight but wasn't sure what to leave. He paused and, before he could decide, the wagon moved off. Shit! Now he would have to take it all. And the others had nearly reached the rocks.

Fire erupted from all around the massive circle simultaneously, in a blaze of light, noise and smoke. The men who were still in exposed positions threw themselves onto their belt buckles on the desert sand, easy targets for the enemy.

All of 1 Section had reached the shelter of one of the massive stone pillars except Angus. They looked back now and saw him.

He lay still, head down, as though he'd already been shot, thinking, Shit, shit, shit. He could feel something like rain, and knew it was rounds. The rough sand bit into his cheeks. He dared to half look up once. All round him the desert danced with bouncing rounds. He put his head back down and knew that one of the rounds must hit him. They could not all miss him. His body was rigid with expectation. He wanted to yell and shout against his helplessness.

He heard helicopters overhead.

'Thank Christ! Where have they been?' roared Angus on PRR.

Dave responded.

'Don't get excited, McCall. There's nothing much they can do to help us, not with a hostage trapped inside.'

'Move forward, Angry,' shouted Sol's voice into his ear. 'It's just as safe as lying there.'

'I shouldn't have carried so much weight,' he moaned. He heard his own voice, whimpering a bit. He was going to die. So he might as well die courageously. The Families Officer might as well stand in his dad's hallway and say that Angus had died a heroic death. He began to stagger to his feet but the mortars he was carrying pulled his left side down and the rest of his body with it. Ping. A round whistled just over his shoulder. Good thing he hadn't stood up, then, or that one certainly would have got him. Except that now he was stuck here, giving the ragheads some easy target practice.

A few moments later he felt someone tugging on his arm.

'Get up, you lazy bastard, stop sleeping on the job.'

Jamie Dermott. Pulling him to his feet, grabbing some of the weight off him and firing the gimpy while the pair of them staggered across the desert together.

Angus didn't have time to think, feel surprise or be grateful. His whole body and mind were focused on running in Olympic time to the rest of the lads by the rock. It wasn't until they arrived safely and he slumped down, his mouth open, the breath never enough to fill his empty lungs, sweat pouring down his body, that relief began to seep from every pore. And then he understood that Jamie had saved his life.

He said: 'Fuck, Jamie. I mean, fuck.'

Jamie was red-faced and gasping too.

'Don't mention it,' he breathed.

'I could feel the fucking rounds scrape against my helmet! One missed my shoulder by that much . . .'

'You must have been just outside the flipflops' arcs of fire,' said Mal. 'I didn't think you could get here alive.'

Angus stood up, still red and panting, and reached for his water tube. He let out a roar.

'What's the matter, Angry?' asked Sol. 'Are you all right?'

'My fucking Camelbak's empty!'

Sol took a look.

'A round went through it,' he reported.

'Fucking, *fucking* hell! I'm thirsty!'

Sol handed him a bottle of water.

'There isn't anyone else in this whole platoon, Angry, who would moan about a round hitting their Camelbak instead of their vital organs.'

The heavy machine guns on the WMIKs were pounding at the other side of the shrine and the mortar men were busy. Sol's section put down fire where they saw muzzle flashes. But most of their rounds were bouncing off rock or getting lodged in the bank.

Dave was pinned down back at the Vector. The boss spoke to each of his section commanders in turn and confirmed that they had all their men up against the rocks. Sergeant Somers of 2 Platoon, on the other side of the shrine, was not so lucky. His Vector drivers had stopped further back and the men in one wagon had been too slow. They had debussed right into the contact. The bank was highest here and the enemy had taken advantage of this to feast on them. Dave saw CSM Kila rushing off in a wagon to deal with the casualties.

'I can see what's happening from back here better than you can,' Dave told his corporals. 'The choggies are firing through cracks in the rocks so you can forget firing back at them. A few insurgents are exposed on top of the ridge . . . See how many you can get.'

'Just look up there,' came the boss's voice.

Dave looked up. High on the top of a rock, like a man who had just taken the elevator to the roof of a skyscraper, was the silhouette of an insurgent with a weapon that was probably a Kalashnikov.

'Did he fly there? And with that weapon, too?'

'Ropes. Or they've carved steps up the back of the rocks.'

The man was kneeling down and lifting his weapon, capitalizing

443

on the natural advantage of his position. Dave guessed he was aiming at Kila's casualty evacuation. He jumped out of the Vector with his SA80. It took just three shots. The body did not fall but remained slumped over the machine gun.

'Rule One,' Dave told it. 'The chances are that the best firing positions are the most exposed. Now let them try getting you down from there.'

1 Section edged cautiously around the rock to the base of the ridge, checking for figures at the top of it. They reached the place Sol had chosen for them to breach it. Now they were close it looked steeper.

'Fucking hell, they can just pick us off one by one as we climb up,' said Finn.

Sol paused, frowning.

From out by the Vector Dave could hear firing from all around the rocks but the acoustic was as strange as the place. It echoed back across the desert until it was impossible to pinpoint where the noise was coming from or to estimate the size of the enemy inside.

'I'm going to move closer in with the Vector and cover you as you go up the bank. I'll deal with any of them waiting for you at the top. But only you can see what's on the other side.'

Sol said: 'Everyone fixed their bayonet?'

The driver turned to Dave.

'Did you say something about going in closer again?'

'Yeah. Shit, I wish I'd thought of keeping the sniper rifle back here with me. That's what happens when you don't get proper information on an operation beforehand.'

'Do I have to move forward?'

'Just a bit. Turn it sideways on if that makes you feel safer.'

The Vector's move brought a hail of fire.

'Fucking hell,' said the driver, as he swung the vehicle round. 'Did you save me from those IEDs in the Green Zone just to get me shot up out here in the middle of nowhere?'

'OK, then, stop.'

'I'm watching you,' said the boss from the next wagon. Dave glanced across the desert. The next wagon was far away.

He leaped out, went to the side of the vehicle and got himself into a good position. He drew so much fire from the enemy that he was forced backwards. He tried again and there was more fire. The third time he told 1 Section: 'Let's get on with it. Up the bank now. Fast.'

He had to steel himself against his own instinct to duck back behind the Vector as rounds tore up the desert around him. He watched Sol go up first, followed by Mal.

A bearded man appeared with an AK47 at the top of the rim, his back against a rock to optimize his arc on the soldiers as they scrambled up the bank. Dave fired off ten rounds and the man fell.

'Wrong weapon, wrong place. You'd have done better with a pistol at that distance,' said Dave, falling back for a moment with relief.

The next time he looked, another insurgent was standing at the top of the bank holding a pistol. Dave shot him.

'Right weapon, wrong place,' he told the dead man.

Sol, Angus, Mal, Jamie and Binman were flat on their belt buckles on top of the bank now, firing into the shrine, while Finn and Streaky, who had been covering from below, were scrambling up behind them. Beneath them, a man with an AK47 appeared. He was at ground level and had emerged from 1 Section's previous position around the rock.

'Shit, how did you get there?' asked Dave, as he fired. 'We're supposed to be surrounding you, not the other way round . . .'

Sections 2 and 3 were also fighting their way into the shrine just around the rock circle, covered by a WMIK. The company was closing in at all points, tightening the net on the insurgents within the shrine, increasing the rate of fire until the noise and its echo sounded like one long, continuous blast.

Dave knew he would soon have to get his platoon more ammo. He told the reluctant driver to move closer. The boss was giving orders to the men inside the rock circle now. He was instructing them to use grenades to move forward. Did this mean that Martyn had been rescued already? Or were they so heavily outnumbered by the enemy that they had been forced into a risky strategy?

The fighting advanced into the heart of the shrine and Dave was able to make his way to the rocks and up the ridge unimpeded. Inside the circle were bushes and hillocks and ridges and giant boulders but mostly there were soldiers. Dave could see how rapidly they were pushing back the Taliban fighters. He could see some of his men in good firing positions. 3 Section were well situated around boulders, 1 Section were back a bit but Jamie with the gimpy was perching on a ledge where he could just drop machine-gun fire into the insurgents' line.

'You're doing well, Dermott, but you're a bit exposed . . .' Dave began.

He stopped speaking because he saw the RPG. After that everything fragmented into a series of snapshots. The Taliban grenade, tearing through the air like a deadly dart, cutting a path towards Jamie. The grenade appearing on the other side of Jamie and exploding thirty metres beyond against a rock in a mass of flame and smoke. Jamie continuing to blast away for a few seconds on the machine gun. Jamie staggering. Jamie falling, Bergen first, at the side of the ledge.

Dave let out a roar. Standing on the ridge he was one of the few soldiers high enough to see what had happened. The roar of battle and the roar of his own denial echoed around in his head as he heard his voice, crisp and clear, reporting the incident. He ordered McCall and Sol Kasanita back to help carry the casualty outside the rocks where CSM Kila and the medic were waiting.

The next snapshots were out of focus. Sometimes he replayed them in the wrong order. McCall's white face. Sol loading the bleeding body of Jamie onto the stretcher: 'He's still alive, Sarge!' Dave's own hand shoving Jamie's autojet of morphine into his leg. Staggering down the ledge and up the bank with the stretcher, feeling that his arms would break with the weight and knowing that something was breaking inside him. Jamie's body moving with each jerk and bump of the stretcher as though deeply, deeply asleep.

'C'mon, Jamie, for fuck's sake, c'mon!' Angus McCall. His face a horror mask. 'You didn't run out into the desert to save me just so this could happen to you . . .'

The enemy's main escape route was past the gatehouse and across the desert to the hills but Finn picked up talk of a tunnel system. And as he watched the number of insurgents diminish, he knew this must be right. The noise level was dropping. The air had been thick with cordite and smoke but it was thinning now. The Taliban couldn't be seen surging across the desert. So there must be some other way out of the shrine.

'We'd drop a five-hundred-pounder if it wasn't for Martyn,' he told Streaky and Binman, who happened to be close by. 'Let's hope they haven't got him down in a tunnel with them.'

'It's just like they're melting,' said Streaky.

'Maybe they're all dead,' Binman said hopefully.

But Finn and Streaky shook their heads.

The soldiers were ordered to start looking for a tunnel system. Finn and Streaky searched in the great shadows of massive boulders but the earth was hot, dry and solid.

'I just want to kill the fuckers!' said Mal. 'They're like rats, running down a rathole. I want to go after them and kill them.' He had the hungry, alert look of a man for whom the fighting had ended too soon. A lot of the men did. A few were fighting each other. But Finn didn't feel that way. He felt tired and defeated.

'This operation was Marty's last hope. And we fucked it up.'

Mal glared at him.

'We did our best.'

'What's the Jedi here for? Why haven't they sorted this out?'

'What do you want them to do? Pull the poor old bastard out of a hat along with a white rabbit?'

There was a shout. A tunnel under the rocks had been found and officers were developing a plan to send men down.

'Hold firm, 1 Platoon,' came the boss's voice. 'It sounds as though you're going to be covering from up here.'

Finn lit a cigarette while he waited for orders. He decided to check out the gatekeeper's vegetables. When the doors on the wagons had slowed so that the SAS men could hit the ground on their arrival here at the shrine, Finn had got a clear view of a vegetable garden in the gatekeeper's compound. It had been well watered and well ordered and there was probably something good to eat. Could you grow carrots in Afghanistan? Finn loved raw carrots and had stolen many from allotments.

'Where you going?' demanded Streaky, appearing at his side.

'I feel like a little snack from the garden out there. Care to join me in a bit of thieving, Streaks?'

They sneaked around to the small, solid house. It looked

deserted. Outside there was a thin irrigation channel, which fed the vegetable garden. There were no carrots but there were grapes. Finn picked a couple.

'Mmm, Streaky. Just try these.'

The grapes were small. Sweetness exploded in their mouths.

'Oooh, juicy!' Streaky picked some more.

A goat hung its head in one corner and nearby was the doghouse. There was no barking from inside it.

'What do people do with their dogs in this country if they never put them in their kennels?' asked Finn. Streaky was busy munching and so he answered his own question. 'Put their hostages inside.'

He walked towards the small ornate kennel.

'The Jedi will have searched there,' said Streaky, reluctant to leave the grapes.

'I know,' agreed Finn. 'I'm just nosy.'

He approached the house carefully in case one of the huge Afghan fighting dogs he had heard about was asleep in there. Crouching, in case the dog bounced out on him, he pulled open the door.

The first thing he saw was a pair of legs. He thought they must belong to a dead body since they did not move at his arrival. His heart thumping, he squatted down and peered up the legs and saw they were attached to Martyn Robertson.

'Fuck me! Marty! I was looking for you. But I didn't think I'd find you.'

Martyn lay with his eyes half open.

'Oy! You alive, mate?'

He still did not move. Finn felt for a pulse.

'Shit, Marty! Don't be dead!'

'Hi, Huckleberry Finn,' Martyn said weakly, without surprise.

'Hey! They've all gone looking down a hole for you!'

'Uh-huh. Well, I've been down a few holes.'

Streaky looked over from the vines.

'Finny?'

Finn turned and gave him a thumbs-up.

'Go and get someone!'

'Is it him? Is it Topaz Zero? I know this is a joke, Finny!'

'Find someone. They won't believe me if I put it out on PRR.'

Streaky ran over to the doghouse to make sure this was no wind-up. Then he rushed out of the garden and back inside the rock circle. The first person he saw was an SAS man with a mug of tea in his hand.

'He's here! He's fucking here!'

The man smiled at him kindly.

'Oh, yeah? And what's your name, kid?'

'Bacon, sir. Streaky Bacon.'

'You must be the only fucking bacon in Afghanistan. Got a mate called Pinta Lager?'

'He's *here*. Martyn! Topaz Zero! The hostage! He's over *here*!'

Back in the doghouse, Finn was trying to help Martyn to his feet.

'Shit, Martyn! They were going to kill you in two days' time.'

'I sort of hoped I'd die soon anyway, just to ruin their fun.'

'While we're waiting for the others, let's talk about that job you were thinking of offering me . . .'

Martyn's face creased itself into something that might have been a smile.

'What odds did you give on finding me?'

'Hundred to thirty at the beginning, shortened down to fifteen to eight when we found your last doghouse in town. Then this morning on the way here I was offering eleven to eight! That was generous but nobody took me up on it. Ha! In five minutes they'll all be kicking themselves, eh, Marty?'

Martyn said: 'You've got yourself that job, boy.'

Finn looked round and saw Streaky advancing with a disbelieving SAS man still holding his mug of tea.

'It's all over. You'll be all right now, Marty, old mate and future boss. The cream of the British Army's come to save you.'

The stretcher was red, painted with Jamie's blood. Two medics seized it and were almost immediately working with a tourniquet and dressings along his left side, where his arm and his leg should have been, except there wasn't an arm and there wasn't much of a leg and Dave wasn't even sure there was a lot of left side.

'Jamie, Jamie, the fucking bastards got you again – they got you again! Don't let them finish the job this time! Come on, Jamie, for Chrissake!' Whose voice was that? His own?

449

He wanted Jamie to open his eyes. He wanted it with a desperation that took over his whole mind and whole body as if he could will Jamie's eyes to open if he wanted it hard enough. He was Jamie's sergeant. Now he was ordering him to live.

'It's not over till it's over,' said one of the medics, without looking up, as he reached for another bandage.

Dave was certain it would soon be over but he refused to look at that certainty. He clung to the medic's words instead. His hand held Jamie's wrist and searched for a pulse. He couldn't feel one.

'It's there but it's very, very faint,' said a medic. 'Did you see what happened?'

'RPG. Went straight through him.'

'No one can survive that,' said Iain Kila.

'It didn't detonate,' Dave said.

'Well, fuck me!' said Kila.

'It certainly touched him but it went straight on and then hit some rocks about thirty metres later.'

'He's in with a chance, then.'

'This man survived a round from an AK, he survived a round from a machine gun . . .'

The other medic said: 'The grenade sliced his left side off but there's a chance it missed his vital organs. He must have been squatting over the gimpy because it went through the top of his leg and the bottom of his arm. But he can live without an arm and a leg . . .'

'A few centimetres further left and he'd certainly be dead,' said the other.

'MERT will be here in four more minutes,' reported Kila. 'He'll be at Bastion inside the golden hour.'

Dave leaned over the stretcher, looking at the unmoving face.

He tried to imagine Jamie without an arm, a leg and God knew what other body parts. Always trying to hide the pain. Making the best of it. Loving Agnieszka as she pushed him around in a wheelchair. Some people can live like that, Dave thought. But Jamie can't.

If Jamie heard what the medic just said, then he can hear me now.

Dave moved close to the thin face. Eyes closed, it showed no pain. He grasped the still fingers.

'Shit, Jamie Dermott,' he said softly. 'You're the last man I can afford to lose. But I know that you're a soldier through and through. And, Jamie, you're the best. You've lost half your body. But you could never be half a soldier. I understand if you want to go now. So go, if you must, mate. You've done a great job soldiering. You've got a lovely kid. You've got a wife who does truly love you – I know that for a fact, whatever you think. So, if you want to, go peacefully. Good luck. I'll never forget you.'

Of course Jamie did not respond. He couldn't.

'Not looking good!' said one of the medics suddenly.

'Are we losing him?'

'Can't be . . . but we are.'

Dave closed his eyes and fell back to let the medics do their work.

'No! No way!'

'See for yourself!'

'Shit! I thought we had him!'

'Resuscitate.'

'Clear, everyone, please.'

Dave turned his back, walked away and stared out at the endless expanse of desert. His face stung. His eyes stung. Sand in his mouth, sand in his eyes, sand in his heart.

A Chinook had already arrived for the casualties. Another arrived for Martyn almost immediately and the hostage was taken aboard by the waiting medics.

The OC was there.

'Martyn is very important but since he is a T3 we must ask him to wait while we load a T4.'

Finn could not stop grinning. He had been clapped on the back by everyone around him and he and Streaky had already told the story again and again of how they had gone to steal grapes and found Martyn.

He heard that there was a T4 and wondered briefly who it was, but he was really looking for Dave. Where was he when Finn was enjoying a bit of glory for once? And it would be nice to have Sol, Angus and Jamie here offering a few words of congratulations, too.

The group of soldiers around the Chinook fell suddenly silent. Finn turned to see his mates approaching. They were carrying a stretcher. The body on it was covered. So this must be the T4. Even then it did not occur to Finn that there had been a death in his own section. It was only when they were close enough for him to see their faces that he suddenly felt cold. His buoyant, triumphant mood turned inside out and left all the raw places exposed.

Dave and Sol were covered with blood. Dave looked bruised, as if he'd been in a fistfight. Sol's white eyes were red. Huge tears spilled down Angus's face.

Finn looked at the men who surrounded him. Among them were Streaky, Mal and Binman.

That left one man.

Billy Finn's mouth fell open, his eyes sprang out, his body was drained so that he swayed a bit. He saw the boss, features frozen, white-faced.

'No. No. Not Jamie, no,' he shouted.

Boss Weeks closed his eyes. He nodded.

The body was loaded onto the helicopter in silence. There must have been the ground-shaking thump of Chinook rotors and the roar of its engine. But afterwards not one man could remember anything but silence.

Chapter Sixty-eight

AGNIESZKA STOOD MOTIONLESS IN THE BEDROOM, STARING AT herself in the mirror. When Darrel came in, she looked up at him. Not his real face, but the one in the mirror. He stood behind her and their mirror eyes met.

'I've thought about you the whole time I've been away,' said Darrel.

That's what Jamie always said when he got back. And he would be back in a few weeks now. But then he would go away again. Loving Jamie meant saying goodbye. It meant waiting, waiting, waiting for him to come home.

'I know you're scared. I know this is a big step for you, Aggie.'

Her eyes met her mirror eyes. They were frightened. She felt frightened. She felt no sexual excitement. She just wanted to be touched and loved and cared for and not to be alone. She didn't want to be a woman in an endless expanse of snow.

'It will be all right. I promise. I'll take good care of you.'

He began to kiss her neck. She tensed.

'No, no, that's no good,' he murmured. 'Melt a little, Aggie.'

She tried to relax. He stroked her gently. He massaged her back and rearranged her hair. And then he began to kiss her again.

Dave was leaning against the wagon. He thought he should get the lads moving, unloading, sorting things out. But everyone just wanted to stand very still.

The officials and VIPs buzzed around them, making a big noise about Martyn's rescue. The SAS men were being wholeheartedly congratulated. Only the soldiers from the base did not speak.

The OC, who had initially disappeared into the ops room, had re-emerged now and was walking over to the men. His face was expressionless. His walk was slow. He dragged his feet through the dust as though they weighed a lot. He surveyed the quiet soldiers and then raised a hand to stop everyone else talking.

The OC cleared his throat.

When he spoke his voice was loud and grave.

'I am very sorry to tell you that Rifleman Jamie Dermott, a loved, brave and highly proficient member of 1 Section, 1 Platoon, died at 1000 hours today. The medics treating him said that it is a testament to his courage and tenacity that he survived with such serious wounds for as much as thirty minutes. Less than an hour before his death, Rifleman Dermott ran into the desert under intense fire to help another man in his section out of danger. It was an action typical of a soldier who served all those around him without thought for his own safety. He died in action, shot through by a Rocket Propelled Grenade, having already remarkably survived two enemy rounds on two previous occasions. We will miss him and mourn him.'

Dave closed his eyes. The loss was so immense that you couldn't put a fence around it, you couldn't estimate its size, you couldn't even begin to get to the edges of it. Because death was endless and so was loss. And even when he was an old man, many years from now, Dave knew that it would not have ended then.

The OC looked at him.

'Sergeant. Would you please lower the flag in recognition of the death of Rifleman Dermott?'

Dave walked across the base to the flagpole. He was loaded down with invisible kit. It weighed more than any ammo. His body wanted to sink beneath it. He could hardly carry this immense burden and he almost stumbled once or twice. He reached the pole. Slowly, very slowly, he lowered the flag. The base was silent, the desert was silent, the distant hills were silent, and he knew that this was Jamie's silence he was hearing now, a silence without end.

*

'God, what am I doing?'

Agnieszka lay in bed, crying.

'For Chrissake, Aggie!' Darrel's voice was tender and then exasperated. 'You enjoyed it, didn't you?'

'Yes. But that make it worse.'

Darrel sighed and rolled onto his back. They lay next to each other, not touching.

'I was trying to make you happy!'

Had she really thought that Darrel could drive away her fear and loneliness? Had she really thought that having sex with him would put right everything that was wrong? Her body was convulsed with sobs. She loved Jamie. And she had been unfaithful to him. Now she felt lonelier than ever and she even knew what the snow was. It was loss. She had gained nothing tonight and lost everything. Because she loved Jamie, even when he wasn't there.

'Aggie?'

Darrel reached for her but she pulled away.

He sighed.

'Do you want me to go?'

She did not reply. She felt the bed rearrange itself as he climbed out. When he dressed, she could hear his anger and resignation from the way he pulled on his clothes. Before he left he leaned over the bed.

'Aggie, call me when you want to talk.' He kissed her cheek. 'I don't understand you.'

'Darrel, I very sorry. It not your fault.'

'Yeah.'

She heard him go down the stairs and close the door. She listened for the sound of his feet on the pavement. The house felt cold. She heard, at the bottom of the hill, a car starting. It pulled away rapidly.

Luke started to scream. She went to him. He would not stop. Finally he had a fit.

Maybe that was why she didn't hear the car. But she heard the doorbell. Darrel. Back to reason with her. She wouldn't let him in.

She pulled the curtain to one side. It was not Darrel and the car outside was at first unfamiliar. She stared down at the figure on the doorstep. Something very cold, like a splinter of ice, ran through her. It started in her scalp and made the hairs stand on end and, as it moved down her neck and her shoulders, on down to her toes, the tiny hairs on her body bristled. The Families Officer. On her doorstep in the night. At that moment, the world froze and this time she knew it might never thaw.

Chapter Sixty-nine

DAVE WENT TO 1 SECTION'S TENT TO CLEAR JAMIE'S THINGS AND found Binns and Bacon already hunched over them. Anger rose up inside him as if it had just been waiting for an excuse.

'What the fuck do you two think you're doing!'

They looked up guiltily.

'We're just sorting something out, Sarge,' said Binman.

'Sorting what out, exactly?'

Streaky was embarrassed: 'Something we were doing with Jamie, Sarge . . .'

Dave could hardly contain his anger. 'You don't go through his things! I do that! You've got no right to sift through a dead man's stuff!'

Binman looked too shocked to speak. Bacon said: 'Sarge, we were making a story with Jamie for his kid, see, so his baby wouldn't forget his voice. And it was almost, almost done. And we wanted his babymother to have it all finished off so . . .'

'See,' said Binns, 'we didn't want it to end suddenly. If it ends nicely his kid can listen to it over and over . . .'

'That's right, Binman's right,' said Streaky. 'If it's finished they'll be able to listen to it and he'll always have his daddy speaking to him . . .'

Dave felt his angry heartbeat slow.

'So, what is this story?'

Bacon produced a small digital recorder. He flicked a switch. Suddenly the tent was filled with Jamie's voice.

'*And so the little frog hopped towards the place where he knew his mum and dad were waiting for him and would wait for ever if they had to. Just one more mountain to cross and he would be there.*'

Dave sat down on the nearest bed and put his head in his hands. Binns did not move. Streaky turned away, his arm across his face as though shielding himself from a blow. There was a long silence.

At last Binman said, his voice hoarse: 'See, we do the sound effects and we thought we could finish it by . . .'

'All right, all right, lads,' said Dave, getting up. He had to cough to clear his voice and then cough again. 'You do that. You finish it. I won't interrupt you. I'll just take the rest of Jamie's stuff.'

He left the tent as quickly as he could.

He wanted somewhere private to open Jamie's personal things. It was an unpleasant but necessary job to remove any letters from girlfriends or pornography or anything else a bereaved widow might not want to see. Not that there would be anything like that here. Jamie had loved Agnieszka and only Agnieszka.

There were letters and photos and a notebook. Dave felt intrusive looking through the notebook. It contained lists and a few sketches: of Luke, of some trees by a river and one of a GPMG. And there was a bit of poetry, love poetry, which he had written or copied from a book.

He delved a bit further in the bag and found some more pictures of Agnieszka. And then something small and hard. Another iPod? It felt like a phone but it couldn't be. He pulled it out. It was. It was a cellphone.

Dave was shocked. Someone else must have put it there! Jamie, of all people, would never sneak in something that threatened everyone's safety. Except here it was.

He switched it on.

There were messages to Agnieszka and from Agnieszka. The last one had been sent a few days ago.

He read: *I love another man now.*

Chapter Seventy

'WE'VE BEEN THROUGH A LOT TOGETHER, ASMA,' SAID GORDON WEEKS.

They were alone in the ops room. The Foreign and Commonwealth Office men had flown out into media frenzy at the hostage rescue, congratulating themselves on a successful mission. The colonel and his staff had gone. Kila and Jean were walking the perimeter together. The OC and the 2 i/c were in the cookhouse and the boss was manning the radio. He hoped there would be no calls.

'Yeah,' she agreed. 'I didn't like you at first.'

'Really? How could you not like Gordon Weeks?'

'Because you were such a prick when we were interviewing those two detainees and I pulled out my pistol. Did you stand there wittering on about the International Convention on Human Rights or did I imagine that?'

He gave her a withering look.

'You imagined it.'

'Bet you wanted to, though.'

He could not suppress a smile.

'I did disapprove.'

She rolled her eyes.

'Sometimes you have to do the wrong thing to get to the right place. A bit like your blokes shooting a wounded insurgent in a ditch?'

He decided not to reply. Something was coming through on the OC's printer and he busied himself retrieving it.

'Another press cutting from London. *SAS SHOOTS ITS WAY*

459

OUT OF HOSTAGE CRISIS.' He put it on top of *UK SPECIAL FORCES RETRIEVE HOSTAGE IN BLAZE OF GUNFIRE.*

'I did tell you that it was a man in my platoon who actually found Martyn?'

She threw back her head and laughed. He watched her happily.

'You've told me at least three times, Gordon. But did I tell you that it was thanks to me we worked out Martyn was at the Early Rocks?'

'You! No, you didn't tell me that!'

He was ridiculously pleased and proud, as though he had worked it out himself.

'It was really exciting but I wasn't allowed to talk about it at all.'

'Not even to me?'

'Not even to you. Remember I said that I kept picking up talk about a holy place and that's when your blokes went and searched all the mosques?'

'And then you worked out that the holy place was the Early Rocks!'

'Yes. Because they said something about a pregnant woman there. That's how I knew. The last time we saw Asad' – her voice faltered; Asad had not been mentioned by either of them since their argument after his death – 'he said the shrine was special for women who wanted a boy child. To Asad it was all unIslamic traditional nonsense, of course. Anyway, we put the place under aerial surveillance and . . .'

The boss beamed.

'Well done, Asma! Well done!'

'. . . and the SAS rescued the hostage!'

'Oh no they didn't.'

She smiled again. He looked at her face, allowed his eyes to linger on its gaunt beauty, and felt that not seeing her every day was going to be hard.

'Asma, I hope we'll meet when we're back in England.'

She sat very still.

'If you want to.'

'Do you want to?'

'I think you'll change your mind when you're back with your friends again,' she said softly. 'In fact, I know you will.'

460

'No!' He didn't want to change his mind. He'd rather change his friends. It was true that Asma wouldn't fit easily into his circle. But here at the FOB he'd stepped outside that circle for the first time in his life. Now he saw no reason to step back into it.

'Asma, you live close to London so maybe we could . . . well, perhaps go to the theatre and have a nice meal . . .'

'I'd like that. I've never been to the theatre.'

She watched him try unsuccessfully to hide his surprise. She laughed again and his face lit up with pleasure, even though he suspected the laughter was at his own expense.

She leaned across the desk and, to his amazement and delight, took his hand.

'Gordon, it won't be the same in England. Here we've been through a lot together and we can see all the things we've got in common. Soon as we're back there, all we'll see are the differences.'

'What differences?'

'C'mon, Gordon.'

'Before you decide you hate people because they live in a farm-house, you should come and see it.'

She sniffed. 'I bet it smells of furniture polish.'

He smiled. 'Only on Wednesdays when Mrs B from the village has been in to clean.'

'Are you kidding?'

'Yes. Come and see my home. I think you'll like it. I could teach you to ride . . .'

'No thanks. And I can guarantee you wouldn't like my home. Luckily my parents haven't spoken to me for three years so there's not much chance you'll ever see it.'

Her touch was very light and her hand so small he could scrunch it up in his fingers if he wanted to. He held it carefully.

'I thought you lived in a flat in Luton now.'

'Yeah.'

'I might like that.'

'Well . . . yeah . . .'

'And I live in the officers' mess, not my parents' house.'

'What are you saying, Gordon?'

'Can't we start from here? From who we are now?'

'Not sure who I am. If I've learned one thing from this tour, it's that. I was born here in this country. I'm Pashtun. I can leave my family and change my surname but that's still who I am underneath.'

Weeks said softly: 'That's one reason Asad meant a lot to you.'

'When I met Asad and his family, I realized I sort of knew them even though I'd never met them. At first it was scary. Now I have to live with it.'

She let go of his hand and got up. So he must have blown it. Because she was walking out.

But no, she was walking around the desk to where he was sitting, bending down and kissing him on the lips. It wasn't a very long kiss. When it was over he wanted more. His lips looked for hers but she pulled back and wagged a finger at him.

'You've had plenty of chances to engage the enemy, Gordon.'

'But now I'm returning fire.'

Laughing, she turned to go. 'Got to initiate those contacts sometimes! Let's see if you do any better in England.'

Dave booked an early slot when the satellite phones were finally re-opened after Jamie's death. He wanted to break the news to Jenny himself. But when she answered he could tell at once that she already knew.

'Who told you?'

'Adi, of course.' She was sniffing back tears. 'Plus it was on the TV news when they were going on and on about the SAS rescuing the hostage.'

'What did they say?'

'That a soldier in the regular army had died during the ambush. Then Adi rang to say who. I was shocked, Dave. But the first thing I thought was: thank God it wasn't you.'

'You liked Jamie,' he said.

'Yeah. A lot.'

'Who's with Agnieszka?'

'No one. I tried. But she's sort of frozen. It must be the shock.'

'No one's there! Not even her bloke?'

'She said she wanted to be left alone. So Adi's taken Luke and I think the Families Officer's going back soon. Dave, listen, I want to call the baby after Jamie. Do you think Jamie's an OK name for a girl these days?'

'I don't know. At the moment it just makes me think of Jamie.'

'Some people spell it J-a-i-m-e for a girl.'

'Let me think about it.'

'Dave. Are you all right?'

Dave felt a stabbing pain in his chest area. There was a long silence. Jamie's silence, again.

'Not sure,' he said at last.

'I always knew he was your favourite.'

'We're not supposed to have favourites.'

'But sometimes people do. And Jamie was yours.'

'He was badly wounded but he didn't die at first so I let myself hope for a few minutes. Even though I knew there wasn't a chance.'

'You were right to hope,' said Jenny. 'Miracles can happen.'

'Not this time. He was so badly maimed that it was probably better not to live.'

'He would have wanted to live for Agnieszka.'

'She's a bitch.'

'Oh, Dave, she's really suffering. And we don't know for sure she was messing about.'

'She had another bloke. And Jamie knew about it too. Because she told him.'

'No!'

'Jen, he had a mobile phone here. It's unbelievable that Jamie would take a risk like that. But he did. I found it. And there was a message on it from her, which he must have got just before he died. Saying she loved someone else.'

There was a long silence.

'Jen?'

'He had that mobile phone because she asked him to and because he loved her a lot.'

'Yeah, and she loved him so much she sent him a message like that.'

'No! Agnieszka didn't send it to him.'

Dave suddenly grew suspicious.

'You *knew* he had that phone?'

'It was the Taliban who sent the message. Agnieszka never would have done it.'

'But the Taliban didn't know she was messing about!'

'She might not have been! The Taliban didn't know anything about her, they just wanted to hurt him. And he read it and believed it . . .'

'How the *fuck* do you know about all this, Jenny?'

'Don't be angry with me, Dave. I promised not to tell you before. But now Jamie's dead, I suppose I can.'

Chapter Seventy-one

THE TIME TO LEAVE THE FOB DREW NEAR. TAREGUE MASUD MADE lemon meringue pie by popular request. People cemented friendships and gave each other addresses and phone numbers. Men who had argued or fought with each other suddenly became mates. Posters were swapped, photos traded, and Masud did a roaring trade in Sin City T-shirts. The OC announced that Martyn was inviting the whole company to dinner at a London hotel soon after their return.

They were scheduled to depart in the afternoon. The men piled their stuff on their cots ready to grab it when the helicopter landed. Some were taking a last look around FOB Sin City. They saw the advance party of the company who were replacing them huddled by the wagons looking miserable, pale and lost.

'We were like that six months ago,' said Angus. 'I reckon I was a different person back then.'

Finn said: 'I think I'm going to miss this place.'

'I know I will,' said Angus. 'I don't want to go. It's like leaving home. 'Specially because it won't be the same now.'

Sin City was to remain an FOB but there would be no more civilians. The oil project was abandoned, Taregue Masud was leaving with R Company and the number of troops here were to be doubled.

'What you going to say to your old man when you get back, then?' Finn asked Angus. 'Going to tell him that his boss from the Jedi still cooks a fucking good lemon meringue pie?'

'Nah. I'm keeping my mouth shut. He wants to be a war hero, so let him be. It costs me nothing.'

Finn nodded. 'Big of you, Angry. I think you got bigger since you came here. Come on, let's have one last sniff of the Cowshed so we'll remember the whiff for ever.'

They passed Mal.

'Feeling nostalgic, mate?'

'I'm thinking about women. Women with curves who don't walk around wearing sheets wrapped all over their bodies. And I'm just wondering how quickly I can pull.'

'Tell the birds you're a war hero. That should do it.'

'You going straight up to Manchester?' asked Angus.

Mal shook his head. 'Nah. My family reckons it's better for me to stay in barracks and they'll come down and see me.'

Angus brightened. 'You hanging around in barracks, too? I was thinking of doing that.'

They looked at each other and grinned.

'We can go out on the pull together then,' said Mal. 'What you doing, Finny?'

'I'll go and see which of my babymothers has got room for me. That's probably the bed where I'll start. After that, who knows?'

They got to the Cowshed and found Streaky and Binns there.

'Come to inhale the last whiff?' asked Mal.

'Mmm,' said Streaky, breathing deeply. 'If they could only bottle it.'

'Think we'll come back here? On our next tour?' asked Binns.

They looked at each other. No matter how much they wanted to go home, a part of them didn't want to leave this strange place. Although no one would admit it.

'Yeah, maybe,' said Angus. 'Maybe we will come back here.'

They heard the throb of rotor blades.

'Come on, come on, come on,' roared Sol's voice at the door. 'What are you all doing here? Get your kit and get out to that Chinook!'

'Here we go!' said Mal, taking a last look around. 'This is it.'

When the Chinook finally took off, the men were silent. Dave felt as though he was leaving Jamie behind in this desolate place. Or maybe its desolation had crept inside him and he was taking it with him. He looked down at the base's right angles, etched in the desert landscape in hesco. He saw the shining gym equipment, the thick mud walls, the tents, the isoboxes, the hardware and all the men of the incoming company racing to grab the best cots.

It was raining when their plane touched down in the UK. As the men disembarked they felt its soft patter on their faces and the coolness of the breeze in their hair. The weather here was kind and forgiving. It didn't want to pin you to the ground or whip you into exhaustion or scrape at the inside of your throat or fry you all day and then freeze you all night. The damp air of Brize Norton was the climate of home and it welcomed them.

It took a long time for their baggage to come through. Dave watched his men's faces as they waited and waited by the circling carousels. They hardly moved. They were expressionless. He'd personally switched himself off, like a TV, to make the journey bearable. He wanted to be at the FOB. And then he wanted to be home. He didn't want the bits in between. He hadn't even wanted a few days in Cyprus.

The carousels sprang into life and so did the men. There were a few goodbyes. CSM Kila was saying a fond farewell to the monkey woman. And the boss was all over the other one, the Intelligence Corps girl.

Kila caught up with Dave when they were loading the last bags onto the bus and a few lads were having a quick cigarette before boarding.

'Think you'll see her again?' asked Dave.

'She's gone up to Edinburgh. And guess what, I've got family in Glasgow. So we'll be meeting next weekend!'

Kila raised his eyebrows suggestively. Dave laughed at him.

'Good luck, mate.'

They boarded. Everyone was given a can of beer. They drank it in silence. The bus started to go and Dave sensed how restless and worried the men were. People had been phoning and writing to their loved ones for six months, yearning for their families and the luxuries of home and now, thought Dave, after all that longing, it was about to happen. And it was terrifying.

'I told Shaz not to meet me at the camp,' said Dean Somers, the sergeant of 2 Platoon, who was sitting next to him. 'I'll get a lift and hook up with her and the kids at home.'

Dave turned to him.

'Can't handle it, eh?'

Somers reddened. He dropped his voice: 'I'm not fucking crying in front of my men, mate.'

'They'll be too busy trying not to cry to notice you.'

'All right, I'll put it another way. I'm not fucking crying in front of the missus.'

Dave said: 'I'm allowed to cry. I've got a baby I haven't even met yet.'

'Who you going to kiss first, then?' asked Somers. 'That's the other fucking problem, innit? They're all standing there, you can't hug them all at once.'

'Jenny,' said Dave decisively. 'Jenny is definitely first. And she'll probably be holding the baby so that's two birds with one stone. Then I reckon I'd better make a big fuss of Vicky before I take the baby . . .'

'You've got it all worked out, then?' said Somers. 'See what I mean? It's better to go home and ring the doorbell and walk into your own hall and do the shit there.'

'I haven't got it worked out really. Because my mum and stepdad might be there too. And maybe my mother-in-law.'

'Well, the mother-in-law goes right to the end of the line!' said Somers. 'Mine would.'

'Yeah. But we've leaned on her a lot lately, and she's been there for us.'

'If she's anything like mine, she'll make sure you know it. Is it true you're leaving?'

'No,' said Dave. 'I just have to pretend I'm thinking about it.'

As the bus neared the camp the atmosphere was as tense as before any fire fight. Everyone stopped talking. There was complete silence. They turned into camp and then it seemed like a long time before they finally arrived in the square. It was crowded with people in bright colours, holding banners and placards, smiling and waving. Everyone strained to pick out their own family group. On the bus, men's faces broke into smiles. Dave felt a thousand tiny strings from all over his body pulling at some knot behind his eyes. Oh, shit. Get a grip on yourself.

Jenny, accompanied by the children, Trish and Dave's parents had arrived early in two cars.

'Christ, Mum, don't do the banner thing,' said Jenny.

'Vicky wants to, don't you, love?' said Trish firmly and Vicky nodded. Jenny and Dave's mum exchanged agonized glances.

'Dave hates that kind of fuss,' muttered Jenny.

'He's been off doing what he likes for six months, he can just put up with it,' said Trish, as though Dave had been away on holiday. 'Anyway, he won't hate it if Vicks is waving her banner, will he, darling?'

Vicky grinned. She knew her daddy was coming home. She knew her daddy was a man. She just wasn't sure which man he was. But she was prepared to get caught up in the excitement anyway.

'I'll hang around for him while he does all his unloading,' Jenny said. 'It'll take an hour or so and you lot won't want to wait that long.'

'All right, love,' said Dave's mother, 'don't you worry about the baby, just stay with Dave.'

'We'll have the food on the table when you two get back,' his stepfather said.

It seemed the bus would never appear, but the carnival atmosphere persisted. Some people passed around union jacks. Children ran in small circles and then larger ones, in and out of the waiting adults. Some mothers, wives, but especially girlfriends, wore new clothes and carefully applied makeup. As they waited longer and longer their feet began to ache in the unaccustomed heels, their makeup ran or smudged or wore off and their hair required re-brushing and rearranging.

Jenny fed the baby and watched as the tiny eyes closed and she fell asleep. Jenny just hoped that she didn't need another feed or a nappy change or a little shout at exactly the moment the bus came in. She laid her in her pram without waking her. Then it was back to waiting and looking and waiting and wanting.

She caught sight of Steve Buckle in uniform, standing with the rear party.

'Just a minute,' she said.

She went over to Steve.

'Leanne here?'

'Not sure.'

'Come and stand with us then. Because Dave might not see you over there and he'll be pissed off if he misses you.'

Steve looked around at the other men.

'I'm not sure . . .'

'Oh, come on,' she said.

Steve touched a red-haired lad on the arm. 'Jen, this is Ben Broom . . . he's still on crutches.'

Jenny gave Ben a broad smile.

'I've heard all about you, Ben. Can you hobble over here to my family? I know Dave's going to want to see you when he gets off the bus.'

Steve and Ben didn't look too confident walking through the crowd. Jenny moved ahead of them, clearing as much of a path as she could.

As they arrived back with the family, Leanne appeared, a twin hanging on each leg. They saw their father and ran to him.

Steve's face lit up. 'Batman! Robin!'

Jenny looked at Leanne. She grinned back. 'He's doing okay with the boys, anyway.'

'How about you?'

Leanne bit her lip.

'We're managing. Most of the time. Today's hard for us, of course, because Steve should have been one of the lads getting off the bus.'

'It was big of you to come,' said Jenny. 'Big and brave.'

The crowd was getting impatient.

'How much longer?' children asked.

'Soon, soon,' their mothers said.

And then, there it was.

This moment, when the first bus pulled into the square, had been anticipated, imagined and longed for so many times that, when it happened, Jenny felt it was the rerun of an old movie instead of something that was really taking place.

She saw Dave disembark and she waited for him to find her in

470

the maelstrom. She saw him walking through the crowds. And she knew that there was only one face in that crowd for him and it was hers.

She waited as he threaded his way through the people, waited for him to see her. More waiting. It had been six months of waiting, she was good at it now. And she was not going to cry. She was going to smile. It was very important to smile and not cry.

Their eyes met and she never did know if she smiled or cried or did both at once. She felt his arms around her and his lips on hers. Completely enveloped by him she felt something deep inside her weaken. The weighty animal of anxiety she had been carrying around every day for six months, invisible but ever present, loosened its hold on her and slunk quietly, rapidly away. Dave was here, they were both safe, they were a unit standing together again, instead of two people fighting different battles far apart.

When they drew back and each examined the face they had thought about but not seen or touched for six months, they saw how much change there had been and they both knew how hard they would have to work to understand the changes and adapt to them.

Dave smiled. He was thinking that he had missed the joy at his baby's birth. But now he had it tenfold.

'Stop crying,' he told Jenny.

'I can't.'

'You are so beautiful. I forgot how beautiful.'

Then there was Vicky, smilingly held aloft by a man she didn't recognize but who her mum seemed to like a lot. He held her while he gazed at the sleeping baby. Next came Trish. Dave knew his mum and stepfather would understand why they had to be last. They were crying when he got to them. He held them both close to him in a double embrace.

Jenny pulled his arm and he turned and saw Steve. This was so unexpected that Dave stared for a moment without comprehension.

'Christ! Steve!'

He gave his mate a bear hug and then feared that he had literally knocked Steve off his foot. He drew back.

'It's OK! I can stand. I can run. I can probably run as far as you!' said Steve.

'Shit! You're looking so good! Put on a few pounds . . .'

'That's the fine food at Headley Court.'

'You can run, you can really run?'

'I'll race you. Now don't throw your arms around Ben because he'll fall over.'

Dave hugged Ben gently.

'The last time I saw you . . . well, you were a lot of spectacular shades of red, Broom. Now you're just the one . . .' He tousled Broom's hair.

'I'm getting my new leg soon, Sarge,' Broom said proudly.

'Shit!' said Dave. 'This is a fantastic surprise.'

'So did you put my leg in your Bergen, mate?' asked Steve.

'Er . . . what?'

'My leg. From the cookhouse freezer. You did bring it?'

For a moment the smile faded from Dave's face.

'Oh . . . so you heard about that . . .'

Steve started to laugh, then. So did Dave, partly with relief. He was still laughing when he put an arm around Leanne and planted a huge kiss on her cheek.

'You're looking good, Leanne!'

But by now Jenny had picked up the baby and handed her to Dave. He stared into her eyes and simply loved her. It wasn't complicated. It wasn't maybe. It was love.

'Yeah,' said Dave to the baby. 'Yeah. I'd like you to be called after Jamie.'

Jenny was watching him. She said: 'How you've changed, Dave.'

He smiled. He looked around the field of men and their families, at the banners and the tears, the wounded and the whole, the joy and the relief. He thought he heard the same phrase on every pair of lips. The men were saying it about their wives, about their children. The families were saying it about their men. Everyone, in Wiltshire and Helmand, had faced experiences that only those who were with them could understand. The words echoed around the people, the buses, the buildings, the barracks, the banners and the monument to the men who hadn't come home, until it seemed to Dave, his new baby named after his dead friend in his arms, that these were the only words he could hear. You've changed, you've changed, you've changed.

About the author

Andy McNab joined the infantry as a boy soldier. In 1984 he was 'badged' as a member of 22 SAS Regiment and was involved in both covert and overt special operations worldwide. During the Gulf War he commanded Bravo Two Zero, a patrol that, in the words of his commanding officer, 'will remain in regimental history for ever'. Awarded both the Distinguished Conduct Medal (DCM) and Military Medal (MM) during his military career, McNab was the British Army's most highly decorated serving soldier when he finally left the SAS in February 1993. He wrote about his experiences in three books: the phenomenal bestseller *Bravo Two Zero*, *Immediate Action* and *Seven Troop*.

He is the author of the bestselling Nick Stone thrillers. Besides his writing work, he lectures to security and intelligence agencies in both the USA and UK. He is a patron of the Help for Heroes campaign.